Jimi Hendrix
Electric Gypsy

Harry Shapiro is the author of WAITING
FOR THE MAN: DRUGS AND POPULAR
MUSIC, ERIC CLAPTON: LOST IN THE
BLUES and GRAHAM BOND: THE
MIGHTY SHADOW.

Caesar Glebbeek is Founder of the Jimi
Hendrix Information Centre.

D1471836

Also by Harry Shapiro

Slowhand: The Story of Eric Clapton
Waiting for the Man: The Story of Drugs and Popular Music

*Caesar Glebbeek is Founder of the Hendrix
Information Centre*

JIMI HENDRIX
ELECTRIC GYPSY

Harry Shapiro
and Caesar Glebbeek

Mandarin

'Hey Joe – this one's for you!'
H.S.

For Jimi
C.G.

Ahoy Hallen, Rotterdam, Holland, 10 November 1967
(autographed at the Rheinhalle, Düsseldorf, W. Germany, 12 January 1969)

A Mandarin Paperback

JIMI HENDRIX: ELECTRIC GYPSY

First published in Great Britain 1990
by William Heinemann Ltd
This edition published 1992
by Mandarin Paperbacks
an imprint of Reed Consumer Books Limited
Michelin House, 81 Fulham Road, London SW3 6RB
and Auckland, Melbourne, Singapore and Toronto

Reprinted 1992 (twice), 1993, 1994, 1995

Copyright © by Harry Shapiro & Caesar Glebbeek, 1990
Front cover photograph of Jimi Hendrix
is copyright © Gered Mankowitz

A CIP catalogue record for this title
is available from the British Library
ISBN 0 7493 0544 4

Printed in England by Clays Ltd, St Ives plc

Contents

Preface and Acknowledgements

At a distance of some three years, it is almost impossible to recall the moment at which this book was born. The project rapidly became so monumental that the overwhelming feeling was trying to stay afloat in a sea of information. However, looking back through the purple haze, I can remember sitting in a cottage in Cornwall replete with cream tea, imagining I could write a dramatic reconstruction of Jimi's life – stunningly titled 'Jimi'. Digging around for some background information beyond what had already been written, I contacted Caesar Glebbeek who runs the Hendrix Information Centre. That conversation sparked off a correspondence which lasted six months. During that time two things became clear; one, 'Jimi' would never be written, and two, there was a more important job to be done. What you have now are the fruits of our combined labour.

The aim was to produce the most detailed account of Jimi's life and work yet published. In particular, Caesar and I wanted to demonstrate the international character of Jimi's appeal beyond America and Britain, to give due weight to his talents as a songwriter, and, perhaps above all, to get the story as straight as possible from the mountain of information at our disposal. Throughout we have tried to use Jimi's own words to express his feelings about his life and music and the world around him as he saw it.

The cornerstone of this book was the archive of the Hendrix Information Centre founded by Caesar nearly twenty-five years ago. Its size is awesome, containing over 10,000 articles and reviews and several days' worth of tapes – interviews, whole concerts and studio sessions – plus a bank of additional information detailing many aspects of Jimi's life from birth to death. In addition, there were a whole host of other libraries and archives to visit and we would like to thank the staff of the following: BBC Sound Archives, London; BBC Written Archives,

Reading; Board of School Trustees, Vancouver, British Columbia; Chicago Public Library; Genealogical Library, London; Genealogical Library, Salt Lake City, Utah; Harborview Medical Center, Seattle; Houston Public Library, Texas; King's Lynn Public Library, Norfolk; Library of the City of Pasadena, California; Nashville Public Library; National Sound Archive, London; Newspaper Library (British Library), London; Public Health Vital Statistics Division, Seattle; San Francisco Public Library; Seattle Public Library; Seattle Public Schools Archive; UCLA Libraries, Los Angeles.

It is surprising just how many people who figured in Jimi's life have never been interviewed before for a biography. Actually it isn't all that surprising. After Jimi died, many were buttonholed by journalists seeking sensational stories. They refused and have remained silent for twenty years until now. Other key people were simply never asked. For all their help we would like to extend our thanks to: Keith Altham, Lulu Appleton, Al Aronowitz, Anne Bjørndal, Benorce Blackmon, Mark Boyle, Leo Branton, Pearl Brown, Randy California, Ed Chalpin, Chas Chandler, Neville Chesters, George Chkiantz, Jimmy Church, George Clemens, Parker Cook, Mick Cox, Monika Dannemann, Dave Dee, Lee Dicker, Alan Douglas, Kathy Etchingham, Bruce Fleming, Freddie Mae Gautier, Dolores Hall, Eddie Hall, Nancy Hall, Dorothy Harding, Al Hendrix, Leon Hendrix, John Hillman, Hugh Hopper, Frank Jeffery, Johnny Jones, Melody Jones, Angie King (formerly Burdon), B.B. King, David King, Larry Lee, Gary Leeds, Jimmy Leverton, Buzzy Linhart, Emeretta Marks, Jim Marshall, Dave Mason, Roger Mayer, Jane de Mendelssohn, Buddy Miles, Colette Mimram, Dee Mitchell, Mitch Mitchell, Zoot Money, David Montgomery, Lawrence Moore, Claire Moriece, Buck Munger, Henry Nash, Kirsten Nefer, Claude Nonette, Walter Price, Bernard Purdie, Mike Quashie, Margaret Redding, Noel Redding, Vicky Redding, Dr Seifert, Carol Shiroky, Chris Stamp, Gerry Stickells, Trixie Sullivan, Juma Sultan, Jerry Velez, Geno Washington, Chris Welch, Herbert Worthington and Robert Wyatt.

We received very few outright refusals for interviews. Where this happened, it was invariably due to a prior commitment to personal projects. Two such cases were Eddie Kramer and Billy Cox. Their refusals are cause for particular regret – everything we knew about them (confirmed by those we spoke to) revealed them to be two of Jimi's most trusted friends. Thus we had to resort to secondary sources to give them a voice in this book and we hope we have done justice to their intentions.

A whole army of people across the world gave unstintingly of their time and effort in a whole range of activities. Some helped set up interviews, pointed the way to those we were seeking, or offered snippets of information to fit into the grand puzzle. Others translated articles from French, Finnish, German, Swedish, Italian and Spanish. A number of people did additional research for us in some of the establishments listed above. We received marvellous assistance in compiling the discography and locating pictures and we were given free access to all the other Hendrix archives in Europe and America.

Thanks are due to Ben Valkhoff in Holland and Bill Nitopi in America for assistance in trawling for rare photographs and general picture research. In addition we owe a debt of gratitude to all of the following: Charlie Angel, Steve Barker, Mike Barich, Anders Berglund, Paul de Bie, Peter Blecha, Jan Blom, David Hugo Boarman, Mark Bogard, Gene Bowen, Veronique Brooke, Ralph Brooks, Carol Brown, Peder Bundgaard, Joe Cabot, Alan Clayson, Darell Clingman, Judy Collins, Michael Collins, Ian Coomer, Paul Day, Roy Dean, Fred Dente, Michel Doncque, Michael Fairchild, Carol French, Shane Gates, Tony Glover, John Goddard, Keith Grant, Finn Jensen, Jess Hansen, Justin Harrison, David Haslam, Richie Havens, Nona Hatay, Andrew Crawley, Ayako June Hendrix, Peter Herzig, Phil Hilborne, Graham Howe, Sami Hurmerinta, Sören Karlson, Francis King, Michael Krogsgaard, David Lands, Paul Lane, Kees de Lange, Alan Lowe, Jeff Marsho, Eugene McFadden, Jean-Yves Mogureou, Charles Shaar Murray, Joe Musella, Maureen Neller, David Noonan, Christian Nötzli, Tim O'Brien, Alain Oddou, George Odell, Anders Øgren, Hugh Padgham, Bruce Pates, David Pearcy, Maurizio Percivalle, Håkan Persson, Bruce Pilato, Cliff Richmond, Steven Roby, Mike Ross, Jay Ruby, Edward Rye, Markku Salo, Peter Schertser, Gerhard Schinzel, Barbro Schörling, Mats Schörling, Louis Schwartz, Roy Simonds, Norman Smith, Ron Theisen, Pim Thiemans, Barbara Thomas, David Thomas (not related), Steve Tibbets, Eleanor Toews, Diego Tremonti, Bill Uhrie, Els Valkhoff, Kenneth Voss, Charles White, Fred Wiebel, David Worthing and Thomas Yeates. We would also like to extend our gratitude to our agent Mic Cheetham and editor Jane Carr for all their advice and encouragement.

A special mention for John Tobler, the man without whose name no decent set of rock biography acknowledgements is complete. But he is to be thanked as an author in his own right, as a kindred spirit who offered a sympathetic ear to bend during times of trouble.

It would be no exaggeration to say that this book could never have been written, indeed could never even have been contemplated without the love, support and encouragement of Kay. She has suffered all the isolation which is the lot of the writer's partner, she put up with so much hair-tearing on my part that it's a wonder I've got any left and she still willingly read the manuscript, offering perceptive comments. The debt I owe to her is boundless. Just as I actually started writing the book, my son Joseph was born. He too played his part by offering me a glimpse of life on the road without ever having to leave the confines of my tiny room. How so? By keeping me up all hours of the night, after a day at work and an evening in front of a word processor. Thank you, Joseph – I dedicate this book to you.

Harry Shapiro
Harrow, 1990

My special thanks go to my friends Tony Brown, Ben Valkhoff and Bill Nitopi for their support and research assistance prior and during the years it took to put this book together. Last but not least I would like to thank the kind people who looked after my animals and house during the many months I was abroad for interviews and research; Ida, June & Frank, and Rose & Colum. I dedicate this book to James Marshall Hendrix . . . forever in our hearts.

Caesar Glebbeek
'Aquarius Cottage', June 1990

The authors would like to pay a special tribute to the work of Tony Brown of the Jimi Hendrix Archives in England. Tony has been a Hendrix researcher for many years and his tireless efforts made a major contribution to the production of this book.

The authors would also like to thank the following:
Bella Godiva Music Inc. and the Estate of Jimi Hendrix for permission to reproduce Jimi's published and unpublished song lyrics. International copyright reserved 1990.
Meatball Fulton/ZBS Media for extracts from the Meatball Fulton Interview. Knockabout Comics for *The Adventures of Fat Freddy's Cat*, copyright Gilbert Shelton. Macmillan Ltd for the extract from *Deep Blues* by Robert Palmer. Pan Books Ltd for the extract from *The Life and Times of Little Richard* by Charles White. Mirror Group Newspapers for *Fan* comic. *Debris* magazine for the *West One* interview. *Guitar Player* magazine.

Preface to new edition

Since *Electric Gypsy* was first published in September 1990, much new evidence has emerged concerning the last few hours of Jimi's life. This, in turn, led me to reassess the material already in my possession with the net result that, although the research is still in progress, Chapter Fourteen has been partially rewritten. In addition, a selected update section has been added to the discography to reflect the surge of new Hendrix releases – for this I would like to thank Tony Brown of the Jimi Hendrix Archives and Mike Williamson. I would also like to acknowledge the assistance of Michael Fairchild in making various corrections and emendations.

Harry Shapiro
August 1991

Introduction *Hear My Train A'Comin'*

Tuesday 19 December 1967 – a bitterly cold day in Leicester Square, in the heart of London's West End. Just off the square at 12 Great Newport Street is the top-floor studio of photographer Bruce Fleming. The Jimi Hendrix Experience has just completed a photo session to be included in a promotional film called *See My Music Talking*.

Drummer Mitch Mitchell and bassist Noel Redding split. Bruce Fleming's job of creating the 'right' image for the group is finished for the day. But the film's producer, Austin Marshall, has a different image in mind – he wants to 'clear away' Jimi's public image, the strobe lights, the amps, the fuzztone, the phasing and the feedback, and set this gentle genius against a plain white background and hear how he plays a simple blues.

Director Peter Neal produces a 1960 Zemaitis twelve-string acoustic guitar specially strung left-handed for Jimi. Austin Marshall is apprehensive. Jimi takes the guitar and looks at it as if it's going to bite him: 'Twelve-string – shit, what the hell am I gonna do with that?' 'Um . . . well,' says Austin, 'we just thought . . . as a contrast to the rest of the movie you might play a sort of slow, quiet blues. Please?'

Jimi perches on a high stool, brings out a tortoiseshell pick and begins to play. The camera rolls, barely five minutes of film left in the can. But Jimi's nervous, he's a perfectionist – even this impromptu jam has to be right. 'No, I want to do it again. Hey, stop that film there. Stop it for a second. I was scared to death. Can I do it just one more time? Can I do it just one more time?'

A brief three-figure motif tumbles down into a Mississippi Delta moan drone blues in B:

Well I wait around the train station
Waitin' for that train

Waitin' for the train, yeah
Take me, yeah,
from this lonesome place
Well now a while lotta people put me down a lot 'a changes
My girl had called me a disgrace

Dig
The tears burnin'
Tears burnin' me
Tears burnin' me
way down in my heart
Well you know it's too bad, little girl, it's too bad,
too bad we have to part (have to part . . .)

Dig
Gonna leave this town, yeah
Gotta leave this town
Gonna make a whole lotta money
Gonna be big yeah
Gonna be big yeah
I'm gonna buy this town
I'm gonna buy this town,
an' put it all in my shoe (might even give a piece to you)
That's what I'm gonna do, what I'm gonna do, what I'm gonna do

This was certainly not the 'right' image, not the 'Wild Man of Borneo' or the 'Mau Mau' of a hundred racist headlines. Here was Jimi 'inside out', the Jimi that resided in the eye of the storm, the real Jimi, the Jimi who was not ashamed of his cultural heritage, who didn't regard country blues as 'old cotton-pickin' nigger slave music'. Jimi had large hands, enabling him to reach for impossible chordings, and he cradled that acoustic guitar, concentrated love on his face, picking at the strings with airbrush sensitivity. It was a moment of rare public calm during a career that was seemingly stuck in overdrive. A little chuckle at the end: 'Bet you didn't think I'd do that.'

Then it was all over. The equipment was packed up and Jimi Hendrix, Electric Gypsy, walked off alone in his skimpy clothes apparently indifferent to the cold.

As the film's narrator, Alexis Korner, said, 'The *real* blues singers are preachers at heart. . . . They very much want to stand up on stage and tell people what they are and what they do. If you feel that's the way you'd like to be, well, good. If you don't, never mind, but don't tell *me* what to do. *That's* the attitude of the bluesman.'

Freedom of action was Jimi's credo, his religion – he often auto-

2

graphed photos with the legend 'Stay Free.' Truth and perfection made up the rest of his Holy Trinity, his personal grail, which he sought with a relentless spirit through the dense forest of lies and compromise which constitutes the music business.

Rheinhalle, Düsseldorf, 12 January 1969

It's easy to be wise in hindsight; the quest was likely to be a chimera. Yes, he died young – along with Buddy Holly, one of the major 'what could he have done if he'd lived' rock deaths. Yes, it was tragic. And yes, the candle that burns brightest often burns shortest. But through all the tough times (and there were plenty of those), Jimi kept his faith, his dedication and often as not his sense of humour. Jimi Hendrix took the music way beyond the place where he found it. Nobody has yet caught up with him. Probably nobody ever will. The only thing to do is to hear the music, listen to the lyrics and try to appreciate something of what Jimi was all about. If, having read this book, you reach back into your record collection for another listen, then all the effort will have been worth while.

One *Cherokee Mist*

The Cherokee Indians, Yun Wiya, the Real People, were thought by other tribes to have come from the skies. They inhabited the region of Southern Allegheny and the Great Smoky Mountains and adjacent areas of Virginia, North and South Carolina, Georgia, Tennessee and Alabama. They were one of the five 'civilised' tribes and more than any other had tried to advance their civilisation to promote peace and harmony between the native Americans and the whites. They were unique among the tribes in having a written language, even their own newspaper, the *Phoenix*. Within months of a Cherokee genius named Sequoyah inventing their alphabet, virtually every Cherokee who was neither too young nor too old could read and write.

They had schools, libraries and mills; they farmed and owned livestock. They had an elegant religion, appealing creation myths where everything in the Cherokee cosmology had its place, down to the smallest insect. Their social structure was sophisticated and they lived comfortably with much grace and beauty. Ultimately none of this would save them.

They had an unfortunate habit of being on the wrong side during wars between the whites – with the French against the British, with the British against the Americans in the War of Independence, and later with the South against the North in the Civil War. Much resentment built up against them which was used as part of the justification for what happened to the Cherokee nation.

What the pioneering white man wanted was land – Indian land – all of it. The Cherokees occupied some seven million acres of southern state heartland. Land grabbing had been going on for decades, but the discovery of gold on Indian land in Georgia sealed the fate of the Cherokee. The state of Georgia did everything to speed up their departure. In 1831, the Cherokees petitioned the Supreme Court that attempts to move them were unlawful. They failed. Indians were played off against their brothers as some sold out their land to whites. In 1835, Congress ratified a fraudulent treaty signed by a minority of Cherokees ceding everything to Georgia. Three years later, 7000 soldiers marched on to Cherokee land to enforce the removal of the whole nation westwards into what is now Oklahoma.

The soldiers attacked en masse one supper time when they knew all the families would be at home. Many Cherokees were killed defending their homes; nearly 1000 escaped to the mountains. Finally, around 17,000 Indians started on what has passed into Indian history as the 'Trail of Tears'. Some took six months to reach halfway – nearly a third, mainly the very young and the old, died of severe cold, drought, exhaustion, fever, measles, pleurisy and whooping cough.

Once they arrived, their well-ordered society collapsed as the nation broke up into warring factions with Mafia-style revenge killings of those who had broken the Blood Law by selling land to whites. Many did survive and prosper, especially in North Carolina, but the Golden Age of the Cherokee nation was over.

Those who fled to the Great Smoky Mountains to live in caves were not the only Indians to escape the Trail of Tears. Kindly white Georgian families suddenly acquired long-lost relatives with deep suntans who had to cease living as Cherokees, but who never forgot emotionally or spiritually who they were and passed that feeling down the generations. Many Cherokees had already intermarried with whites or blacks and so were less vulnerable to state terror. Even John Ross, the Cherokee chief at the time of removal, was seven-eighths white.

One full-blood Cherokee princess who remained in Georgia married an Irishman named Moore. They had a son, Robert. A half-breed living in a white world could not aspire to great heights of achievement; as an adult he found work as a cleaner and settled down to married life with a black girl called Fanny. On 19 November 1883, they had a daughter. This was Jimi's paternal grandmother, Nora Rose Moore. It was Nora's destiny, rather than that of *her* grandmother, to be a zig-zag wanderer.

In the days before radio, television and cinema, the only forms of popular mass entertainment for Americans were the travelling shows – medicine and tent shows, circuses, minstrel shows and vaudeville. Vaudeville evolved from all the previous forms, the last entertainment of its kind before the electronic age of popular entertainment took

6

over. Vaudeville companies comprised singers, comedians, actors performing monologues and melodramas, various speciality acts – and a chorus line. Nora Moore took to the road as a dancer in a vaudeville troupe, criss-crossing the country, stepping out for raucous audiences, the men who came to ogle at the unprecedented display of female flesh on show, unknown outside the disreputable burlesque of seedy bars and saloons.

The troupes came and went; many of the smaller companies could not compete with the large, extravagantly staged shows of the early part of this century and they collapsed – leaving their artists and stage crews stranded wherever the money ran out.

Around 1911, Nora, then twenty-nine, reached Seattle on the Pacific north-west coast with her current troupe. It turned out to be the end of the road – the company went bust. But she didn't really care – it was time to settle down after years of constant travelling, living out of suitcases, one-night stands in one-horse towns. Her husband Ross Hendrix agreed.

Bertran Philander Ross Hendrix was born in Urbana, Ohio, on 11 April 1866, almost a year to the day after the end of the American Civil War. His mother, like Nora's, was called Fanny. Fanny Hendrix (or Hendricks as it was originally spelt) was a poor mulatto woman who had been married to a man named Jefferson Hendrix. But by the time Ross was born, when she was forty years old, Fanny was living alone. Some time in August 1865, she conceived Ross by one of the wealthiest white men in Urbana, one Bertran Philander Ross. He is listed in the Census for 1870 as a grain dealer with a real estate valued at $135,000. How their paths crossed is unknown. The most likely explanation is that Fanny was in Mr Ross's employment when she was perhaps raped or seduced. Perhaps, too, she took her revenge by giving her baby the father's name, an unusual mouthful by any standards. Anybody living in the district would have known who the father was. However, it would seem that Fanny's son gained no material benefit from his 'privileged' beginnings.

For blacks after the Civil War, the promise of living in a land where slavery had been abolished and where all men were created equal quickly evaporated. Ex-slaves were now free to be exploited by the share-cropping system, tied to the land and permanently in debt to the white farmer, free to live in abject poverty and free to be lynched. Of the northern states, Ohio's anti-black laws were among the most severe, mainly through white fears that freed slaves would come flooding across

7

Ohio's southern borders with Kentucky and Virginia. When he was old enough, Ross Hendrix didn't hang about to be persecuted or worse, he left Urbana and headed for the big city. Somewhere along the way he got married and found a job as a special constable in Chicago before leaving home once more to join a vaudeville troupe as a stagehand. On the road, he got married again, this time to Nora Moore.

Bertran Philander Ross and Nora Rose Hendrix Seattle, 1911

Ross wanted to leave 'Jim Crow' America, Land of the Free, altogether – so in 1912 he and Nora headed north out of Seattle on Highway 5 for the 175-mile journey across the Canadian border and on to Vancouver in search of a new beginning. They settled down to family life. In 1913, Nora gave birth to her first son Leon Marshall; Patricia was born the following year, Frank in October 1918, and finally on 10

June 1919 Jimi's father, James Allen (Al).

Al Hendrix, now seventy-one, lives in a well-to-do suburb of Seattle. The walls of his large, comfortable home are adorned with mementos of his famous son. Thieves have stolen the gold discs, so the private collection of guitars and tapes are securely locked away. Surrounded by photo albums and family documents, Al recalls his childhood when money was always tight: 'My dad, he met this guy, Mr Cohen, I think his name was, and got this job out there on the golf course – that's the only job I known him to have.' Ross was strict with his kids, but Al, being the youngest, got away with more than his sister and brothers. His experience of family life was positive. 'We were always together and I was well taken care of.'

Then in March 1932 tragedy struck; aged only nineteen, Leon ruptured his appendix and died of peritonitis. Ross died exactly two years later in March 1934. The family began to break up; Pat got married, but stayed in Vancouver, Frank embarked on the first of four marriages and Al, a boy of fifteen, had to try and make his way in the world.

Al's school career was undistinguished; he had no particular skills at that time and could look forward to little else other than poorly paid manual work around Vancouver and Vancouver Island. 'I shined shoes, worked in barber's shops.' His talents were in his fists and in his feet.

When Ross had been a black policeman in Chicago, he needed to be able to take care of himself. He passed that instinct to his son Al, who, at only just over five feet, needed some self-protection anyway to deal with the rough and tumble of adolescence. And from his mother Nora and brother Leon he came to love dancing as a mode of individualistic expression and high passion.

> I came to Seattle around 1936 to fight in the Golden Gloves. It's a
> big fight tournament that they have . . . fighters come from all over the
> United States. This guy asked me whether I'd like to go down there . . .
> and make $25 a round. I said, 'I'll go for that.' I didn't know then that the
> Golden Gloves was all amateurs – and they don't get paid anyway. I was
> a lightweight. I fought at the Crystal Pool on First Avenue.

Al got to the finals even though 'I didn't have no killer instinct. . . . to be pounding on and on the guy and he'd be hangin' on the ropes and they'd be yellin' at me to hit him some more. I mean, the guy did nothing to me.'

Big-band jazz was another matter. Duke Ellington came to Vancouver in 1938 when jitterbugging was all the rage.

> We used to have jitterbugging contests. But they used to separate the whites from the blacks for the contests, because the whites thought they wouldn't have a chance against the blacks. Once four of us entered the contest: Buster Keeling, Alma, myself and Dorothy King. We were the couples in the black group. They had a hundred dollars for the prize. . . . Man, I picked it up real quick. I mean, shoot, I had all the timing, because I used to do a lot of tap dancing. We went down and put in an application for the contest. That night there were only two black couples in the thing. I thought we had it made.[1]

Unfortunately, they didn't have it made, because at the last minute the two girls chickened out and $100 went down the drain – an awful lot of money especially when you weren't working.

Al could see that he had to do it alone. He went out and performed solo, dancing to the rhythms in his own head because the white band he fronted around the night spots in Vancouver didn't have the first idea what swing was all about. He'd do guest spots with the touring vaudeville shows that hit town, dancing solo, adding improvisations to the dance crazes of the day, pounding the boards in an outsize zoot suit that hung from his muscular frame. Size was no obstacle except that Al had problems finding partners for the more acrobatic routines.

Al's size also proved a handicap to getting the good jobs on the railways in Vancouver, one of the few areas of employment with halfway decent wages. Eventually he'd had enough; he thought about New York and Chicago, but dismissed them both as 'wild, cold-blooded'. Finally, he decided to retrace his parents' footsteps and landed back in Seattle.

Not that living there was any easier; Al did not find the streets paved with gold. He was living in the worst lodgings trying to keep body and soul together. But there was always the dancing to keep the spirit alive. One night he danced with the Louis Armstrong band and gave it his best shot – every routine in the book, Ballin' the Jack, Eagle Rock, the Georgia Grind, a flash of Charleston and jitterbugging. With the crowds in their evening finery cheering and clapping, that was probably the highlight of his dancing career. But though he never became a professional, dancing did change his life. For it was through his love of dancing that he met the sixteen-year-old Lucille Jeter.

Lucille was one of eight children born to Preston Jeter and his wife

Clarice. Born in July 1875, Preston came from Richmond, Virginia. He worked as a longshoreman and down the coal mines near Whitesville, just south of Charleston on the Coal River. Emancipation came slow to such places and working in the mines was virtual slave labour. After a run-in with some local rednecks, Preston fled, changing his name as he went (Preston Jeter was not his real name) until he reached Boston. There he was befriended by a white doctor who put him through college to better his prospects. But a black with an education was still a black as far as employment was concerned, so he finished up in Washington State working in the Rosslyn mines. Little is known about Clarice, except that she was born on 17 January 1894 in Little Rock, Arkansas.

Their situation as a black couple was not uncommon – they had a large family with little money coming in. When Clarice fell ill for a period of time, Preston couldn't (or wouldn't) look after the children, so they were fostered out to a German family in the north of Washington State. They were the only black kids in the neighbourhood, but they were treated very well. Even so, this kind of separation had its impact on all of them. Lucille's sister Dolores says, 'This is why we all married young – to have kids, have a family and all be together, but it didn't work out quite that way.'

Lucille was born on 12 October 1925; she was very pale, so pale that her family were afraid that she'd run off at the first opportunity to make her way in the white world. But Dolores and the rest of the family adored her. 'She was just a sweet little girl.' And she was hardly more than a little girl when Al came into her life. 'We met at a friend's house,' he recalls, 'a girlfriend of hers happened to bring her by where I was staying. I thought she was kinda young at the time. We went to a dance that night, it was a Friday . . . Fats Waller was playin'.' Lucille was small with fine delicate features and a frail constitution arising from a bout of pneumonia caught as a baby, which hospitalised her for weeks. But on the dance floor she was a jitterbugging whirlwind, a local champion in her own right, lithe, smooth and fast. Al had found his perfect dancing partner. He later went to her house to ask if he could see her again. They lindyhopped through 1941, the prospect of a whole lifetime of good times stretching out before them – until in December the Japanese bombed Pearl Harbor.

In the immediate aftermath of the declaration of war, there was enormous uncertainty, fear and apprehension – nobody knew what would happen, other than perhaps a feeling that nothing would be the same again. Under these circumstances and with the draft beckoning, the progress of relationships accelerated. There was no time for prolonged courtships. Al had been working at a foundry and suffered a hernia which put him in hospital. But Uncle Sam was not to be denied; early in 1942, Al received his draft papers. On 31 March 1942, Al – nearly twenty-three years old – married Lucille, still seven months off her seventeenth birthday. They had another reason to tie the knot – Lucille Jeter was pregnant.

Two *The Night I Was Born, the Moon Turned a Fire Red*

Al went into the army very soon after they got married – they didn't even have the chance to live together before he left. He did his basic training in field artillery in Oklahoma, then 'They sent a bunch of us to Georgia [Fort Benning] on account of they didn't know where to put us. We just lollygagged around in the barracks doing nothin', though we were getting paid.'

On 26 November 1942, around 5 p.m., Lucille was admitted in sub-zero temperatures to King County Hospital, Seattle. At 10.15 the following morning, after a long and difficult labour, she had a son weighing about 8 lb with lots of hair, big eyes, a pale complexion like her own and one-sixteenth Cherokee Indian. Lucille named him Johnny Allen Hendrix – only later would his name be changed to James Marshall Hendrix, known as Jimmy.

By the time his son was born, Al was in Alabama – in the stockade. Under army regulations, Al was entitled to furlough for the birth of his child. 'I asked my commanding officer about going home. "No chance," he said. "You live too far away . . . and don't think about going over the hill." ' Al was angry and despondent and his superiors had in mind what Al might do. 'I was back there in the barracks and they came by and said, "You're going to the stockade." I asked my sergeant later about why when I hadn't done anything and he just said, "General principles." I was in there when I got the telegram from my sister-in-law [Dolores] about him being born.' Al says he was locked up for about two months with no trial, but no loss of pay either, denied his freedom simply to prevent him going AWOL to see his son.

Meanwhile back in Seattle, all was not well. Lucille had been living at home for part of her pregnancy, then she moved in with Dorothy Harding, a friend of her sister Dolores. Dolores herself was living at the family home with two kids of her own and there simply wasn't enough room for Lucille and her expected baby. Lucille was at Dorothy's when Johnny Allen was born, but eventually had to move out of there as well because Dorothy had two kids and space was tight.

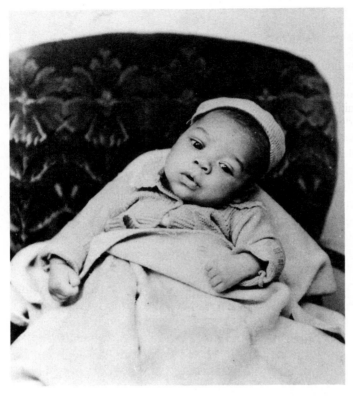

Johnny Allen
(at 2 months
and 3 weeks)
Seattle,
20 February 1943

From there, Lucille moved around a succession of seedy hotel rooms and rooming houses in downtown Seattle. Her father's heart gave out in June 1943 and Clarice sold the house to be with her daughter and help look after the baby. Lucille had such a transient existence because of a bureaucratic bungle by the army; she received no money from Al for nearly a year after he had been drafted into the service. By the time the money did come, she owed everybody in the world and the money evaporated, even though she was doing some waitressing at the Farwest Café to try and make ends meet. But there was another, more deep-seated problem. Lucille Jeter, the typical teenager hell-bent on having a good time around the Seattle nightclubs and dance-halls, had been transformed into Mrs Lucille Hendrix wife and mother, and she was just too young for the responsibility.

Lucille's mother was doing cleaning for a local family whose daughter, Freddie Mae, was twelve years old at the time.

> We lived on the corner of 21st and East St John Street. Mrs Jeter, Lucille's mother, came over to our house to clean – she was almost like a member of the family. One day when it was snowing, Mrs Jeter arrived at the house and had this baby in her arms, about two weeks old, with its little legs sticking out and it was cold, the baby's legs were just blue. My mother [Minnie] said 'What in the world have you got there?' Mrs Jeter said she had Lucille's baby, that she hadn't seen Lucille for a few days and so she had to bring him. My mother was always taking in foster children, so she took the baby in. I remember her going on at Mrs Jeter because she and Lucille lived clear across town on 21st and St James', yet Mrs Jeter had just brought him in a little blanket. He had wet so much and it was so cold that the diaper had frozen and the urine made pockmarks on his skin. Mrs Jeter had no diapers or bottle.
>
> My mother bathed the baby and I put olive oil on him and cuddled him to get him warm. He whimpered, but not too bad. My mother made up some milk in a bottle, but he was a little hesitant at first and she asked Mrs Jeter, 'Does he breastfeed?' 'No, she hasn't been home, so I've been giving him whatever milk was around.' Mrs Jeter was going to take him when she'd finished the house, but my mother said, 'No, you're not taking him anywhere. Leave him here and tell Lucille to come and get him. I want to see why she's leaving this baby in this kind of fix.' Mrs Jeter said, 'Well, she's gonna be mad.' 'Well, let her be mad.'
>
> I can't tell exactly when Lucille came. It wasn't like the next day or two, but maybe even a month or two. When she *did* come, my mother said to her, 'It's a shame to leave this baby with your mother and I'm gonna take this baby and keep him.' And Lucille said, 'Okay.' It wasn't any big deal for her.

And that's how Johnny Allen Hendrix started his life – often with Minnie, sometimes with Mrs Jeter and sometimes with Lucille. But Lucille was a hard drinker and Freddie Mae's mother wouldn't hand Johnny over to Lucille unless she was sober. Lucille was unprepared and unwilling to play the dutiful woman waiting for her man to come home from the war. She fell in with a bad crowd and in the words of a million R&B songs was 'running around town'. Always emotionally susceptible to the attentions of the 'handsome rogue', the sort who made a career out of mistreating women, she was often seen in the company of a black guy named John Williams (not his real surname).

Originally from Kansas City, Williams found his way to Seattle to work on the docks. Seattle like Kansas City was 'wide open' with a reputation for low life which stretched back to its earliest days as a timber town when the loggers would come down from the forests to be relieved of their money by hookers, pickpockets and conmen. Seattle 'boasted' the very first Skid Road or Skid Row, named after the path cut through the forests for mules to bring the logs out. This was the sort of town where the John Williamses of the world could breathe. Dorothy Harding, who helped look after Lucille when she was pregnant, is unequivocal in her feelings about this man. 'He was a slime.'

Once he arrived on the scene, Dolores Jeter and her mother had a hard time keeping track of Lucille and her baby. 'He would take my sister and the baby all over the country, everywhere. There was a [housing] project down in Vancouver [Washington State, not Canada]. I went to see her down there and the conditions she was living in – it was a mess. We tried to get Lucille to come and live with us, but she stayed down there with him. Another time, we had to go and get the baby because Lucille was in hospital. This man had beaten her half to death.'

Although he was not physically abused, Jimi's frequent moves as a baby from one cold, damp lodging to another also took its toll on *his* health.

> I had pneumonia when I was young and I used to scream and cry every time they put the needle in me. . . . I can remember when the nurse put on the diaper . . . I remember she was talkin' to me. She took me out of this crib . . . and then she held me up to the window, this was in Seattle, and she showed me somethin' up against the sky. And it was fireworks and all that. It must have been the Fourth of July, you know. 'Cause then I remember her putting the diaper on me and almost stickin' me with you know. . . . I remember I didn't feel so good . . . and I had a bottle and all kind of stuff and then she held me up to the window and I was lookin' and the sky was just whew-whew-whew.[1]

With his round cherub face and gorgeous staring eyes, little John-ny Allen had the whole neighbourhood drooling over him. If Lucille couldn't or wouldn't look after him, there were plenty around who would. Johnny had been taken up to Vancouver to see his grandma Nora and on his return to Seattle spent some time with one woman called Walls, another called White; Dolores took him in and so did one of Lucille's other sisters, Nancy. Tired of trailing after her daughter,

Clarice Jeter bought another house some time in 1944–5, took charge of the baby and told Dolores, 'I'm gonna take care of him now, I've got a pretty good job. I think I can make it.' 'Next thing I know,' says Dolores, 'some friend of my mother had taken him to California.'

Clarice Jeter had a friend called Mrs Champ whom she knew from the Pentecostal Church, to which a large sector of Seattle's tightly knit black community belonged. Entranced by the little boy, Mrs Champ offered to take him on a two-week trip. However, the two weeks became two months as two-year-old Johnny was spirited around Mrs Champ's home state of Texas. She then took him back to her own home, a low-rent housing project called Savo Island Village in Berkeley, California. Meanwhile, Al Hendrix was on his way home.

Stuck out on the Fiji Islands, Al relied on Dolores to keep him informed as to what was going on. He also sent her money for Lucille and Johnny. Al says he received letters from Mrs Champ about his son, so it was obvious to him that Lucille was not caring for Johnny as Al would expect. However, this by itself doesn't explain why Al was actively considering divorcing Lucille while he was still in the army. What helped him decide to 'give it one more shot' was 'the $25 I had to pay the attorney'. And what prompted him to consider such action in the first place was information he received about his wife's involvement with John Williams – not from Dolores, who denies telling him, but possibly from Nora. Once Al was back, Williams would come up to Al and Lucille in the street blatantly trying to get Lucille to go with him. In response Al gave Williams a taste of the Golden Gloves. Al, a proud man, is very reticent about John Williams; all he says is, 'Yeah, he was around.'

Knowing that his son was in California, Al tried to get a discharge down there, but eventually had to settle for Seattle, arriving there on 11 November 1945.

Contrary to what Al says, Dolores claims Al knew nothing about his son going to California until he turned up at the Jeter house expecting to see him, and says Al blamed her for 'giving his son away'.

The letters Al received from Mrs Champ suggested that she was not over-anxious to give up his son. Anticipating trouble, he obtained a copy of the birth certificate to prove his paternity, but under pressure from his mother and sister, who hadn't seen him for years, he spent a few days in Vancouver before setting off for California.

Mrs Champ had a daughter, Celestine, to whom Johnny had grown very attached. 'They got used to him,' says Al, 'and didn't see why I should take him away from them. They sure were in love with him.' On a more pragmatic level, Mrs Champ was reluctant to hand the boy over because the arrangement had been that she would hand him back to Lucille. Moreover, from Clarice she probably knew of Johnny's desperate existence in the Seattle slums and perhaps hoped to fend off Al's obviously legitimate claims by pointing out to Al how much better life now was for Johnny, even though Al was home. But Al had the law on his side. Here was the son he had gone to the stockade for and he was not going to give him up. Johnny Allen went with his dad to catch the train home. On the trip, the little boy's excitement got the better of him and he got his first taste of Al Hendrix discipline as he raced up and down the train. Unaware of the true significance of this journey, he bawled back, 'I'll tell Celestine.' 'Well, you do that,' said Al, as he sat there ruminating on the fact that, while he finally had his son, the marriage that had hardly started was on the verge of collapse.

Back in Seattle, with no idea where Lucille was, Al moved into an apartment on Oregon Street and then into Dolores' place on 10th

Avenue. Through the grapevine, Lucille heard that Al was home and they got together again, living in Dolores' apartment for a year or so. 'It was like they were on honeymoon,' says Dolores, 'it was the first time they got to live together. They went out every night, they had a good time and I do believe that was the only good life that Jimmy enjoyed. He had love and affection and we were like one big happy family.'

Johnny Allen
with his father
Al Hendrix
Seattle, Winter
1945

One thing Al was not happy about – he had not been consulted over his son's name. On 11 September 1946, Johnny Allen was renamed James Marshall, the 'Marshall' being in memory of Al's brother Leon Marshall, who had died in 1932. Johnny became Jimmy (Jimi being a later artefact of his stage persona). Why did Al change the name? 'I didn't care for "Johnny",' hardly surprising given what he knew about John Williams. It is quite possible that, in naming her son Johnny Allen,

Lucille was actually honouring the two loves in her life. Later Lucille even suggested to Jimmy that Al was not his father. However, by that time, Al and Lucille had irrevocably split and such a comment has to be seen in that light.

Johnny Allen
Seattle,
mid 1946

But, back in 1947, things were looking good. Even though regular work was hard to find, Al was living off what he called his 'rocking-chair money' from the army. The Hendrixes got their own place in the Rainier Vista Housing Project, and in January 1948 another son was born, Leon Morris, who Al says 'came out of the blue'. In September, Jimmy started at the kindergarten attached to Rainier Vista School.

The honeymoon lasted on and off for about three years. Al was working at all kinds of menial low-paid jobs while at school under the provisions of the GI Bill, trying to improve on his eighth-grade education

Lucille Hendrix
Seattle, 1948

and training to be an electrician. None of this suited Lucille's hankering for the good life, so she was out at every opportunity, leaving Jimmy and Leon in her mother's care. Al was angry that Lucille was not the conventional wife and mother he expected, Lucille was going stir crazy and Mrs Jeter was bawling at Al because Lucille was running around. Money was another contentious issue. Poverty had taught Al frugality and the value of money. 'He was very tight with my sister,' says Dolores. 'I'll tell you the real reason why they split up – she would have stayed with him if he hadn't been so tight.' Amid a torrent of tears and angry words they separated. With their mother gone, Jimmy and Leon spent the summer of 1949 in Vancouver with Al's sister Pat. They stayed through the start of the school year and for a couple of months Jimmy attended one of Al's old schools in Dawson Street. Jimmy and Leon had to return to Seattle when Pat's husband Joe died and there was one last attempt at reconciliation between Al and Lucille. They were all together again for the Christmas of 1949, but the festive spirit soon palled.

It was the same old story – Lucille drinking and disappearing for days on end. On one occasion Al and the boys went looking for her. They found Lucille with another guy, but she came home with them. An almighty row erupted in the car and Lucille jumped on the brake and gas pedal at the same time. Leon says that 'The car jumped forward and then stopped short and me and Jimmy flew into the front seat. Now Mum was crying and telling us she was sorry . . . she hugged us and loved us up. That was the best love I ever got from her. Probably Jimmy too.'[2] Al and Lucille separated for the last time and the divorce came through in December 1951. Al was given custody of Jimmy and Leon and another brother Joseph born in 1949. Jimmy and Leon stayed with Al, but Joseph was soon fostered out. Several years later, Al had a traumatic meeting with Joseph in the street, when Joseph refused to acknowledge him. The birth records show two more children born to Lucille before she was divorced from Al – Cathy Ira (27 September 1950) and Pamela Marguerite (27 October 1951). In both cases, Al was cited as the father on the birth certificates. Cathy was born sixteen weeks prematurely, weighing only one pound ten ounces at birth. Incredibly she survived to be adopted.

Jimmy and Leon still saw Lucille. 'She'd come by,' says Al, 'and promise lots of things – she'd do this and she'd do that and Jimmy, he'd say to me, "Why does Mamma always tell me she's gonna do this and that when she knows she's not gonna be able to do it?" And

I said, "Well, she means well – she wants to do it." I didn't talk bad about her to him, 'bout the hard time she gave me, 'cos he *knew* that.' Al did get annoyed by these visits, however, because they were often late at night when he had work and the boys had school the next day. Lucille usually came with a bottle in one hand, hanging on the arm of her latest boyfriend. In fact, Leon says that he and Jimmy saw their mother many more times than Al ever knew about. 'We weren't supposed to see her – we'd walk over to her house. Dad used to *threaten* to send us to our mum if we were bad, but we had more fun with her. . . . She'd give us all the love she had for a few days, then she'd be gone for a few months.'

Jimmy with
his brother Leon
Seattle, 1950

Meanwhile, Jimmy was at school in Seattle. From late 1949 until his parents were divorced, he went first to the Rainier Vista School and then Horace Mann Elementary on East Cherry Street and 23rd Avenue.

The school records reveal that Jimmy started out as a regular attender, becoming more 'tardy' as music came into his life. His grades were generally below average; he actually did badly at music; his best subject was art. 'I used to paint at school. The teacher used to say, "Paint three scenes," and I'd do abstract stuff like the Martian sunset. No bull.'[3] According to Leon, Jimmy sent some car designs to Ford and won some awards.

Leschi Elementary School class photo (Jimmy is in the second row from the bottom, third from the left, with his friend James Williams to the left of him) Seattle, June 1955

Out of school, Jimmy ran in the streets like most kids. After another spell at the Rainier Vista School, Jimmy went to Leschi Elementary on 32nd Avenue and became close friends with a boy named James Williams. Together they'd play in Madrona or Seward Park, go off to Boy Scouts, help each other on their adjacent paper routes shouting out their private nicknames – Jimmy was 'Henry' (from Hendrix), James was 'potato chips' – because that's all he seemed to eat. Jimmy was often out with his dog Prince and little Leon in tow.

> He'd take me out, we'd be gone till sundown, man. Al was often none the wiser because he was out so much as well, although every so often a complaint from the neighbours about child neglect would bring the Welfare around.
> In the summer time about three in the morning, we would all go and knock on each other's windows and all start heading downtown to pick up fruit from where the fruit picking was and get doughnuts. It was like a routine in the summer. Then we'd get a bus and go pick some butter beans for an hour and get a dollar. Sometimes, we'd get down late and miss the bus. The freight yards were right there and so we'd wait until one of the trains started up and we'd ride out for free to the bean field. We'd make a few dollars until noon, then go swimming. We were vagabonds, there was always somebody to feed us – we stayed with anybody. Jimmy was my whole world – my only friend.

At weekends, Al would sometimes take Jimmy and Leon to the Atlas Cinema in the Rainier Vista Project. They saw *Prince Valiant*, a swashbuckling adventure movie, released in 1954, based on a cartoon character about a dashing Viking. Jimmy named his dog Prince after seeing the film. But his very favourite was *Flash Gordon*. Leon recalls,

> You could see the string holding up the rocket ship, but it was fantastic for us. Dad used to give us a nickel for popcorn and ten cents to get in. That's where Jimmy got his nickname Buster – everybody called him Buster [after the *Flash Gordon* actor Buster Crabbe]. We would dress up in the cape and helmet. . . . Jimmy even jumped off the roof one time – he actually thought he could fly. Jimmy would tell me all about the stars and the planets and make up stories and do drawings.

As a kid, Jimmy had a passion for science fiction; in his later songwriting, planetary references would proliferate. The nature of the universe would take on great significance for him within his own personal cosmology, his view of the world and his place in it. As a

25

youngster, Jimmy was in a sense creating a parallel universe to give expression to his already fertile and creative imagination.

Racing through the streets of Seattle's black district, wire hair stuffed inside his helmet, cape flying, he was no longer the shy, confused little boy with sad eyes who couldn't understand why his mother was here one minute and gone the next. He was on the Planet Mongo to save Earth from Ming the Merciless. And with his paints he could recreate the battle for control of Neptune or the bleak landscape of his imaginary home on Jupiter. These were *his* worlds where there were no nasty surprises.

Jimmy with his
football coach
Seattle,
29 November 1956

Back down on the ground, Jimmy found he was excellent at sports. At Leschi he was a regular for the Fighting Irish football team and when he moved on to Meany Junior High in September 1955 he played for the Capitol Hill Rough Riders. 'We had Chinese, Japanese, Puerto Ricans, Filipinos – we won all the football games.'[4]

Al tried to make it as a single parent, and all those close to the situation give him credit for seeing that when he had charge of the boys they didn't go hungry, they had shoes on their feet and they went to school. Jimmy himself knew how hard it was for Al and later told Freddie Mae, 'He might not have had all the education in the world, but he cared for us.' But life was tough; Al was out of the house for long periods of time and this severely limited the chances of Jimmy and Leon having a proper family life.

Al was forced to rely on others to care for his sons, either on a daily basis or for longer periods when there just wasn't enough money coming in or when Al felt he couldn't cope. His sister Pat came down from Vancouver to live in for a while, but Jimmy often stayed with Al's brother Frank and his wife Pearl, at Freddie Mae's house, with Dorothy Harding and with two family friends, Bill and Ernestine Benson. Pat's daughter Gracie looked after Jimmy and he also took trips to see Nora, of whom he was particularly fond: 'My grandmother is a full-blooded Indian [sic]. . . . She used to make clothes for me. And everybody used to laugh at me when I went to school, you know, the regular sob story.'[5]

The family income was depleted still further by Al's fondness for gambling. Leon notes with some bitterness, 'He'd take a chance on the machines and give us no money.' Al was sometimes out of the house longer than need be either because he was out all night playing cards, leaving Jimmy in charge, or says Leon, Al would walk to GI school, 'because he wouldn't spend the bus fare'. Leon goes on to recall a temporary housekeeper/baby-sitter called Edith who looked after him when Jimmy was in school and Al was at work; 'I used to wait for Jimmy to come home every day because this woman was really mean to me – she wouldn't feed me or anything. As soon as Jimmy left to go to school in the morning I was . . . apprehensive.'

Edith had been drafted in to keep the Welfare people off Al's back. Leon says, 'The Welfare had been comin' to our house for years – there had been complaints. They started staying longer – me and Jimmy had to go to another room, but we could get the gist – we were going to foster homes.' Leon was fostered out on a number of occasions from the age of eight. He even stayed with Lucille for a while.

The pattern seemed to be that when Al got into difficulties Jimmy usually stayed with him but Leon went, even though the family consensus is that Al was actually fonder of Leon than Jimmy. Al himself admits that he was harder on Jimmy because he was the eldest. But then again, being older Jimmy was more practically self-sufficient, so from Al's point of view would need less looking after.

Leon never understood why he was being fostered out. 'The only thing that kept me going was that Jimmy would come and visit me. . . . I went to the Wheelers – they were a rich black family and had about eight kids there. They treated us real good – I called her "Mom" and Jimmy would come over every other day at least.' That was one of seven homes in which Leon was fostered.

All this disruption and insecurity meant Jimmy grew up quiet and introverted. In his formative years, he had not been allowed to form strong emotional attachments. No sooner did he get used to somebody than they were snatched away from him. This pinball existence between family and friends, however unavoidable and however much he was loved, made him ultimately aloof and fearful of emotional commitment – an attitude sometimes rationalised by the adult Jimi as 'freedom'. At the same time he was desperate to find people to trust, whom he could talk to and who would listen to what he had to say.

Being somewhat reserved himself, Al could make the situation worse, failing to attune himself to his son's sensitivity and not really appreciating that Jimmy's tentative character was a product of his dislocated beginnings. Dorothy Harding recalls one incident when Jimmy was about three years old.

> We were over at somebody's house and Al was there with Lucille
> and the two boys. Jimmy was small and he was learning to tie his
> shoes and they'd been trying to teach him. And he was so nervous.
> Al was watching and Jimmy was trying to get it right. But he was so
> nervous that he kept getting it wrong. Al screamed at him and I said,
> 'He's just a baby, you'll make him nervous, you'll have a problem.' 'It
> ain't a problem,' said Al, 'he's just hard-headed like his mother.'

But Dorothy was right – Jimmy was painfully shy and for many years he stuttered.

The end of the union-imposed colour bar at the Boeing factory in Seattle meant Al got a job there briefly as a cleaner. He worked in a steel mill, a local market and he pumped gas. But he could never get any work as an electrician because 'of the prejudice', Leon claims. Another problem was that Al was always being called up to school, either because Leon was misbehaving or because Jimmy was being 'adventurous'. An employer would only put up with this kind of absenteeism for so long, if at all.

Al moved house in accordance with his constantly fluctuating circumstances, which explains why Jimmy went to so many different schools. Under the GI Bill, Al even had his own house for a while, but he lost it in 1956 because he couldn't pay the bills. The electricity was cut off and it was horsemeat hamburgers for dinner. This was a particularly bad time for Al and the boys. Leon was fostered out, Al and Jimmy moved into a rooming house owned by a Mrs Mackay and then into what has been described as a 'shack' on Yesler Way. During that year, Jimmy left Meany Junior High on 20 February, started at Washington Junior High on Columbian Way three days later, left Washington in the June and was back at Meany for the start of the fall term in September.

Meany Junior High School
Seattle, April 1958

After leaving Al, Lucille had resumed life with her drinking friends and bore a fifth child, Alfred. She had another run-in with John Williams. Dorothy and Lucille's mother Clarice had managed to get Williams convicted under the Mann Act for taking Lucille across state lines without authority when she was still a minor. Williams had been sentenced to five years, but swore revenge on Lucille's family. Dolores takes up the story.

He was away a long time and I forgot about it. Then one day, I was on the way to the store and I saw this Cadillac and I wondered who it was. . . . I had this funny feeling. Everybody knew about Williams' threat to get us and the word was out that he was going to be released. Lucille was scared to death. We knew he would come looking for Lucille at Mom's house, so she stayed across the street at Al Longacres'. He rented the back of this duplex. Lucille said, 'What we gonna do if he comes?' Al Longacres said not to worry and produced a gun.

Dolores was right about the Cadillac.

John Williams sent this friend up to my [Dolores'] house and rang the bell.
   'What do you want?'
   'We're looking for Dolores. Do you know her?'
   'No, I don't.'
   'Don't she live here?'
   'No, I don't think so. She may have done years ago.'
   'Do you know Lucille?'
   'No, I don't, but let me call my husband and—'
   'Oh, no, no, that's okay. I just wondered.'
   He went away, but they turned the car around, went right back up the street and straight over to Longacres' house. They knew. Lucille told me later they knocked on the door and she was holding Joe and Pammy hoping they wouldn't cry otherwise that was it. They knocked on Al Longacres' door.
   'A friend of Lucille's wants to see her in the car.'
   'She's not here.'
   Then John came running up shouting, 'I know she's here, I know she's here, and we're gonna take her back to Kansas City. [On release Williams had been ordered to leave the State of Washington.]
   'Over my dead body.'
   Al produced the gun.
   They were shocked and backed away. They got into their car, drove off and we never heard of them again.

On 23 December 1957, Lucille married a longshoreman, Bill Mitchell. She dropped out of the life of the Hendrix family, but one member, who does not wish to be named, says she last saw Lucille 'sitting on the corner of 3rd and Yesler, eating some Jello out of them little cartons that you buy from the store, with three kids – the youngest would have been about three years old.'

Lucille spent periods of time in hospital because of her frail constitution and, according to Dorothy, 'On account of the different treatments she'd got from different people. . . . Jimmy saw her in hospital. I think he sneaked down there to see her, he didn't want his dad to know it. He told me he'd go down there and take her cards he'd made at school.'

During 1957, Lucille was in hospital again. This time, Al's sister Pat, on a visit from Vancouver, took Jimmy to see his mother. He said little but just stared. Pat feared that Lucille would look very ill, but she actually appeared in good spirits with her hair nicely cut. It was the last time Jimmy saw his mother. Lucille was discharged, but never took care of herself – even though she already had cirrhosis of the liver, she carried on drinking. On 2 February 1958, the state of her liver caused her spleen to rupture. She haemorrhaged and died.

There are conflicting stories about the funeral. Al says he couldn't go because he didn't have a car (which in truth sounds rather lame), but that Jimmy and Leon could have gone if they had wanted to. They certainly did ask him about going, but others (including Leon) say that Al refused permission. In fairness, Al had every reason not to want to go himself, particularly as Lucille's husband and the Jeter family would all be there. But anyone from that group or Pat (who also went) would have been only too glad to take Jimmy, if not Leon, who was only ten years old at the time. In any case, Jimmy could have gone by himself – he was already fifteen years old. The fact that he didn't lends weight to the story that Al said no, because Jimmy always respected his father's authority and would not have gone against his wishes. Jimmy was never one to bear a grudge, but Dorothy Harding says tersely, 'Jimmy never got over that.' She said to Al, 'What you throw into the lives of your children will come back in your face.'

Jimmy was devastated by his mother's death, but he internalised the grief, and in that he was very like Al. The message of living with his father was that most things were best left unsaid. One night in August 1967, during a concert at the Saville Theatre in London, he dedicated 'The Wind Cries Mary' to her; occasionally he mentioned her in an interview. 'I remember when I was only four and I wet my pants and I stayed out in the rain for hours so I would get wet all over and my mum wouldn't know. She knew though.'[6] But his feelings were to find true expression in the lyrics of his songs and it would be no exaggeration to say that she was the major poetic inspiration of his life.

She came to him in dreams. After one, he wrote his most poignant ballad, 'Angel'. The images of another he recounted in an interview with journalist Meatball Fulton in December 1967:

My mother was bein' carried away on this camel. And there was a
big caravan, she's sayin', 'Well, I'm gonna see you now,' and she's
goin' under these trees, and you could see the shade, you know, the

leaf patterns across her face when she was goin' under. . . . You know
the sun shines through a tree and if you go under the shadow of a tree
. . . shadows go across her face . . . green and yellow. . . . She's sayin',
'Well, I won't be seein' you too much anymore, you know. I'll see you.'
And then about two years after that she dies, you know. And I said,
'Yeah, but where are you goin'?' and all that, you know. I remember
that. I will always remember that. I never did forget . . . there are
some dreams you never forget.[7]

Lucille represented a sense of danger, excitement and fun, and
there was always a side of the adult Jimmy that wanted to be
around dangerous outgoing women. Lucille was also a free spirit,
unencumbered by convention or social expectation, 'doing her own
thing' before the phrase became fashionable, albeit in the company
of men who usually took advantage of her and at the expense of her
own children. But she was Jimmy's mother, that's all he knew or cared
about. He was grateful for any love she could give him. Lucille became
a powerful legend in his life, full of mystery and fantasy.

Jimmy had heard many stories of his wandering ancestry – about life
on the road in Nora's vaudeville troupe, about the nomadic existence
of the Indian – lives where things were done and said and then left
behind. Just around that top bend there were new dreams or ambitions
to realise, choices to make down by the crossroads. It could be a journey
to nowhere, the search for the lost chord that is never found, but the
gypsy spirit had carried through three generations and wasn't going
to stop at Jimmy. His wanderlust was closely linked to his obsession
with getting away from Seattle, the city which came to symbolise the
uncertainties and insecurities of his childhood. He rarely spoke about
his childhood to anyone – this was Jimi at his most revealing: 'I ran
away from home a couple of times because I was so miserable. When
my dad found out I'd gone, he was pretty mad with worry.'[8] 'I stayed
mostly at my aunt's and grandmother's. There were family troubles
between my mother and my father. My brother and I used to go to
different homes because Dad and Mother used to break up all the time.'[9]
Those close to Jimmy knew that his desire to get away was
deep-seated. It was not a child-like reaction to being told off or
the child who wraps his possessions in a handkerchief, makes a big
display of leaving only to return for tea. People like Dorothy Harding
knew that, when the time was right, Jimmy would be gone for good.
He was over at her house – he would have been about eight years

old, just as his parents' marriage was breaking apart for the last time. Dorothy was baby-sitting for Al and Lucille and they were late.

The kids and I and Jimmy were sitting on the porch – we sang songs and popped some popcorn. But it was getting late and I said, 'Jimmy, I'm going inside to give the kids a bath and put them to bed, but I'll be right back.' So I did all that, the kids said their prayers and went to bed. I came back out and Jimmy was crying. It shocked me so bad. I put my arm around him and I said, 'What's the matter, baby?' And he was sniffin' and I said, 'What's wrong? Tell Aunty Dorothy.'
    'Aunty Dorothy (sniff), when I get big I'm going far, far away. And I'm never comin' back. Never.'
    I just didn't know what to say. I hugged him and tears were running down my cheek, and I said, 'Let's sing a song, a church song,' and I told him about the Scriptures and said to him that 'Things happen in your life that you don't like – but you know what? Children can be stronger spiritually than their parents and one day you're going to reach down and help your parents up.' He looked up at me and said, 'Really?' I said, 'Yeah – you're really smart and you've got a good heart.'

Jimmy was fifteen years old when his mother died. Before the year was out, his passport away from the bad memories was at hand. That year, he got his first proper guitar.

Three *Spanish Castle Magic*

Music was always an integral part of Jimmy's childhood, something he absorbed into his subconscious well before he made tentative steps towards flexing his own musical imagination.

Visits to Nora in Vancouver would be punctuated by reminiscences of her time in the chorus line and by Indian tales of wonder where music and dance played such an important part in the magic and ritual.

Music meant good times – the happy days when his parents were together, looking after him and brother Leon during the day and dancing at night. Al and Lucille were serious dancers; little routines might be tried out at home to the sound of Al's record collection. There were the rent parties of the project housing estates and red-light-district apartments where Jimmy spent so much of his early childhood. The sound of Duke Ellington and Count Basie and the R&B stomp of Louis Jordan, Joe Turner or Roy Milton would fold back through the night air as people laughed and drank and danced till the sun rose. Music was fun.

Even music with a message was fun – the music he heard in the black Pentecostal Church that was central to the lives of those Jimmy regarded as family. He often sang hymns with Clarice and his aunt Dorothy at the Church of God and Christ on 23rd and Madison. As a boy Jimmy was once thrown out of church for wearing a suit with tennis shoes, which soured his personal experience of organised religion. But he couldn't help but notice, as he once remarked to Freddie Mae, that the people in the church seemed to be having such a good time. And that was the key to Pentecostalism, a joyous celebration of the Lord, in stark contrast to the formality of white church-going or the austerity of black Baptist fundamentalism. The Pentecostalists had holy dancing and music in their church and sang songs which very much reflected the everyday experiences of the poorer working-class blacks who mostly made up the congregation. The singers of the Sanctified churches including the Pentecostalists had no moral problem with using instruments normally associated with secular music nor having secular musicians playing on their records. Jug-band sounds, harmonica, guitar and tambourines all had their place. In singing about the black experience on Earth, the Pentecostal singers were riding in dangerous tandem with the bluesmen, the purveyors of the devil's music, but this did not seem to worry them half as much as it worried the Baptists and the Methodists. As Charles Keil notes in his classic study *Urban Blues*, 'The sacred music of lower-class Negro churches does not stay put. . . . even from week to week some new songs may be added and old songs rearranged for maximum impact,' and he wonders whether black church music is 'that much more conservative than secular forms'.[1]

But, for Jimmy, looking and listening were not enough – he wanted to get involved. Even as an eight-year-old, there were sounds locked up in his head with no means of escape, because there was no money to buy an instrument. This was the lot of many black kids aspiring to be musicians; Jimmy took a time-honoured route and played out his fantasies with a broom.

The broom played an important part in the history of blues guitar. 'Many Mississippi blues singers began to play music with a homemade instrument known by some as a "one-strand on the wall". Children who could not afford a guitar took a wire from the handle of a broom and stretched it on the wall of their home. A hard object such as a stone raised and stretched the wire at each end to its proper tone, and as one hand plucked the beat, the other slid a bottle along the surface to change the tone.' That's how Elmore James, king of the bottleneck guitar, started out and so did B.B. King:

> I guess that was kind of a normal thing for the average kid to do because instruments weren't very plentiful in the area where I grew up. When we felt a need for music, we'd put the wire up. We would usually nail it up on the back porch. Take a broom wire.
> They had a kind of straight wire wrapped around that straw that would keep this broom together. So we'd find an old broom or a new one if we could get it without anybody catching us. You'd take that wire off of it and you'd nail that on a board or on the back porch.[2]

Jimmy, however, never progressed to getting sound out of his broom. When Al went to work, 'I used to have him clean up the bedroom while I was gone. When I came home, I'd find broom straws at the foot of the bed. I'd say, "Didn't you sweep the floor?" "Oh, yeah," he'd say. But he'd be sitting at the foot there, strumming the broom like he was playin' guitar.' Leon recalls some fraught scenes: 'Dad, he'd come in yellin' and screamin', veins poppin' out of his forehead, "brooms cost money!! I told you about them broom things on the floor. Tie that broom back together again!" Jimmy did as he was told that time, but he kept right on singing the notes and pretending to play. He'd walk down the street with a broom, even take it to school. Everyone thought he was crazy.'

When Jimmy was at Horace Mann Elementary in the early fifties, a social worker tried to get him a guitar paid for out of the school funds for needy children. She could see Jimmy was so obsessed with playing that *not* to have a guitar was actually damaging him psychologically. After about a year of watching him hold on to that broom all day, she talked to the school about providing Jimmy with a guitar to assist his development. The school authorities were less than convinced that Jimmy was in psychological need of a guitar. So he experimented with sound using another old trick of would-be musicians everywhere. He cut a hole in a cigar box, stretched a piece of elastic across the 'soundbox' and attached something resembling a neck to one end. From that he graduated to an old ukulele with one string found by Al when he was clearing out somebody's garage.

Jimmy worked out a number of songs on his ukulele, like Henry Mancini's 'Peter Gunn', but perhaps one of the most influential songs of the period for Jimmy and many other budding guitarists was a novelty song with a calypso lilt, 'Love Is Strange' by Mickey and Sylvia. The song was a top-twenty hit in 1956 on RCA's Groove Label, an attempt by Elvis's record company (along with their 'X' label) to infiltrate the world of the independents. But 'Love Is Strange' was their only major hit and the experiment collapsed in 1960. Mickey was Mickey 'Guitar' Baker, a blues player and one of Atlantic Records' top session musicians. Sylvia was Sylvia Vanderpool, who later founded All-Platinum and Sugar Hill Records. 'Love Is Strange' was important for a number of reasons. First, Sylvia's vocal phrasing, particularly on words like 'ba-bee', was picked up by Buddy Holly (another big favourite of Jimmy's at the time) and incorporated into his own distinctive vocal style. Second, Mickey Baker's solo on the song was probably the first blues guitar solo most white teenagers would have heard. In that respect, because of Al's record collection, Jimmy would have been one jump ahead and less hampered than he might have been by the absence of black radio

36

in Seattle until 1958. Of course, there was no chance of hearing Muddy Waters or T-Bone Walker on any white radio station. The song was also a prime example of using the guitar to simulate the dialogue between a man and a woman. Having sung as a duo all through the song, towards the end, Sylvia's call is suddenly answered by the ringing voice of Mickey's guitar. Baker's single-string dry-toned solo enthralled Jimmy. 'After he heard that,' says Leon, 'he really started to look for some outlet, playing songs and figuring out things on one string.'

Jimmy was a great Elvis fan – he particularly liked 'Love Me Tender' and, along with 15,000 other loyal fans, saw Elvis at the Sicks Stadium in Seattle on 1 September 1957. Elvis drove on to the stage in a Cadillac, walked to the mike and at the end asked everybody to get on their feet for the national anthem. Once they were up, he grabbed his guitar, switched into gear and growled on the beat, 'You ain't nothin' but a hound dog . . . ' The crowd went wild, Jimmy clapping and foot-stomping in time to the music. Leon recounts meeting another giant of rock 'n' roll that year – Little Richard. Nineteen-fifty-seven was the year Richard Penniman decided that his ability to bring an audience to its feet and stir the power of collective emotion should be used in the service of the Lord. He quit the music business halfway through a tour of Australia and headed back to the States, to Seattle to see his mother and take up a new career as a Baptist preacher. 'One day there was this big Cadillac parked out in front of the house,' says Leon. 'Jimmy and I ran out and there was Little Richard himself sitting in the back seat. He had one of those doowop rags around his head and he had stopped just to see us! His mother lived around the corner and she knew how crazy about music we were. . . . We all went to the same church then, Goodwill Baptist at 14th and Spring.'[3]

Getting the feel for live music and picking away on one string was okay as far as it went, but if Jimmy was ever to learn properly he was going to need a 'real' guitar. A card-playing friend of Al's had an acoustic guitar. While they were engrossed in their game, Jimmy would sneak the guitar out on to the porch to see what he could do with it. 'I didn't know I would have to put the strings round the other way because I was left-handed, but it just didn't feel right. I can remember thinking to myself, "There's something wrong here." One night my dad's friend was stoned and he sold me his guitar for five dollars.'[4] But Jimmy didn't have five dollars so it was down to Al, who, claims Leon, was less than willing to pay up. 'My aunt Ernestine *made* him – actually cussed him out. "Al Hendrix – you're gonna buy this guitar for five dollars." ' Al tells it differently: 'Jimmy told me about it and I said "Okay" and gave him the money. He strummed away on that, working away all the time, any spare time he had.' Al tried to get Jimmy to play right-handed, but Jimmy was a natural left-hander and once Al was out of sight Jimmy flipped back to playing the way he felt comfortable once he'd sorted those strings out. 'I changed the strings around, but it was way out of tune when I'd finished. I didn't know a thing about tuning so I went down to the store and ran my fingers across the strings on a guitar they had there. After that I was able to tune my own.'[5] In his early teens, Jimmy had been fooling around with a bass and some drums belonging to friends. 'But when I was fifteen, I decided the guitar was the instrument for me,'[6] and he rapidly became highly proficient. His aunt Dorothy recalls, 'When I lived up on 25th and Raye, he came over to visit and he was sittin' there with Roberta, my oldest daughter, and talkin' and I remember him telling her that he wanted to be a musician. That was the first time I heard this.'

Jimmy absorbed music from wherever he could find it – records, radio, he even sat at the feet of an old-time bluesman who played on the porch a few blocks from Jimmy's place. The old guy picked out country blues songs – a favourite artist was Big Bill Broonzy. Like Jimmy, Broonzy's first instrument was fashioned from a cigar box – a fiddle on which he played country songs where he grew up in Arkansas. Not until he was nearly thirty years old did he take up the blues when he moved to Chicago in 1920 and learnt guitar. He played rags, dance songs, country reels and even led a five-piece band with horns. For his slow, melodic blues numbers, he was often accompanied on piano by Black Bob. Jimmy always had a soft spot for ballads and some of his finest moments as a songwriter came from a love of romanticism.

Up to now, Jimmy had been playing on his own, patiently learning, experimenting, building a rapport with the instrument. Jimmy and his guitar became inseparable; it became a part of him, an extension of his mind and body, the gateway to his soul. You could even say the guitar was him, defined who he was, gave him the identity and self-esteem he lacked through all the dislocations and rejections in his life. The guitar was to be his place in the world, his voice. What he wanted now was some power, to throw that voice far and wide.

He had always been fascinated by electronics. He once took Al's radio to bits. 'Why did you do that? Why did you do that?' 'Just to see how it works, Dad.' But he desperately wanted an electric guitar. 'First I had to prove that I could play a couple of songs on a guitar of a friend, but I did get that thing still.'[7] Al was persuaded to take Jimmy down to Myers Music Store on 1st Avenue and buy him a white Supro Ozark guitar. At the same time, Al bought himself a C Melody saxophone so he could play along with Jimmy. After years of never really understanding Jimmy, he had finally found some point of contact. He could see that his son was as serious about his music as Al had been about dancing. They played duets after a fashion, but Al soon realised that Jimmy would be far better on guitar than he ever would be on saxophone. Jimmy still had a problem – what use was an electric guitar with no amplifier? An answer soon presented itself and it gave Jimmy his first opportunity to play in public for the music lovers of Seattle.

There is a long tradition in America that associates important cities in the history of popular music with the underworld; New Orleans, New York, Chicago and Kansas City were 'centres of excellence' for jazz and blues, where the music provided the entertainment for gamblers, hookers and their clients and the patrons of speakeasies, bars and saloons. Seattle was founded on the rough no-compromise frontier world of logging. The red-light district named 'Down on the Sawdust' was up and running almost as the first trees fell. And while hardly in the same class as New York or New Orleans, Seattle had a reputation as a tough spot to play because of the competition.

In March 1948, eighteen-year-old Ray Charles arrived in Seattle from Florida. 'It was cool when I got to Seattle. . . . The town was wide open. And the entertainment business was in something of a boom. Competition was fierce. Many cats had just left the armed-forces bands. . . . There were lots of musicians roaming the streets who'd blow your ass off the stand if you gave them half the chance.'[8] Among his many jobs, Charles played piano in Bumps Blackwell's band which also featured Quincy Jones on trumpet. Blackwell went on to produce Little Richard while Quincy Jones became one of the most prolific and successful figures in contemporary pop. His credits include a slew of award-winning film scores and production of Michael Jackson's *Thriller*.

Through the fifties, the best music in Seattle went on after hours in clubs like the Rocking Chair, the Esquire and the Palomar Theatre. The Washington Social Club played host to the blues acts like Muddy Waters and B.B. King, which tended to attract the over-thirties crowd. The younger kids were not really interested in the blues. They went to see the hot R&B artists like Little Willie John and Hank Ballard, both discovered by Johnny Otis and by now recording stars with King Records. Clyde McPhatter was another big favourite. These acts played Birdland (among others) supported by the most popular of the local bands: the Wailers, the Dave Lewis Combo, the Checkers, the Frantics, the Playboys and Jimmy Hannah and the Dynamics, all playing the raucous mixture of blues, jazz and rock which typified the 'North-west Sound'.

The clubs were largely integrated, but there were two musicians' unions for blacks and whites and the white bands tended to play north of Denny Street. The black clubs Jimmy frequented were mainly situated in the Central District in an area bounded by Union Street, Jackson Street and Madison Street. An important exception was the Spanish Castle, traditionally a roadhouse hosting big-band jazz, out near the airport on Highway 99 and immortalised by the Jimi Hendrix Experience on their second album *Axis: Bold As Love* in 'Spanish Castle Magic'.

James Thomas lived on 21st Avenue. One day during the school summer vacation of 1959, James and his nephew Perry were practising on guitar and piano when they were interrupted by a bunch of teenagers who wanted to join in. They were James Woodberry, who sang and played piano; two sax players, Webb Lofton and Walter Harris; a guitar player, Ulysses Heath Jr, and a rather quiet kid who played bass on a six-string guitar – Jimmy Hendrix. The boys played in James' house and he was impressed; he said they should consider forming a group. They said they already had it, the Rocking Kings, and went off to bring back their drummer, Lester Exkano. Jimmy had already played some local gigs with the band, although his first one was out of Seattle in a small town called Kent at the National Guard Armory on 36th Avenue. 'We earned thirty-five cents apiece. . . . In those days I just liked rock 'n' roll I guess. We used to play stuff by people like the Coasters.'[9] What they needed now was a manager to get them decent playing gigs and somewhere to practise regularly. James Thomas took them on, but only after checking things out with the respective parents. Jimmy was right when he told James that he doubted if his dad would be happy about him playing in public and neglecting his school work. However, Al consented to let Jimmy have a go and the first time Jimmy went round to formal rehearsals at James Thomas' house was probably the happiest day of his life so far.

The best part of any day for Jimmy was rehearsing with the Rocking Kings. The first gig arranged by James Thomas was a party on 21st

Avenue followed by a dance at the Polish Hall on 18th Street which paid $65. Both gigs were a huge success, everybody went wild to the sounds of the Coasters, 'Searchin' and 'Yakety Yak'. Playing these gigs gave Jimmy some insights into the nature of performance. He continued his education in the clubs watching how musicians whip up audiences, get them screaming, shouting and stomping with carefully orchestrated peaks in the show just like he'd seen the Pentecostal preachers do in church on Sunday. The feeling was exactly the same, only the gods were different. Jimmy saw a ranting rock 'n' roll tenor-sax player called Big Jay McNeely, who would play sax lying on his back while his band went through a dance routine wearing shirts that glowed in the dark. McNeely had a major R&B hit in 1959, 'There Is Something On Your Mind'. The sax players were the guitar heroes of their day and McNeely's act was a blueprint for the game plan that Jimmy himself would use later on. Jimmy was also impressed by the power of the horn itself, its range, the way it cut through the rhythm section, soaring and swooping to the climax of the song, and he incorporated horn sounds into the matrix of his own style and technique.

During the rehearsals with the Rocking Kings, he learnt some basic technique from Ulysses Heath and they would sit trading ideas and licks. Every day, Jimmy would turn up at James Thomas' house to practise. There he had access to an amplifier and that for Jimmy was a revelation. Now he could experiment, not only with the licks and phrases and rhythms that were the guitarist's stock-in-trade, but with the very fabric of sound itself.

While Jimmy took much from the horn players that he saw, his reverence was reserved for the blues guitarists, and in that he was very different from his contemporaries. 'The first guitarist I was aware of was Muddy Waters. I heard one of his old records when I was a little boy and it scared me to death.'[10] But he was a keen disciple of a range of blues-guitar styles including B.B. King, Jimmy Reed, Elmore James and John Lee Hooker. He was also a big fan of boogie pianist Roscoe Gordon and singer Bobby 'Blue' Bland.

Jimmy also listened and learnt from guitarists who were living and working locally, in particular Guitar Shorty, who hailed originally from Los Angeles, but moved north and married a Seattle girl. He played West Coast blues in the style of Lowell Fulson and like most blues guitarists would put on an exhibition of guitar gymnastics to excite the audience.

In turn Jimmy was more than ready to show a beginner a few

licks. Benorce Blackmon went to school with Leon and was himself trying to learn guitar.

> When I started really to play guitar, Leon used to tell me all the time, 'My brother can beat you playing.' . . . I remember seeing Jimmy around, but I didn't know who he was. . . . he was on his bicycle with all these fox-tails and all these flashes and mirrors on it. . . . when he came by he was dressed in black. . . . he was a funny cat. . . . back in those days he was always kind of stand-offish, you know, you could never get really too close to him. . . . I'm sitting on my mother's front porch and here comes this guy up the hill. He started playing my guitar and I said, 'Hey, man, show me that,' and he just started to show me things . . . and I found out who he was and he was real nice, always showing you stuff. . . . he was always showing everybody his stuff. Jimmy was always playing. . . . my mother used to drive me away from the porch some time 'cos he would just pop up and come to play. . . . he'd just be standing on the porch waiting to play.

Benorce also knew other guitarists around town like Pernell Alexander and Sammy Drain. 'Sammy and Jimmy played so much together. I used to go by Sammy's house and we would stand outside and they used to practise all the time. . . . they developed a style . . . not that feedback stuff, the pretty stuff. . . . it was all original. . . . when you heard Sammy play, man, you'd hear Jimmy.'

All in all, Jimmy was like a musical sponge. He absorbed ideas about playing from any source available to him. His own visions were just beginning to take shape, but he was not so arrogant as to presume he had learnt it all, even though he was streets ahead of the other guys. On the contrary, right throughout his life, he could hear another guitarist and, no matter how bad or derivative that player, Jimmy would hear something that he could be complimentary about and possibly utilise himself.

Over the weeks and months through 1959 and into 1960, the Rocking Kings continued to win acclaim wherever they played; in 1960, they came second in the All State Band of the Year contest. Their biggest break came when they got a residency at Birdland doing the teenage dance nights on Wednesdays, Thursdays and Sundays. Here Jimmy suffered his first setback in the music business. One night, he left his guitar on the stand and somebody stole it. There had been trouble with Al about Jimmy playing three nights a week and now Jimmy would have to tell his father that, through his own carelessness, the guitar Al had bought him was gone. Al recalls, 'He didn't tell me about it for a long time. He said he left it over at James Thomas'. I dropped him over there and said to bring his equipment home and that's when he told me he'd got it stolen. So I says, "You're gonna have to do without a guitar for a while." '

Poor Jimmy didn't know what to do – it was like losing an arm for him not to have a guitar and he cut a very sad figure both in school and out. Mary Hendrix, wife of Al's brother Frank, took pity on him and bought him a new guitar down at Myers' store. Al was not pleased: 'He came home with the guitar and I asked where he got it and he told me that Mary had told him she could get it on her credit down there at Myers'. I told him to take it right back down there because I said if I can't get you one, you're not gonna have one.' Eventually Al relented and Jimmy got another guitar, a white Danelectro which he painted red.

Jimmy didn't confine his playing to the Rocking Kings; he was in and out of bands all over Seattle including the Velvetones. Leon recalls, 'Jimmy would walk right across town if somebody said he could probably play there.' Although Jimmy was never boastful about his playing prowess, his obvious talent left some resentment and jealousy in its wake. Nor could Jimmy stomach doing the same old rock 'n' roll riffs with orchestrated dance steps night after night. He knew all that stuff inside out; he wanted to play different and look different. Leon would often call in when Jimmy was practising with a band, 'but they were really starting to get on Jimmy's nerves, because he was getting freaky – he'd tie feathers on his guitar and the others would object. Then he started painting it. They started not letting Jimmy practise. But everyone knew he was the best even then and he was soon back. People started coming down to see what was going on – the rehearsals turned into parties.'

When he wasn't playing with the Rocking Kings, he would hang around in the clubs, hoping for a chance to play. During the time when Jimmy was without a guitar after it had been stolen, he got a chance one night to do the last song with a band, but the guitarist said, 'I'm not going to let him play guitar because he's left-handed.' 'No problem,' said Jimmy. The guy stood to one side smirking, the band started an R&B song and Jimmy started playing brilliantly right-handed; he didn't even turn the guitar upside down. Sometimes they would give Jimmy a half-bar lead solo and Jimmy would take off and then apologise, 'Sorry, I just had to do that.'

If the beginnings of Jimmy's showmanship annoyed some people, James Thomas urged him to develop it. The Rocking Kings played their biggest gig to over 2000 people at an outdoor picnic at Cottage Lake. This event was possibly the first time that Jimmy started his guitar gymnastics in public, playing behind his head and between his legs, which received a very enthusiastic response from the large crowd.

When as Jimi Hendrix he played the Monterey Festival in 1967, some (white) critics objected to the antics, complaining that Jimmy was 'Uncle Tomming' for the white audience. This showed complete ignorance of the tradition of showmanship in the blues. It was done for effect, to grab attention especially for outdoor gigs like the one Jimmy played at, where there would be many distractions for the audience. An element of showmanship was expected by black audiences. If you just stood there like a dummy, they booed you off. Charlie Patton was one of the greatest and most influential of all the early Mississippi singers. His half-brother Sam Chatmon recalled, 'Charlie Patton was a clowning man with a guitar. He'd be in there putting his guitar all between his legs, carry it behind his head, lay down on the floor, and never stopped picking!'[11]

Equally influential was Tommy Johnson, whose performances 'were spectacularly acrobatic. He'd kick the guitar, flip it, turn it back of his head and be playin' it,' remembers Houston Stackhouse, a bluesman who played with Johnson in the late twenties. 'Then he'd get straddled over it like he was ridin' a mule, pick it that way. All that kind of rot. Oh, he'd tear it up, man. People loved to see that.'[12]

These bravura performances on guitar in the twenties were later to be popularised in particular by T-Bone Walker and by the lesser-known Johnny Jenkins, star guitarist in the Pinetoppers, the band which gave Otis Redding his first break down in Macon, Georgia in the late fifties. Like Jimmy, Jenkins was light-skinned and 'Hollywood Handsome'. Speedo Sims, Otis's road manager, recalls one steamy night in the Deep South. 'We played this place and the guitarist, the way he did his act, he fell on the floor just playing his guitar and looking up and this white girl just literally walked over and stood over him with her legs apart and she's going . . . you know . . . all that stuff.'[13] And this was a hall used by the Klan!

Getting to gigs with the Rocking Kings could be a hit-and-miss affair. They had a chance to tour British Columbia and Alaska, but they never made it across the border because their VW bus borrowed from James Thomas' sister broke down. The bus was towed to Bellingham, where they played in the street for the Western Washington College because the college hall was too small. The police moved them on, but they did get to play inside for the college kids – all for just the cab fare back to Seattle and a free meal. Disenchantment set in and the band split, leaving a nucleus of James Thomas, Webb Lofton on sax, Lester the drummer and Jimmy. James took over the vocals and added his nephew Perry on piano and Robert Green on bass. The band was renamed Thomas and the Tomcats and gave Jimmy his first chance to play regular guitar instead of being stuck playing the bass parts with only occasional lead spots. They picked up where the Rocking Kings left off, rehearsing and playing all over Washington State.

As far as money was concerned, Jimmy was definitely his father's son. When he was much younger Jimmy and Leon 'went to the Parade and Dad gave us a specific amount of money and we were supposed to bring a dime home, "one bar of candy and one ride". This white kid was talking to Jimmy and the guy talked Jimmy into trading the dime for the nickel because it was bigger. When we got home, my dad really bawled him out about it.' These kinds of lessons Jimmy did not forget – and the money he was (or wasn't) getting in the early bands he played in always bugged him.

The Tomcats had a gig at Moses Lake airforce base about 200 miles from Seattle. The deal was $35 plus travel costs. They travelled in two cars, but one broke down and the repairs came to more than had been allowed for travel. All the band chipped in the extra except Jimmy, who said it wasn't his responsibility and that he needed all his money to get home. With that he got out of the car and started to walk the five miles to the next town in the freezing cold carrying his guitar and amplifier. The rest let him walk for a bit and then hauled him back in. The band played the Annual Seattle Picnic and Fair. This time Jimmy was charged $5 for the hire of a red jacket as part of the stage uniform and he made nothing out of the gig. Jimmy complained bitterly to Al, who just told him to put it down to experience. Jimmy had just learnt the first rule of the music business – the musicians get paid last and least.

Meanwhile Jimmy had been enrolled in Garfield High School on 23rd Avenue, not far from James Thomas' house. He continued to excel at art, but as far as Jimmy was concerned school was a thing of the past. All he wanted to do was to play music. He dropped out at the end of October 1960 without graduating. The official reason given for his departure was 'work referral and age'. Jimmy always told a different story: 'They said I used to be late all the time, but I was getting As and Bs. The real reason is that I had a girl

45

friend in art classes and we used to hold hands all the time. The art teacher didn't dig that at all. She was very prejudiced. She said, "Mr Hendrix, I'll see you in the cloakroom in three seconds, please." In the cloakroom she said, "What do you mean talking to that white woman like that?" I said, "What, are you jealous?" She started crying and I got thrown out.'[14]

Jimmy's school attainment records clearly show he was not getting high marks, although Leon maintains, 'He probably could have got straight As at school, but he wasn't into that.' Jimmy had never been able to settle at school because of his constant changes of address – at least ten different locations in as many years: playing music killed off any lingering enthusiasm he might have had for school. We will never know if Jimmy could have been a high academic achiever, but undoubtedly he had an immense innate intelligence best expressed by his brother Leon, who says that Jimmy 'knew all the answers. Never read a book.'

Once Jimmy had dropped out of Garfield High School, he needed work, but as Al remarks, 'That was before the civil rights thing and it was hard for blacks to get into certain jobs.' By that time, Al had finally found his niche as a landscape gardener. He was turning work down and needed a labourer. After failing to find a regular job, Jimmy eventually joined his father. But this didn't work out too well. Jimmy hated doing manual work and hated having to take orders. He actually thought Al was exploiting him. 'I had to carry stones and cement all day and he pocketed the money. . . . I ran away after a blazing row with my dad. He hit me on the face and I ran away.'[15]

Al did work for a music teacher, Melody Jones. Jimmy told her he was going to be a musician. She told him about her days as a piano player in the mob-owned clubs of New York, like the Cotton Club, and through their conversations he learnt much about the history of jazz. Sitting in her immaculate garden, this cheerful old lady, who still plays piano in Seattle, remembers Jimmy as a 'nice young boy, nice manners, quiet, never spoke loudly'. Not quiet enough for Al, however, who told him off for too much talking and not enough digging.

Jimmy was beginning to assert his independence. He never lost his respect for Al, but was not prepared to accept his word as the law. He began to develop a key aspect to his character crucial to any understanding of his music – a belief in the fundamental virtue of freedom of action. His personal philosophy was mirrored in the whole ethos of the sixties – 'Do your own thing', or as Aleister Crowley wrote, 'Do what you will, shall be the whole of the law.' It was his talent as a musician that gave Jimmy a measure of self-confidence rarely found in somebody with his kind of disrupted background, although as with many creative artists he was never satisfied with what he achieved. But music wasn't the only source of this self-confidence. If Lesson One in the music business for Jimmy was 'Getting paid is a hassle,' Lesson Two was 'Getting laid isn't.' Even before he took up guitar, Jimmy was never short of girlfriends. His father helped keep them at bay: 'The girls would come by on Sunday to go to church or something with him. He'd ask me who was at the door and I'd say, "Oh, some little girl wants ya. . . ." He'd say, "Oh, don't tell her I'm here." "Jees, Jimmy, she looks awful good to me." ' Once he started playing around town, he quickly built up his own entourage of female fans dazzled by his good looks and 'little-boy lost' charm.

On New Year's Eve 1959, Jimmy had been sitting in his room with his old schoolfriend James Williams. When they were still at Leschi School in 1954, they had rehearsed a song together to sing at a school concert. Now, on this bitterly cold December evening, they sat together again making music.

James was singing 'Memories Are Made of This', with Jimmy doing the accompanying vocal. Later, Jimmy was to become very self-conscious about his singing voice. But Leon is adamant when he says that at that time 'He didn't mind singing out of tune and lookin' you straight in the eye.' James was crooning away and Jimmy stopped to make a phone call. He was phoning Betty Jean Morgan, his then steady girlfriend. The call was to make up for not taking her out as he didn't have enough money. Jimmy put his hand over the receiver and beckoned James over to listen to the conversation. ' "Now what are you going to give me to eat when I come over? . . . Go on, tell me everything. . . . some eggs soft boiled, oysters and clams, raw on the shell, lots of butter and toast." James was confused, Jimmy nearly convulsed with laughter. . . . He hung up and James asked what that was all about. "That's what a woman gives a man for his sex," Jimmy replied, 'that's love food that builds up the potency." '[16] Jimmy was growing up and he had largely left his best friend behind. After their evening together, Jimmy and James walked to the Kingfish Café. Jimmy borrowed some money for food and James left him sitting at the counter. They never saw each other again.

Jimmy knew all about women and all about song, but wine had just about passed him by. During his time with the Rocking Kings and the Tomcats, he was never known to smoke or drink. During the intermissions the other guys would sneak off for a little taste of this and that, but Jimmy invariably stayed behind and practised on his guitar for the second set. Once he was talked into trying a little wine and spent the rest of the evening bouncing off the walls. However, he was game for a spot of juvenile delinquency. 'When I was a kid I often nearly got caught by the cops. I was always gone on wearing hip clothes and the only way to get them was through the back window of a clothing store.'[17] One night Jimmy and a friend climbed in the back of Wilner's store and helped themselves to sweaters, shirts and slacks. But next day, either in a fit of remorse or from a realisation that they would have to account at home for their new outfits, they dropped the clothes into the needy box at Garfield School. The store owner found out who the culprits were, but didn't press charges as the goods were recovered and he got some free gardening from Al.

Jimmy walked the streets with his guitar playing to the air as he had done with his broom. The butt of many good-humoured jokes from the street kids, he was considered something of a freak, an outsider. However, the members of the Seattle gangs, the Counts and the Cobras, the 'cool guys on the block', all respected Jimmy for his individuality. Apart from his soft spot for clothes, Jimmy generally stayed out of trouble. He was never going to run with the pack, although he was always prepared to stick up for himself and had his fair share of street fights. But in a crowd Jimmy stayed on the edges, content now and again just to go along for the ride. And that was his big mistake. On 2 May 1961, Jimmy was arrested for taking a motor vehicle without permission. Three days later, according to police records, Jimmy was caught again riding in a stolen car and this time 'I spent seven days in the cooler. . . . But I never knew it was [stolen].'[18] Jimmy was locked up in the Rainier Vista 4-H Youth Centre before being taken before the court. He was given a two-year suspended sentence because the Public Defender informed the judge that Jimmy was actively considering joining the army. According to Jimmy, the row he had with his father, when Al hit him, and the lack of job prospects sent him off to Uncle Sam. 'Because I didn't have a cent in my pocket, I walked into the first recruiting office I saw and went into the army.'[19] Jimmy was going to be drafted anyway, but volunteering rather than waiting for his draft papers meant that he could choose his posting. Jimmy very much wanted to be a Screamin' Eagle – a parachutist in the 101st Airborne – and shortly after his court appearance he was accepted.

First he had to say his goodbyes. He told James Thomas he would need to find himself another guitarist. Jimmy would be missing a three-date gig at the Annual Seattle Seafair Picnic and Dance and possibly his first chance to record. The Tomcats had been working on a song called 'Drive, Drive'.

Then he had to see Betty Jean. She had a sister called Maddy, who went out with Leon. 'Betty Jean was the only one who got a ring and a promise.' This isn't quite true, but Jimmy gave Betty Jean an engagement ring at a street dance, a few days before he left for his eight weeks' basic training at Fort Ord in California.

Jimmy was on the brink of the freedom he always craved, the chance to get away from Seattle even if he wasn't yet a professional musician. Jimmy was true to the words he sobbed out to his Aunt Dorothy that summer evening on her back porch. Apart from a few brief furloughs during National Service, never again would he go back to Seattle by choice.

Four *Hope You Brought Your Parachute With You*

Tuesday 31 May 1961, RA 19693532 James Marshall Hendrix arrived at Fort Ord on the West Coast to do his bit for the stars and stripes. Jimmy was too late for Korea and too early for Vietnam, but that same year J. F. Kennedy was telling the nation in his inaugural speech as President: 'We live on the edge of danger. . . . I believe that Americans are ready to be called to greatness.' The 'danger' was the Soviet Union and inside two years JFK would be threatening nuclear war if the Soviets refused to take their missiles out of Cuba.

Jimmy, although a genuine patriot at this time, was less concerned with the Red Menace than whether or not he would come through his eight weeks' basic training without going bankrupt. On 8 June: he wrote home the letter reproduced on pages 51-53.

Jimmy addressed the letter to 'Mr and *Mrs* James A. Hendrix' and in a curious show of formality added the salutation at the beginning of the letter: 'Dear . . . ' So who was *Mrs* Al Hendrix? Jimmy was being diplomatic here – he was talking about Willene, whom he mentioned in the letter. She and Al had known each other for years while Lucille was still alive and, some time after Lucille died, Willene moved in with Al on 26th and Yesler. She was married herself at the time, with a daughter Willette, but her husband was away either in the army or simply not around. Al and Willene had been planning to get married and Leon, who was living at home when Jimmy went into the army, called Willene 'Mum'. However, it would seem that at some point her husband returned and plans for nuptials went out of the window. On 11 August, it was back to 'Mr James A. Hendrix' and 'Dear Dad':

How are you? Fine, I hope. How's Willene, Willette, Leon etc . . . and Grandma? Everything's same as usual except we hardly do anything now. The Company left last Saturday morning at 0800 and everyone

June 6, 1961

RCT E-1 James Hendrix RA19693532
HQ + HQ Co 11th BG, 3rd Bat. 4 PLATOON
Fort Ord, California

Dear Mr. + Mrs. James H. Hendrix —

Well. . . I know it's about Time for me to write — We had a lot of things to do down here though — How's everybody up there? Fine, I really hope — the weather here is pretty nice except that it's pretty windy at Times because the Ocean is only about a mile away — I can't say too much because we have to Clean the ~~barrack~~ barrack up a little before we go to bed = I just wanted to let You know that I'm still alive although not by very much — Oh, the army's not too bad So far. It's so so although it does have it's "Ups and downs" at Times — All, I mean All my hair's cut off and I have to shave — I only shaved two Times so far counting tonight since I've been here —

51

I won't be able to see you until about
2 months from now — That's if I'm
lucky — We're going through Basic
Training, That's the reason — Although
I've been here for about a week, it seems
like about a month — Time passes pretty slow
even though we _do_ have alot to do —
How's the gardening business? I hope it's
doing fine — I believe it's more expensive
being in the Army than it is living as
a civilian — So far we had to get —
1. 2 laundry bags 1.00 each, 2 a block hat 1.75,
  2 locks .80 each, 3 Towels .50 each, Stamping kit 1.75,
Haircut 1.00, Shoe polish kit 1.10, Shaveing razor and blades,
and lather .1.70, insignias .50. So I guess this
isn't all that good, finacially, as I first thought.
$10.60 — that's about what it is. And, we
have to buy way more than that before
we're actually set for awhile, and we
don't get paid until JUNE 30th A61. And
So I would like to know if you might be
able to send about 5 or 6 dollars —

We have to buy so much stuff right away and payday is pretty far away. They only gave us $5.00 when we first came and all that's gone except $1.50 and that isn't going to last a minute around here — I can and will pay you back at the end of this month when we get paid if you could send it — After we get situated, things will be way better — It's just this first mixed-up month that messes us up — So I really must close now — Please, if you have time, write back or have Willene to write back and tell me what's going on up there —

I've everybody my love,
"Gramma", Gracie,
Willie May, Uncle Frank,
Betty, ect---ect-----

To Mr + Mrs. James A. Hendrix

from

James with love

Please if you can send a few dollars as soon as you can — Thank You except 4 of us are going home. The silly reason us 4 are still here is that we're still waiting for our orders to come in. They told us what we get and where we're supposed to be going. I'm supposed to be going to Ft. Lee, Virginia at a clerical and typing school. They might just change that when my official orders come in. . . . Some people wait about 2, 3, or 4 days, others weeks or maybe even months – I hope that doesn't happen to me – it gives you a feeling of time being wasted although it *does* count. Anyway, I want to hurry and get home – Well, I . . . probably might miss the whole summer. . . .

Jimmy asked Al to send his love to Betty and put a p.s.:

"How did you get in this line?"

He signed the letter 'Love always, Your son James', and doodled a guitar under his signature.

Early in September he went home on furlough, arriving back in camp on the 12th, when he wrote again to Al. He lost his bus ticket and missed the bus looking for it, so he missed his check-in time at the camp. He had to report to the Military Police, who finally brought him back: 'I've been gone [from Seattle] only 4 or 5 days and it seems like at least 2 weeks already – time is crawling by so slow it seems. . . .'

When he went home on leave, somebody who had been reading his letters must have made some joke about Jimmy falling into the army way of expressing time, for example 0800 instead of eight o'clock. In this letter he says: 'I'm writing this in the supply room now, by myself – it's 11.05 p.m. not 23.05 (smile).' He ends:

Give everyone my love including Betty Jean, the sweet thing. And Willene + Willette – Everybody – and I will try and write real soon.
Take it easy,
Love from your son
James

Tell Gramma I said 'Hi and lots of love'

Jimmy seems quite homesick in these letters; he wrote as soon as he got back to camp, even though the only news he had to tell was about losing his bus ticket. For all his wish to leave Seattle, this was the first time that he'd actually been away from home. Despite all the traumas, he was very attached to a number of his family, and being away from them all threw into relief what they actually meant to him.

There was a gap of six weeks to the next letter because, as Jimmy explained, he was involved in training the next batch of basic trainees: 'the 8 week cycle we just had, had 325 men in it and we were working pretty steady.' Jimmy *was* writing to Seattle during this period, but not to Al:

the reason I was writing Betty is because she just kept writing and [if] I would've missed, she might've started thinking something. One time I did miss writing her, there was so much work and so many hard-headed recruits to be bawled out and I couldn't possibly keep up at the rate she was writing to me. And so when I missed writing her, she wrote again and said a whole lot of stuff about 'you're fooling with someone else down there – California girls are tuff [strong], I know and I know that there's some down there around where you are – you better write and leave those "saphires" alone or you better not come up here to see me.'
I still didn't get a chance to write. . . . I could tell by her letters that her emotions change about 2 or 3 sometimes 4 times as she writes. Sometimes a few lines might sound pretty cheerful, then a few more lines might sound real sweet and 'you know', then a few more lines still might start sounding kind of mad and then calm down again.

Fortunately for Jimmy, he had not forgotten Betty Jean's birthday on 23 October: 'But I already told her that I won't be able to get her anything until around the early part [of] November.'

Jimmy also apologises for not sending any money, because he has to buy two pairs of jump boots and four sets of tailored fatigues plus twenty Screamin' Eagle patches: 'You know what that represents? The 101st AIRBORNE DIVISION, Fort Campbell, Kentucky, yes indeedy – And I have to be there at 5.00, November 8th – my orders for that just came in yesterday.'

Jimmy had been kicking his heels at Fort Ord for a full three months after the end of his basic training, waiting to find out where he would be posted. And finally his ambition was realised. The rest of this letter makes it clear that Jimmy wanted an army experience tailored to his own requirements. He desperately wanted to graduate from the jump school at Fort Campbell and saw it as a challenge: 'I wouldn't mind breaking a leg or something if I can come out wearing that Screamin' Eagle patch and those airborne wings. It's a proud out-fit.' But after that he just wanted a cushy clerk's job, doing one jump a month for an extra $55 in his pay packet. He was adamant that 'I really don't want to be in that infantry stuff if I can help it. . . .' And he was also sure that he would be 'leaving that Rangers mess alone (smile).'

The very next day, he wrote again having received a letter from Al that morning. At home Leon had been moved out, presumably after Willene left, but was back again:

I just received your letter and I'm so glad to hear that you're doing OK and that Leon and you are together. That took me by surprise and I really am so happy about that, because I know that it does get, or I should say, it did get pretty lonesome around there by yourself. That's the way I feel when I start thinking about you and the rest – and *Betty*. Tell Leon to do what he's supposed to because just as you used to tell me, it pays off later in life. . . . I'm happy too about you getting a TV. And I know that you are fixing the house up 'tuff'.

Keep up the good work and I'll try my *very* best to make this AIRBORNE for the sake of our name. I'm going to try hard and will put as much effort into this as I can. I'll fix it so that the whole family of Hendrix's will have the right to wear the Screamin' Eagle patch of the U.S. Army Airborne (smile).

Take it easy, and when you see me again, I'll be wearing the patch of proudness, I hope (smile).

To Daddy Hendrix from your son, love James.

p.s. Don't tell Betty what I said about her in that last letter – she might get mad (smile).

He arrived at Fort Campbell on 8 November and wrote to Al on the 13th:

Well, here I am, exactly where I wanted to go in the 101st Airborne. We jumped out of a 34-foot tower on the third day we were here. It was almost fun. We were the first nine out of about 150 in our group. When I was walking up the stairs to the top of the tower, I was walking nice and slow, just taking it easy. There were three guys who quit when they got to the top of the tower. You can quit at any time. They took one look outside and just quit. And that got me thinking as I was walking up those steps, but I made up my mind that whatever happens, I'm not quitting on my own.

When I got to the top, the jump master snapped these two straps onto my harness and slapped me on the butt and said right in my ear 'Go, Go, GO.' I hesitated for a split second and the next thing I knew I was falling. All of a sudden, when all the slack was taken up on the line, I was snapped like a bullwhip and started bouncing down the cable. . . . While I was sliding down, I had my legs together, hands on the reserve, my chin tucked into my chest. I ran smack dab into a sand dune. Later they'll show us how to go over it by lifting our feet, of course, but my back was to it.

Before Christmas, Jimmy was ready for the real thing, if it is possible ever to be 'ready' to jump out of an aeroplane a mile up in the air. He later recalled the adrenalin surge of parachuting both for the film *See My Music Talking* and in this interview with *New Musical Express*:

The first jump was really outta sight – like you're in the plane and some cats had never been up in a plane before – some people were throwin' up. You had a big bucket, a big garbage can sittin' in the middle. It was great. At the beginning the plane is going rrrrrrrr – this roarin' and shakin' – you can see the rivets just jumpin' around. Talk about 'What am I doing here?' In a split second, a thought went through me like 'You must be crazy.' And it's almost like a blank, and like cryin' and laughin'. In fact the sergeant said 'Who's this joker?' . . . But all the time you're thinkin', 'What am I doing here?' By that time, you're just there at the door and there's this rush and you're out like that and just – oooooooooh.

In *New Musical Express* he was quoted as saying, 'It's the most alone feeling in the world and every time you jump, you're scared that maybe this time it won't open. Then you feel that tug on your collar and there's that big beautiful white mushroom above you and the air's going sssssshhhh past your ears. That's when you begin talking to yourself again.'[1]

He took mid-air shots of jump-school training to send back home. He

Ford Ord,
California,
20 June 1961

wrote on the back of one of them: 'This jumping business is the most thrilling I ever did before. It's just as much fun as it looks, if you keep your eyes open (smile).'

Like any creative artist, Jimmy wanted to express his feelings about his everyday experiences. Strangely, however, when Jimmy went into the army he left his beloved guitar in Seattle. This is extraordinary considering how inseparable he was from his guitar back home. A later musician acquaintance claims that Jimmy told him he just forgot to take it, which seems highly unlikely. Why Jimmy did leave his guitar behind has never been satisfactorily explained. But it is reasonable to assume that he was biding his time to see how army life panned out, where he would be stationed after his basic training and, most important, how secure personal possessions were. After all, Jimmy had already lost one guitar through carelessness and money was just as tight as ever, as his letters home clearly demonstrate. Not that Jimmy wasn't playing; he would borrow instruments from other musicians on the base, and once again his talent caused resentment. When he wasn't practising on a real guitar, he'd be playing air guitar around the camp.

On 17 January 1962, Jimmy wrote home to Al asking him to send his guitar 'as soon as you can – I really need it now – it's still over at Betty's house.' Shortly afterwards, a package arrived at the camp for Jimmy – his red electric Danelectro guitar on which he had inscribed Betty Jean's name. He took his guitar to bed with him, standard bluesman practice, but in the rather narrow community of army personnel, it marked Jimmy out as 'unusual'. He was never one of the regular guys and kept himself to himself, much as he had remained apart from street life in Seattle. However, the army was a closed institution and anybody who stood out was bound to be a target for the more bone-headed recruits. They attacked him through the one possession he held most dear – his guitar. They hid 'Betty Jean' and made him beg for her back and even set on him one time, a humiliation which he did not suffer again thanks to an ex-Seattle buddy who came into the barracks and sorted out Jimmy's assailants.

With or (more usually) without an amplifier, Jimmy was always trying out new sounds, new ways of playing. His latest challenge was to translate the sounds of jump school – the roar and shudder of the planes, the pre-jump tensions and the incredible rush as you leap to oblivion – into the sounds of music. Up in the skies, Jimmy cut loose from earthly trappings and he let his ego slip away in the reverie of free-fall. He wanted to share this experience with the world through the sound of his guitar. But he had to keep the symphonies of the air locked away for some years to come, when he would have the technology at his disposal, the freedom to express his own intensely personal brand of music and an audience to listen to it. Until then, Jimmy had a lot of dues paying ahead of him.

One wet day in November 1961, a group of servicemen were running for cover on the camp as the rain hammered down. Private Billy Cox sheltered outside Service Club No. 1. He heard somebody playing guitar and went in to investigate. He followed the sound – 'somewhere between Beethoven and John Lee Hooker' – to a little practice room where he stood and watched the skinny kid with the red guitar. Jimmy didn't notice him at first, but then he looked up and Billy introduced himself. He told Jimmy he played bass.

Born in West Virginia, Billy had come from a musical background. His mother was a classical pianist while his uncle played sax with Duke Ellington. Billy tried his hand at trumpet, sax, piano and violin, but more than anything he wanted to play bass. Influenced by Ray Brown and Charlie Mingus, he played upright bass at school in Pittsburgh and studied music. Like Jimmy, he had already played in groups before he joined the army.

Jimmy and Billy hit it off at once and they stayed firm friends. They complemented each other perfectly – Jimmy, the wandering adventurer, always ready to go out on a limb and try the unorthodox while Billy was much more cautious, weighing up the pros and cons before taking action.

With the rain beating down outside, Billy proposed to Jimmy that they get a group together. Their five-piece band entertained the soldiers in Service Clubs 1 and 2, but they also did some outside gigs at the Pink Poodle Club in nearby Clarksville. The outfit didn't last long; Jimmy and Billy cut it down to a trio and brought in a drummer from Toledo, Gary Ferguson. For a short while they even drafted in a Major Charles Washington to play sax. He recalled that Jimmy had his guitar restrung for a left-handed player but that:

> somehow [he] would manage to pawn this guitar before a gig and the band would have to repossess it. Nothing else could be used, he had to have this specific guitar. . . . It appeared that Jimmy was never really with us. He did a lot of concentrating on his music and a lot of the small talk that the typical group of guys would make – he would not enter into it. . . . we would look over at him occasionally and there he is staring . . . you never did get to know him that closely. . . . [2]

This band went further afield, taking in some of the other army bases around North and South Carolina, but it too was short-lived. Jimmy and Billy went back to a five-piece and they started gigging as the King Kasuals round the same army and small-town club venues.

As Jimmy was picking up the threads of his musical career, life in the army was fast losing its shine. Jimmy did win his coveted Screamin' Eagle patch and in late January 1962, he was promoted to Private First Class. 'I made it,' he wrote home, 'in eight months and eight days!' But he also wrote to Al in March about 'pushing Tennessee around all day with my hands . . . push ups' and talked in a later interview about doing 'exercises in wet sawdust in temperatures six degrees below zero'.[3] During his army days, Al had always accepted that 'orders were orders' even when it meant missing the birth of his son, but Jimmy was a soldier of a different stripe. He resented the authority and the fact that he had to make his own opportunities to play: 'Army people tell you what to do all the time. . . . the Army's really a bad scene. They wouldn't let me have anything to do with music. They tell you what you are interested in and you don't have any choice. The Army is more for people who like to be told what to do.'[4]

In the best tradition of *MASH*'s Corporal Klinger, Jimmy went to see the army psychiatrist on more than one occasion, but eventually he decided on a much simpler route to freedom: 'one day, I got my ankle caught in the sky hook just as I was going to jump and I broke it. I told them I'd hurt my back too. Every time they examined me I groaned, so they finally believed me and I got out.'[5]

Jimmy got his discharge papers through and was all set to go home during July 1962 to see his family and Betty Jean. Then:

One morning I found myself standing outside the gate of Fort Campbell on the Tennessee–Kentucky border with my little duffel bag and three or four hundred dollars in my pocket. I was going back to Seattle which was a long way away, but there was this girl I was kinda hung up on. Then I thought I'd just look in at Clarksville which was near, stay there that night and go home next morning. . . . I went to this jazz joint and had a drink. I liked it and stayed. People tell me I get foolish good-natured sometimes. Anyway, I guess I felt real benevolent that day. I must have been handing out bills to anyone who asked me! I came out with sixteen dollars left! And it takes more than that to get from Tennessee to Seattle! So, no going home, 'cos it's like two thousand miles. . . . I first thought I'd call long distance and ask my father to send me some money – he's a garden designer and does all right. But I could guess what he'd say if I told him I'd lost nearly four hundred dollars in just one day. Nope. That was out. All I can do, I thought, is get a guitar and try to find work here. Nashville was only twenty miles away – you know, big music scene. There had to be something doing there.

Then I remembered that just before I left the Army, I'd sold a guitar to a cat in my unit. So I went back to Fort Campbell and slept there on the sly that night. I found the guy and told him I just had to borrow the guitar back.[6]

Jimmy left the army about two months before Billy. They agreed that Jimmy would stick around the area until Billy got out, then they would make their way as musicians together. Jimmy sat out the time in Clarksville. His decision not to try and make it back to Seattle finally killed his relationship with Betty Jean, which anyway had been under strain since Jimmy had gone so far away. Joyce Lucas was one of the new women in his life. Once Billy left the army around September 1962, she and Jimmy, Billy and a couple they'd met all lived for a brief time in a rented house. But nothing was happening musically, so Jimmy and Billy took off for Indianapolis in a decrepit 1955 Plymouth. Jimmy had a beat-up car in Seattle 'but a girlfriend wrecked it. She ran it straight through a hamburger joint.'[7] This one fared no better. It broke down and they had no money to repair it. What they had, they spent on a rented room and shared bowls of chilli to keep body and soul together. When the money finally ran out, they slept in the car. Not noted for its vibrant music scene, Indianapolis had nothing to offer two struggling musicians, so they headed back to Clarksville to put together another version of the King Kasuals, learning some hard lessons about the music business in the process. As Jimmy said later, 'I went to Clarksville where the group I was with worked for a set-up called W&W. Man, they paid us so little that we decided that the two WWs stood for Wicked and Wrong.'[8] 'This one-horse music agency . . . used to come up on stage in the middle of a number while we were playing and slip the money for the gig into our pockets. They knew we couldn't knock off to count it just then. By the time the number was over and I got a chance to look in the envelope, it'd be maybe two dollars.'[9] The first incarnation of the Kasuals managed to land a spot playing the Del Morocco, one of the top R&B clubs in Nashville. Jimmy and Billy decided to try their luck there again.

In 1962, Nashville was in the middle of a transition from being the provincial capital of a small country-music scene to an internationally recognised recording centre on a par with Los Angeles or New York. However, its R&B and blues scene was severely restricted. Nashville's only claim to fame in this area was WLAC, a powerful, 50,000-watt radio station owned by the Life and Casualty Insurance Company. In the mid-forties, the station sold cheap late-night selling time to Randy's Record Store, a mail-order shop in nearby Gallatin. Randy Wood pitched his selling at the rural and small-town black population who had difficulty getting the new R&B records. Gene Nobles was the first DJ to host the nightly blues show featuring the sounds of Roy Brown and Muddy

Waters. He was succeeded by John 'R' Richbourg and William 'Hoss' Allen. Other record shops went in with Randy Wood to sponsor the John R shows while Hoss Allen plugged cosmetics. The impact on the mail-order businesses of the record shops was dramatic – Jerry Wexler of Atlantic Records was to say that Nobles, Richbourg and Allen were extremely influential in turning white kids on to black music. In Nashville itself what live black music there was centred on Jefferson Street: the New Era, the Del Morocco (numbers one and two in the club pecking order), the Baron, the Steal Away, the Wigwam and others.

On arrival in Nashville around October 1962, Jimmy and Billy went to see the manager of the Del Morocco, who fixed them up with some accommodation upstairs in a place called Joyce's House of Glamour. When the money was even tighter than usual and they couldn't pay the rent Jimmy slept under the stars, 'in a big housing estate they were building around there. No roofs and sometimes they hadn't put floors in yet. That was wild!'[10]

Jimmy was often seen strolling around the streets of North Nashville, guitar slung around his neck, for which he became known as 'Marbles' (as in 'he's lost his . . . '). Billy Cox would knock on his door in the mornings to wake him up; 'there he was laying on his bed with the same clothes that he had on the night before, his guitar laying on his stomach or alongside him. He was practicing all night long.'[11]

There were racial tensions to deal with, but he played it all down and made a joke out of it. This was Jimmy's whole approach to the race issue – for him it wasn't an issue, despite a number of personal humiliations he was to suffer, even when he became famous. This 'world citizen' stance, a political one, even if he didn't acknowledge it, was to get him into deep water later on with black militants. 'Every Sunday afternoon, we used to go down town and watch the race riots. Take a picnic basket because they wouldn't serve us in the restaurants. One group would stand on one side of the street and the rest on the other side. They'd shout names and talk about each other's mothers. That'd go on for a couple of hours and then we'd all go home. Sometimes, if there was a good movie on that Sunday there wouldn't be any race riots.'[12]

Jimmy was much more interested in the ladies. He was still seeing Joyce Lucas, another girl called Florence Henderson and a barmaid at the Baron club, Verdell Barlow, a brief flirtation which ended abruptly when her husband, nicknamed 'Treacherous', went for her with a piece of two-by-four. Jimmy even had his own unofficial fan club in Nashville, who called themselves the Buttons because they mended his clothes, made sure he was fed and had somewhere to lay his head. Finding a bed was no trouble, getting Jimmy out of it was a different story, as Billy Cox recalls. 'We had a job . . . at the Del Morocco. . . . I think we went on at nine. Nine o'clock, no Jimmy. Ten o'clock, no Jimmy. We're starting to get a little worried, so I run up to the house where he lives. [I] knock on the door, he says "Come in." I go in, he's lying there and I go, "Hey Jimmy, you're late for the gig." He says, "I dreamed the gig was cancelled so I went back to sleep." '13

One night Larry Lee, a young guitarist from Memphis, came strolling into the Del Morocco looking for a soul mate – somebody else who couldn't play.

> At the time, I think I was about the worst guitar player in Nashville and I was searching for somebody in my category, somebody to talk to. I saw the King Kasuals and they had these two guitars, Jimmy was on the far right. Everyone else I saw just looked too advanced for me. . . . the cats who could play wouldn't give you the time of day. Jimmy caught my eye 'cause he looked like the cat I was looking for. So I sat down and watched him the whole set. . . . He was just doing nothing with that guitar, man. His guitar was an old Kay with strings about that high and I was sure that Jimmy was somebody in my calibre that I could talk to. . . . I needed a friend who couldn't play and I *thought* it was Jimmy.
>   So I left the club. . . . I stayed about two blocks from the Del Morocco. . . . I was so happy to see him up there that I think I went back home. . . . When I came back to the club after a few days, I introduced myself to him and I saw he needed a string . . . so I ran home and got him an E-string. He had another guitar, a new Epiphone, and I couldn't believe this was the same cat that I'd seen and I said 'Wow, he's tricked me!' And that's when I found out he really *could* play!

Unlike the other 'cats who could play', Jimmy was generous with his time in helping another guitarist develop his own abilities. However, graduating from the Hendrix School of Guitar Playing could be nerve-racking for an inexperienced musician like Larry Lee. 'What really got me was . . . that Jimmy would see a girl dancing and he would drop his guitar and take her to a room and he would always ask me to come and sit in and that kinda got my nerves up. I wasn't a lead-guitar player when I met Jimmy. . . . this is how I got my chance to express myself.'

Jimmy was playing his guitar through a Silvertone amp given to him by the Del Morocco boss and he was playing it *loud*. For Larry Lee 'a lot of the time it was just magic, man'. Jimmy always had his ears

The King Kasuals (Jimmy, Billy and Leonard Moses)
Jolly Roger, Nashville, Tennessee, spring 1962

open for new ways of producing sound. Jimmy Church was sometime lead vocalist with the Kasuals; 'one time we played in Clarksville and the speaker busted and it started to make a major change and Jimmy said, "Listen to the sound, man, listen to the sound, it is different, don't change it, man . . . listen to the sound . . . listen to the sound." '

But Jimmy was not regarded as the hottest R&B guitar in town; that honour belonged to the lead guitarist with the Imperials, Johnny Jones, although Larry Lee believes people had it all wrong. ' . . . I was more impressed with Jimmy than Johnny. They were afraid even to speak of Jimmy – "He's a mad man" – but I just saw something in Jimmy. . . . He had a sound that was more fluid than Johnny, he played more natural, he got more into it . . . he had a lot of nerve with his guitar.

65

I see him play out in the barn, in somebody's kitchen . . . he would never stop playing. . . . He had a one-track mind once he got going.'

But Larry also says that Johnny was Jimmy's idol and Jimmy would often go and sit all night in a club and just watch Johnny Jones playing guitar. Jimmy was actually quite sensitive about his would-be rival; Jones had a better guitar and bigger amps and Larry reckons that Jimmy did not play Nashville's top R&B club, the New Era, much if at all because he was self-conscious about having inferior equipment. One night though, when Johnny Jones was playing at the Baron, Jimmy and Larry decided to go down and show him who was the best on the block. Johnny was sitting up at the bar in between sets, when in comes Jimmy and Larry puffing and blowing from rolling the amp down the street while Jimmy tried to keep his guitar safe. 'What are you two doing?' says Johnny. 'We're gonna kick your ass, big man,' they said. 'This is the night.' So Johnny and Jimmy take to the stage: Johnny lets rip full blast from his amp and, quite out of character, Jimmy puts a bass tone on his amp and plays sweet, mellow B.B. King. Everyone starts laughing, but Larry Lee was not amused. 'Jimmy comes off the stage and I said, "Man, what the hell was that? You embarrassed me. We rolled this shit all down the street like a fool and all you do is put a bass tone on the amp." "Oh man," says Jimmy, "I was trying to get that B.B. King sound." ' Meanwhile Johnny Jones had eaten Jimmy alive and the pair left the club with their tails between their legs. 'We laughed about it when we got out, but it was embarrassing.'

Perhaps Jimmy did have some vague intention of 'kicking ass' that night, although possibly Larry Lee wanted to see it happen more than Jimmy because he was frustrated on Jimmy's behalf that he wasn't getting his due recognition as a guitar player.

But, however technically adept, it was a fact of life that, if Jimmy was to cut it down south, he had to try and develop some kind of stage act. Jimmy Church reiterates what's already been said about the importance of performance for the blues guitarist: 'You were no guitar player if you didn't do that . . . it was no gig!' Jimmy had tried some of this stuff in Seattle and he could see it got a good reaction, although he was still reticent about it all: 'some cat tried to get me to play behind my head because I would never move too much, you know. I said, "Oh man, who wants to do all that junk?" And then all of a sudden you started to get bored with yourself.'[14]

However, there was no doubt that Jimmy got a kick out of being flamboyant. Billy Cox made him a long cord so that he could go offstage into the audience. 'The club wasn't that big . . . so he could even go out the front door and play on the sidewalk. A lot of people at that time didn't know whether to clap or to walk out, but they knew he was good.'[15] Billy says Jimmy was already utilising feedback as part of the performance by walking back into the club trailing his 75-foot cord with the Radio Shack quarter-inch plugs on it and playing the guitar on top of the amp.

Jimmy also found out about playing with your teeth: 'the idea of doing that came to me in a town in Tennessee. Down there you have to play with your teeth or else you get shot. There's a trail of broken teeth all over the stage.'[16]

If audiences knew instinctively that Jimmy could play, they never got the chance to pass comment about his singing. Back in Seattle he had not been that self-conscious about his voice. When he left, Leon says Jimmy was ringing him up from time to time to sing him songs down the phone. But, once he got in with the pros, it was a different story. Jimmy did not have the sweet, strong wide-ranging gospel-inspired vocal sound expected of singers in blues and R&B bands, and other musicians didn't mince words. 'I never did hear him doing any singing,' says Johnny Jones. 'Once when you heard him sing, you'd know why he wasn't a singer.' Jimmy never had any confidence in what turned out to be his very evocative vocal style – even when Bob Dylan proved you could busk through it with a voice like a blocked drain.

To make ends meet Jimmy and Billy backed artists like Nappy Brown, Carla Thomas, School Boy and Ironing Board Sam. Jimmy also played with Larry Lee in Bob Fisher and the Barnevilles on a package tour with the Marvellettes and Curtis Mayfield. Larry Lee was employed playing bass on his guitar and helped Jimmy get the gig. Jimmy had no amp with him and used Curtis Mayfield's for the Bob Fisher set. Curtis Mayfield was a star who used the best equipment; Jimmy had never had access to such good gear before and really put this amp through its paces. At one point, Jimmy played a long wailing note that crashed through the sound barrier and all but melted the amp. Larry Lee says Curtis Mayfield didn't want any other guitarists around when he was playing, especially a wild one like Jimmy. When it was time to play behind Curtis Mayfield, Jimmy had to leave the stage. 'Ladies and Gentlemen, Curtis Mayfield and the Impressions' – thunderous applause. Curtis plugs in – nothing. Jimmy's standing off-stage mildly amused as the great man moans, 'What happened to my amp, man?'

Apart from trashing his amplifier, Jimmy learnt much of the art of resonance and pulse in music from playing on the same bill as Curtis Mayfield, whose tasteful guitar-playing punctuated by clipped percussive chops greatly influenced the more melodic aspects of Jimmy's guitar-playing.

Now that he was down in the Deep South, when he wasn't earning a few dollars churning out chart-hit riffs Jimmy was trying to soak up as much blues power as possible. However, unlike Memphis, Nashville was not a blues town, so there was precious little opportunity for him to see the premier blues artists performing live. He had to be content with records on the juke-box in cafés or sitting around with Billy Cox wherever they were staying, listening to music, eating strawberry upside-down cake, enthusing as Albert King wrung another hot lick out of 'Lucy' and trying to learn it there and then. He would sit with Larry Lee trying to teach him how to play like B.B. King, and every musician he met up with in Nashville tells the same story of Jimmy bending their ears to the sounds of the blues.

Around Christmas 1962, Jimmy decided to take a break from Nashville – somehow he made it 2000 miles in the middle of winter all the way to Vancouver. Around the festive season, he might have felt a bit homesick, but he didn't go to Seattle; instead he travelled on to see his beloved Grandma Nora and Aunt Pat.

One night Jimmy walked into a club called Dante's Inferno, where the club owners, Bobby Taylor and Tommy Chong, were fronting a Motown-inspired band called the Vancouvers. Jimmy already knew some members of the band and he joined for the short time he was in Canada. From playing soul guitar, Tommy Chong teamed up with Richard 'Cheech' Marin in an improvisational group called City Lights before moving to Los Angeles for a rock/comedy career extolling the virtues of dope.

Early in 1963, Jimmy wound his way back to Nashville to pick up his career playing behind any blues, soul or R&B artists who hit town or slumming it round the clubs with the King Kasuals. Socially, Nashville was good for Jimmy; he hung around with Billy Cox and Larry Lee, they joked and laughed together, went with all the girls, made up nicknames for each other – Jimmy was 'Woody Woodpecker', Billy was 'Charlie Chicken'. But Jimmy wanted more out of his musical relationships than who could fart the loudest. He wanted the guys he played with to grow with him, to hear what he was hearing. But this was really a forlorn hope because Jimmy was too much of an individual, as Jimmy

Church observes: 'He wasn't really a band player. . . . he would take a solo [and] forget he was in a band. . . . it looked like he wasn't gonna quit.' Partly this was to do with Jimmy's sense of the competition all around him which certainly sharpened him up technically; 'You really had to play, 'cos those people were really hard to please. It was one of the hardest audiences in the South. . . . they hear it all the time. Everybody knows how to play guitar. You walk down the street and people are sitting on the porch playing more guitar. . . . That's where I learned to play really . . . Nashville.'17

But as far as musical direction was concerned Johnny Jones makes the point that even Jimmy didn't really know what he wanted; he just knew that he wasn't going to find it in Nashville. Resplendent in a Bo Diddley hat, Johnny Jones sits in the stifling hot kitchen of a Memphis fried-chicken joint and opines, 'He wanted freedom in his playing, he wanted to be able to express himself and not by anybody's format or roots. . . . he could play . . . [but] he was seeking a direction. . . . it takes a lot of time to find yourself.' Jones says you could hear Jimmy's confusion in his playing. It was quite abstract in parts, the phrasing would seem disconnected, as if Jimmy was searching for the lost notes to join everything together. 'He was just like a little bird trying to fly, you fly a little piece . . . until you get it down and make it connect, man.'

There was a problem here for Jimmy as Charles Keil notes in *Urban Blues* about the plight of the aspiring young blues player of the early sixties:

Let us assume that . . . his blues are distinctive. He has moved a step away from his basic B.B. King guitar licks . . . and he has a few original lyrics up his sleeve. Let us further suppose that he has been working with some small-time rhythm and blues bands . . . in his late teens and early twenties. He knows that . . . [club] owners don't pay musicians much and sometimes don't pay at all. Our young bluesman may have considerable 'savoir faire' . . . but he is still as malleable and helpless as a newborn babe in the hands of the music industry. . . . It doesn't take him long to discover that most record companies won't touch an urban blues singer with a twenty-foot pole.18

This could have been written specifically with Jimmy in mind – he was even writing songs at this point, although perhaps he would never have put himself forward as a singer. As an unknown black guitarist struggling to make a name for himself, he had no choice but to be a hired gun. 'I learnt how not to get an R&B group together. The trouble was too many leaders didn't seem to want to pay anybody. Guys would get fired in the middle of the highway because they were talking too loud on the bus or the leader owed them too much money.'[19] He hadn't been back in Nashville from Vancouver long when one of the many soul/R&B package tours rolled into town headed up by Sam Cooke and Jackie Wilson and compered by a showbiz jack-of-all-trades, 'Gorgeous' George Odell. Odell performed many functions – MC, valet, promoter – he also had his own band, which played a set and backed up the solo stars on the bill.

As his name suggests George Odell was a showman. He wore outrageous clothes and a silvery wig, a self-promoter with a sharpened awareness of stagecraft. Larry Lee watched Odell in action:

> He was the kind of cat who needed no rehearsal, you know . . .
> he would just say 'Where's my band, man?' and the promoter would
> get some cats and he would go up there and put on a show, man.
> Jimmy learned from a cat with that much courage to show that the
> power they had in themselves would get them through. . . . He knew
> people's natures, how to make them happy. . . . it was a second nature
> kind of thing and it made Jimmy powerful when he ran into George.

Jimmy and Billy went to see Jackie Wilson at the Hippodrome in Nashville and got talking to Gorgeous George. Billy Cox was wary of the man with a silver tongue to match his wig and opted out, but Jimmy wanted the chance to move around. So in the spring of 1963, Jimmy went on the road as George Odell's guitar-player.

Jimmy spent the next two years travelling on what was rather patronisingly known as the 'chitlin circuit'. Chitterlings were pig intestines, the cheapest meat available, a staple part of the black community's 'soul food' diet. B.B. King, for one, regards the term as derogatory. 'I still play a lot of those places, and some of those that can't afford me I wish I could still play.'[20] These tours were crucial to black artists like Sam Cooke, Solomon Burke, Jackie Wilson and James Brown, who unlike their white counterparts received virtually no media exposure (TV, film and so on). It was their fans' only chance to see them.

When he first came to England, Jimmy claimed he had actually played behind most of the top soul acts of the day. This was a slight exaggeration, a bit of poetic licence to boost his credibility. But he certainly did tours with many of the big names and learnt a lot from the likes of Solomon Burke and Jackie Wilson about manipulating and teasing audiences to a climax, techniques in the Pentecostal tradition of 'house wrecking' where preachers could whip up an audience to the point where people fainted or spoke in tongues.

But he realised, too, that a frenzied audience could be detrimental to the music. Watching Sam Cooke, he observed, 'I'd have learnt more if they'd let Sam finish his act. But they were always on their feet and cheering at the end and I never heard him do the last bit.'[21]

While he might have learnt much about stagecraft, he picked up little about music that he didn't already know. Each singer on the bill would get no more than about twenty minutes to run through the hits. If Jimmy tried any trick playing to relieve the boredom, he'd be glared back into line for taking attention away from the star. But the threat of dismissal was no big deal unless you were owed money. If you got the sack on a Friday, you'd be back playing with someone else by Saturday night.

If onstage was boring, offstage was even worse. The bus might get into town early in the morning after a drive of several hundred miles. If there was nothing going on in town, much of the time would be spent backstage playing cards, boozing, smoking grass or out in the parking lot or down an alley for some quick sex. None of this was Jimmy's style – he preferred to sit by himself practising or perhaps swapping ideas with any musician who'd care to listen. His aloof nature meant nobody got to know him very well and so he could find himself targeted for trouble. The Womack Brothers (the Valentinos) were on this first tour of Jimmy's – Bobby was also Sam Cooke's guitarist. En route to Minneapolis, Harry Womack left some money in a dressing-room and it went missing. Jimmy was the only one around and, not knowing him at all, Harry Womack blamed Jimmy for the theft, something Jimmy hotly denied. Harry lost a week's money in the theft and was now flat broke. He swore revenge. Unlike all the other musicians, Jimmy kept his guitar with him on the bus instead of stowed away in the luggage. When he was asleep, Harry Womack slipped the guitar from Jimmy's hands and tossed it out the window.

George Odell took Jimmy under his wing – the next tour was a non-playing job helping George valet for Hank Ballard and the Midnighters. But Jimmy brought a guitar along just in case, wrapped up in a potato sack. The main act on the tour was Little Richard and his band the Upsetters; assistant tour manager was Henry Nash, who gave George permission to bring Jimmy along as his assistant, not even knowing he was a musician. 'When the concert was over, you would always have an "after show" at some local nightclub. One night in Greenville, South Carolina, he asked if he could sit with the Upsetters.' Once he played (on a guitar with only five strings, incidentally), Nash realised this was no errand boy with fantasies of being a musician. 'He possessed something other guitarists didn't. . . . he did what an audience was looking for. . . . he had good ears.'*

Jimmy travelled all over America during the rest of 1963, but wound up back in Nashville as winter set in. He often went back there, to his friends and the familiar surroundings, to recharge his batteries. But he never hung around for too long. A New York promoter breezed into the Baron one night when Jimmy was playing with Larry Lee, got talking to Jimmy and convinced him he could make him a star in New York. Larry says Jimmy took little persuading. 'He was in kind of a rut, he wasn't going nowhere. He had big dreams, he always had big dreams, and he always said he was gonna be famous and have a thousand guitars laying around in the house, and he always said he had some songs, but he never brought them up. . . . he said, "I got these songs, man," but nobody would be paying attention. . . . It was cold, he didn't have a coat, so I told him to take one of mine. . . . he did write me one letter from New York, he asked me to come up there. . . . he said New York is just a big country town and we can take this town, man. Jimmy had no responsibility, he was just foot-loose and fancy free. I knew it couldn't be that easy in New York.'

* Henry Nash confirms that, contrary to other sources, Jimi did not actually play with Little Richard until 1965.

Five *Dusty Boots Cadillac*

Wearing Larry Lee's coat to ward off the winter chill, Jimmy headed off into the wilderness of empty promises across which all musicians have to trek. Inevitably the promoter's schemes came to nothing and Jimmy was left stranded in Harlem with no work and little money.

To grasp the inner meanings of life in black America, one must put his finger on the pulse of Harlem. (Roi Ottley, 1943)

At the turn of the century, Harlem was a real-estate dream – lavish plans were drawn up for expensive, high-quality housing for rich white folks. Property prices spiralled out of control, followed by a crash. White landlords tried to cut their losses by renting out to black families and the whites fled. Harlem went through good times in the twenties, but never really recovered from the Depression. The white residents may have left, but the economic heartbeat of the world's highest concentration of black people in one six-mile urban area – some 500,000 by the mid-sixties – was still white. Harlem, the seat of black nationalism, was colonised by white landlords and white-owned retail outlets. Most of the profit was taken out of this 'city within a city'.

The black journalist and playwright Sylvester Leaks wrote that Harlem was 'a six-mile festering black scar on the alabaster under-belly of the white man's indifference . . . a privileged sanctuary for that unholy trinity of rent-gouging landlords, graft-grabbing cops, and usurious loan sharks; for silver-tongued pimps and phony prophets, thieving politicians and vendors of sex and religion, fake healers and fortune tellers and atrocious pedlars of narcotics death.' In between the 'dingy-dirty cluster of roach-crawling, rat-infested brownstones and tenement flats and housing projects', poor voices were raised from the area's 256 churches. 'Some of their ministers drive flashy cars

73

and live in fancy homes, [while] misery stalks the streets and the blues are the only antidote to atavistic pain.' Yet in Harlem 'the lust for life is infectious; one feels its accelerating rhythm and demoniacal beat of life the moment he enters the enfolding confines of her streets; here $34,368,000 worth of liquor is purchased annually in 168 liquor stores, exclusive of the untold millions spent in bars. And the unpretentious purchasers thumb their noses at their maligners and shout at the top of their voices, "It ain't nobody's business if I do!"'[1]

Like his father coming down to Seattle from Vancouver looking for the 'big chance', Jimmy found New York a tough place for a strange face. Harlem, in particular, would eat a country boy alive. 'Seattle? Where's that, man?' He hung around all the main music places along Harlem's Broadway, the soul of the community, 125th Street, an unbroken run of cafés, bars, restaurants and music clubs: Small's Paradise, the Palm Café, Sugar Ray's and Frank's. During the golden days of Harlem in the twenties and thirties, Small's would play host to piano battles between Willie 'The Lion' Smith, Fats Waller and James P. Johnson. When bebop came along, there were sessions all over Harlem where Charlie Parker, Dizzy Gillespie or Thelonius Monk might show up. But as the fifties gave way to the sixties, interest in jazz waned and Harlem ceased to be one of the focal points for innovations in black music. Work became much harder to find and Jimmy was just one of a legion of musicians desperate for a gig or even the chance to sit in with a house band. He might have starved, but his good looks came to the rescue once more – he was spotted by a Harlem-wise foxy lady named Fayne Pridgeon, although everybody called her Fay.

One night, Fay was sitting in the Palm Café dressed to kill, painted-on skirt, high heels and stacked-up hairdo. An ex-girlfriend of Sam Cooke, she often hung out there – the famous Apollo Theater was just a few doors up and the Palm Café played host after hours to many of the top black musicians. Lounging at a table, she got talking to this handsome young guy with a long 'process' hairstyle who could, she thought hungrily, still be in his teens. He looked too innocent to be the kind of Harlem fast talker she was used to dealing with, besides which, with his black pants worn at the knees, he didn't exactly look the part of a 125th Street hustler. And once he started talking in his soft, whispery, almost spacey kind of voice, she knew her instincts were right. They talked and talked and finally left the café, talking all the way down to where Fay's mother lived on Central Park West. 'My mother cooks continuously,' Fay told *Gallery* magazine, 'life is one big meal for her.' Although he ate very sparsely, even when he could afford to, Jimmy loved home-cooking and he was certainly hungry now. Afterwards, Jimmy and Fay lay around, she played some of her mother's blues records, Muddy Waters and Lightnin' Hopkins, and Jimmy took out his guitar and played along with the music. Eventually, Mrs Pridgeon got tired of having them lazing about and kicked them out. They went back to the Hotel Seifer where Fay was staying with a girlfriend:

> nobody was home so we hopped in the sack. He was shy . . . he was extremely shy. . . . After that first night . . . he just moved in with me. It wasn't hard because he was carrying all his possessions in his guitar case. . . . The average day consisted of us waking up at noon . . . but not actually getting up for at least a couple of hours. Jimmy loved fooling about with his guitar in bed, and he always slept with it. I used to think of my competition not as a woman, but as a guitar. Many times he fell back asleep with it on his chest. Any time I tried to remove it, he woke up and said, 'no, no, no, leave my guitar alone!' . . . All our activity took place in bed. . . . He was well endowed you see. . . . he came to the bed with the same grace a Mississippi pulpwood driver attacks a plate of collard greens and corn bread after ten hours in the sun. He was creative in bed too. There would be encore after encore . . . hard driving and steamy like his music. There were times when he almost busted me in two the way he did a guitar on stage.[2]

Fay would sometimes wind Jimmy up by suggesting in 'mid-stream' that he wasn't the greatest thing since sliced bread. Jimmy would take his revenge. One time Fay woke up to find Jimmy sitting at the foot of the bed 'wearing nothing but an attitude', in the process of tying her to the bed. The look on his face scared the life out of her. He tied her mouth up, made love to her and then left her still bound and gagged while he went off to some rehearsal. When he came back, he undid her and began talking about the session he'd just come from as if nothing had happened. When they weren't in bed, Jimmy and Fay were cadging meals from Mrs Pridgeon, who had decided that Jimmy was a bum. She told her daughter 'not to bring that long-haired nigger around here' and tried to convince Jimmy that Fay was only going through a phase and not to get too involved. But Jimmy became very fond of her and extremely jealous. Here was a strong, vibrant, exciting woman like his mother and he didn't want to lose her. If she got out of bed he demanded to know where she was going. At one club in Harlem where Jimmy was playing, somebody was pestering Fay for a dance. Jimmy leapt off the stage, dragging his guitar and amplifier with him, and whacked the guy on the head with the guitar. Meanwhile the lead was wrapped round the tables and everyone was falling over it. However, another version of this story, which appeared in a black magazine in the mid-1970s, told how it was Fay who was on the receiving end of Jimmy's guitar.[3] This was one of the strangest contradictions in Jimmy's character. Boy and man, he was universally regarded by everyone who knew him as the kindest, most retiring and polite person you could wish to meet – by rock and roll standards he was a saint. Nobody who knew him can possibly believe that the Jimmy *they* knew had any kind of violent streak in him. However, there is enough evidence later on to suggest that Jimmy was prone to sudden uncontrollable bursts of anger and that much of this was directed against women whom he otherwise cared for very much. As he said himself, 'no matter how sweet and lovely you are, there are black and ugly things deep down somewhere.'[4]

Work was very hard to come by; Fay's connections meant Jimmy could often borrow a guitar when he did have a gig, while his own was in and out of the pawnshop. They went round all the music places together and Fay would feel very sorry for Jimmy watching him struggle just to be allowed to sit in. After a rejection he would come back to the table with a certain look in his eye and tell her he'd try again in a minute. She in turn tried to dissuade him from further humiliation, but he kept on pushing. If a band did say yes, it was often only so they could have a laugh at Jimmy's expense by messing up behind him, changing the key, dragging the beat or whatever. Jimmy would turn round disgusted and leave the stage. If he got a halfway decent chance, he'd steal the show with his tasty repertoire of stage antics, easy guitar skills and the amp set at 'loud', one of only two settings Jimmy ever bothered with. The other was 'off'.

Nevertheless, around Christmas 1963 he did get his first chance to record. En route to New York, he stopped over in Philadelphia and was hired for some sessions with a sax player called Lonnie Youngblood. When Jimmy became famous, a number of Youngblood recordings appeared on albums purporting to feature him on guitar. In 1986, a New York district court ruled that many of these recordings were faked, in that Jimmy did not appear at all. But in among all the frauds were some genuine sessions, some of which were verified by the Copyright Office as having been recorded in 1963. Thus tracks like 'Wipe the Sweat' and 'Under the Table' represent Jimmy's earliest recordings. Across these and other tracks, Jimmy's distinctive vibrato is unmistakable and, just turned twenty-one years old, his blues guitar style was astonishingly mature, combining the subtlety of B.B. King and the attack of Albert King. One song, 'Fox', paced and phrased in the style of Curtis Mayfield, is virtually a blueprint for 'Little Wing'. 'Go Go Shoes' from the same sessions shows that Jimmy was equally conversant with all the chunky chord patterns of soul and R&B, which, unlike his later white contemporaries like Eric Clapton and Jeff Beck, was such an integral part of his playing.

Through Sam Cooke, Fay was well known at the Apollo – she once got Jimmy backstage to meet the great man himself. She may also have been instrumental in securing a spot on Amateur Night as there was a three- to four-month waiting list. Every Wednesday night at 11 p.m., a handful of hopefuls would gather at the side of the stage in sheer terror. The Apollo audience was merciless in the treatment it meted out to anybody who had the effrontery to go on that hallowed stage and fail. If you were lucky, they just booed and heckled. But if the second balcony didn't like you, watch out for the bottles and the chairs! And that wasn't all. If the audience took a dislike to a performer, a backstage nemesis known as Junkie Jones would rush on stage to the sound of a blaring siren and shoot the poor unfortunate with blanks.

When his turn came, Jimmy went up on stage touching the lucky stump of the Tree of Hope that stood on the side as he went. The stump used to be a tree around which out-of-work artists would congregate near the Lafayette Theatre, the Apollo's main rival. Booking agents noticed this and came to sign people up. When the tree was cut down in 1933, the largest bit went to the Apollo. Performers who failed to touch the stump were sent off to do so by the MC. But Jimmy didn't forget and he went up there and played. When everyone had done their stuff, the MC brought out all the contestants, held his hand over each one and the winner was judged by the length of the applause. Most of the winners of Amateur Night were singers – Sarah Vaughan, James Brown and Gladys Knight were among a number of famous past winners. But King Curtis, one of the hottest R&B sax players in the States, had won and Jimmy followed in his illustrious footsteps by walking away with the much needed $25. But the offers didn't exactly flood in after his night of glory at the Apollo and he was back begging for a play with the house band at the Palm Café.

Then, in March 1964, Jimmy's luck turned; in the Palm Café audience one night was Tony Rice, a friend of the renowned Isley Brothers.

As boys, Ronnie, Rudolph and Kelly Isley toured with their family as a gospel group, before moving to New York and singing on their own in clubs and bars. They recorded unsuccessfully with two minor labels in 1957 and 1958 until RCA snapped them up in 1959. Their biggest RCA hit was 'Shout', which gave Lulu her first hit record in the UK, but, unhappy with RCA's staid approach, they moved to Atlantic in 1960 and then to Wand in 1962. This brought them a top-twenty hit with a cover of 'Twist and Shout' which inspired the Beatles' version. United Artists became their sixth label in as many years, but finally in 1964 they moved to Teaneck, New Jersey and formed their own T-Neck label distributed by Atlantic.

When Tony Rice saw Jimmy, the Isleys were looking for a new guitarist. Tony told the Isleys to look no further; he said Jimmy was the best guitarist he'd ever seen. Ronnie Isley was somewhat sceptical, especially as Tony had estimated Jimmy's age as fifteen or sixteen. Ronnie reeled off every great guitarist he'd like to have in the band, including Curtis Mayfield and Sam Cooke's guitarist Bobby Womack; to each one, Tony said Jimmy was better. The Isleys had to see for themselves. They went down to the Palm. Unfortunately, by then, Jimmy had been frozen out for playing too loud. So Ronnie invited Jimmy up to their rented house in Englewood, New Jersey over the weekend. 'I've got amplifiers and the band will come over and we'll have some fun.' In those days, Jimmy's guitar rarely seemed to have a full set of strings – if he broke one, he didn't have the money to replace it. Part of the deal, if Jimmy came over, was that Ronnie Isley would go out and buy him a new set of strings. Jimmy turned up as arranged and Ronnie kept his promise. 'I came back and Jimmy put the strings on and said, "Do you mind if I tune up a little?" When he tuned up it was just like when he played – wonk, woonk, wheee! Well, we played some of our tunes, he knew them all from our records, and we hired him that afternoon.'5

The first priority for the Isley Brothers was to record a single on their new T-Neck label. The song was 'Testify', further testament to the two sides of Jimmy's guitar style – churning, hard-hitting rhythm chords and fluid blues-inspired solo breaks. As Jimmy began to develop his own 'cry', rhythm performed many functions in his music. Built on symmetry, it gave the music a sense of roundness and balance and tied it down to its roots. Conversely, the rhythmic structure promoted, in the words of musicologist Carl Seashore, a feeling of luxury, freedom and expanse.

Once 'Testify' was recorded, Jimmy went on tour with the Isley Brothers. Jimmy loved going to new places; the first date was at the Uptown Club in Montreal and then down to Bermuda, where the Isley Brothers were especially popular. They were booked to play a baseball stadium. The gig had been sold out for weeks and those who couldn't get tickets were standing on the hillside overlooking the stadium. For this date, the Isleys' backing band were supporting the local acts on the bill. Ronnie was in the dressing-room with his brothers 'when we heard what sounded like a riot going on and we figured one of the local acts must have had a big hit. But this guy came into the dressing-room and said, "Who's that out there?" So we all peeked and there was Jimmy down on his knees biting his guitar and the crowd were just going crazy.'[6]

The black R&B and soul-music scenes were distinguished in part from white rock 'n' roll and most of jazz in that they were dominated by solo singers or singing groups with back-up bands whose composition was in a state of constant flux. These singers were part of a black 'show' tradition and they jealously hogged the limelight and deeply resented any sideman trying to steal it away. In this, the Isleys appeared more relaxed and content to give Jimmy his wings even when he was playing behind them. They were also shrewd businessmen – Jimmy had great 'novelty' value. Jimmy himself was aware of this, but the arrangement was mutually rewarding: 'when I was with the Isleys, they used to let me do my thing, because it made them more bucks. . . . '[7] As we shall see what applied to 'uppity sidemen showing off' also applied to band uniforms – mohair suits, white shirt and tie and shiny shoes were de rigueur. Any embellishments might detract from the star. A ruffled shirt was a Communist plot at the very least. Here again, the Isleys appeared more easy-going where it helped to enhance the visual impact of the show. Jimmy might wear a chain belt with another chain hanging down, perhaps a scarf on his arm or leg. Once he got going on stage, he would be a blur of hair and metal.

None of the Isley band members could say they really got to know Jimmy – they called him 'the Creeper' because he moved around so softly, like a will o' the wisp. All they could discern for sure was that, onstage or off, his passion for music was total and absolute. Sometimes Jimmy would stay up at the Isley family home with Marvin and Ernie Isley, the younger brothers who would eventually join the band. Ernie saw something of how Jimmy and his guitar could almost be said to be one entity, how his mind focused on little other than music. Jimmy would stand in the living-room gazing out the window singing guitar phrases softly to himself. Marvin might interrupt his train of thought.

'Hey Jimmy, want some orange juice?'

'Um, yeah, okay, Marvin.'

'Want any ice in it?'

'Um, nah, no ice.'

'I'm making a peanut-butter and jelly sandwich – you want any?'

'Uh, no thanks.'

'Hey Jimmy, when do you know when to change from one string to another?'

'Well, you see, Marvin, it's like this – you tune the strings this way and . . . '

'And he'd just sit down,' says Ernie, 'and explain it all. . . . he played *all* the time, *all* the time. It wasn't like a thing you were listening to though, it was a simple observation – like the sun is shining, Jimmy's playing his guitar.'

Jimmy was a natural talent, but he did not take his gift for granted – he worked ceaselessly to perfect it. 'Jimmy would practise phrases over and over again, turn them inside out, break them in half, break them in quarters, play them slow, play them fast. . . . '

Jimmy would even use the guitar to do his talking for him: 'How are you doing, Jimmy?' 'Bading dada dooo' on the guitar. 'Is it cold outside?' 'Wheeooooow.'[8]

Everyone in the band and the other acts in the show all knew not to mess with the left-handed guy. Some musicians tried to compete like the Isleys' organist Gene Friday. He would dance and move about as he played, but Jimmy outflashed him at every turn and was almost uncharacteristically ruthless in showing Friday just who the boss man was.

Few musicians outside those he played and jammed with saw the sweat that went into honing his art, while even those around him could only imagine the source of his burgeoning talent and wild ideas.

In fact, Jimmy was developing as a conduit for the mystical source of musical genius that would eventually flow through him. The best musicians 'get out of the way' of the music to assist this flow, they become 'invisible', somehow out of reach, intangible and unknowable. Jimmy's transparency is partly shown by the slew of nicknames which attached to him during his career. To the Rocking Kings, he was 'Cupcake', because he always bought one on the way round to James Thomas' house to practise. Fresh out of the army and working in Nashville, he was 'Marbles', now 'the Creeper'. Later, in the Experience, he became 'the Bat' because, when touring, he spent most of the daylight hours cooped up in a hotel bedroom, curtains drawn, until showtime. Jimmy didn't have a ready persona that people could grab hold of, so they made up nicknames, stereotyping one particular character trait. As far as the source of his skill was concerned, Jimmy was as bewildered as anybody. He eventually came to terms with his gifts, believing in the healing power of his music and his own mission to bring that power to the world. But back in 1964 he was perhaps a little frightened by the energies released in his playing. At one point during that year, Jimmy backed the Chicago bluesman Tommy Tucker, whose big hit was 'Hi Heel Sneakers'. Tommy asked him once where all the sounds were coming from; 'I don't know, man, I just don't know.'

Jimmy could have guessed that if he went back to Seattle something bad would happen. He arrived there on tour with the Isley Brothers. He met up with an old girlfriend and disappeared into the night saying that he'd catch up with the band the following day for the trip back to New York. However, he missed the bus and then had his guitar stolen. He finally rejoined the band in New York and had to explain that their star guitarist now had no guitar. Kelly took Jimmy down to Manny's Music Store on 48th Street and bought Jimmy a new guitar – a Fender Duosonic, the first Fender guitar Jimmy ever owned.

In the history of the electric guitar, two names stand out – Les Paul and his great rival Leo Fender. The earliest electric guitar was produced by Rickenbacker for use with lap steel guitars. More popular was the ES-150 made by the Gibson company of Kalamazoo, Michigan. Introduced in 1935, it was closely associated with jazz guitarist Charlie Christian. In fact, ES-150 was the name of the pick-up – the guitar itself was still acoustic. The innovation was to have a guitar with the pick-up already attached. The first truly electric guitar was introduced by inventor Leo Fender. He named it the 'Broadcaster', but had to change it to 'Telecaster' as Gretsch already had the name for a range of drum kits. This was the first guitar whose whole design and concept was geared for use with amplification. The completely solid body and double pick-ups meant previously unattainable levels of sustain were now possible. In 1952, after a long struggle to persuade the company, Les Paul teamed up with Gibson to market the guitar which still bears his name. Both the Gibson and Fender companies extended their ranges through the fifties and early sixties, but Leo Fender always seemed to stay one jump ahead. He invented the electric bass guitar, and with it the name 'Fender' became as ubiquitous as 'Hoover' or 'Biro'. But his *pièce de résistance* was the Stratocaster, a contoured-bodied three-pick-up model which first appeared in 1954. The guitar has amazing flexibility – Buddy Holly, Hank Marvin, Eric Clapton are just a few of the musicians who have been associated with the Fender Strat. But one man was to make the Strat scream beyond Leo Fender's wildest imagination – Jimi Hendrix. In 1964, however, the idea of *Jimmy* Hendrix owning a Fender Stratocaster was just a crazy dream.

By a strange coincidence, as Jimmy was trying out his new Fender, he was nearly discovered by Les Paul. As well as being a guitar technician, Paul had pioneered multi-tracking in the studio, and also performed. Les Paul and singer Mary Ford recorded two number-one hit songs in the early fifties. One night, Les Paul and his son Gene decided to stop by the Lodi Club in New Jersey on their way to Columbia Records in New York. Gene went in first to see who was on. He soon reappeared telling his father to get in there double quick. 'I went in and stood in the doorway to listen. I was really impressed by what I heard. Yes indeed, that dude was really working his guitar over. He was bending string, playing funky as hell. I'd never seen anyone so radical.'9 They had to press on to New York, but afterwards Les Paul says he tried unsuccessfully to track Jimmy down. Invariably, there is another version of this story. According to Hendrix researcher Bill Nitopi, Les Paul actually told him that when he saw Jimmy in the club, he left immediately, his ego rather bruised by seeing a left-hander playing such stunning guitar. You pays your money and you takes your anecdote!

By October 1964, Jimmy decided to quit the band and took the opportunity of a stopover in Nashville to jump ship. Although the Isleys were very reluctant to let him go, there was no real friction; he recorded with them again in New York in 1965, although Jimmy did claim later that 'if our shoelaces were two different types we'd get fined five dollars'. This may have been literally true or Jimmy's way of expressing the straitjacket he found himself in, the band uniform being a metaphor for his lack of freedom. However relaxed the Isleys were, they were still his employers, who could tell him what to do, where to go, what to play and what to wear. To Jimmy it appeared that he'd swapped one uniform with a Screamin' Eagle patch on it for another one posing as a mohair suit.

So Jimmy was back in Nashville, hanging out once again with his old friends. While he was moving about the locality, he had two musical encounters which, while not tremendously significant in themselves, highlighted the barrenness of his onstage playing experiences at this point in his career. Sitting in a soul-food restaurant opposite the Stax recording studio in Memphis, he met up with Steve Cropper, lead guitarist for the Stax house band which under the name of Booker T and the MGs had scored a massive hit with 'Green Onions' in 1962. Cropper himself was a players' player – as clean, simple and uncluttered as the Fender Telecaster he always used. Other guitarists admired his tasteful, inventive, soulful style achieved without distortion or high-pitched soloing. A skilled songwriter, arranger and producer, the Mississippi white boy went on to cowrite 'Dock of the Bay' with Otis Redding and 'Knock on Wood' with Eddie Floyd, and handled the distinctive brass arrangements on many Stax recordings including 'Soul Man' by Sam and Dave.

Jimmy and Steve got talking. Jimmy said he had a song he wanted to record, so Steve took him across the street, set things up with the engineer in the studio and Jimmy laid down a demo accompanying himself on guitar. Nothing happened with it and the demo never resurfaced, but Jimmy obviously revelled in the chance of a one-to-one encounter with a musician of Steve Cropper's calibre. 'Steve Cropper turned me on a million years ago and I turned him on millions of years ago too, but because of different songs. . . . after [the demo] we messed around the studio for 4 or 5 hours doing different little things, it was very strange. He turned me on to lots of things. He showed me how to play certain songs and I showed him how I played "Mercy, Mercy" or something like that.'[10]

Back in Nashville, he met one of his big idols at an audition – Albert King. Despite the age gap, Jimmy and Albert got along fine and found they had much in common. Both were left-handers with large hands capable of squeezing the very life out of strings and bending them two at a time a whole step up across the fretboard. Albert King tended to tune his guitar down, slackening off the strings slightly to make them easier to bend, a trick Jimmy adopted. B.B. King says this goes back 'before I was born' and seems to have originated with Hawaiian steel guitar players on the islands. Jimmy and Albert both had a keen interest in interpreting horn sounds for the guitar. Many of the sides Albert King cut for Bobbin Records in the late fifties had big-brass arrangements which weaved in and around his instantly recognisable guitar sound. Rhythm, too, was an important part of both players' musical vocabulary; Jimmy had messed about on drums as a kid, while Albert had actually

83

had a spell as a drummer in Jimmy Reed's bands. Albert showed while Jimmy watched and then they went their separate ways. The next time they met, Jimmy was a star.

There was no school for blues guitar players – the classrooms were the bars, clubs, outdoor hops, rent parties, trains, band buses, backstage areas and studios where bluesmen sat and traded licks, tricks and ideas. Jimmy would meet up with another of his idols, B.B. King, out on the package-tour circuit. 'Jimmy was kind of quiet, shy, he didn't open up too much, but there were questions we all ask one another, you know, how do you do this and why do you do that. . . . we had small discussions on this and that.' Later still, Jimmy was in Chicago and dropped by the mecca of electric blues, Chess Records – along with Sun and Atlantic, probably one of the most important labels of all time. Their roster of blues artists was peerless, headed by Muddy Waters, Little Walter, Howlin' Wolf and Sonny Boy Williamson. And if that wasn't enough, Bo Diddley just walked in off the street, while in 1955 Muddy Waters introduced this guitar player who had been to reform school for armed robbery and was now a car-factory worker and part-time hairdresser – Chuck Berry. Chicago blues was a 'citified' sound, in other words, not the smooth urban blues style of a B.B. King, but a more raucous, raw-edged, nasty gut-bucket sound roughed up and boosted by amplification – in essence, little changed from the Mississippi country-blues style of the 1920s and 1930s, Deep Blues. This was the blues of Muddy Waters that he brought to Chicago from the Stovall plantation where he worked in Clarksdale, Mississippi – a blues of primeval, almost supernatural intensity whose power affected Jimmy deeply and whose influence on his music cannot be overestimated.

From October through into December, he went with Gorgeous George out on another tour headlined by Sam Cooke, but either by accident or design Jimmy missed the bus in Kansas City and the tour went on without him. On 11 December, Sam Cooke was shot dead by Bertha Franklin, desk clerk of the Hacienda motel in Los Angeles, who claimed Cooke attacked her. Shortly after, Jimmy arrived in George's home town of Atlanta with an address in his pocket, hoping George would find him some more work. And that's how Jimmy, now calling himself Maurice James, landed the gig with the King of Rock 'n' Roll himself, Little Richard. Through playing those after-hours sets with the Upsetters, Jimmy was already a known quantity to the Little Richard organisation. He wrote home to Al on 25 January 1965 from Lafayette, Louisiana, en route to the West Coast:

Little Richard told his biographer Charles White,

I first met Jimi Hendrix in Atlanta, Georgia where he was stranded with no money. He had been working as a guitarist with a feller called Gorgeous George. . . . My bus was parked on Auburn Avenue and Jimi was staying in this small hotel. And so he came by to see us. He had watched me work and just loved the way I wore these headbands around my hair and how wild I dressed. . . . So he came with me. He wasn't playing my kind of music, though. He was playing like B.B. King, blues. He started rocking though and he was a good guy. He began to dress like me and even grew a little moustache like mine.[11]

Hosea Wilson was one of the road managers at that time: 'Jimmy was a really strong rhythm guitar player. He was a hell of a talent . . . you could tell even then. The thing is that when Jimmy was with the band, he wasn't on the band stuff. . . . he was all quiet to himself.'[12] Jimmy would have been impressed by Little Richard's refusal to compromise on his own individuality – he was a black from the redneck South, but had been overtly gay since his teenage years. Disowned by his bootlegging father, he ran away from home. His father was later shot dead in a fight. Against all the odds, he had survived to become a major artist wearing outrageous clothes and a pompadour that looked like the leaning tower of Pisa.

However, there was one big problem for Jimmy playing with Little Richard. He hated wearing band uniforms and going through little dance routines by rote. Jimmy threw himself into playing and wanted to freak out when he felt like it. Conflict was inevitable.

Richard's brother Marquette denies that he kept Jimmy out of the limelight. Little Richard himself said later that sometimes the audience would be screaming for Jimmy and not him. He might have been magnanimous about this in retrospect, but it is hard to imagine him swallowing this for too long, especially at a time when he was trying to re-establish himself after years out of the business – since Jimmy saw him in Seattle back in 1957. The arena for conflict in these situations was fairly predictable – stage appearance.

> Little Richard didn't want anybody to look better than him. I was the best of friends with Glyn Willings, another guy in the band, and we used to buy the same old stuff and wear it on stage. After the show one night, Little Richard said, 'Brothers, we've got to have a meeting. . . . I am Little Richard and I am the King of Rock 'n' Rhythm and I'm the one who's going to look pretty on stage. Glyn and Jimmy, will you please turn in those shirts or else you will have to suffer the consequences of a fine.' He had another meeting over my hairstyle. I said I wasn't going to cut my hair for nobody. 'That'll be a five-dollar fine for you.' Everybody on the tour was brainwashed.'[13]

Jimmy was so unhappy with the situation, he went AWOL when they reached Los Angeles. Meanwhile a young black musician from Memphis called Arthur Lee, who was working the local clubs, was looking for a guitarist for a song he'd just written. 'I wrote a song for a chick . . . Rosa Lee Brooks. And I started working this out with her. And then this cat tells me he knows a guy who can play guitar. See, I wanted this Curtis Mayfield feeling . . . like he does in "People Get Ready" . . . that certain guitar feel. And this guy tells me there is a cat in town who can play that trip . . . and that was Jimi Hendrix. . . . He was working with Little Richard at the time, that was the first time I saw him.'[14]

The song was called 'My Diary' b/w 'Utee' released on Revis Records. 'My Diary' was a fairly predictable slow soul ballad with plenty of tremolo on the mellow guitar tone – a ubiquitous guitar sound that was in demand on most of the soul ballads of the day. Arthur Lee was in the process of forming Love, the thinking man's flower-power pop band of the sixties – Hollywood seedy and San Francisco transcendental meets Memphis raunch. Around the time of this very uncharacteristic recording, Love were debuting at a fly-blown dump called Brave New World. Jimmy and Arthur remained friends and later recorded a complete album together.

Little Richard was also in the studio needing Jimmy's services on his new single 'I Don't Know What You've Got But It's Got Me'. Again Jimmy turned in his impersonation of Curtis Mayfield as he had done for Arthur Lee. Lee's effort had been something of a throwaway, whereas Richard was in need of a hit. His last single 'Bama Lama Loo' was very much in the vein of his previous recordings. But black music taste had been changing – soul was what everybody wanted to hear and so Little Richard duly obliged. The record was released in October 1965 on Veejay Records, but although it made number twelve in the R&B chart, it hardly dented the *Billboard* and *Cashbox* Hot Hundred charts and 'Bama Lama Loo' turned out to be Little Richard's last important hit.

Jimmy with Little Richard and members of the Upsetters and the Kingpins
Paramount Theater, New York City, 17 or 18 April 1965

While on leave from Little Richard's band, Jimmy did a few gigs with Ike and Tina Turner. The story goes that Ike soon dropped Jimmy off when he could see the reaction Jimmy got from women and had visions of him turning on the charm with Tina and the Ikettes. A stint with Sam and Dave was also short-lived, Jimmy committing any one of a number of transgressions which could get him fired. He picked up with Little Richard again in St Louis, but things went from bad to worse and the situation came to a head when they reached New York in the spring of 1965.

From 17 to 19 April, they had three dates lined up at the Paramount Theater, alongside a number of artists including King Curtis and two British acts, the Hollies and Sandie Shaw. Sitting in the audience for the first night was a black model, Pat Hartley, who became a friend of Jimmy's; 'the curtain opens and there's a huge gold throne and lots of red carpet and out come two belly dancers who couldn't belly dance their way out of anywhere . . . in amazing costumes. These four guys come out and one of them was Jimmy and he was really gorgeous with his long hair and played electric guitar in between "the bellies".'[15] But the star of this show, a comedian called Soupy Sales, took exception to Little Richard trying to upstage him and actually managed, by the greatest of ironies, to get Little Richard thrown off the bill.

One of Little Richard's four brothers, Robert, claims that he fired Jimmy.

> He was always late for the bus and flirting with girls and stuff like that. It came to a head in New York, where we had been playing The Apollo and Hendrix missed the bus for Washington D.C. I finally got Richard to cut him loose. I believe when you're paying people, they've got certain obligations. . . . So when Hendrix called . . . I gave him the word that his services were no longer required. We had some words, I explained why we were doing this. I was running the road for Richard and I didn't accept that kind of bullshit.[16]

Jimmy on the other hand wrote to Al from New York saying he had left Little Richard precisely because 'he didn't pay us for five and a half weeks, and you can't live on promises when you're on the road, so I had to cut that mess loose'.

So Jimmy was back where he started – in New York, no money and looking for work. But he realised he couldn't just sit around; he'd done a lot of playing and his technical ability had grown apace. Now he desperately wanted to record his own material and have a shot at forming his own band. He started hawking his own material around record companies in New York. What he had to offer is unknown, although he once said, 'When I was younger I used to write protest songs that were bitter.'[17] At eighteen he was writing poetry, which although repetitious in places was some distance from the 'moon/june' doodlings which most adolescent poetry aspires to. The following example attempts to capture the speech rhythms and cadences of a Harlem hipster – with Shakespearean pretensions perhaps:

> Blessings on thee little square
> O barefoot hag with uncombed hair
> With thy solid peg-legged pants
> And thy solid hep cat stance
> With thy cheeks so fine and mellow
>
> Kiss thy cheeks so fine and mellow
> I was just a little square
> Like the cat with unconked hair
> Now I'm hip to the chicks
> And far from a drip
> The cats on the square
> Call me Joe Ad-Lib
> To show how the cats will rap your
> Scratchings if you're not into
> Their latchings
> Stached at the main crib
> Crib on the hep cat square
> When I just hit this trip
> I was laughed for a square
>
> I'm telling you Jack
> These cats are on with half a chance
> They'll give you the gong
> The hats with the gats
> And the scopes with them gapes
> Pitch a fog very dim
> Over some dregs
> My first encounter with some of these frills
> When I was down at Joe's I was flatched to the gills

She had a candied cutie
Over a solid coke frame
I was so loaded to the gills
I didn't get her name.

The writing here is sufficiently developed to indicate that Jimmy was probably trying to sell songs a cut above the often banal soul lyric. The response he got is shown in a letter he sent home dated 8 August 1965, which neatly sums up the point he had reached in his career:

I still have my guitar and amp and as long as I have that, no fool can keep me from living. There's a few record companies I visited that I probably can record for. I think I'll start working toward that line because actually when you're playing behind other people you're still not making a big name for yourself as you would if you were working for yourself. But I went on the road with other people to get exposed to the public and see how business is taken care of. And mainly just to see what's what, and after I put a record out, there'll be a few people who know me already and who can help with the sale of the record.

Nowadays people don't want you to sing good. They want you to sing sloppy and have a good beat to your songs. That's what angle I'm going to shoot for. That's where the money is. So just in case about three or four months from now you might hear a record by me which sounds terrible, don't feel ashamed, just wait until the money rolls in because everyday people are singing worse and worse on purpose and the public buys more and more records.

I just want to let you know I'm still here, trying to make it. Although I don't eat every day, everything's going all right for me. It could be worse than this, but I'm going to keep hustling and scuffling until I get things to happening like their supposed to for me.

Tell everyone I said hello. Leon, Grandma, Ben, Ernie, Frank, Mary, Barbara and so forth. Please write soon. It's pretty lonely out here by myself. Best luck and happiness in the future. Love, your son. Jimmy.

For all his shyness and self-effacement this letter shows that Jimmy not only had a supreme confidence in his own abilities, but was totally convinced, when the reality of his daily existence denied it, that he was a coming talent waiting to happen. Only later did the doubts creep in, when the accolades were heaped upon him whether he played well or not.

Jimmy had been back with Fay since the end of his time with Little

Richard, which meant the usual round of cadging meals and hopping from one seedy hotel to another to avoid paying the rent, hoping his gear wouldn't be locked in the room until they did. Therefore, with money at a premium, Fay was less than pleased with Jimmy when he went out and spent their last few dollars on the new Bob Dylan album *Highway 61 Revisited*, released in August 1965.

On a number of levels, Dylan had a profound effect on Jimmy. At the most superficial level, and contrary to what Jimmy had been told by record companies, Dylan showed there was a market among young people for 'serious' songs which actually made you think. This came as a revelation to Jimmy, so used to laying down music almost exclusively in support of love songs whose vocabulary ranged from sentimental to crude. The difference, of course, was that Dylan's market was one particular sector of the white record-buying public, while Jimmy's material was being assessed for its sales potential to a black audience.

In his letter to Al, he had complained that 'people don't want you to sing good. They want you to sing sloppy.' Well, at least that was confirmed by hearing Dylan's half-spoken nasal slur – although in fact Dylan was using his voice as an *instrument* rather than as a vehicle for the clear enunciation of his lyrics. At the risk of making a virtue out of necessity, this technique added a meaning to the songs which extended beyond what the words actually said, and relied instead on the tripartite tensions set up between lyric, voice and any additional instrumentation. With the range and colour of sound that Jimmy could introduce into this formula, in his hands the effect of this technique was stunning. But Jimmy's comment about sloppy singing is nonetheless puzzling. Soul and R&B lyrics may on the whole have been mundane, but the biggest chart hits in these genres were sung by stellar vocal talents like Otis Redding, Jackie Wilson, Solomon Burke, Wilson Pickett, the Supremes and so on, where accusations of sloppy singing were hardly appropriate. As a black singer you could be sweet or diamond hard, but to please an audience steeped in a religious and secular vocal tradition going back to the earliest days of slavery and beyond, you had to be pure and strong. Jimmy knew he could never compete vocally at this level, although ultimately his voice was much underrated not least by Jimmy himself. But listening to *Highway 61* in 1965 put out by a major record company, perhaps he realised he didn't have to.

At a more subliminal level, Dylan had a significant impact on the development of Jimmy's lyrical devices. He sketched out a blueprint for Jimmy's poetic imagery and provided the primary colours for Jimmy to paint in the broad strokes on his own emotional landscape. To paraphrase David Bowie, Bob Dylan sat behind Jimmy's eyes and guided in him what he saw. But, perhaps more importantly, he lodged himself in Jimmy's soul to articulate what he felt.

Highway 61 was not Jimmy's baptism of fire with Dylan; once in a black club Jimmy had marched in with a copy of Dylan's first album under his arm and asked the DJ to put on 'Blowin' in the Wind'. The DJ obliged, but Jimmy nearly got lynched by the dancers for interrupting their music. When he brought the new album home to Fay, he couldn't believe it when she told him she'd never even heard of Bob Dylan.

With isolation and alienation as the album's predominant theme, he would have heard much on *Highway 61* with which he could relate. Partly to educate Fay, he played the album until light shone through the vinyl, dragging her across the room to hear this verse or that refrain.

When Dylan sang of loneliness and a life without direction in 'Like A Rolling Stone', one can imagine Jimmy's eyes shining, and him thinking, 'Yeah, man, I know what you're sayin',' and then perhaps letting out a characteristic giggle at the line 'scroungin' your next meal'. He would have sat thoughtfully ruminating on 'Ballad of a Thin Man', reflecting on *his* sense of always feeling like an outsider, *with* people but not really *of* them, sitting on the other side of the barrier that was his guitar, while across the great divide many looked on and saw a 'weirdo', somebody who had lost his marbles walking around the streets singing guitar phrases to himself, playing the instrument back to you when you spoke to him like a ventriloquist's dummy, sleeping with it, talking to it, protecting it. He would have pondered on the aural pyrotechnics of 'Desolation Row', Dylan's bleak analysis of American society where there are no broad answers and where catastrophe is inevitable when people deny the possibility of it ever happening. 'The *Titanic* sailed at dawn', but as it went down the band played on. Yet amid this and others of Dylan's apocalyptic visions was a hope, some wreckage to cling on to, that through individual development, an 'unwarped perspective', as Dylan critic Michael Gray put it, might remain, that losing values was okay if false values were revealed in the process, that there could be history after Armageddon. Jimmy wanted the new life built on music and spent all his short life trying to show people how this might be done.

Dylan had psychedelic insights which Jimmy was not yet party to and a political outlook that Jimmy was never comfortable with, but what he didn't 'understand' in a crude sense, he 'felt', and so paradoxically 'understood' more about Dylan than any literary analysis could reveal.

In his own writing, Jimmy would reiterate a number of Dylan's key metaphors, principally the sea, the road, the rain and the themes of alienation and apocalypse woven into the fabric of many of Dylan's mid-sixties recordings. Jimmy was also to pay direct homage by recording and/or playing live, 'Like a Rolling Stone', 'All Along the Watchtower', 'Drifter's Escape' and 'Can You Please Crawl Out Your Window?' He brought his own art to bear on these songs – the fine detail of his sound paintings, creating for his audience enhanced and multi-dimensional visions from Dylan's catalogue of the human condition.

Fay listened, humouring Jimmy in his schoolboy enthusiasms for this white guy whose songs she couldn't understand and whose music she couldn't dance to. The fight they had about Jimmy spending the money and the virtues or otherwise of Bob Dylan showed Jimmy that, as much as he wanted and needed Fay, she was part of the Harlem scene which Jimmy had tired of. He had to concede that she was part of his past, not his future.

Jimmy would always run away from an argument and it got to the point with Fay where he was communicating with her via letter because 'it seems that this is the only way I can express myself and say what I want to say without being interrupted and without starting an argument'. But the fighting carried on and they split up, although they remained good friends over the years.

Jimmy had never been at ease in Harlem. Quite apart from being cold-shouldered most places he tried to play, he never felt himself one of the 'brothers' and consequently was tagged as somebody who had an 'attitude'. During his time with Fay, they stayed in a house occupied by friends of hers who became quite close to Jimmy, Arthur Allen and his twin brother Albert. Albert explains: 'he was very self-conscious about himself . . . about the things he wore, because he was kind of different you know, kind of freaky, especially in comparison to a lot of brothers at that time. He was very sensitive to the places that he liked to be in. . . .'18

Dylan was in essence the catalyst in energising Jimmy to move out of Harlem. He couldn't see much hope of being able to record his own material on a black record label and felt that Dylan's own

93

London
end of April or May 1967

milieu, the bohemian, artistic community of Greenwich Village, would be more receptive, more open and liberal-minded, more ready to accept individuality. As Albert Allen puts it, 'He figured people would tolerate him a little bit more . . . because he would just blend in with the crowd. Which he didn't because he always stood out, he was always a stand-out person. We used to call him the wicked witch from the East, because of the hat he used to wear.'

But being bohemian and free wasn't going to feed him, and Jimmy still had to try and earn a living on a 'have guitar – will travel' basis. In November he wrote home from Boston to say he was on tour with Joey Dee and the Starlighters, who for a long time were the house band at New York's Peppermint Lounge with a number-one hit in 1961, 'Peppermint Twist'.

In between touring Jimmy was still on the look-out for a recording opportunity plus any session work he could pull to earn a few bucks. Standing in the lobby of a dump called the Hotel America on West 47th Street Jimmy got talking to Curtis Knight, a musician from Fort Scott, Kansas who was visiting the small recording studio located on the ground floor of the hotel. Knight had been in New York for about eighteen months, having made his way across country from Los Angeles. He played guitar and sang and, after some time bumming around the clubs, he formed a band called the Squires doing the usual mix of blues and soul for the drinking/dancing-club circuit. Knight was introduced to a record producer Ed Chalpin who ran Studio 76 on the corner of 51st Street and Broadway. With soul music taking off in a big way, Chalpin thought he might be able to groom Knight for stardom and signed him up for record production and management.

When they first met, Knight says that Jimmy was 'between' guitars, having pawned his last one yet again to eat and pay his rent. Knight went off to get a second guitar he had and an amp, Jimmy went back up to his room on the seventh floor to await Knight's return. When Jimmy started playing, Knight was speechless, but his brain was still working – with Jimmy in the Squires, who knew where it might lead to? The Squires were gigging three or four nights a week and Jimmy had little or no work, so he jumped at the chance for some regular money when Knight offered him a job. To cash in on the fad for 'protest' songs, Knight had 'rewritten' 'Like a Rolling Stone', given it a black slant, calling it, 'How Would You Feel?' Armed with this and his new friend, the guitar ace, Knight headed for Studio 76 and Ed Chalpin. When the producer heard Jimmy, he lost no time and on

15 October 1965 Jimmy signed a single-sheet contract with Chalpin's company PPX Enterprises. Jimmy knew nothing from nothing about the music business and the repercussions of those fateful strokes of the pen reverberated down through the years.

Jimmy was signed for three years to 'produce and play and/or sing exclusively for PPX'. He would get only minimum scale for any arrangements, no control over the release of any recordings and no financial help for equipment save what he could salvage from the 1 per cent royalty he would get once PPX had recouped all the studio expenses. In exchange Jimmy got $1 'and other good and valuable consideration', although what this meant in practice was not spelt out. But what it all meant in the short term was that Jimmy could be used as a session musician without getting session rates.

On the snowy night of 26 December 1965, the Squires played an old hang-out of Curtis Knight's, George's Club 20 in Hackensack, New Jersey. The crowd were in good festive mood, encouraged by Knight's stage announcement that the gig was being recorded. 'What are you goin' to do for the people, Jimmy, on Christmas plus one?' 'A little thing called "Drivin' South",' Jimmy drawls back. On the strength of 'Drivin' South', 'California Nights', Howlin' Wolf's 'Killin' Floor' and other recordings with the Squires during 1965–6, Jimmy could now lay serious claim to being among the finest blues guitarists in America. And certainly there was nobody in England to touch him, even though at the time Eric Clapton was burning down the houses with John Mayall's Bluesbreakers. The pick of the live recordings, the diamonds in the rough, show that Jimmy had the blues idiom entirely within his grasp and the only question to be asked was – where would he go from here? Even Jimmy himself acknowledged his progress for in a card home dated 13 January 1966 he wrote, 'tell Ben and Ernie I play the blues like they NEVER heard!'

That fateful Paramount Theater gig with Little Richard had been Jimmy's introduction to the great King Curtis, the most sought-after sax session musician in the States whose pile-driving R&B sax can be heard on the Coasters' massive hit 'Yakety Yak'. Before he was tragically stabbed to death in 1971, Curtis had worked with musicians representing just about every style of popular music including Buddy Holly, Sam Cooke, Aretha Franklin, Andy Williams, Lionel Hampton and Duane Allman. King Curtis had his own band, the Kingpins, with some of New York's finest, like guitarist Cornell Dupree and drummer Bernard 'Pretty' Purdie.

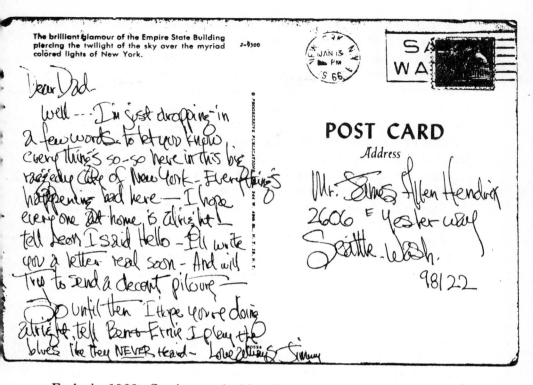

The brilliant glamour of the Empire State Building piercing the twilight of the sky over the myriad colored lights of New York.

POST CARD

Address

Mr. James Allen Hendrix
2606 E Yesler Way
Seattle, Wash.
98122

Dear Dad—

Well --- I'm just dropping in a few words to let you know every thing's so-so here in this big raggedy City of New York — Everything's happening bad here — I hope every one at home is alright — tell Leon I said Hello — I'll write you a letter real soon — And will Try to send a decent piture — So until then I hope you're doing alright, tell Ben + Ernie I play the blues like they NEVER heard — Love always Jimmy

Early in 1966, Curtis was looking for a second guitarist – Jimmy auditioned and got the gig. Cornell Dupree already knew of Jimmy from his days with the Isley Brothers:

It was in Wildwood, New Jersey. . . . there was King Curtis, Fats Domino, the Isleys and a bunch of other acts at the different clubs. Jimmy and I stayed in the same hotel for about a month and during that time we got acquainted. He was very quiet and shy, but we'd talk – we found out we were born under the same sign for instance. We used to sit in our rooms and do a little pickin' together.

At the time [Jimmy joined the band] Curtis was trying to . . . expand it. There was one particular gig I remember where Jimmy and Billy Preston were on the gig together, which was *really* something.

We played opposite – and also behind – Chuck Berry . . . upstate at one of the colleges. Jimmy just stole the show. . . . when he felt the spirit I mean he would go out and *perform*. . . . It was just those magic moments, I guess, when he felt like it and he did it, because he didn't do it all the time – it wasn't planned. But he stole a few shows.

With gigs lined up, Jimmy had to learn fast. 'In a couple of days,' recalls Bernard Purdie, 'he knew everything, so he didn't have any problem. . . . he really picked up very easily.' Purdie and Ray Lucas would alternate on the drum chair, Purdie generally sticking to the studio while Lucas went out on the road. 'We didn't even have time to rehearse before the gig that night [at Small's Paradise, where King Curtis had a residency] and on a lot of songs that Jimmy didn't know, the bass player had to whisper the chords to him. But I never in all my fucking life saw anybody pick up songs as fast as Jimmy did that night.'

Musically the Kingpins were probably the best bunch Jimmy had ever played with, but there was no opportunity to stretch out and jam, so really it was situation normal for Jimmy, however good the band was. Inevitably, Curtis was a stickler for the proper wearing of the band uniform and you could only take off your jacket if he did. The material was the standard crop of current US and by now UK chart hits. 'Stand by Me' by the Drifters was a big favourite, and of course the Coasters' 'Yakety Yak'. Curtis expected the band to do all those unison movements from the shoulder, which Jimmy tried to avoid by moving as far up the stage as possible without being spotted.

Jimmy could justifiably feel he was getting nowhere – formula gigs with King Curtis and dates with Curtis Knight which afforded at least some limited opportunity to freak out and lay down some blues, the odd recurring date and otherwise starve unless a nice girl took him home and fed him. To his credit, however, fed up as he was, he remained a professional, as Bernard Purdie explains: 'Jimmy was well liked by everyone because he did his job. . . . there were no problems and he had no hassles with the people and that was the best part – he *really* did his job.'

But around the spring of 1966 he thought if he was going to starve, he might as well do it on his own terms. One story has it that he was fired by King Curtis for not wearing the cufflinks in his shirt properly, insisting that the shirt cuffs should be folded over his jacket sleeves. It seems unlikely that Curtis would sack one of his star players on such a flimsy pretext, nor is there any accompanying story that he owed Jimmy money. Bernard Purdie does not recall any particular aggravation, so likely as not Jimmy just upped and left.

I had these dreams that something was gonna happen, seeing the number 1966 in my sleep, so I was just passing the time till then. I wanted my own scene, making *my* music, not playing the same riffs.[19]

Jimmy's relations with Curtis Knight had also soured because Jimmy wanted to leave the Squires, but the only guitar he had belonged to Knight, who wasn't about to let Jimmy walk off with it. Jimmy was rescued by his new girlfriend, his first white girlfriend, a blonde named Carol Shiroky, who everyone knew then as Kim, speaking here for the first time on life with Jimmy. 'I met him at a friend's house and he was sitting in the middle of the living-room on an amp strumming and I didn't like him. I thought he was on an ego trip, it was like "Hi" and that was that.' The next time she met him was at the newly opened club called the Cheetah, where the Squires were the second act to be booked. 'He came over to the table and he said, "I wanna tell you something, but I bet you're gonna laugh." I said, "I won't laugh." He said, "No, you're gonna laugh." "*I promise I won't laugh!*" "Well, I wanna kiss you on your knee." So, of course, I laughed. I mean how many people tell you they wanna kiss you on your knee? Three days later we moved in together. It was like an instant fire kind of thing.'

Living with him in the Lennox Hotel, it didn't take Carol long to realise Jimmy was someone a bit different.

Jimmy always used to say he was not from this planet, he was from somewhere out in space. That was his great line when he got in a crazy-ass mood, 'I'm not from this planet.' Hey, listen, you know he wasn't your average Joe, let's face it. You know what he ate for breakfast? Spaghetti and garlic! I said, 'What do you want for breakfast? Eggs?' '*Eggs?* Damn, I want spaghetti and garlic – no sauce!'
He was having a lot of problems with Curtis, he was unhappy, having fights about not being paid – or not being paid – a pittance, you know, just enough to keep him fed.

One night after another row, 'He came in roaring. He woke up in the middle of the night, got up, wrote two verses of a song, threw it at me and went back to bed. Never finished it, never put it to music and I never found out what the fight was about either.'

My friends of fashion
Turned out to be my enemies of thought.
They don't dig the way I'm thinking
They say they adore my chequered bell-bottoms
And wine-coloured socks
But in reality one of us is faking.
So what do I do after thinking about you

And your beautiful long-haired friends?
I just hope and pray that someday
They'll all begin to appreciate the bag I'm livin' in.

In New York, there were two distinct strands of music. Back in the early sixties Joey Dee and the Starlighters had set the trend for bars and dance-halls to have their own favourite house band doing chart hits and standards. Jordan Christopher and the Wild Ones packed them in at Arthur's, with Dow Jones and the Industrials at Trude Heller's. The Cheetah, which opened in April 1966, was one of New York's first 'mixed media' discos, raving to the sounds of Mike St Shaw and the Prophets. The Squires played there and like many of the punters and performers, the band got themselves rigged out in look-alike cheetah skins. The Purple Onion in Greenwich Village and Ondine's on the Upper East Side were other dance venues that Jimmy played with Joey Dee, the Squires and Carl Holmes and the Commanders, who'd had one twist album out on Atlantic in 1963. Folk singer Richie Havens was opening at Cheetah's when Jimmy was there with Carl Holmes not long after the club opened.

> That's how I met [Jimi]. . . . I walked in the door, it's early at night
> . . . it's empty. This place was a ballroom and there were about fifty
> people there. . . . I see this guy standing on the stage biting his guitar.
> Like what the heck is he doing, what is that, you know? And I look for
> the other guitar player 'cause I'm saying . . . he can't be making those
> notes. Where's the other guitar player? No other guitar player! I was
> up under that stage, man, and it's only about three feet from the floor.
> . . . I was on my knees trying to look under the guy's guitar saying,
> '*What* is he doing?'

The other strand was loose folk-rock based in Greenwich Village and centred on clubs like the Cafe Au Go Go and the Bitter End on Bleecker Street, the Night Owl Café on West Third Street, the Bizarre and the Golden Bug, and on MacDougal Street South, the Café Wha?

The Café Wha? was a basement club under the Players' Theater where Ed Sanders and the Fugs performed anarchic, speed-driven rock-poetry satire every night. The basement opened up in the early afternoon – admission was free and you could sit there all afternoon for the price of one item on the menu. Those who played were really auditioning for a spot on the bill in the evening – it was called a hoot –

anybody who had the guts to get up and play did it. The club was right down the pecking order of the Village clubs, a hierarchy headed up by the Gaslight, right across the street from the Café Wha?. The contrast couldn't have been more marked; all the top names like Tim Hardin, Dylan, David Van Ronk and the fêted blues artists like Mississippi John Hurt, Sonny Terry and Brownie McGhee were Gaslight regulars. You never heard of anybody who played the Café Wha?, but with the weekend cover charge at only $1 it was a good place to go to spot new talent when you didn't have much money.

It was here in the heart of Greenwich Village that Jimmy (now calling himself Jimmy James) concentrated his efforts at finding work for himself and his first band. This he called initially the Rainflowers and then, in honour of Junior Parker's band, Jimmy James and the Blue Flames. But first he had to leave Curtis Knight. Carol couldn't understand why Jimmy was so unhappy but still carried on playing in the band. The answer was simple: 'Because it's his guitar.' 'Two days later I went out and bought him a white Fender Stratocaster.' Jimmy finally had his hands on his dream machine – his very own Fender Strat. 'That was the love of his life and he filed down the frets on the strings, because he'd reverse the order of the strings, and he sat there for hours and hours filing the frets. So the strings would fit in reverse. Curtis never forgave me for that, he didn't talk to me for a long time.' So Jimmy had a way out. A black singer, 'King' George Clemons, recalls seeing Jimmy in a club around mid-May unplug his guitar at the end of the set with the words, 'That's the last time I play this shit.'

The Café Wha? was especially useful for Jimmy precisely because it wasn't fashionable. He could work out his material and sharpen up his stage presence in front of an audience, but one that was extremely tolerant, often because most of them were the next performers waiting to go on.

The line-up of Jimmy's band was fluid, and included a fifteen-year-old guitarist who'd run away from home in Los Angeles, Randy Wolfe. He was in Manny's Music Store on 48th Street buying a guitar and saw this tall thin black guy standing there playing a new guitar. While he was listening to Randy, Jimmy got really excited about what the young kid was doing. He invited Randy down the Café Wha? to play with him that night – his first solo gig. They spent fifteen minutes in the dressing-room, which at the Café Wha? was the boiler-room – and Jimmy taught Randy 'Hey Joe', 'Like a Rolling Stone', 'Wild Thing', 'Shotgun' and a few other songs. 'We played together for about three months. . . . the band made about $60 a night and Jimmy split it equally four ways. . . . The bass player in the band was named Randy also; and because he was from Texas, Jimmy called him Randy Texas and me Randy California. So that's how I got my name.' Later that year, Randy California returned home to form Spirit with his stepfather, drummer Ed Cassidy. The sales assistant that day in Manny's Music Store was Jeff Baxter of Steely Dan and Doobie Brothers fame, who played bass in the Blue Flames a couple of times.

Carol recalls Jimmy dubbing Randy Texas 'Robin' – Jimmy, of course, was Batman. 'Jimmy *loved* Batman. He sat on the edge of the bed and read every word that came on the screen, the old Adam West series, he would live for Batman.' She goes on, ' "Wild Thing" was born in the Hotel Lennox. He came home one night and asked me if I'd heard that song. It was on the radio a day or so later, he came flying out of the bathroom, butt-assed naked, hair in rollers, listening to the radio, picked up the guitar and started playing it. He loved that song, he listened to it once or twice and that was it – music came so easy to him.'

Soon Jimmy was doing six nights a week at the Café Wha?; he wasn't living with Carol then – they'd had a number of arguments. 'You couldn't hold him down. If you tried to hold him down that's when you lost him. There were nights he didn't come home and I knew he was in someone else's bed and I would never question him, because if I did he'd be gone.' But Jimmy remained in contact with her as he did most of his ex-girlfriends and she was down at the Café Wha? regularly to watch him play. Her recollection is not $60 a night, but $7 for the whole band.

> They used to put him on at the close, at the end of the evening, 'cos he would go off, the last song would be forty-five minutes of feedback and freak everybody out. We'd all be sitting there, the place would be dark, they'd be mucking about with the lights and he would just get lost in himself. We would leave there exhausted.
>
> He got very frustrated very easily if things didn't go right – I saw him lay down on the stage and cry during a performance. I've seen him walk offstage because he broke a string and leave the other guys sitting there like 'Okay, what do we do now?'

Jimmy was picking up some influential friends in the Village. John Hammond Jr, son of the man who signed up for Columbia Billie Holiday, Pete Seeger, Bob Dylan and Bruce Springsteen, in one lifetime, was a prominent torch carrier for the revitalised interest in the blues among the young urban white middle class. Having recorded his first blues album for Vanguard in 1963, he went up to Canada and brought back with him a band called the Hawks who had been backing rockabilly singer Ronnie Hawkins. By the time Hammond met Jimmy, the Hawks had been lured away by Bob Dylan and become the Band, but not before playing on Hammond's 1965 album *So Many Roads*, songs from which Jimmy was performing onstage with the Blue Flames.

John Hammond was working the Gaslight.

> One night between shows . . . my friend who was working the Players' Theater . . . came over and said, 'John, there's this band playing downstairs that you've got to hear. This guy is doing songs off your old album, and he sounds better than you.' So I thought I'd check this out. I went down there . . . and he was playing the guitar parts better than Robbie Robertson had. He was a really handsome black kid, playing with these guys who could barely keep the beat. . . . He was playing a Fender Stratocaster upside down and left-handed – one of those things that just boggles your mind. I just could not believe it – playing with his teeth, and doing all those really slick techniques that I had seen in Chicago on the south side on wild nights. But here was this guy doing it, and he was fantastic playing blues. [20]

Jimmy felt it was about time for some 'up-market' exposure and, once he and John Hammond had established a rapport, he asked him if he could help at all. Work was not that easy to come by – as Jimmy himself graphically indicated. 'We'd get a gig once every twelfth of never. We even tried to eat orange peel and tomato paste. Sleeping outside them tall tenements was hell. Rats running all across your chest, cockroaches stealing your last candy bar out of your pocket.'[21] It so happened that John had a gig coming up at the Café Au Go Go. They rehearsed together and opened there about two weeks later. This was the classiest club on MacDougal Street, the place where all the visiting English musicians showed up, the place where the Beatles, the Rolling Stones and the Animals all got their first sight of the most accomplished, most visually exciting blues guitarist they had ever seen.

The word was out to all the hot-shot guitar players in the Village to check out this black guy who played a Strat upside down. *The* name guitarist on the block was Mike Bloomfield, who played with Paul Butterfield as his regular gig, but had been called up by Dylan for *Highway 61*

Revisited. 'I thought I was *it.*' Mike saw Jimmy for the first time when he was still at the Café Wha?. 'Hendrix knew who I was, and that day, in front of my eyes, he burned me to death. I didn't even get my guitar out. H bombs were going off, guided missiles were flying – I can't tell you the sounds he was getting out of his instrument. He was getting every sound I was ever to hear him get right there in that room. . . . I didn't even want to pick up a guitar for the next year.'[22]

The Loft on Hudson Street was a general hangout place for musicians to drop by and jam or just get stoned. Guitarist Roy Buchanan came by – he and Jimmy blasted each other into the night racing ahead of the music on speed. Smoking dope to keep mellow and snorting methedrine to keep going was as natural as breathing for the tight community of musicians. Jimmy kept his speed crystals in a baby's bottle, always a source of great amusement. It was no big deal. The only time Jimmy ever met Dylan, at the Kettle of Fish on MacDougal Street, they were both completely stoned. Asked about what should have been an auspicious event, Hendrix could only recall, 'We just hung about laughing. Yeah, we just laughed.'[23]

Through Carol, Jimmy met Mike Quashie, six foot two inches and fifteen stone of Trinidadian singer and dancer who introduced the limbo dance to America and consequently had his face on the front of *Life* magazine in March 1961. Fire-eating and fire-walking were also part of his repertoire and Jimmy was interested to talk to Mike about West Indian and African voodoo and obeah. Carol says about Mike and Jimmy, 'They were very tight together.' Jimmy took a fancy to Mike's colourful scarves and 'borrowed' one or two to wear on stage tied around his arm or leg, something he'd been doing for quite some time now, when 'rules' about uniform had allowed. Mike was also a source of ready cash for Jimmy when he needed it, which seemed like all the time. But Jimmy more than paid Mike back when he hit the big time; Mike's expensive hospital bills were often settled by his good friend. Mike had thought Jimmy was a pimp the first time he saw him strolling around Carol's hotel room in pink and yellow curlers.

Mike says that the club owners in the Village didn't like Jimmy that much because he wouldn't feed their egos, asking for special billing or going on at certain times. 'He never had time to open up to all these assholes. He said, "I have no time for all this bullshit." ' Jimmy just turned up in time to do the show, did it and left. But Jimmy was never impolite, he just backed away from situations. 'He hated to say "no" to anybody,' says Carol. 'He would kind of dance around the issue, he didn't like the word "no" for some reason. It was like, "I'll get back to you" or "I'll let you know." ' Mike concurs: 'You could never pin him down. If anybody ever say they pin Hendrix down. . . . If Hendrix say "yes" to you, you have to know which "yes" is really "yes" and which one is "no". Boy, what a guy.'

Inevitably, Jimmy got to know some of the women in the Village who were part of the music scene. Emeretta Marks was in the original cast of *Hair*. 'I saw him in the Village a lot. I used to sing with the Blues Project.' Then there was Jeanette Jacobs. She had come from a background as disturbed as his own. 'He used to grab drinks out of my hand and say, "You've had enough." His mother used to drink. "Please don't drink, you're the only girl who could make me cry apart from my mother." He said to me, "You're going to have all the clothes you want when I'm a big star." He'd take down the addresses of clothes shops, and say, "You can have this, and that. . . . "'24

After Carol, Jimmy's next regular girlfriend was Diane Carpenter. She was only sixteen years old when they met and she lived with Jimmy in New York for about six months. During their time together, she allegedly conceived a daughter by Jimmy named Tamika, who was the subject of a later paternity suit. Diane's daughter was never formally recognised as Jimmy's child, 'because, I was told, my daughter was black'. But many years later Al Hendrix sent a photo and wrote on the back 'with love from Gramps', which Tamika, now in her twenties, has cherished ever since.

With so many of the best musicians in New York, music capital of the States, *and* some of the biggest names in British pop all seeing Jimmy and enthusing wildly, something *had* to happen sooner or later. The story goes that Linda Keith, Keith Richard's girlfriend, had taken a special interest in Jimmy. With the Stones on tour, Jimmy became a regular visitor to her hotel suite grateful for the access she gave him to food, money, and records. Linda knew Chas Chandler, bass player of the Animals, who were about to embark on their farewell tour of America commencing in late June/early July of 1966. She also knew that once the tour was over, Chas would be looking for an opportunity to manage and produce his own acts in partnership with the Animals manager, Mike Jeffery. Linda had already taken a record producer down to the Café Wha? to see Jimmy. He looked, listened, shrugged his shoulders and walked out – another black guitarist struttin' his stuff – so what? Undaunted, Linda persuaded Chas to go down and check out Jimmy for himself. Now bluff Newcastle Geordies are not easily impressed, but when Chas saw Jimmy he knew he was on to something. One of the songs Jimmy played when Chas saw him was 'Hey Joe'. By coincidence this was the very song that Chas wanted to cover in England to launch his business career.

The song had chequered origins. It was first recorded by an LA band called the Leaves in 1965 and was called 'Hey Joe, Where You Gonna Go?' They rerecorded it in 1966, shortened the title, smoothed out some of the rough edges and took it to number thirty-one in the *Billboard* Hot 100 during June 1966. The song was credited to one Chester A. Powers, a Greenwich Village songwriter whose real name was Dino Valenti, later of Quicksilver Messenger Service. But the real author was an obscure West Coast folk singer, Billy Roberts. The Leaves' 1966 version of 'Hey Joe' was a fast, breathless folk-rock bash in the style of the Byrds. But Jimmy took his cue from another version released in the same year by singer Tim Rose. Rose had been in an early-sixties folk group with Mama Cass Elliot and somebody actually called James Hendricks. Rose slowed the song right down to a more controlled tempo with a vocal that brought the previously buried lyrics to the fore with Bernard Purdie snapping out the drum rolls behind. This was the version Chas wanted to record and thought Jimmy would be ideal.

As Chas stood and watched Jimmy playing to the tables and chairs one afternoon at the Café Wha?, he thought, 'There's got to be a catch somewhere. How come nobody has signed him up yet?' Well, he was right – there was and they had. Not only Ed Chalpin of PPX, but also Juggy Murray of Sue Records and anyone else who gave Jimmy the chance to record by waving a piece of paper in front of his face. Chas quizzed Jimmy closely about this. Jimmy told him who he would have to buy out. Unfortunately Jimmy failed to mention Ed Chalpin. Chas asked Jimmy if he fancied coming to England, where he could have his own band and record. Jimmy played it very cool. After all, he'd heard all the bullshit before. So he asked questions about the equipment in England and what the musicians were like. The clincher was that Chas promised to introduce him to Eric Clapton.

Chas said he would be in contact after he finished the Animals tour. He got back to New York in early September, but 'It took me about four days to find Jimmy,' and this time he brought along Mike Jeffery. For his part, Jimmy was surprised to see Chas again, not really believing all the talk about going to England. But here Chas was, large as life, saying 'Let's go.'

Jimmy had some idea about bringing Randy California along, but Chas was against this, partly because Randy was so young, but also because Chas didn't believe there was room for another lead guitarist in Jimmy's band. Billy Cox says Jimmy contacted *him* about going. But generally nobody knew what was afoot – Jimmy didn't even write or phone home to Seattle to tell Al what was going on. The collective memory of friends and other musicians is that one minute 'Jimmy James' was slouching around the Village gigging where he could – the next moment he was gone. When they saw him again, he was Jimi Hendrix.

Have passport, will travel . . .

Six *If My Daddy Could See Me Now*

At 9 a.m. on Saturday 24 September 1966, Jimmy stepped off his first-class Pan-Am flight on to the tarmac at London's Heathrow airport. In his guitar case was everything he possessed, one Fender Stratocaster, a change of clothes and a jar of Valderma cream for washing his face.

Travelling with Chas and Jimmy was Terry McVay, the Animals' roadie, who carried Jimmy's guitar through immigration because he didn't have a work permit. Immigration put Jimmy through the mill; no work permit meant his entry stamp was cancelled. After a lot of talking by Chas, the authorities were finally conned into believing that Jimmy was a prolific songwriter on a visit to collect royalties. They issued a new stamp and a seven-day non-work permit – otherwise Jimmy might have been back on the next flight to New York. But that wasn't the only deception – Jimmy's passport was issued under false pretences. The passport form that Jimmy filled out in New York needed a character reference from somebody who had known Jimmy for a long time. Chas didn't want the hassle of chasing back to Seattle to find somebody, 'So this New York writer I knew forged all the passport papers for us . . . like, "Yes, I've known this man eight years, yes, he's a good character. . . ." '

With Jimmy now safely out of the airport, Chas wanted to introduce Jimmy to the London music scene as soon as possible. He also had a number of phone calls to make and, after spending a couple of months in America, was in urgent need of a decent cup of tea. The answer was to stop by at the home of organist Zoot Money, who lived in Gunterstone Road, Fulham, in West London, on a direct route from the airport. Zoot's house was a crossroads for any musicians coming in and out of London. There were a handful of British musicians like John Mayall, Graham Bond, Alexis Korner and Zoot who, while never being big stars with hit records in their own right, were nevertheless catalysts on the music scene. The best musicians passed through their bands.

At the time Zoot had his Big Roll Band, an R&B outfit heavily influenced by Ray Charles, James Brown and Jimmy Smith and driven along by Zoot's 'Hail fellow well met' desperado exuberance. Living in the basement flat of his house was lead guitarist Andy Somers, who later found fame with Police. Jimmy and Chas rolled up at the house around eleven o'clock in the morning.

Most of the Big Roll Band's gear was set up, so during the day Jimmy, playing a white Telecaster, jammed with Zoot, Andy and the others until the gear had to be packed up for that night's gig. Jimmy tried unsuccessfully to play through Zoot's hi-fi, gave up and carried on using his host's acoustic guitar. Zoot offers this first impression of Jimmy: 'When I heard him play it was obvious that all forms of blues or black music had sort of gone through him. He was able to play all forms of blues, gospel, whatever you want to call it.' Meanwhile Zoot's wife Ronnie stood with eyes out on stalks taking in this black vision playing in her living-room. She rushed up to the top-floor flat to tell Kathy Etchingham, the stunning nineteen-year-old girl who lived there. 'Ronnie came running up to my flat and said, "Kathy, you gotta come down, Chas has just brought this guy back from America and he looks like the Wild Man of Borneo." So I said, "All right, I'll come down." But I wasn't so keen to get out of bed and by the time I got down they were leaving, so I didn't meet him. But Ronnie said they were all going down to the Scotch of St James that night.'

The contrasting reactions of Zoot and Ronnie Money encapsulated the impact Jimmy was to make within weeks of arriving in London – the men were knocked out by the music, the women by the body. Both would be entranced by the man.

The Scotch of St James, decked out in tartan, was located at Mason's Yard among a maze of cobbled streets and mysterious alleyways, near St James's Square and the Houses of Parliament. The owners were Louis Brown and John Bloom, later to be at the centre of a financial scandal when his Rolls Razor washing-machine company collapsed.

It was appropriate that the seat of elitist political power should be nearby, because the Scotch and other clubs like the Cromwellian and Blaises in Kensington and the Ad-Lib in Leicester Square were all very expensive locales for the young bluebloods of the London social scene. There, they could rub shoulders with the new aristocracy: pop stars, fashion designers, models, photographers and, for a touch of excitement, the odd East End gangster. These clubs and others like them were really the last vestiges of 'Swinging London' from its heyday during 1964, when Carnaby Street was the most famous thoroughfare in the world. London fashion and music was beginning to change; the 'underground' and 'flower power' would soon be de-rigueur subjects for Sunday newspaper colour supplement treatment. So the clubs were something of an anachronism, but much loved by musicians as private places for a drink and a jam and by the newshounds as deep wells of hot gossip.

The crowd packed into the tiny club stood amazed as Jimmy did his stuff, but Chas didn't want him up there too long because of the work-permit problem. So by the time Kathy arrived with Zoot and Ronnie Money, Jimmy had finished.

> When we got in there, there was a group in the corner on a rostrum and there was Jimmy and Chas and they all waved and said, 'over here.' So we all introduced ourselves and Jimmy leaned over towards me and said, 'I want to tell you something,' and I said, 'What is it?' and I put my head forward. He kissed my ear and said, 'I think you're beautiful.' Anyway, we're all sitting there having a drink and a fight broke out between Ronnie Money and this girl who I didn't know from Adam just sitting with the group. She turned out to be Linda Keith. Plates started flying across the table. Everybody said, 'Let's go,' so I stood up and Jimmy grabbed my hand. Chas said to me, 'Take him back to the Hyde Park Towers Hotel,' 'cos Jimmy wouldn't have known how to get a taxi or anything. He'd only just arrived that day. So we jumped in a taxi and he was terribly polite, I've never met anyone more well mannered in my life.

The Hyde Park Towers Hotel near Bayswater station was a well-known establishment for musicians to stay in. Chas and his Swedish girlfriend Lotte had rooms there and Jimmy was also booked in. 'Eventually the others turned up, by which time we had a rapport going. We all gathered in the reception area and Jimmy said to me, "Will you come outside a minute, I want to talk to you." And he gave me all this excuse about this girl, how he hardly knew her at all, how she was Keith Richard's girlfriend and he didn't want to interfere – and please don't go. So I didn't. And that's how it all started.' They went back to join the others in the cocktail bar. 'I'll never forget this, Jimmy said, "Shall we go to my room?" We got up and everyone said

Jimi and
Kathy Etchingham
Jimi's flat,
London, first week
of January 1969

"Goodnight, Kathy, goodnight, Jimmy," and we went off to his room. The next morning we were in bed, Linda Keith burst into the bedroom, grabbed his Stratocaster and ran out with it. She phoned up later on and said to Jimmy, "you gotta get rid of her and I'll come back and you can have your guitar." ' Kathy made herself scarce while Jimmy negotiated the return of his guitar. Later he phoned her at the flat in Gunterstone Road and asked her to come back to the hotel. 'We started going around all the time together and I moved into the hotel with him. We were absolutely flat broke, didn't have a bean. We would wake up in the morning, sit in bed with the tea and toast, talking and talking. Then we'd wander round the shops. He used to come with me to visit my friends. We just drifted around. I showed him all the sights, but we spent much of our time in an enormous embrace – we were very much wrapped up with one another.' Jimmy and Kathy were together for the best part of three years, the longest female relationship Jimmy ever had.

Within days of arriving Chas had kept his promise to Jimmy about meeting Eric Clapton. Chas bumped into Eric and Jack Bruce, then in the throes of establishing Cream, told them about Jimmy and they said to bring him along the following night, 1 October, to the Polytechnic of Central London where Cream were playing.

Jimmy duly turned up with Chas, but Ginger Baker was none too happy about somebody jamming with their new band, *his* vision, on such an important date. The deal was that Jimmy could play if Eric stayed on the stage. Jimmy started off playing Howlin' Wolf's 'Killin' Floor', which Eric said later he'd always had trouble with. 'I'll never forget Eric's face,' says Chas, 'he just walked off to the side and stood and watched.' What Eric witnessed scared him – and very soon afterwards every other guitarist in London – to death.

On another night Jeff Beck went down to Blaises. 'I heard this sound blasting up the road. I got out the cab, went in and there was Jimmy. I just couldn't believe it. He was singing "Like a Rolling Stone". I knew the tune, but the way he treated it was something else. He was going crazy and the people were going crazy. After that everyone was blown away. I have been ever since.'[1] As he was leaving Blaises he met Pete Townshend coming in and told Pete what he had just seen. Townshend went in to see for himself. Jimmy was putting on a show, feedback howling through the amp – in fact very much like Pete's own performance with the Who. But at the same time he realised that Jimmy was taking this whole idea somewhere else, to another dimension. Out of the blue he got a call from Eric Clapton, who, Pete says, had never spoken to him before, to see if he wanted to go to the cinema. Although they didn't actually talk much, it was understood that the only item on the agenda was Jimmy Hendrix. Jimmy would turn up at a club in the evenings with Chas and Kathy and just sit in with whoever was on. Very soon, other musicians were making a point of finding out where Jimmy would be on any given night. Clapton and Townshend saw Jimmy at every possible opportunity, except twice when the particular club was so full that even *they* couldn't get in.

In a very short while Jimmy's name was on the lips of all the clubland cognoscenti: Paul McCartney, Brian Jones, John Lennon and Mick Jagger in particular became enthusiastic and influential admirers. For the time being, Jimmy was their secret and they revelled in the knowledge that an outstanding black American bluesman needed to come to England to establish his career. There was a long tradition among English music fans of taking up 'lost causes' in black music: New Orleans jazz, Dixieland, bebop, cool jazz, country blues and reggae. At one time there was a better selection of reggae records to be had in London than in Kingston, Jamaica.

But, like any religious converts, the new devotees could be furiously purist to the point of narrow-mindedness. When Big Bill Broonzy visited Britain in the fifties, he left his electric band behind and came on like 'an ol' nigger from the plantation', picking out his mournful acoustic country blues because he'd been told that's what people wanted to hear. Muddy Waters, on the other hand, would have no truck with such kowtowing. He came in 1958 with his brash, nasty, citified Chicago blues band wearing shiny suits and had the critics running for the toilets with their hands over their ears. Much of this disapprobation came from those who appeared threatened by black blues musicians who refused to conform to some romantic vision, almost racist in its concept and definitely patronising, although hands would have been thrown up in genuinely aggrieved horror at such suggestions. Jimmy, too, would be subject to tasteless racial stereotyping even more blatant, leaving in the minds of the public a crude character outline. But all the musicians needed to know was that Jimmy played like a dream and he was playing for them – as Mick Jagger said, 'He was ours.'

An obvious priority for Jimmy was to get his own band together as soon as possible. Chas had no particular musicians in mind, while Jimmy knew nobody – it was just a question of seeing who was free and asking them to try out.

On 28 September, Jimmy was issued a work permit valid until the end of the year. On the same day an out-of-work rock 'n' roll guitar player walked into the offices of the Harold Davidson agency to ask about auditions for Eric Burdon's New Animals, which he'd heard tell of on the grapevine.

Approaching his twenty-first birthday, Noel Redding had travelled up from his home town of Folkestone on the Kent coast. He was very dispirited, set to give up playing altogether and become a milkman. This seemed to be his last chance.

Noel Redding
Rheinhalle,
Düsseldorf
12 January 1969

Since turning pro in 1962, Noel had been on the road with the Lonely Ones and the Loving Kind, playing support to many of the major pop bands of the period including the Hollies, the Beatles and Manfred Mann. He earned his spurs travelling the length and breadth of Britain and on the notorious club circuit in Hamburg. The Loving

Kind released three singles which all flopped and they seemed to be working harder and harder for less and less reward. So with warning words from manager Gordon Mills about his 'non' future ringing in his ears, Noel walked out.

He was told to go to the Birdland Club for an audition and saw Chas, who was helping Eric Burdon put the new band together. 'Noel turned up with the same haircut as Jimmy's and asked to join the Animals and I said, "Well, that seat's gone [to Vic Briggs of Brian Auger's band], but I got this guy in from America looking for a bass player." He was pink [broke] then, so he said, "I'll do anything." '

In the rehearsal room with Jimmy that day was Mike O'Neill, pianist with the Gladiators, and ace drummer Aynsley Dunbar, who curiously had only just joined John Mayall's Bluesbreakers about two weeks before. They ran through a couple of numbers including 'Hey Joe', and Chas asked Noel to come back next day, sending him on his way with five shillings (25p) for his fare. On his return home to Folkestone, he told his mother Margaret, 'I met a guitarist who's going to be the greatest guitar player ever and I think I'm gonna join the group.' Next day, Noel went back to the Birdland, but found nobody there, so he headed for ANIM, Mike Jeffery's office in Gerrard Street. There, Mike offered Noel the job playing bass, which Jimmy confirmed a few days later by a phone call from Chas. Noel was quite happy to switch to bass – apart from obviously needing the work, he recognised immediately that nobody *else* was going to play lead guitar in a band with Jimmy Hendrix. But Jimmy also had a very clear idea what he wanted from a bass player. He had been playing bass on the guitar back in the days of the Rocking Kings, so was very familiar with the possibilities of the instrument. He knew what he wanted to hear, what the feel and pulse should be. There was a distinct advantage in having a novice bass player unencumbered by fixed ideas about the instrument. Besides, Jimmy liked Noel's curly Afro hairstyle – it indicated an appealing streak of individualism. All in all, the right face in the right place at the right time.

The evening of Noel's audition, Jimmy sat in with the Brian Auger Trinity at Blaises. In the audience was Johnny Halliday, 'the French Elvis' and a major European rock star in the early to mid-sixties. By 1966, his career had lost much of its momentum, mainly due to the Beatles, but he was still hugely popular in France. He had a tour coming up there and invited Jimmy if he could get his band sorted out.

So they had to find a drummer. A number had been auditioned including Aynsley Dunbar, but nothing had been finalised. Then at the beginning of October, R&B organist Georgie Fame, who'd had two UK number-one hit singles, 'Yeh Yeh' and 'Get Away', decided that a new direction was needed and broke up his band, the Blue Flames. Drummer Mitch Mitchell got a call from Fame's manager, club owner John Gunnell, 'who said go and have a play with a guitarist Chas had just brought over from America. I think the offer was about two weeks' work in France.'

Mitch Mitchell
afternoon rehearsals,
Royal Albert Hall,
London,
24 February 1969

Born in West London in 1947, John 'Mitch' Mitchell had been involved in show business since boyhood. As a teenager, he went through drama school and appeared in a number of films, TV shows (*Whacko* and *Emergency – Ward 10*) and adverts (as an 'Ovalteeny').

Tap-dancing was part of his theatrical training, a skill he shared with at least two other master drummers, Steve Gadd and Buddy Rich. Music was his other passion. On Saturdays, he worked at the music shop run by Jim Marshall, whose amplification systems helped define the sound of sixties rock. In between acting work, Mitch, largely self-taught, deputised in a host of bands including Screaming Lord Sutch and Johnny Kidd and the Pirates. He eventually chose drumming over acting and turned professional with the Riot Squad, a mod band, whose clean-cut shirt-and-tie image belied their outlandish stage act with painted faces and exotic props. Organist Jon Lord was a member before going off to form Deep Purple. Mitch got fed up with Riot Squad 'silliness' as he once put it, and the endless club grind which the band could never seem to break out of, and moved into lucrative but boring session work. That was until three days' work with the Pretty Things rekindled his enthusiasm for touring. He joined Georgie Fame and stayed with him until the band broke up.

Mitch had heard nothing about Jimmy, so he didn't really know what to expect, least of all to see Jimmy getting ready to play in a Humphrey Bogart Burberry trenchcoat. They played through some soul material for about four hours. 'It was like going through a bit of Wilson Pickett, James Brown,' but still Chas and Jimmy couldn't decide. The choice was between Mitch and Aynsley. Both were highly proficient, technically accomplished musicians with exciting, busy styles ideally suited to driving what would probably be a three-piece band. Even that had not been finalised; bassist Dave Knight (later of Procol Harum) was auditioned to see if Noel playing rhythm guitar would work. It didn't and the idea was dropped. Finally, Chas says, 'We actually tossed a coin and it came down for Mitch.' It was a new playing experience for Mitch. 'It felt good to have the amount of freedom to play whatever you wanted within a small framework of people. It was the first time I'd worked in a trio *and* been able to play loud.' And how did Mitch feel about playing with a bass guitarist who had never played bass before? 'I was a little blasé maybe about Noel's playing to some degree, but he took care of business. I think he always wanted to be a guitarist more than a bass player, but he certainly held things down more than adequately.'

With the band in place and a tour coming up, a name was needed. Jimmy had reverted back to 'Hendrix', which apart from being his real name was more hard-edged and dramatic than 'James'. It was agreed that Jimmy's name should be included and Chas came up with the idea of a novel spelling to attract attention and hopefully make people remember it. So 'Jimmy' became 'Jimi'. The name Experience came up in conversation – Jimi Hendrix and the Experience? No, the Jimi Hendrix Experience. In truth, it was a forlorn hope that concert promoters *would* get the name right – every possible spelling variation of 'Jimi' and 'Hendrix' appeared on the walls or in adverts, certainly in the early days. One roadie swears he saw a poster in America during 1967 announcing 'The Garry Henpecked Exposition'.

The decision by Chas to dispense with 'and the' was probably intuitive rather than calculated, but still symbolic of how the management at any rate viewed the situation. Deleting 'and the' gives a sense that Jimi Hendrix *is* the Experience and not *part* of the Experience. In other words, Chas and Mike saw Noel and Mitch as employees who had been brought into a manufactured band to play behind Jimi Hendrix, whom they were managing. Even Mitch at the start thought all he was doing was a two-week stint in France and says, 'The first idea was that Chas brought Hendrix over and there would be an employed backing band.' Moreover, although they called Chas and Mike 'managers' the contract they all signed in October 1966 was not a management contract, but a production deal whereby Chas and Mike were record producers – Jimi alone signed a management contract in December. But there was nothing in this production contract to indicate differential status between Jimi and the others – the individual members were 'to form a group of musical performers known as the Jimi Hendrix Experience'. Mike and Chas took 20 per cent plus further percentages for royalties and publishing. The band would share 2.5 per cent of the royalties from record sales between them. The terms were hardly favourable for the band, but of course nobody knew what was going to happen. Twenty per cent of nothing was nothing. But ultimately the stakes became astronomical and to this very day the recriminations over the status of Noel and Mitch in the Experience – and consequently the money due to them – have been rancorous.

Rehearsals continued, although nobody was happy with the dinky thirty-watt Burns amplification provided by the manufacturer. 'We did our best to get rid of them,' says Mitch. Their best was to bounce the gear down flights of stairs and drop it off balconies, causing great offence to Noel's finely developed sense of thrift. But if nothing else, the amps were sturdy. Finally they contrived to have it all stolen, to be replaced by more powerful Marshall gear. But money was a problem; there was no income and proceeds from the French trip would probably not cover the road expenses. Chas says he had to sell about five bass guitars to keep going and to borrow money from John Gunnell because the funds that should have been coming from Mike Jeffery, the business manager, were, according to Chas, 'tied up in one ridiculous case after the other somewhere in America' – a reference to a shower of litigation involving the Animals' chequered business past. With the Animals, Chas played mainly Gibson bass guitars, the most expensive on the market. Allowing for the sale of five with a second-hand value of about £150 each, that would have raised about £750, around £4500 at today's prices, so a not inconsiderable sum of money to play around with. According to Marianne Faithfull, Chas approached Mick Jagger to 'co-sponsor' Jimi. But, for all his enthusiasm for Jimi, Jagger apparently ran a mile from the idea.[2]

Nevertheless, the whole point of the partnership was that Mike would be putting up the money – it could not all have been tied up in America because he had business interests in Spain. Which is precisely where he disappeared to after the contract was signed in October. Not for nothing was he known as the Scarlet Pimpernel.

Rock management was a new game in the sixties and the key players like Robert Stigwood (Cream), Andrew Oldham (Rolling Stones), Kit Lambert (the Who) and Brian Epstein were very different in the way they did business and nurtured their charges. Stigwood and Oldham were overreachers, shooting for the moon, trying to create the kind of media empires now controlled by the likes of Rupert Murdoch. But, unlike Stigwood, Oldham also wanted to be 'one of the boys' and was flattered if autograph hunters thought he was with the band. By contrast, Epstein was more paternalistic and emotionally involved. But one thing they and Kit Lambert all had in common was a thirst for self-publicity, for being known and recognised as powerful and influential trendsetters in their own right – the force behind the stars. But Mike Jeffery was very different. As manager of the all-girl group, Goldie and the Gingerbreads, and more significantly of the Animals, he stayed in the background. Few photos of him exist and he was rarely seen without his prescription dark glasses. He was probably the most mysterious and elusive manager of any big-name rock act – those who were close to him remain fiercely loyal. His personal assistant throughout his time with Jimi was Trixie Sullivan. 'I liked Mike very much, he was really something special. He was an incredibly talented man and could see talent in other people. He was shy and always stood back. But he was one tough guy, and bloody clever.' Even his legions of enemies thought him charming and amusing while at the same time completely untrustworthy. Chas Chandler has few kind words to say about Mike, but concedes, 'He was great fun, fantastic sense of humour, and you couldn't help liking him.'

Mike was born in Peckham, South London, in March 1933, the only child of Frank and Alice Jeffery, both Post Office employees. According to his father, Mike did a little above average at school with an aptitude for school sports and was never without friends. He finished his schooling in 1949 and went to work as a clerk for the Mobil Oil company. Then in 1951, aged eighteen, he was called up for National Service. For most men, this meant two wasted years, but for Mike, never happy as a pen-pusher, it was a turning point. His exam success in science helped him into the Educational Corps and, when his spell of duty ended, Mike signed on as a full-time professional soldier. Drafted into the Intelligence Corps, his army career from then on, not surprisingly, becomes a matter for conjecture. He later told tales of undercover work in Egypt during the Suez crisis of 1956, when President Nasser closed the Suez Canal to shipping; of being primed for counter-espionage work against the Russians; and of murder, mayhem and torture in foreign climes. Some, if not all, of this was done for effect, often to demonstrate to impressionable young musicians that he was not a man to be trifled with. But this does not mean that the whole saga was elaborate fantasy. His father says Mike rarely spoke about what he did – itself perhaps indicative of the sensitive nature of his work – but confirms that much of Mike's time was spent in 'civvies', that he was stationed in Egypt and that he could speak Russian. In fact, Mike jokingly suggested to Trixie that all the office accounts should be in Russian so the Inland Revenue couldn't read them.

On leaving the army, Mike decided to continue his academic education and took off for Newcastle University to read languages and sociology. In his own way, Mike was very charismatic – his charming manner, elegant pinstripe suit, enigmatic dark glasses and his 'mature' student status earned him a flock of admirers. They eagerly patronised the dances he began to arrange for fellow students around 1958 at a local hall usually given over to ballet lessons. When the dances became successful, the woman running the hall incredibly managed to squeeze Mike out – not that he cared much: he had his eyes set on new horizons. College hop dance promotions had given him a taste for the entertainment business and in the years immediately following his honours graduation Mike opened the Downbeat club, the Marimba (which burnt down in mysterious circumstances) and the Club A Go Go. Mike's clubs were the top venues in Newcastle for visiting bands like the Rolling Stones and he gave new talent a start, most spectacularly the Animals, eventually becoming their manager. To be a club owner in Newcastle (or anywhere else for that matter) you had to be tough and ready to deal with violence from drunken punters, protection rackets and the goons hired by rival club owners to cause trouble. Thugs arrived at the door in many guises – some polite, impeccably dressed, driving fast cars, others who dispensed with the niceties and started negotiations with a crowbar. All learnt to beware the smile on the face of the tiger that was Mike Jeffery. He certainly had his own 'boys', but stories abounded of the gun he carried around and of the way he once dealt with eight guys, one armed with an axe, before calmly walking off to hospital to be patched up.

Mike's empire began to grow; he worked with the ferocious Don Arden to establish the Animals in London and invested in real estate and clubs in Spain. Mike's army training stood him in good stead. The successful intelligence officer needs a highly developed sense of self-preservation, finely tuned paranoia, bags of native cunning, the acting talent of Olivier, the deviousness of Machiavelli and the ability to throw up a smokescreen where fantasy and reality merge into the fog of confusion. This enables the smart operator to make his killing and quietly slip away. All in all, a perfect grounding for the would-be rock manager.

Chas and the rest of the Animals were convinced that as their manager Mike had robbed them blind – they had the fame while he had the fortune. But Chas was no fool either – he could see the lie of the land and once the Animals had disbanded sought a partnership with Mike. They worked out a deal for the new acts they wanted to sign. 'I was gonna be given half of Eric Burdon and the Alan Price Set and he was getting half of Jimi Hendrix.'

The day after they signed the contract, the new Jimi Hendrix Experience flew off for their four-date tour with Johnny Halliday. 'We got a few Marshall bits and pieces,' says Mitch, 'we had no road manager and I remember seeing these amplifiers with no covers on them [in the days before flight cases] being literally thrown into the cargo hold.' They could only hope that Marshall equipment was as resilient as the Burns gear they had tried unsuccessfully to destroy.

They were only on stage for about fifteen minutes and, with no original material, played 'Hey Joe' (planned as the first single release), 'Killin' Floor' and odd soul standards like 'Land of a Thousand Dances', 'Respect' and 'Have Mercy'. Jimi was most reluctantly singing lead vocals and was less than happy about his stage clothes; the as yet uncrowned king of high psychedelic fashion was trussed up in a blue two-piece suit and white shirt. 'The jacket had a big vent up the back,' says Kathy, 'and Jimi hated it.' Jimi's first concert review appeared after the 13 October gig at the Novelty cinema in Evreux. 'Johnny Halliday's latest discovery . . . was a singer and guitar player with bushy hair, a bad mixture of James Brown and Chuck Berry, who pulled a wry face on stage during a quarter of an hour and also played the guitar with his teeth.'3 But the highlight of this brief showcase tour was the 14,500 sell-out concert at L'Olympia in Paris, where the Experience went down a bomb.

In between shows, Chas would hold debriefing sessions analysing their performance and he would sit with Jimi in the audience watching Johnny Halliday. 'He was one of the all-time great manipulators of an audience. As a performer he was unbelievable. You've never seen a guy stick an audience in the palm of his hand the way Johnny did. He had that marvellous nerve of doing nothing at the right time except pose. The tricks became part of the Hendrix Experience.'

Back home, Mitch and Noel were on £15 a week and doing sessions to make ends meet. Jimi turned up at Little Richard's London hotel, prior to Richard's gig at Brian Epstein's Saville Theatre, to borrow $50 from his former employer. Even so, Jimi was doing better than Mitch and Noel – at least he was getting his rent paid. On 6 December, he and Kathy had moved into Chas and Lotte's new flat, previously owned by Ringo Starr, in Montagu Square, off Baker Street.

As much as anyone could say they 'knew' Jimi Hendrix, Chas probably got to know him better than most in the coming months. During the day, they sat around discussing the future, listening to music, playing games of Risk (a war boardgame), Jimi drinking wine mixed with Coca-Cola, chain-smoking menthol cigarettes, reading science fiction lent by Chas, writing scraps of songs and preparing his breakfast with his guitar still strung round his neck. Chas looked after Jimi. One night Chas and Lotte, Mike with his girlfriend Nancy, and Jimi with Kathy were all in a Soho bar. Two guys at the bar were having a go at Jimi. 'They both followed us outside,' recalls Kathy. 'One of them hung back, but the other one kept going on. Chas turned round and tried to warn the guy off. But he wouldn't listen. Chas turned back to us and said, "Take care of Lotte," and then completely laid out this guy in a most astounding way. It took Jimi aback; he'd never seen anything like it even in New York. He certainly wasn't expecting anything like it in England. Chas totally protected Jimi.' Jimi's relationship with Kathy also deepened beyond the first flush of physical excitement. By now Kathy had given up her job with a frozen-food company and spent all her time with Jimi. 'We had a lot in common. I had a difficult background and so had he. He took me under his wing as well as me leading him through London life. I introduced him to people, opened doors for him, and he did the same for me.'

Finale!
L'Olympia, Paris, 18 October 1966

Shortly after returning from France, the band went into the De Lane Lea studio in Kingsway and recorded two songs over different sessions – 'Hey Joe' and 'Stone Free', written by Jimi, who, tentative as ever, had wanted 'Killin' Floor' on the B-side. But Chas was adamant. 'I told him, "There's nothing going on the B-side but one of your own songs," because I used up all my money doing "Hey Joe".' Besides, it was important that Jimi proved himself as a songwriter. Unlike the early days of the Beatles and the Stones, it was now essential that bands write and perform their own material in order to secure recording contracts. Chas was also insistent that Jimi could not have everything turned up to 'pat pending' in the studio because the equipment was not designed to handle such volume levels. This was the source of one of the very few rows he had with Jimi. That day, Chas had been trying to sort out Jimi's work status, 'and I had his passport and all his details on me in the studio'. With the argument rising to crescendo 'I just took his passport out and I said "Well, there you are – fuck off then." He started laughing and that was the end of it. All the time I spent with him, it was a lot of laughs. He was a very funny dude.'

Produced by Chas and engineered by Dave Siddle, 'Hey Joe' built on Tim Rose's arrangement accentuating the menace inherent in the lyrics, starting with open strings in unison and then playing fourths against the open string – now a stock item in all heavy-metal repertoires – with the mournful female backing vocals provided by the Breakaways. The song did not feature Jimi's playing as much as everyone who knew him might have liked, but it was perfectly suited to Jimi's vocal delivery. 'Hey Joe' had given the Leaves a hit record in the USA, so was a relatively 'safe' song to launch on the UK market.

His extraordinary guitar playing and sensational public image have tended to obscure Jimi's excellent song-writing capabilities. Many of his songs operated on at least two levels or had more than one message to impart – he later said to close friends that he had to wrap up his metaphysical and spiritual intent in simplified language or through commonplace metaphors in order to get the material accepted by the record companies, and probably by most of his audience as well.

Jeff Beck cites 'Stone Free' as his favourite Hendrix song. 'It's just a really great Jimi Hendrix driving rhythm . . . and the solo, the way that burns in. If somebody's talking to me and that comes on, I can't listen to them.'[4] 'Stone Free' tackles Jimi's pet subject – freedom of action – from three points of view. The first is geographical claustrophobia and the obsession with constant movement:

> Every day in the week
> I'm in a different city.

The second is his distaste for those who try to force their opinions on other people or who mock anything or anybody out of the ordinary:

> They talk about me like a dog
> Talk about the clothes I wear
> But they don't realise
> They're the ones who's square.

And the third rails against any woman who thinks she can tie him down emotionally:

> A woman here, a woman there
> Try to keep me in a plastic cage
> But they don't realise
> It's so easy to break.

What is interesting in the song is that although it was written before Jimi was famous – as a travelling musician he had already had to deal with two contrasting hassles of his life-to-be: asinine comments about his appearance and the legion of women hanging round his legs whether he wanted them there or not – Jimi was quite old fashioned and very shy when it came to women. His New York friend Mike Quashie observed that if he saw somebody he liked in a club, for instance, he would go through a whole routine of asking somebody to ask the girl if she wouldn't mind joining him at his table and he would be terribly polite and charming. Some of Jimi's peers, however ('like Led Zeppelin', says Mike laughing), adopted a somewhat more neanderthal approach to courtship.

Convinced he had a hit record on his hands, Chas went round to Decca records with the demo only to be shown the door with the words 'Sorry, he hasn't got anything.' Chas was stunned – hawking a demo around London was not part of the plan. There was no time for all that because there was no money coming in – both were being borrowed. Then, as with so many stories of success coming on a wing and a prayer, fortune smiled. One night, Jimi was having another blow at the Scotch of St James. In the audience was the Who management team of Kit Lambert and Chris Stamp, brother of actor Terence Stamp. 'Jimi got up and jammed. Kit and I could see this guy was something special and we wanted to get involved. We checked it out and found he had a manager, we couldn't produce him, so the only thing left was a record deal.'

The Who were signed to Decca (probably that was why Chas went there), but the company was essentially a very conservative and staid classical music label with no real commitment to pop music whatsoever. They had turned down the Beatles, given Chas the brush-off and it had taken the best of Kit Lambert's eccentric hustling to get a deal for the first Who single 'I Can't Explain' in 1965. Lambert and Stamp wanted their own label, Track, and approached Polydor for backing, but Polydor too were very cautious about the idea. They were in the process of trying to convince Polydor when they saw Jimi.

Chas desperately needed this deal, but he played his cards close to his chest. For their part, Lambert and Stamp had a shrewd idea that Jimi's heavy acid blues was the coming sound for '67, whereas their own band was too closely associated with the passé era of the Mods. Hence they wanted Jimi, not the Who, as their first signing for their new label Track to show Polydor they were up with the trends. Negotiations went on for some weeks. 'The deal really hinged,' says Chris Stamp, 'on what we guaranteed to do with Jimi. . . . I mean we guaranteed *Ready, Steady, Go.*'

RSG was one of the most popular and important British TV pop shows of the sixties. Producer Vicki Wickham and director Michael Lindsay-Hogg only booked the acts they liked, and fortunately their taste was impeccable. The Rolling Stones, the Animals, the Kinks and the Moody Blues all had their TV debuts on *RSG*. The show also regularly featured top black acts from America: Stevie Wonder, James Brown and Ike and Tina Turner. But with a semi-permanent residency, the darlings of *RSG* were the Who, so Lambert and Stamp had every reason to feel confident about getting Jimi on the show. Eventually a deal was struck: 'Hey Joe' would be released on Polydor and, if it did well, Polydor would finance Track Records, and future Experience recordings would be released on the new label.

While deals were being struck, the band needed to keep rehearsing. Whatever its pedigree, club owners were unwilling to put on an untried act. With no dates in England, another European tour was set up – this time in Germany, at the Big Apple in Munich. Rock history has often claimed that Jimi's career took off in England. But it was the early concert tours around Europe where Jimi first won acceptance beyond the coterie of musicians, particularly in Scandinavia, Germany and France.

Rehearsals for this tour and later for their *RSG* appearance were disrupted because Mitch still had session engagements to fulfill. (John

Banks of the Merseybeats sat in for the *RSG* rehearsal). However, the tour got underway, four dates in Germany, this time accompanied by their first roadie Gerry Stickells, whose main qualification was his van. 'I knew Noel, he comes from down in Kent where I came from, and he fixed me up with the job. As far as I was concerned, it was purely temporary, I was on my way to Spain to work in a bar.' Gerry's 'temporary' job lasted until the day Jimi died and beyond.

German fans were witness to Jimi's first act of auto-destruction, which came about entirely by accident, as Chas recalled in 1968. 'Jimi was pulled offstage by a few over-enthusiastic fans and as he jumped back on stage he threw his guitar on before him. When he picked it up he saw that it had cracked and several of the strings were broken – he just went barmy and smashed everything in sight. The German audience loved it and we decided to keep it as part of the act when there was good press about or when the occasion demanded it.'5

Back in London, Jimi made his first call home to Al to tell him about his good fortune. Unfortunately, this did not quite work out as Jimi had hoped. He telephoned at 1 a.m. Seattle time, but his big mistake was to call collect (reversed charges). According to Jimi, Al's first question was: 'Who had I stolen the money from to pay for the crossing?'6 Dorothy Harding says Al told her he bawled Jimi out for calling him collect and instead to put it all in a letter, while Jimi was crying down the phone, begging his father not to hang up. Later Jimi had an altogether more amicable conversation with his father on the phone, passing it over to Kathy to say a few words just to verify his story.

The success of 'Hey Joe' was absolutely vital – 1966 was still a time when the band without a hit record got nowhere. First the press needed to be primed for the single release; Chas also wanted to whip up some enthusiasm for the band among club owners to get some gigs. John Gunnell had recently reopened the Bag O'Nails club in Kingly Street off Regent Street and it was there that Chas hosted an expensive press launch for the band. Keith Altham worked on the *New Musical Express* and knew Chas and the Animals from their earliest days in London. Chas had been giving Keith the big build-up on Jimi since the summer – now it was November and Keith was going to find out what all the fuss was about.

Big Apple, Munich, between 8 and 11 November 1966

It was a lunch-time reception and I remember going down into a cellar thinking, 'Do I really want to be down here with it being such a beautiful day outside?' They came on and played at fairly considerable volume for a small club like that. But Jimi was, I think, almost too much, to be absolutely honest. . . . he was overwhelming in that small space. You knew something special was going on, you knew the guy was obviously a brilliant guitarist. But, by the time he had gone through about four or five numbers, it was very difficult to take in as a journalist. I kept thinking that this was maybe just a bit too clever, this guy should be in an avant-garde jazz group or something, although what he was playing was fearsome in its delivery and obviously rock oriented.

Keith decided he had heard enough; Jimi was obviously good, Chas was a mate, so he would help if he could with sympathetic write-ups when things got going.

I was on my way out when they started into a version of the Troggs' 'Wild Thing' and that *did* kick me. . . . what Hendrix was doing with that basic, very simple framework was so extraordinary. I came back and sat down and at that point he really did get me and I thought this guy is doing something on another planet. You could see the visual thing of the three of them and the way he looked was sufficient in its impact to mean that people were going to look twice at them when they saw pictures in the paper or saw them on stage. And even if it was too clever for the Monkees aficionados, it was going to cause a stir. I can remember them walking off, he left his guitar playing on the stage. . . . it did create quite an impact, but it wasn't something that initially made me think, 'Oh, this guy is going to be a super-mega star.'

Subsequent to the reception, in a piece headlined 'Mr Phenomenon!' *Record Mirror* enthused about the performance, predicting that Jimi would 'whirl around the business like a tornado' and conducting Jimi's first interview. Right from the off, Jimi made it clear that he did not want to be associated with any particular genre of music, having his music neatly tied up and labelled for consumer convenience. 'We don't want to be classed in any category. If it must have a tag, I'd like it to be called "Free Feeling". It's a mixture of rock, freak-out, blues and rave music.' Asked about playing with his teeth, Jimi was unconcerned; 'but I do have to brush my teeth three times a day!'[7]

From the point of view of getting gigs, the launch was a disaster – it doesn't appear that any offers were forthcoming. They did play their first UK club date the following day, supporting the New Animals at the Ricky Tick club out near the airport, but this had already been

advertised in *Melody Maker* on 19 November, nearly a week before the reception. Then again, booking a potentially big act too early into small venues could backfire. If the band breaks quickly, then they may find themselves committed to playing a host of low-prestige dates which could damage their credibility.

Jimi's twenty-fourth birthday was on 27 November. He could look over the past twelve months with some satisfaction. A year ago he was scuffling around with Curtis Knight sharing his candy bars with the rats. Now he had his own band, recordings in the can, a single set for release, fans in Europe and good press coverage in England. But it could all still go horribly wrong – the next four weeks could be make or break.

On 16 December the release of 'Hey Joe' b/w 'Stone Free' in the UK on Polydor Records coincided with Jimi's UK TV debut on *Ready Steady*

Go. Lambert and Stamp had cut it very fine – the following week's show was the last *RSG* ever broadcast. The Experience performed 'Hey Joe' live, but that would not necessarily guarantee a hit record – the song would not get crucial airplay unless it got into the top forty. To help the record on its way, seed money was laid down. In Johnny Rogan's book about pop managers *Starmakers and Svengalis*, Tony Martin, a former employee of *New Musical Express*, claims that he hyped 'Hey Joe' into the charts, a service he says he also performed for Don Arden and Kenneth Pitt to get the Small Faces debut single 'Watcha Gonna Do About It' and David Bowie's 'Space Oddity' respectively into the charts.[8] Both Chas Chandler and Chris Stamp deny any knowledge of this, but it was very common practice in those days and the claim is confirmed by Trixie Sullivan. 'There was a guy who used to come around, all the business used him. He knew all the record shops, so he would go round and buy records to make the numbers up.'

Chart-hyping was simple – the charts were compiled by the British Market Research Bureau from lists supplied by 'chart shops' around the country. Everybody in the business knew which shops these were, so it was a question of bribing a shop assistant to add a few ticks or look the other way while the fixer did it. Another method was to buy up singles just from the chart shops to produce a biased read-out for the charts. A single was once hyped up as far as number eight, but usually all that was necessary or possible was a single in the bottom reaches of the top forty – then it would get some airplay and after that it was down to the quality of the record. This kind of service did not come cheap – Don Arden spent nearly £15,000 in two years. It should also be said that the pirate radio stations operating at that time from ships anchored in the North Sea probably had just as much impact on Jimi's early chart success as any manipulation of the statistics. These stations, together with Radio Luxembourg, which gave Jimi a great deal of air time, commanded huge teenage audiences and many Hendrix fans can thank DJs like Kenny Everett, Stuart Henry and Emperor Rosko for their introduction to Jimi's incendiary music.

Although Jimi was now on first-name terms with some of the biggest names of pop, he never let this go to his head and remained painfully shy. Chas's birthday was on 18 December and he had a party at the flat. The 'few friends' Chas invited swelled to forty and the place was packed. Eric Burdon, Mitch, Zoot, Alan Price, Bill Wyman and Brian Auger were among the guests. *Melody Maker*'s Chris Welch was there. Always a Hendrix enthusiast, he recalls that amidst all the throng, 'Jimi

Forest Gate Centre, Woodgrange Road
London, E.7   Tel. (01) 534 6578/9

BILLY WALKER'S
FABULOUS OPENING WEEK

GRAND OPENING NIGHT Wednesday, 21st December

| 7.30 - 11.30 p.m. | **THE WHO** | Gentlemen 17/6 | Ladies 15/- |

Thursday, 22nd December

| 7.30 - 11.30 p.m. | **THE EASYBEATS** | Gentlemen 12/6 | Ladies 10/- |

Friday, 23rd December

DAVE DEE, DOZY, BEAKY, MICK & TICH

| 7.30 - 11.30 p.m. | | Gentlemen 15/- | Ladies 12/6 |

GALA CHRISTMAS EVE — Saturday, 24th December

ERIC BURDON & THE ANIMALS

| 7.30 - Midnight | | Gentlemen 20/- | Ladies 20/- |

BOXING DAY, FOR ALL THE FAMILY
Monday Afternoon, 26th December

THE JIMMI HENDRIX EXPERIENCE

| 2.30 - 5.30 p.m. | | Gentlemen 5/- | Ladies 5/- |

Monday Evening, 26th December

THE PRETTY THINGS

| 7.30 - 11.30 p.m. | | Gentlemen 12/6 | Ladies 10/- |

spent most of the time at the party huddled in a corner on the floor.'

On New Year's Eve, Jimi and Kathy, Chas and Lotte and Mitch went down to Folkestone where Noel's mother, Margaret Redding, lived. Noel's sister Vicky came home the next day. 'I remember looking up the stairs and seeing Jimi – and the charisma – I couldn't take my eyes off him. . . . he was so polite and charming and shy.' Her mother agrees: 'The man had something special about him. When Jimi was there, you wouldn't look at anybody else. . . . you could feel his presence. . . . I liked Jimi very much indeed . . . there was always this warmth.'

The previous evening, everybody explained to Jimi what 'First Footing' was all about and he went out and brought the coal in to bring luck for the coming year. The signs were promising. *Record Mirror* thought 'Hey Joe' would be a hit 'should justice prevail', while *NME* declared the song to be 'guttural, earthy, convincing and authentic'. In the first British review of an Experience concert at Blaises, Chris Welch declared that 'Jimi looks like becoming one of the big club names of '67'. Most important of all, the charts published on New Year's Eve showed 'Hey Joe' at number twelve in the R&B chart and number thirty-eight in the national singles chart.

All together now!
Big Apple, Munich, between 8 and 11 November 1966

Seven *Are You Experienced?*

Haha. Now I'm not stupid Jimi anymore but Mr Hendrix. (Interview, Munich, 16 May 1967)

I want to be the first man to write about the blues scene on Venus. (*New Musical Express*, 28 January 1967)

One thing I hate, man, when these cats say, 'Look at the band, they're playing psychedelic music' and all they're really doing is flashing lights on them and playing Johnny B. Goode with the wrong chords. It's terrible. (*West One*, February 1967)

Nineteen-sixty-seven was the year it all happened, the year it all came together for rock music, the marching sound for a generation of white middle-class youth who thought they could change the world with flowers and acid. Hunter Thompson wrote, 'There was a fantastic universal sense that whatever we were doing was *right*, that we were winning . . . our energy would simply prevail. . . . we all had the momentum, we were riding the crest of a high and beautiful wave.'

It was the year of *Sergeant Pepper*, the Monterey Pop Festival, the first issue of *Rolling Stone*, the Summer of Love, the Human Be-In at San Francisco's Golden Gate Park, Scott MacKenzie, 'A Whiter Shade of Pale', kaftans, bells, beads, army greatcoats, swirling colours, posters, tie-dye T-shirts, Liverpool eclipsed by London as centre of the pop universe, the Apple boutique, Haight Ashbury, Portobello Road, Pink Floyd's debut single and album, UFO club, Middle Earth, *Oz*, *International Times* – a psychedelic soup of social criticism, hedonism and Eastern religion diffused and vulgarised for public consumption, a state of mind bought over the counter and analysed to death. What is often forgotten is that, behind the scenes, it was business as usual. True, pinstriped suits gave way to flowery shirts and hair below the ears and 'man' dripped off the lips of many a record company executive. But if one hand held the joint, the other held the pen, proffered encouragingly to the next hapless musician with the immortal words 'Just sign here, son, and we'll sort it all out.'

Early club gig (possibly Bag O' Nails, London 11 January 1967)

The appearance of 'Hey Joe' in the charts and of the band on *RSG* and *Top of the Pops*, set the rock 'n' roll circus in motion early in 1967 with interviews, photo calls, recording sessions and an ever-growing list of club dates which, if you include all the travelling time between gigs up and down the country, meant that they very rapidly found themselves with no free time. It had taken the best part of four months for the momentum to pick up; now it was relentless. Jimi received the kind of across-the-board media attention in England that would have been impossible in America where there is no national TV, radio or press, simply because the country is too big.

Chas wanted to establish Jimi's image as mean, moody and magnificent, so photos of Jimi were chosen to make him look ugly. The press duly obliged. *Disc and Music Echo* had the dubious honour of being the first to dub Jimi 'The Wild Man of Borneo'. Not to be outdone, *New Musical Express* began their January piece headlined 'The scene's wildest raver': 'The most obvious thing about Jimi Hendrix is that he's not pretty.' But the subtext of Jimi's media image was far from ugly, as Eric Clapton candidly said in 1968: 'Everybody and his brother in England think that spades have big dicks. And Jimi came over and exploited that to the limit, the fucking tee. Everybody fell for it. . . . I fell for it.'[1]

But once the interviews got under way, Jimi was always very forthright in his thoughts and feelings about both music and whatever situation he found himself in at the time. And right now Jimi was hungry.

He told Mike Ledgerwood of *Disc* that his biggest fear was 'Sitting right here. You can't last forever. I hope I won't lose my gigs. If I write something about three or four in the morning, I can't wait to hear it played. It's even a drag to have to wait for the other cats to arrive. It's like almost being addicted to music. Music makes me high onstage. And that's the truth!'[2] He didn't think twice about dismissing 'Hey Joe' as 'really a cowboy song', a record that 'isn't us. The next one's gonna be different. We're working on an LP which will be mainly our own stuff,'[3] even though 'Hey Joe' was by January in the top ten, and still climbing, eventually peaking out at number four the following month.

At the International Racing Car Show at Olympia on 12 January, Jimi mimed on the pirate Radio London stand. The songs were never broadcast, but miming was a real pet hate of Jimi's and was guaranteed to put him in a bad mood. As he told *NME* after this event: 'It's so phoney. . . . I felt guilty just standing there holding a guitar. If you want to scream and holler at a record you can do that at home – I'm strictly a live performer.' In the same interview, he was disarmingly frank about his perennial hang-up: 'I know I can't sing – I'm primarily a guitarist.' But somehow in the knowledge that he was a man whose time had come (and playing along with the early PR which knocked a few years off his age) he stated, 'I've been working with myself and my ideas for 21 years. Now I want to find out from everyone else if they are any good.'[4]

Highlights of their January dates included breaking the house record at the Marquee Club (with a queue rumoured to stretch 600 yards) and playing their first date at Brian Epstein's Saville Theatre on Shaftesbury Avenue. Cream were in the audience that night listening to Jimi do a souped-up rock 'n' roll version of B. B. King's 'Rock Me Baby', 'Like a Rolling Stone', 'Wild Thing', 'Hey Joe' and one of Jimi's compositions, 'Can You See Me?' Eric Clapton later related to *Rolling Stone* how Jimi's performance that night inspired Cream's most famous song, 'Sunshine of Your Love':

> he played this gig that was blinding. I don't think Jack [Bruce] had really taken him in before. I knew what the guy was capable of from the minute I met him. It was the complete embodiment of all aspects of rock guitar rolled into one. I could sense it coming off the guy. And when he [Jack] did see it that night, after the gig he went home and came up with the riff. It was strictly a dedication to Jimi. And then we wrote a song on top of it.[5]

Coincidentally, Jimi used to play this same song as a dedication to Cream, one of *his* favourite bands, unaware that he was in fact playing his own dedication.

The success of 'Hey Joe' convinced Polydor to bankroll Track Records and on 11 January, the same day that the band went into De Lane Lea to start work on the next single 'Purple Haze', Chas and Mike signed a contract with Lambert and Stamp's production company New Action. In exchange for a £1000 advance and the promise of a promo film for every single, Jimi was obliged to provide four singles and two albums for every year of the contract. There are some significant points about this contract. The Jimi Hendrix Experience was not signed directly to Track Records; in fact none of the band signed the New Action contract at all. The terms of the October contract left Chas and Mike free to arrange recording and publishing deals. Also production company contracts put ever more distance between the artist and the money. In this case, New Action paid Chas and Mike an 8 per cent royalty on record sales; they didn't actually pay anything to the band – this was left to whatever arrangements had been made between the band and the managers. In fact, the contract stipulated that a written consent from any artists involved should accompany each recording to confirm that the producers, Chas and Mike, were free to hand over the material. Chris Stamp says Track, or rather New Action, did get one letter from Jimi okaying the whole deal (which was not exactly what the contract required), but neither Noel nor Mitch was asked to do likewise. According to Chris Stamp, once this was settled, Mike Jeffery did a deal with Polydor whereby all the rights to the Experience's work would revert back to him and Chas once the Track deal lapsed.

Imperial Hotel, Darlington, 2 February 1967

Mike then turned his attention to America. Using his network of contacts built up through the years, he went there in January to land a recording contract. What he came back with about two months later, incredibly for an unknown band which had never played in America or had any record releases there, was a $150,000 deal with Warner Brothers netting him 2 per cent producer royalties with 8 per cent for the band plus a fat advance. Finally there was money in the bank. Question was – whose?

The band knew nothing about contracts and deals. They in common with most musicians left that to the management. Dave Dee (of Dave Dee, Dozy, Beaky, Mick and Titch) simply says, 'None of us were interested in money, 'cos it was all so new and exciting and all we wanted to do was go on stage and play and become famous. If you ask anybody who came up through that period in the sixties, nobody really thought what was possible on a financial basis, only when it was too late. I don't think the Experience was any exception to the rest of us.' Probably not, but Noel at least was unhappy about the weekly wage and complaints to the office pushed this up to £30 by mid-February. 'We hated to complain, but it became obvious that unless we did, nothing happened. Like most musicians, we hated to speak up, preferring to avoid any form of upset. It's nearly impossible to play music when you're upset. We'd mumble and complain until we were desperate and forced into confrontation.'6 There were also mumblings in the ranks that the management allowed the band to be billed just as 'Jimi Hendrix'.

Sitting in a London club one evening, Jimi was being interviewed by *Beat Instrumental* in the company of John Mayall's ex-girlfriend Chrissie Charles. At one point Eric Clapton came in and joined them. This was probably the first time that Jimi and Eric had talked properly. There was great mutual respect but, keenly aware that people were making comparisons all the time, they were a little wary of each other. Eric did become rather exasperated living in Jimi's shadow. 'Everybody's obsessed with Jimi Hendrix – and if anybody else dares to play a blues guitar phrase they're accused of copying him!'7 The journalist let the tape run after the interview was over. The conversation strung out over a range of subjects – romance, money and the future – as they all got progressively more drunk. Jimi hit on his favourite theme, the monotony of existence when you stagnate, the dreariness of 'walking on the same street, go to the office, regardless if you make a million dollars . . . but still, catch yourself, you know for a second, you're walking the same street for thirty years . . . everything is exactly the same. . . . if I get a gig doing £500 a week and if I get bored, I'm gonna quit, man, and go to something else. . . . I wanna see the North Pole. . . . I wanna see the mountains they say they have at the South Pole.

Blue Moon, Cheltenham, 11 February 1967

. . . I wanna see Moscow.' Brought up in the fifties with Reds under beds, Jimi was cautious about Communism: 'I wanna witness a slight bit of pain of what I hear about, which might not come about 'cause it might be all propaganda, but anyway, I don't wanna witness it for too long. . . . '

Jimi waxed lyrical about women, told Chrissie what lovely hair she had, said how he fell in love a thousand times a day: 'There's no pain in falling in love for a second or even for three minutes. . . . '

There was a lot of laughter and giggling and then Jimi hit a reflective patch: 'I find out – even when I get sober – I find that I tell more of the truth on my own self when I am like this than when I'm sober. . . . music and life goes together so closely. . . . Music, man, it means so many things. It doesn't mean necessarily physical notes that you hear by ear. It could mean notes that you hear by feeling or thought or by imagination or even by emotion. . . . '

The mood swung round again and Jimi, whose main interest in coming to England was meeting Eric Clapton, could now reach across to him declaring, 'I kissed him, Eric Clapton, I kissed him . . . I kissed the fairest soul brother in England.'

The journalist asked Eric what would happen when he was forty-five years old: 'When it stops . . . then you can work out what you wanna do, but I mean, it's a sick thing to be a young guy and be worried about being old. . . . '

Jimi, on the other hand, had more definite ideas about the subject, not imagining that his fame would last too long. 'Maybe, try my best to get real estate and maybe a few clubs and manage a few groups that have creative ideas and minds.'

Most of the stage-managed interviews were formulas for the times – influences, early playing days, comments about his 'way out' appearance and so on. Often these interviews were syndicated, versions of the same appearing in a number of newspapers. Of more interest were the interviews he gave to 'alternative' publications such as *West One*, the student magazine of the Polytechnic of Central London. He was asked about psychedelia and Donovan and in an oblique reference to the Move's stage act, he said, 'There's this cat smashing a car when he might be singing a song about "I love you baby" – now what does that have to do with it? Now if he was saying the car is evil and the music is in the background and he's out there reading poetry with his little green and gold robe on, that might have some meaning. Singing "love is strange" while smashing an M.G. up is just stupid.' Of Donovan he said, 'He's nice, kinda sweet! He's a nice cat in his own groove, all about flowers and people wearing golden underwear. I like Donovan as a person, but nobody is going to listen to this "love" bit.'[8]

In one sweep, Jimi succinctly demolished British art-school pseudo-surrealistic Dada rubbish: 'We are the eccentric English – now we've got some money, let's be mad.' Even Cream had a stuffed bear on stage at the beginning. And from the standpoint of his black working-class cultural background and his profound sense of individualism, he exposed the shallowness of flower power even before it had really taken off in Britain. In an interview for the Sunday *Observer* in 1989, Frank Zappa made a distinction between the sixties hippy and the 'freak':

Hippies were basically a uniform and conformist group. They had a special costume . . . they had their own special language . . . their own culture, their own folk ways, and they had their own ideas of what was a good time. In my mind, a freak would be a person who basically exists as an individual, who has his own individual style. . . . [Freaks] were mutants that stood out from the rest of the community. Though a freak may have long hair and a hippy have long hair, they are *not* the same kind of person.[9]

In some ways, Jimi was *psychedelic* (meaning 'mind expanding') before any journalist had heard the word. Still in the States, he was playing blues guitar like nobody had heard, driving audiences wild with his stage act and, when he could get away with it, tying scarves to his arms and legs. Jimi might have been 'repackaged' for a white audience, but nobody invented him.

The band continued gigging in England through February and into March. Journalists around the country were awestruck; nobody had quite seen anything like it before and this review was typical:

Last night at the Plaza, Newbury, the Jimi Hendrix Experience roared and romped their way through an hour and a quarter's worth of music that shattered the senses both aurally and visually.
    Resplendent in red corduroy trousers and antique waistcoat, Jimi proceeded to show just how many positions it was possible to play the guitar in, at the same time showing his very own professional skill which must rate him as one of the most outstanding newcomers on the scene since Jeff Beck or Eric Clapton.
    Outstanding for the Experience on drums was Mitch Mitchell. . . .
    Throughout the evening, Jimi showed flashes of on-stage humour for which he must be given full credit. 'Hey Joe' . . . was introduced as being written by Mickey Mouse; after a sudden frenzy of excitement in which he attacked his amplifier with his guitar (not a new idea, but somehow done refreshingly) he announced 'Anyone wanna buy an ole guitar? This one don't tune so well.'
    The finish came suddenly, in an excess of violence. Mitch Mitchell attacked a cymbal stand and it broke into pieces, then distributed his drum kit round the stage and finally squirted the other two with a handy

The Pavilion, Bath, 20 February 1967

water-pistol. The bass-guitarist locked his guitar in its case and then kicked it about over the stage. Jimi attacked his huge amplifier with his guitar, breaking all the strings and nearly toppling the amplifier onto his hand. He then squatted on the guitar with both feet and rocked to and fro. Thus the evening came to its conclusion in a storm of feedback, flying microphones and water-pistols.[10]

From England, they travelled to France and Belgium for a couple of club dates and some TV work, five days back in England and then a flight to Schiphol airport for their first visit to Holland. Like everywhere he went, Jimi caused any number of heads to turn – a tall black guy with Indian features and Afro hairstyle, wearing a Victorian military jacket with gold buttons and threads. Not exactly a common sight on the streets of Amsterdam. The band were there to record a TV show, *Fanclub*. They rehearsed their new single 'Purple Haze', due for release in England on their return. They played so loud that staff fled the studio and plaster came down from the ceiling at the Hotel American some fifty yards away. Jimi refused to turn it down, so was told he would have to mime 'Hey Joe' instead. Jimi was outraged at such a suggestion and stormed out. He returned later to do the show, the producer convinced he had Jimi's agreement to toe the line. Wrong. The cameramen had specific instructions to focus exclusively on Jimi's head, showing him 'eating' his guitar. The female announcer duly announced Jimi as 'the guitar eater' – and Jimi stood there hardly moving at all. He did 'Stone Free' and then walked straight off and out of the studio, on his way to play and get drunk at the home of 'underground' writer Simon Vinkenoog.

On 17 March 1967 Track Records made its debut with 'Purple Haze' b/w '51st Anniversary'.

'Purple Haze' kicks off with the best-known two-note riff in the history of rock – the interval of a tritone or flattened fifth, condemned by the Spanish Inquisition as *Diablo in Música*. Playing the note was supposed to call up the devil, so composers of religious music were banned from using it. 'Purple Haze' was more guitar-oriented than 'Hey Joe' and, for most budding guitar players, the first real indication of Jimi's range and inventiveness, how he could be a lead, rhythm and bass player all at once, with vocals thrown over the top. Above all, the song is a fine example of the inherent freedom in Jimi's playing, where 'feel' was far more important than polished technique. The use of open string techniques, the flattened fifth intervals, hammer-ons and pull-offs in single-note runs creating modal sounds and the famous 'Hendrix Chord' – the sharpened ninth – all contributed to the dirty, raw, metallic, angular sounds of this and many other Hendrix songs. The sharpened ninth chord is particularly interesting because it demonstrates how Jimi would embellish chords to add new colours to the music, often derived from his own roots in black music. Much of the

Roundhouse, London 22 February 1967

To see or not to see . . .
Hamburg, between 17 and 19 March 1967

pulse of black music is encapsulated in the seventh chord and that's how an R&B guitarist would have originally played it. When black sounds became more funky, ninths were added, and what Jimi did was to sharpen those ninths for a different sound again.

Apart from some reverb, 'Hey Joe' had no technical effects on it; 'Purple Haze' features not only a Fuzz Face distortion pedal, again to rough up and muddy the sound for a good grunchy feel, but a unique gizmo called an Octavia. The second guitar heard during the solo is played through an Octavia invented by an electronics wizard called Roger Mayer.

When he first met Jimi, early in 1967, Mayer was working for the Royal Navy Scientific Service and so could only be identified in articles by nicknames (like 'Roger the Valve'). From his Admiralty work on sound distortion and his love of guitar came the ideas for the earliest fuzz-tone boxes used by Jim Sullivan (for example, P.J. Proby's 'Hold Me'), Jimmy Page, Jeff Beck ('Heart Full of Soul' and other Yardbirds singles) and Keith Richards ('Satisfaction'). The Octavia was a device for raising or lowering guitar notes by a whole octave. With it, Jimi could add various forms of distortion, second harmonics and any amount of sustain. Jimi would always have his Marshall amps turned up full and would play every part of his Fender Strat possible (often modifying the guitar itself by removing the selector spring to get five pick-up positions), removing the back plate to tap the string tensioning springs, and bending springs themselves with the tremolo arm and behind the nut. None of this was random or ill thought out – the chord embellishments, the effects, his remarkably precise control of feedback, the volume, all combined to make the Hendrix sound his very own.

The lyrics to 'Purple Haze' were written upstairs in the dressing-room of the Upper Cut Club on Boxing Day 1966. A year later, Jimi told interviewer Meatball Fulton that he thought it wrong that songs should be restricted in length: 'You know the song we had named "Purple Haze"? . . . That was about . . . it had about a thousand words and it didn't . . . Oh, it gets me so mad 'cause that isn't even "Purple Haze", you know.'[11] Interviewed for this book Chas emphatically denied that 'Purple Haze' was reduced in length. However, without reference to any specific titles, Chas has gone on record as saying that songs were cut down: 'In the initial stages, I changed a lot of the lyrics. He would come up with a lyric on a song and I would make suggestions . . . and in general editing down. His songs tended to be six, seven minutes and we got them down to three and four minutes. We all felt it improved them.'[12]

Purple Haze all in my brain
Lately things don't seem the same
Actin' funny, but I don't know why
'Scuse me while I kiss the sky.

Purple Haze all around
Don't know if I'm coming up or down
Am I happy or in misery?
Whatever it is, that girl put a spell on me!
Help me, help me. . . .

Yeah, Purple Haze all in my eyes
Don't know if it's day or night
You got me blowin', blowin' my mind
Is it tomorrow or just the end of time?

147

'Purple Haze' has become known as one of the archetypal psychedelic drug songs of the sixties, with lines like 'Purple Haze all in my brain' and ' 'Scuse me while I kiss the sky' (a line often rendered in concert as ' 'Scuse me while I kiss this guy', with Jimi pointing at Mitch). But how accurate an interpretation is this of the song? Undoubtedly, it would have been professional suicide for Jimi to have admitted the song was about drugs – banned from the airwaves, concert cancellations and so on. But nobody can recall seeing Jimi take LSD before the Monterey Pop Festival in June, six months after the song was written, even though he was regularly in the company of renowned indulgers like Eric Burdon (known as the 'Space Cadet') and Brian Jones. Jimi told *NME*, 'I dream a lot and I put a lot of dreams down as songs. I wrote one called "First Around the Corner" and another called "The Purple Haze", which was all about a dream I had that I was walking under the sea.'[13]

If we really are only left with a fragment of the lyric (and none of the rest has ever surfaced), then the scope for interpretation is perforce limited, but there are clues to other strands in the song. Jimi often told a story about a girl who tried to ensnare him with voodoo during his early New York days to the point where he had to see a doctor, and this is very likely expressed in the line 'Whatever it is that girl put a spell on me', and indeed most of the first two verses.

As well as utilising real-life experiences in his songs, Jimi incorporated images and themes from his reading of science fiction and mythology. One book known to have influenced Jimi in this way was Frank Waters' *Book of the Hopi* (1963) describing in great detail the rituals, ceremonies and legends which comprised the Hopi Indian religious world-view. The basis of Hopi genesis mythology is the creation of four worlds, the fourth world being that now inhabited by humans. The other three were probably allegorical interpretations of the migrations made by prehistoric tribes up from South America to the North American homelands. The first phase of the dawn of creation, the birth of the first world, was 'Qoyangnuptu', the time of the dark purple. It was fashioned by an entity named Spider Woman, the Hopi 'Eve', but with god-like powers, gathering the earth and mixing it with the liquid of her mouth (the sea). So the first world of the Hopi Indian was born in water, where the light above was diffused and became, to those brought into existence by Spider Woman, a Purple Haze.

The song was the first example of Jimi's explorations of the possible which are inherent in the impossible. Who can kiss the sky or proceed further when 'just' faced with the end of time? He would later tell friends how as a child, feeling detached from the real world because nothing in the real world was secure enough to hold on to, he would lie in bed and somehow find himself floating away, looking down on himself, knowing he wasn't asleep, but drifting through the mists of another dimension, the astral plane, looking for something he could never identify.

Every time he was asked about this song, he gave a different answer. The likelihood was that even he couldn't be positive about the initial inspiration. 'He likes this girl so much, that he doesn't know what he's in, ya know. A sort of daze, ah suppose. That's what the song is all about.'[14]

Jimi had lyrical ideas running through his head the whole time; he scribbled them down in the middle of the night, on napkins in restaurants, on the back of matchboxes, just odd lines, words, though sometimes a whole song might come. He often said scraps of lyrics were scattered in a hundred motel rooms throughout America. 'Purple Haze' was almost certainly a pot-pourri of ideas neatly parcelled up into one song. Like any creative artist, Jimi was intrigued by the visions he had under the influence of LSD, but the degree to which such visions informed his music overall is arguable. Quite simply, there was so much of it about in the mid- to late sixties that for anybody using it regularly, as many musicians did, the novelty soon wore off. What was initially profound became mundane, and acid was relegated to a drug for relaxation rather than inspiration.

'51st Anniversary', the B-side of 'Purple Haze', was a comprehensive tirade against holy deadlock directed at any woman who thought she could get Jimi Hendrix down the aisle. However, the first verse about being 'old and happy and they settled down' shows that it can work if you stick at it long enough. It's the early years that are tough when:

> a thousand kids run around hungry
> 'Cause their mother is a louse
> Daddy's down at the whisky house
> That ain't all.

Jimi's own experience of his parents' marriage would have certainly prejudiced his attitudes towards any long-term emotional attachment to one woman, clearly expressed in the last two verses of the song. Not only does he not wish to be tied down, but to the seventeen-year-old girl (Lucille's age when she married Al) he says, 'Life for you has just begun.' If she wants to get married 'You must be losing your . . . sshh, hmmm . . . mind. Let me live, let me live a little while longer.'

He told Eric Clapton that night in the club about this song: 'the first part is just saying the good things about marriage or maybe the usual things about marriage. . . . And the second part of the record tells about the parts of marriage which I've seen. I just see both sides, but I just really want to witness the first side.' 'Purple Haze' entered the UK charts at thirty-nine and raced up to three. Two singles – two hits.

Faculté de Droit d'Assas, Paris, 4 March 1967

We wondered about the bill before the tour started, and it's certainly true that any reception we get from the fans is more of an after-effect. . . . All the sweet people follow us on the bill, so we have to make it hot for them. (*Disc and Music Echo*, 15 April 1967)

It takes a perverse kind of Tin Pan Alley thinking to conceive of a show comprising the Walker Brothers, Engelbert Humperdinck, Cat Stevens and Jimi Hendrix. Yet this, the Walker Brothers' Farewell

Tour, was the package put together to play the country's cinema venues throughout April. The artist roster was drawn up in January, so despite their recent successes the Experience would be appearing way down the bill. But this was the band's first official tour of the UK and so it was important for publicity purposes to be noticed. The Finsbury Park Astoria (later the Rainbow) was the first date. Journalist Keith Altham was backstage on the night of 31 March before the show.

> There was a clutch of us in the dressing-room. Chas, Jimi and I were all talking. Various things were being discussed about what they could actually do that night to grab some headlines and capture people's attention. I think it was simply because I had a variflame lighter, I said, 'What would happen if we set light to his guitar?' I kind of said it as a joke and Chas said, 'That's not a bad idea.' I said that you would never get away with it, I mean, they are solid-bodied guitars, you could light a bonfire under it and it would take fifteen minutes to catch. And Chas said, 'Well, if we use lighter fuel it will just burn the lighter fuel and won't burn the actual guitar.' So we tried a few experimental runs in the dressing-room and it worked.

The Experience took the stage for the second show sandwiched between the Californians and Engelbert Humperdinck, who closed the first half. The short set comprised two new songs destined for the first album, 'Foxy Lady' and 'Can You See Me?', plus 'Hey Joe' and 'Purple Haze'. The final song 'Fire' was also new and, at the climax of the song, Jimi touched the lighter to the petrol-soaked guitar. At the third or fourth attempt – whoosh – flames leapt up in the air, the audience gasped and compere Nick Jones rushed on to the stage and burnt his hand trying to douse the fire. Keith Altham takes up the story: 'It caused an enormous bloody row with one of the security officers in the theatre – he threatened that Jimi would never work on his cinema circuit again. He came storming round afterwards looking for the guitar as evidence of what had happened.' Contrary to reports at the time, the promoter Tito Burns was actually in on the stunt; he took the guitar from Jimi and hid it under his coat as he left the theatre. 'But before doing so, he put his head in the dressing-room and tore Jimi off a strip – "You're never going to work for me again if you pull a stunt like that" and so on, so that it looked good in front of the security officer.' In truth there was far more press mileage to be made out of the controversy surrounding the onstage fire than the fire itself.

Once the tour was underway, some provincial papers got starchy about Jimi's stage performance. The *Lincolnshire Chronicle* complained that 'His movements were far too suggestive for an audience mostly in the 14–18 age group', and this fed nicely into the hype that Jimi was about to be thrown off the tour for being obscene if he didn't 'tone down' his act. It was also good PR to suggest that every star hated all his rivals. Apparently, Scott Walker *was* miffed at what he saw as a crude attempt to upstage his group's farewell tour, but press stories about dressing-room rows and attempts to sabotage the Experience's stage act by turning on the lights, cutting guitar strings and the like were all deliberately placed in the papers, again to build up the 'Big Bad Jimi' image. In truth, according to Walker Brothers drummer Gary Leeds, this very disparate bunch of artists inhabiting totally different musical worlds got on very well and were all good drinking mates. To earn a few extra pounds, Noel played guitar offstage for Engelbert Humperdinck; Gary knew Mitch from Riot Squad days and he also became good friends with Jimi. As with Billy Cox and Larry Lee from Nashville days, Jimi always valued the friendship of those who knew him before he was a superstar – and in April 1967 Jimi was still a way from being an international celebrity. 'Whenever I went into their dressing-room, we'd laugh and talk and joke.'

While there was little in the way of malicious sabotage – there were plenty of jolly japes on the road to dissipate the boredom of what Jimi called in a letter to a fan 'this silly tour'. Cat Stevens was somewhat aloof from all the schoolboy mayhem, but everyone else freely indulged in letting off fire extinguishers and sending toy soldiers across the stage during an act. Jimmy Leverton, an old friend of Noel's, was Humperdinck's bass player. 'Cat used to come on and do "Love My Dog", "Matthew and Son" and "I'm Gonna Get Me a Gun", at which point Noel and Mitch sprayed him from the back with water pistols. Humperdinck sacked me for hanging out with "undesirables"!' The ultimate sin as far as Mitch was concerned was for anybody to mess about with the set-up of his drums. He allowed his kit to be used to save change-over time between acts. Needless to say, every drummer moved bits of kit to suit himself and, having put up with this for the whole of the tour, on the last afternoon Mitch struck back. He hung the Cat Stevens/Walker Brothers second drummer on a coathook, so he actually missed a number, and then put stink bombs under the bass drum and hi-hat pedals knowing that the drummer would have to sit there through two sets before he could move. He also let off smoke bombs on the coach from Birmingham to Lincoln. After all, says Mitch, 'Man's gotta have a little fun.'

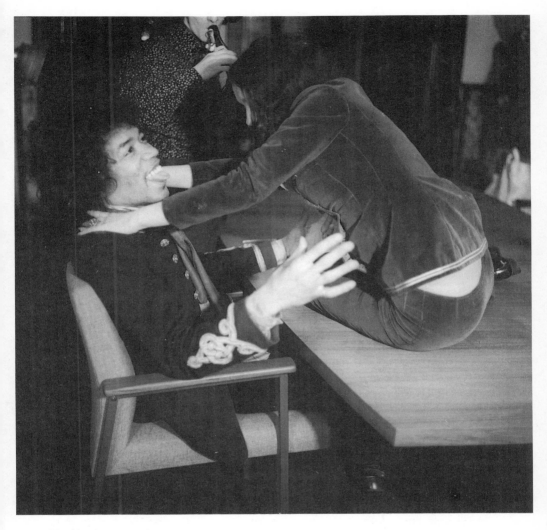

The Hamburg strangler . . .
Between 17 and 19 March 1967

Each date brought with it its own excitement. In Cardiff, Noel and Mitch were chased by fans, couldn't get back in the theatre and had to scale some scaffolding to reach safety. In Blackpool, Jimi got scalped by a girl wielding a pair of scissors and then spent the night walking the streets when the hotel refused the whole band entry. At another gig, a guy nosedived out of the balcony during the Experience's set

153

and hit the speakers on the way down, 'just to shake hands with us', said Jimi afterwards.

Of course, few of the audience were actually there to see Jimi. In Bolton, the band played only three songs for the second show because of the poor response during the first show, while in Birmingham Hendrix fans were outnumbered by a battalion of middle-aged women armed with flasks and sandwiches waiting for Engelbert and tut-tutting during Jimi's performance. But Jimmy Leverton says eventually 'people were going berserk. They should have changed the billing – once the Experience had done their bit during the first half of the show, everything else after that was an anticlimax.' In Carlisle they did change the running order; Jimi came on after the interval that night:

> Soon the chants of 'Jimi' 'Jimi' drowned the compere's voice and the curtain lifted to screams of ecstasy from the Cumbrian fans. One young girl . . . ran down the main aisle and managed to vault over the orchestra pit into Jimi's own arms. A Carlisle corporation bouncer named Ginger Watson gently escorted her offstage and the ABC cinema echoed to the haunting sound of 'Hey Joe'. . . . In the following numbers only 'Purple Haze' was distinguishable in the screams and cries of delight from the 2000 fans. Jimi did a good impression of making love to his guitar on stage and then proceeded to pluck the guitar with his teeth. . . . [The] St John's Ambulance Brigade were busy reviving young girls who had either fainted or become hysterical. As the curtain came down . . . Nick Jones tried to keep his composure and prepare the audience to greet Engelbert Humperdinck, only to be drowned out by the continuing screams for Jimi. [15]

After the chaos of the opening night, Gary Leeds says the promoters were petrified at the thought of what was being cooked up for the last night. The answer was 'nothing much' and the Granada Tooting was still standing when the tour came to an end. To put the Experience in a package like that was bizarre to say the least, but from a PR point of view they couldn't lose. For a start, there would be lots of attention because it was the Walker Brothers' Farewell Tour. Many of Jimi's fans who had bought the singles would now have a chance to see him – the show was designed to impress and excite, and Jimi did not let them down. Finally, of course, any public disapproval of Jimi's act was heaven-sent publicity. What better way to get young people to patronise a concert and buy records? But the icing on the cake was setting fire to the guitar. It was a stunt that Jimi would have cause to

Fringe Boutique, Carlisle, 7 April 1967

regret and only did it on two further occasions throughout his career. Nevertheless, by the end of the tour on 30 April, the Jimi Hendrix Experience were stars and every sub-editor's dream.

> Sure, the tour was good experience, but our billing position was all wrong. I was setting the stage on fire for everyone else. . . . that Engelflumplefuff hadn't any stage presence. He never got anything going. Stopped it all stone dead. . . . we did Dylan's 'Like a Rolling Stone' and 'Wild Thing', but we're not going in for any of this 'Midnight Hour' kick – no gotta, gotta, gotta because we don't have ta, have ta, have ta. (*NME*, 13 May 1967)

On 5 May, the Experience's third single, 'The Wind Cries Mary' b/w 'Highway Chile', was released in the UK. Mitch says the band tried various takes of the song, cleaning it up to the point of sterility, neutralising much of the creative spark of the first take. Eventually they went back to that for the released version. 'Mary' demonstrates that Jimi could adopt an almost technical approach to the construction of chord patterns and embellishments. The song also captures the mood of the Curtis Mayfield/Bobby Womack guitar style with sliding fourths and open tuning which so informed the more melodic aspects of Jimi's playing. Where there might have been a wailing R&B sax solo, there is a clear, ringing compact guitar solo, played virtually straight with only one bend.

> After all the jacks are in their boxes
> And the clowns have all gone to bed
> You can hear happiness
> Staggering on down the street
> Footprints dressed in red
> And the wind whispers Mary
>
> A broom is drearily sweeping
> Up the broken pieces of yesterday's life
> Somewhere a Queen is weeping
> Somewhere a King has no wife
> And the wind it cries Mary
>
> The traffic lights they turn blue tomorrow
> And shine their emptiness down on my bed
> The tiny island sags downstream
> 'Cause the life they'd lived is dead
> And the wind screams Mary

Will the wind ever remember
The names it has blown in the past
And with its crutch, its old age and its wisdom
It whispers 'No, this will be the last'
And the wind screams Mary.

The song was written in the wake of a cataclysmic row between Kathy (whose middle name is Mary) and Jimi. Although they cared a lot for each other, 'Jimi and I used to have terrible rows. We'd fight like cat and dog, screaming and shouting. But at the end of the day, there was not a thing Jimi would have done against me.' Kathy cannot remember the source of this particular row, but seems to think it all started when Jimi accused her of using dirty pans to cook with. 'I hit him with a frying pan, plates and glasses went flying, we smashed the kitchen up. It was a horrific argument, really nasty stuff. He locked me in the bathroom for absolutely ages and wouldn't let me out. He went out and left me locked in the bloody bathroom. Eventually Chas's girlfriend Lotte let me out. I stormed outside and Jimi was sitting there in his black cloak. I got into this taxi and he called out "where are you going?" ' Kathy went to see her best friend, Eric Burdon's wife Angie. 'When I got back, he had done most of the clearing up and he had the whole song written out.'

By contrast, 'Highway Chile' is a joyful autobiographical stomp, starting with a typical guitar/bass harmony line. Jimi marches through the song in search of the All-American Dream: 'Yeah, his guitar is slung across his back / His dusty boots is his Cadillac', unperturbed if he's called a tramp because he knows 'it goes a little deeper than that'.

'Mary' was well received – 'A beautiful record,' said *NME*, 'the best showcase yet for Jimi's inherent feeling for the blues. Shades of Ray Charles, Percy Sledge and the singer's own distinctive quality . . . thought-provoking . . . a subtle flowing accompaniment, with some delicious guitar work, make this a quality blues-ballad. Not normally commercial, but with his current popularity, Jimi should notch another hit.'[16]

Two days after the single was out, the Jimi Hendrix Experience headlined the Saville Theatre for the first time. Penny Valentine of *Disc* noted in her review how Jimi had grown in confidence since the first time she saw him perform in London only a few months before: 'he stood on the stage and played, a quiet dynamic force. He said little to the audience and seemed incredibly humble. . . . he is now

Star Club, Hamburg, between 17 and 19 March 1967

And the guitar cried . . .
Star Club, Hamburg, between 17 and 19 March 1967

confident and entirely at ease . . . feeling much more at home with his success. . . . To his friends he smiled gently and said, "When I played in my backyard at home kids used to gather round and heard me and said it was cool. I wanna thank you now for making this my home." '[17] Jimi was in fine spirits that night as the band went through their core routine of songs for this period. Even when he started having trouble with his guitar, something guaranteed to annoy him, he could joke, 'Man, is Eric Clapton in the house? Ask him to come up here.'

The great non-conformist was a guest at the Variety Club of Great Britain's 'Tribute to the Recording Industry' bash on 9 May at the Dorchester Hotel in Mayfair, attended by such rock rebels as Sandie Shaw, Harry Secombe, Tom Jones, Val Doonican and Vince Hill. Under any other circumstances, Jimi would have been lucky to get a job washing up, let alone be walking in through the front door holding an invitation in embossed lettering.

159

Jimi with Gerry Stickells
Star Club, Hamburg, between 17 and 19 March 1967

The rest of May was spent hopping around Europe: one day in
Paris doing TV; back in England for three club dates, during which
time 'Mary' entered the singles chart at twenty-five; and three days in
Germany including a return to Munich's Big Apple. After the gig, Jimi
and the band were interviewed by *Bravo* magazine, which headlined

the article 'I'm not their fool anymore' with Jimi in a very self-confident mood.

> Jimi: 'I don't care about what the critics say!'
> *Bravo*: '. . . the critics say you are a genius, Jimi. Why don't you want to hear about this?'
> Jimi: 'They are the same people who first laughed. . . . I don't think they understand my songs. They live in a different world. My world – that's hunger, it's the slums, raging race hatred and [the only] happiness is the kind that you can hold in your hand, nothing more!'

At the end, the interviewer asked Jimi how he explained his transition from hobo guitarist to fêted genius. 'Haha,' said Jimi with that special look in his eye, 'Now I'm not stupid Jimi anymore, but Mr Hendrix.'[18] From there they took on Scandinavia for the first time – two dates in Sweden and one in Denmark before flying on to Finland.

On 22 May, the band landed at Seutula airport in Helsinki, Finland's international airport, which the Beach Boys had thought was somebody's private airstrip!

As usual, mouths fell open as they passed through customs, but they got through with no hassle. The Experience were there to record a TV show with Cat Stevens with a gig at the Kulttuuritalo. Producer Antti Einiö asked Jimi if he wanted to perform the four songs required from them live or using playback. Jimi told him to forget about miming; he said in any case he could never remember lyrics nor how the songs were performed when they were recorded. All of which was true – Jimi had terrible recall for lyrics and musically never performed the same song twice in the same way. Not that the lyrics mattered much in concert; the volume was so loud and venue acoustics then were so poor that few could hear the words anyway. Even on stage, with no monitoring, the band had great difficulty hearing each other.

Taking their cue from the more disreputable British papers, the Finnish pop press weighed straight in against Jimi. The day before the concert *Helsingin Sanomat* headlined its piece 'NEW MADMAN COMING TO HELSINKI', continuing to run Jimi down as someone who 'didn't have the strength to become a myth like . . . Donovan'.

The shooting schedule for the TV programme broke down immediately – Cat Stevens was an hour and a half late, the Experience's gear was still in the truck and the band were fast asleep. The producer was running round like a lunatic trying to make something, anything, happen.

Eventually, he got the band up and then had to hump the gear from the truck into the studio himself with the help of one of the stagehands – only to be told that (somehow) Jimi had agreed to mime, so all the gear had to go back again.

Finally the band were on stage, but Jimi soon started complaining that the lights were too bright. He tried to look away from them and then stopped again at the end of the second song because he said he couldn't remember the words. It was the director's turn to go crazy. It does seem most unlikely that Jimi would have happily agreed to mime – it was something he always felt very strongly about. He arrived in Finland very tired and probably just gave in to pressure, even though the live option had been offered. Eventually they managed to get the four songs on tape – all mimed.

Back at the hotel, there was a press conference. Jimi was quiet and uncommunicative with the reporters, hardly surprising when faced with questions like 'How do you like ohukaiset [Finnish pancakes]?' 'Is that music?' Jimi asked.

The concert that night was not a sell-out; those in attendance were the die-hard enthusiasts of British blues and rock and also lovers of modern jazz and classical music who the night before had watched Karlheinz Stockhausen. In the early sixties, Otto Donner was one of Finland's leading composers of contemporary classical music. He later wrote:

> For me it was an important coincidence that a day before Hendrix
> played in Kulttuuritalo, I heard Stockhausen's Musica Nova concert.
> . . . Stockhausen and Hendrix work in many ways with the same
> material and same equipment. But Stockhausen has fallen into sterile
> observation of sound material whereas Jimi Hendrix creates vital music
> from that material. . . . The way Hendrix uses feedback, extended notes,
> humming of amps and echo effects and the way he mixes them with so
> vital [a] blues guitar . . . makes him an artist who in complexity can be
> compared to most of the serious composers.

After the show, talking in the dressing-room, Chas said he wanted to go out for a meal at a place he'd heard about called Kalastajatorra. Sue Lemstrom was a part-time DJ, still at school, who had managed to get backstage. She tried to dissuade Chas because this was the smartest hotel and restaurant in Helsinki, which would not take kindly to long-haired psychedelic waifs turning up to dine. But Chas would not be put off; he asked Sue to make the reservation on the phone and to

Kulttuuritalo, Helsinki, 22 May 1967

say that famous English artists were on their way.

They pulled up outside in a taxi. The doorman took one look and shook his head. Dressed up in his suit and tie, Chas went in to try and sort things out. Not a hope. Meanwhile outside, the band were being sworn at in Finnish and then English by a group of drunken middle-aged men. The band ignored them. Eventually, the biggest and baldest of the bunch came up to Jimi yelling, 'I'm sorry, I'm sorry.' 'So you should be with a haircut like that,' replied Jimi.

Next day the Madman and his cohorts flew out of the same tiny airport and somehow never managed to return to Finland. They headed back to Sweden again, where 14,000 people saw their concert at the Tivoli Garden in Stockholm, nearly twice the crowd which had recently seen the Beach Boys.

Hotels gave them the usual trouble; this time they were refused a second night in their hotel and couldn't find anywhere that would accept them as ordinary paying customers. Disgusted, they flew on to Gothenburg and two days later back to Germany. By now, the ridiculous scheduling of gigs, TV shows and so on was beginning to

Stora Scenen, Gröna Lund, Tivoli Garden, Stockholm, 24 May 1967

get everybody down. Jimi was particularly tired and fed up. Noel recalls that his absolute worst memory with Jimi was during this brief stop-over in Kiel when Jimi was so drunk at the Star Palace that Noel had to tune his guitar for him, making excuses in German to the audience that Jimi wasn't feeling well.

Back in England, the band headlined 'Barbeque '67', a rock extravaganza at the Tulip Bulb Auction Hall in Spalding, Lincolnshire – support bands included Cream, Pink Floyd, the Move and Zoot Money. Four thousand people packed themselves into what was now a large cattle auction shed, hot and fetid because all but one of the sliding doors were

'Barbeque 67', Spalding, 29 May 1967

shut and there were no windows. Thousands of tickets had been sold, far more than the venue could hold; the promoters disappeared leaving the kids to fend off police dogs sent in to sniff for drugs. Anyone who fainted didn't even have enough room to fall down. Things weren't much better onstage. Probably because of the heat, Jimi had trouble getting his guitar in tune and the Marshall amplification he was using didn't work properly. He started to play, but had to stop because the sound was so awful. The crowd, already edgy and restless because of the terrible conditions, started to jeer. Jimi yelled back, 'Fuck you. I'm gonna get my guitar in tune if it takes all fucking night.' Germaine Greer witnessed this chaos and later wrote:

> They . . . didn't even care whether 'Hey Joe' was in tune or not. They just wanted to hear something and adulate. They wanted him to give head to his guitar and rub his cock over it. They didn't want to hear him play. But Jimi wanted, like he always wanted, to play it sweet and high. So he did it, and he fucked with his guitar and they moaned and swayed about, and he looked at them heavily and knew that they couldn't hear what he was trying to do and never would. [19]

Jimi finished up ripping the strings out of his guitar one by one, smashing what was left to bits and kicking the amps over. This fused all the lights in the hall and plunged it into darkness.

This was Jimi's first taste of the two major difficulties he would face playing live on stage. First, because of the volume level and the autodestruction routines, the equipment was largely incapable of withstanding the pounding of a Jimi Hendrix concert. The problem was compounded by the unavailability then of protective cases for the equipment – it was often damaged in transit even before it reached the stage. Also Jimi's constant and rigorous use of the tremolo arm on his guitar frequently threw it out of tune. Always striving for perfection, Jimi found all this immensely frustrating. Nor could Jimi ever come to terms with audiences who came to see him put on a show rather than listen to the music. Jimi actively enjoyed being a showman and loved the adulation that went with it – but only when *he* wanted to perform, not each and every time the audience screamed for it. For Jimi, it was a dilemma he never really resolved. Taken together with his preference for working in the studio and the punishing touring schedules to which he was subjected once he did go out on the road – live performances were not always the positive experience he would have wished.

Offstage, too, May ended on something of a sour note. A palace revolution was brewing over the fact that the band never seemed to have any money even though they had been working almost continuously since January with several gigs paying £300 a night and had records in the charts. Noel wrote a letter to Chas and Mike which they all signed and there was a showdown in the office. The outcome was typical; the band got cash-in-hand to smooth it all over until the next row. Around this time, there was an oral agreement between Jimi, Noel and Mitch that all income would be divided on a 50–25–25 basis with Jimi taking the biggest share, rather than Noel and Mitch being on a wage. Nothing was ever put in writing, but it didn't really change anything. Once all the multifarious expenses were deducted, the cake would be down to a slice and it was then a matter of dividing up the crumbs.

Noel did most of the talking at these meetings; neither Mitch nor Jimi would say much. Given his poor background, it would have come as no surprise for Jimi to have been money-hungry, once he realised that his natural talent could put him on Easy Street. But in fact he was always very cavalier about money, genuinely unconcerned so long as he had freedom to create music. At this point, when he had very little hard cash in his pocket, a fan up in Hull asked him to autograph his wage-packet. Jimi had to ask him, 'What's a wage packet?' The day after 'Purple Haze' was released, Jimi was at a press reception in Hamburg at Danny's Pan folk club. When asked what he was going to do with his money, Jimi turned to Chas saying, 'When am I going to get my money . . . is there any money?' Everybody laughed and Jimi went on to say that he hadn't got any money, but when he did he would buy his father a house and (so it is claimed by the photographer who organised the press reception) bring his mother back to life.

June was destined to be a crucial month for the band. The success of their first album *Are You Experienced?* was just as important as 'Hey Joe' becoming a hit, because the music was ideally suited to the growing stereo album market, in both Britain and the States. The album had been recorded mainly at De Lane Lea with Dave Siddle again at the desk and Chas producing. But Chas had then taken the masters to Olympic Studios to be mixed by a young South African engineer named Eddie Kramer, who later became profoundly important in the process of realising on disc the sounds in Jimi's head. (For studio details of this and all other recordings, see Discography, Appendix 1.) Technical problems caused delays; its release on 12 May came only a week after 'The Wind Cries Mary'. Chas was none too pleased with

Hamburg, between 17 and 19 March 1967

Track Records over this, fearing that too much product on the market at once might damage album sales. He need not have worried – by 10 June, the album was number three in the album charts. In all probability, only *Sergeant Pepper* prevented the Experience's debut album from going to number one.

The album received universal acclaim. Keith Altham's review for

NME on 20 May was typical: 'Hendrix is a new dimension in electrical guitar music, launching what amounts to a one-man assault upon the nerve cells. The LP is a brave effort by Hendrix to produce a musical form which is original and exciting.' *Are You Experienced?* fully justified Jimi's claim that his music should not be categorised – the music ranges across all the genres of popular music, from R&B to free jazz.

Jimi had great difficulty conveying his feelings to those few around him (usually women) prepared to listen to him. As Jimi said himself, 'Ever since I can remember, I have been moody. I can't help isolating myself from the world. Sometimes I just want to be left alone. People think I'm funny. I'm sorry, I can't help it.'[20]

Thus Jimi's lyrics speak his thoughts and he tended to unpack his heart in his songs. They were confessionals of his beliefs and opinions, ecstasies and loneliness, a map of his emotions with music styles chosen to match the sentiments expressed in the lyric. Music is performed here as knowledge – from the songs you can learn something of their creator.

The introduction to 'Foxy Lady', which kicks off side one, is a stone killer – F bent to F# and the whole guitar shaken with side vibrato sending up a scream with the adjacent strings followed by a slide into the same chord pattern as 'Purple Haze', the sharpened ninth signalling the start of a relatively straight-ahead R&B macho stomp, although lyrically Jimi managed to avoid the worst excesses of rock's schoolboy sexism. In fact, Jimi tended to put women on a pedestal and this song is out of step with most of Jimi's catalogue. His anthems of love were not usually such crude updatings of the Wilson Pickett leer. The song feels like Jimi shaking the last of the chitlin' circuit off his boots, laying down pure funk soul where, as Evan Eisenberg has observed in *The Recording Angel*, 'funk suggests the following [dialectic]: music having started out as ritual, having then become a thing, now becomes a *thang*. The difference is profound. A thing occupies space, a *thang* occupies time and preoccupies people. A thing above all is private, a *thang* can be shared. As *thang* music is again communal and celebratory. Again it is spirit: again it is ritual. . . .'[21]

Against this background, the driving pulse of the song 'Foxy Lady' can be seen as a celebratory declaration of the emotional power of the community of women, rather than (or as well as) a private missive directed at one woman in particular. In the ritual of lustful cat-and-mouse games, the woman has certain influences and knows it, the original meaning of 'foxy' being 'cunning' rather than 'sexy':

> You know you're a cute little heartbreaker
> And you know you're a sweet little lovemaker

– rather than 'you *are*' and so on. Jimi often wanted more out of a relationship than just sex. While in Leeds on the Walker Brothers' tour, he wrote this in reply to a female fan named Bil whom he'd never even met:

> Regardless of what people think about you, me or our group – just so long as you have your freedom of mind, freedom of speech and thought – Don't let nobody turn you off from your own thoughts and dreams – I am *very* interested in seeing you – I believe I would really love to talk to you for a very long time. You seem *very* different from other girls who may write to us. . . . I believe your mind is really and truly together. BUT!!! Don't call yourself stupid any more in LIFE. . . . This is your life – you must die by yourself, so for heaven's sake, live for yourself and no one else. . . . Love you forever, Jimi Hendrix

A later note to her asked for a photo, so this wasn't a 'come-on' to some beautiful girl he wanted to bed. With this in mind, there is perhaps a little more to 'Foxy Lady' than offering sweeties to schoolgirls for nefarious purposes. To a limited degree it is more to do with self-determination and moving on from what you are good at in a familiar environment to taking up new challenges. Jimi will be your guide.

The strangest waltz in 3/4 that Mantovani never played, 'Manic Depression' is a sound poem in psychosis, an angry cry of despair and rage at a world full of misery and pain, in sum 'a frustrating mess'. Jim Morrison was certain that 'We want the world and we want it now'. Jimi's not so sure: 'I know what I want, but I just don't know how to go about getting it' – is the world worth having in the state it is in? Is it even worth being around? This is as good an indication as any that Jimi did not share the acid anarchy of many of his peers and fans. Jimi had only one safe refuge, his own Eldorado, 'music, sweet music'. Snap that thread and the only way to go is 'all the way down'.

'Manic Depression' is characterised by a low riff with Noel's prominent bass part and behind the anguish is Mitch's spiralling drum patterns culminating in an Elvin Jones-inspired percussive wash as the whole edifice crumbles into madness. Mitch tended to strain at the leash somewhat with the ballads like 'Mary' and later 'Angel' – he was much more at home generating rhythmic waves for Jimi to

Stora Scenen, Gröna Lund, Tivoli Garden, Stockholm, 24 May 1967

ride on, as Jimi himself peaks out in mania with long-interval bends, feedback and vibrato in the solo before crashing down into depression.

In his early days, Jimi went back to Nashville to see his old friends like Billy Cox and Larry Lee, to find his bearings before venturing out again on another desperate package tour. Jimi's 'safe house' in music was 'Red House', a blues song which he endlessly improvised on and embellished both in the studio and onstage. Although the song was one of the very first to be recorded by the Experience back in November 1966, they had rarely played it in concert up until then, so this was the first taste for many fans of Jimi Hendrix as bluesman. 'Red House' is a shining example of Jimi's easy blues guitar style. Even on record, the song has a jam feel to it, Jimi casually throwing out streams of melodic blues runs. The song is in B major although, as Jimi always tuned down half a step, it comes out in Bb major, a stately blues in 12/8 time allowing space for all kinds of lead intricacies and rhythmic details which bring guitar transcribers out in a cold sweat. Us mortals can just lie back and enjoy. At the end, Jimi calls out 'How's that one?'

Lyrically we have unrequited love, the theme of a thousand blues songs, although with a difference. Here Jimi is not over-bothered that the locks have been changed – there is always his first love to go back to who *never* lets him down or betrays him: 'That's alright, I still got my guitar!' And he has a second string, 'Because if my baby don't love no more / I know her sister will.' The lady in question, according to Jimi's brother Leon, is Betty Jean, with a reference to her sister Maddy, who both lived in a house painted red.

However *The Book of the Hopi* may again hold the clue to a deeper meaning beyond mere 'woman trouble'. In Hopi legend hundreds of stories exist about the mysterious Red City of the south, a religious and cultural centre possibly in Mexico or Central America known as Palatkwapi, which translates into English as Red House. The city was built in three sections, the first section four storeys high in a rough pyramid shape being reserved for ceremonial purposes. Initiates into the ceremonies were taught in this building by spirit people, Kachina. The more knowledge gained, the higher up the building an initiate would progress. On the fourth storey they learnt about the planets and the stars. They also learnt about the 'open door' in the top of their heads, how to keep it open and so converse with their Creator. But what happens if you lose faith, turn to evil ways and take the left-hand path away from light and love – 'Wait a minute something's wrong, baby / The key won't unlock the door' – your spirit cannot break away, you are no longer free. Jimi's ultimate nightmare realised.

Jimi had an amazing capacity for coming up with one fist-clenching rock riff after another, 'Can You See Me?' being one example among many. But he often had a surprise up his sleeve – he stops this song dead in its tracks with a reverbed Hank Marvin-style one-note bend.

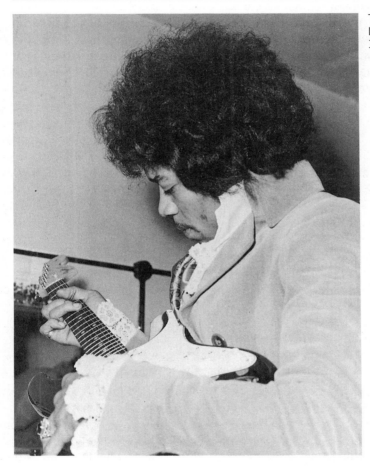

The Astoria,
London,
31 March 1967

Sitting low in the saddle and characteristically hunched over the kit, Mitch really puts his shoulders behind this one, especially as he drives Jimi into the solo which sounds like the jump-off point for an extended jam, but gets pulled up sharply and back in harness for the first verse.

> Can you see me, yeah, begging you on my knees?
> Oh yeah, can you see me, baby?
> Baby please don't leave, alright
> If you can see me doing that
> You can see in the future of a thousand years.

The lyric implies repressed emotions and the inability to communicate which often proves the downfall of relationships. Nobody can see a thousand years into the future nor hear a train coming from a thousand miles off – so the woman is not hearing or seeing Jimi in his misery, either because she doesn't want to or because his blaming, crying and singing is internalised.

Jimi flicks the toggle switch on his Stratocaster between the neck and middle pick-up in 4/4 time while sustaining the chord to take the listener into 'Love Or Confusion'.

> Is that the stars in the sky or is it rain falling down?
> Will it burn me if I touch the sun, yeah, so big, so round?
> Will I be truthful yeah, in, eh, in choosing you as the one for me?
> Is this love, baby, or is it, uh, just confusion?

The F chord with an open G string produces the raga-like drone effect, making this song very much 'of its time'. Jimi's insistence that his voice be kept back in the mix gives it a spectral, ghostly quality, the voice of his own thought processes as he wonders whether he has found truth and love or just more betrayal. Emotion tells him one thing ('My heart burns with feeling . . . '), logic another ('Oh, my mind is cold and reeling'). Dominant use of feedback with vibrato and heavy distortion mirrors this dilemma. Springsteen songs tell of late-night rides in '55 Chevys to think things through. Jimi kick-starts a Harley Davidson into the double-time solo and heads out for the sun to see if it's hot to the touch (put it all down to Experience), to put names and sounds to the emotions or colours in his mind and soul. He burns through the song, coasting into neutral, a note whammies off into the distance, the problem unresolved.

In many of his early songs, Jimi gave violent expression to a volcano of repressed energy, a bubbling, seething force building up over time with no outlet. The escape valve was the formation of *his* band, recording *his* songs, releasing a torrent of molten feelings – depression, frustration, lust, mania, anger and love. If Jimi *was* taking acid in late 1966/early

1967 when the songs on the album were recorded, then the fruits of much of the writing were in spite of LSD rather than a product of the psychedelic imagery it induced. Little of it has the feel of an ego at sea, even one drifting in the hell of a bad trip, let alone floating in transcendent beatitude. The conscious feeling is sharp and defined and often in torment, no more powerfully expressed than in 'I Don't Live Today', one of Jimi's most desolate songs.

Mitch's native American drum pattern is the cue for Jimi as the reservation Indian to lay his plight before the world.

> It matters little where we pass the remnant of our days. They will not be many. A few more moons: a few more winters – and not one of the descendants of the mighty hosts that once moved over this broad land or lived in happy homes, protected by the Great Spirit, will remain to mourn over the graves of a people once more powerful and hopeful than yours.

So spoke Chief Seattle of the Dwarmish on handing over his people's land to the governor of Washington State in 1854.

In a sense, the films *Soldier Blue* and *Little Big Man* were prequels to the song, telling of the inhuman treatment of the Indians meted out by American soldiers last century. 'I Don't Live Today' reflects on the modern-day barbarities of Indian life on the reservation as Jimi may have experienced or heard tell from Grandma Nora Hendrix. These are lives blighted by poverty, unemployment and alcohol – lives with no present, no future and a past written out of the history textbooks.

> Will I live tomorrow? Well I just can't say,
> Will I live tomorrow? Well I just can't say
> But I know for sure, I don't live today.
> No sun coming through my windows
> Feel like I'm living at the bottom of a grave.

Four guitars play the solo, two with wah-wah, one with distortion, while the fourth dominates with a ringing sitar effect as the sound is propelled to a climax, known in those days as a 'freak-out', not a term Jimi was happy with. 'I wrote this song called "I Don't Live Today". . . . it's a freak-out tune. I might as well say that because everyone else is going to anyway.' He then goes on to explain pointedly that 'freak-out' was old Californian lingo for humping in the back seat of a car – '[laughs] I'm being frank that's all, so I guess I'll get deported soon.'[22] In other words, a singularly inappropriate description for his song.

> It's such a shame to spend the time away like this . . . existing
> Oh, there ain't no life nowhere.

With 'May This Be Love', the mood switches from sonic assault to a plaintive ballad, rather spoilt by the switch to the chugging rhythm of the second verse, but then into a sublime solo full of subtlety and invention. Listen to the echo repeats, sliding glissandos and reverse raking on the strings to give aquatic effects. Like so many composers before him, Jimi realised instinctively that many of the characteristics of music, the variations in mood and tempo, fluctuating rhythms and changing colours, are shared by water, as ocean, river, lake, stream or waterfall. Thus whether the composer is creating for a classical or electronic orchestra, the palette of sounds available is inherently symphonic.

Jimi used water imagery both literally and metaphorically – here he makes an allusion to one's inner calm which can so effectively negate external chaos, putting problems into perspective:

> Waterfall, nothing can harm me at all
> My worries seem so very small
> With my waterfall.

Jimi expects ridicule, but keeps faith with his beliefs:

> Some people say 'day dreaming is for all the lazy minded fools
>   with nothing else to do'.
> So let them laugh, laugh at me
> So, just as long as I have you
> To see me through, I have nothing to lose
> Long as I have you.

Poetically and musically, 'May This Be Love' is Jimi at his most spiritual.

With 'Fire' we are back to a great R&B hook: heavy-duty funk, snappy drum breaks, guitar–bass unison, low-note riffs and carefully placed single- and double-note bends. Jimi's soloing could be wild, but was never uncontrolled. The mundane routine of 'man chats up woman' was itself inspired by an even more ordinary incident. When Jimi arrived at Margaret Redding's house in Folkestone for Christmas 1966, he was greeted by a roaring fire in the grate. Always under-dressed for the climate, Jimi, ever polite, asked if he could stand in front of the fire to warm himself from the cold December night air. The German Shepherd dog was in the way, hence one of Jimi's most famous lines, 'Oh, move over Rover and let Jimi take over.'

> it lasts about seven minutes and it's instrumental and, eh, these guys come from another planet, you know. And the third stone from the sun is Earth and . . . they observe Earth for a while and they think the smartest animal on the whole Earth is chickens. . . . And so . . . there's nothing else there, so they just blow it up at the end. . . .[23]

It is possible that the inspiration for this song ('Third Stone from the Sun') came from an old Louis Jordan song 'Ain't Nobody Here But Us Chickens' in the sax-dominated blues-band style popular in Seattle when Jimi was starting out. The story tells of a party held by the chickens that keeps the farmer awake, 'a metaphor for a black house party that the farmer – perhaps the landlord, maybe the police – wants to quiet'.[24] In turn, Jimi's song inspired a Donald Duck cartoon (see Discography, Appendix 1).

Speeded up to 66⅔, the slowed-down vocals on 'Third Stone from the Sun' are revealed as an interstellar communication:

> 'Star fleet to scout ship, please give your position. Over.'
> 'I am in orbit around the third planet from the star called the Sun. Over.'
> 'You mean it's the Earth? Over.'
> 'Positive. It is known to have some form of intelligent species. Over.'
> 'I think we should take a look.'

The images of science fiction – battles on distant planets, visitations from UFOs and near-future Armageddon on Earth – were regularly employed by Jimi to highlight what he saw as the essential hopelessness of the human condition bereft of any spiritual values. 'Third Stone from the Sun' was the first of these; lesser-known examples include two unreleased songs, an instrumental, 'South Saturn Delta', and 'Valley of Neptune', and 'Somewhere' from the album *Crash Landing* released after Jimi's death.

A case has been made suggesting that Jimi was moving towards jazz when he died, claims made largely on the basis of some jams he had with the likes of Tony Williams, John McLaughlin and Larry Young and a tentatively planned collaboration with Gil Evans. Such claims miss the point that Jimi's breadth of vision put him beyond such categorisation. In the sense that freedom was the watchword of his playing, the freedom to improvise and embellish on standard themes and forms, Jimi was innately a 'jazz' musician (as well as being a quintessential blues musician), if only because that is where the most open attitudes lie in modern popular music. Jimi had a 'jazz' mind even if he wasn't a prospective jazz musician.

Jimi had a particular liking for free-form jazz. 'I like Charlie Mingus and this other cat who plays all the horns, Roland Kirk. I like very different jazz, not all this regular stuff. Most of it is blowing blues and that's why I like free-form jazz. The groovy stuff instead of the old-time hits – like they get up there and play "How High is the Moon" for hours and hours – it gets to be a drag.'[25] About Kirk specifically, Jimi said, 'I really would like to meet Roland Kirk and I'd like him to play with us. If people read this they'll say, "That guy must be joking," but I really think we're doing the same things. We have different moods and I think some of the moods are on the same level that Roland Kirk is doing.'[26]

Jimi later got to jam with Roland Kirk and, like Jimi, Kirk was accused of gimmickry because he played three instruments at once – the stritch, a kind of straight alto sax; the manzello, which looked like an alto sax, but sounded like a soprano; and a tenor sax plus a number of sirens and whistles, all to create drama and excitement. Kirk retaliated by saying that he did everything for a reason – he was just translating the sounds he heard in his head. Jazz musician and critic Ian Carr called him a complete original performer, one of the great improvisers, whose style carried in it the whole history of jazz from New Orleans to avant-garde. Much the same can be said of Jimi Hendrix, encompassing blues, R&B, rock 'n' roll and free jazz.

Another kindred spirit of Jimi's within free-form jazz was Ornette Coleman, whose musical history was not dissimilar to his. Self-taught, Coleman did the R&B circuit in the South before moving to New York, scuffling around from one dive to another in search of work. There he suffered similar humiliations from other musicians. He had a very unorthodox concept of music which essentially was non-harmonic with no chords, although it was nonetheless very blues-oriented. This profoundly original musician was mocked as a charlatan who couldn't play. But he closed his ears to everything but the music and like Jimi practised endlessly in solitude, obsessed with atomising what he was playing: 'I used to play one note all day and I used to try find how many different sounds I could get out of the mouthpiece. . . . I'd hear so many different tones and sounds.'[27]

The sentiments Ornette Coleman expressed in the liner notes to his fifties album *Something Else* Jimi carried forward into the rock idiom of the sixties: 'The creation of music is just as natural as the air we breathe. I believe music is a really free thing and any way you can enjoy it, you should.'

'Third Stone from the Sun' exhibits a more clearly identifiable jazz lineage in the influence of Wes Montgomery on Jimi's playing and in the way that Jimi invokes John Coltrane's 'sheets of sound', shooting sparks off Mitch Mitchell in the Coltrane/Jones mode with Noel the source of unity.

Feedback is achieved by turning everything up full, hitting the guitar any way you want and then (but not inevitably) facing the speakers as close as possible. In the hands of a novice, this creates a banshee wail of uncontrollable noise. With all the equipment up full, anybody who touched Jimi's guitar would start up this incredible hurricane of sound. But strangely, when Jimi took hold of it, nothing happened – as if the savage beast knew who was the beastmaster. In 'Third Stone', we have the best example of controlled feedback in the Hendrix catalogue, where Jimi used the tremolo arm on the guitar to alter the pitch and intensity of the notes and create rhythmic patterns.

The song has two short verses spoken by Jimi. The second promises that although the Earth is going to be blown to pieces, it might even be worth it because 'you'll never hear surf music again'.

'Remember' is probably the weakest track on the album, although as Charles Shaar Murray reminds us, 'It's all topped off with a magnificently offhand arpeggiated chord guitar solo, the sort of thing that most British guitar-hero bluesbusters wouldn't have known how to *start* to play.'[28]

        If you can just get your mind together
        Then come on across to me
        We'll hold hands and then we'll watch the sun rise
        From the bottom of the sea
        But first, are you experienced?
        Have you ever been experienced?
        Well, I have
        I know, I know you'll probably scream and cry
        That your little world won't let you go

But who in your measly little world
Are you trying to prove that
You're made out of gold and eh can't be sold
So, are you experienced?
Have you ever been experienced?
Well, I have . . .

Trumpets and violins I can hear in the distance
I think they're calling our names
Maybe now you can't hear them, but you will (ha ha)
If you just take hold of my hand
Oh, but are you experienced?
Have you ever been experienced?
Not necessarily stoned, but beautiful.

The album's title track is a majestic setpiece of declamatory anthem rock. Mitch's military snare raps out behind the startlingly contemporary hip-hop scratch sound-effects of tapes running backwards punctuating Jimi's condition for being your guide ('If you can get your mind together'). To what? Sexual ecstasy? Altered states of consciousness? Or just finding yourself, taking time out to view what you're doing from the outside, 'from the bottom of the sea', letting go of the daily grind of the 'measly world'. It is all there for the taking. The secret is being at peace with yourself – 'not necessarily stoned, but beautiful'.

As we have seen, some Scandinavian commentators equated Jimi's music with avant-garde classical composition, an extreme music challenging order, control and purpose. However, this is not necessarily anarchic; Jimi's value set was quite traditional. Nevertheless, many of the songs on the album assault the senses. In mirroring the barbarity and savagery of the world as he saw it, the violent frenzy of Jimi's songs shocks and disturbs. Jimi always felt 'different', somehow apart from his environment, hence he couched his observations in terms of the outsider, the stranger in a strange land – be it above, in the skies, or below, underwater. But, even out in the cosmos, Jimi shows us only the cold edge of an alien technology which fights intergalactic battles and annihilates planets.

Perhaps ultimately, Jimi's songs of war and peace, irrespective of whether the conflict was interpersonal or interplanetary, reflected his own inner turmoil, the hope and despair of the spirit guide or the wanderer of the waste.

Paris, 3 March 1967

In March 1967, two young Hollywood entrepreneurs, Ben Shapiro and Alan Pariser, booked the state-owned Monterey Fairgrounds for 16–18 June to stage a festival showcasing the best of 'serious' rock music.

Since 1964 when the Bay Area cognoscenti got wrecked on LSD-spiked orange juice to the sounds of the Warlocks (later the Grateful Dead), community events in San Francisco centred on rock music had been hugely popular. The culmination of these 'pre-rockbiz' events had been the Human Be-In of January 1967 where thousands of young rock fans packed into San Francisco's Golden Gate Park to hear the cream of local rock talent headed by Jefferson Airplane. This was the first rock festival to attract media attention and a prime demonstration that mass gatherings of under-twenty-fives did not have to end in murder and mayhem. The fact that California's leading underground chemist Augustus Owsley had parachuted 100,000 free doses of LSD into the park to undercut the black market almost certainly guaranteed peace and love, even among the Hell's Angels present. Entrepreneurs like Shapiro and Pariser noted two important points about the new music: it drew hordes of kids and most of them came from the affluent white middle class.

They managed to raise $50,000 and hired LA publicist Derek Taylor who had worked for the Beatles to help put the show together. But they soon ran into trouble. When John Phillips of the Mamas and Papas turned down $5000, they realised that even in 1967 $50,000 did not buy you a three-day music festival of crowd-pulling acts. In fact, Phillips had turned down the money because he didn't like the 'Colonel Parker' feel to the whole enterprise – and the group could afford to pick and choose their gigs. Together with Paul Simon, who had also been approached, John Phillips turned the whole thing around and suggested a non-profit-making festival, organised by the artists themselves with acts playing for expenses only and the proceeds going to charity. Shapiro and Pariser agreed. Largely for publicity purposes, a Board of Governors was set up including Paul McCartney, Mick Jagger, Brian Wilson and Smokey Robinson. But even though they played little if any part in the formal organisation of Monterey, it was McCartney who suggested that no international music event of this kind would be worth the name without Jimi Hendrix.

So on 4 June, with their debut album galloping up the charts, the Experience played a 'farewell' concert at the Saville Theatre – the last gig before flying out to Monterey. Jimi delighted the audience (including

Paul McCartney) by launching into 'Sergeant Pepper's Lonely Hearts Club Band', from the album which had gone straight in at number one in the charts. He ended the gig by smashing a guitar handed to him for the finale of 'Are You Experienced?' and hurling it into the audience. Inscribed on the back of the white Fender was a poem written by Jimi:

> May this be
> Love or just
> Confusion Born out of
> frustration wracked
> feelings – of not
> being able to
> make true physical
> love to the
> Universal gypsy Queen
> True, free expressed music
> Darling guitar please
> rest. Amen

In Britain and Europe, Jimi had proved himself. There was no doubt that he had the potential for international stardom – but first he had to crack America. And for Jimi that task held a special significance. Unlike all the other artists who had spearheaded the British Invasion since 1964 – Jimi was going home.

Eight *No More Surf Music*

Just because you have curly hair or wear bells and beads, you're not a love-in person. You have to believe in it, not just throw flowers. It's the feeling. And someone who wears a stiff white collar can have it. (*Fabulous 208*, 4 November 1967)

In five years I want to write some plays and some books. I want to sit on an island, my island, and listen to my beard grow, and then I'll come back and start all over again as a bee, a king bee. (*Newsweek*, 9 October 1967)

Festival expenses for the Monterey artists included the cost of first-class travel. The Experience started out as they meant to continue by travelling to Heathrow in Mike Jeffery's Rolls-Royce. Jimi scanned the airport bookstalls for a science-fiction novel (Asimov being a current favourite) and charmed anybody who didn't gawp or mutter, but who, like the passport official, had the common decency to say 'Hello' to him. Once in the air, the TWA air hostess paid Jimi an inordinate amount of attention, even for a first-class passenger, sitting down with him to discuss music. Jimi spent much of his time flicking between the different in-flight music channels, taking a perverse delight in Al Jolson and Bing Crosby, but a more serious interest in Bach.

When they landed and were whisked away in a Cadillac, Jimi didn't even bother to check in at the hotel, but headed straight for the Colony record centre off Broadway and came back with about half a dozen albums.

That evening they all visited Jimi's old stamping ground in the Village. They ate at the Tin Angel and moved on to the Café Au Go Go. Keith Altham was travelling with the band to file a report for *NME*. Feeling he ought to do something 'American', 'I had a root beer . . . it was disgusting. I sat there sipping, and there's a black guy sitting on a stool playing a guitar, about 150 people in the club, and they weren't paying him a lot of attention. Me, I was hypnotised by him . . . he was singing a song about the Ku Klux Klan. . . . it was Richie Havens before he became well known.' Havens asked the audience how, having finished one war in the Middle East (the Arab–Israeli Six Day War), they were going to stop the one in Vietnam. Somebody shouted out, 'Send over twelve Israeli officers!' Jimi didn't pay much attention, but did tell Keith that people would be hearing a lot more from Richie Havens. Nor did Jimi play that night; instead they went to see the Doors at the Scene club before returning to the Buckingham Hotel where they were staying. Jimi strolled through the Village in a multi-coloured floral jacket, white trousers, emerald-green scarf and gold medallion inscribed with the words 'Champion Bird Watcher'. Which was fine until they tried to get a taxi, as Keith explains:

> You had three chances of not getting one in the Village. One, if you were a weird-looking hippie. Two, if you had long hair. Three, if you were black. And he made it on all three counts. Not only would they not stop for him, they would try and run him over, so we would have to hide him in doorways, go and stop a cab and even then the cabby would tell him to get out. We had to get out of a couple of cabs and I'd get a bit humpty about it. But Jimi would say, 'Just get out and don't say a word.' But of course, a year or two later, when he was a superstar, they couldn't do enough for him.

In the meantime – welcome home Jimi! Soon after they arrived in New York, Mike Jeffery did one of his disappearing acts, only to reappear just before they left for an overnight stop in San Francisco prior to flying on to Monterey.

A number of problems beset the organisation of the 'First International Festival of Music'. Right from the start, John Phillips brought in his own producer, Lou Adler, who was the real operational force behind Monterey. Ben Shapiro deeply resented his intrusion and, after a number of showdowns, Shapiro dropped out.

The famous Haight Ashbury district of San Francisco was already awash with disaffected teenagers on the run from home. Monterey's Mayor, Minnie Coyle, and Police Chief Marinello visualised a plague of runaways swamping the town and needed some convincing by a suave and attentive John Phillips. He helped assuage their fears and doubts by assuring them that the Festival was aimed at an older audience and undertook not to book 'teeny' pop bands who might attract young kids, or bands likely to incite revolution from the stage.

This may partly explain the rather strange look of the programme, heavily weighted in favour of laid-back Californian acts with only a nod to the pop mainstream, East Coast bands and black music. This in itself was another source of resentment, as bands from other parts of America believed the California music 'mafia' was keeping everyone else out of what was obviously slated to be an important opportunity for exposure. For this reason too, the agents and managers of the big-name acts forced upon the organisers complete unknowns as part of the deal. Hence a singer from England, Beverley, and an LA band, the Paupers, were able to line up with the likes of the Mamas and Papas and the Who. To be fair, the lack of black acts was not entirely the organisers' fault: Chuck Berry inevitably would not play for free while the hotel in San Francisco which had booked Dionne Warwick would not release her for the show. The Rolling Stones could not have appeared either because both Mick Jagger and Keith Richard were denied work permits on account of their pending trial on drug charges. On the other hand, the Beach Boys refused to appear, partly over concern as to the ultimate destination of the proceeds. In fact, the Festival had a severe image problem in the eyes of California's radical spokesmen. One of the Grateful Dead's managers even arranged an anti-Festival on the football field of the Monterey Peninsula College. To try and counteract any 'bad vibes', Derek Taylor issued a press release saying that part of the money would go to a local movement known as the Diggers. Founded on an anti-property, self-sufficiency ethos, their activities included giving away free food grown on their own farm and running a soup kitchen and free clothes store. However, the Diggers, a powerful voice in the local community, were not impressed. They asked why a dollar was being charged to gain admittance to the normally free showground area, declaring that Monterey was just another piece of traditional rock 'n' roll business with a spurious 'alternative' veneer.

And they were right. The promoters needed the financial backing of the record companies to put the Festival on in the first place. In return, Monterey provided the companies with a supermarket of unsigned rock talent to give the monolithic corporations the youth credibility they now realised they needed. Managers like Chas and Mike were not enthusiastic about Monterey just because it might be the dawning of the Age of Aquarius – this was pure business. If Jimi went down well, they would have an international star on their hands. Monterey promised to be a festival of two worlds. Out front, many of the audience believed they were participating in an event that would help revolutionise society.

Backstage, the executives were looking to revolutionise their trading balances while the managers lusted after big advances – which they got. Caught literally in the middle were the musicians, trying to keep everybody happy.

The locals' unproven suspicions about the concert finances never really subsided, particularly when it was revealed that Adler had banked $400,000 from ABC television for the film rights. But, to his credit, Adler got the whole show on the road inside six weeks – artists' booking, staging, lighting, sound, travel arrangements, accommodation, security and concessions. For those who couldn't get on to the site, there were activities outside the arena: a playground, projection room, a stage for impromptu acts, demonstrations of closed-circuit TV and the Moog Synthesiser of Dr Robert Moog. Forty shops and booths opened up for business, fresh from the poor takings of the Magic Mountain Music Festival held in Marin County the week before Monterey. Pickings here were expected to be much richer. At the beginning of the week, the crew set up the staging plus all the sound equipment donated by engineer Wally Heider. On Thursday 15 June, the first of the 'love people' arrived. By Friday, the trickle became a torrent – the roads were blocked north and south by cars, many carrying 'straights' who had come to see the 'weirdos', Hell's Angel bikers and hitchhikers, many dressed as cowboys or Indians mingling with those self-defined as hippies. By the time John Phillips formally opened the Festival at 9 p.m. on the Friday evening, 30,000 people were inside the showgrounds, of whom only 7,500 could actually get into the arena.

Over the weekend, the numbers climbed to an estimated 90,000. Police Chief Marinello drafted in reinforcements, but they weren't needed. They kept a low profile, virtually ignored all the drugtaking and most stood down before the weekend was over. If anybody felt harassed, it was the festival organisers. By Saturday night, Derek Taylor had vanished altogether, leaving a notice on his door saying 'I cannot relate to your problem.' But those who were there and have since written of that weekend all talk of the totally benevolent atmosphere, how you got a contact high just from being there surrounded by stoned, happy, laughing faces. People spoke of tribal connections and collective unconscious experience. Robert Christagu wrote that the weekend was dominated by a 'mood of sanguine goofiness'. Certainly as the Festival wore on, increasing numbers of policemen meandered about wearing sloppy smiles, not unconnected with the marijuana smoke that hung like LA smog over the site and, of course, Owsley's special gift to the people. In some respects, the cultural significance of Monterey was the audience, not the music. The audience was getting off on itself and a majority of the 1200 journalists who had been issued press passes were there to watch them do it. It was Disney time for rock 'n' roll.

Very generally, the concert programme was broken down into 'pop' on Friday evening, Californian bands on Saturday and the 'superstars' to end the proceedings on Sunday. The black and R&B acts like Otis Redding, Lou Rawls, Booker T and the MGs, Johnny Rivers and Hugh Masekela were sprinkled across the weekend like parmesan on spaghetti. There were a number of guest MCs including rock manager and promoter Chet Helms and Peter Tork of the Monkees. Mickey Dolenz was also there. The Monkees had been keen to play, to establish some kind of musical credibility, but were no doubt barred because of the audience they might attract. Inevitably, at such events rumours of who might play flashed around the site. Paul McCartney was spotted, and Brian Jones, resplendent in gold-lamé coat dripping with crystal, lace and beads, 'wafting around . . . looking like the Ghost of Christmas yet to come' as Keith Altham puts it, which lent weight to stories about the Beatles and the Rolling Stones. Dylan was on everyone's lips and minds. All rumours proved unfounded and David Crosby, sitting in with Buffalo Springfield, was all that came from speculation about all-star jams. Charity or no charity, each band was there to make its mark with its own material using its own personnel.

The Experience were not due on until the Sunday night. Until then they had a high time being rock stars – in every sense of the word. Noel sat next to Brian Jones on the flight over and had his first taste of LSD. In his report back to *NME*, Keith Altham wrote, 'Noel Redding and Mitch Mitchell . . . plunge in and out of the pool with hot and cold running girls in tow.' Jimi spent much of his time in the company of Brian Jones, Eric Burdon, who played the opening night with the New Animals, and Buddy Miles, the black drummer/vocalist with Mike Bloomfield's new band Electric Flag. Jimi and Buddy actually went way back; when Jimi came to Montreal with the Isley Brothers, Buddy was there drumming with Ruby and the Romantics and they hung out together briefly. Many of the musicians wanted to try 'Purple Haze' acid and something new on the streets from the House of Owsley that made LSD look like sherbet dip – STP.

The letters were supposed to stand for 'Serenity, Tranquillity and Peace', but the STP experience could be anything but peaceful. STP, also known as DOM (2,5, -dimethoxy 4-methyl-amphetamine), is, as this formula indicates, part of the amphetamine family rather than a genuine 'hallucinogenic' like LSD. It has properties similar to both and is a more powerful relative of MDMA or 'Ecstasy'. It first appeared at the Golden Gate Be-In in January 1967 in ten-milligram doses. Three milligrams is enough for an eighteen-hour trip – ten had people freaking out for a week and many finished up in Bay Area hospitals convinced they were never coming down again. However, Jimi himself did not seem to suffer any ill-effects from using the drug.

As well as chewing the fat with musician mates, soaking up the atmosphere and generally having a good time, Jimi had one specific task he had set himself. He needed another Fender Strat for his stage act. He hadn't bothered to pick up one in New York and couldn't get one in San Francisco, presumably because it was an overnight stop and none of the music shops were open. Eventually he found what he wanted in Monterey. Eric Burdon observed him outside his motel room during Sunday. 'He crouched down in the sun, a silver conch belt around his hips, white calf-length boots, gypsy waistcoat, a purple shirt, the box of coloured inks and oils alongside his guitars. He was quite alone. I stood and watched a minute. It was like a Navaho dream – the warrior before the hunt.'[1]

Jimi had four Fenders on the ground in front of him. Eric watched long enough to see him paint black swirls on one white Fender and yellow on another. One of these guitars would be that night's holy sacrifice. Jimi and Eric shared some marijuana. 'I'm looking forward to tonight, man,' said Jimi. 'I'm so high, living on my nerves. The spaceship's really gonna take off tonight.'[2] Jimi took it easy in the afternoon, sitting in the audience watching Ravi Shankar, trying to absorb some of that master musician's inner calm. The only hassle of the day came later. Jimi got into a frank and fearless exchange of views backstage with Pete Townshend as to who would follow who on stage. Neither band wanted to follow the other. Earlier in the year, the Who had followed Jimi on stage at the Saville Theatre and Townshend was not about to repeat the experience. The key element of visual excitement in both bands was the same, namely autodestruction. The impact could not be the same second time around in the same evening. They reached stalemate; eventually John Phillips tossed a coin and Jimi lost – the Experience would have to follow the Who. Without a word, Jimi stood up on a chair and played some absolutely blistering guitar while everyone else stood around with their mouths open. Then he climbed down and quietly said to Pete, 'If we're going to follow you, I'm going to pull out all the stops.' Which is not quite how Eric Burdon received the story from Mike Jeffery. He told Eric they had pulled off a coup by negotiating that the Experience would follow the Who.

Jimi was very anxious about playing in America in his new persona, actually quite concerned about what those who knew him before would think about the transformation from tuxedo to psychedelic finery. Even Jimi was a little unsure about the military jackets and jazzy shirts when he first arrived, but all the gear now sat very easily on his shoulders – it symbolised just how far he had moved on, but he didn't like to think that this progress would be attended by yet more mockery and criticism of the type he had endured for so long.

Downstairs, beneath the stage, was a small warm-up area with some VOX AC 30 amps set up for the guitarists to plug into for tuning up. Jimi hooked up his Fender and started whacking out this riff. Buddy Miles started a hand-clap beat, Mitch beat out quiet patterns on the wall, Chas and Mike joined in – until promoter Bill Graham stuck his head in and told them all to shut up. Not surprisingly, the Who went down a storm. Rock critic Ellen Sander, one of the poor unfortunates shoe-horned into the press enclosure, wrote that the Who left the audience 'crazed and nobody would sit down. A shiver of apprehension snaked through the air. There was a feeling of something uncontrollable with all its good and frightening implications. Later festivals would stand or fall on that moment.'³ Although Jimi had lost the argument, he couldn't be expected to go on straight away, so the Grateful Dead took the stage. Once the debris of the Who had been cleared away, out came Peter Tork to discourage people from breaking down the fences at the back of the arena by announcing that, contrary to rumour, the Beatles were not on the site. From the stage, Phil Lesh, the Dead bass player, mischievously suggested to loud cheers that, as it was the last night, what difference did it make? Let the people in! Tork slunk off, leaving the Dead to relax the crowd with the delicate interplay of guitar work between Jerry Garcia and Bob Weir. It was the calm before the storm. The announcement begins: 'And now the next act, one of the hottest bands from England. It's led by an American – Jimi Hendrix. And here to introduce him – he's all the way over from London – Brian Jones of the Rolling Stones. Ladies and gentlemen, Brian Jones!' Then Jones said, 'I'd like to introduce a very good friend, a fellow countryman of yours . . . he's the most exciting performer I've ever heard – the Jimi Hendrix Experience.'

Jimi hit the stage – looking eerily like Little Richard, wearing the same kind of ruffled shirt he had not been allowed to wear only two years before, with red pants, feather boa and hair pushed up almost in a pompadour. This was the sideman's revenge. Jimi was on the verge of outstripping all those who had given him the sack or who'd scorned his music.

The band crashed into a full-tilt version of 'Killin' Floor'. Jimi did the arm sweeps along the neck, the tongue wagging to match the vibrato sound and faced the speakers for feedback. And that was just the first number. They went straight on to 'Foxy Lady', then Jimi addressed the audience: 'I tell you what, let's get down to business [takes off feather boa] . . . I don't want anyone to think I'm P. T. Barnum [the audience laughs]. It's really outtasight here . . . Right now we'd like to dedicate this song to everybody here with any kinda hearts and ears. Goes something like this . . .'

He digs deep to dredge up the heavy opening chords to what? 'Wild Thing'? 'Like a Rolling Stone'? Jimi keeps them guessing. Audience reaction at the start had been a little muted as they tried to assimilate what Jimi was setting out before them. But now Jimi was taking them with him, his confidence was growing and his talk became less gabbled: 'Like I said before, it's really groovy. I'd like to bore you for six or seven minutes and do a little thing . . . 'Scuse me a minute and let me play my guitar . . . Right now we'd like to do a little thing by Bob Dylan and that's his grandmother over there [points to Noel], a little thing called "Like a Rolling Stone".' That does it, he's mentioned a homage to their hero – audience and artists are now humming on the same wavelength.

The way Jimi plays it, the song almost becomes a soul bump and grind – the starship is now in hyper-drive, the band are playing their socks off. Jimi was riding the surf, brushing aside mistakes that he had the confidence to announce – an easy half-turn to Noel: 'I know I missed a verse, don't worry.'

As a prelude to 'Rock Me Baby', Jimi gives the audience a quick lesson in the blues, demonstrating how B.B. King might have played it. But 'We've got our own "Rock Me Baby" that goes something like this here. The words'll be wrong, but that's alright.' Mitch's arms nearly came off during 'Can You See Me?', propelling the band to the climax of the set, while Noel adopted the bass man impassivity of a Bill Wyman or John Entwhistle and did his job extremely well through 'Hey Joe', 'Can You See Me?' and 'The Wind Cries Mary'.

Monterey International Pop Festival, 18 June 1967

Jimi built up the atmosphere for the grand finale. He took an enigmatic sideswipe at media hype: 'You know, everybody says that, man, but this is something else, man, like, it is no big story about we couldn't make it here so we go over to England and America doesn't like it because, you know, our feets too big and we've got Fat Mattress and we wear golden underwear. It ain't no scene like that, brother, you know, it's just, dig, you know, laying around and went to England and pick up these two cats and now here we are. Man, it's so groovy to come back here this way and, you know, really get a chance to really play, you know. . . . I can sit here all night and say thank you, thank you, thank you, but I could just as well grab you man and ohhhhh. . . . one of them scenes, but I just can't do that. . . . so . . . I'm gonna sacrifice something here that I really love, okay. . . . don't think I'm silly doing this, 'cos I don't think I'm losing my mind. Last night, oh, man, God. . . . this is it for everybody, this is the only way I can do it. So we're gonna play the English and American anthem combined, okay? . . . Oh, don't get mad. I want everyone to join in too, alright. . . . don't get mad. . . . There's nothing more I can do. . . . '

Jimi made the guitar sound like it was revving up for a highway burn to hell and back. Mitch started pummelling the life out of his Premier drum kit and, with Jimi's guitar now wildly out of tune, the band tumbled into 'Wild Thing'. He did the whole routine, every trick in the bag – guitar playing between his legs, on his knees, behind his back, even somersaults. He faced the equipment, humped the speakers, rammed the neck into the front of one for maximum screech factor. He sat astride the guitar and whammied it into submission. He stepped to the rear of the stage, came forward once more and ejaculated lighter fuel all over the guitar. It was a bit of a put-on, a jive, because it was all pre-planned. But from the audience point of view Jimi had no more to give to them, so he made the ultimate sacrifice. Flames shot up, Jimi smashed the still-burning guitar to bits and flung them out into the crowd. The amps and guitar remnants squawked their death throes. Audience stunned. Goodnight.

With the sounds of the arena screaming in their ears, the band left the scene of triumph and desolation to a tumultuous backstage reception – smiling faces, nodding heads, back-slaps, fives on fives, a kiss for Jimi from Andy Warhol actress and singer Nico, Hugh Masekela's ecstatic cries of 'You killed them, man! You killed them.' From his position in the lighting box at the back of the arena, it took Chas about twenty-five minutes to get backstage; Mike Jeffery was already there, amid all the celebrations, going potty over a broken mike stand. The Experience was saved from a further tongue-lashing by a brash New York publicist, Michael Goldstein, who dragged Mike away and persuaded him into letting him represent the Experience for three months. The band had other detractors: Warner Brothers record executives were there to see what they had spent all their money on sight unseen. They saw the Who smash all their gear up first, so Jimi didn't get many marks in their eyes for originality. Overall, they probably felt a bit like EMI when they realised what it meant to have the Sex Pistols on their books. The critics were divided: the *LA Times* said that when Jimi left the stage 'he had graduated from rumour to legend', but the East Coast guys, who appeared ignorant of the meaning of 'performance' for a black musician and his black audience, saw nothing much other than a Spade routine, a psychedelic Uncle Tom, a 'vulgar parody of rock theatrics', as one put it. What they failed to appreciate (apart from the tradition of black performance of the blues) was that for Jimi back to Charlie Patton the 'theatrics' were a response to the sheer joy of playing the blues, the exuberance born of the feeling. Which was why it could not be turned on and off like a tap – you could only do it if you felt it – something few would ever understand. It was a pity that the audience should have been subjected to the tranquillising harmonies of the Mamas and the Papas, who closed the show, rather than being left to come down on their own from the Hendrix speed experience. What Jimi did that night was to sum up all the music that preceded him at Monterey – deep bluesman, funky soul brother, folk poet and psychedelic guitar hero – and announce his arrival as the universal fusion artist.

A certain amount of mythology has grown up around the various events in Jimi's career which time has hardened into 'fact'. One such myth is that the Experience had no other gigs set up for America, only Monterey, and that all their subsequent work came out of their barnstorming appearance at the Festival. Not so – even before they left England a series of dates at Bill Graham's Fillmore West was announced both in the British pop press and by Jimi himself to a Swedish journalist. Straight after Monterey, the band flew to San Francisco for six nights (two shows a night), plus a free open-air gig on the back of a lorry in Golden Gate Park. After the first Fillmore show, Jefferson Airplane found themselves in the same position as the Who – only worse. They were supposed to be the headlining band, but there was no way they could go on after Jimi. So they ducked out altogether and Bill Graham paid the Experience a $2000 bonus plus an antique engraved watch each for the change in status to top of the bill. From there, they flew to Los Angeles for some recording at the TTG Studio in Hollywood. It was probably a combination of their performance at Monterey and twelve Fillmore sets that promoted the flow of work offers; TV, radio and club dates on both the West and East Coasts.

But, directly as a result of Monterey, Jimi was the instant toast of the LA rock elite in much the same way as he had been acclaimed in London. Peter Tork invited him up to his estate in Laurel Canyon, where other guests included Cass Elliot, Judy Collins, Joni Mitchell, David Crosby and Mike Bloomfield. Jimi also went to Steve Stills' house in Malibu for a jam session involving Buddy Miles and the Buffalo Springfield bass player, Bruce Palmer, among others. Steve Stills set up his amps, 'we took some acid and just went. We played quite literally for twenty hours straight. We must have made up about fifty songs, but there was no tape running. We just played for the ocean.' The music brought the cops, but this time not to cause trouble. ' "Would it be okay if we parked across the street and listened? . . . we don't care what you're doin', we just want to listen. And if one of our sergeants shows up, someone'll sound a siren which means just cool it for a few minutes." So me and Hendrix jammed with the sheriff's protection! And that night I really started to learn how to play lead guitar.'

Another resident of Laurel Canyon was Devon Wilson, from Milwaukee. On the streets since fifteen, this stunningly attractive black girl had been 'befriended' by just about every musician she came into contact with. Initially, she seems to have been an out-and-out groupie, but was far too streetwise and clever not to move rapidly up the 'hierarchy' to become a rock lady seen in all the best dressing-rooms, receptions, clubs, parties and beds. She was very much a scene-maker in her own right. Jimi's friend from the Village, Emeretta Marks, introduced Jimi to Devon; this was the beginning of a complex relationship. Jimi was never particularly communicative in social situations, but Devon had an instinctive feel for Jimi's needs in any given circumstances. Right now he wanted a break from the post-Monterey whirlwind of gigs, interviews, phone calls, publicity and attention. She took him up to her house where Houdini used to live. For the next day and a half, the last thing on Jimi's mind was escaping.

Since arriving on the West Coast, the band had been working and partying non-stop. Noel says that by the time they made their LA debut at the Whisky A Go Go on 2 July, 'We were tired and too stoned to care. We could hardly stand up and it didn't help to know we had a

10 a.m. flight to New York the next day.'⁴ None of which seemed to bother club owner Elmer Valentine: 'I had Sam and Dave playing . . . and they were stiffing. I asked them if I could put Jimi on with them. The people started lining up. . . . Sam and Dave arrived that night, saw the crowd and thought it was for them. When Jimi finished his set, the place cleared out. . . . *Nobody* stayed for Sam and Dave.'⁵ Another case of the sideman's revenge.

A few days earlier, the band had a try-out for their next single, 'The Burning of the Midnight Lamp', but it didn't work too well and the track was left unfinished. With East Coast gigs coming up, there was no time to keep working at it, so Jimi gave up. Their failure to make progress by Jimi's standards had frustrated and depressed him and he was in low spirits as they boarded the plane for the 2000-mile journey across America. At that point the song had no lyrics. 'I wrote part of the song on a plane between LA and New York. . . . There are some very personal things in there. But I think everyone can understand the feeling when you're travelling that no matter what your address there is no place you can call home. The feeling of a man in a little old house in the middle of a desert where he is burning the midnight lamp. . . . you don't mean for things to be personal all the time, but it is.'⁶ Lack of sleep and the fall-out from over-indulgence acted to exacerbate negative feelings. Whether it *was* a waste of time is a subjective judgement. But there was nothing subjective about probably the main reason for Jimi's despair: Mike Jeffery had booked them on a nationwide tour of America – with the Monkees.

They had known about this since the first night of their Fillmore West gigs. Chas recalls,

> We got back to the hotel and Mike Jeffery phones up: 'I've done it, a great deal, a nationwide tour.'
> 'Oh yeah, who with?'
> 'The Monkees!'
> 'Are you out of your fucking mind?'

Jimi was sitting there as Chas hurled further invective down the phone at his partner. Jimi couldn't believe it. After playing themselves into the vanguard of the new contemporary rock-music scene, here they were taking a giant step backwards, playing in a Walker Brothers-style package tour with yet another audience hardly out of nappies. Jimi had *this* to say about the Monkees before he returned to America: 'It's so embarrassing, man, when America is sending over the Monkees.

Oh God! That kills me. I'm so embarrassed that America could be so stupid as to make somebody like that. They could at least have done it with a group that has something to offer. They got groups in the States starving to death trying to get breaks and then these **** come up.'[7]

Jimi with Peter Tork of the Monkees during a sea trip on a cruiser
Miami, Florida, 9 July 1967

Even now knowing Peter Tork did not make this project any more bearable. In fact it was Tork who appears to have set the ball rolling, wanting to have some 'real' musicians on the tour, of the kind he was used to hanging out with in Laurel Canyon. Mickey Dolenz was also a fan of Jimi's, having seen him in London, and he too was keen on the idea. The motivation for having Jimi on the tour was the same as wanting to play Monterey – an attempt to break out of the sub-teen market, appeal to older teenagers and gain the acceptance of the rock establishment. And as Monkees producer Tommy Boyce said, 'It was a personal trip. They wanted to watch Jimi Hendrix every night, they didn't care if he didn't fit.'[8] Tour promoter Dick Clark reluctantly agreed and the wheels were set in motion for the inconceivable to happen.

For his part, Mike thought he'd brought off a coup. Whatever one thought of the Monkees, in America only the Beatles were more popular and, to his way of business thinking, it would be worth sacrificing musical integrity for the media exposure. It also proved that Mike really only saw Jimi and not the rest of the band. In some quarters Jimi had 'teeny-bopper' status irrespective of the music he played. Two girls wrote in to *Record Mirror* in August saying, 'If anybody has any material on Jimi Hendrix, the Walkers (especially Gary) or Peter Tork of the Monkees, please send' etc. Warner Brothers thinking was no different. Stan Cornyn, a Warner Brothers executive, said, 'In those days [at Reprise] anything beyond Dean Martin fell into one category. And the Monkees and Jimi Hendrix were beyond Dean Martin. So nobody at the time in Burbank had any feelings of absurdity in pairing them. After all, they both played loud.'[9] Chas was particularly annoyed because he had been trying to set up an agency deal with Frank Barsalona, one of the best agents for rock bands in the country. When Barsalona left Creative Artist Management to form his own Premier Talent agency, he changed the nature of the business. He did not get involved in the package tours which were such a bad deal for the artist. These were set up on the basis that no rock performer's career lasted more than eighteen months, so you bled them dry while the going was good and it didn't matter what dodgy promoters and self-seeking disc jockeys were employed to run the shows. Barsalona, on the other hand, saw that rock had a future and that the artists had to be nurtured and given a chance to develop. His reputation grew as the agent who had the best bands working for the best rates and he took full advantage of the rapidly expanding ballroom and arena circuit developing around the country willing to play host to rock.

The Experience flew into New York to be greeted by the same old nonsense – their hotel refused them admission, so they checked into Loew's Motor Inn on 8th Avenue. As ever Jimi was quite cool about the funny looks and loud comments the band always attracted, but Mitch was less philosophical. As he told a *Melody Maker* journalist, 'It's ridiculous people standing laughing at us at New York airport when they were dressed in ill-fitting Bermuda shorts.' At the famous Chelsea Hotel, a woman mistook Jimi for the bell hop and told him to pick up her luggage – a sobering reminder perhaps that out in the wide world he was just another black guy.

However ecstatic their reception on the West Coast, because of the size of the country coming to New York was like starting over again. As Mitch observes, the early gigs went well: 'The Scene club was very, very good for us. That was more or less an underground circuit [instead] of going to do teeny-bopper shows . . . not what the band was about at all.' The Experience also played the Rheingold Festival in Central Park, co-headlining with the Young Rascals, who were playing to their home crowd, in front of 18,000 people. Even so, it was the Experience who won the night while the Young Rascals were actually booed during one number.

But after the up came the down – on 8 July they flew to Jacksonville, Florida for the start of the Monkees tour.

The tour moved north into North Carolina. Mike Nesmith recalled to *Guitar World* magazine a strange vision of Jimi at the tour hotel there:

> The hallway was lined with probably five or six on either side of these stereotypical southern police with the big beer belly and different colour blue shirts. . . . I was standing in the hallway for no particular reason, just couldn't sleep or something. A door opened and there was this eerie kind of blue-red light that came from it because of the exit sign over it. Hendrix appeared in silhouette, with this light in the back of him. . . . And he took a step forward and it was like it was choreographed. Noel and Mitch came up on either side of him and they made this perfect trio; it looked like the cover of *Axis*. They started walking down, and none of those guys was very big, and all those cops were like 6'5" and Hendrix just started walking down the hall with these pinwheels in his eyes. And to see him walk under the nose of these cops and these guys lookin' at him going by was something to see. They didn't know what in the world had landed. . . . It was pretty spectacular, wall-to-wall hair brushing against pot bellies. . . . Jimi was in absolute control. [10]

From there they moved on to Forest Hills in New York State.

Around this time, the Experience doubled their road crew to two with the arrival of Neville Chesters, who had been working for the Who and Robert Stigwood. Because Gerry Stickells was relatively new to the trials and tribulations of being a roadie, Noel had offered the more experienced Chesters a job every time he fell out with the Who. Eventually after a major post-Monterey dust-up, Chesters quit for good, rang Noel from New York to see if the job offer was still open and joined the Experience.

> The whole set-up of the tour was farcical in its way. The Monkees had their own plane with the Monkees logo painted on the full length of it and the staff had these suits with 'Monkees' on them. The Monkees

management tried to keep them apart from other artists, but it didn't really work 'cause Mickey Dolenz was a complete lunatic. . . . he had gone out and spent a fortune on his camera gear and took delight in photographing everything. . . . It was a hideous tour. We stayed in the same hotel in New York, the Waldorf, where the Beatles had stayed. When the Beatles were there, they cornered off four blocks; when the Monkees were there they cornered off four yards! It just didn't happen – there were 50 kids outside instead of 5000. But it was great, because everything was on expenses and we had two floors in the hotel. We were on one floor and the Monkees had the entire floor above us. Even for us to get passes to go upstairs through security was quite difficult. . . . they were quite strict. They just tried to hype the whole thing up.

There was no great rivalry. I think a couple of them were a bit, you know, 'We are the Monkees'. Dolenz and Tork were okay, Mike Nesmith was a bit off it and David Jones always tried to be above it all. He was from Manchester and he had this dreadful northern accent and everyone who was around who was English just mimicked him, poor lad. . . . We had this water-pistol fetish, it was who could get the best water pistol. The police outside the Waldorf tried to hustle us into the limousine and, of course, we were nobody. Anybody who came out the hotel, everybody gathered around and this girl tried to make a dash for it. This policeman went up to sort of stop this girl. Mitch had this water pistol, it was like a machine gun and you put half a gallon of water in it. He just started firing it at this girl and, of course, the policeman got in the way – completely soaked him.

Onstage, life was less amusing. The band did 20–25-minute sets; sometimes they went down okay, but overall the reception ranged from muted to hostile. Jimi became increasingly depressed and made no attempt to hide it. With an unresponsive audience who regarded the Experience as little more than a noisy interlude, it didn't take much to wind Jimi up – a broken string or a buzzing speaker cabinet. He would turn his back on the audience, refuse to sing, rush through songs at break-neck speed or just play sloppily. This annoyed Noel intensely and he accused Jimi of being unprofessional. Matters went from bad to worse, and eventually Jimi refused to carry on.

Beforehand, Chas had arranged with Dick Clark that, if things didn't work out, then the Experience could leave the tour without being buried in an avalanche of litigation. However, they needed to concoct a story for the press.

This took a while to arrange and in the immediate aftermath there was some confusion as to what had actually happened. The band's final gig with the Monkees was on 16 July. A week later Jimi phoned the *NME* to say that they were off the tour.

Firstly they gave us the 'death' spot on the show – right before
the Monkees were due on. The audience just screamed and yelled for
the Monkees. Finally they agreed to let us go on first and things were
much better. We got screams and good reaction, and some kids even
rushed the stage. But we were not getting any billing – all the posters
for the show just screamed out – MONKEES. Then some parents who
brought their young kids complained that our act was vulgar. We decided
it was just the wrong audience. I think they're replacing me with Mickey
Mouse. [11]

The publicity team headed by Michael Goldstein 'developed' this
business about outraged parents and announced that a right-wing
women's group, the Daughters of the American Revolution, had
demanded that Jimi be taken off the tour. Not wishing to offend the
parents of the kids who made millions for the Monkees organisation,
Jimi was pulled. It was a good story, and the press wanted to believe
it because it fitted Jimi's image. Nobody seemed to think it strange
that the DOAR didn't issue any sort of press statement themselves
– unless, of course, certain journalists knew it was a put-on. Like the
burning-guitar affair, there was much more publicity to be gained from
being thrown off the tour than being on it. It became enshrined in the
Hendrix mythology and was only repudiated after his death.

Mike Jeffery, however, was not best pleased by the turn of events.
Chas and Mike were on a collision course. 'It took all day and night to
convince Jeffery that we had to get off the tour.' Finally Chas made a
most interesting and mysterious threat which he won't elaborate on.
'I said, "Just remember one fucking thing. Jimi is signed to me and
you don't have a fucking contract with him." ' Mike apparently then
disappeared off to Spain again.

From mid-July, Jimi, Noel and Mitch were back in New York
City. They re-recorded the new single at the Mayfair Recording
Studio and played some important club dates at the Café Au Go Go
and the Salvation in the Village, a club with strong Mob connections.
After-hours Jimi got into some serious jamming with old friends like
John Hammond down at the Gaslight on MacDougal Street.

He came in with a wad of money, I remember. Charles Otis had
loaned him some money before he left [in September 1966], so Jimi
paid him back. Charles told me Jimi pulled out a roll with hundred- and
thousand-dollar bills and said 'Here, man, take what you need,' and
Charles took the $40 he had loaned Jimi and said, 'No, that's cool,
man' – but it sure impressed Charles forever.

201

At one point Eric Clapton was in New York as well and both of them jammed with us for two nights in a row at the Gaslight. It was amazing. . . . What were the two of them playing? *Blues*, man, straight, heavy blues. [12]

John Hammond was not the only 'memory of things past' that crossed Jimi's path in the summer of 1967. He spent some time with Fay Pridgeon and Albert and Arthur Allen. He was looking very prosperous and they were amazed to hear what had been happening since they last saw him. Jimi said he had brought them a present. He called it 'acid' – Fay didn't know what he was talking about at first until somebody mentioned LSD. Jimi tried to suggest that they should take less than him because they wouldn't be used to it – but not wanting to appear 'out-machoed' Arthur kept up with Jimi until they were all very far gone. Fay couldn't handle it and started freaking out, believing that her new baby was in some kind of danger. She rushed out of the apartment to call in the neighbours. Arthur recalled: 'She just went hysterical. So Jimi and I we ran in the bath tub, jumped in the shower, pulled the shower curtains . . . and she's hollering . . . the whole building's inside [the apartment]. "Damn," said Arthur, "how we gonna get out of here, what are we gonna do?" Fay was talking wild: "Get these niggers out of here." She didn't even know us, you know.'

Curtis Knight says he met up with Jimi at the Gorham Hotel in New York, after the aborted Monkees tour. There, Jimi went along to Mike Jeffery's room to get some money and was told to go away. A few days later he was in the Gaslight with a big roll of money paying off an old debt, but Knight maintains that this rebuff from Mike sent Jimi to Ed Chalpin to borrow some money. They went out to have dinner on the corner of 43rd Street and 11th Avenue in Manhattan. There Ed told Jimi the good news – he was going to sue everybody in sight because Jimi was still legally under contract to him. In fact, he had already started proceedings; a notice in the London *Evening Standard* dated 4 July was headlined 'Jimi Hendrix sued for agreement breach' and went on to say that PPX had issued writs against Polydor and Track to stop them recording Jimi until the PPX contract expired in October 1968. Writs would also be issued against Warner Brothers.

Even so, Jimi agreed to do some recording for Chalpin. Together with Curtis Knight, they went into Chalpin's studio during which time the following dialogue was recorded:

Jam with Tomorrow
(left to right: Junior, John 'Twink' Adler on drums –
one hand visible – Jimi on bass, Keith West)
UFO, London, 28 April 1967

Jimi: 'You can't, you know . . . like if you use it you can't put my name on the er . . . thing . . . right?'

Curtis: 'No, no, no. Hell, no.'

Jimi: 'Now, listen, huh . . . he can't do this, all right . . . okay?'

Ed: 'Go ahead.'

Jimi: 'Edward, can you hear me?'

Ed: 'I hear.'

Jimi: 'In other words, you can't, you know, like you can't use my name for any of that stuff . . . right?'

[Someone mentions a song called 'Gloomy Monday'.]

Ed: 'I can't hear you loud enough.'

Curtis: 'You can't use his name for any of this.'

Ed: 'Oh, don't worry about it.'

Jimi: 'No, but . . . '

Ed: [Laughs.]

Jimi: 'No, seriously though, seriously though . . . '

Ed: 'It's our own tape, don't worry about it.'

Jimi: 'Huh?'

Ed: 'I won't use it. Don't worry . . . '

They recorded about six tracks, but the question remains as to why Jimi did it in the first place. Curtis Knight claims it was to get back at Mike for not giving him any money and because he and Jimi had such a good time the last time they recorded together. Perhaps Jimi thought it might help smooth things out if he did some more work for Chalpin. He was obviously unclear about the status of the contract – Jimi was telling Chalpin that he couldn't use his name, whereas Chalpin's case was that he had a perfect right to, despite his assurances in the studio that he wouldn't. To that extent, doing more for Chalpin could actually have made matters worse, because it could have been evidence that Jimi was committed to the agreement. After the issue of writs, the second shot in the war was fired. Ed Chalpin was tied in with Capitol of America. Capitol's sister company in Britain was Decca, who tried to release Curtis Knight's version of 'Like a Rolling Stone' called 'How Would You Feel?', featuring Jimi, as a spoiling tactic in advance of the new Experience single 'The Burning Of The Midnight Lamp'. Under threat of counter-litigation from Track/Polydor, the release set for 13 August was cancelled.

Meanwhile in August the Experience notched some more nights at the Salvation, five nights at the Ambassador Theater in Washington (where Jimi was arrested for jaywalking) and then back to Los Angeles for a prestigious gig on the 18th supporting the Mamas and the Papas at the Hollywood Bowl. However, it was not a triumphant return to the West Coast for Jimi. In Noel's words, 'We died a death' – and the reason was simple. The Mamas and the Papas were headlining and so it was the wrong audience – the Monkees tour all over again. Prior to the gig, Jimi gave an interview to a local paper *Open City* – a clear and lucid exposition of his modus operandi:

ON SEXUAL AND VIOLENCE SHOWS ON STAGE [sic]
Everybody thinks we do it every single time we perform. . . . we don't depend on this, you know. Like I've burned the guitar three times out of 300 gigs we've performed. That's a small percentage.

A lot of people think what I do with my guitar is vulgar. I don't think it's vulgar sex. . . . It's a spontaneous action on my part and a fluid thing. It's not an act, but a state of being at the time I'm doing it. My music, my instrument, my sound, my body – are all one action with my mind. What people get from what I do is their scene. It's in the eye of the beholder. You know, if you lick girls' bicycle seats every morning before they go to school – then you should really think that what I do is masturbation of the instrument. . . .

It might be sex or love to certain people in the audience when I'm playing, but to me – it just gets me stoned out of my mind when I'm playing. It's like a contact high between the music and me. The actual music is like a fast lingering high.

ON DESTROYING THE OLD SCENE WITH NEW SOUNDS
I'm not here to destroy anything. Don't forget there are other people still around making those nice, sweet sounds. You've still got the Beach Boys and the Four Seasons to hang on to. . . .

WANDERING THROUGH THE PADDED JUNGLES OF ELECTRONICS
We're using amps just like anybody else. All the sounds we produce are strictly from guitar, bass and drums. On records – we might overdub, but here again the sound is still guitar, bass and drums, basically. The feedback you hear is from a straight amp – and a little fuzz thing I had built. We don't even use an oscillator. That could really blow a lot of minds, but it just doesn't interest me that much right now.

We improvise an awful lot. Like we don't really rehearse a thing. It's a spontaneous performance. For instance, one of us is in a rock bag, another is just jazz, while I'm on the blues. We are all doing our separate things together. Rehearsals are only to see how the amps sound or something technical like that. Spontaneity is what I could best term it. We are constantly growing in this spontaneity. We have other sounds to make, other singles and LPs to cut.

Critics are already classifying us on the basis of ten months . . . one album and perhaps one or two concerts they've heard. I think it's time for these people to understand that we are not always in the same bag with each performance. How can you be – when you are constantly reaching, improvising, experimenting? It's impossible. It is just going to take time to reach these labelers with our sounds. It's like Cowboys and

Indians. All Indians are bad because they've got the clap – so nowadays something different like the Experience comes along and a lot of the labelers are frightened by it. It's not easily classifiable, but they sure as hell are going to try. So quite naturally, they're going to start little rumours about people they don't understand, like 'Jimi Hendrix is sullen, he's always stoned, he drinks watermelon juice with his coffee, he uses shower curtains for toilet paper.'

ON GOING TO ENGLAND

. . . You must remember that Jimi Hendrix U.S. didn't really have a chance to do anything because he was playing behind people, man. People say I had to go to England to make it – that's not true. Like, I had enough respect for a performer to know that I would have to simmer down with what I wanted to do before I went on stage to back him. Like what would have happened if Little Richard started doing his thing and I got all fired up and started doing mine in front of him – playing the guitar with my teeth, or start burning up the amp? I was bored to death really as a back-up man, but I had respect for the people I was playing for – so I got out and did my own thing.

IS HENDRIX'S MUSIC PSYCHEDELIC?

There are only two songs on my album that would give anybody the horrors, if they were on a trip – 'Are You Experienced?' and 'May This Be Love'. But they are actually peace of mind songs. They are just relaxing things like meditational shades. As long as you can get your mind together while you are listening to them – they've made it with you, man.

TEENYBOPPERS

They're good, groovy I guess. All their screaming and sexy moving and squirming doesn't really bother me at all . . . but sometimes they scream in the wrong parts. Like when I cough. . . . you don't let the squeals get you uptight. You can't work by screams. I mean, you don't perform according to how they scream.

HENDRIX ON SOUL

A Spanish dancer has soul and grace. Everybody has soul. I really don't like the word in connection with the Experience. I like the words 'feeling' and 'vibration'. Like playing together. We play together in free form – yet everybody has a chance to do his thing, to express his own feeling. I get very hung up on this feeling bag. The sounds of a funky guitar just thrill me, go all through me. . . . I can get inside it, almost. I'm not saying that I play that good, but I'm just explaining my feeling towards it and the feeling towards the sound it produces.

HENDRIX ON DETROIT AND WATTS

Well, quite naturally, I don't like to see houses being burnt. But I don't have too much feeling for either side right now. . . . Maybe I'll have more to say later when I get more political.*

* The riot in the Watts black ghetto of Los Angeles in August 1965 was the most serious outbreak of urban violence in America since the end of the Second World War. In 1967, there were more riots in the black ghettos of many major cities. Eighty-three black people were shot, mainly in Newark and Detroit.

. . . Right now I'm scared. Like, soon I'll be going into another bag with a new sound, a new record, a new experience. We'll go exactly the way we feel. I don't know which way that'll be, nothing will be intentional. It'll just happen. We won't do anything with gimmicks, music-wise. We're not going to try and keep up with trends, because we've got a chance to be our own trend. [13]

The day after Jimi gave that interview, the new single, 'The Burning Of The Midnight Lamp' b/w 'The Stars That Play With Laughing Sam's Dice', was released on Track Records in the UK. Much of the song was written at 30,000 feet en route from Los Angeles to New York and finds Jimi in an introspective and melancholy mood.

> The morning is dead and the day is too
> There's nothing left here to lead me, but the velvet moon
> All my loneliness I have felt today
> It's a little more than enough to make a man throw himself away
> And I continue to burn the Midnight Lamp, alone
>
> Now the smiling portrait of you
> is still hanging on my frowning wall
> It really doesn't, it really doesn't bother me too much at all
> It's just the eh ever falling dust that makes it so hard for me to see
> That forgotten earring laying on the floor
> Facing coldly towards the door
> And I continue to burn the Midnight Lamp, all alone
> Burn!
> Yeah, yeah
> Lonely, lonely, lonely
> Loneliness is such a drag!
>
> So here I sit to face that same old fireplace
> Getting ready for the same old explosion
> Going through my mind
> And soon enough the time will tell
> About the circus in the wishing well
> And someone who will buy and sell for me
> Someone who will toll my bell
> And I continue to burn the same old lamp, alone
> Yeah
> Darling, can you hear me calling you?
> So lonely
> Gotta blow my mind
> Yeah, yeah
> Lonely, lonely . . .

The Burning Of The Airport Lamp. . .
Kloten airport, Zurich, 30 May 1968

The song is 'the feeling of [a] man in a little old house in the middle of a desert where he is burning the midnight lamp'.[14] The man is trapped by his history, entombed with the everlasting flame that burns . . . among dead memories. It hurts, however much you try and deny it.

The house in the desert becomes a metaphor for Jimi's own suffocating frustration at failing to produce the song he wanted in the studio, failing to communicate or being a victim of failed understanding. The time for reflection on the plane leads Jimi to consider the downside of being the electric gypsy: the circus comes to town and moves on leaving no trace that it had ever been there – no roots, no home, no love. But Jimi keeps his own flame of love – ultimately the lamp is a beacon. Jimi calls out to anyone who cares to listen.

Jimi plays the harpsichord to pick out the opening melody: 'It just came to me, that's all. . . . we were recording our last LP, just messin' around. I can't play no piano or harpsichord, I just picked out different little notes and started from there.'[15] He also introduces the wah-wah pedal, one of his most evocative guitar effects, a sound forever associated with Jimi Hendrix. It's a simple device for changing the tone of a guitar – heel down for a muted tone, toe up for a crisp bright treble. It can be used rhythmically to accentuate a beat and to make the guitar sing, as Jimi does on 'Midnight Lamp'. Just as he hits the solo he lets out a fatalistic moan of 'Burn!' and then plays that fire out on guitar – slices of slashing wah-wah guitar, echoing Jimi's own plaintive cries of 'Lonely, lonely', plummeting down to 'Loneliness is such a drag!'

'The Stars That Play With Laughing Sam's Dice' was hardly commented upon at the time – dismissed as a good-time joke with lots of guitar to fill up the B-side. Nobody seems to have asked Jimi about it. Only later has it been suggested that the song refers to the hallucinogenics STP and LSD. The mood changes abruptly from the A-side. Jimi here is Captain Trips, your tour guide and courier through what is ostensibly 'outer space', but is in fact 'inner space'. Jimi addressed the passengers:

Alright everybody together now. Away we go. . . . Thank you very much for coming. . . . We'd like to bring to you our one and only friendly neighbourhood Experience Maker. . . . The Milky Way express is loaded. All Aboard! I promise each and every one of you won't be bored. . . . Oh, I'd like to say that there will be no throwing cigarette butts out the window. . . . Thank you. . . . Now to the right you'll see Saturn. Outtasight. Really outtasight. And if you look to the left you'll

see Mars . . . I hope you brought your parachute with you. Hey! Look
out! Look out for that door! Don't open that door! Don't open that door!
(Oh but, that's the way it goes) . . . and now we're coming to the Milky
Way section. . . . If you look around you'll see a few minds being blown
hahaha. . . . It's happening baby. Yeah, I hope you're enjoying your ride
– I am!

Jimi was developing into a seasoned traveller in the mental terri-
tories of psychedelic experience. No mind tourist he. Like so many
others, from his use of mainly LSD flowed an interest in the occult
sciences, I Ching, astrology, numerology and colour as sound. But
like any traveller who knows the roads, Jimi also knew the potholes.
He had tried to persuade Fay and her friends not to take as much as
he because they weren't used to it. The passenger on Jimi's joyride
did not heed the warning about opening Aldous Huxley's Doors of
Perception without due regard to the dangers of sensory overload
– and he certainly didn't have his parachute.

The single was released to mixed reviews, although most were
agreed that it was not the stuff of commercial hits, whether they liked
it or not. Reviewing it for *Melody Maker*, Bruce Johnston of the Beach
Boys thought a lot of the fire and humour had gone out of Jimi's music.
'The best passages are when the drums are rock steady and Jimi and
his guitar are cooking. But there is a great deal of record time devoted
to jews harp noises and other extraneous effects.' However, he did
concede that 'in three separate build-ups the overall effect is hypnotic
and reaches an interesting Wagnerian climax. . . . '[16] *Record Mirror*
thought it was Jimi's best single to date while by contrast a reviewer
for Nottingham's *Guardian Journal* commented sadly, 'seldom have I
expected so much from a record and been so disappointed.'[17] The
critics were proved right: 'Midnight Lamp' was Jimi's first single not
to reach the top ten, peaking at eighteen in the UK charts. But Jimi
didn't seem to mind: 'That song was the song I liked best of all we
did. I'm glad it didn't make it big and get thrown around.'[18]

To compensate, a week after the release of 'Midnight Lamp' in
England, 'Purple Haze' and 'Are You Experienced?' both entered the
Billboard Charts. The American version of the album on Reprise had
different tracks from that released on Track. Warners decided to include
Jimi's singles 'Hey Joe', 'Purple Haze' and 'The Wind Cries Mary' at the
expense of 'Remember', 'Can You See Me?' and, most unfortunate of
all, 'Red House'. Warners' marketing people also had a new cover done.
The original was shot by photographer Bruce Fleming with Jimi in his

favourite black shirt with red roses bought in the King's Road by Kathy, who had to borrow the money from Angie Burdon. Mitch and Noel are rather subserviently posed at Jimi's feet, looking like elfins to the Grand Vizier in his spreading cloak. In fact, Bruce preferred another shot he took in black and white without the cloak spread wide, but he was overruled by one or all of Chris Stamp, Kit Lambert and Chas. The American cover was more 'democratic' – all the band were standing and looking uniformly horrible, distorted by fish-eye lens photography and blue tints against the all-American down-home background of Kew Gardens – once they'd persuaded the 'parky' to let them in for the shoot.

Unfortunately, by the time the band had made an impact on America's national chart, they had flown back to England, whereas it might have made more sense to do a tour. It is true that a trip to Europe had already been arranged, but the reasons for going home were as much for personal as business reasons. Jimi almost certainly did not want to leave, but Chas had recently got married to his Swedish girlfriend Lotte, Mitch was due to get engaged to *his* girlfriend Carolyn, while Noel and Mitch both felt they needed some respite from the madness of life on the road in America.

Their return to England on 21 August was marked by both comedy and tragedy. Coming through London airport, Mitch was relieved of a tear-gas gun by customs. Noel defended his colleague bravely to the *Daily Mirror*: 'It was only a very small gun.' Venue owners slept more soundly in their beds that night.

Jimi did some TV recordings three days later for *Top of the Pops* with Alan Price. As the 'live' acts on the show, both were there to sing the vocals over backing tracks to their respective new singles so as not to contravene the Musicians' Union ban on miming. As Jimi waited for the intro to 'Midnight Lamp', Alan Price's 'The House That Jack Built' was played. Said Jimi on the show, 'I like the voice, man, but I don't know the words!' and to a journalist later on: ' "Burning of the Midnight Lamp" is difficult enough as it is and I was all cued up ready to say the words nice and clear. This really threw me, man – mass confusion.'[19] Alan Price was quite happy – he got a second plug.

On the 27th the band were due to play two shows at the Saville Theatre. After the first show, they went back to Chas's flat only to hear that Brian Epstein had died after taking an overdose of barbiturates, possibly one of the most dangerous drugs of its kind

Saville Theatre, London, 27 August 1967

because of the very small margin between a safe and a lethal dose. The second show was cancelled, although many felt that Brian would have wanted it to go ahead as scheduled. Earlier in the year, Brian had been interviewed by New York DJ Murray the K: 'Many of your listeners probably won't know about Jimi Hendrix, who by the way is nothing to do with me. He's broken through big now. I suppose to the general public in England it looks an overnight success, but no star is born overnight and he's a great performer. . . . He plays guitar with his teeth . . . with his amplifier. He bashes it about, but it's not a gimmick thing . . . it's just that he can play with his teeth, he's an ace guitarist.'[20]

During September and October, the band kept live work down to a minimum so time could be spent in the recording studio working on the second Experience album, *Axis: Bold As Love*. They played seven gigs in Sweden including two 8000-ticket sell-out shows at the Tivoli Garden in Stockholm. Flushed from the enthusiastic reception, it was something of a let-down to be hustled out of the restaurant of their Park Avenue Hotel in case they caused offence to Princess Alexandra, due to arrive shortly after them. Even when it was established who they were, the hotel manager tried to keep them out of the way. As recompense for the embarrassment, the British Ambassador to Sweden, Sir Archibald Ross, bought them all a drink at the bar. They did some TV and radio work in Sweden and Germany and some 'showbiz' events like the 'Guitar-In' at the Royal Festival Hall on 25 September in aid of the Liberal Party. They played the Saville Theatre again on 8 October, where they performed Dylan's 'Can You Please Crawl Out Your Window', and during the finale, 'Wild Thing', Jimi jumped all over Noel, wrestling him to the ground.

With most pirate stations banned and off the air, BBC Radio One, the corporation's 'pop' station, started its first transmission on 30 September. A week later the Experience went into the BBC studio to record the first of two sessions for the *Top Gear* programme hosted by ex-pirate DJ John Peel. The fruits of these sessions appeared on the Hendrix Radio One sessions album released in 1989. And what fruits! 'Drivin' South' in particular probably represents one of the Experience's finest pieces of ensemble playing led by some breathtaking guitar that swoops, dives and motors on relentlessly. If the word 'tight' means anything in music, then 'Drivin' South' was a peerless example. Compared to the well-oiled roadster of the Experience, Curtis Knight's rhythm section sounded like a battered pick-up with two flat tyres. One can only gasp at the fact that this track, along with most of the others, took over twenty years to see the 'official' light of day when in the interim such dire material 'credited' to Jimi has flooded the market.

During that same session, they also laid down Jimi's tribute to Muddy Waters, 'Catfish Blues', featuring a drum solo by Mitch. This was before the heyday of the drum solo when every drummer, however awful, felt obliged to beat his kit to a pulp for twenty minutes. Mitch's expansive style, like Keith Moon's, made soloing largely redundant. But when he did play a solo, the vehicle was often a slow blues like this one, necessitating an awkward kick down into a slower time at the end.

They also played a very different version of 'Midnight Lamp', which had just entered the UK charts, with no additional instrumentation or background vocals. The final song was a throwaway version of 'Hound Dog' with Noel and Mitch baying in the background. It turned up as warm-up number during sound checks for the Albert Hall gig of February 1969, and that's really where it belonged – the boys having a bit of private fun. Stevie Wonder was in the BBC studio that same day waiting to be interviewed. He was so nervous that the Experience let him sit in on drums to calm him down and they jammed on the Temptations' 'Ain't Too Proud to Beg'.

Popladen, Högbo Bruk, Högbo, Sweden, 8 September 1967

The new album *Axis: Bold As Love* was recorded at the Olympic Studios in Barnes with Chas producing. The engineer was Eddie Kramer, who had impressed everybody with his sensitive mixing of Jimi's earlier recordings. At the time there were very few engineers around who had any feel for rock music at all. Either they worked with classical orchestras or they went through a daily grind of pop songs and advertising jingles.

Eddie Kramer came to England from South Africa in 1960. His first studio job was at Advision learning the basics of tape editing, disc-cutting and the operation of tape machines. He moved to Pye, where he supplemented his income by building a PA system for fellow South African Manfred Mann, then of the Mann-Hugg Blues Brothers. He started up his own studio, KPS: 'I really cut my eye-teeth on that, learning how to record under very adverse conditions.'[21] KPS was sold to Regent Sound and Eddie stayed on as manager until he was head-hunted by Keith Grant, studio boss of Olympic. Eddie quickly accepted the engineer's job.

He joined a very creative and enthusiastic team comprising Keith Grant, chief engineer Dick Swetenham, Phil Brown and George Chkiantz, who joined the studio in December 1966, a little after Eddie. Although it would be correct to describe George as a tape operator, this does him a disservice as he was a very accomplished electronics expert, a Heath Robinson artisan of sound using any components that were to hand. He is one of those credited with developing the art of phrasing, the 'panning' effect first heard on the Small Faces single 'Itchycoo Park', and he cites *Axis* as the first time he had got this to work in stereo.

Jimi needed somebody who could fly with him, who would try crazy things just for the hell of it. It was pure delight for creative studio technicians to hear somebody say, 'I want the sounds of underwater,' or be asked to recreate intergalactic warfare.

But as important as Eddie was to the tangible realisation of Jimi's music, the contributions of others such as George Chkiantz and Roger Mayer warrant due recognition. Roger made possible many of the sounds Jimi was able to coax and wrench from the guitar. Jimi had an unmatched ability not only to master new technology, but to 'humanise' it, take away the cold edge and give it warmth, depth and expression. Roger Mayer provided much of that technology. 'I spent a lot of time with Jimi privately, hanging out and talking about the sounds and maybe bringing a few [fuzz]boxes around the flat so he could jam in private. And we would get some general ideas of what we were trying to accomplish in the way of sustain and tone. We were normally using colours to describe the sound.'

In the early recording days of the Experience, Jimi had been quite taciturn in the studio and generally went along with what Chas

215

Mariebergsskogen, Karlstad, Sweden, 9 September 1967

suggested. But with every visit to a studio, Jimi's confidence grew, as Eddie Kramer explains:

> There were no meetings in advance and Jimi created things in a very loose sort of fashion. *He* knew in his own head what he wanted to do and how he wanted to create – he had pages and pages of lyrics to choose from – but he knew *exactly* what he was doing. Every overdub, every backward guitar solo, every double-tracked thing was very carefully worked out . . . in his own head . . . in a very private sense. I was not to know what he was going to do until he walked into the studio. I don't think anybody else did.[22]

> Take any of the backwards guitar solos – and there are quite a number of them. When the tape was put on backwards – and it is played backwards, with the music rushing by you – Jimi knew where he was on every inch of that tape. It didn't matter where you started it. And he knew exactly in his own mind as he was doing the solo what it would sound like afterwards. The point is the man had a firm grasp of what he was doing and what its end result would be.[23]

Roadie Neville Chesters gives another insight into the way Jimi worked in the studio during the *Axis* recordings: 'He was doing the lyrics as the sessions were going. . . . they would start to lay [tracks] down very roughly and it would all come together and then Jimi would have to go into the control room or he'd go somewhere and sit down. Then you'd see him writing things and he tried them in his mind and played them. . . . it was, I suppose, very natural. I think they did a bit of rehearsing, but very, very little. . . . '

Eddie always regarded Jimi as a special client and always went out on a limb technically whenever Jimi came in. Eddie had done some work with black musicians in South Africa and also loved avant-garde jazz – these were his points of reference for a Jimi Hendrix session. 'There was nothing he wouldn't try. He was wonderful in the studio, he was such a funny guy. There was not a moment when we weren't laughing or carrying on. Because, to him, recording was fun. . . . '[24]

Well, perhaps a few moments. There were some very strong characters gathered together in that island universe known as a recording studio. Concentration was fierce, intense – the outside world did not exist and they worked relentlessly to push through mystical barriers, on to pure moments of creation. Eddie was tough and ambitious; he had some very fixed ideas about problem-solving which George Chkiantz did not always share. Neither now did Chas and Jimi always see eye to eye in the studio.

'Everybody who was around Jimi looked to him,' says Neville, whose job it was to set the gear up in the studio. 'There was undoubtedly something about his manner that when he was working you didn't question what he was doing. I remember a couple of times on *Axis*, Chas, you know, was sort of questioning things, "I think you ought to do it like that," and Jimi would say, "Yeah, yeah," in a subdued voice and then he would do it how he wanted it anyway.'

Jimi didn't exactly ignore Chas nor was he humouring him, but somehow at the end of the day he seemed to have his own way. They rarely actually argued, but there could be tension if Jimi wanted to do take after take, perhaps to perfect a solo or include lyrics which made a song excessively long in Chas's opinion. Neville remembers that 'Chas used to find us things to do so it wasn't apparent in front of us, but I do recall a number of times he and Jimi having fairly harsh words about how things ought to be done. It must have infuriated Chas that we always went along with Jimi, who would sort of look round and everybody would say, "Yeah, you ought to do that." ' As the producer, who had to take a 'world-view' of what was going on, Chas had one eye on the budget. In any case, he was a man proud of the fact that 'The House of the Rising Sun' had been recorded for £4 over lunch-time and was still a smash hit all round the world. Much happier on a stage than in a studio, Noel shared Chas's exasperation with Jimi's insistence on carrying on until it sounded right to *his* way of thinking. Noel quickly tired of Jimi's recording technique and also resented Jimi showing him what to play.

Mitch, on the other hand, says Eddie Kramer, was another story altogether. 'Mitch had the ability to almost read what Jimi was thinking. Even though Jimi would dictate a lot of things to play . . . where to put accents . . . and where to fit fills – it was generally left up to Mitch's imagination, which was pretty vivid. Jimi would never cease to be amazed at Mitch's ability to play ridiculous things.'[25]

Perhaps the only thing Jimi was not at all confident about was his singing. He didn't want anybody even to watch him sing. Eddie Kramer had to dim the studio lights to put Jimi in the shadows while he laid down vocals.

In the studio, Jimi was keen to recreate the power of his live performances, which meant cranking everything up to melt-down. The strain this put on the studio equipment was immense. Olympic boss Keith Grant ordered all the expensive BBC microphones they normally used to be locked away when Jimi came in. Other studio economies meant that when it came to headphones, says George Chkiantz, Jimi was uncharacteristically not master of the technology.

> The trouble poor Jimi had getting the cans off. We had these unbelievably uncomfortable cans, they were really naff. All of us kept pleading to Keith about getting new ones. He said, 'Look, we lose about fifty pairs of cans a week out of this place and I've gone out of my way to get the nastiest, most uncomfortable I can find. Their only attribute is that they are loud and they don't blow up – and people *still* nick them. If you think we are going to buy good ones, you are out of your mind.' They were like World War II wireless operator phones and by the time Jimi had finished a session, he'd turned round so many times it was like *The Mummy*. These cans with wires and clips round the ears would catch in his hair and he'd go crazy.

Whatever conflicts there may have been between competing forces in the studio, these never actually got in the way of working. In fact, they could be a positive influence in improving the finished outcome. What *did* get in the way were the hangers-on. In keeping with all studios, whenever a name band was in one of the rooms, musicians from the other one would put their head round the door to see what was going on. Often they were co-opted on to the session doing background vocals or assorted percussive effects. This wasn't a problem. The real hassles were two-fold. There are those who hang around on the fringes of the rock business currying favour with musicians by bringing in drugs, and this was certainly a problem during the *Axis* sessions, especially for people like Noel lounging around the studio with not much to do during takes. And, with Jimi around, the other problem was the women – eager to get a private view of the Great Man.

Olympic Studios was situated on the first floor of an old cinema. On one side of the studio were double doors with a sheer drop to an alleyway below for winching in gear. Around 10.30 one evening when George Chkiantz was locking up after an Experience session, he went to shut these doors and found a girl hanging precariously on to the outside hinge. Jimi would send women off to restaurants to wait for him and then forget about them, and, in general, strangers wandering through a studio full of expensive equipment were a security nightmare which for a technician like George Chkiantz 'got in the way of my peace of mind'.

Trouble was, Jimi was pathologically incapable of saying 'no' to anybody who wanted to come down to the studio. But the open-door policy of Jimi's studio world was not all negative. Although self-conscious about his singing, he liked to put on a show even in the studio for people to enjoy – confirmation of his own assertion that his act was not essentially a gimmicky put-on to please the paying customers, but something he did when he felt like it.

Once in New York, at a time when he was the highest-paid rock artist in the world, Jimi got into conversation with a taxi-driver who said he played bongos. Sure enough, down came the guy at Jimi's invitation to jam. He wasn't any good, the studio costs meter ticked on relentlessly, but this guy got the thrill of his life playing with Jimi Hendrix, and Jimi was happy to indulge him. This was real 'man of the people' stuff and earned him a lot of respect.

If *Are You Experienced?* was the rocket blasting off into orbit, then *Axis: Bold As Love* saw the rocket drifting in orbit surveying the wonders of the universe. The album has a softer, more mystical feel to it, the vocal textures are more subtle and the effects used imaginatively.

> It's made with stereo in mind and I hope everyone can dig it in stereo because that's what it's all about. The album was made over a period of sixteen days and we all helped in producing it with Chas Chandler, and I mixed it with him as well – so it really is us.
>   We've tried to get most of the freaky tracks right into another dimension so you get that sky effect like they're coming down out of the heavens, you know. [26]

In creating the first album, Jimi appears to have sublimated much aggression and pain, airing some major internal grievances. The lighter, less frantic approach of *Axis* allows Jimi's gentle humour and occasionally self-conscious reflective philosophies to float more readily to the surface.

The impression is of an artist less ill at ease with newfound status who has settled into a highly creative mode. The songs are full of dreams and colours, a romantic poet's perception animated by lyrical precision and tight orchestration and underpinned by a depth of musical vision. Notwithstanding Jimi's pulled punches on *Axis*, one reviewer of the album asked how a man as gentle as Jimi could produce such violent music. But this is at the core of romanticism: an unending revolt against convention, authoritarianism, insincerity and moderation, an extreme assertion of the self, a celebration of the value of individual experience.

Jimi's flat, London, late March 1967

A pity then that *Axis* should start the way it does. The intro to 'EXP' suggests 'Stone Free' then stops abruptly for Mitch to announce,

'Good evening, ladies and gentlemen. Welcome to radio station EXP. Tonight we are featuring an interview with a very peculiar-looking gentleman who goes by the name of Mr Paul Caruso on the dodgy subject of "Are there or are there not flying saucers or UFOs?" Please, Mr Caruso, please could you give us your regarded opinion on this nonsense about spaceships and even space people?'

Mr Caruso [a.k.a. Jimi]: 'Thank you. As you well know, you just can't believe everything you see and hear, can you? Now, if you'll excuse me, I must be on my way.'

Mitch splutters and gasps in disbelief as a wall of white-noise guitar feedback and microphone static pans manically across the speakers. Interplanetary voices calling through time to harmonise with the music of the spheres – or a horrible din? Even ardent Hendrix fans tend towards the latter.

Then a shock – the easy triplet jazz feel of 'Up from the Skies', a good example of Jimi's debt of honour to the traditional styles of popular music that informed his earliest exposure to music.

'Up from the Skies'. Yeah well, like people layin' up in gray buildings and so forth is dusted away. And people run around shoutin', 'Oh, love the world, love the world!', you know. We love everybody! . . . Even when you go into people's houses, people must respect the time sequence. . . . Like why keep livin' in the old, in the past? These buildings ain't goin' to be there for all that long, so why be like that?[27]

Against the background of delicate wah-wah and Mitch's brush-work we hear a song which best demonstrates the contrast between the first two albums. The aliens in 'Third Stone from the Sun' are preparing to destroy the planet, whereas Jimi as alien is concerned about what has happened to the place since the last time he passed through. He may even have foreseen the Greenhouse Effect.

I have lived here before, the days of ice
And of course this is why I'm so concerned
And I come back to find
The stars misplaced and the smell of a world that's burnt
A smell of a world that has burned

222

Yeah, well, maybe, maybe it's just a change of climate
Oh, I can dig it, I can dig it baby, I just wanna see.

So where do I purchase my ticket?
I just like to have a ringside seat
I wanna know about the new mother Earth
I wanna hear and see everything
Yeah
Aw shucks,
If my daddy could see me now.

The Jimi Hendrix trademark of guitar and bass in unison has the immediate effect of locking up a song in a strong rhythmic voice. This is particularly evident on 'Spanish Castle Magic', another powerful Hendrix riff with some unusual chord progressions and a large number of note bends in the solo ending with a crazy double-stop.

The song partly celebrates the Spanish Castle club in Seattle ('No, it's not in Spain'), located right out of the city ('it's very far away'). But 'castles in Spain' is also a concept comparable with Utopia or El Dorado, and so the song becomes an invitation to journey with Jimi on the back of a fantastical dragonfly to some kind of promised land – 'just a little bit of daydreaming here and there'.

Right at the end, Jimi's insecurities about his voice manifest themselves as a vocal aside, 'I can't sing a song', and there are a number of such incidental vocals throughout the album, many of which are unfortunately inaudible.

There is a triptych of head-on boy–girl songs on *Axis*, two of which are 'Wait Until Tomorrow' and 'Ain't No Telling'.

Well, I'm standing here freezing inside your golden garden
I got my ladder leaned up against your wall
Tonight's the night we plan to run away together
Come on Dolly Mae, there's no time to stall
But now you're telling me that ah . . .
I think we better wait till tomorrow

Oh, Dolly Mae, girl you must be insane
So unsure of yourself leaning from your unsure window pane.
Do I see a silhouette of somebody pointing something from a tree
CLICK BANG what a hang
Your daddy just shot poor me
And I hear you say, as I fade away
We don't have to wait till tomorrow

So from verse one to three, Romeo climbs the balcony only to be wasted by Daddy Montague.

'Ain't No Telling' reverses the scenario:

> Well there ain't no
> Ain't no telling baby
> When you will see me again
> But I pray it will be tomorrow

Both songs have interesting points of guitar style. In the first, Jimi plays sliding sixths notes in unison with the background vocals, a much favoured feature of Steve Cropper's playing. On 'Ain't No Telling', Jimi uses his favourite chord patterns and lots of third-finger vibrato for which you need Jimi's long, strong fingers.

His ballads represent the most endearing part of the Hendrix legacy, none more evocative than 'Little Wing', covered by musicians as diverse as Eric Clapton, Gil Evans and Sting.

> Well she's walking through the clouds
> With a circus mind that's running round
> Butterflies and zebras
> And moonbeams and fairy tales
> That's all she ever thinks about
> Riding with the wind.
>
> When I'm sad, she comes to me
> With a thousand smiles, she gives to me free
> It's alright she says it's alright
> Take anything you want from me, anything
> Anything.
>
> Fly on little wing
> Yeah, yeah, yeah, little wing

Talking to a Swedish journalist in January 1968, Jimi said of 'Little Wing',

it's based on a very, very simple Indian style. . . . I got the idea like when we were in Monterey and I was just lookin' at everything around. So I figured that I take everything I'd see around and put it maybe in the form of a girl, or somethin' like that, you know, and call

224

it 'Little Wing', and then it will just fly away. Everybody's really flyin' and they're really in a nice mood, like the police, and everything was really, really great out there. And so I just took all these things and put them in one very, very small matchbox, you know, into a girl and then do it. It's very simple, but I like it though. . . .

Musically, 'Little Wing' is structured to lay a gossamer touch across the whole song from the arresting opening statement and the haunting glockenspiel to the use of a Leslie speaker cabinet for the guitar. The speaker baffle rotates, creating a doppler effect of rising and falling waves of sound. Jimi plays the song almost like a pianist with the thumb fretting the bass notes like the pianist's left hand, while the fingers of the fretting hand correspond to the right. The song fades on a magical solo after only two minutes and twenty-five seconds. Even live, 'Little Wing' was hardly any longer – he said what he wanted to say and stopped.

'If 6 Was 9' bears out Frank Zappa's comments quoted earlier about the difference between hippies and 'freaks' in the sixties, with Jimi clearly siding with the freaks:

> Alright, if all the hippies cut off all their hair
> I don't care, I don't care
> Dig, 'cos I got my own world to live through
> And I ain't gonna copy you

The background vocal intro carries the words 'sing a song, brother', tied into the line 'If the mountains fell in the sea' – which is exactly what happened when the second world of Hopi creation mythology collapsed – and there is a hint of another dedication to the American Indian woven into the fabric of a freedom song.

Jimi was interested in the esoteric significance of colours – the 'vibratory' power of colour that lies behind expressions such as 'green with envy', 'seeing red' and 'feeling blue'. As a lead-in to the last verse, with Mitch racing round the kit, Jimi introduces colour symbolism to reinforce the enigmatic nature of his lyrics ('there ain't nobody knows what I'm talkin' about'). He speaks of 'purple, red, yellow and green' where (in ancient scripts) purple rays make the individual a self-ruler, red is the colour of the pioneering spirit, green is the ray of balance and harmony, only achieved through struggle and conflict, while yellow is the colour of creativity. The final occult reference in the song is located in the title itself: in the *I Ching* commentary, 6 is one of the numbers of Earth, 9 one of the numbers of Heaven. The scenario then is one of primeval chaos, but Jimi is going in his own good time:

> I'm the one that's gonna have to die
> when it's time for me to die
> so let me live my life the way I want to.

The women in Jimi's songs are primarily angels and madonnas. Many appear to be his mother Lucille invoked as a saviour and redeemer. Some are more obliquely mother-figures – strong, wilful heartbreakers for Jimi to lose his mind over. 'You Got Me Floatin' ' typifies these sentiments, although the line 'And I kiss you when I please' indicates that Jimi did not always confer the freedom of action on his girlfriends that he wished for himself.

Of interest is Noel's use of an eight-string Hagstrom bass played in counter-point to the guitar during the solo. The additional four strings are tuned an octave higher, giving the effect of a guitar doubling on bass.

The occasional dips from major to minor modes accentuate the essential pathos of 'Castles Made of Sand', a sharply observed reflection on life's bitter ironies.

> Down the street you can hear her scream 'you're a disgrace',
> as she slams the door in his drunken face
> And now he stands outside and all the neighbours start to gossip
> and drool
> He cries 'oh girl, you must be mad, what happened to the sweet
> love you and me had?'
> Against the door he leans and starts a scene, and his tears
> fall and burn the garden green
>
> And so castles made of sand fall in the sea, eventually
>
> A little Indian brave,
> who before he was ten played war games in the woods with his
> Indian friends
> And he built a dream that when he grew up he would be a
> fearless warrior Indian Chief
> Many moons passed and more the dream grew strong,
> until tomorrow he would sing his first war song and fight his first battle
> But something went wrong, surprise attack killed him in his sleep
> that night

London, September 1967

And so castles made of sand, melts into the sea, eventually

There was a young girl, whose heart was a frown
'cause she was crippled for life, and she couldn't speak a sound
And she wished and prayed she could stop living, so she decided to die
She drew her wheel chair to the edge of the shore,
and to her legs she smiled 'you won't hurt me no more'
But then a sight she'd never seen made her jump and say,
'Look, a golden winged ship is passing my way'
And it really didn't have to stop, it just kept on going

And so castles made of sand, slips into the sea, eventually

Sand was a favoured metaphor of Jimi's for the temporary nature of existence, of time slipping away, how nothing can be taken for granted – love, loyalty, family bonds, friendship. Jimi's whole childhood had been spent in a state of uncertainty and transition – different homes, different schools, different carers and a mother who was here one minute and gone the next. The irony is acute: not solid castles built *on* sand which might shift, yet still remain intact, but a castle made *of* sand and so therefore fatally flawed from the moment of creation. Utopia is a mere illusion as the castles in Spain crumble away.

Noel makes his songwriting and lead-vocal debut with 'She's So Fine'. Working with Jimi provided a fund of frustrations for Noel, not least the fact that Jimi showed little enthusiasm for recording Noel's songs and none at all for playing them on stage. Noel had 'She's So Fine' on *Axis* and 'Little Miss Strange' on the next album (*Electric Ladyland*), but they were only crumbs from the master's table and as George Chkiantz says, 'Jimi didn't exactly kill himself to help with "She's So Fine" in the studio.' The song itself is an unremarkable piece of psychedelic pop not dissimilar to 'Happy Jack', a chart hit for the Who earlier that year. Noel's songwriting led one writer to comment rather unkindly that Noel should 'quit while he is behind'.[28] But if 'She's So Fine' did not live up to the title, Noel's playing throughout the album certainly did, exerting a gravitational pull on the music, a rhythmic rendezvous point for Mitch and Jimi.

Mike Stern, one-time guitarist for Miles Davis, said this of Jimi's playing on 'One Rainy Wish': 'His playing is so lyrical. It has that same singing quality that I dig in Jim Hall's playing or Wes Montgomery's playing. But the thing about Hendrix was that he had that sound, he could achieve that lyrical feeling with a fatter sound on his Strat than you could get with a regular hollow-bodied jazz guitar.'[29]

The song creaks with radical harmonies and rhythmic concepts, not least the fact that the verse is in 3/4 time while the chorus is in 4/4. As with 'Castles Made of Sand', 'Wait Until Tomorrow' and 'Ain't No Telling', Jimi engages the bridge and middle pick-ups simultaneously for that 'nasal' sound. The overall filigree guitar style provides a gentle aural wash to complement Jimi's word painting – one of Jimi's many songs born out of a dream.

It's only a dream, but I'd love to tell somebody about this dream
The sky was filled with a thousand stars
While the sun kissed the mountains blue
And eleven moons played across the rainbows above me and you
Gold and rose, the colour of the velvet walls that surrounds us.

Originally planned as the single release to follow 'The Wind Cries Mary', 'Little Miss Lover' is the third of Jimi's declamatory love songs on the album, although as usual he is reluctant to commit himself unreservedly:

Excuse me while I see if that gypsy in me is right
If you don't mind.
Well, he signals me okay
So I think it's safe to say
I'm gonna make a play.

Mitch produces another of those thrilling patterns that mirror the guitar and bass parts as he does in 'I Don't Live Today', while Jimi reintroduces Roger Mayer's Octavia for the lead break, gets a percussive feel with wah-wah and muted strings – and includes every string bend in the book.

From all viewpoints, 'Bold As Love' is the album's tour de force – an Olympian battle of passions whose strategy is mapped out more self-evidently in colours than Jimi let slip in 'If 6 Was 9'. The turbulence of the song accelerates as it moves from the third to the first person. The conclusion has to be that love comes in many hues, love is hard work and to get properly involved takes commitment and courage. Just ask the Axis.

Anger he smiles, towering in shiny metallic purple armour
Queen Jealousy, envy waits behind him
Her fiery green gown sneers at the grassy ground

Blue are the life-giving waters taken for granted,
they quietly understand
Once happy turquoise armies lay opposite ready,
but wonder why the fight is on
But they're all bold as love, yes, they're all bold as love
Yeah, they're all bold as love
Just ask the Axis

My red is so confident that he flashes trophies of war and ribbons
    of euphoria
Orange is young, full of daring,
but very unsteady for the first go round
My yellow in this case is not so mellow
In fact I'm trying to say it's frightened like me
And all these emotions of mine keep holding me from, eh,
giving my life to a rainbow like you
Well I'm eh, yeah, I'm bold as love
Yeah, yeah
Well I'm bold, bold as love (hear me talking, girl)
I'm bold as love
Just ask the Axis (he knows everything)
Yeah, yeah, yeah

Yeah

'Well, uh, like the axis of the Earth, you know. If it changes, well, it changes the whole face of the Earth like every few thousand years, you know. It's like love in a human being; if he really falls in deep enough, it will change him. You know, it might change his whole life. So both of them can really go together.'[30]

The idea of the Axis may yet again have come from Jimi's reading of *The Book of the Hopi*. The life forms on the first world of the nine universal kingdoms were created by Spider Woman, who instructed one of her assistants to 'go about all the world and send out sound' to echo the sound of the ultimate creator Taiowa.

All the vibratory centers along the earth's axis from pole to pole
resounded to his call; the whole earth trembled; the universe quivered
in tune. Thus he made the whole world an instrument of sound, and
sound an instrument for carrying messages, resounding praise to the
Creator of all.
    The living body of man and the living body of the earth were

constructed in the same way. Through each runs an axis, man's axis being the backbone . . . which controlled the equilibrium of his movements and functions. Along this axis were several vibratory centers which echoed the primordial sound of life throughout the universe. . . .

The rather abrupt editing of the coda takes us into Mitch's solo/fill, 'flanged' by Eddie Kramer, an effect achieved by manipulating one of two tape decks running simultaneously and mixing the signal. Jimi arpeggios and phase-solos his way through the coda, taking the spaceship in stately and regal fashion out of orbit and into the stratosphere.

Unlike the previous album, the covers of both the UK and American versions were the same, except the latter had the lyrics printed inside. Roger Law, later of *Spitting Image* fame, did the head drawings of Jimi, Noel and Mitch. But these were then superimposed on top of a multi-coloured Indian religious motif poster which Track Records art director David King says he bought in the Indica bookshop in London. Thus, even if claims made at the time that the cover cost £3000 were true (which seems doubtful), precious little of this appears to have been spent on original artwork.

Axis: Bold As Love was released on Track Records on 1 December to uniformly ecstatic reviews:

Hendrix: Fantastic Second Album
One of the most incredible things about Jimi is that something as deeply personal as his music should appeal to so many people. Honesty must be the answer and it's nice to see it on the winning side. (*Disc and Music Echo*, 16 December 1967)

With Jimi the Music Is 3-D
It's too much. Amaze your ears, boggle your mind, flip your lid, do what you want, but please get into Hendrix like you never have before – it's just too much. (*Melody Maker*, 9 December 1967)

A Vivid Listening Experience
Jimi and the Mitchell–Redding duo have produced something very special. A hit LP with no doubts. (*Record Mirror*, 2 December 1967)

The album was not released in America until January 1968 and it took until April for a qualified review from *Rolling Stone* to appear, by which time the band were well into their first US tour.

Jimi Hendrix may be the Charlie Mingus of Rock, especially considering his fondness for reciting what might loosely be called poetry. But his

231

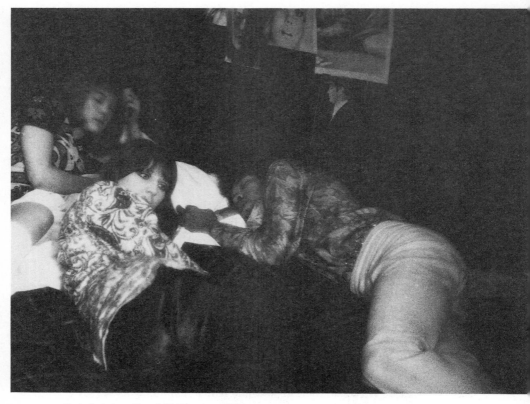

Paris, between 9 and 12 October 1967

songs too often are basically a bore, and the Experience also share with Cream the problem of vocal ability. Fortunately both groups' instrumental excellence generally saves the day and Hendrix on *Axis* demonstrates conclusively that he is one of rock's greatest guitar players in his mastery and exploration of every conceivable gimmick. Uneven in quality as it is, *Axis* nevertheless is the finest Voodoo album that any rock group has produced to date.[31]

By the time *Axis* was released, the Experience were nearing the end of their second UK tour. The venue size was about the same as on the Walker Brothers tour; the difference was that for the first time the Experience were headlining. The tour started at the Royal Albert Hall on 14 November with a large supporting cast for this and all the subsequent dates of the Move, Pink Floyd, Amen Corner, Outer Limits, the Nice and a new band from Ireland managed by Chas Chandler and

232

Mike Jeffery, Eire Apparent. Their road manager was Dave Robinson, who founded Stiff Records.

Waiting backstage to go on as the star attraction, it finally dawned on the Experience that they were now superstars. A year later, Chas told *NME*, 'Noel and Mitch were shaking like leaves and even Jimi was petrified to go on stage. They realised that they were part of something bigger than themselves and I had to get a bottle of Scotch to restore some courage all round.'[32] Hugh Nolan's review of the concert for *Disc* highlighted how much the pop scene in Britain had changed in the year or so since Jimi had come to Britain and, in becoming successful, how much a part Jimi had played in turning the music business around.

> Way back in 1966, a bill consisting of the Jimi Hendrix Experience, the Move and the Pink Floyd would probably have had little impact. But on Tuesday last week exactly that bill packed the vast Royal Albert Hall. . . . A funny thing pop, isn't it?
> Hendrix . . . it seems . . . can do no wrong, [his] hysterically exciting act provides what must be the most crashing, soulful, thrilling finale any pop bill could hope for – short of perhaps the Beatles, who don't play on pop bills any more.

The Albert Hall seemed packed with nothing but Hendrix fans. There were honourable mentions for Mitch and Noel, 'but it was Jimi the crowd was screaming for, and it was Jimi they got, doing every trick he knows . . . and always managing to produce very beautiful sounds'.[33]

However, for a number of reasons, not all the gigs were such an unqualified success. They were torn apart by enthusiastic fans in Sheffield and got a good reception in Glasgow, but audience reaction was poor for both shows in Blackpool and nothing went right at all in Chatham, the very day *Axis* was released. Before the gig, the local paper declared 'POP FEVER GRIPS THE TOWN' and announced that tickets for the second show had sold out. Problems started on the night, when the band couldn't find the hall and then played out the first show to a small audience who 'had to put up with insults about its size, "thank you, both" was a typical on-stage comment, but [it] was still expected to applaud with enthusiasm'.[34] Better times were had at the Belfast gig in Northern Ireland: Jimi was presented with a cake to mark his twenty-fifth birthday; he telephoned a fan in hospital who couldn't make the gig because of a bad asthma attack and sent him a souvenir; and Noel got Gerry Stickells arrested by planting a hotel ashtray in his case.

After thirty-two shows in twenty-two days, the tour ended in Glasgow on 5 December. The band played only one more major gig that year, at the Olympia Exhibition centre in London on 22 December, headlining over the Who, the Move, Pink Floyd, Eric Burdon, Graham Bond and Soft Machine. Jim Marshall, who supplied the band's amplification, was at the rehearsal for this concert, where the electricians threatened to go on strike if Jimi didn't turn the volume down. 'I said to Jimi, "You gotta stop," and then he turned it up again. In the end the shop steward said, "Everybody is out, there will be no show tonight!" And I said to Jimi, "I think this chap is really serious, there's not gonna be a show." But Jimi thought it was very funny. . . . it did quieten down a bit, though.'

'Christmas On Earth Continued', Olympia, London, 22 December 1967

Christmas Day was Noel's birthday, so Jimi spent the day at Noel's family house in Folkestone, but the rest of Christmas with Bruce Fleming, his wife and some of their friends. Bruce invited Jimi when

234

he realised that for all the number of people that would hang around Jimi's neck dragging him to this party and that reception during the year, nobody had actually invited him anywhere for Christmas. Bruce recalls a fun few days. 'We got to talk a lot – architecture, painting, all sorts. He was into everything. . . . we just had a brilliant time and a lot of laughs. . . . Americans like Christmas and we had turkey, the whole thing. He was very radical in his opinions and in his ideas; a very original thinker, very laid-back, very quiet, very funny. . . . he had a beautiful sense of humour.'

From the interviews Jimi gave during the latter part of 1967 came a flurry of revelations that he was already tiring of the *Sturm und Drang* of the Jimi Hendrix act (which for him was several years old) and thinking beyond his current music and band format. To Bob Farmer of *Disc* he said, 'I know we'll have to change some way, but I don't know how to do it. I suppose this staleness will finish us in the end.'[35] He commented to the *Manchester Independent*, 'You can only freak out when you feel like it. I used to feel like freaking out a lot, but, man, if I did it all the time, I'd be dead two years ago.'[36] By Christmas, he was going public on a plan to shake up the band:

I'd like to take a six-month break and go to a school of music. I'm tired of trying to write stuff and finding I can't. I want to write mythology stories set to music based on a planetary thing and my imagination in general. It wouldn't be similar to classical music, but I'd use strings and harps with extreme and opposite musical textures. . . . I'd play with Mitch and Noel and hire other cats to supplement us.[37]

But Jimi would find himself up against powerful forces in his quest for sea-changes in his career – not least the dynamism of his own stage presence, which burned with the heat of quasi-religious ecstasy deep into the souls of fans like the girl from Yorkshire who had this memory of Jimi printed by *Fab 208* magazine on 23 December 1967:

The violent colours of the spotlights paled into insignificance beside the colour of the man beneath them. He stood there, tall and slim, surveying his followers. His long, upstanding hair framed the beautiful, sensitive face and I longed to reach him.
    I looked through the smoke and the silence and saw only Jimi. He began to sing, his velvet-toned voice falling like raindrops on to the hushed curtain of the crowd. This was his destiny. This was my life.
    My eyes begged to close, but I could not move them from his face.

235

I watched his long fingers caress the guitar shaft. I watched as he tore at the strings viciously with his teeth.

I watched as the words flung themselves out of his throat and hung above us somewhere. I watched Jimi being torn to shreds by his music; his skin and his mind stripped away, leaving the skeleton of his dreams shining white and brittle in the raw darkness. I wanted to comfort him, go up to him, but I was helpless, I could not move.

Then he stopped singing; stopped the sensuous movements of his lithe body; stopped time. I saw his eyes close in an admission of his tiredness and I knew he was going.

Suddenly the lights glared and I was alone. My heart reached the stage and curled around his still-remaining shadow and brought him back inside me. Then I could breathe again. Then I could go home.

Dutch TV recordings for *Hoepla*
Vitus Studio, Bussum, 10 November 1967

Nine *Alive, But the War Is Here to Stay*

We'll keep moving. It gets tiring doing the same thing, coming out and saying, 'Now we'll play this song', and 'Now we'll play that one.' People take us in strange ways, but I don't care how they take us. Man, we'll be moving, 'cause, man, in this life you gotta do what you want, you gotta let your mind and fancy flow, flow, flow free. (*New York Times*, 25 February 1968)

There's only *two* kinds of music . . . good and bad. (*Beat Instrumental*, January 1968)

Lorensberg Cirkus, Gothenburg, 4 January 1968

On 3 January 1968, the band landed at Torslanda airport, Gothenburg in Sweden for a brief four-date tour. They checked into the hotel Opalen. After the concert, Jimi and Mitch went out nightclubbing. They ended the evening at the Klubb Karl, returning to the hotel around 2 a.m.

According to Mitch's police statement, there were friends waiting for them when they got back to the hotel and they went off to Mitch's room. Some quiet conversation followed and then Jimi went crazy and started smashing up the room.

Jimi himself told the police that he had drunk only three beers and two whiskies and that he thought somebody had spiked his drinks, although he also told them that he went a bit mad when he'd had too much to drink. He said he felt strange when he got back to the hotel, couldn't handle having people around and just wanted some peace and quiet. What Mitch has to say sort of confirms this: 'When he checked into a hotel, it wasn't like being in America where you got security on the floors of the hotel. People would turn up and say, "Let's have a party," you know, like in Sweden, they could only drink by licence a couple of times a year! So it's "Excuse me, we're just coming back from doing a concert, you know, do you mind leaving us alone. *We* might have some guests." '

Around 4 a.m., a guest in the room below Mitch's complained to Per Magnusson, the night receptionist, about noise in Room 623. The door was locked – Magnusson let himself in with the pass key. On the other side of the door was total devastation. Save for the telephone, not a single piece of furniture, fitting or fabric was intact and there was blood everywhere. Magnusson saw that the window was broken and thought somebody had jumped out. But Jimi was lying on the bed, his right hand bleeding heavily from smashing his fist through the pane. Having sat on Jimi while he calmed down, Mitch was now sitting next to the bed beside him. Magnusson put the commissionaire on guard outside and went to phone the police. Two policemen arrived and tried to arrest Jimi, but he put up a spirited resistance and reinforcements were called in. It took five of Gothenburg's finest to get the cuffs on before Jimi eventually quietened down. He was charged with criminal damage and then taken to hospital to have his hand attended to. The hotel made no claim for damages because Chas handed over 8000 Crowns (about £500) for repairs.

The police put an immediate travel ban on Jimi, telling him he had to report to the police station at 2 p.m. every day until the court hearing. However, there must have been some arrangement

Reporting at the police station (Gerry Stickells on the right),
Gothenburg, 9 January 1968

made, because on the 7th the Experience played two shows at the Tivoli in Copenhagen. Not surprisingly, Jimi was very subdued. Amplification troubles and the pain in his right hand added to the problems. According to the Danish newspaper *Expressen*, Hanson and Carlsson, the Swedish support act, got a better reception from the crowd than Jimi. The Experience returned to Sweden for a gig in Stockholm the next day, during which they flexed their muscles on some of the more melodic and less strenuous material from *Axis* – 'Little Wing' made its live debut and what would be a rare outing for 'Up from the Skies'. The band went home, leaving Jimi and Chas to deal with the authorities. On 16 January, Jimi was fined 3200 Swedish Crowns (£200). Including the amount Chas had paid the hotel and out of total gig money for the four dates of around £2000, they lost one-third on account of Jimi's little outburst.

> I think pop groups have a right to their own private lives. ... people should judge them by what they do on stage ... their private life is their own business. ... You can't expect artists to be goody-goodies all the time. ... any kid that does something bad because a certain pop idol did it would probably have done it anyway. (*Music Maker*, February 1968)

Despite the success the band had achieved, they were still playing in Europe for little more than £500 a night. The big pay-outs could only be had in America; the rest of January was spent gearing up for their first headlining tour of the USA.

The warm-up gig for the tour took place at a favourite venue for the Experience, the Paris Olympia. Their first tour together with Johnny Halliday had ended in triumph there in October 1966. The following October they were back – Jimi announced from the stage, 'We're having a little anniversary thing today. I'd like to say thank you very much for last year for letting us play here instead of booing us off the stage, you know, you gave us a chance – so thank you very much.' Jimi was in good form that night: 'I'm gonna say something in French: "Je vous aime beaucoup," right? Oui. I can say "Eiffel Tower," yeah, listen to that. . . . '

He even joked his way through equipment hassles. After the second song, 'Foxy Lady': 'Well, this guitar is no more good. Do you want it?' he says to the audience. 'Here, take it.' Later into the set, he still hadn't got his guitar troubles sorted out: 'We're gonna try a little blues again until my guitar gets fixed 'cos we're gonna stay *until*

Stora Salen, Konserthuset, Stockholm, 8 January 1968

L'Olympia, Paris, 9 October 1967

my guitar gets fixed, until I play. . . . ' And lets a little lick shoot from his fingers. 'I really hope we get a chance to play here again.' On 29 January 1968, Jimi got his wish.

There is a hum of expectation in the audience – cries of 'Jimi' dot the auditorium. The band take the stage in front of banks of Marshall amps and speaker cabinets.

Jimi starts a run, notes drip like rain. He stops, then accelerates, playing lead, bass and rhythm all at once, signalling Noel and Mitch into Howlin' Wolf's 'Killin' Floor'. The pace is frenetic, Jimi is reaching higher and higher up the frets, racing ahead of Noel and Mitch's pounding rhythm. He holds the song in tension at the end with some vicious note bends and lets go of the reins for the crashing finale.

242

Like to go ahead and do a song that goes something like this here.

> I wish I was a catfish
> Swimmin' all in the deep blue sea
> I'll have all you pretty women
> Fishin' after me

Jimi lends his own considerable weight to the density and passion of Muddy Waters' classic declaration of sexual bravura, emulating the shimmering metallic vibrations of Waters' Telecaster rasp. The song, originally called 'Still a Fool' when Muddy recorded it in 1951, was a hybrid culled from two other Mississippi Delta blues – 'Deep Sea Blues' by Tommy McLennan and 'Catfish Blues' by Robert Petway. When he recorded it for the BBC in October 1967, Jimi turned it into a blues suite called 'Experiencing the Blues', incorporating another Muddy Waters song, 'Rollin' and Tumblin' '. Jimi told *Hitparader* magazine, 'I liked Muddy when he had only two guitars, harmonica and bass drum. Things like "Rollin' and Tumblin' " were what I liked, that real primitive guitar sound.'[1] In Paris 1968, this suite winds down (after Mitch's solo) to the end on the riff of Willie Dixon's 'Spoonful'.

Most people believe that, to be a good blues musician, one has to suffer. I don't believe this. I just like the sound of the blues. When I hear certain notes, I feel real happy. (*Cheltenham Chronicle*, 11 February 1967)

The Mississippi Delta stretches 200 miles from Memphis, Tennessee to Vicksburg, Mississippi. This flat land of cotton and soyabeans was home to the greatest blues singers, Son House, Charlie Patton, Robert Johnson, Muddy Waters, Howlin' Wolf and B.B. King, master craftsmen of the purest and most deeply rooted of all blues strains – Delta blues. On first appearance, a simple enough musical form, but as Robert Palmer observed in *Deep Blues*,

The fact of the matter is, Delta blues is a refined, extremely subtle and ingeniously systematic musical language. Playing and especially singing it right involve some exceptionally fine points that only a few white guitarists, virtually no white singers and not too many black musicians who learned to play and sing anywhere other than the Delta have been able to grasp. These fine points have to do with timing, with subtle variations in vocal timbre and with being able to hear and execute, vocally and instrumentally, very precise gradations in pitch that are neither haphazard waverings nor mere effect. We're talking here about

L'Olympia, Paris, 29 January 1968

Johnny Allen Hendrix
Seattle, 15 January 1946

Kentucky, 21 December 1961

Jimi's grandmother Nora
celebrating her 95th birthday in Seattle

Jimi and Al Hendrix
Center Arena, Seattle, 12 February 1968

Taken Dec. 21, 1961

Dear Dad~

Here's a picture
I took dureing Jump
School – look at those
body positions! –
this jumping business is
the best most thrilling
I've ever did before –
It's just as much fun
as it looks, if you
keep your eyes open (smile)

Your Loving Son
Jimmy
Mar. 5, 1962

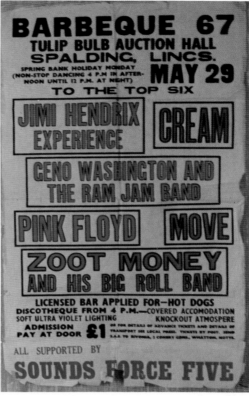

BARBEQUE 67
TULIP BULB AUCTION HALL
SPALDING, LINCS.
SPRING BANK HOLIDAY MONDAY
(NON-STOP DANCING 4 P.M IN AFTER-
NOON UNTIL 12 P.M. AT NIGHT)
MAY 29

TO THE TOP SIX

JIMI HENDRIX EXPERIENCE   **CREAM**

GENO WASHINGTON AND THE RAM JAM BAND

PINK FLOYD   **MOVE**

ZOOT MONEY AND HIS BIG ROLL BAND

LICENSED BAR APPLIED FOR—HOT DOGS
DISCOTHEQUE FROM 4 P.M.—COVERED ACCOMODATION
SOFT ULTRA VIOLET LIGHTING   KNOCKOUT ATMOSPERE
ADMISSION
PAY AT DOOR **£1**

ALL SUPPORTED BY
SOUNDS FORCE FIVE

Jimi and Little Richard
Fillmore, San Francisco,
between February and early April 1965
Roger Mayer, Mitch, Jimi, Noel and Michael Goldstein
Tucson, Arizona, 6 February 1968

And all that for just one pound!

Hyde Park Towers

41-49 INVERNESS TERRACE · LONDON W2

TELEPHONE: BAYSWATER 9461 (5 LINES) · TELEGRAMS: "HYTOW" LONDON W2

Is that the stars in the sky or is it rain coming
down
would it burn me if I touch the sun, so big
so round —
must there always be these colors, without names,
without sound
would I be lying if I said you're the one

techniques that are learned and methodically applied, are meaningful in both an expressive and purely musical sense, and are absolutely central to the art.[2]

Anybody listening to Jimi against all the pre-eminent blues masters like Muddy Waters could not fail to realise that he was one of the chosen few who had both learned and then applied himself to the art of the Delta blues.

Possibly as a product of his days backing R&B and soul artists who never let the pace of a show drag, Jimi was always apologising on stage for taking a minute or two between songs to retune his guitar. 'We really care for your ears' became a Hendrix catchphrase. On stage that night in Paris, he throws in some falsetto singing and general play-acting while he sorts himself out. On the other hand, he gets annoyed at any audience interruption during melodic interludes or as he wound up his guitar during the intro to 'Foxy Lady'. He issues a friendly warning, 'We got this song here goes something like this. You all have to be as quiet as bunnies.'

Jimi announces 'Red House' and adds that Noel Redding will play guitar. Noel said in interviews that he played Keith Richard's guitar for the occasion. But the lead playing that follows is not Noel, but Jimi – Noel is playing the bass strings of a six-string guitar, recreating the song as recorded for the *Are You Experienced?* album.

'Drivin' South' has its live debut – a very different version from the Radio One sessions, much more of a free-form jam than the relentless and well-ordered flash down the freeway of a few months ago. They do a quick burst of 'Spanish Castle Magic' to tune up, go through 'The Wind Cries Mary', 'Fire' and 'Little Wing'. 'I'd like to thank you very much, huh, like I'm having trouble with this raggedy guitar here, but we'd like to do this last song for you anyway dedicated to everyone here.'

Jimi sets up waves of feedback and distortion – chaos at the end of the world – effects achieved by manipulating the springs at the back of the guitar with his right hand and using the tremolo arm with his left to get a booming sound. The crowd roars its approval as Jimi hits the two-note riff intro to 'Purple Haze'. This was the end of the second show. On the plane at Le Bourget, change at London airport. Next stop – New York.

All the misgivings of Warner Brothers executives on seeing Jimi at

Monterey evaporated when they saw how his records were selling. *Are You Experienced?* had sold over 1 million copies, stayed on the chart for two years and eventually sold 2.2 million copies. Record shops had shifted 100,000 copies of 'Purple Haze' and the advance orders on *Axis* would put it straight into the top twenty. Even Warner Reprise's top artists like Frank Sinatra and Dean Martin never got within a shout of Jimi's sales figures. Mike Jeffery was gearing up for a big American operation to capitalise on Jimi's growing stature there as the major league artist reflected in these sales figures. He set up Jeffery and Chandler Inc. in New York staffed by his assistant Trixie Sullivan and Bob Levine, a former road manager for touring British bands like Herman's Hermits. Gerry Stickells was now spending less time on the road in order to perform the necessary task of co-ordinating increasingly complicated tour arrangements from behind a desk in the office. Mike Jeffery also employed the law firm of Steingarten, Wedeen and Weiss, dealing mainly with Steven Weiss, who had a good track record of establishing British bands in the States through his links with the Harold Davidson agency in London. Weiss was one of a growing band of younger professionals who eschewed the sober blue pinstripe for the leather jacket and shades aimed at instilling confidence in rich fashionable clients. He captured Mike's interest in the idea of handling concert promotion himself instead of losing anything up to 15 per cent of the gate receipts to agencies.

The Experience flew to America as part of another 'British Invasion' of pop bands. Touchdown was delayed due to bad weather, causing mayhem on board as Neville Chesters explains:

It was a pretty riotous flight. . . . we went up to 39,000 feet. . . . we flew [over New York] for about twenty minutes. The whole plane was just a complete litter of gear and everybody was mucking about . . . bits of baggage everywhere. It got out of hand because everyone was cheesed off. Suddenly it came over the loudspeakers that we had a slot to land and as I recall we plummeted out of the sky down to about 10,000 feet in seconds. Everything in the plane went up the aisles and over the seats. We levelled out and some people were just green.

I was the only one who was smart, I'd got a white suit on and everybody else were complete hippies. We all went through customs and they said, 'Excuse me . . . ' Strip-searched the lot of us.

Michael Goldstein, the American PR man, had organised a press reception dubbed 'The British Are Coming' at the Copter Lounge on top of the Pan-Am building in Manhattan. The British pop invasion was supposed to land in a helicopter next to the Copter, but the stunt misfired because the bad weather that caused the late arrival stopped everything flying. One of the stars, Eric Burdon, leading the New Animals, missed the plane altogether and was still in London. Nonetheless, the press were there in droves, fighting each other to get photos and interviews with the man they had all come to grab a piece of – Jimi Hendrix. One journalist would battle to get Jimi into a quiet corner only to see another mike shoved in front of Jimi's face.

One of the more unlikely interviewers that day was Jay Ruby, then assistant professor of anthropology at Philadelphia's Temple University, on sabbatical studying various social aspects of rock music and buttonholing Jimi on behalf of *Jazz and Pop* magazine. He asked Jimi about the comparison people made between him and Eric Clapton. 'That's one thing I don't like . . . the notes might sound like it, but it's a completely different scene between those notes.' Ruby asked Jimi for his definition of the blues. 'You can have your own blues. It doesn't mean that folk blues is the only type of blues in the world. I heard some Irish songs that were so funky – the words were so together and the feel. That was a great scene. We have our own type of blues scene. We do this blues on [*Axis*]. . . . It's called "If 6 Was 9". That's what you call a great feeling of blues. We don't even try to give it a name. Everybody has some kind of blues to offer, you know.'

Just before Christmas, American journalist Meatball Fulton conducted an interview with Jimi in London. Talking about singles Fulton asked Jimi: 'Are you satisfied with the recording technique generally?'

'No, not at all.'

'What about the LPs? Same thing?'

'No, not at all. Worse even on the LPs. It makes me so mad. . . . we record it and everything and then all of a sudden something happens and it just comes out all screwed up. You just get so mad, you just don't want to know about any more. Like our next LP, every track's gonna have to be right, or else, you know. . . . '

'It really depends on the engineer, then?'

'It depends on so many things . . . the cutting of it. . . . You can get in there and mix and mix and mix and get such a beautiful sound and when it's time to cut it, they just screw it up so bad.'

'I don't understand.'

'I know. I wouldn't understand that either. . . . it comes out all bad 'cause they go by levels and all that. Some people don't have imagination. . . . When you cut a record, [because] of the really deep

247

sound, the depth, you must almost remix it right there, the cutting place. And ninety-nine per cent don't even do this. They just go "Oh, yeah, turn it up there, make sure it doesn't go over there, make sure it doesn't go under" and there it is. It's nothing but one dimensional.'

Fulton asked Jimi whether he got enough time in the studio, to which Jimi replied, 'Our new LP was made in sixteen days, which I'm very sad about.'

At the Copter Lounge press reception Jimi made the same point to Michael Rosenbaum of *Crawdaddy* magazine about the next LP being just the way he wanted it 'or else' and was very noncommittal about *Axis*. In this respect, Jimi was a PR nightmare, openly unhappy about the album he was there to promote, although nobody noticed this enough to comment in their subsequent articles. Jimi was rare among musicians at this time in wanting to be involved in the whole process of creating and recording music, right up to the cutting stage. His obvious displeasure with the time-scale for *Axis* and the corruption of the music on its way to vinyl lends some credence to a strange story told to the authors by a studio technician who wishes to remain anonymous. Shortly after *Axis* was finished, it was revealed in the press that the final stereo mixes for side A had gone missing – left in a taxi or stolen from Chas's flat, nobody knew for sure. The studio guy claims Chas told him he was certain Jimi had taken them. Apparently the tapes were sitting on a stool in the studio waiting to go for production – Jimi came into the control room and after that nobody saw them again. What's more, they have never resurfaced, remarkable when you consider that virtually every squeak Jimi committed to tape is somehow accounted for. The likelihood is that the tapes were stolen to be destroyed: if these interviews are anything to go by, it would seem that the only person who could possibly want that to happen was Jimi.

After the chaos of the press call, Jimi, tired of the blandness of English cooking, fancied some good traditional 'soul food'. With Al Aronowitz (who had interviewed him for the *New York Times*), Mike Jeffery and his girlfriend Nancy Rainer, Jimi escaped to the Pink Teacup on Bleecker Street in the Village. Meanwhile back at the hotel, according to Soft Machine roadie Hugh Hopper, Noel was making the startling discovery that American soap floats and announcing this to anyone who would listen. This was Hugh's first trip to the States: 'Up to this point in my life, I had always thought of America as being an extension of Britain, but it was a country as foreign as Germany or France.'

Brian Jones, Jimi and Kathy Etchingham at a party for the group Grapefruit
London, 19 January 1968

Somebody in the audience: 'Are you better than Eric Clapton?'
Jimi: 'Are you better than my girlfriend?'
(Fillmore East, 10 May 1968)

The tour proper started the next day with the first of four nights in San Francisco, the first at the Fillmore headlining over John Mayall, Albert King and Soft Machine and the next three at the Winterland. Janis Joplin with Big Brother and the Holding Company were added to the bill on the last night.

The gigs were a tremendous success. Michael Lydon reviewed the Fillmore concert and Jimi's rise to fame for the *New York Times* in an effusive article headlined 'The Black Elvis?' The question mark indicated that while James Brown held that title for black youth in America white youth were just waiting to hand that crown to Jimi. Promoter Bill Graham was so pleased with the sell-out performances that he gave all the boys an antique gold watch each. Graham was less enamoured of Soft Machine drummer Robert Wyatt, who had called him a fascist. Wyatt explains, 'I wasn't really used to that sort of very bossy, heavy-handed pushing around . . . someone who comes on like a fucking war general.' Hugh Hopper recalls, 'This was not tactful, we were told, as some of Graham's family had died in Auschwitz. We were packed off to wait at the next town . . . while the row was smoothed over.' Hugh had another potentially explosive situation to deal with over the equipment. Neville Chesters, the Experience roadie (incredibly for such a major tour, the *only* roadie), had flown to the Fender factory before the tour started to get their new equipment sorted out. What nobody had told him was that gear was to be used both for Jimi and the Soft Machine. Given that roadies protect their own band's gear like broody bears, this, says Hugh, 'could have been disastrous . . . but we worked it out. In fact it was fairly disastrous anyway, because it wasn't the right gear for Hendrix. It was too clean. . . . '

Over those four nights, Jimi renewed his acquaintance with Albert King, playing to his first white audiences. Albert recalled meeting Jimi again in an interview with *Musician*: 'The first time I saw him after he left Tennessee was here in San Francisco. He had this hot record out. . . . I hadn't seen him in about five years. So I went back in the dressing-room and saw him and we laughed and talked and hugged one another. I was glad to see him.'

But, proud man that he is, Albert was conceding nothing to nobody when it came to playing the blues. 'That night I taught him a lesson about the blues. He had a row of buttons on the floor and a big pile of amplifiers stacked on one another. And he'd punch a button and get some smoke. And punch a button and get something else. . . . Then when he'd get through playing, he'd take his guitar aside and ram it through his amplifier or something, you know [laughs]. But when you want to really come down and play the blues, well I could've easily played his songs, but he couldn't play mine.'

The tour moved on to Arizona to play in the gymnasium of the State University and the VIP club in Tucson, described succinctly by Neville Chesters in his personal diary of the tour as 'Not a bad show. Shit place.'

On 9 February the band were back in California at the Anaheim

Winterland, San Francisco, between 2 and 4 February 1968

Convention Center. Jimi was backstage with his British PR agent Les Perrin, waiting to go on. 'Jimi was dressed in mauve trousers, a wide-brimmed brown-topped black hat with brass-ringed holes with matching material woven in and out. He had brass-buckled shoes, a flowered shirt and a metal-worked waistcoat.' Les was wearing a grey business suit, white shirt and a tie embroidered with the insignia of the ancient Fleet Street journalists' club, the Wig and Pen. 'We were standing in the entrance and people were coming in and just staring at him. He turned to me and out of the corner of his mouth said, "Hey, man, Les, all these people standin' here starin' at yuh; ah wouldn' have it – ah'd stare right back!" '3

On stage, the atmosphere was less light-hearted. Jimi was unhappy with the new Fender amplification system and at the start of the second show an amp fused. Jimi was so upset that he only sang occasional words on the next four songs before quitting the stage altogether. A grim dressing-room scene followed, Noel furious with Jimi for blowing the gig and everyone abusive about Fender. As Hugh Hopper indicated, the equipment just wasn't right for the band, neither robust nor loud enough. Jimi cranked it all up beyond the point of no return and it expired. Given that Jimi was the best possible advert for their guitars, it had taken all Gerry Stickells' immense powers of persuasion to prise a measly four guitars from Fender for the tour, so the band were not well disposed towards the company in the first place.

Salvation (which proved only temporary) appeared in the form of Buck Munger from Sunn amplification, who catching the whiff of anti-Fender feeling leapt in and promised a free set-up for the next night at the Shrine in Los Angeles.

The company was based in Oregon and named after Norman Sundholm, bass player with the Kingsmen, whose fifteen minutes of fame came with the three-chord hit 'Louie Louie', the song without which no heavy rock band set was complete.

As Sunn's artist relations man, it was up to Buck Munger to 'see in' the new equipment with the Experience in the hope of getting a contract signed. Sunn also worked with the Who; Pete Townshend had Sunn gear and this according to Buck strongly influenced Jimi in wanting to try it out. It was a curious rivalry thing – whatever Pete was using Jimi wanted the same. 'As soon as Jimi got all his equipment, he went directly to the volume and turned it all the way up to 10. . . . we assumed that maybe a third or two-thirds of the power is the maximum ever gonna be required. But because of the approach Jimi had to this thing, I'm in the middle, talking to an engineer on the phone in Oregon who's saying "Nobody does that, tell him not to do that!" And I'm saying, *"You* tell him not to do that!"'

What the engineers at Sunn did was to recalibrate the gear so that when Jimi turned it up to 10, he was in fact only getting two-thirds power. But the sound was clean and undistorted, so Jimi knew straight away that something was up. As soon as he sussed this out, it was the beginning of the end of any relationship with Sunn. Noel was happy with the sound, but Jimi relegated the gear to a monitor system and went back to using Marshalls.

But the promise of new gear after the Anaheim fiasco cooled Jimi out and the next day he was in a much better mood, especially as some old friends came around to see him. Electric Flag were one of the support bands and during the afternoon soundcheck he had a jam with Buddy Miles. Dave Crosby and Peter Tork spent the evening sitting on top of the amps. Backstage Flag guitarist Michael Bloomfield marvelled as Jimi casually fooled around on guitar. 'He was taking the toggle switch

252

of the guitar, tapping the back of the neck and using vibrato, and it came out sounding like a sirocco, a wind coming up from the desert. I have never heard a sound on a Hendrix record that I have not seen him create in front of my eyes.'4

Jam with Harvey Brooks
Shrine Auditorium, Los Angeles, 10 February 1968

The show was promoted by a 'mixed media' organisation called Pinnacle. At the time, Los Angeles was in the throes of emerging from the shadows of San Francisco and New York as centre for everything that was 'happening' in music and art. Nobody was more 'happening' than Jimi Hendrix.

The Experience played against a backdrop of slowly transmuting kaleidoscopes of coloured lights projected on to a screen showing computer-generated films. Gene Youngblood of the *LA Free Press* wrote, 'There is only one word for Hendrix – inspiring. He's an electric religion. We all stood when he came on and after he hurled his guitar at the screen in a cataclysmic–volcanic–orgasmic finale, we fell back limp in our seats, stunned and numbed. . . . To say that Hendrix has stage presence is like calling *The Enterprise* a dinghy.'

The equipment worked fine that first night, Jimi felt good and it showed in his music. The dressing-room afterwards was a much happier place – the Sunn engineer breathed a (short-lived) huge sigh of relief.

Man, that Seattle thing is really something. The only keys I expected to see in that town were of the jailhouse. (*Sunday Mirror*, 11 February 1968)

Jimi must have looked at the gig sheet for 12 February with some trepidation – 'Center Arena, Seattle'. He hadn't been home or seen his father or the rest of his family for close on seven years. There is no evidence that he'd even phoned or written in the previous eighteen months. His father had remarried a Japanese woman, Ayako, who had a little girl, Janie, neither of whom Jimi had met. Nor could Jimi be too sure what kind of reception he'd get from Al. Back in September 1967, Jimi had told a German interviewer in Berlin, 'I'm scared to go home. My father is a very strict man. He would straight away grab hold of me, tear my clothes off and cut my hair.'5

He was greeted at the Seattle airport by Al, his brother Leon and his new family, Ayako and Janie. There was a quiet press reception at Al's house, Al answering the questions from Seattle reporters while Jimi retired to a corner of the room with Leon and his friends.

Jimi was in subdued mood for the concert sponsored by local DJ Pat O'Day. He would have been even more subdued if he had heard that the guy handling the promotion for O'Day, on hearing that Jimi was black, allegedly said, 'God, I hope we don't attract a lot of coloured people!' The concert itself was covered by among others Tom Robbins of Seattle's 'alternative' paper *Helix*, who had made this allegation about racist slurs. Robbins reported that Jimi played the concert absolutely straight, 'no copulating with his guitar . . . no shoving the mike up the drummer's arse'. As Robbins suggested, the most likely explanation for Jimi's low-key performance that night was the presence of his family in the front row, Al beaming at his now-famous son. Jimi would have wanted to impress his new stepmother and he was always anxious that Al would approve of what he was doing. In any event, just being in the city would have made him feel uncomfortable.

Robbins was, incidentally, less than complimentary about Jimi, calling his singing 'mannered', his guitar chording 'bulky and coarse', his

254

Jimi and his stepsister, Janie
Center Arena, Seattle, 12 February 1968

changes 'amateurish and contrived' and his sound 'shallow', although he graciously conceded that what Jimi allegedly lacked in content he more than made up for in style.

Jimi had one more engagement to fulfil – he was supposed to receive his High School Diploma at his old school Garfield and the keys to the City of Seattle. Somehow, he made it to Garfield by eight o'clock the morning after the gig. First, the principal Frank Fidler made a speech, then DJ Pat O'Day made some comments and called Jimi to the microphone. He mumbled something about being glad to be home and then dried up completely, hastily asking if anybody had any questions. But the school was about 85 per cent black – these kids didn't play his music and so hardly knew who Jimi Hendrix was. After a long embarrassing silence, a girl asked, 'How long have you been away from Seattle?' Jimi thought for a while, said, 'Oh about two thousand years.' Then another student asked, 'How do you write a song?' Jimi said, 'Right now, I'm going to say goodbye to you, and go out the door and get into my limousine, and go to the airport. And when I go out the door, the assembly will be over and the bell will ring. And as I get in the limousine and I hear the bell ringing, I will probably write a song. Thank you very much,'[6] and walked straight out of the building. Garfield school assembly was hastily dismissed. Jimi didn't get his Diploma or the keys to Seattle because it was Lincoln's birthday and City Hall was closed. Lincoln had been dead for over a hundred years – you would have thought the authorities would have known that no such key ceremony could have taken place that day.

a peace of mind is a quiet
Piece of behind - is that yours
I'm scratching? it sure aint
a piece of mine —

The band spent 15–18 February in Texas ('the last chance we'd get to have a good time before things got serious', says Hugh Hopper), being organised by Bob Cope, a flamboyant rock promoter who favoured a powder-blue cowboy outfit and boots and was often heard shouting orders from behind the wheel of his Ford T-Bird. Hugh remembers him with affection:

> He was a great guy – he looked after his artists, buying meals for the whole entourage and taking care of all the trivial things which if left undone make life a pain for a band on the road. But if anyone went against him, he dropped like a ton of bricks. His famous catchphrase was 'I'll sue you.' I heard it ring out loud and clear within minutes of meeting him at the airport when Noel pressed the emergency stop button on the escalator taking us down to the waiting limos. Cope was bringing up the rear and hadn't seen Noel race to the bottom with his normal giggly schoolboy look. The whole lot of us lurched to a sickening stop and then struggled to stay upright as Noel pressed the re-start button.

Cope indulged crazy English musicians, but not the poor guy who had the audacity to be late with the concert programme – sued with clinical efficiency to within an inch of his life.

Saturday 17 February was something of a red-letter day for Jimi and the band. *Axis* had entered the *Billboard* chart the previous week and was shooting up towards the top twenty. With *Are You Experienced?*, the band left America for Europe without any chance of touring to promote the album. The timing now was perfect with several weeks of the tour still to go. That day, *Disc and Music Echo* in Britain published its annual poll – Jimi was voted the best musician in the world. 'Nice to win,' he said. 'But we've only just begun.' In the evening, the Experience played the Will Rogers Auditorium at Fort Worth, Texas and walked away with a cool $25,000, their biggest pay-out to date. Mike and Chas had opted for percentages of the gate money to top up the fees and the gamble paid off. As the tour progressed, word of mouth meant sell-outs everywhere and the money rolled in.

But the Fort Worth gig was significant for another reason – for the first time, the band had separate dressing-rooms. Ostensibly this recognised their superstar status, but it was also indicative of the deteriorating relationship between Jimi and Noel.

Being on the road for any length of time is a very strange experience. No less than the office, shop or factory floor, for the musician the road, the stage, the dressing-room and the studio all constitute his place of work. And in this job he is thrown together in a very intense, close-knit environment surrounded by all the pressures of the business with those with whom he may have little in common other than membership of the same band. Imagine working, eating, drinking, relaxing and travelling with

257

your workmates for twenty hours a day, every day for months on end, and no sight of your family. Under these circumstances, you either cut yourself off completely or you come to rely very heavily on the other band members as surrogate family with all the emotional turmoil that can bring. Drugs and alcohol can make a difficult situation impossible.

As professional musicians, they worked while everyone else was at play and, while the audience was working, they were asleep. But that sleep was often taken when they weren't tired, because of the travel itinerary, the show times, the press and photo calls, the recording dates, the interviews, the sound check, the airport strike or whatever. The same went for waking up. If they were lucky, they got to eat. And however awful they felt, when the lights went up, they had to be THE JIMI HENDRIX EXPERIENCE for two shows a night, the demonic super-beings the press and audience were all expecting.

Hawaii, first week of October 1968

If they felt bad, there was no ringing in sick, taking days off (unless it was in the schedule) or turning up a week later with a sick note from

258

the doctor. In general all sorts of horse dope was pumped into musicians to get them on stage. And in between bursts of hyperactivity could come periods of stupefying boredom; hours spent in airport lounges, hotel rooms, dressing-rooms, recording studios, trains, boats, planes and cars. So there were drugs for going to sleep, waking up, being superman and not being bored. Drugs were also used to wind down after the adrenalin surge of a great gig or to keep the buzz going or conversely to deal with the post-show trauma of a bad one. 'Chasing' one drug with another was common practice – some speed or cocaine to counter-balance the sleeping pill; a tranquilliser to take the edge off the stimulants and so on. Finally, musicians playing high-energy rock in the sixties like the Experience felt they had to be stoned to put themselves in touch with the audience, many of whom would arrive for a concert totally out of their heads. An interesting variation on the myth of the junkie musician turning hordes of impressionable youngsters on to mind-numbing drugs.

During 1967, the Experience travelled all over Europe, Britain and America playing 255 shows, recorded two albums and did umpteen of everything else listed above. And now they were doing it all over again in 1968 under the glare of being one of the biggest rock bands in the world. In such a working environment, it was very easy to jump on a chemical carousel just to survive. This is not an excuse – this is just the way it was. Everyone in the band was smoking dope, tripping on LSD and for dessert snorting a good noseful of another hallucinogenic drug called DMT. Noel was also into drinking in a big way and picked up the habit of popping amyl-nitrate capsules under his nose – equivalent in sensation to being hit in the face with a brick. Mitch was a walking chemist shop. Neville Chesters recalls the band signing up with a Harley Street doctor: 'prior to going anywhere, Mitch used to go and get his stocks. He had an airline bag with three compartments for sleepers, leapers [amphetamine] and creepers [Mandrax or Quaaludes]. The airline bag went everywhere, the pills cabinet!'

Even at its most benign, LSD is an introspective drug and its effects are very much dependent on the mood and expectation of the user. If you are feeling bad, LSD can give you the horrors. Too much speed causes a restless edginess which can tumble into paranoia over time while, as we have seen, the effects of the booze were equally unpredictable. Drugs were also not always what they seemed – even if you were the Jimi Hendrix Experience didn't mean you were automatically given or sold top-quality goods. All it meant was that you paid even more for it than Joe Sucker on the streets.

What all these drugs did to the already precarious internal dynamic of the band was to increase the outbreaks of moodiness by a number only understood by higher mathematicians. It is against this kind of background, common to all touring bands, that the relationship between the members of the Experience should be viewed.

The three members of the Experience were very different characters. Noel was the schoolboy prankster, boyish in looks and outlook and, of the three, he probably had the most trouble coming to terms with the adulation. He was certainly more sensitive than Mitch to aggravation on or offstage and found Jimi's mood swings very hard to handle. For some reason, Jimi was unhappy after the Fort Worth gig. Neville Chesters and Hugh Hopper were packing up the gear when Noel appeared. 'He came out in tears to talk to Neville. Hendrix hadn't liked the gig and Noel had gone into the dressing-room to say something and Hendrix said sort of "I don't need any fucker to talk to." It may have been because it was Noel or maybe just his general feeling, but Noel took it really personally and he was actually in tears.'

Mitch was different again – still a practical joker, but much harder and more self-sufficient, more sanguine than Noel about the ups and downs of life on the road and far less of a worrier. He was never much into 'friendships' as far as work was concerned – the quality of the music and being on a 'good gig' was more important than getting on with people all the time. He was less bothered than Noel about spending time in the studio and more easygoing about the money side of things, which infuriated Noel, who always had to take the lead in challenging what he saw as an unfair division of the spoils. Thus Jimi was probably closer to Mitch than Noel, although as Chas notes, 'Noel ended up with a lot of influence over Jimi when the chips were down. At the end of the day, Jimi would take Noel's opinion, I think. . . . If Jimi got pissed it was always Noel who would calm him down.' Jimi and Mitch sometimes found Noel rather hard going and would deliberately miss flights to avoid travelling with him. Noel thought this was just Jimi and Mitch being 'cool' and not running for flights. From Noel's point of view there seemed to be a fund of frustrations in being part of the Jimi Hendrix Experience – hassling over money, the way the band was billed and publicised, Jimi telling him what to play and not doing his songs – sources of friction which success only served to exacerbate.

Like first-class travel, fast cars and room service, easy and unlimited access to banned substances was regarded as one of the perks of the job, the reward for living the life and providing the audience with a vicarious thrill. Equally valued as part of the benefits package for the itinerant musician were the groupies. In London, the groupie scene was restricted to a hardcore of a dozen or so, who hung around the musician elite. America was very different. With every hotel, restaurant, airport lounge and bar looking the same as the one you left 500 miles ago, sometimes you could only remember where you had been in terms of who you had been with. As Jimi said, 'What I don't like about being on the road is that you only remember each town by the broads. Like the blonde broad with the mole, she's from Frisco – things like that.'[7]

Invariably in America the queues formed for Jimi – he was hardly ever seen without a woman or six on his arm. They would be backstage, in the studio, in his bed when he got back to the hotel or hanging about waiting for him to emerge, presenting themselves like forbidden fruit. 'Like if I get up at seven o'clock in the morning and I'm really sleepy, but then I open the door and see someone that appeals to me. First of all I think "What in the world is she doing here?" or "What does she want?" . . . She says, "Uh, maybe can I come in?" And I'm standing there and really diggin' her, you know, she's really nice looking, about nineteen or twenty, beyond the age of so and so. I say, "Oh well." I'll probably stand there and then there I go, I'll be bitin' into an apple maybe.'[8]

More than one of Jimi's male friends has reported finding naked women draped all over Jimi's bed wherever he was staying and joining in the fun – not so much the organised orgies of Zeppelin or the Stones – just Jimi being Jimi. People wanted to come down to the studio, sit at his table in a club (and expect him to pay), come to his hotel, borrow money or whatever. And Jimi invariably said 'yes', because it was a lot less bother than saying 'no'.

But Noel and Mitch had their admirers too – nothing would give Noel greater pleasure than to snatch a girl from under Jimi's nose. The likes of Noel, Mitch and Jimmy Page all shared an image of the English rock star that had American groupies (black and white) drooling – a mop of hair framing elfin little-boy-lost features on a wafer-thin body that looked like it would blow away in a strong wind.

Pamela Des Barres (Miss Pamela) was a member of the GTOs (meaning many things, including Girls Together Outrageous), a bunch of LA groupies 'adopted' by Frank Zappa and given a chance by him to record an album *Permanent Damage* featuring the talents of Jeff Beck, Nicky Hopkins, Rod Stewart and members of the Mothers of Invention. Their aim was to rule the LA groupie scene, saving the biggest and the

". . . please . . . please help me. they're trying to take me away . . . for . . . for a crime that I just can't help . . . A crime they say I committed to make people happy sad, indifferent, deaf, climax, cry, laugh, life, intertaintment . . . "forget your life and fancy, young slave You belong to us, Ha Ha Ha" . . . Please Gold & Rose . . . please help me . . . . . . " !

best for themselves. Miss Pamela had the hots for Mr Redding. One of her diary entries read:

I CAME! How do you like that? I phoned Noel (nervous and sweating) and he invited me over 'anytime'! I dressed quickly . . . and split. We got along fantastic, but he must have thought I wanted to be platonic because after two hours I had to seduce him and we soon wound up in his room. . . . Lovely romance, we played around for a while and then he made love to me. AMAZING! I was totally under his control. He put me in a hundred positions and did stupendous things! It's doubtful that anybody could surpass his proism. It was like being caught in a web, unable to free myself – wanting to get more tangled. . . . Noel said, 'That, my dear, is what you call a fuck.'[9]

262

Pamela had an acquaintance in Chicago – Cynthia, part of another groupie set-up, also enjoying Zappa patronage, but not as recording artists. She had a different gimmick. Cynthia and her friend Diane were the Plaster Casters, dedicated to the preservation of the rock-star penis for posterity. They would suck Mr Rock Star to attention, plunge his dick in a flower vase of slimy white goo called alginate, yank it out the moment said member went soft, pour plaster in the hole that was left and wait for it to harden. Zappa, needless to say, wanted to put their handiwork on display in a major art museum.

Cynthia and Diane were waiting for the Experience after their Chicago Opera House gig on 25 February. They put their proposition to an amused Jimi, who readily agreed. Like Pamela Des Barres, they kept a diary. About Jimi, they wrote:

> We need a ratio 28:28 (a much larger than normal amount of mix) and found this just barely sufficient. He has got just about the biggest rig I've ever seen! We had to plunge him through the entire depth of the vase. . . . We got a beautiful mould. He even kept his hard for the entire minute. He got stuck, however, for about fifteen minutes, but he was an excellent sport – didn't panic. . . . I believe the reason we couldn't get his rig out was that it wouldn't GET SOFT!

Jimi actually fulfilled the myth of black sexual potency, although, as black comedian Dick Gregory once remarked, the worst thing that could have happened to blacks was integrated toilets, because the myth that *every* black was hung like a horse was the most powerful weapon they had.

Pamela discovered that Cynthia was a rival for Noel's affections. She sneaked a look at the diary to read about Noel: 'It moulded superbly, we applied some baby-oil to his hair and he only got stuck for five minutes. I had been counting aloud before we thrust Noel into the mould and when I announced the crucial moment he got panicky and began to get soft, thus instead of mightily diving straight in, we had to shove it and pound it in, and it twisted like a worm.'[10]

After Chicago, the Experience played the Factory in Madison, Wisconsin – the address given to the roadies Hugh and Neville conveniently left out the name of the town, the slip of paper shoved under their bedroom door just saying 'The Factory, Wisconsin' – and thereafter to the Scene club in Milwaukee. Hugh and Neville found the Factory, but wished they'd missed the Scene. Neville wrote in his diary, 'Another bad club, terrible, had to carry gear through hotel lobby, up in the elevator, through the club's kitchen and then carry it the full length of the club. It took us three hours just to get the gear on stage.'

But Jimi (who didn't have to carry the gear) much preferred these small venues. As he told Buck Walmsley of the *Chicago Daily News*, 'Right now when it comes to actual playing, I like to do really funky clubs. Nice sweaty, smokey, funky, dirty, gritty clubs, 'cause you can really get to the people then. All this stuff where you stand 2000 miles away from the people and all that – I just don't get any feeling at all. But I guess we can't do that for the rest of our lives. We'll just have to play these other scenes too. Just so long as there are people there.'

The gear arrived late for the gig in Columbus, Ohio and again at Clark University in Worcester, Massachusetts, where Jimi was interviewed and filmed by Tony Palmer for his film *All My Loving*. The reason why the gear was late for these and most gigs, and why Hugh could say Texas was the last time he and Neville had some fun, was all to do with geography, planning (or the lack of it) and because all the gear went by truck instead of plane. After the Texas gigs, they all flew to Philadelphia where, as Hugh explains, the equipment received its usual sensitive handling: 'Amplifiers would come off the plane with their innards hanging out, drum cases crushed. It sometimes looked like the loading crews had held an Olympic meet with equipment-destruction as the favourite event.'

In Philadelphia, they hired a brand new U-Haul truck, saying they would drop it off in New York in about ten days' time. This was said in good faith, but not until about seven weeks and over 8000 miles later did U-Haul get their vehicle back. Word of mouth and good press coverage meant the office in New York were constantly adding new gigs to the itinerary. Hugh calls it the VW tour for the shape of their travel across the map of America. In fact, it was worse than that. Draw a map of the tour by linking the venues, and it looks like a spider half-crazed on acid has staggered aimlessly across the page. 'There would be times I would be loading the gear at one o'clock in the morning, that I'd taken out the truck only a couple of hours before, in this strange place, in the middle of nowhere, to go somewhere else. Some nights we checked into the hotel maybe for an hour, just to get a shower. I was really starting to get disoriented and feeling strange.'

Neville, fuelled up on speed (*without* which, says Hugh, his roadcraft was erratic to say the least), drove the van in all weathers and with an ever-increasing load of equipment as Jimi went through Fender and

264

Sunn amps together with Marshalls and Sound City, which he had flown in from London. All this gear had to be loaded and unloaded for every gig. Nor were they best pleased to be carrying around the fruits of the Experience's mad shopping trips. On the road, the band were addicted to buying things – movie cameras, radios, hi-fi and 'novelty items'. 'But Noel was the winner for the craziest things,' says Hugh. In a department store,

I came across him seriously discussing with a girl in cosmetics the relative virtues of different hair tints. He ended up buying jet-black dye and appeared two hours later in the Hilton restaurant with black eyebrows and moustache. A sort of hysteria gripped us all and most of the tour applied what was left of the dye to various parts of their anatomies. It grew out very quickly leaving two-tone eyebrows, lashes, sideburns and moustaches all over the place.

Another time Noel couldn't resist buying the joke violin case designed to carry two bottles of booze, playing cards and a set of poker dice. Where did all this junk finish up? Noel carried the violin case around for a few days and then we never saw it again. Some things were handed to us to look after and transport from gig to gig. The truck, already overloaded, now took on extra unnecessary cargo.

Nor, recalls Hugh, was Neville shy of the odd prank to keep you on your toes. It was on the way to Toledo . . . or was it Muncie? . . . then again . . .

I sat beside him in the truck waiting as he took the necessary charge of speed to get us and the music of rock's greatest guitarist to the eager fans of wherever it was. As soon as the powder was down his throat, his body gave a great shudder and shrank into the corner of the seat. I looked at his face and was horrified to see a contorted, staring mask. His hand went to his throat and he was making gurgling noises. I thought 'Jesus, he's dying, he's been poisoned.' He kept it up for a couple of minutes, while I went through all the emotions around being alone in the middle of America with a man dying of drug abuse. Then suddenly his face dissolved into a grin: 'Really got you going, didn't I?' I was too relieved even to hit him.

Jimi had hardly seen the inside of a studio since January, but on 13 March he went into the Sound Center studio in New York to record among other songs 'My Friend'. Played out to the sounds of the bar-room (with help from Steve Stills, Ken Weaver of the Fugs and a New York friend Paul Caruso) the tune is a loping blues, paced like 'Mannish Boy', lyrically obscure in places, but strongly autobiographical.

265

Community War Memorial, Rochester, New York, 21 March 1968

Jimi plays the saloon-bar lush, pouring his sorrows into his glass – bad times in Harlem, the Swedish bust, 'sand' once again the metaphor for betrayal and his depressing if realistic conclusion that the only person you can trust is yourself.

Hey, look out for my glass up there, man!
That's my drink, man, that's my drink, alright . . .
Make it a double, or eh . . .
Somebody has to sing
Somebody will sing?
Somebody will sing, right?
(I don't know!)

Y'all pass me that bottle,
and I'll sing you all a real song
Yeah!
Let me get my key, ahum!

Well I'm looking through Harlem
my stomach squeal just a little more
A stagecoach full of feathers and footprints,
pulls up to my soap-box door
Now a lady with a pearl-handled necktie
Tied to the driver's fence,
breathes in my face,
bourbon and coke possessed words
'Haven't I seen you somewhere in hell,
or was it just an accident?'
(You know how I felt then, and so:)

Before I could ask 'was it the East or West side?'
my feet they howled in pain
The wheels of a bandwagon cut very deep,
but not as deep in my mind as the rain
And as they pulled away I could see her words
Stagger and fall on my muddy tent
Well I picked them up, brushed them off,
to see what they say,
and you wouldn't believe:
'Come around to my room, with the tooth in the middle,
and bring along the bottle and a president'

And-eh sometimes it's not so easy, baby
Especially when your only friend,
talks, sees, looks and feels like you,
and you do just the same as him
(Gets very lonely up this road, baby)
(Yeah, hmm, yeah)
(Got more to say!)

267

Well I'm riding through LA (huh),
on a bicycle built for fools
And I seen one of my old buddies
And he say, 'you don't look the way you usually do'
I say, 'well, some people look like a coin-box'
He say, 'look like you ain't got no coins to spare'
And I laid back and I thought to myself, and I said this:
I just picked up my pride from underneath the pay phone,
and combed this breath right out of my hair
And sometimes it's not so easy
Especially when your only friend
talks, sees, looks and feels like you,
and you do just the same as him

I just got out of a Scandinavian jail,
and I'm on my way straight home to you
But I feel so dizzy I take a quick look in the mirror,
to make sure my friend's here with me too
And you know good well I don't drink coffee,
so you fill my cup full of sand
And the frozen tea leaves on the bottom
Sharing lipstick around the broken edge
And my coat that you let your dog lay by the fire on
And your cat he attacked me from his pill-box ledge
And I thought you were my friend too
Man, my shadow comes in line before you
I'm finding out that it's eh not so easy
Specially when your only friend
Talks, looks, sees and feels like you,
and you do the same just like him

(Lord it's so lonely here, hmmm, yeah)
Yeah!
(Pass me that bottle over there . . .)
Yeah, yeah, okay . . .

Back out on the road, Experience gigs were invariably 'eventful', none more so than the show at the Public Music Hall in Cleveland on 26 March.

The fun started as soon as Neville and Hugh arrived in the truck. They pulled up to a loading ramp and a stagehand appeared. For once, it looked like they were going to get some help unloading. No such luck.

'You got a card?'

'A card?'

'Yeah, a card. Union card. Teamsters.'

'No, but we're Brit—'

'If you're not 'filiated, you can't unload. 'Fact you shouldn't even drive that truck in here. There ain't gonna be no show tonight.'

Hugh was over the moon – a rest at last! But conscientious 'the show must go on' Neville was rushing around trying to find Gerry Stickells and the promoter. Hugh sat in the truck observing first Gerry, then the promoter trying to get the stagehands to co-operate. The temperature was rising rapidly when the band arrived, blissfully unaware that, as things stood, the gig was cancelled. After nearly two hours, it was agreed that there *would* be a show so long as nobody but the stagehands touched the equipment. At one point in the negotiations, the union men weren't even going to allow anybody on the stage before the show except them. Mitch went up the wall because he was extremely particular about the placing of his kit. If a cymbal stand was a fraction off the mark, he'd know it. Neville Chesters is certain they finally had to pay the union off to get the gig on at all. Setting up took ages – the Teamsters didn't know what half the gear was for, let along where to put it. Meanwhile back in a dressing-room, Neville really did take too much this time. He swallowed a whole packet of cold-cure ephedrine tablets as a substitute for speed and could hardly stand up. Instead of Hugh getting an evening off, he found himself doing double the work, showing the crew where to put everything.

Midway through the show, the MC Chuck Dunaway stopped proceedings and asked everyone to look under their seats as there had been a bomb scare. Said Jimi from the stage, pre-empting a song he was due to record five days later, 'Nobody but Jimi burns a house down.'[11] Then at the end the crowd rushed the stage. 'Shouting "Stoned! Stoned!" his listeners surged forward, clawing at the kicking feet of the policemen who ringed the footlights. After the performance, the fans shredded curtains, ripped doors off their hinges and generally wreaked the worst havoc on the Music Hall since it was battered three years ago by the Beatles.'[12] At least no equipment was lost that night – theft was a perennial problem on the road; Jimi lost any number of guitars to friendly faces who 'helped' Neville and Hugh, which is why, despite the aggravation, they preferred to work unaided by 'fans'. More than once, either Neville or Gerry had to wrestle a fan to get a guitar back.

'Some lucky guy in Columbus, Ohio,' says Hugh, 'has a guitar of Jimi's – we accepted his offer of help because the stagehands had a desperate need to leave ten minutes after the show had finished. On his second trip from stage to truck, he disappeared. Maybe I do him wrong – he could have had a close encounter of the worst kind and will turn up in years' time in the Mexican desert with a baffled look on his face and carrying a 1968 Fender Stratocaster tuned to E flat.'

The most spectacular example of fan versus roadie came in the aftermath of another riot, this one in Montreal on 2 April. Neville's diary entry for this gig read, 'Riots! They had to get extra police in to keep the kids back. Right at the end some guy jumped on the stage and stole Noel's mike and stand. Suddenly all the lights were on in the hall and there was complete chaos – kids everywhere all over the stage.' Looking back on that gig Neville recalls that 'the stage was ten to twelve feet off the ground. . . . out of the corner of my eye I saw this guy climbing up this little rail at the back of the stage and picked my toolbox up, everything I owned was in this blue toolbox, and he picked it up and ran up the stairs. I ran across the stage and by this time he jumped and it was all slow motion – he saw me, I went for him, he hopped over the rail. I heard the crash as I hopped over, but it was too late for me to stop. I just plummeted to the floor. . . . I nearly broke both my legs.'

Amid all the chaos, Jim Morrison tried to get on stage. British soul star Geno Washington saw what happened next: 'The place was fuckin' packed, the people are going ape shit, Jim Morrison is drinking his drink and staggers up to the front of the stage, "Hey Jimi! Jimi! Let me come up and sing, man, and we'll do this shit together." So Jimi goes, "That's okay, fella, I can handle it myself." And he said, "Hey, do you know who I am? I'm Jim Morrison of the Doors." "Yeah," said Jimi, "I know who you are – and I'm Jimi Hendrix." '

On 4 April the band were playing two shows at the Civic Dome in Virginia Beach, Virginia. During the afternoon, the Experience with some of Soft Machine were sitting in a bar. Mark Boyle, who designed the Soft's light show, was also there: 'The woman serving the drinks told us that Martin Luther King had just been assassinated and there were these guys at the bar drinking the health of the assassin. You immediately find yourself wondering what your role should be. You want to go in there and do something, you're so outraged. And I remember turning and looking at Jimi, who was just staring away into space as if nothing had happened. Of course, I realised that these guys were just waiting, trying to promote some reaction from Jimi and us, so they could beat us up. I was terrified. I felt I'd grown twenty years older in two minutes.'[13]

270

Dr King had gone to Memphis to lead a dustmen's strike. He leant over a balcony to say to the Reverend Jesse Jackson, 'Be sure to sing "Precious Lord" tonight and sing it well.' Those were his last words – James Earl Ray shot him and drove away in a white Ford Mustang. Ray was later picked up by the FBI.

As the news spread, black communities all over America rose up in spontaneous displays of anger. In New York, Mayor John Lindsay was stoned by a crowd in Harlem; in Detroit, two policemen were shot; there was burning and looting within 300 yards of the White House; and in Tallahassee, Florida, a white youth was burned to death.

By the strangest of coincidences, the next scheduled Experience gig was in the heart of the black district of Newark. Everybody was nervous about doing the gig. They were hanging about at the hotel waiting to see if there would be any concert at all. The word came that it was on. The limo driver was adamant: 'Jimi sits up front with me or I don't go.' With the white guys slumped uneasily in the back, the car made its way cautiously to the Symphony Hall on Broad Street. The truck was unloaded in silence in a back street behind the theatre. Neville gave Hugh the keys to lock up and disappeared through the stage door.

> I checked all the truck doors and picked up the last piece of equipment, a chrome mike stand, and turned to follow him. But the stage door was locked fast with no outside handle. I shouted and pounded to no effect. Great, here I am in Newark, on the night that one of the world's best-loved black men had been shot and I've got to walk around to the front doors of the theatre (nearly half a mile as it was in the middle of a block), by way of some very dark streets with only my pale face showing. I looked down at the shiny mike stand in my hand thinking that if anything happened it might be some defence . . . then, Christ! I suddenly realised what it might look like from a distance in the semi-darkness, either to a prowling cop or a lunatic sniper – a rifle! I plodded round the block with a sort of fatalistic resignation and I swear there was a hum in the air that was more than the noise of the traffic.

Outside the theatre, Newark was like a ghost town, armoured cars on the street corners, sporadic gunfire in the distance. But inside, the place was packed. Because the bands had taken so long to get there, it had been decided to collapse the first and second shows into one. There was a very strong feeling that some conspiracy was abroad to eradicate any prominent black figures or pro-black politicians – first JFK, now Martin Luther King, could Jimi be next? Tragically,

271

a month later, the answer came – Bobby Kennedy. But, sitting out in the auditorium that night doing the lights for Soft Machine, Mark Boyle wondered what he could do should some lunatic rise out of the darkness with a gun. 'It was terrifyingly crowded.' He need not have worried.

Hendrix came out to enormous applause and said, 'This number is for a friend of mine,' and he abandoned completely his normal set. The band played an improvisation which was absolutely hauntingly beautiful. Immediately everyone knew what this was about. This was a lament for Martin Luther King. And within minutes the whole audience was weeping. . . . Old redneck stagehands came on the side of the stage and they were standing there with tears running down their faces. The music had a kind of appalling beauty. Harrowing music. When he came to the end there was no applause. He just put down his guitar, the whole audience was sobbing, and he just walked quietly off the stage.

If we are arrested every day, if we are exploited every day, if we are trampled over every day, don't ever let anyone pull you so low as to hate them. We must use the weapon of love. We must have compassion and understanding for those who hate us. We must realise so many people are taught to hate us that are not totally responsible for their hate. But we stand in life at midnight, we are always on the threshold of a new dawn. (Martin Luther King, Montgomery, Alabama, 1955)

Hawaii, first week of October 1968

Ten *Have You Ever Been . . . to Electric Ladyland?*

I don't ever think I'll ever get a chance to do all the things I really
want to do as far as music wise. (*Go Go Girl*, 20 January 1968)

After Newark, the Experience played one more gig, in White Plains,
New York State, before flying to England for a short rest. Neville
Chesters also took a holiday, but never went back. He'd been with
the band since the Monkees tour, and although that had been only
nine months before, in another sense it was a different era.

> Things weren't actually going that well with the group. By that time
> [April 1968] I think that was the early days of it. I am sure Mitch and Noel
> were getting, you know . . . hundreds of people were hanging around
> Jimi, you could not speak to him, you couldn't get anything together and
> everybody was getting angry with each other. . . . so psychologically, I
> had the feeling that it wasn't going well. We had a good time, we had a
> *great* time, and it was due to end for some reason. . . .

The band returned to New York about two weeks later to begin
work on Jimi's most ambitious project to date – the double album,
Electric Ladyland. As we have seen, in interviews with Jimi at the
back end of 1967 and into early 1968, he gave clear notice as to how
he wanted his recording career to progress. First, he was looking to
use additional musicians; second, he wanted more control in the studio;
and third he wanted more time . . . 'or else'. But there would be a price
to pay – further estrangement from Noel, but, more seriously, a split
with Chas Chandler.

They went into the Record Plant on West 44th, one of New York's
most sophisticated studios, and virtually block booked it for the next
three months. Jimi established a pattern for the recording of his next
album. In the evening, he would be jamming at the Scene, the Café

A Go Go, the Salvation or the Generation. Since the American tour started, Jimi had taken every opportunity to show up at these clubs for a blow – between then and the end of the sessions for *Electric Ladyland* in July, he shared the stage with Jeff Beck, Eric Clapton, B.B. King, Paul Butterfield, Roy Buchanan, Larry Coryell and Muddy Waters to mention a few. Not all the jams were a success – Howlin' Wolf put Jimi down badly at the Scene. Jimi was very hurt – Wolf was one of his idols. But, this aside, Jimi was always at his most relaxed out of the public spotlight with nobody expecting him to put on a show. Rick Derringer, then playing with the McCoys, recalls Jimi coming down to the Scene club to jam after their set was over. 'Jimi was very nice and a true gentleman. A lot of other guitar players would get up and jam with Jimi. Most of them would take the spotlight and continue playing until somebody said "Shut up!" Jimi would always encourage other people to play and jam, but would always wait until the very last before he played his thing. . . . My guitars were stolen once from the Scene and Jimi lent me four of his guitars, but they were all backwards. That was the only problem.'[1]

Ted Nugent recalls another jam session at 1 a.m., this time at the Generation.

Hendrix came walking in, pulled a blue Strat out of the case, plugged it into a Fuzz Face fuzzbox and a rolled and tucked Kustom amp and all by himself started playing shit that was unbelievable. I was mesmerised, totally in shock. He did this for about 45 minutes and then B.B. King, Al Kooper and a bass player joined in. B.B. signalled for me to come up and we jammed until 6 a.m. It was the most overwhelming excitement that a guitar player could stand. It was an earth-shattering experience.[2]

Jimi expressed his love of jamming to *Eye* magazine:

Any chance we have, we jam. That's what playing is all about . . . when you're creating music with other musicians. That's what you live for. You can't express yourself by jabbering and talking all the time. And half the people don't know how to jam nowadays. They don't play together . . . they don't really think about the other person. That's what jamming is about, it's playing *with* everybody. . . . We have a certain little crowd which is great. We'd like to bring in other jammers, but then after playing a while you feel the flow that goes through the music and you can follow each other, and finally you get to where, jamming, you can be more together than on a record you might have worked on for two weeks. Like changes of key and timing and breaks and licks, it can be one of the most beautiful things if you have time to hit it.[3]

275

Jimi's favourite haunt was the Scene, just up the block from the Record Plant. Once the Scene closed in the early hours of the morning, it 'reopened' in the studio, as blues guitarist Johnny Winter explains: 'I first met Jimi at the Scene. . . . we jammed together there a good bit. . . . what we would often do after the club closed is go over to a studio where he had recording time booked regularly, and play around with things, maybe play for several hours, and then some other day listen to the tapes to pick out the good parts for ideas to work into songs.'4

Jimi was determined to get involved in the whole recording process; a Record Plant engineer told *Rolling Stone* in 1972, 'I recollect watching him at the board one night long ago, adjusting the sound like Captain Video at the space deck. Fiddling with equalisers to get more highs and lows, some echo button here, setting dials there, throwing switches, calling plays. Satisfied, he got up and walked into the studio with the others. Before he even picked up his Fender, the engineer jumped into the just-vacated seat and started to retwist everything.' 'Let's get this shit right.' Jack Adams from the Plant told the same interviewer,

> Jimi knew nothing about the board. . . . But he was brilliant alright. . . . sometimes he and the band would come in and jam all night. One song would blend right into the next one, but later on he'd remember every single one. . . . On remixing, he'd have such a set idea of what he wanted a record to sound like that he'd remix a song *300* times. No fooling. We'd remix a song for ten hours, all night, all week. I'd get tired and say to hell with it, I'm going home. He'd smile and ask if he could phone me up if he had a question. Then, about ten the next morning, the janitors would phone up and say, 'Hey, get this guy outta here, we gotta clean the place up.'5

Eddie Kramer was asked to come over from England to engineer the album, a duty he shared with the Record Plant's own Gary Kellgren. Jimi enjoyed a close working relationship with Eddie Kramer; he played around on the board, but he knew he had to bow to Eddie's technical expertise. With *Electric Ladyland* 'It became apparent that we [were] into the next era because things started to get a lot more complicated. We were spending a lot more time in the studio [and] Jimi had much more time to develop his ideas.'6

Jimi was in his element; the studio was the centre of his creative universe – for the first time the finances allowed Jimi to use the studio, not only for actual recording, but for trying out new guitar effects and sounds, to perfect solos, go off in a corner to compose, arrange and write, conduct electronic experiments with Eddie at the console or just as a rehearsal room to jam with friends, picking up new ideas as he went along.

Mixing with Eddie Kramer
Record Plant, early May 1968

True to his word, apart from the jamming with whoever happened to be around from the Scene club that night, Jimi invited other musicians to take part in the actual recording sessions to add colour and variety to the sound and broaden the scope of the music – Stevie Winwood and Chris Wood from Traffic, Al Kooper, Jack Casady, bass player with Jefferson Airplane, and keyboard player Mike Finnegan.

Jimi was moving further and further away from the original concept of the Experience as a three-piece band and how its music would be produced, and inevitably there was conflict. Noel just refused to sit around all day while Jimi did the 100th remix of the solo he'd just played for the 200th time. He also resented other musicians on the sessions and the fact that Jimi would take no advice from anybody on the songs nor show much interest in Noel's material, although Noel did get one of his songs on the album. Sometimes Noel turned up and there would be nobody else there, so he'd work with Gary Kellgren on songs of his own. This led him to consider perhaps getting out of this unhappy situation once and for all and forming a band of his own. In this, he was encouraged by both Chas and Mike – think of the earning potential of a band fronted by the ex-bass player of the Jimi Hendrix Experience!

For his part, Chas had a number of problems with the way his relationship with Jimi had changed, which he sums up by saying, 'He just wasn't listening any more.' And it is true that Jimi had changed, or rather the circumstances had changed to allow Jimi the kind of freedom in his music that he always craved. It's as if Jimi was suddenly let off the leash. From what he said in interviews, he was never happy with the way the music had been created, except of course that it was the hit albums and singles produced by Chas which now gave Jimi the financial clout to go his own way. They were also at odds over the stage presentation of the band. Mitch says that Chas's early idea 'was to have a back-up band for Jimi with patent-leather shoes, white jackets and so on. Jimi had other ideas. . . .'7 Jimi undoubtedly felt that Chas had retained a 'pop' image of the band which in no way sat easily with him now – if it ever did.

Right from the start, Chas felt he had no control over the recording of the album, and indeed walked out of the early sessions. 'Jimi would turn up in the studio with a dozen hangers-on who you've never seen before in your life. . . . you used a sort of shorthand conversation in the studio when there's nobody around, but when there's an audience around, people get uptight. . . . it changes the atmosphere in the studio. He wanted to go over and over songs, some things he'd got in the first take. I just couldn't communicate with him. I felt like an alien.'

One of these 'hangers-on' was Devon Wilson. She was determined to become indispensable as his personal assistant and social secretary. She would do anything to curry favour with Jimi, even procuring women for him, despite her obsession with becoming the only woman Jimi took to his bed. Years on the streets fending for herself had made Devon a powerful figure in her own right. Jimi admired her strength and was grateful for her help. But at the same time he was wary of her, knowing the unscrupulous side to her nature, the side that would spike drinks to put some competitor out of circulation for a while. Jimi had two idealised women in his head: one was the strong, benign mother-figure who would come to shelter him from the storms of life; the other was similar in intent, but different in conception – a vision of unquestioning sweetness who would construct an aura of peace and calm around him. Devon didn't fit either image. In fact Jimi treated her more like a male friend than the woman he would want to spend his life with, and it is doubtful if he ever loved her in the traditional sense of the word.

Jimi had moved around different hotels in New York, but now had his own apartment on 12th Street which Devon had found for him. She also 'found' him a Jewish–Moroccan woman called Monique, who although married spent a lot of time with Jimi while her husband was away, decorating his flat out in neo-Moroccan style, designing his clothes and generally 'looking after him' as so many women had done in the past. She in turn introduced him to some friends of hers, Colette Mimram and Stella Douglas, who had a boutique on East 9th Street. In the company of these women, Jimi 'got' culture – they took him to art galleries and expensive restaurants. Devon also had her 'role' to play in the studio, deciding who could come down, where they should sit and so on. She was often found in the control booth and her propensity to try and direct operations was a problem for Chas, supposedly the producer.

Drugs were also creating problems as far as Chas was concerned. 'Drugs didn't get in the way of shows and it didn't get in the way of recording, but I thought it was getting in the way of his brain . . . mainly acid, it was fucking madness, it had to stop.' Chas says Jimi was bringing all kinds of spaced-out weirdos to Chas's New York flat. Lotte, Chas's wife, was pregnant by then and became scared by these late-night visitations. Eventually Chas refused to let Jimi in if he had these acquaintances in tow.

Drugs also formed a wedge between Chas on the one hand and Mike Jeffery and Jimi on the other. Chas says Mike and Jimi were 'acid buddies'. Mike related to drugs on two levels. The late R & B star Graham Bond spent most of his professional career in music battling against the business. He dubbed all managers, agents, promoters, record company executives and so on as 'beaks'. But more lethal than these in his opinion were the 'freaky beaks'. These were the very same people, but with long hair, kaftans, the best drugs and all the lingo who pretended they were on your side. In Graham's terms, Mike Jeffery was a freaky beak. He certainly proffered drugs to musicians to distract them from asking awkward questions about money. Mick Cox was the guitarist with another Jeffery/Chandler band, Eire Apparent. 'With Mike it was, "Oh, come in, guys. Hey, try some of this!" Very soon instead of asking for money, it was, "Oh yeah . . . er . . . nice wall you've got, Mike." That went on so much.'

Less easily explained is that although right-wing by instinct, Mike had a need to feel part of the 'radical sixties', to wear the mantle of being 'right-on' among the younger people who surrounded him in the business. He bought himself a house in Woodstock in upstate New York, the rural retreat for the city's wealthier artistic and musician community. Albert Grossman, who managed Dylan and Janis Joplin, was a neighbour who also helped Mike with concert promotions, where he lacked experience. Much more than Chas, Mike wanted to hang out and get stoned and be hip and so on. According to Trixie Sullivan, Mike gave Abbie Hoffman $10,000 for the Yippies. Even though Hoffman was an accomplished hustler, and Mike was always fascinated by anything involving covert action and subterfuge, any movement acting more counter to Mike's interests is hard to imagine. And it was this aspect of Mike's character which, Chas says, finally brought matters to a head.

Mike was friendly with a guy in his fifties named Jerry Morrison, whose real name was Gerald Herbert Breitman. As a PR man and manager, Morrison had been involved with a number of artists, including Louis Armstrong and the band leader Harry James. He also said he'd worked for five years as PR man for Papa Doc Duvalier, the much feared leader of Haiti. Morrison left the island rather quickly after declining Duvalier's offer of his daughter in marriage. According to Chas, Morrison had some scheme to overthrow Papa Doc using mercenaries which, under the influence of their acid haze, Jimi and Mike were going to fund jointly. Timothy Leary was fond of saying 'Two acid heads are better than one' – each tending to support the other's delusions in a mutual conspiracy of non-criticism: 'I won't-break-your-euphoria-if-you-won't-break-mine'. But as far as Chas was concerned that was it. Jimi was off in his own world, Mike he hated anyway, he was sick of New York and neither he nor his wife Lotte wanted their child born there. Before the summer was out, arrangements were made for Mike to buy out Chas's share of the partnership for the healthy sum of $300,000, plus 'future considerations', although in practice this didn't happen until the winter. He still came to gigs and because of these unspecified 'future considerations' retained financial interests in the affairs of the band well beyond the summer of '68.

Looked at from another angle, Jimi's alienation from Chas and Noel was in part his 'rediscovery' that he was an American, that he could feel comfortable in New York whereas neither Chas nor Noel ever could. Jimi had known the city since late 1963, but the place never held many fond memories for him until much later. Now, he could move about the city as a celebrity, he had regular jamming times, a studio to work in, a nice place to live and beautiful women to look after him. As much as he loved London, in New York he had a sense of being 'at home'.

However, in hindsight Jimi made a major miscalculation in allowing a situation to develop where Mike eventually became his sole manager. Jimi wanted to keep things uncomplicated – he would look after the music while Mike took care of the money. However, it wasn't as simple as that. In the first place, Noel had been querying for some time whether the money really was being cared for properly. Getting nowhere with Chas or Mike, Noel complained to Trixie. She says she suggested to Noel that he bring in his own accountant if he wasn't happy, but nothing happened. Jimi knew there were problems, but he always had what he needed – as many guitars as he wanted, the latest gadgets and effects from Manny's New York music store, cars, unlimited studio time, and all road, leisure and living expenses. The bills just went straight to the office.

The real problem for Jimi in having Mike as his sole manager was that Mike was a businessman. His prime directive was making money and the means of achieving this as far as Mike was concerned – lots of touring and quickly produced commercial records – was fundamentally at odds with the way Jimi wanted to work. Nor was Mike the best person to look after Jimi's general health and well-being, because he was always off nurturing his other business interests. Keith Altham puts it like this: 'The managers, people like Brian Epstein and Chas Chandler, they had flair and imagination and they involved themselves on a personal basis with the artist.' But what happens if you haven't got somebody like this? 'It's okay if you are a really strong character. If you are not, then I think you run a huge risk by putting your life in the hands of somebody whose real business is looking after the business and not looking after the person. It's easy to make Mike Jeffery the villain of the piece [but] he didn't pretend to be much more than what he was – a business-oriented manager. Jimi elected to have that kind of representation and when he lost Chas, he lost a very important part of his direction and care.'

Despite Jimi's increasing disenchantment with touring, it was that which prevented the Experience starship from plummeting into a decaying orbit in mid-1968. Whatever hassles there may be out on tour, most musicians quickly start climbing the walls when the gigs dry up. This was certainly the case with Noel; there was just too much time to brood on insults, injustices and frustrations imagined or otherwise. On a good night, anger was sublimated in the frisson of making powerful music and differences set aside in the headlong rush to get smashed after the gig.

Mike Jeffery, too, wanted the band out on the road, keeping the cash coming in to offset the ever-mounting costs of studio time taken up in recording the next album. It was important, too, to keep the band in the public eye, play new venues and maintain interest in the records that were still in the charts and selling well. For Mike, the earning power of the Experience was taking on increasing significance as other bands in his stable like Soft Machine and Eire Apparent didn't look like taking off financially. Worse still, he had finally split with Eric Burdon with a torrent of Animals litigation still pending.

The Experience had some outstanding dates to fulfil in Europe. Prior to leaving, they headlined the Miami Pop Festival held over two days at the Gulf Stream Race Track in Hallandale, Miami.

The event was masterminded by twenty-two-year-old Michael Lang, originally from Brooklyn, who had opened Florida's first 'head shop'. But his cherubic hippie appearance and shy manner hid a very sharp businessman. Captivated by the success of Monterey, he pulled together a group of investors under the name Joint Productions whose purpose would be to stage a series of rock concerts at the Gulf Stream Race Track near Miami Beach. The bill for this first three-day event included the Mothers of Invention, John Lee Hooker, Arthur Brown, Chuck Berry and Jimi. Day one was a great success. Twenty-five thousand came to watch bands playing on three flat-bed trucks brought in so there would be no waiting between acts – one would be warming up while the other was performing. A firework display heralded the grand finale – a forty-foot-high peace symbol blazing in the sky.

Unfortunately, that was the last thing to blaze at the Gulf Stream Track apart from tempers – part of the second day and all the third day were washed out by rain storms. Nobody wanted to play for fear of electrocution and the event was cancelled. Then came the ticklish problem of payment. Joint Productions were out of pocket by $60,000. Lang had hired an ex-cop from Fort Lauderdale to guard the takings. He in turn took on some of his own men to assist. When it became clear that the festival had lost heavily, this group attempted to stop a Brinks security truck taking what money there was to a local bank. The cop's idea was that he and his men would lock themselves in the counting room to make sure they got paid in cash before any money was taken out of the grounds. They reached the room the same time as the Brinks men, who had come with Michael Lang to collect the cash – all of it. Both the Brinks men and the security force were armed. Also in the office waiting for payment was Gerry Stickells accompanied by Jimi, Noel, Mitch and the Eire Apparent guitarist Mick Cox, who takes up the story:

> We're sitting there waiting, 'Where's the money?' 'Oh, we've got to wait until my partner arrives.' And he's got this big guy with him carrying a gun. Then the Express [Brinks] wagon pulls up outside, guy comes upstairs and *he's* got two others with him, both carrying guns. And the guy says, 'You are gonna pay the boys the rest of the money?' The other one says, 'No, no, there's been a change of plan. We're not gonna pay them, it's gonna be sent on.' So the first one says, 'Sorry, we've got to pay them now.' 'No, we're not.' Then they all get out their guns and they're facing one another. 'Well,' says the second one, 'my guys have got more armoury than you have . . .' And there's this whole number going on where they're going to shoot each other – it was all an act, but we didn't realise then.

Whether or not this potential shoot-out between Brinks and festival security ('the boys') was a charade to get out of paying is hard to say, but Michael Lang disappeared to New York while things cooled down. His next venture was Woodstock.

Back in Miami, events had left the band short of ready cash and neither Chas nor Mike was around to bail them out. Everyone was booked into the Castaway Hotel where a jam took place in the downstairs club with Jimi, John Lee Hooker, Frank Zappa and others. Trixie calls it 'incredible . . . music like you've never heard, everyone played each other's instruments. Brilliant.' Time came to pay the hotel bill. Mitch, Noel and the others sneaked out of the hotel and into the limousine. Trixie and Jimi were not so fortunate: 'The manager kept us locked in the room as hostages. We had to get through the bathroom window.'

But even the clouds of Miami had a silver lining, as Eddie Kramer explains: '"Rainy Day, Dream Away" was written in Miami. . . . I was in the back of the car, we were pulling away from Gulf Stream Park . . . the bloody thing was rained out, and then he started to write it right there.'[8]

Hey man,
take a look out the window and see what's happening
Hey man it's raining!
It's raining outside man
Oh don't worry about that brother
Everything's gonna be OK
We'll get into something real nice, you know
So just lay back and groove on a rainy day
Yeah . . . yeah I see what you mean brother,
lay back and groove

Rainy Day, Dream Away,
let the sun take a holiday
Flowers bathe and-eh see the children play
Lay back and groove on a Rainy Day
Well I can see a bunch of wet preachers,
look at them on the run!
The carnival traffic noise,
it sinks to a splashing
Even the ducks can groove,
rain bathing in the parkside pool
And I'm leaning out my window sill digging everything,
and-eh you too!

Rainy day, rain all day
Ain't no use in gettin' uptight
Just let it groove its own way
Let it drain your worries away
Lay back and groove on a rainy day (hey)
Lay back and dream on a rainy day

The Experience's short tour of Europe consisted of three dates in
Italy and two headlining a package in Switzerland with John Mayall,
Eric Burdon, Traffic and the Small Faces. En route to Italy, Noel met
Eric Barrett, roadie for the Nice, and offered him the job of replacing
Neville Chesters. Eric said he would think about it, staggered home
drunk from Blaises at 4.30 and three hours later got a call from Gerry
Stickells asking him to make up his mind. Eric was soon on the plane
to Milan.

He was thrown in at the deep end – much of the gear was in
pieces from the US tour and he felt the keen edge of Jimi's intolerance

at equipment that kept breaking down. Sick of Jimi's abuse, Eric almost left there and then. But Jimi apologised and Eric stayed with him right to the end of Jimi's life.

Much of the pre-publicity in the popular press for Jimi's visit to Italy was ludicrous, if predictable; one paper actually wrote that 'mothers showed his picture to children who didn't eat their meat'. Once they spoke to him, the press were forced to concede that the man they had billed as some unwashed child-molester was actually very polite, took three or four baths a day and carried a beauty case with hairpins for his perm, lotions and perfumes. 'THE YOUNGSTERS GO WILD FOR THE UGLY MAN WITH A PERM'.

Since I've been to Europe, I've met one in a hundred people who let me talk about what I want to. Everybody asks me how old I am, if it is true I have Indian blood, how many women I have had, if I am married, if I have a Rolls or more of those jokes. The people who dig me, don't want this at all. They want something different, to feel something inside, something real – revolution, struggle, rebellion. (Interview with Gigi Movilia, Rome, May 1968).

Jimi often had trouble with fluctuating power supply when he played in Europe; at the Teatro Brancaccio in Rome, the amplifiers blew every fuse in the place and the concert only went ahead because all the lights (including those in the toilets) were switched off and, much to his displeasure, Jimi had to make do with one less amplifier. The best playing experiences were often unscheduled; after the gig they all went down to the Titan club for a jam and just about every rock musician in Rome turned up. Noel and Jimi swapped guitars for two hours of R&B. Then Noel and Mitch walked off to get friendly with the local girls, leaving Jimi on his own to invite anybody up on stage to play with him.

In between the gigs in Italy and Switzerland, Noel and Mitch flew back to London while Jimi went all the way home to New York for three days to attend meetings about Ed Chalpin's lawsuit, before returning to Zurich. Before they all split up, the band had a meal at the airport. Noel's sister Vicky had come along for the trip. 'Jimi gave me some money to pay the bill and said, "Give the change to the waitress." I considered that the waitress wasn't very good and there was about £25 left over, which was a bit much, so I gave her £5. We got on the plane and I gave £20 back to Jimi and he went berserk, he really told me off.'

Teatro Brancaccio, Rome, 24 or 25 May 1968

While Jimi was on his way back to Europe from New York, the rest of the British package with Noel and Mitch were coming in on another flight from London. Keith Altham travelled with them:

Jesus Christ! What a plane load that was. Bloody hell! The plane was flying at about 18,000 feet and the crew and passengers were at 24,000 feet. The first thing that happened to me, I was sitting in the seat and Noel thought it would be quite amusing to snap an amyl-nitrate capsule under my nose. I thought I was dying and that was the beginning of the trip. I remember Stevie Winwood at one point on his hands and knees in the aisle trying to unscrew an ashtray because somebody had stubbed out a joint which still had a lot of smoke in it. He'd run out and was trying to dismantle the ashtray. People had hold of the internal address system: 'Will Keith Altham report to the tip of the north wing where he's urgently required.'

The Experience flew into a Europe convulsed by waves of political turmoil. In April, thousands of West German students rioted at the attempted murder of left-wing student leader Rudi Dutschke, by a gunman who claimed he was trying to emulate the assassination of Martin Luther King. Attacks on the Berlin offices of the right-wing German newspaper publisher Axel Springer were replicated in Italy, Holland and Britain. In May, Paris saw some of the worst street fighting since the end of the war and, before the summer was out, the democratic dreams of the Czech people would be crushed by the Soviet Union.

The first of the two concerts at Zurich's Hallenstadion was played out in an atmosphere of simmering unrest. During the New Animals' set, the Hell's Angels arrived. Keith Altham had a grandstand view:

They came in all their Nazi paraphernalia and coal-scuttle helmets with their bikes revving at the far end. They made for the stage in a flying wedge shape with people parting like the Red Sea in front of them. This bare-chested monster in leather and chains who looked about eight feet tall from where I was, tried to get into the photographers' pit. The steward was pointing to his badge and you could see him trying to say, 'No, no, you've got to have one of these.' This Neanderthal looked down on him, took the badge out of the steward's blazer and stuck it in his bare chest. The steward waved him into the pit!

Jimi was into 'Stone Free', the second song of his set, when the audience started hurling beer mats and bits of chair leg on to the stage in protest at police brutality. The promoter came on stage to warn that

287

Kloten airport, Zurich, 30 May 1968

the concert would end if the trouble didn't. The rest of the gig passed off without further serious incident – but afterwards the trouble moved on to the streets, as Richard Neville described in *Playpower*:

> After Paris student uprisings spread with a velocity and a geography difficult to document fully. Although the fact that the insurgents are usually described as students meant little even in Paris, a great proportion were aimless youths, beats, travellers and criminals.
>
> Take, for example, what happened when 10,000 young people attended a Jimi Hendrix concert in Zurich. The music – the usual delirious, steamy mixture of black power and masturbation – ended after midnight; public transport had closed down and to keep warm, people made bonfires out of garbage. Without warning, Zurich's police force attacked, swinging their truncheons and unleashing their dogs. The police violence and brutality . . . so shocked the staid city elders that they gave the victims permission to use an empty chain store as a meeting place.[9]

Two nights of rioting put 200 in hospital and 250 behind bars. Youth leaders gave the city two weeks to find them a permanent site for a youth centre. Nothing happened and, when the deadline was reached, police removed people from the store by force. 'I don't know why the police react in this kind of way,' said Jimi to Keith Altham. 'Maybe because there is such a low crime rate in this country, they have to find something to do. Any kind of action seems to make them overenthusiastic.'[10]

Hallenstadion, Zurich, 30 or 31 May 1968

After the gig, while the youth of Zurich did battle with the guardians of law and order, Keith Altham and the lads from the bands staged their own riot. 'It was absolute chaos. . . . there was a dreadful party at some club [the Crazy Girl] where one of the journalists I was with, Richard Green, "The Beast", insisted on jumping on to the bar to sing "Deutschland, Deutschland Über Alles". At which point, the good old Zurich fuzz, who had done their level best to make the visiting musicians' stay as miserable as possible, burst into the club and starting fighting everybody.' Our gallant band of British rock stars made their excuses and left.

Both Keith Altham and Richard Green filed reports back to *NME*, but neither mentioned that back at the Hotel Stöller, 'Gentle Jimi', as Keith dubbed him in his article, was only prevented from appearing stark naked in the foyer brandishing an axe by the ever-alert Gerry Stickells, who rugby-tackled him on the landing before he could get to the stairs. Earlier the hotel manager had called in the police to have a girl removed from Jimi's room. Telling a reporter from *Neue Presse* to 'go to hell' was indicative of the mood which may have sparked off Jimi's impersonation of a Viking.

> Gentle Jimi is still king of the guitar and was warmly received at every performance although he struck me as a little jaded on stage. Hardly surprising when you consider he has just finished an American tour of 47 cities in 57 days. He has two albums high in the best-selling charts in the US and is now one of the highest-paid pop artists in the world. . . .

Keith briefly interviewed Jimi, who asked, 'How is it in London? I bet they think we're dead over there, don't they? I'm looking forward to getting back and locking myself in my toilet to play my records. I've forgotten what most of them sound like.'

There was a brief stop-over in England to tape some songs for the Dusty Springfield show. Jimi flew back to New York to continue working on the album, leaving Noel and Mitch kicking their heels in London. Much of their time was spent hanging around the office in Gerrard Street. Now no rock manager wants his band getting the low-down on all the wheeling and dealing, hence a surprise offer of a holiday in Majorca. In the sun and out of the way. Of what?

A number of business matters were coming to a head in the spring and early summer of 1968. Ever since the middle of 1967, when Ed Chalpin first issued writs against Polydor, Track and Warner Brothers, there had been a cat-and-mouse game in progress over the release by Chalpin through Capitol Records of material Jimi had recorded with Curtis Knight. Two singles were released in 1967 by Capitol, 'Hush Now' and 'How Would You Feel?' Track Records forced Decca, Capitol's British arm, to withdraw the second single, but strangely put it out themselves. Then in December, an album *Get That Feeling* was released. In March 1968, after a very expensive case involving a whole posse of lawyers the High Court in England ordered Decca once again to withdraw a Curtis Knight record as it misleadingly suggested by the cover that Jimi took a major role. But a similar court action in America failed; all Capitol had to do was change the cover. By then three more albums had been released. Jimi was unequivocal in his condemnation of *Get That Feeling*: '[The] Curtis Knight album was from bits of tape they used from a jam session, bits of tape, tiny little confetti bits of tape. . . . Capitol never told us they were going to release that crap. . . . You don't have no friend scenes, sometimes makes you wonder. That cat and I used to really be friends. Plus I was just at a jam session and here they just try to connive and cheat and use. I knew Curtis Knight was recording, but listen, that was just a jam session.'[11]

Curtis Knight, naturally, does not see it like this at all: 'There were never any hard feelings whatever between Jimi and me. If there had been, would he have recorded with me when he came *back* from England, when he was already a success?'[12] That was the whole point, of course; undoubtedly, Jimi was very naive to have allowed Chalpin to tape anything, even if he thought it was just a jam, but the only reason Ed Chalpin wanted to release stuff anyway was precisely because Jimi *was* a success. Otherwise *Get That Feeling* would have sunk without trace and with it would have gone any hope Chalpin had of making Curtis Knight a star. As it was, it all came to nothing anyway – the only winner was Ed Chalpin.

Dire though all these recordings were, Chalpin *was* legally entitled to release them and theoretically entitled to be recompensed for Jimi breaking his contract. The question really was whether a court of law would deem this contract a fair one for Jimi to have signed. But it was never put to the test; Chalpin pressed his suit against Warner Brothers in America, who rolled over and settled. Why? Possibly because, having seen Jimi's earning potential, they didn't want to take any chances of lengthy litigation putting a freeze on their ability to release his material and earn them far more than they could ever lose in court. There was also a risk that the court would find in favour of Ed Chalpin and declare all subsequent agreements null and void. So Ed Chalpin received a very favourable settlement.

He got a 2 per cent 'override' on the first two albums and the as yet unfinished third, *Electric Ladyland*, plus complete rights to Jimi's fourth album (with a guarantee of $200,000), plus he could carry on marketing his Curtis Knight tapes unhampered. And, because nobody thought to get him to sign a worldwide release (which he might have refused to do anyway), he was still free to sue Track, Polydor and also the French label Barclay.

Mitch says they could have worked on *Electric Ladyland* for a year and it still wouldn't have been finished to Jimi's entire satisfaction. Track Records in England, now desperate for some product from Jimi (there had been nothing since the release of *Axis* in December 1967) put out *Smash Hits*, which reached number four in the UK album charts in early June. By the end of July, the recording sessions in New York were just about complete.

In April, Chris Welch of *Melody Maker* in an interview with Mitch pondered on the fact that most of the top British bands like the Who, Cream and Traffic seemed permanently Stateside – to which Mitch replied in a quote used for the headline, 'Let's face it, America is where the big money is.' In pursuit of more of it, another major tour of the US was lined up for the Experience starting at the end of July, but they returned to England to play the *Melody Maker*-sponsored Woburn Music Festival on 6 July supported by Marc Bolan and Steve Took (as Tyrannosaurus Rex) and Family among others. While Jimi was in England, he was interviewed by the paper – Jimi was in no mad rush to release the album:

> People were starting to take us for granted, abuse us. It was that what-cornflakes-for-breakfast scene. Pop slavery really. I felt we were in danger of becoming the American version of Dave Dee – nothing wrong with that, but it's just not our scene.
>
> I was tired of the attitude of fans that they've bought you a house and a car and now expect you to work the way they want you to for the rest of your life. But then we couldn't just say 'Screw them,' because they have their rights, too, so we decided the best way was to cool the recording scene until we were ready with something that we wanted everyone to hear. I want people to hear us, what we're doin' now, and try to appreciate what we're at. [13]

Jimi made no apologies for having been out of the UK since the previous Christmas. The money was better, there were far more venues to play than in England and, besides, 'I'm American. I want people there to see me. I also wanted to see whether we could make it back in the States. I dig Britain, but I haven't got a home anywhere. The Earth's my home; I've never had a house here. I don't want to put down roots in case I get restless and want to move.' Jimi gave no indication of any dissension within the Experience, but there were clues: 'I'd like to see Mitch and Noel getting into things that make them happy. Noel is on the English pop and hard-rock scene and is writing some good songs these days. Mitch is becoming a little monster on the drums. . . . He's the one I'd worry about losing. He's becoming so heavy behind me that he frightens me!'

The article also mentioned that Jimi was due to visit Majorca – 'It'd better be a gig or I'm not going,' said Jimi. Well it was, after a fashion. It was really another mini-holiday before the big push through America. They played the opening night of Mike's new club, Sergeant Pepper's, and Jimi literally brought the house down, by ramming the neck of his guitar into the ceiling tiles.

The contrasts in Jimi's life as a black superstar could be stark. From Spain, the band flew back to London for a few days. Evenings were spent in Blaises, South Kensington, where, as in all the clubs he frequented, Jimi would be an honoured guest. All heads would turn as he came into the club, the DJ might announce his presence, people would fight to sit next to him. If somebody was stupid enough to get up, six more would tussle for the spot.

After London, the Experience landed back in the States at JFK airport in New York. There they ran into Jerry Lee Lewis – Jimi approached him and offered him his hand in admiration for Lewis' contribution to rock 'n' roll. The Louisiana-born star ignored him. Next stop was Los Angeles, to receive some gold discs at the Warner Brothers offices – more tangible evidence of Jimi's success. From LA to Louisiana – the Deep South, Jerry Lee's home state, to start the tour. The arrangement was to play the first gig in Baton Rouge, then fly to Shreveport, but they all missed the flight, so they drove instead. They stopped to get something to eat. Jimi wouldn't even get out of the car. Here he was just another nigger. And he knew it. Fêted as the greatest rock guitarist in the world, acclaimed as a dionysian superstud and refused service at the tattiest redneck lunch counters – Jimi Hendrix was treated as superhuman and subhuman, but rarely just human.

Ten dates into the tour and having travelled through Texas, Illinois, Iowa, New York and Maryland, they found themselves back in the South, in Atlanta, Georgia.

Eire Apparent and Soft Machine had been the main support bands up to then. Now another name appeared on the hoardings – Vanilla Fudge. Formed in New York in 1965 as the Pidgeons, Vanilla Fudge had a minor hit in 1967 with a slowed-down baroque version of 'You

Keep Me Hanging On' with gothic organ and drone guitar sounds. Their debut album gave similar treatment to 'Eleanor Rigby', 'Ticket to Ride', 'Bang Bang' and 'People Get Ready'. On the strength of this and subsequent efforts, they became labelled as one of the first 'heavy' rock bands. They were also apparently controlled by the Mafia.

Robert Wyatt of Soft Machine recalls Mike Jeffery coming to see them rather sheepishly.

> He said, 'I know you got your time sorted out for your act, but we've got a fourth group on, so you got to cut it down to twenty or twenty-five minutes. We didn't really want these guys, but anyway, don't make a fuss.' And then the Vanilla Fudge arrive accompanied by, and I kid you not, two geezers straight out of *The Godfather* with scars down their cheeks. Everybody, including Mike Jeffery, was frightened, that's the word for it. [Apparently] Mike got a call:
> 'The Fudge haven't made it on the West Coast, they would like to join your little tour.'
> 'Oh, no, sorry, we've got our package tour.'
> 'You don't understand what I'm saying. The Fudge would like to join your tour, you don't want any trouble. The Fudge join your tour.'

Once on the tour, La Cosa Nostra did a good chaperone job as Mick Cox observed: 'They [the Fudge] weren't allowed to do anything at all, you know like talk to under-age girls, smoke, drink, take anything. They had to be white as white. The first time they arrived on the tour, they walked up to Dave Robinson [Eire Apparent roadie] and said, "We're using your gear. Ours hasn't arrived yet." '

In fact, out of sight of their minders, Vanilla Fudge were just as big dopers as any other band. They'd given all their stuff to the roadies to bring with the gear across the desert, in case they got stopped and searched. One of the roadies took everything he'd been given, jumped out the van and was never seen again. The other roadie couldn't drive, so all the gear was left stranded in the desert.

> Dave Robinson says, 'Oh no, you're not.' And so this guy just walked up to him, ripped his shirt off, pulled out a gun and pushed him up against the wall.
> 'Right, we're using your gear.'
> 'Yeah, right, sure you are.'

By whatever name you wish to call it, organised crime has a long association with popular music. In the twenties and thirties all the major jazz acts played at clubs owned by mobsters – one of the most famous being Owney Madden's Cotton Club in Harlem. But for the crime syndicates, the history of jazz might have been very different. Mob-controlled brothels, bars, speakeasies, clubs and up-market night-spots were bread and butter to many famous black jazz artists like Louis Armstrong, King Oliver and Fletcher Henderson who couldn't get gigs at fashionable white venues like the big New York hotels. As most of the gangsters were immigrants, they felt an affinity both with struggling white musicians from their own cultural groups and with black musicians from the South. There was also an age affiliation; in 1925, Legs Diamond, Lucky Luciano, Vito Genovese, Al Capone, Meyer Lansky and Carlo Gambino were all under thirty. Capone would arrive at one of his clubs, request his favourite songs and leave $100 tips for the musicians.

After the Second World War, the Mafia (in particular New York's Anastasia family) latched on to juke boxes as a source of revenue and again had a significant role in popular music history by spreading southern R&B north of the Mason–Dixon line. Anastasia controlled both the location of juke boxes and what music was played in them:

> The mob kept its own 'charts', constantly shuffling boxes so popular titles got the most exposure. It didn't matter what label the record was on, who was singing or what colour he or she was. If an R&B or country song was big in one region, it was shipped to another. Eventually the most popular R&B records made their way to the neighbourhood soda shops up north, frequented by America's newly affluent teens.[14]

Given the extent of criminal involvement in most aspects of the American leisure industry and the amount of money generated by rock, it would have been surprising if organised crime had *not* secured a piece of the action. From the sixties onwards crime syndicates in America controlled venue blue-collar workers through the Teamsters Union, trucking and stadium concessions to the point where it was said nobody toured America without making 'arrangements' first to ensure the shows were staged and the gear didn't finish up in Alaska. The Mafia have also been implicated in payola scandals, but the degree to which they have actually controlled record companies is open to question. Indirect associations abound, however, and this brings us right back to Jimi, or rather Mike Jeffery.

Mike often dropped hints that he had friends in heavy places, although people like Chris Stamp of Track Records were sceptical: 'Mike could go into quite detailed fantasy.' Indeed, the evidence is circumstantial, although it becomes more compelling as the story goes on.

For openers, Mike's efforts had resulted in Jimi being one of the first rock acts signed to Warners' Reprise label, established solely for the benefit of Frank Sinatra to lure him away from Capitol Records. At a Warners reception for the band subsequent to the signing, Neville Chesters saw somebody sidle up to Mitch: 'I remember overhearing a conversation between Mitch and some very strange-looking gentleman who gave Mitch a telephone number and said, "If you're ever in trouble in America, you ring that number."'

Nor were Vanilla Fudge an entirely unknown quantity to Mike. Their affairs were handled by the Experience's lawyer Steve Weiss, with whom Mike had worked closely for some time. Moreover, it was one of the Fudge management who got Mitch out of a sticky situation with the police.

On 18 August, the Experience were playing Tampa, Florida and staying at a reasonably smart hotel with a big lake at the back. Mick Cox decided to sample the facilities.

Me and Noel go out in one of those little paddle boats, and of course Mitch had to have a speed boat. Mitch is buzzing up and down doing ninety miles an hour, flooding the boat, and then he goes straight for the jetty and smashes it to bits. Within minutes, there's these police cars coming from everywhere, all the lights on, sirens going, they've all got guns – and they arrest Mitch. The guy who's handling Vanilla Fudge just comes walking out of the hotel and walks up to the guy who is obviously the head cop. He has a few words with him and they all drove off – it was unbelievable! I've no idea what he said, but there was a lot of police there. . . . that was a real insight I think into some of the things that went down.

In this instance 'connections' paid off – later they took on an altogether more sinister aspect.

With Vanilla Fudge on board, the tour proceeded through August and September, playing to ever larger crowds. The Experience were now almost exclusively a stadium rock band, rarely appearing in front of less than 5000 people.

But, as the crowds increased, so Jimi was becoming less inclined to be subservient to their demands and began toning down his perfor-

Singer Bowl, Flushing Meadow Park, Queens, New York, 23 August 1968

mance. Even though he maintained that his choreography was always spontaneous, he realised that he had made a rod for his own back. Kathy Etchingham says of his dilemma, 'He started to hate his image. He would sit at the end of the bed almost in tears, trying to explain to me how he felt, how he was fed up with his stage act and what people expected of him.'

Those reporting on this second leg of the American tour noted the change and most reacted sympathetically. At the Washington Ballroom, during 'Foxy Lady' a man dressed in a chicken suit rushed on to the stage and attacked Jimi, who fell against the drums, before a dozen cops leapt on the man and dragged him off. Jimi got up laughing and carried on. Apart from a sideswipe at the amp during 'Wild Thing', his nose dive into the drums was just about the limit of his gymnastics that night and the answer to the question on everyone's lips, 'Will he burn it? Will he burn it?', was 'no'.

Hullabaloo magazine published this review by one of its readers, suggesting perhaps that some of Jimi's fans at any rate might be receptive to change and were more sensitive to his needs than he perhaps gave them credit for:

> No, he didn't burn it. But the evil guitar-burner didn't let us down either. His soaring guitar lines . . . were a thrill. 'The Wind Cries Mary' and 'Red House Blues' gave the eyes of the cult an added vision. (It's nice to note that in spite of the evening's wildness, there was absolute silence during those two numbers.)
> He didn't have to burn it. If he were a superficial performer with no style or poetry to show us, the burning ceremony would have been necessary – a shock at the end of the show to leave a scar. But Jimi Hendrix has style and poetry; his fire is that most important fire: the fire within.[15]

In Dallas, however, it was situation normal:

> the cat sitting behind me yelled, 'Burn it, Jimi! Burn it, man!' But Jimi was good and Jimi stayed beautiful and Jimi did blues . . . Jimi became blues . . . it was 'Red House', and it was good blues. . . . suddenly it wasn't JIMI-HENDRIX-THE-SUPERSPADE-WHO-RAISES-LUST-IN-THE-HEARTS-OF-TEENY-BOPPERS-WHO-JACKS-OFF-HIS-GUITAR up there on stage. . . . it was a damned fine black cat who knew the blues and had the ability to show it. B.B. King, Muddy Waters and T-Bone Walker would have been proud of Jimi's blues. It was black downhome blues . . . not white bastardised blues . . . but real blues . . . and the audience got restless. . . . kids went to buy cokes, people

coughed . . . disappointed that their idol and his phallic, screaming guitar would resort to playing good honest blues. (Wow, he'd better burn his guitar pretty darn quick.) Jimi was trying to show his audience that he was a musician and not a show-off spade.

Then just as everybody was expecting the big climax, Jimi floored them all by playing 'Taps' before giving in with 'Wild Thing' with just a touch of destruction schtick. The 'Taps' Jimi played was commemorating the death of Jimi Hendrix Superspade Psychedelic Dervish and telling the world that Hendrix the Musician was here to stay. [16]

The most significant concerts of the tour took place on the West Coast. On 14 September, the Experience made a triumphant return to the Hollywood Bowl where a year before they had been received in stony silence by an audience there to see the Mamas and the Papas. About halfway through the set, with the audience on the verge of hysteria, about fifty fans swan-dived into the pool fronting the stage. Fearful of being electrocuted, Noel made an appeal for people to stop splashing about while Mitch came from behind his kit to offer a towel and a hand-up to some waterlogged enthusiasts. The interruptions took the gig into the early hours of the morning with the promoter hopping up and down threatening to pull the plug.

From 10 to 12 October, they played two shows a night at the Winterland in San Francisco – about fifteen songs out of forty or so played appear collectively on the *Live at Winterland* and *Jimi Hendrix Concerts* albums. Taken together, there were two interesting pointers for the future from these nights at the Winterland. First, most of the songs were done as loose jams, something they probably would not have contemplated anywhere other than in San Francisco. This, incidentally, is how Cream took off in America. They played the Fillmore West with what were then their three-minute songs and when they ran out of material found the audience screaming at them, 'Just play! Just play!'

Secondly, other musicians played with the Experience: Jack Casady on the first night; on the second night, there were Virgil Gonzales on flute for 'Are You Experienced?' on the first show, and for most of the second show Herbie Rich, organist with the Buddy Miles Express.

With the *Electric Ladyland* sessions, Jimi introduced a new pattern to the recording of his material, tying sessions in closely with jamming and not sticking to the trio format. Now there were clear indications in his live performances that Jimi was looking to experiment with a similarly less structured and rigid way of working.

299

Hollywood Bowl, Hollywood, 14 September 1968

During this tour, Jimi had introduced 'Sunshine of Your Love' into the set as a tribute to Cream, who had announced their imminent break-up. He also attended their farewell US concert at the Forum on 19 October. He sat there nursing the information that, since the summer, it had become increasingly obvious that his own band was going the same way. Noel's disenchantment with the Experience set-up had reached the point where he had made contact with some old musician friends to plan the formation of a new band to be called Fat Mattress. The more involved he became with this project, the more estranged he became from Jimi. Later Jimi gave this as the main reason why the Experience split up, because he was unhappy at Noel diversifying his efforts in this way. But the formation of Fat Mattress was really just a catalyst in this situation. By the time Jimi was watching Cream wave their last goodbyes, he had already agreed with Noel and Mitch that they needed a rest from each other.

300

Rehearsals, Honolulu International Center, Hawaii, 5 October 1968

They talked about playing with other musicians: Noel would run Fat Mattress, Mitch was toying with something called Mind Octopus, while Jimi would develop his ideas utilising more flexible line-ups. Hopefully, all this creative energy would feed back into a rejuvenated Experience which would perforce tour less often. When this was first mooted around September, the feeling about this among the three of them was quite positive, because it gave them all something to look forward to and resolved what was a very difficult working situation with Jimi and Noel pulling in opposite directions and Mitch somehow in the middle. How much this was self-delusion is difficult to say – like a 'trial separation' in marriage as a way of postponing taking a decision about the inevitable.

The fact that by November Jimi didn't seem at all positive in talking to the press when the news broke is perhaps indicative of his true feelings. Interviewed by *Melody Maker* he did not mention that other groups were being planned: 'Mitch and Noel want to get their own thing going – not a group: producing and managing other artists . . . so very soon, probably in the New Year, we'll be breaking the group, apart from selected dates.' Was it the end of Jimi Hendrix as a performer? 'Oh, I'll be around, don't worry . . . doing this and that. But there are other scenes we want to get into.' He talked about the Experience doing gigs all over the world, saying prophetically, 'We're just like a band of musical gypsies moving about everywhere.'[17]

At the time Jimi was interviewed, he had just finished a period of 'time out' away from touring. With a hectic round of recording and touring behind him and a period of worrying uncertainty ahead of him, Jimi desperately needed a break. During October, he rented a house in Benedict Canyon, Los Angeles and buzzed around the town in the company of his old running-mate Buddy Miles. He put in some recording time at the T.T.G. Studios in Hollywood, while evenings were mainly spent at the Whisky A Go Go and a new club, named in his honour, the Experience. Jimi's face was painted around the entrance – his mouth was the doorway.

The owner of the club was Marshall Brevitz, who had some involvement in the Miami Pop Festival fiasco. His club was in trouble because the Whisky was operating some kind of blacklist, telling any musicians who played at the Experience that they would be barred from the Whisky. To show there were no hard feelings, Jimi made a point of playing at the Experience every night for a week and getting this announced on the radio. Jimi and his friends ran up a bar bill of about $1000 which kept the club afloat, and Jimi insisted Brevitz keep all the entrance money.

My eyes are very bad and sometimes you might go into a club and you might not see somebody and they might get all funny – 'Oh, you're big time now, you won't talk to me.' (*Go Go Girl*, 20 January 1968)

Jimi was a sucker for fast cars and had Gerry Stickells drive 3000 miles across America from New York with a brand new Corvette sports car. Jimi wrecked it taking a corner too fast near his house, the very day Gerry arrived. 'I had to rush down there and say to the cop it was me driving because Jimi didn't have a licence. . . . he couldn't see a bloody thing, he couldn't see to the next traffic light. He had glasses, but he would never wear them.'

This was the latest in a number of incidents resulting from Jimi's seeming inability to keep a car on the road. When he first arrived in London in 1966, he wrapped Chas's car round a tree and just walked away and left it. In early October 1968, just before the Winterland shows, the band did a show in Hawaii and, during their seven-day stay, Jimi wrote off another brand new sports car on the island of Maui. Neither did Jimi cotton on to the notion of actually parking a car. Whenever Jimi was in New York, Gerry spent much of his time down at the car pound: 'It was a nightmare. Whenever he saw some place where he wanted to stop, he would just leave the car right there and walk off.'

Having protected Jimi from one prosecution, Gerry had to intervene once again to head off a far more serious charge – that of grievous bodily harm against a girl.

In April, Mitch told *Downbeat* magazine, 'Some nights we can be really bad. If we smash something up then it's because that instrument which is something you dearly love, just isn't working that night. It's not responding and so you want to kill it.' In the same interview, Jimi further likened the process to the love–hate relationship: 'It's just like maybe you feel at times when your girlfriend starts messing around. You might feel that you wanted to do that, but you couldn't but with music you do, because an instrument can't fight back.'[18]

In common with many blues guitarists, for Jimi his guitar took on female characteristics – he called one 'Betty Jean', duetted with it in classic 'call and response' mode, slept with it, manipulated it on stage in ways that can only be described as erotic and, often as not, as he said above, he took his obscure object of desire and smashed it up. On occasion, Jimi dangerously blurred the distinction between guitar and woman.

Bakersfield, California, 26 October 1968

Stories of Jimi being violent provoke general disbelief among those people who knew him, and who maintain that he could never deliberately hurt anybody. And it is true that a public figure like Jimi would always be vulnerable to allegations such as this from those seeking publicity or money or both. However, Trixie Sullivan maintains that, where women were concerned, 'He wasn't that nice to them. The only one who ever stood her own ground was one lady called Kathy [Etchingham].' Gerry's story is that this particular incident took place at the girl's house. She made a complaint and the police arrested both Jimi and Gerry, who was there to try and sort things out. '[They] gave us a right bollocking and it had nothing to do with me! "You can't do this sort of thing, you'd better go and apologise to the girl." So I drive over to her place and he says, "Don't worry, I won't do anything, I promise." So I'm sitting in the car while he goes into the house and he didn't come back. So I go into the house to see what's going on and he's busy giving her one! I said, "For Christ's sake, Jimi, get out of here!" and I dragged him away.'

It was a supreme irony that while the Experience was on the point of breaking up, Jimi's greatest recorded achievement hit the streets. Released in October, *Electric Ladyland* shot up the charts in Britain and America. But when British record retailers saw the twenty-one naked women who adorned the British cover, the row that followed almost pushed the music aside: 'STORM OVER JIMI'S ALBUM – STORES REJECT SLEEVE AS PORNOGRAPHIC' and 'TITS 'N' ASS LP BROWN-BAGGED IN ENGLAND'. David King was Track Records' art director. 'We wanted to make it a kind of untouched cover – I asked David Montgomery to take the photographs and make [the women] look like real people.' Apparently the original photos had 'very pretty pink tones, but with cheap printing it came out all black and grotty'. As one of the women, Reina Sutcliffe, complained to *Melody Maker* at the time, 'It makes us look like a load of old prostitutes. It's rotten.'

The photo sessions had been conducted the previous November in London. Jimi was supposed to have been in the shot but never showed up, which is why the women (paid £5 a head and an extra £5 for those who took their knickers off) are holding pictures of him instead. The inside of the gatefold sleeve showed Jimi against a background of smoke and flame, again organised by David King. 'The photo session was held at the Roundhouse and they literally built a bonfire. Jimi was standing very close to a twenty-foot wall of flames.' King was also picture editor for the *Sunday Times*; the shot was originally scheduled for a Hendrix feature which never appeared, so it was used for the cover instead. According to King, the photos of Noel and Mitch were very much an afterthought, dropped in at the last minute and then enlarged slightly to head off what would otherwise have been a major row.

Obviously the question of the cover came up in interviews. Jimi flatly dissociated himself from it: '. . . I don't know anything about it. I didn't know it was going to be used.' With no control over the English cover, Jimi tried to influence Warners' art department and wrote to them. He wanted to make liberal use of shots that Linda McCartney (then Eastman) had taken in Central Park. Warners reproduced the 'Letter to the Room Full of Mirrors' and made use of Linda's photos, but chose a standard group shot for the cover, not dissimilar to the UK cover of *Are You Experienced?*

Dear Sirs,

Here are the pitcures we would like for
you to use any where on the L.P. cover — preferably inside and back.
with out the white frames around some of the B/w ones.
and with most of them next to each other in diffrent sizes
(INSIDE)
and mixing the color
prints at diffrent
points —

Rough Sketch
of L.P

INSIDE
and OUTSIDE

for instance

Please use color pitcure
with us and the kids
on the statue for front
or BACK COVER — (OUTSIDE)
COVER

and the other
back or Front side, (outside)
cover
please use three
Good pitcures of us.
IN B/w or color

Electric
Lady
Land

OUT SIDE

we would like to make an apoligee for
taking so very long to send this but we have been
working very hard indeed, doing shows AND
Recordings

yes sir!

And please send two pitcures back
to Jimi Hendrix Personal + Private
c/o Jeffery + Chandler -
27 East 37th St. N.Y. N.Y.

after you finishe with them.

Please, if you can, find a nice place and lettering
for the few words I wrote ~~first the~~ named... "Letter ~~the~~
of the room full
on the L.P Cover.
of mirrors."
  the sketch on the other page is a rough
  Idea of course)... But please use ALL the pitcures.
  and the words — Any other drastic change from these
  directions would not be appropiate according to
the music and our group's present stage —
And the music is most important. and we have enough
personal problems without haveing to worry about this simple
clet effective layout. "yes sir!" thank you. — Jimi Hendrix

So what about the *music* between the covers?

The cover announces 'Produced and Directed by Jimi Hendrix'* and as a body of work *Electric Ladyland* (hereafter *EL*) can be regarded as the apotheosis of Jimi's creative achievements. Certainly it was the album he was most satisfied with and over which he had had most control, although not as much as he would have wished. 'We mixed it and produced it and all this mess – but then it's time for them to press it, and quite naturally they screwed it up, 'cause they didn't know what we wanted. There's a 3-D sound on there that you can't even appreciate, because they didn't know how to cut it properly. They thought it was out of phase.'[19]

The songs cover similar ground to previous work, from woman trouble to the fate of the planet, but although the themes are familiar, Jimi's pedagogic tendencies appear temporarily to have receded in deference to an intensified quest for personal meaning and possible redemption. *EL* presaged Jimi's attempt to withdraw from the rock 'n' roll circus during 1969 while he tried to re-evaluate his position and consider his next moves. Thus in constructing the album musically, Jimi shoots for definitive statements as if to draw a line under his music ready for the future. Incorporated into *EL* as discrete entities are virtually all genres of popular music – blues, soul, pop, R&B, jazz/funk, rock 'n' roll and electronic. In particular, partnered by Eddie Kramer, Jimi took the exploration of the symphonic possibilities of rock electronics further than anybody else. And with 'Voodoo Chile', he committed to vinyl one of the finest interpretations of the Delta blues in modern times. *EL* also proved beyond any doubt that alongside all his other talents Jimi wrote some of the best intros in the history of rock.

'And the Gods Made Love' opens the album, a fragment of a sound painting, utilising the taped sounds of Jimi's own voice, a tympanum drum and snare rimshots. The resulting mix is slowed down, reversed and finally replayed as repeating tape echo.

In interviews, Mitch labelled *EL* as a 'concept', a term much in vogue in those days, without actually stating what the concept was. Jimi was more specific – *EL* was dedicated to groupies: 'Some groupies know more about music than the guys. . . . some people call them groupies, but I prefer the term "Electric Ladies". My whole *Electric Ladyland* album is about them.'[20]

---

* This is not entirely fair to Chas, who produced 'Crosstown Traffic', 'Burning Of The Midnight Lamp' and 'All Along the Watchtower'.

TV recordings
Zoniewoud, St Pieters Woluwe, Belgium, 6 March 1967

Jimi's flat, London, February/March 1967

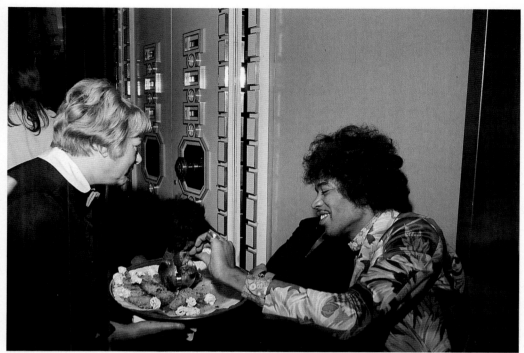

Europa Hotel, London, 16 September 1967
Europa Hotel, London, 16 September 1967

Studio rehearsals
De Lane Lea Music Ltd., London, 23 October 1967

Devon Wilson spent a lot of time with Jimi in the studio and she, for one, would tell Jimi what she thought of his playing and, if she didn't think it was up to much, she'd come right out and tell him to his face – something few others ever did, and it was one aspect of her character that Jimi admired. He often said in interview how much he hated people coming up to him after a gig and telling how great he'd played if *he* knew that by his standards he hadn't. To the interviewer, Jimi mentioned some of his 'electric lady' acquaintances, but wouldn't be drawn about to whom each song was dedicated.

So with 'Have You Ever Been (To Electric Ladyland)', Jimi, harmonising falsetto with himself, takes us on another magical mystery tour in the spirit of 'Spanish Castle Magic' and 'The Stars That Play With Laughing Sam's Dice'. This latest excursion, floating on a melodic cushion of chord patterns similar to 'Little Wing', visits the embrace of the Electric Ladies and their garden of delights.

> Have you ever been,
> Have you ever been to Electric Ladyland?
> The magic carpet waits for you so don't you be late.
>
> Oh, I wanna show you the different emotions
> I wanna learn you the sounds and motions
> Electric woman waits for you and me

These women were often the only people willing to listen to a musician bursting with frustration and anger or burdened with loneliness or isolation after months on the road. Many ended up marrying the musicians they followed around. Whether groupies or more steady girlfriends, Jimi rarely spoke to anyone else about how he was feeling.

> People, they don't give inspiration except bad inspiration, to write songs like 'Crosstown Traffic' and all that, 'cos that's the way they put themselves in front of me, the way they present themselves. (*IT*, 28 March 1969)

> You jump in front of my car when ya, you know all the time,
> that, ninety miles an hour girl is, the speed I drive
> You tell me it's alright, you don't mind a little pain
> You say you just want me to, take you for a drive
> You're just like (Crosstown Traffic)
> So hard to get through to you (Crosstown Traffic)
> I don't need to run over you (Crosstown Traffic)
> All you do is slow me down,
> and I'm tryin' to get on the other side of town

I'm not the only soul who's accused of hit and run
Tyre-tracks all across your back, I can, I can see you had your fun!
But-eh, darling can't you see my signals turn from green to red
and with you I can see a traffic jam, straight up ahead
You're just like (Crosstown Traffic)
So hard to get through to you (Crosstown Traffic)
I don't need to run over you (Crosstown Traffic)
All you do is slow me down,
and I got better things on the other side of town

Yeah, yeah (Crosstown Traffic)
(Yeah) Look out (look out)
Look out baby
Coming through
(Crosstown Traffic)
Yeah (look out, Crosstown Traffic, yeah, look out)
Look out, look out baby (Crosstown Traffic, yeah, look out)
What's that in the street? (Crosstown Traffic)
(Yeah, look out)
(Crosstown Traffic, yeah, look out)

Like the early jazz singers, Jimi scat sings in unison with his guitar the intro to 'Crosstown Traffic', flipping us from space time to boogie time. The jazz-related chordal progressions produce, according to Dave Whitehill, an accomplished transcriber of Jimi's music, a degree of harmonic sophistication almost unheard of in rock at that time. Lyrically, 'Crosstown Traffic' is an R&B put-down of women who in Jimi's terms were 'clingy', using a neat metaphor of the urban transport snarl-up. And with Jimi playing up to a macho-spade image, snarl is exactly the tone.

But *EL* was not entirely concerned with groupies, or 'band-aids' as Jimi called them. With 'Voodoo Chile' Jimi brought the dark secret of the blues to the international stage – the bluesman's historic connections to the underground religion of slavery. Voodoo, a mixture of West African magico-religion and Catholic ceremony, came to the West Indies with the slaves imported by the French. Established in Haiti, voodoo quickly spread under a variety of names throughout North and South America. In the impenetrable, forbidding swampland of Louisiana, for example, voodoo became hoodoo.

Within the black community of the American South, voodoo operated on at least two levels. Led by the Hougan, a high priest of deep knowledge and experience, voodoo worship was an act of political defiance, a secret communications and belief system uniting a people in oppression.

310

At a more pragmatic level, voodoo provided the ordinary citizen with access to the powerful accoutrements of sorcery – potions and charms to be used for good or ill. This sympathetic magic worked through men and women well versed in voodoo lore. These were the 'conjurors', 'root doctors' and 'gypsies', part healers, shamans and witch doctors, and much feared. Among the most potent fetishes were High John the Conqueroo Root (which had to be gathered before 21 September to be effective) and Mojos. High John was combined with any number of objects – cats' claws, hair, teeth, herbs, bones and so on – and wrapped up in a small cloth bag to win back a wayward lover. Mojos were good-luck charms. This 'low magic' of voodoo was celebrated in a number of blues songs, most notably 'Got My Mojo Working', 'Louisiana Blues', 'She Moves Me' and 'Hoochie Coochie Man', which Jimi recorded once with Alexis Korner for his BBC *Rhythm and Blues Show* in 1967 and later as a jam session at the Record Plant in New York with Buddy Miles and Billy Cox.

But the bluesman engaged voodoo on yet another plane – the implications of which made him almost as feared as the root doctor.

The bluesman was a wayward spirit, a drifter down dusty highways, bound by nothing save an obsession with learning the secret of playing music that would strike deep into the soul of his audience. To achieve this, it was alleged, he sought divine (or, if you were a God-fearing Baptist churchgoer, diabolical) intervention and made a pact with the devil. Such claims added to the status of the bluesman as an outlaw in society and were good for business – Peetie Wheatstraw called himself 'the Devil's Son-in-Law'. In fact, the basis of these claims was to be found embedded in a voodoo ritual with its roots in antiquity – a meeting at the crossroads with one of the most feared gods in the voodoo pantheon, Papa Legba. The occult writer Francis King has suggested that Jimi dedicated 'Voodoo Chile' to Akonidi Hini – a Ghanaian occultist and one-time President of the African Psychic and Traditional Healers Association. Jimi was supposed to have been impressed by her occult powers while she in turn believed that the rites she carried out in her ramshackle temple on the banks of the River Zribi in Ghana in some way contributed to Jimi's success – a service she also performed for Bob Marley.[21] But Jimi was no voodoo adept, and the religion did not inform his life as it almost certainly did for Delta blues legend Robert Johnson, whose well-documented songs show that Papa Legba put stones in your pathway and a hellhound on your trail as the terrible price to pay for mastery of the blues.

But even if only metaphorically Jimi is nonetheless infused with the spirit of Legba in 'Voodoo Chile'. The sepulchral tones of Stevie Winwood's Hammond organ add gothic menace to a song brimful of the brooding, fascinating and haunting tensions inherent in this most supernatural of blues.

Well I'm a Voodoo Chile
Lord I'm a Voodoo Chile

(Yeah)

Well the night I was born,
Lord I swear the moon turned a fire red
The night I was born,
I swear the moon turned a fire red
Well my poor mother cried out 'Lord, the gypsy was right!'
and I seen her fell down right dead
(Have mercy)

Well, mountain lions found me there waitin',
and set me on a eagle's back
(Oh Lord)
Well mountain lions found me there,
and set me on a eagle's wing
(it's the eagle's wing, baby, what did I say)
He took me past to the outskirts of infinity,
and when he brought me back,
he gave me Venus witch's ring
Hey!
And he said 'Fly on, fly on'
Because I'm a, Voodoo Chile baby, Voodoo Chile
Hey!

(Yeah)
Well I make love to you,
and Lord knows you'll feel no pain
(Yeah)
Say I make love to you in your sleep,
and Lord knows you felt no pain
(Have mercy),
'cause I'm a million miles away,
and at the same time I'm right here in your picture frame
(Yeah, what did I say now)
'Cause I'm a Voodoo Chile,
Lord knows I'm a Voodoo Chile
(Yeah)

(Yeah, yeah turn it up, yeah)

(Yeah, yeah)
Well my arrows are made of desire
From far away as Jupiter's sulphur mines
Say my arrows are made of desire, desire,
from far away as Jupiter sulphur mines
(Way down by the Methane Sea, yeah)
I have a humming bird and it hums so loud,
you think you were losing your mind, hmmm . . .

(Yeah, yeah . . .)

Well I float in liquid gardens,
and Arizona new red sand
(Yeah)
I float in liquid gardens,
way down in Arizona red sand . . .

Well, I taste the honey from a flower named Blue,
(way down in California)
and then New York drowns as we hold hands
(Yeah)
(Hey!)
'Cause I'm a Voodoo Chile
Lord knows, I'm a Voodoo Chile
Yeah! . . .

Possession is the highest aim of voodoo ceremony, to the point where, rather than communing with God, the Hougan, the high priest, *becomes* God. This is the central theme of the song – from a primeval soup of erotic power, ancient curse, gypsy prophecy and intergalactic communion, Jimi manifests himself as the cosmic force who can travel in both the physical and the psychic plane, through time and space. Although grounded and inspired by the Delta blues form, Jimi takes us through a history of the blues in its broadest sense from Peetie Wheatstraw to John Coltrane via Muddy Waters and B.B. King.

In 'Voodoo Child (slight return)' Jimi carries on the images of unlimited power transcending all the laws of nature:

> Well, I stand up next to a mountain and chop it down with the
>   edge of my hand.
> Well, I pick up all the pieces and make an island
> Might even raise a little sand.

Finally he offers up that terrible challenge:

If I don't meet you no more in this world
Then I'll meet you in the next one
And don't be late.

The long version of 'Voodoo Chile' in the studio, though it sounds
as if performed live in front of a select band of studio hangers-on,
actually had those crowd noises dubbed on later. But Jimi regularly
featured 'Slight Return' in concert and it was up on stage where a
voodoo image of Jimi became most potent. There, on good nights,
he 'hoodooed' his audience, guiding them through his music like the
Hougan guiding adepts through the rituals and ceremonies. With his
clothes, jewellery, feathers, hat and scarf, he looked like a Hougan
and as he snaked his way across the stage he danced like a Hougan
in the throes of serpent worship, the central deity of voodoo, symbol
of life, fecundity and wisdom. The late African percussionist Rocky
Dzidzournu who jammed with Jimi during 1969 used to tell him that the
beat he naturally fell into (especially on much of *EL*) was the exact beat
he remembered from the voodoo ceremonies he witnessed as a child
back in Ghana. Jimi was the root doctor, revered for the spirit within
him, a conjuror of electricity in the service of music. A Magic Boy.

Side B opens with Noel's contribution, 'Little Miss Strange', still
very much in the English Small Faces/Who pop field where he hoped
Fat Mattress would successfully plough its own furrow. Although similar in feel to 'She's So Fine' on *Axis*, the four-guitar harmony structure
makes for a more sophisticated piece.

Al Kooper's keyboard work, Jimi's use of Steve Cropper-style sliding
sixth notes and a tight, yet loose-limbed rhythm section gives 'Long
Hot Summer Night' a less frantic feel than some of Jimi's other R&B
compositions. In his analysis of Jimi's music, Charles Shaar Murray cites
a number of songs, starting with 'May This Be Love' through 'Long Hot
Summer Night' to 'Angel', wherein a mystical woman, 'no geisha, slave
or groupie', is sought by Jimi as his only means of inner peace and
personal salvation. But Jimi's throwaway comment during one concert
when he said, 'Anyway, the other half of man is a woman' suggests
that in some of his songs, under the guise of genuflections to woman-
kind, Jimi was possibly making an oblique reference to the feminine
side of his own psyche.

For example, in 'Long Hot Summer Night' Annie, who is terrified
of the phone, and Jimi, who hated the phone and rarely answered it
himself, appear to be the same person.

Around about this time the telephone blew its horn across the room
Scared little Annie clean out of her mind . . .
And the telephone keeps on screamin' . . .
'Hello', said my shaky voice
'Well, how you doing?' (I start to stutter . . .)
'Can't you tell I'm doing fine?'
It was my baby talkin' way down 'cross the border.

Relief follows panic:

I'm so glad that my baby's comin' to rescue me

At the same time interwoven into the subtext of these and several future songs was a remembrance of his mother Lucille, not voiced in the accusatory tones of Lennon's 'Mother', but as heartfelt yearning for her to return and take care of him.

In 1953 Ray Charles wrote an arrangement for Eddie Jones (alias) Guitar Slim) of a song called 'The Things I Used To Do' which was recorded in New Orleans for the Los Angeles-based label Specialty. Released in 1954, it was the biggest R&B hit of the year, selling over a million copies, and set Ray Charles on his way as a writer of commercial hit records. It was Guitar Slim's only hit, but this Mississippi-born player with an astonishingly intense high-screaming guitar style spawned a number of imitators including Ike Turner and a New Orleans guitarist Earl King. Jimi Hendrix recorded the same song with Johnny Winter at the Record Plant studio in May 1969, Earl King claiming with some justification that Jimi in the late sixties sounded a lot like the Guitar Slim of the mid-fifties. To complete the connection, Jimi also recorded Earl King's one and only hit record, 'Come On Part One', for *Electric Ladyland*.

Earl King, from New Orleans, based his song on the successful hit record of another New Orleans act, Shirley and Lee, who in 1956 struck gold with 'Let The Good Times Roll'. Jimi played 'Come On' during his high-school days and he takes this opportunity for a good work-out, building up the suspense just before the solo with some dramatic ascending parallel chords similar to big-band arrangements during the swing era.

A simple yet effective bass drum/hi-hat figure and some beautiful phased guitar/voice unison harmony introduce 'Gypsy Eyes'. Like so many of Jimi's songs, 'Gypsy Eyes' with its outro fills and solo based on

Beverly Rodeo Hyatt House
360 North Rodeo Drive
Beverly Hills, California

forget of my name... Remember it only as a hand shake... introduction to my Belief which is God... Fire instead the Wives of my Interpreture. Music, Saint Hynotic if you choose. But Thruth and life regardless of your questionable timid ~~peace sacrifice~~ compromises... which I intend to erase.... Which I ~~will~~ erase without hint of reward as I am only a messenger And you a Sheep in process of evolution... Almost at Death with yourself' and On the Stair case of Birth. Soon you may almost forget the Smell of your family...

variations of the blues scale has its own blues heritage – the song is very reminiscent of 'Rollin' and Tumblin'', recorded first by Hambone Willie Newbern in 1929, by Robert Johnson (who called it 'If I Had Possession Over Judgement Day') and by Muddy Waters (who recorded the original song plus a variation called 'Louisiana Blues', his first nationwide hit).

In the third verse, Lucille tells Jimi why she had to get away:

I remember the first time I saw you
The tears in your eyes look like they was tryin' to say
'Oh, little boy, you know I could love you
But first I must make my getaway
Two strange men fighting to the death over me today
I'll try and meet you by the old highway.'

Side B ends with 'The Burning of the Midnight Lamp', which appears well in keeping with the tone of the whole album, even though it had been recorded some eighteen months earlier. The song was never released as a single in the States, which probably explains its inclusion. Jimi was on record as saying that this was his favourite song, but he was never happy with the mono single release because he felt the vocals were lost. Now he had the chance to release it in stereo, although in truth it does not make that much difference.

'Rainy Day, Dream Away' was the first song Jimi recorded with neither Noel nor Mitch present. Instead, he recreates a smoky night-club atmosphere with the help of Buddy Miles, Freddie Smith on sax, Mike Finnegan on organ and Larry Faucette on congas. Together they hit an easy shuffle groove, Jimi throwing in a Charlie Christian lick for good measure. 'Still Raining, Still Dreaming' on side D continues the jam, with an outstanding 'talking' wah-wah solo spanning both tracks.

As 'Rainy Day' fades away, we fade into '1983 (A Merman I Should Turn to Be)', a song of firsts and lasts. Musically, it marks Jimi's first piece of major orchestration, using the full capacities of the Record Plant's studio facilities.

Lyrically, it is the last of Jimi's surreal apocalypses; despairing of mankind, he finally returns to the sea, the source of all life. Most of Jimi's later statements on the human condition were couched in more positive terms related to self-help and the fulfilment of self-potential. Not so here.

Hurrah, I awake from yesterday
Alive, but the war is here to stay
So my love, Catherina and me,
decide to take our last walk through the noise to the sea
Not to die but to be reborn,
away from lands so battered and torn
Forever, forever

Oh say, can you see it's really such a mess
Every inch of Earth is a fighting nest
Giant pencil and lipstick tube shaped things,

Continue to rain and cause scream and pain
And the arctic stains from silver blue to bloody red
as our feet find the sand,
and the sea is straight ahead, straight up ahead

Well it's too bad that our friends, can't be with us today
Well, it's too bad
'The machine, that we built,
would never save us', that's what they say
(That's why they ain't coming with us today)
And they also said 'it's impossible for a man to live and breathe under
    water, forever',
was their main complaint
(And they also threw this in my face, they said:)
'Anyway, you know good well it would be beyond the will of God,
and the grace of the King' (Grace of the King)
(Yeah, yeah)

So my darling and I make love in the sand,
to salute the last moment ever on dry land
Our machine, it has done its work, played its part well
Without a scratch on our body and we bid it farewell
Starfish and giant foams greet us with a smile
Before our heads go under we take a last look at the killing noise
Of the out of style, the out of style, out of style (oooh) . . .

Jimi is the Star Child of Arthur C. Clarke's *2001* and speaks
in a childlike way about the implements of war: 'Giant pencil and
lipstick tube shaped things'. He is also Noah scorned by onlookers as
he prepares for Armageddon: '"The machine, that we built / would
never save us", that's what they say'. Jimi's two favourite metaphors
appear, sand and water – to represent the impermanence of nature
and the mirror of the soul respectively. Jimi sliding into the water is
Jimi turning in on himself and taking a helpmate with him. But in the
phrase 'straight ahead' is a direct reference to Jimi's belief in the power
of positive thinking apparent in his music, lyrics and interviews through
all the rest of his life.

As Jimi moves underwater, '1983' segues into the 'Moon, Turn
The Tides':

So down and down and down and down and down and down and down we go
Hurry my darling we mustn't be late for the show
Neptune champion games to an aqua world is so very dear
'Right this way!' smiles a mermaid I can hear Atlantis full of cheer
Atlantis full of cheer, I can hear Atlantis full of cheer

The fabric of the song is quite sparse, Jimi's raga-sounding guitar never intrusive, while effects are used most imaginatively, a superb evocation of the lush rhythms and cadences of life beneath the waves. Many 'tricks' result just from ingenious use of the guitar and standard studio equipment. At one point the tapes are slowed down and then speeded up again to represent a shoal of fish swimming up to investigate these strange beings that have joined their world. Their curiosity satisfied, they swim away. The seagull noises are headphones that Jimi had feeding back into the microphone with delay tape added later. Eddie Kramer recalled working with Jimi on this track 'for about eighteen hours straight. We mixed the entire thing in one go with no interruption, so it was a complete piece. With all the panning, all the effects, we would rehearse it numerous times, obviously. But it was like a performance . . . a creation of a piece of music . . . a unique experience.'[22]

'House Burning Down' signals the beginning of Jimi's more overtly political stance, particularly on black issues, although, as this song indicates, Jimi never had much sympathy with black militancy as championed by the Black Panthers. The lyric, as with so many of Jimi's songs, scans beautifully as a piece of poetry set to music.

Not everyone shared Jimi's enthusiasm for involvement in the community:

> Well, I asked my friend, 'Where is that black smoke coming from?'
> He just coughed and changed the subject and said,
> 'Oh well, I think it might snow some.'

Jimi gets out there 'in my Jag' to find out what is going down. He asks the question: 'Why did you burn your brother's house down?' And gets the answer:

> We're tired and disgusted
> so we paint red through the sky

But this is not Jimi's way – it is not what Martin Luther King died for:

> I say the truth is straight ahead
> So don't burn yourself instead
> Try to learn instead of burn
> Hear what I say.

But even within the very real world of urban ghetto violence, Jimi cannot resist the notion that extra-terrestrials might intervene from some other world, some Eldorado:

> A giant boat from space landed with eerie grace
> And came and taketh all the dead away.

When *John Wesley Harding* was released in January 1968, Jimi's initial idea was to record 'I Dreamed I Saw St Augustine', but as a song chronicling the passage through dissipation to redemption via guilt, he thought it too personal to Dylan and changed his mind. Instead, he chose 'All Along The Watchtower', where Dylan confronts the chaos of fallen man and emerges from Armageddon chastened but intact, much as Jimi does in '1983'. Jimi's version has to be the premier cover of a Dylan song; Dylan himself loved the new arrangement which enlivened and enriched the lyric. The central section of the song is a solo structured in four parts: straight rock lead, blues with slide on an electric twelve-string (where Jimi sounds as if he is deconstructing the guitar then putting it back together again), a six-string electric through a wah-wah, and finally a chord section ending on a series of ascending unison bends. The song was recorded at the end of January, but, says Kathy Etchingham, 'he didn't do anything with it for ages while he was thinking about it. He didn't dare release it because it was a "Bob Dylan song". He came right out of himself when he did "All Along The Watchtower" and he enjoyed it. He loved that song.'

Nineteen-sixty-eight was the year of the big break-up: Cream, Traffic, Spencer Davis and the Byrds (again!) all disintegrated, while Eric Burdon (New Animals), Janis Joplin (Big Brother and the Holding Company), Al Kooper (Blood, Sweat and Tears), John Sebastian (Lovin' Spoonful) and Graham Nash (Hollies) all split from their respective bands. In an end-of-year review for *Melody Maker* of all this rock carnage, Chris Welch observed, 'Today's scene is moving away from permanent groups and more towards recognition for individual musicians. The trend is going more in the direction of the jazz scene where musicians just jam together as they please.' But, as he pointed out, this would only be possible for the 'extra-talented and financially endowed'. He mused on past super-sessions he had witnessed: 'One recalls the night Jimi Hendrix played "Auld Lang Syne" for half an hour last New Year's Eve and blew several minds.' But, he concluded, a rock scene based on jamming would be unsustainable – even the jazz greats who thrived on jamming did it after hours.

320

Philharmonic Hall, New York City, 28 November 1968

Jimi was an enthusiastic supporter of this trend, but was not so naive as to imagine he could just go out on stage in front of a paying concert audience for an hour or two of unstructured jamming. However, based on his shows at the Winterland in October, Jimi was moving inexorably as a live performer from entertainer to musician.

In concert, Jimi always had a sharply honed sense of the dramatic. As drummer with Soft Machine who toured with the band during 1968, Robert Wyatt had ample opportunity to assess the panoply of theatrical effects Jimi would employ:

> With Jimi it was a theatre piece . . . everything you would expect from the theatre – the drama, the pace, the variety, the build-ups and the drops. He was a master at organising a dramatic event. He wasn't indulgent. Actually he hated the boring bits. . . . he would keep things moving or changing or tighten them up to get the boring bits out. He was ruthless like that with his own material. Didn't let himself get away with anything. He wouldn't break that spell.

On 29 October 1968, a rather special version of 'Red House' was laid down at the T.T.G. Studios in Los Angeles. The song was recorded live with Jimi announcing against the rumble of drums and the swell of Hammond organ notes: "Bout this time, I'd like to present to you the Electric Church – Mitch Mitchell on drums, Buddy Miles on another set of drums, we got Noel Redding playing bass, we gotta whole lotta our friends – we got Lee Michaels on organ, have mercy. We're gonna have a jam right now, we feel very free about these things, we'd like for you all to have peace of mind, just dig the sounds, it's all freedom.'

This was one of the earliest references to Electric Church or Sky Church music. Never very specific terms, they were meant to indicate a loose communion of musicians who would ideally perform untrammelled by the constraints of rote renditions of hit songs. By conceiving this new incarnation for his music, Jimi was keeping faith with his philosophy of performance, a philosophy founded on rigorous self-assessment and commitment to change. The question was, could he take the audience, the management and the record companies with him?

T.T.G. Studios, Hollywood, October 1968

Eleven *Electric Church*

My music is my personal diary. A release of all my inner feelings, aggression, tenderness, sympathy, everything. (*Disc*, 22 March 1969)

Mike Jeffery was not a happy man. By January 1969, the press had got their teeth well into the story that the Experience would be splitting up and all interviews naturally focused on that one theme. The picture seemed confused – the press couldn't get a handle on the fact that Jimi, Noel and Mitch would still play together, but work with other people in between. Perhaps they didn't believe it either. *Disc and Music Echo* headlined its contribution of 11 January 'JIMI HENDRIX GROUP TO SPLIT – EVERY THREE MONTHS!' while referring to Noel elsewhere in the same issue as 'Ex-Hendrix Experience'. However, in *Melody Maker*'s issue of the same day, Chris Welch announced, 'SAVED! The Jimi Hendrix Experience are not breaking up!' For Mike, the picture seemed no less clear; the Jimi Hendrix Experience was his main source of income, there were gigs booked through the first half of 1969, and he was not about to see the band go the way of the other major acts who split in 1968.

Of course, he couldn't physically force them to perform, but the legal stranglehold he had on Jimi was just as effective via a complicated set of contracts signed during 1968 which meant that Mike owned Jimi lock, stock and barrel. Since the summer of 1968, Noel had been writing songs with Neil Landon, with whom Noel had played in the Loving Kind. Another member of that band drawn into this new venture, bass player Jimmy Leverton, recalled that originally Fat Mattress 'wasn't meant to be a band at all . . . just a one-off album', allowing Noel to record his own songs and get back to playing guitar, which he always preferred, to work off some of his current frustrations. However, the project developed to the point where in early 1969 Noel was demanding that Fat Mattress support the Experience as part of the deal whereby he carried on playing with Jimi. But in truth he had no more bargaining power than Jimi. As yet, no deal had been struck for the first Fat Mattress album, which was nearing completion at the turn of the year. And because contracts were often presented for signature when the band were stoned or drunk, dashing for a flight or at business meetings held in office hours when they should have been asleep, Noel could not be sure that somewhere along the line he hadn't signed something tying in any solo work to the current management. Mike agreed to having Noel's band on the tour because of the gimmick value, but just how much of a 'hold' Noel had over Mike on this point is debatable. The most important thing for Noel was to get his band up and running; in any game of bluff and counter-bluff with Mike the outcome was never in any doubt. Of course, avarice is not the sole prerogative of rock managers: the next set of US dates would make the Experience the highest-paid rock band in the world and it would take a great deal of courage to walk away voluntarily from that, whatever the provocations.

One point of dispute between Jimi on the one hand and Noel and Mitch on the other was the time spent in America. The band hadn't toured Britain in over a year and had played only one English gig during the whole of 1968. On this at least Jimi and Mike agreed. America was where the money was and, despite his love of London, Jimi never seemed that bothered about touring the rest of the country. Even so, 1969 started off in England with what became a famous live appearance on the *Lulu Show* on 4 January. Before the show, Chris Welch interviewed Jimi on the roof garden of the BBC. Jimi may have had a twinge of guilt about ignoring his British fans: 'He said, "I'll buy everyone a drink." . . . he was being very generous. I got the feeling he wanted to make up with the British press for things that had gone wrong.'

Later that day, Chris was with Noel and Mitch 'preparing' for the show within the hallowed walls of the British Broadcasting Corporation. 'Mitch and Noel had a little hash which they were trying to get together in the dressing-room and they dropped it down the plug-hole in the sink. One of the roadies with spanners and stuff pulled the pipes off the wall trying to get this bit of hash out.'

Jimi had two numbers to perform. After the first, 'Voodoo Child (slight return)', Lulu did the link to the next:

Jimi and Lulu at the Europa Hotel, London, 16 September 1967

Well, ladies and gentlemen, in case you didn't know, Jimi and the boys won in a big American magazine *Billboard* [massive feedback screech throws her right out] [laughs] the . . . er . . . group of the year. They're gonna sing for you right now the song that absolutely made them in this country – 'Hey Joe' – and I love to hear them sing it.

Jimi used a lot of tremolo arm in the intro which tended to put the guitar out of tune. By the time he started the song he was in trouble, staring hard at the strings. Then he hit a glorious bum note, and grinned hugely across to Mitch as he retuned the bottom string 'on the run'. After the solo, he turned again to Mitch shouting 'Hey hey', went to the mike and brought the song to an abrupt halt: 'We'd like to stop playing this rubbish and dedicate a song to the Cream, regardless of what kind of group they may be in – dedicate this to Eric Clapton, Ginger Baker and Jack Bruce.' They broke into 'Sunshine of Your Love', but it wasn't long before Jimi called out with a smile on his face, 'We're being put off the air'. The producer Stanley Dorfman, realising there was now no time for Lulu's last song and farewells, hopped up and down making slashing strokes across his throat. Jimi explained later, 'It was the same old thing with people telling us what to do. They wanted to make us play "Hey Joe". I was so uptight about it, so I caught Noel and Mitch's attention and we went into the other thing.'[1]

By now, Kathy Etchingham had set up a flat for her and Jimi. He sent over some money and they moved into 25 Brook Street in Mayfair, which Kathy decorated to her own taste, conferring with Jimi on the phone from time to time about colour schemes. Trixie Sullivan wrote to Mike on 10 January:

> Jimi is happy at the moment and in fact has not been out once since his return from America, except to go shopping. He arrived and instead of going to the hotel he went to the flat as he says to 'pick up some clothes', but I think he wanted to see how 'the land was lying'. It seems that Kathy cooked a meal for him, and I know she cleaned the flat so thoroughly that he decided to stay. Kathy says he goes to bed at 11.30 and gets up every morning at 10.30 and looks better than he has ever done. Domestication seems to suit him for the moment. You never know how long it will last.

The flat turned out to be the former residence of George Frederick Handel. Jimi was mightily impressed over this, declaring he would compose here as Handel had done and ordering Kathy out to buy up all Handel's work on LP. In one respect, Handel was the Hendrix of his day – he once attracted an audience of 12,000 just to see a rehearsal in Vauxhall Gardens. Music students would come to visit the flat only to be struck dumb when they found their tour guide to be none other than Jimi Hendrix. When Jimi was away, Kathy shared the flat with singer Madeline Bell and Angie Burdon.

Jimi conducted all his main interviews from the flat during January – and now there was no Chas to hustle Kathy out of the room in case any reporter thought Jimi had a (gasp!) girlfriend. Not that Jimi made any particular allowances for her presence. He told one interviewer, '"You know what really turns me on about London, just watching the girls go by – it's a fantastic city for girl-watchers. They're all so beautiful and so many different nationalities." Kathy was not exactly looking too knocked out with some of the conversation. Jimi gave her a dashing smile and a mumbled apology.'[2]

Invariably Jimi tolerated the stupid questions reporters continued to throw at him, but from time to time he let some of his irritation show through. *Eye* magazine tried to corner Jimi on the 'crucial' issue of fashion – 'Where is fashion going?' asked the interviewer earnestly. Replied Jimi, 'I don't know where fashion is going. I don't care really. Maybe people will wear different colored sheets, the way they used to wear them in olden days. And don't ask me those silly questions!'[3]

In contrast, Tony Norman, who spoke to Jimi for *Top Pops* at the BBC on the day of the Lulu show, gave him the chance to outline some of his plans for the future.

THE FIRST RAYS OF THE NEW RISING SUN

. . . I asked him how he felt about Noel recording with a group he has formed called Fat Mattress. I had heard rumours that Noel was likely to leave the Experience in the coming autumn. Jimi denied this, saying:

'All three of us have individual interests. We work together in the Experience, but we are not tied down to that alone.

'The scene is developing along the line of jazz where cats from different bands always jam together. We are like a band of gypsies who can roam free and do what we want.'

Jimi dismissed *Electric Ladyland* as a thing of the past and announced two forthcoming albums – the first called *Little Band of Gypsies* and the second *First Rays of the New Rising Sun*.

'While I was in America, I went through periods of deep depression seeing the way the country was becoming split strictly in half. Their life is based on material things. The dollar is their God. The people are like pelicans who all think the same. There is no such thing as a colour problem. It is a weapon for the negative forces who are trying to destroy the country. . . . They are striving for dead, useless things, like sending guys round the moon.

'One day I saw a soldier in the street and said, "Hey, how are you?" He just stared at me and said, "Hey, man, are you for real?" He was bringing himself down because he was so full of hate. With enough love and faith these people can find themselves again.

'The Americans are looking for a leader in their music. *First Rays of the New Rising Sun* will be about what we have seen. If you give deeper thoughts in your music then the masses will buy them.

'Life must be positive . . . if your life means something then happiness will follow. Everyone has something to give. Your body is as unimportant as one fish in the sea compared with your soul. I believe you live and live again until you have got all the evil and hatred out of the soul.'

Tony Norman compared Jimi to 'an apostle', saying 'The youth of the world knows Hendrix from the outside, but the philosophy which burns within his soul is of far greater importance to us all.'[4]

Jimi had hardly set foot in his new flat when he was off again to fulfil some outstanding European dates. He returned to Gothenburg on 8 January to play a lacklustre show at the Lorensburg Cirkus. They did a new version of the slow blues number 'Getting My Heart Back Together Again' (also known as 'Hear My Train A'Comin''), but whatever Jimi put into this show, it wasn't his heart. Chas happened to be there with his Swedish wife, Lotte. Backstage, Jimi actually asked Chas to take over management of the band – one of a number of occasions when Jimi asked and Chas said 'No.' To Chas, the band were beginning to sound like three soloists rather than a cohesive unit. 'It was a dire concert. You could just see there was trouble with the band. There was friction, it wasn't together, it just didn't work.' But more than that, he knew better than most how impossible it would be for Jimi to break free from Mike.

The first show of the next night in Stockholm was pretty much the same. The MC came on to announce, 'Time now for a little bit of Electric Church music – yeah, that's how the band like to call their music. And the band – THE JIMI HENDRIX EXPERIENCE!'

But there wasn't anything very sanctified about that first show. The equipment was hopeless from the start and, consequently, a Swedish TV tape shows Jimi looking very sullen and uninterested: 'Hello, how y'all doin'? I'd like to dedicate this show to the American deserters society.' He does a quick burst of 'Taps' and then back to the mike:

Also I'd like to dedicate this show to Eva, who keeps sendin' roses, but we never seen her before. She's a goddess from Asgard.
    We're gonna play nothin' but 'oldies but baddies' tonight, because, you know, we haven't played together in about six weeks, so we're just gonna jam tonight – see what happens. Hope you don't mind – just gonna mess around and see what happens – [off mike] you wouldn't know the difference anyway.

Konserthuset, Stockholm, 9 January 1969

Via a rather messy intro, they stumble into 'Killin' Floor'. The playing is desultory and casual. When Jimi was in this sort of mood, the lyrics were all but ignored – half lines, half verses, verses missed altogether or he didn't sing at all, although he does get the whole lyric out on this occasion. Jimi musters a wry joke: 'Like to do a thing that was recorded in 1733 in the Benjamin Franklin studio – a thing called "Spanish Castle Magic".'

The song and 'Fire' which follows are both delivered flat, fast and joyless. Jimi goes straight into 'Hey Joe' in the wrong key, goes up centre stage to adjust the amps for the nth time, and saunters back to the mike: 'We had a request to do a thing called "All Along the Watchtower", but I forgot the words, so we won't do that one. We've never played that before in person – we only recorded it. I really am sorry.'

He announces 'Voodoo Child (slight return)' instead. Noel, his perm now straightened to fall long over his shoulders, floppy hat pulled over his eyes, throws in a dedication to the support act, a Swedish band called the Outsiders. Jimi turns and asks for a quick confirmation of the song. As a joke, Noel quietly scat sings the opening wah-wah break – nah na nah nah na na nah na nah, nah na na nah – as if to say 'It goes like this, Jimi, remember?' Jimi doesn't laugh.

This song and 'Sunshine' which closes the show are really just jams with a noodling bass solo in each thrown in by Noel to cover for Jimi when he stopped playing. Mitch throughout tries to keep things afloat with judicious pounding of his double bass drum Ludwig kit, but his gratuitous solo during 'Voodoo Child' about sums up the show.

The penultimate song is 'Red House', for which Jimi switches from a black and white Strat to a white Gibson and then proceeds to muff the beginning. He recovers to play some of his finest stuff in the show, even if it is tossed off with disdainful ease.

Sixties bands seemed to be pathologically incapable of working out how they would end a song. The best cop-out was to slow right down until you stopped. Which was how 'Sunshine' and this show finished.

But if the quality of the performances could differ from night to night, they could also vary enormously between the first and second shows. By comparison, the second show that night in Stockholm was a revelation.

'Okay, Mitch,' signals Jimi.

Mitch thunders the unmistakable Cherokee intro to 'I Don't Live Today' and the band take off, not this time three disconsolate soloists, but the synchronised flying wedge of the old days. As the song goes into double time, Jimi bends strings right off the fretboard, stretching the surface tension of the music to its limits without letting it break up altogether.

'I'd like to warn you now – it's gonna be a bit loud. A tiny bit loud because these are English amps and we're in Sweden and the electricity scene is not working out with this Australian fuzz-tone and this American guitar.'

And so it went on – fending off the usual audience idiot shouting 'Wild Thing' between every song. 'You're livin' in the past' and 'Same to you, brother' responds Jimi – improvising lyrics and throwing bits of 'I Feel Fine' and 'Daytripper' during 'Hey Joe'. 'Let's do "Johnny B. Goode"!' shouts Noel to Jimi across the stage. Jimi laughs:

> What do we do next? Oh yeah, I'll tell you what we do. We got
> this LP out called *Electric Ladyland* and there's only one song that we
> remember from it because, I dunno, it's like a diary all these LPs. That's
> why we don't necessarily do them on stage all the time. We just like to
> jam on stage. . . . I'd like to dedicate this song to all those people who
> can actually feel and think for themselves and feel free for themselves
> – a thing called 'Voodoo Child (slight return)'.

Jimi really gets into this – despite the similarity of the shows from one gig to the next, no song is ever played the same way twice. Here, Mitch and Noel drop out as Jimi does a sweet and simple country-blues solo peppered with featherlight tremolo effects. They follow this with one of the best versions of 'Sunshine of Your Love' ever captured on tape, recorded by Swedish radio.

These two shows highlighted the hit-and-miss nature of a Jimi Hendrix concert – one audience transported, the other given a rough deal. How a gig would go was now complicated by Jimi's insistence that most of the songs should be vehicles for jamming and improvisation rather than formula renditions of the records (which he rarely did anyway). Even more so did Jimi have to be on the top of his form for a successful gig – although as he said from the stage earlier that night – nobody seemed to know good from bad. And that hurt most of all.

Eva, whom he mentioned during the first show, was a student named Eva Sundqvist. She had first met Jimi in May 1967 in Stockholm. He was wandering around the streets lost; as she stepped off a tram, he stopped her to ask the way. She later recognised his face on an album cover and thereafter she sent him roses and letters. On 8 January 1968, she met him backstage again in Stockholm and they went off to a party together. Now a year later they met again after the concert and went back to Jimi's hotel. She later testified to a paternity-suit hearing in Sweden that in the hotel room around 5.30 a.m. Jimi became her first lover; she later discovered she was pregnant. She wrote to Jimi in London, but got no reply.

Rheinhalle, Dusseldorf, W. Germany, 12 January 1969

After a concert in Copenhagen, the Experience flew to Germany. Sitting in the auditorium for the second show in Dusseldorf was a young ice-skating teacher from a wealthy German family, Monika Dannemann. She had first heard Jimi on the pirate Radio Caroline and immediately fell in love with the music, although she wasn't too impressed with Jimi the person from what she had read about his violent stage act, his promiscuity and drug-taking. She was staying in Düsseldorf when it

333

was announced that Jimi would be playing there on 12 January. Monika knew a bunch of people from a local discotheque; one of them, who claimed he'd met Noel in Spain, said he would try to get the band down to the disco after the concert so they could take pictures of them. As the only person with access to a camera sporting a flash attachment, Monika was reluctantly roped into this scheme.

Sitting in the Rheinhalle with her brother waiting for the show to start, Monika was surprised to be surrounded by a cacophony of whistling and stamping as the audience grew impatient. She had no idea the band was so popular. Monika was awestruck when Jimi finally walked on to the stage, and almost in spite of herself she couldn't take her eyes off him.

The band did go to the disco afterwards, but Monika didn't want to be part of any 'star trip', so she didn't join in, although she did turn up at Jimi's hotel the following day with her camera. Jimi came into the hotel bar, made a bee-line for Monika, a classically beautiful Teutonic blonde with long hair and a sylph-like figure, and engaged her in gentle, whispered conversation to the exclusion of everybody else. For her part, Monika remained cool, still influenced by what she had read, imagining that Jimi was sizing her up for a trip to the bedroom.

But as the conversation wore on, with Jimi asking about her life, what she did, her likes and dislikes and so on, Monika concluded that she had misjudged him. From her gothic-style cottage on the south coast of England, where she now spends much of her time painting, including many superb images of Jimi, Monika recalled, 'We didn't stop talking for over an hour until they had to leave for Cologne, the next concert. . . . I changed my mind about him. I realised he was a very gentle, kind person, very considerate and not what you would imagine a rock star to be like. So when he asked me to come to Cologne, I agreed. I followed him later in my car. And on the way there I realised I had fallen in love with him.'

Monika met up with Jimi at the Dom Hotel and accompanied him as he was driven to the Sporthalle. Pleased though she was to be with him, Monika was still very wary, believing that Jimi would want her in bed at the first opportunity. She confided her fears to him, but he quietly reassured her that he would never force himself on her and begged her to stay.

Monika stayed, watched the show from the side of the stage and left with Jimi in his car.

The band, Monika, Gerry and his girlfriend plus two of the disco crowd went off to a club where, unusually, Jimi, Noel and Mitch jammed alone together, Jimi taking over on bass with Noel on lead, before moving on to a Chinese restaurant. Eventually they went back to the hotel. After a while, Monika was alone with Jimi. They had a long discussion about drugs. Jimi was pleased that Monika didn't do drugs and himself railed against the use of heroin as a destroyer of the human spirit while expressing sadness that everyone thought he was a rabid junkie, which meant body searches in and out of every airport. Next day, Monika went home while Jimi moved on to Münster for a concert at the Halle Münsterland. She arrived about halfway through the show, drove back to Cologne with him afterwards and they eventually parted with Jimi asking Monika to come to London at the end of February for a concert at the Royal Albert Hall.

Backstage at the Sportpalast, Berlin, 23 January. The mood is light-hearted and jokey.

'Hello, Eric', says Noel, greeting roadie Eric Barrett, who comes into the dressing-room to bring the good news:

'I don't believe this place – there's millions of bloody rockers, millions of them. They couldn't get them to sit down, they're all round the pitch.'

Eric is followed in by road manager Gerry Stickells: 'When the Mothers [of Invention] were here, they were all playing away and like at the end the bass player would stop and clear all the bass gear into the truck. The drummer's still playing away and all the others had finished and gone up the stairs. He just ran!'

'It was Jimmy Black,' says Noel. 'He told me, he said he almost got killed.'

'What is that?' says Jimi to Trixie Sullivan, who is there because the promoter is paying her hotel bill.

'Beautiful stuff,' she says.

Eric chimes in: 'Gimme some.'

'Put your head back then.'

'Don't bust anything', laughs Jimi, who is actually more interested in the booze. 'Hey, is there anything we can get to drink?'

'Lots of booze', says Eric, 'beer in the beer barrel.' And he adds, 'You should do "Hey Joe" and "Boris the Spider" and get the hell out of there.'

The security confirms that trouble is anticipated as Trixie finds out: 'I just walked in the wrong place. I thought it was the entrance to the

Monika Dannemann

stage. There was this tiny box of a room and all these policemen are in there. Do "Foxy Lady" and run.'

Gerry Stickells comes back in: 'Three or four minutes. And for Christ's sake get off that stage a bit quick.'

'Somebody give me a cigarette,' mutters Noel.

Jimi wants to know more. 'What have they been doing, though?'

'They are violently excitable', says Gerry. 'They'll smash everything up – that type you know.' Apparently, the boisterous German bikers had been throwing fireworks. 'The Eire Apparent guitarist [Mick Cox] was playing away, all of a sudden one went bang. He let go of his guitar and everything. Thought he'd been shot!' Gerry recalls the incident with relish and everyone is falling about.

Just then Mick Cox himself appears outside the dressing-room and hears Gerry talking about his misfortune. 'You, was it!' he roars. 'Fuckin' hooligan, Stickells. You tryin' to scare the fuck out of me?'

'No, no, it wasn't me. It was the audience.'

Mick is not convinced. 'I wouldn't put it fuckin' past you, Stickells.'

Then Gerry announces, 'The Albert Hall concerts are both sold out.'

'Already?' say Noel and Trixie in unison.

Jimi cuts in with an impression of his father's drawl: 'We'll have a tour of the Albert Hall.'

Noel calculates. 'That's a Tuesday. Imagine what we'd have done on a weekend. Why don't you get a weekend?' he asks Gerry.

But, as Trixie rightly points out, a sell-out is a sell-out. 'The thing is, you couldn't sell out more than you're selling now.'

Gerry asks if everyone is ready. Noel goes off to the toilet.

'What's that?' says Jimi.

Gerry replies, 'He's having another wee.'

A mass chorus of 'We'll Meet Again' breaks out, dies down and a lone voice strikes up with 'So You Wanna Be a Rock 'n' Roll Star?' Jimi and Gerry get to talking about Jimi's guitars. 'Do you wanna take that one on or you just gonna play with one tonight?'

Jimi considers. 'No, no . . . yeah, I hope I just don't break anything.'

'I'll change a string for you, don't worry . . . Right I'm just gonna see if they're ready.' They are.

Jimi's at the mike: 'Dedicate this to anybody . . . let me tell this to your old lady or either . . . let me tell it to your fire . . .' The Jimi Hendrix Experience is off and flying. But as the last feedback screams of 'Purple Haze' still hang in the air and with the police by now surrounding the stage, the band head for the escape route already worked out by Gerry. Fast.

From the end of January to the beginning of the US tour in mid-April, the Jimi Hendrix Experience was put on ice. There wasn't a venue in Europe, let alone England, which could afford the band now. Also there seemed little point in touring outside America to sell more records because Track and Polydor were holding up all the royalty payments pending the outcome of Ed Chalpin's lawsuit against them. Jimi went back to America for a few days, while Noel took up Mike Jeffery's offer of a flat for some R&R in Spain.

Together again in London during February, there were some recording sessions at Olympic which produced little apart from the first recording of a song Jimi had been working on for many months

I use to live ~~though~~ in a room
full of mirrors — All I see
was me — Repeat
Well I ~~take~~ can't stand it
no more — So I smash the mirror
and set me free —
~~Broke~~ ~~I use to live in a room~~
~~full of mirrors~~

Broken glass all on the floor
Broken Glass in my head — ~~repeat~~
Broken Glass come ~~cut~~ through my
~~~~ dreams fall and cut me
in my bed —

I find a ~~girl~~ sweet little girl
But she say "goodbye, you
don't need me, Repeat
So I go to Detroit to find
an angel and she gives ~~her~~
~~Living~~ ~~of love~~ ~~for~~ ~~Come~~ me her wings
~~the~~ ~~throne~~ ~~free~~ ~~and sets I~~ ~~fly I go~~
it and sets me free.
I use to live in ze room of
mirrors : And I just might

and which he never really finished to his satisfaction, 'Room Full of Mirrors'. The lyric reproduced on pages 338–9 was from an early draft in 1968, but the theme remained the same – a discovery of the world beyond the limited visions of self-centredness.

Noel finished off the Fat Mattress album at Pye, but most of the action was down at the Speakeasy club, jamming with anybody who came in – Dave Mason, Jim Capaldi, Alan Price and Billy Preston, and a plus for Jimi at Ronnie Scott's jazz club, Roland Kirk.

Mike Jeffery was now justifiably only interested in playing prestigious venues for large amounts of money. If they were going to play England at all to assuage a guilty conscience, the obvious choice was the Royal Albert Hall. The concert had been fixed for 18 February, but with all 4500 tickets going within three hours of the box office opening, another was arranged for the 24th.

It was an important gig for the band, their first English show in over six months, and they actually rehearsed for it. Always a rarity, Experience rehearsals were now almost non-existent because Jimi wanted show time to be more free-form. If all he was going to do was use the old songs as jump-off points for jamming, there wasn't much point in rehearsing. It meant that new songs were introduced into the set only gradually whereas if he had held rehearsals, Jimi perhaps might have been able to include new songs more regularly and keep the stage performances fresher, if only for his own enjoyment. But this would only have worked if the band had been putting out new records, so the fans and critics could hear the new material first. Getting across in concert with previously unheard songs was difficult for any band. The trouble was, there were no albums in the pipeline.

Not really a matter of choice, the rehearsal was a necessity, as they hadn't played together for nearly a month, but behind the scenes all was not well. Like any football team, a band needs psyching up for a big gig and Mike Jeffery was not the man for the job. Despite the formal dissolution of his partnership with Mike, Chas was still involved with the band and its individual members. Remember that the buy-out agreement included vague references to 'future considerations' which meant that Chas had some kind of investment in keeping the band together. He also wanted to manage Fat Mattress. Jimi asked Chas to come down and help get things moving.

Afternoon rehearsals, Royal Albert Hall, London, 24 February 1969

When I was a little boy, I believed that if you put a tooth under your pillow, a fairy would come in the night and take away the tooth and leave a dime. Now, I believe in myself more than anything. And, I suppose in a way, that's also believing in God. If there is a God and He made you, then if you believe in yourself, you're also believing in Him. So I think everybody should believe in himself. That doesn't mean you've got to believe in heaven and hell and all that stuff. But it does mean that what you are and what you do is your religion. I can't express myself in easy conversation – the words just don't come out right. But when I get up on stage – well, that's my whole life. *That's* my religion. My music *is* electric church music, if by 'church' you mean 'religion'. I am electric religion. (Interview, London 1969, printed in Royal Albert Hall concert programme notes)

Unfortunately, Jimi wasn't on form for either show. For the first one, Trixie Sullivan virtually had to push him out on to the stage and the playing was rather subdued. If anything, the second concert, on the 24th, was worse. Fat Mattress made their debut that night – Noel had got so drunk with the anxiety of it all that he fell off the stage, calling out 'Carry on, lads' as he disappeared into the orchestra pit. There was a nice touch when some young kids came out on stage to shake Jimi's hand. But only Elmore James' slow blues, 'Bleeding Heart', 'Red House', 'Stone Free', 'Foxy Lady' and a loose shuffle jam version of 'Room Full of Mirrors', with Chris Wood from Traffic and Dave Mason who had just left the band plus Rocky Dzidzournu, were really up to scratch. Mason claims that he and Jimi had talked about him joining the Experience. 'When I left Traffic I was gonna join the band on bass, but that got kinda squashed by Chas Chandler and Mike Jeffery.' Afterward's Noel's mother Margaret went backstage to the dressing-room: '[Jimi] was sitting right against the wall at the end with his eyes shut. I took out my handkerchief and wiped his forehead. He opened his eyes, looked up and said, "Oh, it's you. Could you check on my white guitar?"'

Jimi and Kathy's flat served as Jimi's press office and the time off before America gave journalists time to catch up with him and sample his uncompromising attitude to music. Jimi was also moving into an introspective phase of reassessment. It promised to be a challenging and difficult period as he would be faced by the combined weight of an audience, a management and a set of record companies, united in a desire to keep things as they were. In the broadest sense of the word,

Afternoon rehearsals, Royal Albert Hall, London, 24 February 1969

Royal Albert Hall, London, 24 February 1969

Jimi was a religious person and during this time his belief in *a* god, some kind of Supreme Being that might guide him, began to surface.

IT'S HOW YOU FEEL
I dream about having our own show where we would have all contemporary artists as guest stars. Everybody seems to be busy showing what polished performers they are and that means nothing these days. It's how you feel about what you are doing that matters.

Say, wouldn't it be great to take over the studios like they do in Cuba. We'd call it 'The Jimi Hendrix Show – Or Else'!
A REAL HANG UP
You have to make people identify with the music. You make a record

in the hope that the public may want to buy it, so you have to make it presentable in some way. They have to have an identification mark.

The trouble is that a single has to be under six minutes – it used to be under three which was a real hang up. It's like you used to be able to give them just one page of a book, now you can give them two or three pages – but never the whole book.

The music is what matters. If an audience are really digging you on a show then naturally you get excited and it helps. But a bad audience doesn't really bother me because then it is a practice session, a chance to get things together.

FRINGE BENEFIT

I always enjoy playing whether it's before ten people or 10,000. And I don't even care if they boo, as long as it isn't out of key.

I don't try to move an audience – it's up to them what they get from the music. If they have paid to see us then we are going to do our thing. If we add a bit of the trampoline side of entertainment then that is a fringe benefit, but we are there to play music. If we stand up there all night and play our best and they don't dig it, they don't dig it, and that's all there is to it.

SPIRITUAL MUSIC

Maybe a lyric has only five words and the music takes care of the rest. I don't mean my lyrics to be clever. What I want is for people to listen to the music and words together as one thing.

Generally I don't do other people's songs unless they really say something to me.

If you say you are playing electric church music people go 'gasp, gasp' or 'exclaim, exclaim'. The word church is too identified with religion, and music is my religion. Jesus shouldn't have died so early and then he could have got twice as much across. They killed him and then twisted so many of the best things he said. Human hands started messing it all up and now so much of religion is hogwash.[5]

Jane de Mendelssohn, whose husband Felix had once been editor of Britain's most famous underground newspaper *International Times*, was sent by the paper to interview Jimi.

I think at the beginning I was quite over-awed by him. I was very surprised that, when I got to his flat in Mayfair, he opened the door in the nude. I followed his naked torso up the stairs to the first floor. As soon as he got into the room, he got into bed. Quite a strange way to start an interview with a famous pop star – or anyone else come to that!

Most of the interview was conducted with Jimi in bed and me sitting on the side of the bed. And on his bedside table was the biggest collection of alcohol and drugs, I mean there were three different types of hash, grass, amyl nitrates, pills and lots of different kinds of bourbon and whisky. We just helped ourselves.

He was constantly smoking joints and we were both drinking. . . . I had much less than he did because I wanted to keep the interview together. But also I wanted to get to some level where I could communicate with him. Then at one point he offered me some amyl nitrate and we both went out of our skulls. I remember we finished off the interview in the early evening, but we hadn't finished, so he invited me back the next day and we started the whole thing all over again.

The reason I did interviews at all was that I'm interested in what makes people tick. I get the feeling he was quite insecure. . . . when I asked him about his family he didn't want to talk about it. All the alcohol and drugs were some kind of compensation. Also it was quite clear all along that if I wanted to go to bed with him, I could have just got inside. He never touched me, but it was 'understood', free and easy. But I didn't – it was a question of pride, I didn't want to be seen as a groupie. . . . I came away feeling I'd met somebody.

'Do you get hustled a lot by people wanting bread and banging on your door?'

'Oh, constantly, yeah. I try to treat everyone fairly, but if I did I wouldn't be able to buy another guitar. So therefore I don't go around too much, except when I find a certain little scene going. . . . I stay in bed most of the time or go to the park or somewhere. That's where I write some of my best songs, in bed, just laying there. I was laying there thinking of some when you came in.'

'You've got a reputation for being very moody. I was almost afraid to come.'

'Moody? Oh, that's silly. . . . That's what you're supposed to think. . . . The Establishment, they project a certain image and if it works, they have it made. They knock down somebody else for instance, like saying I'm moody or so and so is evil or saying blah blah woof woof is a maniac or something, so that everybody gets scared to know me. So that's part of the Establishment's games.'

'You were quoted in the *Sunday Mirror* as saying that it was time for a change from the pretty songs the Beatles made, time for something else.'

'Ah, I don't know if I said that. Which paper is that in? *Sunday Mirror*. Well, most of those papers are all screwed up anyway. They come over here and they do their interviews, we turn the cats on, you know, give 'em wine and all that, and they go back and they're so stoned, they don't know what they are writing about. No, I didn't say nothing like that. I wouldn't, there's no reason to.

'If I wasn't a guitar player, I would probably be in jail, 'cos like I get very stubborn with the police. I used to get into arguments with them millions of times, they used to tell me to be quiet and I just *can't* be

346

quiet, there's no reason to be especially if you have something to say. So I'd probably wind up getting killed. But I have to feel those things. I hear about violence and all that, but really for me to say anything about that . . . I can't just jump on the bandwagon just because it might be happening today.'

'It was surprisingly easy to get an interview with you. I mean if you want one with Paul McCartney, it can take weeks to set up.'

'Well, maybe 'cos I'm not Paul McCartney. You get a lot of . . . oh no, I shouldn't say that.'

'Why not?'

'There's a lot of things I shouldn't say . . .'

'Do you sit down and think "I want to say this to them" and then compose the song around what you want to say?'

'Yeah, definitely. . . . A lot of songs are fantasy-type songs so that people think you don't know what you are talking about at all, but it all depends on what the track before and after might have been. Like you might tell them something kinda hard, but you don't want to be a completely hard character in their minds and be known for all that, 'cos there's other sides of you and sometimes they leak on to the record too . . . that's where the fantasy songs come in. Like for instance "1983" – that's something to keep your mind off what's happening today, but not necessarily completely hiding away from it like some people might do, with certain drugs and so forth. . . .'

'But is this awareness actually conscious when you write the song, or do you write it, listen to it and then realise what motivates you afterwards?'

'Well, honest to God truth, on the first LP, I didn't know what I was writing about then. Most of the songs like "Purple Haze" and "Wind Cries Mary" were about ten pages long, but then we're restricted to a certain time limit, so I had to break them all down, so once I'd broken the songs down, I didn't know whether they were going to be understood or not. Maybe some of the meanings got lost, by breaking them down, which I never do any more.

'I've had no time off to myself since I've been in this scene . . . and anything that doesn't have to do with music, I don't think about too much. People just make me so uptight sometimes, but I can't really let it show all the time, because it's not really a good influence on anybody else. . . . Oh no, don't take any pictures now 'cos my hair's all messed up. I just hate pictures. People are always saying "D'you remember that picture that was in so-and-so" and I say "No, I don't fuckin' remember it." . . . Most people would like to retire and just disappear from the scene which I'd *love* to do, but then there's still things I'd like to say. I wish it wasn't so important to me. I wish I could just turn my mind off. . . . But there's so much rubbish going by and for us trying to do our thing, there's so much rubbish said about us. I'd like to get things straight in this interview. I spend most of my time writing songs and so forth and not making too much contact with people 'cos they don't know how to act. . . .'

347

'And do you believe you can change anything, anybody?'

'Well, the idea is trying. But I'm just gonna do it and if it works, great!'

'It's all really down to your music, isn't it?'

'Yeah, that's it, that's what we're talking about. Music. Talking isn't really my scene. Playing is. There's certain people on this earth that have the power to do different things, for instance in the Black Power Movement, they're using it wrongly. . . . Protest is over with. It's the solutions everyone wants now, not just protest. The Beatles could do it, they could turn the world around, or at least attempt to. But you see it might make them a little more uncomfortable in their position. But me, I don't care about my position. What I have to say I'd be glad to say it. You see it comes out in my music and then you have to go through scenes like releasing an LP and you can't release one every month, and you can't do this and you can't do that. And all the public image bit. . . . You find yourself almost running away. You have to grab hold of yourself. People, they don't give me any inspiration except bad inspiration, to write songs like "Crosstown Traffic" . . . 'cos that's the way they put themselves in front of me, the way they present themselves. . . .'6

Jimi and Mitch were back in the States by 13 March, with Noel following a week later, to get ready for the US tour. Jimi got straight into recording sessions at the Record Plant. On 25 March he played there with John McLaughlin and bassist Dave Holland, who made vital contributions to Miles Davis' seminal albums *Bitches Brew* and *In a Silent Way*, both released that year. In a radio interview, McLaughlin recalled, 'We played one night, just a jam session, from two until eight in the morning.' Apart from the jam with Roland Kirk, this was Jimi's first blow with jazz musicians, who had a very different approach to the rock music. Already with a keen appreciation of the subtleties of jazz and always anxious to expand his musical vocabulary, Jimi's session with McLaughlin and Holland gave him the taste for further experimentation.

They were much more atuned to spontaneity in music; Davis' 'Kind of Blue', possibly one of the greatest jazz albums ever made, came out of first-take improvisations on sketches that Miles had put to his musicians only moments before the recording. In contrast, there was a deep appreciation of the different shades and textural potentials of the multiple take: 'Charlie Parker's alternative takes for Savoy have come to be as treasured for their endless invention as Picasso's studies and series.'7 Given how much of Jimi's studio work was committed to tape and given how much of it still exists, it is a shame that many of the multiple versions of songs that Jimi performed remain unreleased. Writers' first drafts usually end up in the bin and few would want such drafts published. Equally true is that Jimi was a perfectionist and might not have wished alternative takes released. Even so much of this material remains vastly superior to much else that has been peddled under Jimi's name and offers as instructive an insight into the creative process as any artist's preliminary sketches.

Royal Albert Hall, London, 24 February 1969

Studio A at the Record Plant, 7 April. Jimi is in with Mitch and Noel. He has decided he wants to re-record 'Stone Free'. *Zygote* magazine has sent Doc Storch for a rare inside view of a Jimi Hendrix recording session: 'Jimi Hendrix dry humps his guitar to an earsplitting climax. In the confusion of overgrown Marshall guitar amps and mike booms, Hendrix's figure is almost lost. In the control room this evening are the usual cadre of hangers-on, groupies, sycophants and musicians.'

349

Using a sixteen-track studio for jamming, as Jimi does, works out to be horrendously expensive; after midnight it's $160 a hour with tape at $120 a roll. When Jimi went into a studio, he could easily leave $2500 behind.

'The session is booked for eight o'clock. In accordance with time-honoured custom, the set-up crew [Eric Barrett and probably John "Upsey" Downing] starts to arrive with the equipment at ten or so, and by midnight the prefatory honks, squeaks and buzzes are over with. The equipment men with their own desultory jokes check out the drums (if Mitch is working) and Hendrix's thirteen guitars, most of which are always at a session. They stack spare Marshall amps along the wall and fiddle with adaptors to permit the British equipment to mate with American plugs.'

Jimi turns up with a small army of women in tow including Devon. In a typical piece of groupie power-play, she heads straight for the control room to claim a seat next to the engineer Gary Kellgren. A guy named Mark appears claiming to be Jimi's 'dealer' and proceeds to lay out the evening's supply of grass and cocaine.

Jimi and Gary are laughing and joking in the control room. Gary leans forwards and flicks the switch on the talk-back mike, so his voice comes over the speakers. 'Good evening, ladies and gentlemen, and welcome to the Record Plant banana boat, freak show and travelling blues band.' Imagining some slight in this comment and eager to show how influential she is, Devon snarls at Gary, 'Do you like your job?' 'No,' says Gary and leaves her totally nonplussed.

Jimi signals it's time to get moving: 'Okay, let's lay it down.' About a third of the way through the song, Jimi calls time-out and goes off to the control room to confer with Gary. Everyone reaches for beer and cigarettes while the groupies subtly jostle one another for pole position near Jimi's chair ready for the next time he needs to come for a conference.

Back out in the studio, they start again, only for the music to come to a grinding halt as a woman appears next to Jimi, hanging drunkenly round his neck. They speak inaudible words near Jimi's mike; Gary considers turning the mike up so everyone can hear what's going on, but thinks better of it. Eric and two other women step forward and lead her out to a couch in the foyer. She is obviously in a bad way – streaked make-up, puffy eyes and torn velvet dress. Earlier on she had fallen down the steps of the Scene and hit her head on the swing doors. She is now slumped semi-conscious on the couch.

Back in the studio everyone is in the control room listening to the takes. Jimi is telling Gary to edit a sixteen-track tape, a very tricky operation where it would be very easy to ruin the master. 'Look, man,' says Jimi, 'just cut it right where I say . . . listen now. Right there. Stop. That's it. Now run ahead to that next part we did and where the drum goes ch-boom, ch-boom, cut it again and put the end of the first part on there.' Gary looks at Jimi as if he is mad, but does it anyway. Only Jimi is not surprised when the playback is smooth with no hint of any 'cut and paste' work.

They start off again on another take, but Mitch and Noel are growing restless. Jimi takes a break, but on his return meets them on their way out. 'Where are you going? I want to know.'

'Man, we've done that number to death right into the ground,' says Mitch and to Storch on the way out he adds, 'But Jimi will keep going back and back over it forever and it'll never get any better than it is now, man, and that's what's wrong with this group.' But Jimi didn't do these endless retakes because of mistakes, but because he was aiming for the sound he heard in his head. Trouble was that nobody else could hear it, so they didn't know what they were striving for. Jimi couldn't explain it, he just knew that when it was right he would know it. The result was deadlock and frustration for everybody.

Jimi stayed on, laying down multiple guitar tracks and listening to the takes over and over again, hoping that Mitch and Noel would come back. They didn't. Jimi gave up around 6 a.m. gathered up his sheafs of notes into his fringed shoulder-bag, grabbed his coat and left, ignoring the girl and leaving the groupies to slink off into the dawn from whence they came.

Mark the dealer gives his own view on why a woman would follow Jimi probably in the sure knowledge of rejection: 'She followed him because she wants what he has inside, the thing he uses to make music. It's the same reason all these chicks follow him around. And they know he'll leave them, he says so and he's not kidding.' Standing over the girl he adds, 'She'd follow him into hell if she thought he'd look after her.'

Storch concludes that perhaps in some respect, Jimi and the groupies are similar. Jimi has this vision of a song which he can't make manifest in the real world of perceived sound. The groupies are living a similar unreality by hoping that Jimi Hendrix will come and sweep them off their feet and declare his faithful and undying love. Neither can understand why they live in pain so much of the time.

The 1969 US tour started on 11 April in Raleigh, North Carolina where Fat Mattress made their US debut. That Jimi didn't want to do the tour at all was clearly shown by his total lethargy when interviewed by a reporter from *Distant Drummer* in Philadelphia prior to what was only the second date on the schedule. Asked if he minded photos being taken, Jimi replied listlessly, 'No, the same shit happens every day, so fuck it.' The interviewer, John Lombardi, did a good job of asking Jimi just about every question likely to get him annoyed, starting with 'why did you cut your hair?' 'I cut it short in protest. There are too many long-haired people running around whose heads aren't anywhere. But I think I'm gonna let it grow again.'

Lombardi suggested that Jimi's success was more due to what he represented (making reference to the cover of *Electric Ladyland*) rather than the music.

'I don't consider myself a success. I haven't even started yet. The scene puts you through a lot of changes . . . you get involved in images. I didn't have nothing to do with that stupid LP cover they released and I don't even want to talk about it . . . it's mostly all bullshit.'

'Well, what about your act on stage? Setting the guitar on fire, going through the motions of intercourse?'

'We did those things mostly because they used to be fun . . . they just came out of us. But the music was still the main thing. Then what happened the crowd started to want those things more than the music. Those little things that were just added on, like frosting, became the most important. Things got changed around. We don't do that stuff as much anymore.'

Lombardi asked Jimi about Jim Morrison, who had just been arrested in Miami for indecent exposure on stage. Jimi didn't want to talk about it, because he didn't know what actually happened.

'We used to try and defend against some of the publicity, but we don't anymore. They just ignore what you say anyway, and the people who know where you're at, know without asking questions. They know from the music . . . I dig music.

'Listen, you want to talk about music. That's what I really know about. I don't want to say nothing about comparisons with other groups, because if you do, that puts you higher or lower than them, and that's just the same old cycle. Our music is in a very solid state right now. Not technically, just in the sense that we can feel around the music and get into things better. We don't have any answers this time, but we'd like to turn everyone on to all we know. . . . we know for instance that Jesus was starting to get it together quite nicely, but that ten-commandments thing was a drag. The bogey man isn't going to come and get you if you don't tie your shoe. You don't have to be afraid to make love to one of your boyfriend's wives. Brand-name religions like Buddhism and Zen are just clashes. The Catholic Church is spreading and vomiting over the earth. The Church of England is the biggest landowner in England. Your home isn't America, it's the Earth, but things are precarious. . . . You know my song, "I Don't Live Today . . . Maybe Tomorrow"? That's where it's at. . . .

'But I want to talk about music. Things were getting too pretentious, too complicated. "Stone Free" – you know that? That's much simpler. That's blues and rock and whatever else happens. People were singing about acid itself, man. Things start to rule you. Images. Drugs. Everyone forgets what happened to God.

'You know when you're young, most people have a little burning thing, but then you get your law degree and go into your little cellophane cage. You don't have to be an entertainer or anything to get it together. You can do the family thing. I've wanted to do that at times. . . . I've wanted to go into the hills sometimes, but I stayed. Some people are meant to stay and carry messages.'

The next logical question was 'You think of yourself as a messenger?' but by then Jimi just wanted out: 'No, man, nothing like that. I didn't want to do this interview because I was tired and I never get any time to myself. I wanted to relax, write a song, but how can you say that to someone?'

This was the trouble – Jimi never thought he could say it, when plenty of others in his position did. Or rather they didn't have to because they had protection. Jane de Mendelssohn of *IT* had mentioned how easy it was to fix up an interview with Jimi compared to other big-name musicians. Fans would just go to his hotel room and meet him – which was great for them, and Jimi was invariably very polite. But he needed space for himself and he never got it. For a musician of his status, the situation was ludicrous.

Jimi concluded the interview when Gerry Stickells came into the room to tell him he had to get ready for that evening's gig at the Spectrum.

'Listen, man', he said to Lombardi,

'I'm tired, but this is what I'm trying to say. If you prostitute your own thing . . . you can't do that. We were having a lot of fun with that stuff we used to do, but the more the press would play it up, the more the audience would want it, the more we'd shy away from it. Do you see where that all fits?

'When I'm on stage playing the guitar, I don't think about sex. I can't

353

make love when a beautiful record comes on. When I was in Hawaii, I seen a beautiful thing . . . a miracle. There were a lot of rings round the moon and the rings were all women's faces.'

As usual the room was full of people. Jimi glanced around and looked back at John Lombardi: 'I wish I could tell somebody about it.'[8]

Jimi moved into another room and got talking to a black girl who said she had a friend in hospital nicknamed 'Beefy' who was a mad Hendrix fan, but couldn't get to the show. Jimi picked up the phone, called the hospital and talked to 'Beefy' for a good twenty minutes. On stage he dedicated 'Gettin' My Heart Back Together Again' to her.

The next gig was in Memphis. Before Jimi left New York he called up his old bass-playing pal Billy Cox, who was still living in Nashville, and asked him to come backstage. After the gig, Jimi had a quiet but intense conversation with Billy, telling how he was unhappy that Noel was spreading his energies with Fat Mattress, which was somewhat at odds with Jimi's press statements implying that the two bands could work in tandem. Possibly, however, this was just a rationalisation to Billy to explain that he didn't want to play with Noel any more. He gave Billy $500 and told him to go back to Nashville and wait. When the time was right, Jimi would call. The band continued to Houston, Dallas and then back to New York for some sessions at the Record Plant. But the most important gig that month was the Forum in Los Angeles. Important enough for a rehearsal.

The Forum was packed to bursting, the crowd on the edge of hysteria as the band took the stage.

> Yeah, okay, okay, then. We're all at church, alright? Pretend there's sky above ya, alright? Yeah. [To Noel] Oh come on, let's get tuned up. . . . This whole show is dedicated to you, ourselves, Murray Roman, the Smothers Brothers, God bless their souls. . . . It'll take us around forty-five seconds to get arranged here. . . . And we want to forget about everything that happened yesterday, last night or this morning. Just forget about everything, but what's going on down now, it's up to you all and it's up to us too, so let's get our feelings together. They talk about some kind of earthquake going on, you know, dig, dig, you know where all the earthquake happening is coming from. It's bad vibrations, man, they get very heavy some time, you know. You wanna save your state? Get your hearts together.

Even though relations in the band were at a low ebb, this didn't mean they couldn't turn in a good set – often the frisson caused by personal aggravations sparked off good music as they tried to outplay each other. They began with the rather ponderous heavy riff of 'Tax Free' written by Bo Hansson and Janne Karlsson and then blew through a range of their standards, extending each one to a jam, taking the set to an almost unprecedented two hours. Throughout, the crowd periodically rushed forward, prompting several calls for calm from both Jimi and Noel as the police began to move in.

'Look,' said Jimi at one point, 'they're going to cut the show short if this keeps up. So just sit down and be cool so these other "people" [coughs] will get off the stage.'

When it was all over, Jimi just put down his guitar, gave a peace sign and left the stage. A lot of people stayed, not believing it was all over. The Los Angeles *Image* commented, 'It will be a long time before this performance is equalled at the Forum – probably as long as it takes the Jimi Hendrix Experience to return there.'9 But critics were rarely neutral about Jimi – they either loved the man and his music or they dumped him as an empty charade. Pete Johnson of the *LA Times* called Jimi's guitar work 'lack-luster and sloppy' and accused him of over-reliance on an 'ageing set of tricks' and a boring rendition of 'Red House'. But, for Johnson, Jimi's main crime was to be a phoney social commentator compared to Country Joe Macdonald, the Fugs or Phil Ochs. 'If Jimi Hendrix has anything serious to say, he is starting late and badly. If he has anything serious left to play, he hid it well Saturday night.'10

To some extent, Johnson had a point, even though his criticisms of this particular concert were unwarranted – there were a number of concerts which were undeniably below par and Jimi had played out his old blues stunts. Nobody knew this better than he.

Financially the tour promised to be an outstanding success – they were being paid upwards of $50,000 for shows generally lasting no more than an hour or so. Three gigs in Philadelphia, Toronto and Madison Square Garden promised $320,000 alone. Potential gross earnings for the tour added up to nearly $1.3 million. Only the Rolling Stones and the Beatles (if they decided to tour again) could command such huge fees. Then disaster struck – the worst thing that could have happened with so much at stake – coming through Toronto airport at 9.30 a.m. on 3 May, Jimi was busted for drugs.

Twelve *House Burning Down*

I want to see desperately ... I want to grab on to anything besides myself. I turn to the world – what has the world to offer me except pats on the back, shaking hands, making plans? (Extract from 'Room Full of Mirrors', unpublished rap)

The law-enforcement tradition of rousting musicians in the search for drugs has a long history. As early as 1933, four years before possession of marijuana was made a US federal offence, the newly appointed head of the Federal Narcotics Bureau, Harry Anslinger, kept a special file on musicians. At the time, the Bureau was virtually the only source of public information on drugs. Through lectures, articles and ludicrous films like *Reefer Madness*, Anslinger almost single-handedly fixed in the public mind the association between drugs, music and the moral decline of the nation's (white) youth. Anslinger was fixated with busting musicians. He tried to set up a system of informants within the music business, but this proved a dismal failure. Even so, as well as satisfying his own vendetta against musicians, the 'star bust', when it happened, provided useful leverage at the annual Congressional hearings to discuss the Bureau's budget.

During the fifties, many of the big names in jazz faced a regular shakedown and several were arrested, including Art Pepper, Lester Young, Hampton Hawes, Thelonius Monk, and Billie Holiday. For the federal or local precinct cop, the sight of a fêted black jazz musician, especially with a white girl on his arm, was too good a chance to miss. Of course, many musicians *were* strung out and it *was* illegal to possess heroin or marijuana, but the system was hideously corrupt and the drug laws provided a very convenient justification for harassment. Anslinger seemed to have a special grudge against Thelonius Monk, whose working life was all but ruined by police action.

Billie Holiday was charged with cocaine possession as she lay dying in her hospital bed wired up to every contraption known to medical science. She could hardly move, let alone be in a state to 'possess' cocaine actively.

But the most invidious way of crippling somebody's career was the infamous New York cabaret card system. If you wanted to play a venue which sold liquor, for more than two days, you had to have a card. Playing New York was absolutely vital for any singer or musician. It didn't matter how well you were known elsewhere, you could forget any kind of national recognition if they didn't know you in New York, home to all the most prestigious night-spots. And you could lose your card for a whole host of reasons, including a drug conviction. But, if you had the money and the connections – hey presto – you could buy it back again. The card system was finally abolished by Mayor John Lindsay in 1967 – just about the time that white pop stars began replacing black jazz musicians as the target for political disapprobation.

However, it was Britain rather than America that led the way in pop-star drug busts. Until about 1960, the drug scene such as it was centred on London's West End – some dope-smoking in the jazz clubs and a handful of heroin addicts mostly known to the police by name. But with the new affluence of young people came a dramatic increase in conspicuous consumption – records, clothes and the use of controlled drugs; amphetamines were banned for the first time in 1964, followed by LSD in 1966. And spearheading this hedonistic free-for-all, and invariably blamed by the press and politicians for all its worst excesses, were pop stars. First on the rack was Donovan – convicted for possession of LSD in 1966, followed by the Stones in 1967, then (gasp! shock!) two of the lovable moptops, John and George, arrested on marijuana charges in 1968. In America, it was much the same – most of Jefferson Airplane and the Grateful Dead had their collars felt, along with Stephen Stills, Eric Clapton and a whole host of others. The rock equivalent of losing your cabaret card was denial of a US (and later also a Japanese) visa. But, despite all the press hoo-ha, the only drugs involved were marijuana and LSD. Nobody among the pop/rock fraternity had been busted for the big boogie drug, heroin. Until now.

Drugs ... it's a very bad scene ... specially when you get caught with it, you know. (Radio interview. Frankfurt, 18 May 1967)

The only incontrovertible facts are that the band came into Toronto from Detroit where they had played the Cobo Arena the night before.

357

They landed around 9.30 a.m. Jimi was asked to open his flight bag by Officer Marvin Wilson, who produced a small glass jar containing three cellophane packs of white powder and a small metal tube stained with a dark resin. When asked, Jimi confirmed that the flight bag was his and he was detained for four hours while a mobile lab was set up to establish the nature of the substances found. The results were unequivocal – the dark resin was hash, the white powder, heroin. Jimi was formally charged with being in possession of controlled drugs, taken to police headquarters and later released on $10,000 bail.

While they were waiting for the results of the lab test, Gerry Stickells phoned the office in New York to tell Mike Jeffery, but he was on holiday in Hawaii. Instead, Gerry spoke to their press agent Michael Goldstein who by greasing a few palms managed to prevent any extensive press coverage until *Rolling Stone* gave the full low-down in its issue of 31 May, some four weeks after the bust. The risk was that if the mainstream press had got hold of the story, their treatment of it would almost certainly be hostile to Jimi – recalling his wild stage act and trying to portray him as some addled junkie. This had to be stopped for two reasons. Most immediately, there was still a highly lucrative tour to finish; some promoters might pull the plug on the concerts, fearful that they would have trouble with local politicians, press and residents' groups. Secondly, and with one eye on the trial, it was important that any prospective juror should not have too prejudiced an opinion of Jimi before the start of the court proceedings – whenever those would be.

On the evening of the arrest, the band were due to play Toronto's Maple Leaf Gardens. They had one piece of luck that day, as Gerry Stickells explains. He was worried that all the paperwork would prevent them doing the show that night. 'The detective said, "Oh, don't worry, we'll get it done as quick as we can. My kids have got tickets for the concert and they'll kill me if I don't get him out."'

Considering the circumstances under which the show took place, Jimi seemed in surprisingly good spirits. He established a jokey, warm rapport with the audience, even throwing in a bit of mock opera to sing along with a concert picked up momentarily by the amps. The playing was well up to standard, particularly a free-form medley segueing from 'Spanish Castle Magic' to 'Third Stone from the Sun', 'Little Miss Lover' and back to the opening riff. Jimi and Mitch traded rhythmic patterns followed by possibly one of Mitch's best solos. Jimi would often ad-lib lyrics to suit the occasion; during a gentle, sparse version of 'Red House' he sang, 'Soon as I get out of jail / I wanna see her.'

Madison Square Garden, New York City, 18 May 1969

So what happened? According to Mitch, they had been warned the night before in Detroit to take extra precautions. 'We were in the Cobo Hall and the word came through the grapevine that there were going to be problems in Toronto. The roadies came round and said, "Just check all your baggage and make sure that there's nothing that could possibly be planted." I made a point of wearing a suede suit with no pockets and no underwear. There was no way they could plant anything on me. So as far as I was concerned, it was a plant. By whom and on whose authority, I don't know.' Mitch also says they were actually met off the plane, escorted to separate rooms and searched.

This is at odds with the account given by Louis Goldblatt of Celebrity Limousines, who was waiting at the airport for Jimi to chauffeur him around Toronto. He told *Rolling Stone* he had witnessed the incident and how Jimi had leant back against a railing and shook his head in disbelief. However, as driver to the stars, Goldblatt had seen similar incidents before at the airport – this one was a bit out of the ordinary. For a start, the Mounties didn't usually wait at the airport to make dope busts. This was the job of customs. Also the whole procedure was carried out in full public view. The usual practice after an initial find was to conduct further searches in private. It would appear that the police had prepared themselves for a show.

Even without such a specific warning, the band could have expected problems in Toronto, because it was a notorious trouble spot for bands coming into the city – customs invariably gave rock musicians a tough time. In any case, it was a golden rule of the road that the star went through any airport clean as a whistle.

In fact, the band had long known that they were under surveillance. Most other name bands had run foul of the law, but the biggest of them all – the Jimi Hendrix Experience – had so far 'got away with it'. In late 1968, when the band had a house in Benedict Canyon, Los Angeles, they received a visit from three detectives who put them on notice that they were being watched from a police-rented house up the Canyon. Noel had been tipped off about the impending visit, phoned Mitch at the Whisky A Go Go and together they cleaned out the house, including Jimi's room, where much to their amazement they found a wide-ranging assortment of drugs – mainly gifts from so-called 'admirers'. The message from the police was clear – 'We're out to get you – but if we don't, somebody else will.'

Prior to the Detroit concert, the band had been back in Los Angeles, staying at the Beverly Rodeo Hotel. A journalist, Sharon

Lawrence, was with the band and became a close friend of Jimi and Noel. She later testified that Jimi was in his room complaining of a headache. Somebody suggested he take some Bromo headache powder and a girl gave him something which he put in his bag without looking at it. This suggests that Jimi did not check his bag in Detroit as advised or that he did check it and thought he was carrying headache powder (although that still doesn't explain the hash). It is unlikely that Jimi would have used the heroin had he found it because, according to Kathy Etchingham, Jimi had tried snorting it a couple of times but, as with most novice users, it had made him sick, so he simply didn't bother again.

However, there is still the question of the Mounties apparently waiting for Jimi as if they knew it would be worth searching him. Anybody trying to plant drugs on Jimi to be sure he got busted in Toronto would have had to do it as close to landing as possible. Therefore it is unlikely that the drugs were planted back in Los Angeles. This lends some credence to Trixie Sullivan's account that a male groupie who was actually travelling with the band in some capacity had planted the drugs (then presumably phoned ahead) in revenge for a rebuffed sexual advance he had made to Jimi. 'He actually put that stuff in Jimi's bag, because Jimi was not that stupid.' If this is true, then it suggests that when Jimi got on the plane to Toronto he *knew* he was clean, because he'd already found the LA stuff in his bag and ditched it. Hence his astonishment at the police finding drugs at the other end.

Later, people started whispering in Jimi's ear that maybe Mike Jeffery had set him up, to bind Jimi ever closer to him and prevent him from going back to Chas. But it doesn't make sense for Mike to risk seeing his main source of income locked away for a possible seven years, the maximum sentence he could have faced. In 1969, the rock business still operated in the belief that it would all be over tomorrow. Few cared about artistic development; most managers signed their bands to the company who would pay the biggest cash advance. The motto was 'Take the money and run'. If Jimi really was put out of circulation for several years, what guarantee was there that anybody would remember him for the comeback tour of 1976? Also, there was very little finished material in the can to sustain the release of the several albums that would be needed to keep up the interest in the intervening years. In fact, according to Jerry Morrison, Mike's 'Papa Doc' sidekick, in the wake of this incident Mike asked him to find a house in upstate New York which would afford Jimi some protection from what Mike perceived as evil New York influences.

But ultimately, however the drugs got there, it was bad news for Jimi, who according to Eric Barrett went around looking 'as if there had been a plane crash'. In a song he later wrote called 'Stepping Stone', Jimi made reference to what happened with even a hint of a possible mid-air plant, 'flying can't be trusted – got busted'.

The rest of the tour continued from Toronto to New York and then down south to Charlotte, North Carolina. After the gig, two fans went in search of a rumoured post-concert party. They phoned Jimi's hotel and were amazed to be put straight through to Jimi's room (he had registered in his own name), where Jimi answered the phone himself. He said he didn't know about any party, but invited them over anyway. They found him subdued, but friendly. He gave them a few minutes of his time – they asked him a few juvenile questions, but were considerate enough to leave quite soon as they could see he was tired. It was just an interlude on the road. Here was the most famous rock star in the world, sitting by himself in a hotel room giving time to a couple of fans writing for the *Inquisition*, a newspaper few had heard of and probably even fewer read. But then this was Jimi Hendrix!

The next night saw them in Charleston, West Virginia giving a pre-gig interview to Ray Brack of the *Charleston Gazette*. Nowadays, Mitch laughs when he remembers the interviews they gave concerning the future of the Experience and the individual projects of each member – 'a figment of imaginations' he calls them. In between some genuine expressions of Jimi's thinking on music is some good old-fashioned bull-shit starting with,

The Experience's last album together should be out in about a month. It's in the can and late this month while they're in New York for a Madison Square Garden concert, they'll spend some time in final mixing on the release. 'We're not sure what the title will be,' Jimi said, 'but I think we'll call it, *The End of the Beginning.*'

Hendrix's first solo album which could appear by fall will show the inevitable 'new side'. In addition to startling departures musically, he plans to introduce a new type of Hendrix song, mystical and full of social comment.

'Music is stronger than politics,' he said. 'I feel sorry for the minorities, but I don't feel a part of one. And I think the answer lies in music. One of the worst statements people are making is "no man is an island". Every man is an island and music is about the only way we can really communicate. Forget about the mass love scene. That's not

also NOEL REDDING

CORA PROMOTIONS PRESENTS

CHARLESTON CIVIC CENTER

Saturday, May 10 at 8:30 P.M. — 1 Show Only

Tickets $3.50 - $4.50 - $5.50

Tickets on Sale Now at the Civic Center, Galperins, Turners, Sears,
Gorbys and Kay Jewelers in Downtown Huntington.

where it is. It's not building understanding. And I wish I could say this
so strongly that they'd sit up in their chairs.

'My songs speak in different ways, but when I say "I", I don't mean
"Me", but rather whoever I can relate to. I have a song on abortion and
a song on Vietnam and a song on just about any problem. And my song
on the campus thing today says the kids are shouting through a keyhole.
They're not being individuals.'

Mitch cuts in while Jimi tunes his Fender: 'We have things we
want to do. Like I want to do a concert at Carnegie Hall with Miles
Davis and Roland Kirk. We're trying to get it together right now. We
just can't go on playing concerts like this. You know, one group goes
on and then we go on.'

Says Jimi: 'I died a thousand times in this group and was born again.
But after a while you have to get yourself straightened out. A person
has to have five to ten minutes to himself every day. After this tour is

over and our album is ready, I'm going to take a long vacation – maybe in Morocco or Sweden or way out in the southern California hills.'[1]

After a gig in Indianapolis, they returned to New York where Jimi dived straight into the womb-like security of the Record Plant. There he wasn't being hassled by policemen, managers, reporters and the like. *He* was in command. One of the first things he did when he got back was to meet up with Billy Cox, who had come up to New York at Jimi's request. The time was not yet right for Billy to replace Noel, as Jimi planned, because there were still a number of concerts coming up, but at least Jimi could work out with Billy in the studio away from too many prying eyes. They had flexed their muscles in late April with some blues jamming – now Mitch help set up something more challenging. Mitch had been sharing a New York apartment with the former Miles Davis drummer, Tony Williams. 'I got him to play with Jimi. Unfortunately it didn't work out too well, but all these people would give each other a try . . . and see what we learned.' At the time Williams was putting together Lifetime, an extraordinary band of all-talents with Jack Bruce, John McLaughlin and organist Larry Young. Jimi had already jammed with Jack and John individually, now Mitch brought Larry to the Record Plant for a session. Part of their collaboration can be heard on the album *Nine to the Universe* featuring a very different Jimi from the one who had to pump out 'Purple Haze' every night. Jimi let loose some wild octave-doubling and generally enjoyed the space to express a different musical vocabulary in the company of another master musician.

Then, the very next night a total change of mood: Jimi brought together Johnny Winter, Stephen Stills on bass and his drummer Dallas Taylor to do Guitar Slim's 'The Things I Used To Do', a good candidate for the blues album that Jimi was also planning. The albino player from the South and the black player from the North had a mutual appreciation society going. 'I was a Hendrix groupie and he was a Johnny Winter groupie.' They jammed at the Scene, owned by Johnny's manager Steve Paul, and hung out some when they got the chance. 'About that time, Jimi was real fascinated with the old bottleneck blues style. So we both went into the Record Plant studios . . . got the engineer to roll the tapes and we just jammed together. . . . You couldn't show that man anything new. It was just a case of Jimi watching how I used a bottleneck when playing. I guess Jimi and I must have played together for at least two or three hours that day.'[2] Steve Stills was so drunk 'I could barely see. After a while Jimi leaned over and nudged me with his guitar. Then he literally moved my hand on the bass. I was a fret off . . . I nearly died of embarrassment.'3

Although Jimi was considering his musical direction, he always remained faithful to the spirit of the blues, if not necessarily its traditional structures.

> When I was upstairs while the grown-ups had parties listening to Muddy Waters, Elmore James, Howlin' Wolf and Ray Charles, I'd sneak down after and eat potato chips and smoke butts. That sound was really – not evil – just a thick sound.
> Guitar is the basic thing for me, voice is just another way of getting across what I'm doing musically. It's hard for me to think in terms of blues any more – so many groups are riding the blues bandwagon. . . . The blues are easy to play but not to feel. The background of our music is a spiritual-blues thing. Blues is part of America.4

By 23 May 1969 Jimi was back home in Seattle in front of 15,000 people at the Seattle Coliseum. The concert went well, Jimi playing with much more enthusiasm than he had the last time he was in town. He was on good form that night, forging a good rapport with the audience as he had done in Toronto. Reporting for the *Seattle Post-Intelligencer*, Janine Gressel noted, 'He gave the sincere impression that without either the musicians or the audience, there would be no "Hendrix Experience", a correct but seldom-acknowledged theory.' Admitting she was at a loss for any original superlatives, she concluded her piece: 'Hendrix's guitar seemed to be an extension of his body; the peculiar positions from which he sometimes played seemed a result of emotion – as if just to hold the guitar could not express his erupting feelings. The impression was that if Hendrix were to have to put down his guitar, the music would have to come from his body – that the instrument was entirely superfluous.'5 Fat Mattress were the support band, as they had been for most of the tour. Their bass player Jimmy Leverton watched Jimi's set from the wings: 'The stadium had a glass dome and a revolving stage in the middle. He was playing his white Stratocaster, playing really blistering guitar. Lightning flashed overhead. The whole place . . . it was a great effect. Steven Spielberg on lights! An awesome experience. "Good light show" said Jimi afterwards.'

Jimi kept up his enthusiasm the following night at the Sports Arena in San Diego. There were no surprises in the set, no new songs, but it was just one of those gigs where everything flowed sweetly, crystallised in possibly his finest rendition of 'Red House' captured on the *Hendrix in the West* album. However, the virtues of the music seemed of little concern to a San Diego underground paper called the *Door*, which bemoaned top-price tickets at $5.50 and the concert gross for the Experience of $35,000, declaring 'That's right, kiddies, our HEROES are screwing us! . . . Hendrix and the others have copped out to the American standard of happiness and success. The incorruptibles becoming corrupt.' So you would have thought that the *Door* would have been rooting for those kids who tried to buck the system, defeat the tainted capitalists and get in free – not a bit of it: 'The second person in this bad-news trinity (greedy bands and the pigs being the other two) is the kids who tried to get in free. . . . Just because these fuck-ups didn't get their heads in the right place to either have the bread or the tickets before the concert, they threw a tantrum.'6 No pleasing some people.

The main part of the tour ended in Hawaii. Jimmy Leverton says that 'Mike Jeffery and the tour promoters weren't going to take Fat Mattress to Hawaii, you know, "What a waste of money, no need for them to go" and it was Hendrix who said, "Come on, they've done the graft, they deserve the perk." That was really nice of him. That was great.'

Offstage they all had a good time, but the first show was a disaster because Jimi was distracted by some amplifer hum. He did six songs, went off for a fifty-minute interval and never reappeared. The second show passed without a hitch, followed by a third to make up for the first, after which Noel flew back to London to sit out the next three weeks before the Newport Pop Festival at Devonshire Downs in Northridge, California for a massive payout of $100,000.

Jimi meanwhile hung out in Los Angeles, making himself available for interviews at the Beverly Rodeo Hotel in Hollywood. The interview with Jerry Hopkins for *Rolling Stone* (conducted on 8 June, but not published until 12 July) made it clear that the original Experience was finished. Before the interview was underway, Jimi must already have told Hopkins that Billy Cox would be his new bass player, because there is no mention of this in the interview transcript prior to Hopkins asking, 'Anybody else besides Billy you can name?' Hendrix answered, 'We're going to have Albert Allen writing songs – from the Twins. He has a brother who's getting himself together now.'

By now Jimi was beginning perhaps to regret using the word 'Church' in describing his new sound as 'Sky Church' (for outdoor gigs) and 'Electric Church' (for indoors). 'I don't like the name "Church"

because it sounds too funky, too sweaty. You think of a person prayin'
between his legs on the ground. So until we find something better, we'll
have to use that, you know.'

Jimi didn't want to be drawn on who else would be in the new
line-up: 'It's best not to harp upon us – the personalities an' all that . . .
the body of the music itself is what counts. That's where we go from.
You'll see what we look like when we get on stage and get ourselves
together.'

However, from what he said to Ritchie Yorke of the Toronto
Globe and Mail and *LA Times* on 19 June, there was going to be
no Hendrix-led supergroup:

> I plan to use different people at my sessions from now on; their
> names aren't important. You wouldn't know them anyway. It really
> bugs me that there are so many people starving, musicians who are
> twice as good as the big names. I want to try and do something about
> that.
>
> Really, I'm just an actor – the only difference between me and
> those cats in Hollywood is that I write my own scripts. I consider
> myself first and foremost a musician. My initial success was a step in
> the right direction, but it was only a step, just a change. Now I plan to
> get into other things.
>
> A couple of years ago all I wanted was to be heard. 'Let me
> in' was the thing. Now I'm trying to figure out the wisest way to
> be heard.

Up to that point, the Newport Pop Festival, held over three days
from 20 to 22 June, was one of the biggest events of its kind.
Artists appearing included Spirit, Joe Cocker, Creedence Clearwater,
Steppenwolf, Jethro Tull, Eric Burdon, the Rascals, Johnny Winter and
the Byrds. Marvin Gaye and Ike and Tina Turner were among some of
the big-name black acts on the bill. Jimi was set to headline the opening
night, but from the off it was clear that just about the last place Jimi
wanted to be that night was onstage in front of several thousand people. Almost certainly, his mood was connected to two recent personal
problems.

The previous day Jimi had had to fly back to Toronto for a preliminary
hearing of his case in front of Judge Robert Taylor. The judge duly
announced that Jimi would stand trial on 8 December on two counts
of possession, dispelling rumours that Jimi might be charged with far
more serious offences such as smuggling or trafficking. Bail was held

at $10,000 and Jimi had a Sword of Damocles hanging over him for the rest of the year.

More immediately, just before the Experience were due on stage, Noel went into the band's caravan/dressing-room to find Jimi surrounded by about eight guys purporting to represent the Black Panthers. Jimi looked scared to death and was very relieved to see Noel. The waif-like bass player wouldn't have stood a chance on his own – fortunately, the visitors left voluntarily.

The formation of the Black Panther Party for Self-Defense in Oakland, California during 1967 was a response by young black political activists who rejected the pacifist stance of Martin Luther King. This approach, they maintained, had patently failed to win for black people the freedoms they demanded as of right by virtue of being American citizens and so equal with the rest of society under the Constitution. In essence, they believed that violent revolution was the only way to wrest such rights from the white establishment – and they had only contempt for any of those few black people in positions of power who would not assist their cause. The Panthers first burst on to the scene on 2 May 1967, when two dozen heavily armed members marched into the California State Assembly to protest at a pending arms-control law. A year later, Martin Luther King was shot by a white man and, so far as the Panthers were concerned, their commitment to armed struggle was vindicated. Most of their battles were against the FBI, who instituted a very sophisticated programme of destabilisation called COINTELPRO to break the Panthers, culminating in a deadly and bloody split between two leading members, Huey Newton and Eldridge Cleaver. What the Panthers needed most was money.

Backstage was a favourite place to try and engage Jimi. Trixie Sullivan recalls one night at the Fillmore West: 'These two black guys came in. . . . they were bloody heavy, I'm not joking, calling Jimi a white nigger and God knows what else. Bill Graham came in and had them thrown out.' 'The Black Panthers were moving in for money,' says Jimmy Leverton. 'I wasn't allowed near it, but backstage, it was real heavy, "Don't go in there," and all that.'

They even called Jimi's flat in London to get at Kathy, knowing Jimi was on tour in America. 'Apparently he'd promised them some money and they wanted me to write the cheque out. And I refused. About a day or two later, they phoned up and said, "Why don't you get your white ass out of his flat?" When I told Jimi about this he went up the wall, he was furious. I had never seen him so mad.' Kathy went to the police, but there was little they could do about it.

As one of the most famous black celebrities in the world, pressure on Jimi to contribute to party funds was inevitable. But Jimi was never that interested in becoming involved in black politics. He used music to make his political statements – songs like 'House Burning Down' and unfinished fragments like 'Peace in Mississippi' and 'Captain Coconut', actually titled 'MLK' (Martin Luther King). If anything, his political sympathies were more attuned to the plight of the American Indian than the black. During one live performance of 'I Don't Live Today', he slipped in an ironic snatch from America's national anthem, 'The Star Spangled Banner'.

However, he was prepared to offer limited support, even for some form of Panther 'positive action', particularly if doing so would earn the approval of the black community, which overall had failed to respond to Jimi and his music. Such approval could be quite important at this stage in his career as he tried to broaden the base of his appeal with a looser, more funky type of sound. Besides, Jimi had never disowned his black roots either musically or emotionally and when the Panthers called him a 'coconut' (dark outside and white in the middle), it hurt. In January 1969, *Teenset* magazine ran an article, 'Jimi Hendrix, Black Power and Money', in which Jimi imagined a role for militancy where peaceful protest about a certain issue had failed a few times: 'then get your Black Panthers . . . not to kill anybody, but to scare them. It's hard to say . . . I know it sounds like war, but that's what's gonna have to happen, it has to be a war if nobody is going to do it peacefully. Like quite naturally, you say, make love not war, and all these other things, but then you come back to reality and there are some evil folks around and they want you to be passive and weak and peaceful so that they can just overtake you like jelly on bread. . . . You have to fight fire with fire.' Whatever Jimi was trying to get across here, one thing was for sure – he was saying it to the wrong magazine. No black kid on the streets was likely to be reading *Teenset*.

Whenever he was in New York, Jimi would renew his friendship with Albert and Arthur Allen, the twins he and Fay had shared a house with in the early days. Arthur had since married Fay and both he and his brother featured in Jimi's future. Arthur tells the following story.

He [Jimi] never talked in terms of colour. He wasn't much of a colour talker. . . . I remember one time we were walking towards 8th Street

. . . we were rapping about a few things. So there was this guy selling Black Panther papers, 'Black Panther, Black Panther, brothers.' So I was walking by, my head was somewhere else at the time. . . . But Jimi picked up on it . . . the first thing he did was he went right over and he bought the paper. First thing, right? So Albert and I we looked at each other and the guy said, 'Oh, wow, brothers, Jimi Hendrix is buying the paper, Black Panther paper, and you're not?' So we said, 'Yeah, well, Jimi Hendrix bought the paper 'cause he wanted the paper. We don't.' But then Jimi looked at us as though he bought the paper like to impress us.[7]

The crowd applauded enthusiastically when he took the stage at Newport but his mood was black. Because of everything that had gone down, he became incensed at those who wouldn't listen while he played some quieter moments, such as the introduction to the slow blues number 'Getting My Heart Back Together Again'. Jimi tried to start the song. He stopped. 'Fuck off.' He started again and stopped. 'Yeah, we hope we're not playin' to a bunch of animals, so please don't act like some. Lay back, okay, 'cos you're really making us uptight, man, you know. It's a bad scene for us to be feelin' uptight, tryin' to give you some good feelin' and all that sort of crap. . . . I'm just tryin' to play guitar, thank you.'

He started to try and explain the song, but gave up. 'You just choke yourselves. Fuck ya.' He played much of the concert with his back to the audience.

Jimi must have felt very guilty about this performance on the Friday night, because he came out to jam on the Sunday with Buddy Miles, Eric Burdon and a new band, Mother Earth, fronted by Joplin sing-alike Tracy Nelson, and played for almost two hours. At one point Buddy Miles said, 'We don't want to overdo it,' but Jimi kept on playing. For the arts editor of the Los Angeles *Image*, it was the most impressive moment in rock he had ever witnessed:

He seems to know the instrument and its nearly limitless possibilities better than any electric guitarist who has ever lived. He [stopped] only now and then to let other performers lay down some business – and he never repeated a riff. His creativity was awesome as he switched styles from blues to jazz to rock to rhythm or whatever, all with ridiculous ease. Hendrix was Wes Montgomery, B.B. King, Eric Clapton and you name it all wrapped in one package of artistic fury.

It was as if Hendrix had broken through to the most profound musical dimension available to mortals and was being guided by the perfect, instantaneous teachings of improvisational composing's most exalted spirit. Man, Hendrix was playing out of his mind.[8]

Since 1968, there had been scenes of civil disorder on the streets of American cities unprecedented in the nation's history. To the established tradition of rioting in black ghetto areas was added white youth protest at the Vietnam War. Confrontation was becoming uglier as police and national guardsmen reacted more violently to what was seen as an orchestrated and direct challenge to the authority of the state. Inevitably, this kind of antagonism spilled over into rock music where the now-popular large festival attracted thousands of young people. Security was obviously essential, to protect the artists against being rushed on stage, the promoter's profits from gate-crashers and the audience from itself. But the quality of policing varied enormously from regular cops to local biker gangs bought off by the organisers to avoid trouble. The bikers were just spoiling for a fight, while the cops, staring blankly ahead, totally bewildered by the sights before them, 'dealt' with their confusion through a grim determination to crack heads as and when they thought necessary. The worst trouble often occurred when the guardians of law and order were confronting those who wanted to get in free, either because they believed rock was the music of the people and *should* be free or because they were broke. Usually both. It was classic *them* and *us*. And, although he would have demurred, one of the most potent images of the US, encapsulating ghetto street-fighter, psychedelic freak and heroic Indian warrior was Jimi Hendrix.

The sparks that flew on stage often ignited audiences already hyped up to fever pitch by Jimi's very presence. Fans threatened to overrun them on many occasions – in Dallas back in April, there was near riot when Jimi played his incendiary version of 'The Star Spangled Banner' and Gerry Stickells always had to give thought to the quickest way out of a venue.

The weekend following Newport, the Mile High Stadium in Denver, Colorado played host to another three-day rock festival. The Experience were headlining on the last day, the final gig of the American tour and another six-figure pay-day. There was the usual problem with people trying to get in free. Friday saw some minor disturbances, but on Saturday with the temperature soaring to 95 degrees, Denver's hottest day of the year, a major incident flared up at the south-west entrance to the stadium. Police hurled tear gas at about 500 would-be gate-crashers, only to have the canisters thrown back, engulfing a large section of the crowd in choking gas. Around 7 p.m. the following evening, the same thing happened again and a two-hour battle ensued between police and those outside in the parking lots. By the time the Experience were onstage, tension snapped and crackled in the night air. But Jimi was feeling good – he'd shared some LSD with a friend, Herbert Worthington, who sat and watched him from the side: 'Jimi started singing "Bold As Love" and I was high, I was so happy, probably one of the happiest times of my life, being with an Angel [Jimi] and having a woman on each arm. I just went into an LSD laugh.' Jimi looked over to Herbert, realised that he too was peaking out on acid, tried to say something to Herbie, but it wouldn't come out. Meanwhile he took three goes to get past the intro.

Jimi with
Herbert Worthington
Hollywood,
28 June 1969

As they were into their last song, a large section of the crowd ran across the field to get close to the band. Herbert was concerned for Jimi's safety. 'The kids started jumping over the fence, they started running towards him and, being high, it just intensified the feeling that

Jimi was gonna get hurt. I ran to the steps of the stage saying, "Don't hurt him, don't hurt him, be careful, be careful." And I looked over to my right and there was a truck backed up and I saw that Noel and Mitch were already in there and Jimi shouted, "Come on, come on." And I ran and got in this truck. There were kids climbing on top, yelling, "We love you! We love you!"' But the real drama of the evening happened before Jimi left the stage: he announced, 'This is the last gig we'll ever be playing together.' To everybody connected with the band, like Gerry Stickells, it came as a complete shock. 'He hadn't discussed it with anybody.'

Soon after the concert, Noel flew to London, announcing he had left the band. He told *Disc and Music Echo*, 'I was planning to leave Hendrix this year anyway, because I was getting very bored. And then on our last tour in America, in fact in Denver, we read about Jimi augmenting the band and rumours about me splitting which even I'd never heard about. So I just quit then.'9

Later he said that before the gig somebody came up to him and asked if he was still in the band because Jimi had been reported as having chosen a new bass player. But once Jimi made his totally unexpected announcement from the stage in front of 30,000 people, that sealed it. After the split in 1968, everyone must have known that the band were living on borrowed time. Mike had cajoled Jimi into carrying on because of all the summer bookings. And now they were over. But it is likely that, once the gravy train had starting rolling again, the unspoken hope among everyone in the Hendrix camp (apart from Jimi) was that it could pick up some momentum and keep running – for a few more $100,000 gigs at least. What annoyed Noel about the band breaking up was not hearing it from Jimi himself, who could never handle any kind of messy confrontation. Making a grandstand play of resigning was really a face-saving device for the folks back home. In truth, there was really no band to resign from.

I can't play guitar any more the way I want to. I get very frustrated on stage when we play. I think it's because it's only three pieces.... We're working on more songs that are very hard, but that are very straight to the point, you know. You can always sing about love and different situations of love, but now, we're trying to get solutions to all the protests, you know, arguments that they're having about the world today. So we'll try to give our little opinions about that, in very simple words, you know. Anybody can protest, but not too many people can offer a decent answer. So we're gonna try and do that, like we did on *Are You Experienced?* ... Every time we come into town everybody always looks towards us for some kind of answer, for what's happening to them. And which is a good feeling, but it's very hard, so therefore I have to live the life, you know, I have to witness all these bad scenes, and all these good scenes, so then I can say, well, what I found out, you know, instead of just reading books and all that. So therefore I'm gonna get all these words together in nice heavy songs, very straightforward songs, you know, and just sock it to 'em, properly. (Radio interview, Stockholm, 9 January 1969)

Jimi had been planning this day for some while, although when it arrived, he was very worried about hurting Noel and whether overall he was doing the right thing. Herbert Worthington recalls Jimi coming into his hotel room the day after Denver and saying, '"I gotta go back to New York, something has come up." I didn't know it at the time that Noel had quit, but I could tell Jimi was very concerned, he was very nervous about it.'

What Jimi had in mind was very different from the powerhouse rock-trio style – it would be more free-wheeling and experimental, loosely constructed with a heavy emphasis on jamming. To fulfil the promise of his Electric Church, he wanted to build a community of musicians around him who would be receptive to his ideas, where he could try things out and avoid head-on clashes of ego. Sun Ra's free-jazz Arkestra was a good model. This was a co-operative based in New York where all money from concerts and sessions went into recording. Sun Ra was a stern disciplinarian but, because of the working environment he created, the loyalty shown him by his musicians was rivalled only by that shown to Duke Ellington. Jimi and Sun Ra shared a musical vision inspired by science-fiction and cosmology employed as a vehicle for their own escape from the parlous state of mankind. In programme notes for a London concert in 1970, Sun Ra said:

I've chosen intergalactic music or it has chosen me. Intergalactic music concerns the music of the galaxies. It concerns intergalactic thought and . . . travel, so it is really outside the realm of the future on the turning points of the impossible, but it is still existent as astronomy testifies. . . . I'm actually painting pictures of infinity with my music and that's why a lot of people can't understand it.

The real aim of music is to co-ordinate the minds of the people into an intelligent reach for a better world and an intelligent approach to the living future.

Jimi was looking for a special kind of musician for his 'Arkestra'. They didn't have to be the best; in fact for Jimi's purposes it was probably

374

important they weren't, if he was to avoid the kind of internal strife that was to tear Tony Williams' Lifetime apart. Jimi was primarily concerned with having guys around him he could trust, which meant for Jimi those who knew him *before* he became famous. As it stood, he didn't really know who he could trust, suffering the special conflict of the celebrity – the desire to confide and the distrust of confidants. This explains why he could be quite candid with reporters while remaining taciturn with his musicians, roadies and management. Even those he might have counted as close friends (mainly women) could never be sure they knew what was going on inside his head.

> The belief comes . . . through electricity to the people. That's why we play so loud. Because it doesn't actually hit through the ear drums like most groups. . . . They got this real shrill sound, you know, and it's really hard. We plan for our sound to go into the soul of the person . . . actually see if they can awaken some kind of thing in their minds, 'cause there's so many sleeping people. (*Dick Cavett Show*, July/August 1969)

Jerry Morrison obliged Mike and rented a house for Jimi where he could put his 'rock star' career on hold for a while. The house was at the end of Tavor Hollow Road near the villages of Shokan and Boiceville in the Woodstock area of upstate New York. The house was set in huge grounds with riding facilities, a swimming pool, gardens and all the accoutrements of celebrity seclusion. The house itself had eight bedrooms, each with its own sitting-room set off with a wood-burning stove. Rare antiques furnished much of the house. Jimi's room had a French antique make-up table, but he created his own environment with beautifully decorated Moroccan rugs brought from his various New York apartments. Jimi loved the house in spite of the $3000 a month rent. If it bought him some peace and quiet it would be worth every penny. All he needed now was his musicians to fill the place.

While he was finishing his commitments with the Experience, Jimi asked Billy Cox to stay in New York, setting him up temporarily with the Buddy Miles Express so he wouldn't starve. Once the Denver Pop Festival was out of the way, Jimi began to move into gear. Jimi asked Billy if he ever knew what happened to Larry Lee, his old guitar buddy from Nashville days – the man who gave Jimi his coat for the freezing trip to New York in 1963. 'Can you find him?' said Jimi. 'Sure,' said Billy, 'I know his mother.'

Larry recalls the day a voice from the past came down the phone.

I just gotten out of Vietnam, I just come from the unemployment office and I got a call from Billy. I said, 'What's happenin', man?' and he said, 'I'm in New York, I'm with Jimi, he's sitting right here.' And I said, 'Oh, oh, can I talk to Jimi?' 'Yeah, he want to talk to *you.*' 'What's happenin', Jimi?' 'We're tryin' to do some things and me and Billy was just thinkin' about you and wonder if you would like to come up here and join?' I said, 'What? . . . *Yeah.* Give a few days to get my business straight.' He said yeah and 'We're gonna send you a ticket and we'll call you back and meet you up in New York.' I was scared, man, I just got out of Vietnam, I just wasn't ready for a lot of things. I went up there and him and Buddy Miles met me in a limo. . . . that was my first time meeting Buddy, that's how it got started.

Jerry Velez was born in Puerto Rico, but grew up in the Bronx. A conga player, he hung around the Scene club, where Jimi heard him play. His sister Martha released an album in 1969, *Fiends and Angels*, backed by an incredible array of talent unnamed on the original cover including Eric Clapton, Jack Bruce, Mitch, Christine Perfect, Brian Auger, Paul Kossoff, Chris Wood and Jim Capaldi. Jerry had given up his apartment in New York and Jimi invited him to stay in Shokan. 'I was one of the first ones up there.'

Jimi wanted to explore some of the subtleties of rhythm, away from the thrashing of large drum kits, towards the light and shade possible with African and Latin American percussion, instruments that laid down a pulse, gave a certain heartbeat feel to a composition, a sound altogether more natural and less frantic. To help bring this idea to fruition, he contacted another conga player, Juma Sultan, an acquaintance from his days in the Village.

Juma was probably the most schooled musician Jimi ever played with on any sort of regular basis. The same age as Jimi, Juma was a grade musician in piano, susaphone and baritone saxophone, sang in a church quartet and took lessons from an African drummer. But things didn't work out too well for him as a youngster. 'I spent seven of my first twenty-one years in jail. . . . I was always into something . . . I had a chip on my shoulder.' Eventually he moved to New York in 1965, gigging as a conga player with some heavyweight company including saxophonists Sonny Rollins and Albert Ayler, Ayler's drummer Sunny Murray and Richie Havens. Unusually for a jazz drummer in the sixties, Murray was not of the Elvin Jones 'Hell for Leather' school. He was more interested in, say, the tonal variations inherent in the cymbal, an approach to percussion with which Juma was very much in tune.

Juma had a forty-acre farm up in Woodstock. '"Why don't you come up to the house and jam?" said Jimi. And so I did and he asked me to play with his group.' Jimi responded immediately to Juma's quiet, thoughtful intelligence. 'Juma looked like an African prince,' says Jerry Velez. 'He and Jimi had a special thing.'

Even before they had settled in at the house, there was a gig to do – Jimi was booked to appear on the *Johnny Carson* Show on 10 July, except that night the black comedian Flip Wilson was the guest host. According to John Delgardo, curator of Carson Productions, this was no coincidence. Carson ducked out of interviewing Jimi because of all the publicity being given to the Black Panthers at the time. Delgardo opines that Carson's concern for his image put Flip Wilson in the host's chair that night. Wilson asked Jimi if he wanted to make any comments relating to his widely reported belief that his performance was a spiritual experience. Jimi said that, because music was his whole life, it perforce became his religion and likened the experience of his music to the gospel church. 'We're trying to get the same thing through modern-day music.' 'Well, Jim [sic], it's my pleasure to extend an invitation to you to whip a light sermon on us.' Jimi then introduced Billy Cox, 'our new bass player', and then had two attempts at 'Lover Man', when the amp blew.

The early days up at the Shokan house were somewhat confused. When Larry Lee first got there, he was alone with Billy, Juma and Jerry. 'We rehearsed as best we could, we didn't have a band. . . . we had some cats from the Paul Butterfield band [living in Woodstock at the time]. . . . we were waiting on Mitch, we were waiting on Buddy. Jimi said he was going into town and some way we didn't see him no more. So we called the office in New York and they told us Jimi was in France or somewhere. So we spent a lot of time up there doing nothing.'

In fact, Jimi, having got permission from the Canadian authorities to travel, had gone to Morocco to join Stella Douglas, Colette and Luna on holiday. He travelled there with Deering Howe, heir to a large American commercial empire, and Michael Jason, a musician friend of Howe's. He hadn't told the women he was coming, he just appeared at the airport when Colette and Stella came to meet Deering Howe off the plane. Jimi and the girls rented an old Chrysler with a driver, travelling across country, staying in Marrakesh, Casablanca and Mohammedia until they came to Essaouria and met up with the Living Theatre. He allowed himself to be ripped off for tourist merchandise, saying that the sellers needed the money more than he did. The local kids followed him everywhere, not only because of his (to them) strange

just over yonder —
here comes some news —
Coming down ~~the mountain~~
like lightning...
~~electric red and blue~~ ...
Straight for me and you —
People of destruction —+
~~————————~~ your time is
~~———————~~ out of date..
people ~~——~~ who's living
Crooked, better start
getting straight

way of dressing, but also because he bore a striking resemblance to a North African superstar called Vigon.

Opinions differ about this trip. Colette who was there says that Jimi had a wonderful time, telling how he would sit poolside in one of the hotels, gently playing Deering Howe's acoustic guitar. 'It was probably the only vacation he really ever had. . . . it was very relaxed and very peaceful and very wonderful. There was no hassle, it was really a lot of fun.'

But Juma Sultan maintains, 'There was some mysterious circumstances behind that whole situation. I think Jimi going wasn't totally by choice.'

Jimi himself told friends later that he did not enjoy himself very much. For a start it was too hot for him and he refused to take off his shirt because he didn't want to get burned. Then there were these men following them about everywhere. Who were they? And why were they still there when Jimi got home? Was Mike Jeffery spying on him? A better guess would be that it had something to do with Jimi's drug bust. The thrust of the prosecution case would be that far from the victim of a fan's thoughtless gift, Jimi was a hardened drug-user. It is possible that arrangements were made to have Jimi followed out of the country to see what he got up to – especially as he was going to Morocco, where the streets were lined with hash.

In dismissing the trip, Jimi may also have been reflecting with sadness on a country much loved by his friend Brian Jones, who had very recently been found floating in his own swimming pool, rendered insensible by the cocktail of drugs in his system.

Jimi had had a good friend in Brian Jones in his early days in London. Carousing round the jazz clubs together, they found common cause in their musical taste, their love of beautiful women and outlandish clothes. Brian had flown to Monterey to introduce Jimi to his own country – and now he was gone, his spirit carried by a swarm of half-dead butterflies released in Hyde Park perhaps to salve somebody's conscience.

Once Jimi came back, life up in Woodstock settled into a very comfortable groove. Jimi started to get the music together. All through summer the momentum had been building for a three-day music festival due to be held in the Woodstock area in mid-August. Jimi had it in mind that he would use the event to showcase his new outfit – named Gypsy Sons and Rainbows. It was a goal to aim for and gave a focus to the rehearsals and jamming.

One problem needed sorting out – who would play drums, Mitch or Buddy Miles? 'Mitch was always hard to get,' says Jerry Velez.

'We didn't know whether Mitch was gonna do the gig and you would hear that Buddy was gonna come back. . . . we were having problems with Mitch.' By which he means Mitch might not show up to rehearsals. Jimi didn't really want to lose Mitch, but Mitch wasn't sure he would be able to fit in with a situation where Jimi's entire stable of companions consisted of 'brothers'. There were other black guys on the scene, friends of Jimi like James Scott (known as Vishwa), who became part of the Shokan entourage. Mitch's discomfort wasn't a racial thing, after all he'd shared a flat with Tony Williams. It was just that there would be lines of communication set up between Jimi and the others which neither Mitch nor any other white person could ever hope to penetrate. Not only that, but there would be a lot of chewing the fat over the old days in Nashville – again nothing Mitch could connect to. Buddy had his own commitments with the Express, but even so, it was never certain that Mitch would be the drummer at Woodstock.

When he wasn't playing or composing (which wasn't often), Jimi liked nothing better than to tuck into the food prepared by the Shokan cook, Claire Moriece. Jimi was never much of an eater, but in her case he made an exception.

> I was cooking for a friend of mine at a dinner party in Woodstock and one of the guests [who turned out to be Jerry Morrison] said, 'I didn't know you were such a good cook. Would you consider it as a job?' I said, 'Yes, it's something I'd love to do.' And they said, 'You know the Woodstock Festival this summer? There are a lot of famous rock stars coming, would you go work for somebody, but we can't tell you who it is until after you get there?' They wanted to drive me there blindfolded as it was a superstar and they did not want anyone to know where they lived.

Like everyone who met Jimi, however brief the acquaintance, she retains nothing but the fondest memories of him. 'My instant impression was what a sweet, humble, funny guy. I don't think that image of him has ever been projected. He felt like he was really lucky and he just expressed gratitude. You never get the essence of that when anyone mentions Jimi.' She cooked all Jimi's favourites. 'I baked blackberry pies and I made lots of different soups. Jimi loved soup and chocolate-chip cookies and corn cakes.'

Jimi, Jerry and the others would go joy-riding in one of Jimi's sports cars. Jerry confirms that Jimi was 'one of the world's worst drivers. He was funny, he'd get behind that wheel and it would be like Mr

Magoo. . . . Oh no, Jimi . . . he'd be trying to miss a pothole and go straight in it. God was with him when he was driving. I remember one time in Manhattan, five o'clock in the morning, daybreak, and he got pulled over. He was a fast talker that guy and he talked his way out of it. We'd have drugs in the car and the guy would go "Thanks for the autograph."'

Jimi fared no better with one horse-power. When they went riding, says Jerry,

Jimi was the world's worst. In the morning, I'd go out and get the horses. The first time I brought Jimi out, he was scared to death. I boost Jimi up and he gets up there on the horse – and all of a sudden the horse knew, he kind of looked up like 'I got a live one here' and started to take off and Jimi's going like 'Jerry! Jerry! Come here!' And I'm laughing all the time, 'cos he looked so ridiculous. Here he was in this great outfit he always had on and the saddle just slipped over on him and he fell down in the shit and knocked the wind out of him. I was laughing so hard I couldn't help him. And that was the last time I could get him on the horse.

Jerry's love of animals was not shared by other members of the household. 'Jerry had two dogs,' says Claire, 'one was a German short-haired Pointer and the other was an *enormous* Great Dane called "Huge Dog". One day, Huge Dog shat in the middle of the floor directly below the staircase. And this was some shit. It really was *huge*. I am not a pet lover, nor was the maid, and we both refused to clear it up. Jerry was gone for days – so everything went on as usual in the house with this great pile of dogshit in the middle of the floor!'

Although Jimi's presence was supposed to be a big secret, the news soon leaked out. The house was secluded, but not secure: Claire did the job of trying to shield Jimi from the most persistent hangers-on, but there were always nameless bodies tripping in and out of the house. 'Jimi had a girl with him who was from Texas. I recall her father was wealthy and she phoned home bragging that she was with a big rock star and he sent the cops! I had to pretend Jimi wasn't home.' One girl was big trouble; she walked eleven miles to give Jimi some beads. Claire gave her a helping hand in the opposite direction. 'I remember driving her in my car, personally escorting her out of the area and she started a fire in the car. There were some real bona-fide nut jobs, I mean the dregs of the earth came to seek him out. At the same time, Jimi would pick up hitchhikers in his flashy silver Corvette car. At one time he picked up a group of people and then went to Woodstock and bought a whole huge bag of art supplies. We started a fire and after dinner everyone sat round and drew. He did a lot of drawings back then.' Later that evening, Jimi grabbed an acoustic guitar and played sweetly into the night for anyone who cared to listen.

To complete the Woodstock ambience, apart from the wall-to-wall women, there were drugs aplenty. 'Everybody did a lot of drugs then,' says Claire, 'there's no question about that. There wasn't too much heroin around then, but there was enough coke and psychedelics. We took mescalin up at the house, but those days were different, people took drugs to get spiritual and Jimi was really a deeply spiritual and wonderful guy.'

When the mood took him, he would wander down to the Tinker Street Cinema in Woodstock for some impromptu jam sessions with whoever showed up – Buddy Miles, Taj Mahal, Paul Butterfield, saxophonist David Sanborn and members of Santana. Formed in 1967 in San Francisco, Santana had already proved that a percussion-dominated outfit with stellar rock guitar soaring over the top could be commercially viable. Their performance of 'Soul Sacrifice' at Woodstock would be remembered as one of the high spots of the festival.

Back at the house, Jimi tried to pull the band together for the concert. Billy had to learn some of the Experience standards like 'Purple Haze', 'Fire' and 'Foxy Lady', less concerned than Noel about being shown what to do, just happy to be there. They even tried out 'If 6 was 9', which Jimi had never played live before. Jimi was also working on some new material. He had the basis of a song in an instrumental with the running title of 'Jam Back at the House'. Like the solo parts for 'All Along the Watchtower', it was constructed in four sections, starting at 'Lover Man' pace, cooling back to a 'Rainy Day, Dream Away' shuffle, and moving on to end with a drum solo and feedback howl. The band ran through a number of versions of another new song called 'Izabella'. Among the scattered notes for lyrics that remain in Jimi's handwriting, is one that reads 'Monika = Izabella', so it is possible that the song was inspired by Monika Dannemann, whom he hadn't seen since February:

> Hey Izabella
> Girl, I'm holding you in my dreams every night.
> Yeah, but you know good well baby,
> You know we got this war to fight.
> Well, I'm calling you under fire
> Well, I hope you're receiving me all right.

Hey, Izabella
Girl, I'm fightin' this war for the children and you
Yeah, yeah, yeah, baby!
All this blood is for the world of you.
All your love!
So I hope you save your love, baby
Then I know the fightin' is true.

Jimi used Claire as a sounding-board for 'Izabella'. 'We had a talk about it and first of all Jimi would ask me into his room and play acoustic twelve-string guitar for hours and hours and he would ask me how I liked it. And then he asked me what I thought of his singing and I said, "What do you mean, it's fine." He was looking for confirmation and affirmation.'

The Woodstock Music and Arts Festival began life in the spring of 1969 as a germ of an idea in the mind of Michael Lang (from the Miami Pop Festival) and his partner, an ex-Capitol Records executive, Artie Kornfeld. The original scheme was to build a studio complex in the Woodstock area, where so many New York musicians now lived, and press launch it with a festival. Lang found two rich young men, John Roberts and Joel Rosenman, looking for some exciting investment potential. Once they started thinking about who they could invite, it didn't take too long for the studio idea to recede in favour of the festival as Lang realised that here was an opportunity to go down in history as host to the biggest rock party ever held. And using somebody else's money.

The relationship between the two sets of partners was always strained. For their part, Roberts and Rosenman became increasingly uneasy as costs began to escalate. They also felt Lang was freezing them out other than as the money men. Lang claimed he didn't want the festival 'vibes' upset by two men in suits being 'uncool' about money. The charismatic Lang was a sharp businessman, much closer in spirit to his backers than either side would care to admit. His answer to all nervous queries about expenditure was 'Don't worry, man, it'll be okay.'

And so it was, until with only thirty days to go the residents surrounding the site at Walkill forced through a change in local legislation and forced Woodstock Ventures out. A dairy farmer, Max Yasgur, sickened by the bad press constantly heaped on young people, came to the rescue and rented out his land in Bethel so the festival could take place. Sadly, as exhaustively documented in Robert Spitz's *Barefoot in Babylon*, the story from then on was one of staff incompetence on

383

the one hand and straightforward greed and extortion by those whose services were bought in by the organisers caught with a crazy deadline breathing down their necks.

As the opening day on 15 August approached, the festival lurched from one crisis to another. On-site organisation was chaotic; an estimated 30,000 people had camped out before any of the security, food or medical aid was in place. Trying to get entrance money from this number was deemed suicidal and it wasn't too long before the whole thing was declared a free festival. Out of an estimated peak crowd figure of around 400,000, probably only those who bought tickets in advance (about 60,000) paid to get in.

Arrangements for the performers were equally shambolic – the managers of several bands asked for money up front because they could sense that the organisers were in trouble. They needed helicopters to fly many of the artists in – all the approach roads were jammed solid as far as the eye could see. Most bands went on several hours late.

Holed up in Shokan, Jimi was unhappy about media reports of the size of the crowd, the Governor of New York declaring the site a disaster area and so on. He hated playing large crowds; Janis Joplin had already complained before her set to her friend and biographer Myra Friedman that such a crowd was too 'abstract' – you could touch only a tiny fraction. Jimi was due to go on at midnight on the Sunday – at four in the afternoon he was still saying he wouldn't do it. Although meagre by Jimi's standards, he was getting the top fee of $18,000 (plus $12,000 for the right to film him) and it was a prestige gig. Mike Jeffery was determined that Jimi would be on stage and he reassured the organisers to this effect.

As far as Mitch is concerned, 'It was a shambles for us. . . . it took us hours to drive up there in a couple of estate cars [including Claire Moriece's Dodge]. There were no facilities for dressing rooms or anything. In the end we finished up trekking across this muddy field for half a mile to this little cottage with no heating, nothing. Playing-wise, you couldn't hear a bloody thing. . . . it was like ten days' rehearsal and I think it shows.'

Eventually they didn't get on the stage until about 8 a.m. the following morning when only about 30,000 people remained. By then, as Jerry Velez euphemistically puts it, they were all 'spinning'. Unlike Mitch, who had seen it all before, Juma was overwhelmed by the occasion. 'It felt like three minutes, I walked out there, the sun was coming up and there was a sea of people, all this good energy, they were coming with the sun and the light, it was overpowering. We could have played for hours more – all the songs the Experience played, we knew them all.'

Juma says that they played that day 'from the freedom of spirit. We did not have a plan, we didn't know what he was gonna play. My position was that if he came out with something I hadn't played before, if I could add my ingredient with continuity I would play. If I couldn't then I wouldn't.'

The Woodstock performance of Gypsy Sons and Rainbows ('We're nothing but a band of gypsies,' said Jimi from the stage) was loose and sprawling, as Mitch suggests, but somehow it didn't seem to matter. Indeed, there were some very fine moments, in particular Jimi's beautiful solo improvisations, the complete performance of which has never been officially released.

Coming out of a scorching version of 'Voodoo Child (slight return)' incorporating 'Stepping Stone', Jimi surged straight into 'The Star Spangled Banner'.

Although he had only recorded the song in March, 'The Star Spangled Banner' had been part of the set for some time. In fact, Woodstock may well have been the anniversary performance; probably the first time he played it was on 17 August 1968 in Atlanta, Georgia. By comparison with live recordings, the studio version which later appeared on *Rainbow Bridge* sounds rather anaemic.

One of the abiding images of the place and time of Woodstock is Jimi, in white-beaded leather jacket, blue jeans, gold chains and a red head-scarf standing centre-stage alone sending out 'The Star Spangled Banner' as a series of shock waves across the audience in the early-morning light. When Jimi performed the song at the LA Forum in April, Pete Johnson of the *LA Times* accused Jimi of cheap sensationalism, his protest lacking the sincerity of politically committed artists like Country Joe MacDonald, Phil Ochs, the Fugs 'or other literate, disturbed performers'. Nevertheless, 'The Star Spangled Banner' has gone down in history as a classic reworking of the national anthem in the service of *us* against *them*. But is this the only interpretation?

From a political point of view, Woodstock, as exemplified by the performance of Country Joe MacDonald, Crosby Stills and Nash and Joan Baez, was a cosy affirmation of affluent, white middle-class angst about Vietnam as a metaphor for the moral bankruptcy of the state. Just being at Woodstock was as close to an act of revolution as most of the audience ever came, that and saying 'pig' to a policeman from 500

'Woodstock Music And Art Fair', Bethel, New York, 18 August 1969

yards off and having Che Guevara on the bedroom wall as a statement of radical chic. Jimi was coming at this from a different angle. Sly Stone and Richie Havens excepting, there were no major black recording artists on the whole bill – and precious few black faces in the audience. Combined with his distancing view of the world (as expressed in songs like '1983'), this gave Jimi something of observer status at Woodstock. Nor did Jimi altogether share the majority youth view on the criminal lunacy of the Vietnam War.

Eric Burdon once remarked that Jimi 'did have a right-wing attitude when he first arrived in England'. Asked about Vietnam in early 1967, Jimi said, 'After China takes over the whole world, then the whole world will know why America's trying so hard in Vietnam.'[10] This brought a wry response from erstwhile music journalist Karl Dallas, writing on behalf of Folksingers for Freedom in Vietnam: 'Jimi Hendrix is right! The Chinese are trying to overrun the world. That's why they've got to be forced to withdraw their troops from Britain, West Berlin, West Germany, Guantanamo in Cuba, Turkey, Thailand and all over Asia. The fact they are in these countries under the American flag shouldn't be allowed to fool anyone. Put that in your guitar and chew it, Jimi!'[11] Undeterred, Jimi told the Dutch magazine *Kink*, 'Did you send the Americans away when they landed in Normandy? That was also interference . . . but that was concerning your own skin. The Americans are fighting in Vietnam for a completely free world. As soon as they move out, they [the Vietnamese] will be at the mercy of the communists. For that matter the yellow danger [China] should not be underestimated. Of course, war is horrible, but at present it's still the only guarantee of peace.'[12]

One might have imagined that several subsequent months of fairly regular use of LSD would have changed Jimi's attitude, making him more at one with the world as his ego dissolved into the melting pot of the global psychedelic unity promised by Timothy Leary. But exactly a year later Jimi was saying this to a Swedish interviewer: 'I will hardly get to Vietnam in time. I will probably go direct to China. This little war in Vietnam is just a preparation for what will come.'[13] If nothing else, it showed that although Jimi was disturbed by some of his LSD visions, taking the drug had a limited impact in changing the way he thought about life.

What Jimi seems to have objected to is the horror of war in general as symbolising man's inhumanity to man and also the way conscription imposes limitations on personal freedom – which explains why some of his Swedish concerts were dedicated to American draft dodgers who fled to neutral Sweden.

So in the light of this, what are we to make of 'The Star Spangled Banner'? Jimi was perhaps telling the audience that if they think sitting in a sea of mud and garbage for three days is going to change anything, forget it. The military helicopters hired to bring in supplies and performers may be 'on our side' (or rather 'your side') today, but what about tomorrow? Forget what is happening thousands of miles away in Vietnam, what about the mess on your own doorstep, policemen beating up kids, black and white, what about the ghettos in flames? How can you possibly imagine that this is the Dawning of the Age of Anything when all that is going on? If you want to progress to a better life, where are the leaders? Who is setting the example? And you only have to realise that within twelve months, there was Manson, Altamont and students shot dead on the campus of Kent State University in Ohio to think that, if this thesis has any validity, then Jimi might just have had a point. Think about how euphoric most (but not all) the media were the next day about the 'promise of Woodstock' and reflect on how unkind history has been to the event since, especially after Altamont. Perhaps Jimi was Woodstock's only true revolutionary. He was certainly the major iconoclast.

But given the level of trouble at some of his recent gigs, Jimi was nonetheless impressed (like everyone else) that so many kids could coexist for so long in less than ideal surroundings without beating each other to death. Claire Moriece says that, as Jimi came off stage, he collapsed from exhaustion. But he was together enough to give this comment to a local radio station about the positive side of Woodstock for him:

> The non-violence, the very, very, very good brand of music, I don't mean good, I mean the very true brand of music, the acceptance of the long waiting crowd. They had to sleep in the mud and rain and get hassled by this and hassled by that and still come through saying it was a successful festival. . . . they're tired of joining street gangs, they're tired of joining militant groups, they're tired of hearing the President gab his gums. . . . They wanna find different direction, they know they're on the right track, but where the hell is it coming from?

Despite all the fun times Jimi had up at Shokan, he was deeply troubled. Life was crowding in on him and the pressure was getting unbearable.

388

Not surprisingly, Mike Jeffery was not pleased with Jimi's continuing association with a bunch of guys he would have regarded as free-loading no-hopers who were putting a brake on Jimi's career, diverting him away from the job of being a high-earning rock star. This was Mike being the insensitive businessman; he had little or no appreciation of Jimi's music and even less interest in how it would develop, so long as it brought in the cash. Claire recalls going with Jimi to Mike's house in Woodstock and hanging around waiting for him to show up. 'Jimi went to play some music and Michael had a record collection like from one end of the wall to the other and Jimi couldn't find anything to play, it was all kiddy pop and bad rock 'n' roll, you know, no real music. There was something that disgusted Jimi about that.'

There was a strong feeling among guys like Jerry, Juma and Larry that Mike's displeasure was being translated in subtle ways into acts of sabotage against them by those in the office and the roadies, which they feel – rightly or wrongly – may also have had racial undertones. 'They would take our instruments like my congas', says Jerry, 'and they would just throw them around like nothing.' Jerry was supposed to be with Jimi on the *Johnny Carson Show*: 'I got a call, there was a fuck-up,' he says vaguely. The same kind of thing happened to Juma; Jimi did the *Dick Cavett Show* in September: 'They were trying to extricate me at that time. Jimi said, 'Show up and I'll pay you for the gig.'' So I show up at the *Dick Cavett Show* and they left my drums at the house. So I went round the corner and got a conga from a friend.' Not that they took it all lying down. Fresh out of Vietnam, Larry Lee was full of aggression and the atmosphere could be very tense. 'They didn't let me play on the *Dick Cavett Show* 'cause they wanted to keep the image steady. Juma sneaked down and played, he wasn't supposed to play. It was supposed to be Mitch, Jimi and Billy, so that our group wouldn't be publicised. After seeing that going on I told Jimi as a friend it might do you more good if I went home [that is, back to Memphis]. This is turning into a disaster. I was in the wrong town.'

Quiet, mild-mannered Billy Cox was finding all this tension and aggravation too much to handle and he didn't know whether to stay or go. Larry says that Billy was 'playing musical chairs on the 747 – Jimi would be looking for him and he'd be calling from Nashville, then he'd come back and we were supposed to do something and Billy jumped another plane.' Larry also blames drugs for much of the paranoia and confusion. 'It was different drugs affecting different people in different ways.' Talking about acid he says, 'It was in some fruit punch and I said,

"Let's have a jam." Jimi picked up a bass and I picked up a guitar and we started to play some of the old numbers we used to play in Nashville and we were just laughing. He stopped laughing, but I couldn't. I laughed at everything I saw, my whole trip was nine and a half hours of laugh. . . . I was hallucinating. . . . that was my first time and I did too much of it. I had a sore throat for a long time. I laughed for *nine and a half hours* and I didn't take that shit no more.'

People see a fast buck and have you up there being a slave to the public. They keep you at it until you are exhausted and so is the public and then they move off to other things. That's why groups break up – they just get worn out. Musicians want to pull away after a while or they get lost in the whirlpool. (*Melody Maker*, 2 March 1969)

For some time, Jimi was telling friends that he wanted to get away from Mike. Jimi was also worried about the money. He knew he had earned a fortune, but was concerned that his taxes might not be paid. Sometimes he had rolls of cash on him, other times he'd be flat broke, borrowing money from Claire. Documents appertaining to his business affairs were stolen by friends out of the New York office and handed to Jimi; one showed that what was supposed to be a $10,000 gig was in fact grossing $50,000. Now, he was also anxious about Mike's plans to build him his own studio – an idea which went back to 1968.

The issue of New York's *RAT Subterranean News* for 19 April 1968 reported the gala opening of a new music club on 7 April in the Village on the site of the old Generation Club. Michael Goldstein sent out invitations to the press, who were entertained by B.B. King, Janis Joplin, Joni Mitchell, Buddy Guy, the Paul Butterfield Blues Band, Richie Havens, Roy Buchanan and Jimi. The club had just been bought by Mike Jeffery as part of his own business expansion, which saw the simultaneous opening of Sergeant Pepper's in Majorca. The club was still called the Generation, although Jimi told one reporter it would be renamed Godiva's.

The original idea was for a club-cum-studio; architect John Storyk was asked to redesign the premises accordingly. While discussions were held and plans drawn up through the rest of the year, Mike's business manager on the project, Jim Marron, commissioned an audit into Jimi's studio costs at the Record Plant. The results confirmed what Mike had felt; because of Jimi's habit of block-booking the studio for lengthy jam sessions at peak rates, expenditure was enormous, amounting to $300,000. At these prices it made sense to abandon the idea of having a studio tucked at the back of a club and open a state-of-the-art studio available to Jimi any hour of the night or day. And there was the prospect now of a very lucrative business venture – all the top bands would want to record there. With the help of Eddie Kramer, John Storyk threw away his drawings and started again early in 1969. Ultimately, the new studio, which Jimi wanted to call Electric Lady, was supposed to be a cost-saving for Jimi. But the budget allocation from his earnings was a hefty $350,000 – Jimi was asked to put in $250,000 up front before a single brick was in place, and in April Jimi signed a memo from Jim Marron authorising the accountant Michael Hecht to transfer $17,000 of his money for the purchase of two Ampex tape machines. By June Jimi began to get cold feet.

With the support of the journalist Sharon Lawrence, he went to see his lawyer Henry Steingarten to tell him he wanted to sever his links with Mike Jeffery. They met Steingarten at the Sheraton-West Hotel on Wilshire Boulevard in Los Angeles. It took a lot of persuading by Sharon to get Jimi to tell Steingarten himself, in his own words, how unhappy he was, how he wanted to be bought out of the studio, how he thought Mike was ripping the Experience off, how he wanted to be released from his contract and so on. Steingarten appeared to be genuinely interested in helping Jimi, but in asking him to gather evidence of Mike's alleged 'crooked dealings' he must have known what an impossible task that was. He must also have realised the 'conflict of interest' implications of all this for his own firm. In all probability, he was just humouring Jimi, knowing that all musicians claim that their managers are ripping them off, and that it would all come to nothing. Which is precisely what happened. Nothing.

As if he didn't have enough to deal with, the Panthers were making a nuisance of themselves up at the house. Jimi did not want to make any direct contribution to the cause of black militancy, but their jibes did galvanise him into some positive action – to present his music to a black audience.

One night Jimi wanted to go to a black club where he could jam. Arthur Allen suggested an old haunt of Jimi's, Small's Paradise in Harlem on 138th Street.

Some band was playing and Jimi sat in, but the *way* he sat in, like he
was afraid, like he was wondering if his hat was alright. He really
wanted to make a good impression in front of this audience of no
more than forty people. But Jimi was very, very self-conscious. And

Harlem, New York, 5 September 1969

he came in and said, 'How's my hat, man, how does my hat look?' So we said, 'Your hat looks alright, man.' 'Do you think they'll mind if . . . ?' Always wondering what we, what other black people thought about his music and him . . . so he wound up jamming and blowing everybody's freaking mind out. . . . every time I seen him play uptown, he played better than I have ever seen him play in my *life*.

Earlier in the year, Jimi had expressed a desire to play the Apollo Theatre, but this never came off because the theatre only booked artists by the week. Instead, he played an open-air gig again on 138th Street with Sam & Dave and Big Maybelle as supporting acts in aid of the United Block Association, which ran a poverty programme unit managing day centres and organising trips. Jimi told the *New York Times*, 'Sometimes when I come up here, people say, "He plays white rock for white people. What's he doin' here?" Well, I want to show them that music is universal – that there is no white rock or black rock. Some of these kids haven't got $6 to go to Madison Square Garden – besides, I used to play up here myself at Small's.'[14] Around 5000 people had gathered in Harlem, but by the time Jimi came on after midnight the crowd had dwindled to about a tenth of that. Arthur Allen stood to the side watching.

Jimi started playing, but he came out with too much noise, he wasn't projecting like he should have. Nobody knew him. 'Get off, so we can hear Big Maybelle.' 'Who is this Jimi Hendrix?' 'Jimi who?' 'Jimmy Witherspoon?' He started making some kind of distortion out of his guitar, feeling the public, like throwing something at them. And the audience replied with an egg, someone threw an egg out a window and it really freaked him out. He started playing like he never played before and blew everyone's mind, had everyone on their toes. And that was his first communication with black people and they dug him.

Those that were left, that is – *Disc* reporter Richard Robinson estimated that only about 200 remained to see the set out, of which about a quarter were white.

But after the gig, Arthur says, Jimi 'felt very up . . . he was happy to turn on even that number of people.'

The gig five nights later at the Salvation club in the Village Jimi was decidedly less keen on playing. As a discotheque the club was a regular haunt for the rich and famous until it ran foul of state laws on drinking and had its liquor licence revoked. Owner Bobby Woods continued to run it as an unlicensed bar, but the club lost its glitzy clientele. A far

Jazz street festival, Harlem, New York, 5 September 1969

---

seedier element moved in, including local drug dealers and some young
Mafia guys from Brooklyn out to establish their gangster credentials
with the Mob hierarchy. They demanded the usual protection money,
but things took a more serious turn when Woods was persuaded to
take on as club manager John Riccobono, a relative of 'Staten Island'
Joe Riccobono, a key figure in the Carlo Gambino family, one of the
most powerful Mafia families in America. Mafia associates were put
on the payroll, large sums of money were going out of the club while
Woods tried rather foolhardily to resist this take-over. He upset the
wrong people and wound up dead a few months later.

Trying to salvage the club's failing fortunes, Woods switched over to a live music policy. Knowing Jimi was a regular in the club, his 'associates' suggested that Jimi perform the opening night. Jimi didn't want to do it – he had a plan of how the band would develop and that didn't include doing small-club dates at this time. But they were insistent, so Mike went up to Shokan to try and persuade Jimi to change his mind. Mike was keen to stay in with these guys. First, it was always useful in the music business to have some friendly muscle on your side, but more specifically the Mafia had been getting concerned over the siting of the new studio, fearful that it would become the focus of unwelcome attention from the police looking for drugs in an area which the Mafia largely controlled. Mike was anxious not to upset anybody and saw the Salvation gig as an easy way to do them a favour. He owed the Mafia and Jimi was the collateral.

Mike did not come alone to the house – he arrived in a limousine with another behind carrying some toughs. Mike and one other went upstairs to talk to Jimi alone, leaving another Italian suit outside. Juma watched all this going on with some trepidation, but also determined that he and the others would stand by Jimi and resist this kind of intimidation. However, 'This guy comes up and put a target up about twenty-five yards away near a tree, pulls out his .38 and pow! pow!, bullseyes every time while the conversation with Jimi is going on.' They did the gig.

Jimi came on to the stage at around 12.15 a.m. with the Woodstock band and, although the crowd were expecting Hendrix pyrotechnics, he stood there calmly, the band working together pretty well, Jimi trading solos with Larry Lee, who according to a reviewer from *Rock* magazine was 'wonderful'. But then 'the set continued with jam-songs and the audience waiting for "Foxy Lady" and "Fire" grew impatient and disappointed. It was sad to see Hendrix, creating a series of superb informal compositions, being condemned by a horde of $10-paying customers who finally chose to walk out.'

All evening the sound system had been playing up and Jimi's vocal mike didn't work properly. They got it fixed so Jimi could do 'Izabella'. He then thanked what was left of the audience, set his guitar on top of one of the amps and walked off.

Jimi had another reason to regret his forced association with the Salvation. In one of the more bizarre incidents of his life, Jimi was kidnapped out of the club one night by unidentified hoods claiming to be the Mafia. He allegedly left the club with these guys to score some cocaine (strange in itself if true, when drugs were being pushed on him all the time) – next thing he knew, he was whisked off to an apartment in Manhattan. The following morning these guys told him to phone Mike Jeffery. Bob Levine took the call in the office and he in turn called both Mike and Jerry Morrison telling them both that Jimi was dead unless Mike handed over Jimi's contract.

Jerry Morrison said that he had connections who owed him a favour. After a couple of days, somebody phoned Morrison, told him where Jimi was being held and said that these guys were street punks with no authority. This wasn't a Mafia hit, just a straightforward hustle. It had happened before – backstage at the Scene club, the band had been threatened if they didn't sign up for yet another supposed Mafia heavy. The name was used to invoke fear – and uttered by the right-looking character, it usually worked.

Morrison said he went with two toughs of his own to the flat, but found that Jimi had already been moved. Suspicion grows when he then says that he 'guessed' they would go to the Shokan house. Would genuine kidnappers really take their victim back to his own house? Sure enough Morrison and his friends arrive, overpower Jimi's kidnappers and find him sitting upstairs calm as you like. The consensus of opinion among the few people Jimi told was that the whole thing was perhaps a set-up either by Jerry Morrison at Mike's behest to screw Jimi up further or by Morrison himself just to show Mike he wasn't the only one with 'connections'. Alternatively, given the amount of interest by gangsters (organised or otherwise) in the money to be made from rock, Trixie Sullivan supports the story that the kidnap was real enough – just the ending has been changed.

The music business in those days was like the Wild West. What it was, the 'junior' Mafia was always trying to move into the music business. The 'older' Mafia wasn't really interested. And Jimi was kidnapped by some guys that were holding him for ransom to get his contract. Mike had his contacts in the music business, which could be quite heavy too. Mike found, or was given an introduction to, people who would go with him to sort it out. And that's exactly what happened. Mike was teamed up with these guys in limousines, they were taken to where Jimi was being held. When they realised who Mike was with, they let him go.

Whoever was responsible, this incident helped put Jimi's growing paranoia over who he could really trust into overdrive.

Jimi still had the house in Shokan, affording some tranquillity when it wasn't packed to the rafters with hangers-on. But he was never one for being completely on his own, he liked the company of perhaps just one woman or a very small group of friends. On a quiet weekend in September, with all the intruders gone, Jimi actually managed to have the place to himself with his musician friends and Sheila Weller from *Rolling Stone.* He was very subdued, holding mumbling conversations with people in between mouthfuls of Claire's chocolate-chip cookies. In the article published in November, Sheila Weller described Jimi as 'vulnerable and boyish'. From time to time Jimi made some aide-memoires in the embossed Moroccan lyric notebook he always had with him. Sheila was surprised at his catholic taste in music from Marlene Dietrich to Schoenberg, Wes Montgomery and Crosby Stills and Nash. But straight on the turntable went *John Wesley Harding*, Jimi playing along gently to 'The Ballad of Frankie Lee and Judas Priest'. Equally surprising, considering how disparaging he was about them in his early interviews, is a photo of Jimi on the bookcase from his early sixties R&B days, process hair-do, silk suit and shiny shoes. Now he doesn't have anything to prove, there's no need to distance himself from those times. 'That's okay,' he laughs, 'I don't try to cover up the past. I'm not ashamed of it.'

But he did seem very humble about the present, wondering if he should try out with some of the more avant-garde jazz musicians. 'Tell me honestly,' he asks someone in the room, 'what do those guys think of me? Do they think I'm jiving?' They listen to some free-form jamming from the night before featuring Juma and Jerry on percussion, Juma on flute and a jazz keyboardist, Mike Ephron. Jimi's reflections on what might be, who he could try out with, what kind of music he could create, leads up to one of his most famous press statements: 'I don't want to be a clown any more. I don't want to be a rock 'n' roll star.'[15]

In not wanting to be manipulated, performing to order, subject to the shifting sands of audience expectations, Jimi was in some esteemed company. The very next month in Paris, Ornette Coleman was telling jazz drummer Arthur Taylor for his book of jazz interviews *Notes and Tones*, 'I don't feel healthy about the performing world any more at all. I think it's an egotistical world, it's about money and clothes not about music. I'd like to get out of it, but I don't have the financial situation to do so. I have come to enjoy writing music because you don't have to have that performing image. . . . I don't want to be a puppet and be told what to do and what not to do.'[16] Because of the system of arts patronage in the nineteenth century, even classical composers could feel trapped; the Norwegian composer Grieg wrote to a friend, 'I don't want to be an organ-grinder. I want to compose what's in my heart.' All of which goes to show how similar are the problems of all creative artists who reach a certain level of fame irrespective of time, place or genre.

It is 7 a.m., they've been up talking all night and just returned from a trip in Jimi's Stingray sports car to see the sunrise at the waterfalls. Back at the house, Jimi goes around emptying ashtrays and tidying up a bit, another unexpected character trait – Jimi hated living in a mess. Then they all catch some sleep before it's time to go down to the Record Plant at 4 p.m. Interestingly, Jimi says they'll do the mixing elsewhere because the studio (which he doesn't name) he says has 'bad equipment [and] likes to take advantage of so-called long-hair musicians'.

On the drive down, a car pulls up alongside with 'If 6 Was 9' blaring out of the car radio. It's a trailer for a new film, *Easy Rider*. 'Have you seen the film?' asks Sheila Weller. No reply. Jimi's curled up in the back seat, foetus-like, fast asleep.

Jimi was trying to get his band together at the Record Plant, but the situation was next to impossible. Mitch was in and out of the sessions and Jimi's relationship with Eddie Kramer was also strained. Eddie was employed by Mike Jeffery, who didn't want to see Jimi rehearsing this band in the studio, so Eddie was always going to be in a difficult situation. Thus Jerry Velez describes Gypsy Sons and Rainbows in the studio as 'a train out of control', although 'it would have its moments'. However, it would be wrong to lay the blame for unproductive sessions entirely at the feet of an uncooperative management. On one session, music was not uppermost in Jerry's mind. 'I brought half a dozen girls, champagne, food, and I crashed into the session and put it on the grand piano. Jimi said, "Hey man, you can't do this, you are interrupting the session."'

By now both Warners and Track were hopping up and down for some new material – Jimi had been promising all kinds of projects to the press, but nothing had been delivered. Fragments of songs were liberally sprinkled through hundreds of hours of tape. In fact, to satisfy his record companies, Jimi would have to produce *two* albums' worth of new songs, because Ed Chalpin had first call on the next Jimi Hendrix album and he too was getting impatient. To plug the gap *Smash Hits* was released in the summer and did very good business on both sides of the Atlantic. Later that year, Track released 'Fire' b/w 'The Burning of the Midnight Lamp' as a filler.

To complicate matters still further, Jimi got involved with Stella Douglas' husband Alan of the jazz label Douglas Records, whom he first met when Devon brought him to a dinner party at the Douglas home. Alan Douglas has remained a controversial figure in the story of Jimi Hendrix, both while Jimi was alive and in the continuing battle over who controls Jimi's music since his death – and there are as many views on Douglas' relationship with Jimi as there are people to proffer them. At one extreme, Claire Moriece claims that Douglas 'had a very bad reputation' among musicians and that 'Jimi hated the man.' Then again, Ira Cohen, who took photographs for Douglas Records, has said Jimi and Alan 'seemed to be in pretty warm and personal contact'.

Certainly Jimi was impressed with Douglas' recording credentials. Douglas had recorded a number of jazz artists including Eric Dolphy and John McLaughlin. Jimi helped him out on two albums, the eponymous *Last Poets* album and Timothy Leary's *You Can Be Anyone You Want This Time Around*, for which he got a rap over the knuckles from Warners. Unlike Mike Jeffery, Douglas knew a lot about music and Jimi found him a sympathetic ear to talk to about developing a new kind of sound for his music.

Alan had rightly surmised that Jimi was bored playing with rock 'n' roll musicians 'in the sense that they were very limited in their capacity to expand the music that he always had the vision for. He, of course, admired the jazz musicians because of their imagination and their capacity to deal with their instruments.' He wanted to develop Jimi's limited connections with jazz and was very keen to team him up with Miles Davis. However, although Miles had a lot of respect for Jimi's music, he still wouldn't even put in a studio appearance for less than $50,000. Miles asked drummer Lenny White if he was interested, 'But I wasn't into Hendrix, so I didn't do it.' Ultimately, the whole idea fell through. However keen Jimi might have been on the plan, he wanted it to happen only on his terms. Juma observed something of this: 'Jimi wanted to work with Alan, but they had artistic clashes. I was in the studio when Alan called Miles and asked him to come in. But Jimi wanted to do it *his* way and it wasn't about Alan's way and that's where the conflict came in.' Miles wasn't keen to be involved in any formal sessions, so he asked for a big fee. But in his autobiography Miles says that Jimi did come around to play in private. When Miles attempted to explain musical theory, Jimi just looked blank, but once Miles played the piece, however complex it was, Jimi picked it up immediately. Jimi tried to sort out other jazz connections on his own. For example, he went to see Quincey Jones, who says he set up a session for Jimi, but Jimi never showed. Miles Davis also says in his book that he lived to regret inviting Jimi over, because, he claims, the subsequent affair between Jimi and Betty Davis was partly to blame for the break-up of Miles' marriage.

Unfortunately, Jimi found himself caught in a 'push me, pull you' game between Alan Douglas and Mike Jeffery which he could well have done without. About Douglas, Ira Cohen observed, 'He was always interested in supporting and doing things, but of course he was also looking for what would be a commercial success.' More forthrightly, Juma adds, 'Jeffery hated Douglas, because Jeffery knew he and Alan were both from the same mould.' Alan worked with Jimi in the studio on versions of 'Izabella', 'Room Full of Mirrors' and 'Stepping Stone', which further isolated Jimi from Eddie Kramer. Alan encroached still more into Mike's territory when 'I became a kind of consultant to Jimi on a business basis – Mike's jealousy with me was on that basis. It was constantly, "There's not enough to deal with what you want," which was not really true, but he fell for it always.'

As autumn gave way to the grip of winter, so Jimi gave way to mounting pressure from without and the realisation within that Gypsy Sons and Rainbows as a working outfit was never going to work. They all met up at the Navada Hotel in Central Park South where Jimi was staying and he told them it was the end of the road. He hoped that they could jam together and that even their musical co-operative named Heaven Research Unlimited could come to fruition. But, for now, everything was on hold.

It has become part of the Jimi Hendrix mythology that he was under pressure to form a black band. There may well have been demand from black nationalists that he should do this, but there is no evidence that he actually complied. With Gypsy Sons and Rainbows, Jimi wanted to hang together with some friends from the less complicated old days, but he still wanted Mitch involved. With his next venture the presence of two black musicians in a new trio format was sheer expediency.

The name Band of Gypsys had been on Jimi's lips for some time. Ex-Hendrix roadie Neville Chesters credits Mitch with its first utterance: 'It was in a hotel one time in New York in 1968. There was always this continual entourage of people going back and forth

400

along the corridor to Jimi's room and nobody ever saw Jimi for two or three days at a time. And I just remember one day Mitch saying, "It's like a fuckin' band of gypsies in here." I remember it quite distinctly.'

Mike Jeffery had an idea that the way to get Ed Chalpin off their backs would be to record a live album and give him that. It would be cheap to produce, but would probably need to contain new material to fulfil the agreement. It was for this reason, says Billy Cox, that the Band of Gypsys came into existence. 'At the time I was there and I think Mitch was in England. He was asked to do it, but I think he wanted to stay in England. Buddy was easily available. So me, Buddy and Jimi . . . rehearsed for a couple of weeks and that was the Band of Gypsies.'[17]

Jimi's twenty-seventh birthday was on 27 November. Devon threw a party for him at an apartment on the Upper East Side of Manhattan. The Rolling Stones came and Devon made a bee-line for Mick Jagger. Back in early 1967, Jimi had tried to entice Marianne Faithfull from under Jagger's nose. Believing Devon was Jimi's 'girl' Jagger played up to these advances and, although it was supposed to be Jimi's party, Devon eventually left with Jagger. Jimi couldn't have cared less. He was too depressed to have much feeling about anything. His relationship with drugs had been changing. Cocaine had come into his life to a greater degree which could only exacerbate his sense of anxiety and insecurity. But more important than any particular drug was that, instead of drugs being used to relax, they were employed to escape. Same drugs, different expectations, more danger.

Carlos Santana was down at the Record Plant in mid-November when Jimi was doing overdubs for 'Room Full of Mirrors':

This was a real shocker to me. He said, 'Okay, roll it', and started recording and it was incredible. But within 15 or 20 seconds into the song, he just went out. All of a sudden the music that was coming out of the speakers was way beyond the song, like he was freaking out having a gigantic battle in the sky with somebody. It just didn't make sense with the song any more, so the roadies looked at each other, the producer looked at him and they said, 'Go get him.' I'm not making this up. They separated him from the amplifier and the guitar and it was like he was having an epileptic attack. I said, 'Do I have to go through these changes just to play my guitar? I'm just a kid!' When they separated him, his eyes were red. . . . He was gone.

To me, it was a combination of the lifestyle – staying up all night, chicks, too much drugs, all kinds of stuff. It was a combination of all the intensities he felt, along with a lack of discipline. In the rock style of life at that time, there was no discipline.[18]

Jimi was caught in the crossfire of warring factions, record producers, musicians, women and businessmen all competing for his money, his time, his body, his soul, his good will, his conscience and his music. Everybody seemed to be whispering in his ear warning him about this person or that person while nobody, least of all the management, was offering him the care and protection his genius and status deserved. And hardly anybody around him heard or chose to hear Jimi's own primeval scream demanding the one request constantly denied him – 'LEAVE ME ALONE!'

On 6 December, Jimi was staying in New York when he heard about the Altamont Festival and the murder of a black kid, Meredith Hunter, by Hell's Angels 'security guards'. It could not have been a more depressing preparation for him, two days before his trial was due to open in Toronto.

On the 7th, Jimi flew to Toronto with his star witness Sharon Lawrence and Jeanette Jacobs, whom he had known since the early days in the Village. He was terrified that as a black rock star accused of possessing drugs, he was on a hiding to nowhere.

On Monday the 8th, Jimi stood impassively before Judge Joseph Kelly dressed in a sober blue blazer and grey trousers bought specially for the occasion. The first witness up on the stand was Officer Marvin Wilson, who had found the drugs, followed by his supervisor and the lab technician who conducted the tests on the substances found. Jimi sat in court, next to his Canadian lawyer John O'Driscoll, reliving the events of seven months ago – a nightmare which had plagued him ever since.

There was no denying that Jimi had had the drugs on him. But in legal terms for 'possession' to be proven the Crown had to show that Jimi knew the drugs were there, so they would want to show that he was a regular drug user who carried his supplies with him.

Jimi was the first witness in the defence case. He confirmed that he received gifts from fans all the time, including drugs; and was often in too much of a hurry to register what he'd had thrust in his hand or baggage. He also perjured himself by declaring that he had outgrown drugs. This was part of the rock-star drug trial game. Juries like to see the mighty humble themselves before the common people. A nice bit of contrition always went down well. It was expected, and defence lawyers knew this. Jimi continued his defence testimony the following day and was then subjected to relentless prosecution cross-examination trying to show Jimi up as a seasoned drug abuser. Holding up the aluminium tube in which the hash was found, prosecuting counsel probed Jimi on what sort of 'gift' was this. What use could Jimi possibly put this to? 'A pea shooter?' said Jimi innocently, amid roars of laughter from the court.

Sharon Lawrence was next on the stand to tell her story about what happened in that LA motel room. She was followed by Chas, who, despite prosecution claims that his testimony was irrelevant, was allowed to confirm Jimi's story about the deluge of gifts from fans. As the judge said in his summing up – if the jury believed Sharon Lawrence's story, then Jimi was not guilty. Eight hours later they came back: James Marshall Hendrix, 'Not Guilty'.

Jimi was ecstatic – 'The best Christmas present I could have,' he told reporters. Only one way to celebrate – get smashed. He went back to New York to the rambling apartment on 57th and 10th belonging to a musician friend of Devon's, Al Brown. Brown's place was one of a number of comfort stations made available to Jimi, a place to relax, get high and get fed. Al Brown had a mouth-watering repertoire of West Indian dishes at his fingertips. A pot of beef, chicken, dumplings and carrots was always on the stove if Al knew Jimi was coming by. They often talked seriously about music, composition and arranging. But that night it was fun time, with Jimi doing his hilarious impersonations of Little Richard and the Harlem drag queens.

It wasn't all doom and gloom in the studio either. Despite the incredible pressure of recent months Jimi was very slowly beginning to regain his creative spark. From his rehearsals with Billy and Buddy at the Record Plant during December came two songs. In 1968, the Experience had tried out instrumental versions of the song which Jimi now, at the end of 1969 with the Band of Gypsys, called 'Ezy Ryder', adding lyrics presumably influenced by the film.

> There goes Ezy, Ezy Ryder
> Riding down the highway of desire
> He says the free wind takes him higher
> Trying to find his heaven above
> But he's dyin' to be loved. . . .

The other song was the seemingly gospel-inspired 'Earth Blues':

Jimi with Jeanette Jacobs (right) plus unknown friend
Toronto Court House, 10 December 1969

Tempe, Arizona, 5 February 1968

Jam session
Wreck Bar, The Castaway Hotel, Miami, Florida, 20 May 1968

Kiel Auditorium, St Louis, Missouri, 3 November 1968

Whisky A Go Go, Los Angeles, 18 September 1968

The Experience joined by Jack Casady
Oakland Coliseum, Oakland, California, 27 April 1969

Well, I see hands and attesting faces
reachin' up but not quite touching the Promised Land
Well, I taste tears and a whole lot of precious years wasted,
saying 'Lord please give us a helping hand'
Lord, there's got to be some changes
Gonna be a whole lot of re-arranges
You better hope love is the answer
Yeah, it better come before the summer

Well, everybody can hear the sound of freedom's beating heart
Sirens flashing with earth and rockets stoning
You better love me like it's gonna be the last time
and tell the child to bury Daddy's old clothes
Yeah, they're talking about getting together, yeah,
together for love, love, love
You better hope love is the answer, baby
I think you better hope it comes before the summer

Everybody, every Sister, every Mama
to feel the light, it's shining bright, baby
Everybody, we got to live together, oh
Right on baby
Feel those Earth Blues coming at you . . .

Don't let your imagination take you by surprise
A Queen and me I, one day, visualise
My head in the cloud, my feet on the pavement
Don't get too stoned, please remember you're a man
Lord, there's got to be some changes
Living together's gonna be a lot of re-arranges
You better be ready, Lord, my Lord
Just hope love comes before the summer

Everybody, got to feel the light
You gotta feel the light, baby
Everybody, we gotta live together
Keep it together, right on together, oh (yeah)

All standing together for the Earth Blues coming at you baby . . .
(Right on)
Feel those Earth Blues coming at you . . .
(Yeah, yeah)
(Yeah, yeah let me hear it)

Meanwhile the Band of Gypsys was to play Bill Graham's Fillmore
East over two nights for the recording of the live album – New Year's
Eve and the first day of the new decade – 1970.

Thirteen *New Rising Sun*

The First Wave of the New Rising Sun is my new life. Everybody has
something to give of themselves and it's not just money. I don't know what's
happening in England, but the dollar bill is God in the States. All those pelican
people just believe in money and nothing else. (*Melody Maker*, 11 January
1969)

All I write is just what I feel. . . . I don't round it off too good. I just keep it
almost naked. . . . what I was trying to do was doing three things at a time,
which is my nature. . . . I hate to be in one corner, I hate to be put only as
a guitar player, or either only as a songwriter, or only as a tap dancer. . . .
I like to move around. (Radio interview, London, 11 September 1970)

After the Band of Gypsys' first show on New Year's Eve 1969, Jimi
walked into Bill Graham's office just killing some time, and he asked
Bill what he thought of the show.

'Mmmm, okay.'

'What was that?'

'I said it was okay.'

Jimi knew there was something more to this. 'Come on, Bill.'

Bill Graham asked his assistants in the office to leave. They closed
the door after them. Bill looked long and hard at Jimi. 'You want me
to tell it the way it is?'

'Yeah, sure, I respect you. We've been friends too long. What is it?'

Bill sighed. 'Well, you were one big giant shuck, man.'

Jimi looked at Bill as if he was crazy. 'What did you say?'

'You were one big shuck from beginning to end.'

'Bill . . . wow . . . what are you talkin' about? Did you hear
that? They went crazy.'

'That's the point, Jimi. You're so big, you're Jimi Hendrix. In my
opinion you are the world's greatest exponent of the electric guitar

and what can be done with it. You're a genius. You humped the guitar, you stuck it behind your back, you picked it with your teeth, with your toes, with your knees. You did everything except one thing. *You forgot to play!'*

Jimi was stunned. 'What?'

'You didn't play. I don't know if you know it, but you could walk on that stage and play "Yankee Doodle Dandy" and do push-ups and they would love you, because you are Jimi Hendrix. But being Jimi Hendrix and having that power – wouldn't it be good to tell them – this is what can be done. And that's who you are – you're so powerful.'

Jimi sat there numb. 'Wow.'

'What? Am I lying to you? What do I do – apologise? Don't forget, schmuck, you asked me what I thought. You are a very powerful person – musically, politically, socially, anyway you want to look at it. You walk around with no socks – they won't buy socks, they won't wear socks. Some guy'll set fire to his house trying to set fire to his guitar *before* he learns how to play.'

Jimi and Bill talked it through some more, but Jimi was not too happy about it. He knew Bill was right, but he hadn't been out there for months, he felt he had to put on a show. When he wanted to, he enjoyed putting on a show. What he objected to was being expected to do it all the time – hence he didn't want to be a circus clown performing to order. Besides, when he did cut down the theatricals or left out songs like 'Wild Thing', the disappointment in the air was tangible. Even the hip Woodstock crowd were shouting out for 'Wild Thing' between numbers.

Jimi was as much upset with himself as with Bill. 'You gonna be around for the second show?'

'Yes.'

The second audience came in. Bill came out on stage and announced: 'On bass Billy Cox, on drums Buddy Miles, on lead guitar Jimi Hendrix. Will you please welcome . . .'

'What followed', says Bill, 'with respect to Carlos and Eric and all those others, was the most brilliant, emotional display of virtuoso electric guitar playing I have ever heard. I don't expect ever to hear such sustained brilliance in an hour and fifteen minutes. He just stood there, did nothing, just played and played and played.'

The audience applauded, not the kind of screeching, cheering heard at most rock concerts, but the resonant, thunderous applause accorded opera singers or great classical violinists or pianists – accolades for high art.

Jimi came to the side of the stage – he was like a big mop of sweat. He walked over to me and said, 'Well (pant, gasp), you satisfied, motherfucka?'

'Jimi, that was brilliant. What can I say? You were magical.'

'Awright. You gonna let me go? You gonna release me now? Thanks.'

And Jimi goes out and does a half-hour of all the schtick, all the garbage, the humpin' and grindin' and kickin', pickin' with his teeth, playin' behind his back. And he comes off and goes to me 'Naaaaaa'.*

It was from the next day's performance that tracks were selected for the Band of Gypsys album released later in June. From the first show came 'Who Knows' and 'Machine Gun', the focal point for the sustained brilliance of which Bill Graham spoke. If one piece of music had to be chosen to exemplify why Jimi Hendrix was the best there was by some considerable distance 'Machine Gun' was it. The quality of the improvisation, the sophisticated techniques employed, the artistry and imagination are staggering.

Jimi announced the song: 'Happy New Year, first of all. I hope we'll have a million or two million more of them . . . if we can get over this summer (heh, heh, heh). Right I'd like to dedicate this one to the draggin' scene that's goin' on – all the soldiers that are fightin' in Chicago, Milwaukee and New York . . . oh yes, and all the soldiers fightin' in Vietnam. Like to do a thing called "Machine Gun".'

Jimi was a hero among black soldiers in Vietnam. In his book *Dispatches*, war correspondent Michael Herr describes coming across a black corporal hunched over a cassette recorder with a big grin on his face as 'Fire' boomed out across the paddy fields above Vinh Long. Jimi had Credentials. '"Say, that Jimi Hendrix is my main man" someone would say. "He's definitely got his shit together." Hendrix had once been in the 101st Airborne, and the Airborne in Vietnam was full of wiggy-brilliant spades like him, really mean and really good, guys who always took care of you when things got bad. That music meant a lot to them. I never once heard it played over the Armed Forces Radio Network.'[1]

But mention of Vietnam as an afterthought was perhaps a further indication that his onomatopoeic evocations of death and destruction were primarily directed at civil unrest in America.

> Machine Gun
> Tearing my body all apart

*It has been suggested that the tapes of the shows don't really bear out Bill Graham's anecdote. However, it is possible that he mixed this up with another of the shows he promoted for Jimi.

Machine Gun, yeah
Tearing my body all apart
Evil man make me kill ya
Evil man make you kill me
Evil man make me kill you
Even though we're only families apart

Well I pick up my axe and fight like a bomber
(You know what I mean)
Hey! And your bullets keep knocking me down

Hey, I pick up my axe and fight like a bomber now
Yeah, but you still blast me down to the ground

The same way you shoot me down, baby
You'll be going just the same
Three times the pain,
and your own self to blame
Hey, Machine Gun

I ain't afraid of your mess no more, babe
I ain't afraid no more
After a while, your, your cheap talk don't even cause me pain,
so let your bullets fly like rain

'Cause I know all the time you're wrong baby
And you'll be goin' just the same
Yeah, Machine Gun
Tearing my family apart
Yeah, yeah, alright
Tearing my family apart

(Don't you shoot him down)
(He's 'bout to leave here)
(Don't you shoot him down)
(He's got to stay here)
(He ain't going nowhere)
(He's been shot down to the ground)
(Oh where he can't survive, no, no)

Yeah, that's what we don't wanna hear anymore, alright?
(No bullets)
At least here, huh huh
(No guns, no bombs)
Huh huh
(No nothin', just let's all live and live)
(You know, instead of killin')

'Who Knows' was essentially a jam featuring the mundane soul/R&B voice of Buddy Miles punctuated by some desperate 'strangled parrot' scat vocalising. Jimi seemed content to fall back on, by his standard, some unremarkable wah-wah licks.

Given how deeply ingrained is the image of Jimi as the hell-raising axe-wielding cocksman, it takes a fair leap of the imagination to comprehend a Jimi Hendrix who felt an increasing need to impart his compassionate vision of human potentiality realised through a love of God. Yet this is precisely the thrust behind 'Message to Love' and 'Power of Soul' (which Jimi called 'Crash Landing' for the show the day before), taken from the second show on New Year's Day. Like Dylan in *John Wesley Harding* Jimi wanted to move away from cynicism and bitterness and towards gentleness and compassion, towards a notion that only by an act of faith can the futility of life be redeemed. Dylan sublimated these passions in 'All Along The Watchtower', which instantly struck a chord deep within Jimi. In dealing with this theme under his own steam, these two Band of Gypsys songs do not quite have the lyrical adroitness common to much of Jimi's poetry. Then again, Jimi may have rightly surmised that, with 'rallying cry' anthems such as these, the message has to be simple and not wrapped up in enigmatic imagery. Typically, however, Jimi did not cosset the songs in drippy psychedelia ('All You Need Is Love' being one of the more obvious examples) but delivered them as gritty, hard-edged funk tunes. Introducing 'Message to Love' in subsequent concerts, Jimi often put on his side-of-mouth drawl to disparage the emptiness of many hippy songs about love. 'Message to Love' is much more 'take it or leave it', but if you take it, be prepared for a struggle. Nothing worth having comes easy.

The other two songs chosen for the album were both written by Buddy Miles – his hit song 'Them Changes' and 'We Gotta Live Together'. Not much to say about either of these, apart from some quite incredible guitar playing by Jimi towards the end of the latter song. At that point, it picks up to double time and the sounds of electronic equipment not yet invented stream out of Jimi's Stratocaster at breakneck speed. Coming after the kind of stuff Jimi could play in his sleep, the contrast is even more startling. The passage is quite short, but it has an eerie abstract quality which almost makes you fear for Jimi, so intense is the execution. Like his free-form work with Larry Young, a window was briefly opened on a side of Jimi's music he never had the chance to develop.

When the album was released in June, Ed Chalpin complained that he had not been given an album up to Jimi's normal standards, even though the album was top five on both sides of the Atlantic and so very profitable. As for the quality, Jimi agreed, but nonetheless he told friends he was very depressed in the wake of the concert that any of his work should be handed over to Ed Chalpin.

While Jimi was rehearsing the Band of Gypsys, Mike was harbouring thoughts about re-forming the Experience. Originally, Jimi had conceptualised the Band of Gypsys in much the same light as Gypsy Sons and Rainbows – just a fluid and developing aggregation of musicians. 'The fact of callin' it Gypsys means it could even expand on personnel or so forth. . . . We would like to plan a tour. We'd like to be on the major festivals. We'll play anywhere where we know it's gonna make some kind of penetration or some kind of impact. . . . I might not even be there all the time. Buddy might not even be there all the time, but the core, the whole, the child will be there!'[2]

Rehearsals at the Fillmore East, New York City, 31 December 1969

Buddy Miles himself says that Jimi was going to ask Stevie Winwood to join the band on keyboards. But as far as Mike was concerned, Jimi's new band was a one-off to get rid of Chalpin and now it was time to get back to serious business. On New Year's Day, he called Noel with plans for a tour. Noel jumped at the chance because life for him in England

411

was falling apart – both his short-lived marriage and his band Fat Mattress had collapsed. Chas had secured a huge advance of $175,000 for Noel's band, who went on a spending spree buying houses, cars and so on. But although they were all friends from the old days, the band never really worked out; Noel found himself increasingly isolated from the others to the point where just as Mike was ringing up saying 'How about a tour?' the other members of Fat Mattress actually dismissed him, saying they would be finding another guitarist. Mitch's life was far less complicated; he'd taken the drum chair in an ad-hoc association, Jack Bruce and Friends, with Larry Coryell – Bruce's first band since the break-up of Cream.

Jimi was always ambivalent about re-forming the band even just for one tour. In late December he told *Melody Maker*, 'I've been thinking about [it] for a long time. All I'm waiting for is for Noel and Mitch to make up their minds and we can get everything fixed.'[3]

But speaking to him backstage at the Fillmore East, *Record Mirror* quoted Jimi as scotching any idea of playing again with the band: 'With Mitch maybe, but not with Noel for sure.'[4] The reason given was the good reception received by the Band of Gypsys. So why say that he would possibly tour with Mitch when Buddy Miles was the drummer? In fact, Jimi was not that happy having Buddy as his regular drummer, because he just wasn't good enough. Jimi needed someone like Mitch to play against. Buddy was fine for jamming at the Scene and socially he was great fun – he and Jimi had some good times together. But as Gerry Stickells observed, 'Buddy was a solid, lay-down-the-beat, rock 'n' roll drummer. Mitch had a certain bit of jazz background there that allowed him to move around a bit, around what Jimi was doing.'

Jimi was always keen to play benefit concerts like the one in Harlem. Another opportunity arose on 28 January at Madison Square Garden – a Winter Festival for Peace, organised by the Vietnam Moratorium Committee. Peter Yarrow of Peter, Paul and Mary organised the talent, who all played for free. The seven-hour bill included among others Richie Havens, Judy Collins, the Rascals and Jimi – a gift to the anti-war effort from New York's underground music community. The show started at 8.30 p.m. and ran like clockwork until the Band of Gypsys came on stage around 3 a.m. Peter Yarrow announced the band: 'I think I can safely say "friends" after the length of time we've been living together. This is certainly the moment I've been waiting for and I'm sure all of you have. Mr Jimi Hendrix and his Band of Gypsys!'

Jimi was given a great reception, but from seeing him backstage before he went on, Johnny Winter knew he was in no condition to play.

> When I saw him it gave me the chills. It was the most horrible thing I'd ever seen. He came in with this entourage of people and it was like he was already dead. He just walked in and even though Jimi and I weren't the greatest of friends, we always talked, always – and he came in with his head down, sat on the couch alone and put his head in his hands. He didn't say a word to anybody and no one spoke to him. He didn't move until it was time for the show. He really wanted to do that gig, but he never should have.[5]

The story goes that Jimi was given some contaminated LSD before he went on stage, although from what Johnny Winter says he was obviously in some distress even before he arrived at the venue. Buddy Miles and others claim that Mike Jeffery gave him the stuff knowing it was bad, because he didn't want Jimi to do a political benefit gig or to carry on playing with Buddy and Billy. However, Mike had gone to the expense and trouble of hiring a film crew for the night, so it seems unlikely that he would deliberately jeopardise Jimi's performance. Jimi himself told friends later that Devon had given him some cola spiked with LSD in some kind of display of power over him. Being a famous rock star was no guarantee of purity when it came to drugs. So it is possible that Devon and/or Mike gave Jimi LSD 'in good faith' if one can put it like that, without knowing what would happen.

Jimi tries to tune up and tell Buddy and Billy about the first number, his voice strange and distant. 'I think it's in the key of D or A or G, something like that.' Somebody in the audience calls out for 'Foxy Lady' and Jimi turns on them, pointing out the 'Foxy Lady sittin'' over there with the yellow underwear stained and dirty with blood'. Billy Cox starts the bass riff to 'Who Knows', Buddy joins in. Jimi is trying to solo in inventive and imaginative ways, but on top of feeling ill, he is getting nothing from Buddy, who plods on relentlessly behind. Billy is almost invisible. Jimi is carrying the song himself. It grinds to a halt.

Jimi starts a new composition, 'Earth Blues'. He all but abandons the lyrics and solos off into space, swooping and diving, almost desperately inspired, leaving the band and the audience far behind. He plummets back to Earth and tells the audience, 'That's what happens when Earth fucks with space. Never forget that, never forget that.' Then Jimi sits

413

down on the stage. Buddy speaks into the microphone: 'We're . . . not . . . er . . . *quite* getting it together. Give us a bit more time because it has been hard and things are not exactly okay yet. So just bear with us for a few minutes and we'll see if we can do something together.'

But Jimi was gone. He left the stage, went back to his dressing-room and sat there hunched over with the stomach cramps of a badly manufactured dose of LSD. The Band of Gypsys never played again. Buddy Miles was fired by Mike Jeffery with the words: 'The trip's over.' Jimi could no more face Buddy than Noel, so, albeit gleefully, Mike Jeffery was probably doing Jimi's dirty work for him.

Meanwhile Mike was also gearing up to announce the re-formation of the Experience. Mitch and Noel both flew in from London and *Rolling Stone* was contacted in order to set up a major interview. John Burks was assigned to the job, but right from the start he was sceptical about the whole thing and felt that the paper was being manipulated to hype up another Second Coming by Jimi. What happened to the Band of Gypsys after all the press announcements in December and successful concerts at the Fillmore? The article published on 19 March was most unusual in that by inference it was clear that the magazine was not *always* going to play the game of keeping the music business sweet in pursuit of exclusive interviews and advertising revenue.*

> The other two cats in the band are Mitch Mitchell and Noel Redding from the original Experience. The Experience is back together again, and everybody's pals and no hard feelings. Considering the attrition rate among rock and roll bands during the past year, this has approximately the news value of a trial separation between Dick & Liz. But this was the big news Hendrix' press agent was eager to Get Across, so this is what we started on, as Michael Jeffery, Jimi's manager, brought on wine and booze.

In the interview Jimi was quoted at greater length than Noel or Mitch, although in fact, he very much took a back seat, particularly when it came to questions about the future plans for the 'new' Experience. Asked about the material they would perform, Noel says pointedly, '"Red House" with *two* guitars.' Away from music, Burks tried to engage Jimi in conversation about his alleged support for black militancy, but any serious comment was broken up by jokey asides from

*This was just about the only time that the rock press in either Britain or America failed to swallow the publicity hype around Jimi. In contrast, the Swedish rock press made more than one statement openly criticising the way Jimi was managed.

Noel and Mitch, which had all three rolling about laughing, successfully deflecting the questioning. They were there to promote the new band. Period. At one point Burks asked, 'How long have I got?' and received an answer probably unique in the annals of rock journalism: 'As long as you want.'

Burks moved on to Jimi's trial in Toronto and his claim in court that he had 'outgrown' drugs. True?

> Long pause, deep look on Jimi's face. 'I don't know . . .' He had said this seriously. All of a sudden he flashed his little-boy grin, 'I'm too . . . wrecked right now . . .' This was Hendrix the comedian. This side of Jimi is the one people love. He does it with split-second timing, a shrug, an eye cast downward, a slightly over-accented word. It's the essence of his charm, and figures, in many ways, in the way he makes music. . . . About dope. 'Oh yes, it's true, it's true. I don't take as much. That's what I was trying to tell them.'

Jimi said he had moved out of the house in Woodstock, to get more time to himself for writing. 'What kind of writing?' asked Burks. 'Mostly it's cartoon-type material. I make up this one cat who's funny. He goes through these strange scenes, you know. You put it in music, I guess. Just like you put blues in music.' Burks points out that it would be easier for Jimi if he could read music to enable him to express the larger concepts that he carries around in his head. So how does he write his music? 'Most of the time I can't get it on the guitar, you know? Most of the time I'm just laying around day-dreaming and hearing all this music. And you can't, if you go to the guitar and try to play it, it spoils the whole thing, you know? – I just can't play guitar that well to get all this music together.'

Jimi's way of constructing songs in the studio was often very ad hoc – just an idea, a riff, a few lyrics and he would build the material up from there. It was easy, it suited Jimi's way of working and it produced some classic rock music. This was how the Experience had worked for all the time they were together from 1966 to 1969 and that, thought Burks, was why they were prepared to play together again, despite all the rumours of bad feeling. But of course, they were all pals together now, weren't they? How this reconciliation had been engineered, Burks considered, it 'was not mine to discover'.

Significantly, there were no concrete plans expressed for the Experience to record new material, and discussion of future releases was rapidly glossed over.

Burks then broached the subject of the Band of Gypsys: 'I asked Jimi what had happened to blow the Gypsys apart.' 'Maybe', he began,

> I just started noticing the guitar for a change. It's like the end of a beginning maybe or something. I figure that Madison Square Garden is like the end of a big long fairy tale. Which is great. I think it's like the best ending I could possibly have come up with. The Band of Gypsys was outtasight as far as I'm concerned. It was just . . . going through head changes is what it was. I really couldn't tell – I don't know. I was very tired. You know, sometimes, there's a lot of things that add up in your head about this and that and they might hit you at a very peculiar time, which happened to be at the peace rally, you know? And here I'd been fighting the biggest war I ever fought. In my life. Inside, you know? And like that wasn't the place to do it.

Maybe his choice of words was odd, but it seems clear that it wasn't just a dose of acid that sent Jimi from the stage that night. Whatever else was on his mind, he had been having some major doubts about this band and whether or not it was ever possible to work with Noel and Mitch again.

The answer came just over two weeks later, when Burks received a call from the press agent to say that Noel was going to tour initially with Jeff Beck (which he never did); Billy Cox would stand in, Noel returning later.

The truth is that Jimi decided he could not work with Noel again and really went along with the *Rolling Stone* charade just to save an argument. Nor was Billy Cox necessarily the automatic choice for bass – others were considered like Jack Casady of Jefferson Airplane, who had played on *Electric Ladyland* and jammed with the band at San Francisco's Winterland in 1968 and again in Oakland in April 1969. Early in 1970, the Airplane were near to collapse – touring had virtually stopped and Casady with guitarist Jorma Kaukonen had been going out as Hot Tuna. But finally Billy was confirmed in the band with Mitch. Noel didn't even know that rehearsals had started without him until he returned to New York in March to rejoin the band.

A week after the interview with *Rolling Stone*, Jimi put his signature on two contracts. The first related to the Electric Lady Studio. Costs for the studio had been soaring. The ceiling had to be three layers thick to prevent the sound leaking up to the cinema above on the ground floor and the contractors unearthed a stream, Minetta Brook, which flooded the foundations. And this was aside from the very expensive specifications for equipment, studio construction and creature comforts.

416

Electric Lady Inc. had already spent $369,000, but Mike Jeffery needed some more money and so he went back to Warner Brothers. Jimi and Mike jointly signed to guarantee a further loan of $300,000 to Electric Lady Inc. The loan was to be paid back over three years (three six-monthly payments of $50,000 plus interest at 1.5 per cent above the base lending rate). The second contract linked to the first related to a film project of Mike's called *Wave* (later renamed *Rainbow Bridge*) to be shot in Hawaii.

Mike had become entranced with the islands after visits with the Experience in October 1968 and May 1969. He would fly out there at any opportunity – once Trixie Sullivan had to reach him by field telephone as Mike was meditating on the side of a volcano on the island of Maui. This was the other side of Mike Jeffery the sharp businessman – the side that smoked dope, dropped LSD and gave Abbie Hoffman $10,000. Mike wanted to build a musician's retreat/studio on Maui and spent large sums of money having plans drawn up by Buckminster Fuller, the American architect, visionary and polymath whose name is inextricably linked with the invention of the geodesic dome. Mike's latest project was to get Warner Brothers to put up some cash for a 'youth movie' to be shot in Hawaii.

The director was Chuck Wein, who had had three previous films produced by Andy Warhol's Factory. Described by *Rolling Stone* in 1972 when the film was eventually released as 'a living breathing piece of late-sixties southern California acid trip memorabilia', Wein (still wearing purple satin trousers) related how Jimi got involved in the project. Wein had been living in New York and sharing a place with Devon Wilson and another friend of Jimi's, Pat Hartley, who appeared in the film. 'I was into reading Tarot cards and one night over at Jimi's apartment I read the cards for Jimi and Mitch Mitchell and Billy Cox. Jimi started to tell me about being from an asteroid belt off the coast of Mars, so I said, "Stop and I'll tell you about it because it's a place I've seen three or four times clear as a bell." And that's the point the deal got on, which was that there was something manifesting that had to be worked out. And that something eventually became *Rainbow Bridge*.' Wein claims that a group of people meditated for several months and travelled astrally to visit those with sufficient funds to finance the venture.

The record books fail to show whether Mo Ostin of Warners received an occult visitation, but he did get a call from Mike Jeffery, who had been swept along by young Wein, who was also allegedly the leading light of a sect of White Witches and thus a being of some power.

A company with the suitably mystical name of Antah Kar Ana Inc. 'owned and controlled by Michael Jeffery' was set up to produce *Wave*, which Warners would distribute. Jimi had already signed as a guarantor of the loan to complete work on Electric Lady. To fulfil this he had to sign an agreement committing him to compose and perform music for the film sufficient for 'at least one full-length long-play album of quality comparable to Jimi Hendrix Experience recorded albums released by Warner Bros. Records Inc.'. Furthermore, Warners would not be counting this album 'in computing the minimum number of albums required to be delivered by Hendrix to Warner Bros. pursuant to the Artist's Agreement [of 24 June 1968]'. Jimi wasn't keeping pace with the agreement as it was; he had put down a lot of song fragments and studio jams since summer 1969, but very few completed songs were in the can. With a few exceptions, his new songs had gone to Ed Chalpin on the Band of Gypsys album and, when it was finally released, the album of *Rainbow Bridge* contained two songs 'My Friend' (see pages 267–8) and 'Look Over Yonder' recorded with the original Experience in 1968 and 'The Star Spangled Banner' recorded in March 1969.

Just about the only piece of 'factual' information from John Burks' *Rolling Stone* article which turned out to be correct was the April start date for Jimi's next tour. Jimi rehearsed the band through early March, but without too much enthusiasm. The Electric Lady studio, *his* studio, was not finished, but was nearly ready enough for Jimi to go and try it out and begin to record some new songs. For the first time in several months, his personal vision was clearing, he was beginning to see straight ahead and felt he could write again – and here he was getting ready for the road once more. The reasons put to him were predictable enough: one, Jimi was in hock to Warners over the studio: two, no royalties were coming from outside America, because of Chalpin's continued pursuit of his case against Track and Polydor in London; and three, Jimi hadn't toured in nearly a year and there was danger he would disappear from view. As if to reinforce this last point, the single release of 'Stepping Stone'/'Izabella' saw Jimi have his first US chart failure since 'Hey Joe' in early 1967 when nobody in America had heard of him. More correctly, the single was withdrawn so quickly because of poor mixing that it didn't have a chance to flop.

The women in Jimi's life at this time had very contrasting person-alities. Devon's social stance was invariably aggressive, desperately clinging on to the only status position she had in life. She was intelli-

418

gent, musicians respected her opinions about music, which were always forcibly expressed, and of course she had tremendous sexual presence and beauty. She was particularly prized by white rock stars and she revelled at the idea of musicians like Mick Jagger and Eric Clapton chasing after her. The 'spear-carriers' of rock, those who hang on the fringes eager to be noticed and bathe in reflected glory, contain many insecure people who could be easily disturbed by a strong personality like Devon. She was rumoured to be a secret member of the Black Panthers, their hot line through to Jimi; she was supposed to practise black magic and spike the drinks of those she didn't like. Many of the other women who frequented the inner sanctums of rock were terrified of her.

Of Devon Wilson and Jimi, Alan Douglas says, 'She understood music, she was very strong, very opinionated. Devon had lesbian tendencies, she had drug tendencies, she was all these things, so that I don't think she had the sensitivity to be the female that Hendrix had in mind as his ideal female. But she was the only one that I have ever seen, you know, get up in his face and tell him when he was fuckin' off and not playing right and he respected her, he respected her a lot.' Jimi's Greenwich Village friend Mike Quashie calls Devon 'the mother and big sister. Very protective.'

Unfortunately, Devon started getting heavily into cocaine and then heroin. 'When he found out that she was strung-out,' says Alan Douglas, 'their relationship changed. He became a little bit suspicious of her motives. But she influenced the business, she would tell Mike Jeffery to fuck off when he should have, she kept all the fools away from him, she was very protective and when the day was over she was a very good friend and served in lots of capacities.'

Some of these 'capacities', however, like drug-supplier, Jimi could do without. As Devon tumbled down deeper into dependent drug use, Jimi's respect turned to pity.

And then there was Kathy Etchingham. She hadn't seen much of Jimi since he left for the American tour in March 1969. But she did make the occasional trip over and Jimi often called her in his darkest moments, and she more than most would lend a sympathetic ear. 'He would cry down the phone after a bad gig and I used to bolster his ego. He didn't have any confidence in himself.' They were both free spirits; Kathy didn't sit at home mooning after Jimi when he was away – she was out enjoying herself. They always had that insecurity with each other which added a certain frisson to the relationship, 'but at the end of the day, we could look at each other from across a room and remember when we didn't have a bean between us. And that's probably the reason why we always came back together.' But geography and time put a distance between them that became insuperable.

During the early part of 1970, Jimi was becoming increasingly distrustful of those around him: he told Juma that for a time he thought the conga player was a spy for the office; he told Billy Cox that he dropped $100 bills on the ground to see who would pick them up; he believed Mike Jeffery would kill him rather than release material that Mike didn't think was commercial enough and he even sought out some disreputable drug connections to enquire about hiring a hit man. Thus it was an unfortunate moment for him to hear the news that the previous November Kathy had got married to a guy called Ray Mayer, who worked for Eric Clapton. Most unusually for Jimi he flew to London on his own, arriving around 10 March to try and talk Kathy into leaving Ray. When he first arrived, he stayed with Ray and Kathy, but soon found that too difficult and moved out to the Londonderry Hotel. About her marriage to Ray, she says, 'I really feel guilty that I had deceived Jimi, he wasn't planning on anything like that. He was devastated. I allowed myself more freedom than he was expecting. We sat up all night arguing about it and he nearly had me convinced. I never really saw him much after that.' Nowadays, Kathy finds it next to impossible to listen to any of Jimi's music. During one conversation for this book she requested 'All Along the Watchtower', only to rip the headphones off in tears moments later.

Jimi went round his old haunts like the Speakeasy and did some recording sessions with friends like Steve Stills and Arthur Lee, trying to find his bearings, some links with his less complicated past, but, says Kathy, 'I went along and after a while I felt completely useless, so I just drifted away.'6 Monika Dannemann says that Jimi phoned her and wanted her to come to London, but she was ill and couldn't make the trip. He must have felt, with great sadness, that there was nothing left for him in London and on 19 March he flew back to New York.

On 23 March Jimi took Billy and Mitch into the Record Plant to record 'Midnight Lightnin'. The last time he had done this song in the studio was at Olympic in London on 14 February 1969. It was St Valentine's Day and Kathy was with him in the studio. Having just come back from seeing her a married woman may have prompted Jimi to record the song again, a slow blues very much in keeping with his current sense of resigned melancholia with one devastating image of

420

dying love, although Jimi does try to inject the odd note of stoicism and even humour in the reference to smoking.

> I get stoned
> I can't go home
> I'm calling long distance on a public saxophone
> My head is achin'
> Lord my mind is breakin'
> Feel I got run over by Captain Coconut and his dog named Rover
> Gotta keep on movin'
> Gotta keep on movin'
> To understand both sides of the sky
> You gotta keep on groovin' yeah,
> Good groovin'
> 'Cause you got your God and so do I
> We gotta keep on lovin'
> Good, good, good, lovin'
> Make love on my dyin' bed
> We gotta stop smokin', stop, stop,
> I mean cigarette smokin'
> Or else I cough myself to death
> And to make love to you baby,
> I wouldn't even have the breath
> We gotta keep movin'
> Keep on groovin'
> Understand both sides of the sky
> Keep on movin'
> Keep on movin'
> You got your God and so do I.

Shortly before the start of the 'Cry of Love' tour as it was dubbed, Keith Altham, now writing for *Melody Maker*, interviewed Jimi at his New York apartment on West 12th Street. Jimi was not well, suffering from swollen glands, and he took some persuading to allow Keith up there. Looking back, Keith recalls Jimi was 'in bad shape. His health was deteriorating and I think the drugs had got a hold.' But Jimi still managed to retain his sense of humour throughout their meeting.

About the new line-up Jimi said rather obtusely,

It was always my plan to change the bass player even back in the days after the Experience when there was no band.
  Noel is definitely and confidently out – Billy has a more solid

421

style which suits me. [But] there's no telling how I feel tomorrow.

I'm not sure how I feel about the Experience now. Maybe we could have gone on, but what would have been the point of that? . . . It's a ghost now – it's dead – like the back pages in a diary. I'm into new things and I want to think about tomorrow, not yesterday.

I wasn't too satisfied with the *Band of Gypsys* album. If it had been up to me, I would never have put it out.

I'd like to play some festivals, but I wish they would break up the events a bit more for the audience. They should make them like three-ring circuses, booths, movies . . . and Freak Shows!

Jimi neatly sidestepped Keith's question 'Whatever happened to the plans for your . . . album *The First Ray of the New Rising Sun?*' by enquiring after the painful smallpox jab Keith had at Monterey. 'The pain went away,' said Jimi. In answering his own question, he'd also answered Keith's. Asked about other guitarists on the scene, Jimi thought that Alvin Lee of Ten Years After should be in the movies: 'The Gene Vincent of the 70s I hear.' He wasn't at all impressed by Clapton working with the white soul duo of Delaney and Bonnie: 'He should be getting his own thing together, not trying to carry other people.' Jimi raised a smile and a laugh for one of the few journalists he had any respect for, who had supported him when he was on the way up, but he quickly had to excuse himself on this occasion because he said he had to go out and buy a cushion to rest his gland.

The first date of the tour was in Los Angeles at the Forum, packed solid with 20,000 Hendrix fans, most of whom hadn't seen him in nearly a year, since the Newport Pop Festival of June 1969. They gave him a rousing reception; The Voodoo Chile, the Magic Boy had returned to weave his spell. The concert had its ironies: Jimi was back on the road touring with a band that was half Experience, half Band of Gypsys playing a mixture of old and new material with Buddy Miles now leading his Express as one of the support bands. Jimi knew his audience well enough; after such a long absence, he carried them along with 'Spanish Castle Magic' and 'Foxy Lady' to open the set, even though Mitch was not up to his snappy best and the 'solid style' of Billy Cox that Jimi said suited him often had the effect of dragging songs back. He introduced 'Lover Man' as 'Getting Your Brother's Shoes Together' with typically quick-talking conspiratorial stage patter about a poor Vietnam Vet coming home and finding his woman in somebody else's bed. 'Getting My Heart Back Together Again' ('Hear My Train A'Comin'), an andante blues, delved deep into the well of blues history,

422

recalling one of the classic motifs of the genre, jumping boxcars, saving up the money for the bus or train or just walking up the long and dusty highway to escape trouble, be it political, social or personal.

> I'm tired of this Jim Crow, gonna leave this Jim Crow town
> Doggone my black soul, I'm sweet Chicago bound,
> Yes, I'm leavin' here, from this ole Jim Crow town
> > (Cow Cow Davenport, 'Jim Crow Blues', 1929)

> Bye-bye Arkansas, tell Missouri I'm on my way up north now, baby
> I declare I'm gonna pack up, pack up now, baby
> And make my getaway
> > (Big Bill Broonzy, 'Make My Getaway', 1951)

> I'm waitin' round the train station
> Waitin' for that train
> To take me
> From that lonesome town
> (Jimi Hendrix, 'Getting My Heart Back Together Again', 1970)

Jimi placed his newest material in the centre of the set, songs like 'Message to Love' and 'Ezy Ryder'. Announcing these songs brought little response, but the applause at the end, although muted through lack of familiarity, was nonetheless warm.

Replacing Buddy with Mitch brought a different dimension to 'Machine Gun'. Instead of the dramatic rat-a-tat-tat snare drum beats, Mitch played military rolls, giving the song a funereal feel, flags at half-mast, coffins draped with the star-spangled banner – the inevitable conclusion to Jimi's angry images of smashed bodies and broken minds.

'On a clear day, you can see forever,' said Jimi as he introduced 'Room Full of Mirrors'. Played live, Jimi had to be three guitarists at once, two lead and one rhythm, and the song nearly broke down in the rush, attenuated and incomplete. He moved into the beautiful flamenco-style improvisation first heard in concert back in 1968 before segueing into what might be called his theme song for the seventies 'Hey Baby (The Land of the New Rising Sun)', Jimi making the guitar sound pitch and sway like waves gently rolling against a deserted sandy beach in early morning. Jimi's eternal mother-figure is on hand to guide him to a promised land, a new beginning.

423

Hey, baby, can I step into your world a while?
'Yes you can,' she said
'Come on back with me for a while
We're gonna go across the Jupiter Sun
And see all your people one by one.'

Another new song 'Freedom', a funk rock song, followed Mitch's drum solo, and then back on to home territory with 'The Star Spangled Banner' dissolving into 'Purple Haze', causing the crowd to rush forward, and finally to loud acclaim 'Voodoo Child (slight return)', seamlessly spliced with a section of 'Midnight Lightnin''.

And, with minor changes, this was pretty much the set they played throughout the tour – going from Los Angeles to Sacramento, then Milwaukee, Madison, St Paul, the University of Oklahoma, Fort Worth and San Antonio, reaching Philadelphia on 16 May. But Jimi had not fully recovered from his glandular problems before the start of the tour and he began to feel sick again, so the next three gigs in Cincinatti, St Louis and Columbus were cancelled. Happily, the fortnight's break

St Paul Civic Center, St Paul, Minnesota, 3 May 1970

424

must have done him the world of good because he turned out to play an absolutely sparkling two-show concert at the Berkeley Community Theater in California, part of which is captured on the *Jimi Plays Berkeley* video.

Everybody is afraid of anything they don't know anything about. I'm nothing but a human being just like everybody else.... The only thing that hangs me up: the very bad laws that are happening. The way the country's being run. You see badness, you can see evil right in front of your face, as soon as you turn on the TV.... I'd have to have a voice; I'd try to use my music as a machine to move those people, to get changes done. Because if people go too long when they get older, they'll realise or they'll get mediocre and fall right into that dead scene, rat-race America. (*New England Scene*, November 1968)

Berkeley had become almost synonymous with student protest since the Free Speech Movement came to prominence in December 1964 'to expose the contradiction between democracy's rhetoric and the Pentagon's reality'.[7] In April 1968, 200 Berkeley students were arrested for protesting against the refusal to credit the lecture course of black activist Eldridge Cleaver. Worse was to follow: in May 1969 one person was killed, another blinded and over a thousand injured when an attempt to turn a vacant lot of university property into a 'People's Park' was broken up by 2500 national guardsmen using helicopters and tanks. The youth of Berkeley were no strangers to violence.

Demand for tickets had been feverish and many hundreds had been disappointed. Outside the theatre on the night, the mood was turning ugly as these unlucky fans milled around without tickets. In true festival fashion, as soon as the doors were open, there was a massive crush to get in free, glass doors were broken and fans scaled the walls, looking for a way in. Mingling with the fans were demonstrators angry at the $3.50 admission charge to see the recently released film of *Woodstock*.

Jimi drove to the Community Theater in the now regulation limo with Colette, Devon and his young friend Vishwa. Because of the cancellations, the band had lost some of the impetus of the tour, so they turned the sound check into a proper rehearsal, running through 'Blue Suede Shoes', 'Power of Soul', 'Machine Gun', 'Message to Love', 'Room Full of Mirrors' and 'Freedom'.

The whole band seemed to benefit from their enforced lay-off,

425

producing an overall sound that can best be described as symphonic. Across the two shows, there were outstanding performances of 'Machine Gun', 'Getting My Heart Back Together Again' and 'Star Spangled Banner'. Theatricals were kept to a minimum, but during a devastating rendition of 'Johnny B. Goode', which brought roars of approval from the audience, Jimi really played with his teeth, the distinctive metallic attack sound of enamel on metal clearly audible on the soundtrack. Jimi's rhythmic sense never deserted him for an instant. His playing was fluid and flawless. A complete performance and beautiful to watch.

With the Band of Gypsys album in the charts and the Woodstock film and album released, the tour quickly picked up momentum through Dallas, Houston, Tulsa, Memphis (where Jimi met Larry Lee backstage and borrowed his guitar for a few songs), Evansville, Baltimore, Albuquerque, San Bernardino, Ventura, Denver, Boston and a re-run of Woodstock, the three-day Atlanta Pop Festival in front of half a million people. Highlight of the Festival? According to *Rolling Stone* it was Jimi playing 'The Star Spangled Banner' against a barrage of fireworks at the end of the second day, Saturday 4 July, although in truth this was just about the worst version he ever played.

Not to be outdone, New York staged its own three-day festival on Randall's Island near Spanish Harlem. The festival almost didn't happen when a permit was refused on the ground that Jimi would incite a riot. Mike Jeffery's threats to bring a suit for racial discrimination saw the necessary paperwork pushed through. However, the festival was hijacked by white radicals, the Randall's Island Collective, who blackmailed the promoters into accepting a whole list of demands which included giving their supporters virtually every job on the site. Nominally in charge of security, the Collective let everyone in for free and the festival began to collapse. Backstage, when it was realised there was no money for the performers, managers were screaming at the organisers, who in turn feared a riot if acts were pulled at the last minute. Jimi's response to having to perform in such a bad atmosphere was to get stoned; it was touch and go whether he would make it. With impending chaos behind and an edgy, tense audience in front, Jimi finally went out to try and play, having first gone through a big scene to get the stage cleared.

News broadcasts were coming through the amps for most of the set; the second song 'Fire' almost fell apart when Mitch and Jimi just lost one another; and there was trouble offstage with the Collective throwing their weight around as to who should be standing there watching. All of this was calculated to have Jimi heading for the limo, but apart from the odd 'Fuck this', he kept his cool and even managed to inject some humour into the rather grim proceedings, by playing a snatch of 'Auld Lang Syne' in the bridge between 'Star Spangled Banner' and 'Purple Haze'. Jimi thanked the crowd at various points for all their support in the past and, satisfied with the smattering of old hits, they responded by calling out for newer songs like 'Machine Gun' rather than the tired pleas for 'Wild Thing'. Unfortunately the finale was spoilt when Jimi tried to dedicate the last song to Devon, Colette, Alan Douglas and other friends he'd arrived with. He didn't get the reaction he wanted, spat into the mike 'Fuck off, these are my friends. Yeah, well fuck you and goodnight,' before hurling an angry version of 'Voodoo Chile', lines of power like 'If I don't see you no more in this world / I'll meet you in the next one / don't be late', now pregnant with menace. With the sound of a thousand radio stations blaring through the speakers – Jimi disappeared.

On 26 July 1970, Jimi flew from San Diego to Seattle to play the Sicks baseball stadium. On this trip back home, Jimi spent more time with his family than at any point since he left for the army. Leon says Jimi did not want to play: 'He said it was gonna rain, and outside, man, it was as clear as a bell.' But Jimi was right, the rain poured down, turning the outfield of the baseball stadium into a soggy grass mat and the infield a wide terrain of mud. Leon stood at the side of the stage. 'You could tell Jimi didn't really want to be up there. It was like he was looking at people, seeing all those who were against him.' The equipment wasn't hooked up correctly, the amps were poorly balanced and Jimi was 'really pissed off'. The stadium wasn't built for live music, an overwhelming echo careened off any available surface. The rain eased off slightly before Jimi came on; the crowd surged forward as he appeared, but were quickly scattered to the stands by another freezing downpour, where the acoustics were even worse.

The next day Jimi talked at some length to Freddie Mae Gautier, whose family had looked after him when he was only a few weeks old. She had seen him the night before at the concert. 'I was so upset, the acoustics were terrible, it was raining. This was Seattle's way of getting back at him. They resented it because he always talked bad about Washington and told how bad he was treated in school. Then, on top of that, his life coming up was nothing but turmoil. He had nothing but bad memories here from a baby right on up. It's a wonder he didn't turn out real bad.' And knowing what Jimi felt about Seattle, she couldn't understand why he agreed to play. 'I said to him, "how come, you're back and you let those people put you on at the Sicks Stadium?" And he said it was a trick. He said, "I started to break my contract, but my lawyers warned me that if I did they'd clean me out." Jimi had put it in writing that they could send him anywhere, but not the State of Washington – if they did, he'd break his contract.'

Jimi had things on his mind that needed talking through with Freddie Mae: 'We talked about life in general, about why people were unkind to each other, about racial discrimination, about Dr King. We talked about him getting married to somebody. He said, "All my friends, they don't stay together. It's hard because I'm out on the road all the time." He didn't remember Lucille and the Jeters too much and he said, "Aunt Freddie Mae, I really need to know a little bit about them."' So she told all the history she knew about his mother and her family. Jimi was quiet, but he listened intently.

I talked to him about his will. I said, 'Have you made provisions? I know you like music, but what provisions have you made if anything should happen to you?' And he said, 'Oh, I gotta will, but it isn't signed.' I said, 'How come you got a will and you haven't signed it?' 'cos money was no big thing to him. And he said, 'Oh, that's like signing a death certificate. That's an omen.' I said, 'Oh, you're too young to be talkin' like that, Jimi.' 'Oh, everything's for my dad, anyhow, it doesn't make any difference.' I told him you had to put that in black and white. I asked him, 'Where is your money? Where is your bank account? Are you taking care of these things?' He said, 'No, no, my manager does.' 'Do you know how much you have?' 'Well, I think some of it's out in the islands [West Indies], but it's no big thing, 'cos whenever I need some, Michael [Jeffery] gives it to me.'

Then we talked about drugs. He brought it up and he said, 'I'm really, really tryin' to get off of this, because it's controllin' my mind and I don't need it.' I said, 'You got that right. But all you can do is really pray about it. You've got to help yourself. It's in your hands.' I asked him about money for buying drugs. He said, 'Oh, I don't hardly have to pay for that. They just give it to me.' I said, 'Yeah, just to be in your presence because of who you are. Those kind of people you don't need. You need to get somebody that cares about *you*. These one-night stands, those people don't care nothing about you. If you weren't Jimi Hendrix, they probably wouldn't turn round to look at you. These people you call friends, they are acquaintances. True friends do not allow you to

Ventura County Fairgrounds, Ventura, California, 21 June 1970

destroy yourself.' Tears came in his eyes and he said to me, 'Aunty, I really want you to do some serious prayin'.' I said 'Jimi, I'm not fanatical about religion, but I do believe in God and I believe he can help you.' He said, 'I'm gonna do better. I've *got* to do better.'

I get this eerie feeling, he had a premonition, that there were some things that he needed to understand, to get right in his own mind.

After about two hours, Gerry Stickells came by to pick Jimi up. Freddie Mae never saw Jimi alive again.

Where Gerry was taking Jimi, he didn't want to go. Leon says Jimi was virtually kidnapped. Even Gerry himself says, 'He didn't particularly wanna do it. He said that quite openly!' although Billy Cox maintains that 'Jimi was looking forward to some R&R there'. The destination was the Hawaiian island of Maui, setting for Chuck Wein's film *Rainbow Bridge*.

The idea was to shoot an antidote to *Easy Rider* showing more of the positive side of the youth movement. Laudable enough, but the end result was a ludicrous farrago of pseudo-mystical acid babble devoid of sincerity. In one interview, Wein said in all seriousness that the cast of non-professional actors 'is made up of the best clairvoyants I could find, people that are into various schools of consciousness and phenomena and had inter-planetary contacts'. The 'plot', such as it is, constructed in a very loose documentary style, follows Jimi's friend, the tough New York–Jewish ex-model Pat Hartley as she travels from San Diego to the Rainbow Bridge Occult Center on Maui. There, she encounters various devotees of surfing, clairvoyance, zen, yoga, meditation, Tai Chi and the odd ufologist. There's a 'stoned rap' involving Pat, Jimi and Chuck Wein, interesting for a slab of Jimi's stream-of-consciousness which, although it is largely incomprehensible, gives a flavour of how the images flowed from mind to music. What is lost in print is Jimi's intonation, timing and the endearing quality of this spontaneous delivery.

I don't know, man, it seems like there's this little center in space that's just rotating, you know, constantly rotating, and there's these souls on it, and you're sitting there like cattle at a water hole and there's no rap actually going on, there's no emotions that are strung out so you're just sitting there and all of a sudden the next thing you know you'll be drawn

430

to a certain thing and the light gets bright and you see stuff, a page being turned and you see yourself next to a Vietcong, you know a soldier being cut down, you arrive on the scene of a soldier being shot down and all of a sudden you feel like helping that soldier up, but you're feeling yourself held in another vibe, another sense of that soldier. It seems like the soul of him, you know, and then you whisk back to the water hole or the oasis and you're sitting there and you're rapping again or eating a banana cream pie and sitting on the grey hardwood benches and so forth and all of a sudden somebody calls out again, but this is without words that whole scene, and all of a sudden the next thing you know you see yourself looking down at the left paw of the Sphinx and the tomb of King Blaaaa and his friendly Phacians and these all-night social workers with mattresses tied around their backs screaming, 'Curb service! Curb service! Curb service!' you know with the Third eye in the middle of the Pyramids. Ah, then we find ourselves drifting across the desert sands dry as a bone but still going towards home and then finally things look up as Cleopatra is here giving you demands, and at the same time begging for fetishes, invent something or else I'll kick your ass. Those kind of scenes, a girl who claims to be Pio Cleopatra. Pio what? And all of a sudden the Hawaiian mountains open up, rise another 13,000 feet, and we go higher and higher and Cleopatra has this beautiful raven hair and what are you supposed to do, man, except lay there and play the part and so I'm laying there playing the part and a grape chokes me almost, but I can't let the choke come out, because, you know, I have to be together, right? So I say, groovy grape wine you have there Cleo. Ah well, I mean let's get it on, forget about all that stuff back there and forget about you and your scene, let's just go up in the hills and relax and live. No, I have the conscience, I must do this, I must do that, I must . . . Oh, forget about it Cleo, man, you're a woman, I'm a man, come on let's get it on. Let's go get ourselves a grape vine out in the valley somewhere on the side of Mt Vesuvius or something. I don't know, hell. No, no, no, my parents, my traditions, my snake, ugggh, you bit me in the ass again, you naughty asp. Then we found ourselves wrapped up in carpets which was fine. And here I am. See, sometimes, it gets to be strenuous for instance, like when to try and clean marijuana with steel, metallic tea strainers. Sin! Sin! You die like a rabbit run over by a Mack truck, sin, but then again, you threw away your wizard's hat and I got a book of matches in my back pocket we can: What's your name? I like you. You know what I mean?

The last section of *Rainbow Bridge* is part of Jimi's two-set concert played at the foot of Haleakala, 'House of the Sun', the highest point on Maui. In 1866, Mark Twain viewed a Hawaiian sunrise from the edge of the crater of Haleakala. The sun rose above the clouds and threw a warm purple glow across the barren landscape of dead lava: 'It was the sublimest spectacle I ever witnessed and I think the memory of it will remain with me always.'

The day was overcast and windy as Jimi, Mitch and Billy took the small stage. The audience was no more than 400 strong, ostensibly 'grouped' under the star signs shown on flags that fluttered in the breeze. When Jimi normally did outdoor gigs, he was faced by an anonymous mass of people with whom he found it difficult to communicate. He was rarely at his best in such circumstances and tended just to play for himself. On Maui, with a club-size audience, Jimi felt more at ease and, although he was initially unhappy about going on, he joked, grinned and laughed through the first set, pulling faces for those right down the front. A rather sloppy 'Foxy Lady' was dedicated to Pat Hartley.

It was a standard set apart from a well-structured heavy riff rock song 'In From The Storm', an unusual song in that Jimi's many paeans to the mystical mother-figure were rarely so forcefully presented:

> It was so cold and lonely
> The wind 'n' cryin' blue rain
> Were tearing me up.
>
> It was so cold and lonely
> The crying blue rain was tearing me up, tearing me up
> I wanna thank you my sweet darling
> For digging in the mud and picking me up.

After a short break, Jimi came back for an hour-long set in marked contrast to the first, far more melodic and dream-like and infinitely more in tune with the ambience of the occasion. Unfortunately, the final edit of the film excluded all but a brief glimpse of the second set, where Jimi is seen playing a Gibson Flying-V rather than his white Stratocaster. To his credit, Wein resisted the temptation to use the kind of tricksy camera techniques for the concert footage that ruined Tony Palmer's film of Cream's farewell performance at London's Royal Albert Hall. Overall, however, the best thing that can be said for *Rainbow Bridge* is that, after seventy-one minutes, it finishes.

Behind the scenes the vibes were not as beatific as the film would suggest. Inevitably, where the 'beautiful people' were involved, arrangements were chaotic. 'They couldn't organise a piss-up in a brewery, to put it mildly,' says Mitch. For their part Jimi and Pat resented the way both Wein and Mike Jeffery were trying to stage-manage what everyone

432

'Rainbow Bridge Vibratory Color/Sound Experiment', Hawaii, 30 July 1970

was told would be improvisational. Pat Hartley recalled later, 'They took us out in the bushes one by one and said, "You're on, baby" and everyone felt compelled to say something magnanimous about the others. . . . Chuck Wein . . . pulled the same shit on Jimi and the first confrontation between the two of them, Jimi told him to fuck off. One night . . . Jimi started telling us a fucking funny story, because Jimi was a fucking funny guy, and just as Jimi got within two lines of the end the Toad [meaning Mike Jeffery] leaps out and says, "Yeah, Jimi, that's what you should do in front of the camera."'[8] The Hollywood film crew insisted upon by Warners were kept hanging around for hours while Chuck, Pat, Jimi and Mike argued back and forth about the filming. Eventually, Jimi stormed off but, fortified with some rosé wine, he turned up later to do his bit.

433

I want to get colour into music: I'd like to play a note and have it
come out as a colour. (*Disc*, 22 April 1967)

The concert was dubbed 'A Vibratory Color/Sound Experiment' and,
about a month before the film was shot, Chuck Wein introduced
Jimi to one of the organisers, Emilie Touraine, who was interested
in translating sound into colour as 'Energy–Sound–Colour-Dynamics'.
Together with Jimi, she bought a horse which was named Axis Bold
As Love and which was never to be ridden. Songs like 'Bold As Love',
'Love or Confusion' and 'One Rainy Wish' declared Jimi's similar interest in the esoteric significance of the Twelve Rays of Colour among
occult and mystical schools of thought. The association between sound
and colour has a long history predating psychedelic experimentation.
Prometheus, composed by the Russian pianist Alexander Scriabin in
1911, called for the projection of colours on to a screen during the
performance. His *Mystery*, for which only sketches remain, was planned
to be a religious experience, a unity of music, dancing, poetry, colours
and scents. Jimi once said, 'Don't hold me up I am but a messenger.'
Likewise Scriabin believed his sacred duty was to sound the final chord
of mankind, unifying it with the Spirit of God.

The main task Jimi had set himself during the summer of 1970 was
the completion of his next album, a double LP, a unity of music and
spirit, a new beginning, the 'First Rays of the New Rising Sun'.

Jimi had been telling his friends for some while that he was in
conflict with Mike over the next album, that Mike was saying a double
album wouldn't sell, that the material Jimi had already recorded wasn't
commercial enough. There is some truth in this; the majority of Jimi's
studio work from late 1969 onwards was mainly jams, as he strove to
rekindle his creative spark. Of the seven or eight new songs recorded
before Christmas, half went as live tracks to Ed Chalpin on the Band
of Gypsys album. What turned everything round from mid-June onwards
was that the Electric Lady Studio was unofficially open for business and
Jimi embarked on his most intensive period of recording for two years.

'I want it comfortable,' Jimi said – and just over $1 million later,
comfortable is what he got – architecturally and technically, Electric
Lady was unsurpassed. A curved mural (which incidentally Jimi hated)
ran the length of the basement complex from the entrance. On Jimi's
instructions, all the walls were curved with red carpet wall-to-wall and
floor-to-ceiling juxtaposed with white walls which changed colour courtesy of a remotely controlled theatrical lighting system. Mirrors and big

434

cushions were dotted all over, the rest rooms were lavishly appointed and a film-projection suite was also available. The studio entrance was policed and monitored by closed-circuit TV. Jimi worked in Studio A, the larger of the two (B was unfinished) with its massive forty-mike input console housed within concrete and fibreglass walls and a huge floating ceiling hovering some twenty feet above the floor, all constructed to allow for variable acoustics. Musicians were convinced that the underground stream flowing beneath the studio, which stopped work for three months when the whole basement area flooded, actually gave the recorded sound a strange and unique resonance. And the cost of all this luxury? The peak-time price when the studio opened was $155 an hour for sixteen tracks. But of course, to Jimi, it was free.

When Jimi was working at the Record Plant towards the end of 1968, he and engineer Eddie Kramer had become estranged in the battle for who controlled the console. But they had settled their differences, Eddie had supervised the building of Electric Lady on Jimi's behalf and now they looked forward to working together once again. In a typical display of Hendrix reticence, he would sidle into the studio and ask Eddie if it was okay to come in. 'Jimi,' Eddie would say in light-hearted exasperation, 'you *own* the place.'

Jimi started work with yet another battle going on in the background. The basic band was Mitch and Billy, but Jimi was also using Juma on congas and all efforts were being made to push Juma aside. Mike Jeffery's *Rainbow Bridge* production company Antah Kar Ana Inc. 'offered me a contract *not* to play with Jimi, so they could have control over me. They tried to buy my farm. I took the contract to my attorney and he said, "take it back and tell them to use it for toilet paper."' Mike knew that if Jimi wanted Juma to play, then there was precious little he could do about it, except try to buy Juma off. But Juma resisted and stayed on, offering as much support to Jimi as he could.

By the end of August, Jimi had several new songs in the can. With its 'sanctified' exhortations to 'keep on pushing', 'Straight Ahead' recalls some of the earlier material recorded and played live with the Band of Gypsys like 'Earth Blues', 'Power of Soul' and 'Message to Love' and recaptures that same driving soul-based feel. 'Freedom' nods to the spirit of 'Straight Ahead', but should really be considered back-to-back with 'Dolly Dagger'. First, because both refer to Devon Wilson. 'Dolly Dagger' is the more overt dedication and in fact Devon was in the studio when Jimi recorded the basic track – he says at one

435

With unidentified party poopers
Minneapolis, Minnesota, 3 May 1970

point, 'Watch out, Devon, give me a little bit of that heaven, eh?' and
she revelled in a song portraying her as a dangerous vamp.

> Here comes Dolly Dagger
> Her love's so heavy, gonna make you stagger.
> Dolly Dagger, she drinks her blood from a jagged edge. . . .
> Been riding broomsticks since she was fifteen
> Blow out all the other witches on the scene.
> She got a bull whip, just as long as your life.
> Her tongue can even scratch
> The soul out of the devil's wife.

In 'Freedom' Devon becomes more of a metaphor for restrictions

436

and limitations on personal freedom, but the nods in her direction are unmistakable: Devon attempting to see off a rival for Jimi's affections – 'you've hooked my girlfriend'; her dubious connections – 'you know the drug-store man'; and Jimi's nickname for Devon, mocking her flirtations with Mick Jagger – 'Better stick your daggers in someone else.' Devon also appears in a version of the song 'Crash Landing' recorded in April 1969:

You don't need me
You just wanna bleed me,
So take out your dagger and cut me free, cut me free, cut me free,
Hey, you don't love me girl, you just try to suffocate me . . .
You don't love me, hey look at ya, all lovey-dovey when you,
   mess around with that needle . . .
As long as you're gonna be all messed up, I don't give a damn,
Slow down, slow down, slow down, bang bang, shoot shoot,
As long as you're your silly self, I don't give a hoot.

Both 'Dolly Dagger' and 'Freedom' are also indicative of the extent to which Jimi was eschewing electronic studio tricks in favour of more instrumentally complex arrangements. 'Freedom' is semi-orchestrated with an arrangement for five separate guitar tracks. The basic track for 'Dolly Dagger' consisted of bass, drums, percussion and rhythm guitar recorded live with the good separation possible at Electric Lady. Over that was the lead guitar and a lead vocal recorded together with more congas. Then fuzz bass, background vocals from Arthur and Albert Allen, 'the Ghetto Fighters', and Jimi, more percussion and foot-stomping. The lead guitar floats over the whole song, locking together all the numerous cross-rhythms established by the multi-tracks of percussion, drums, bass and rhythm guitar.

There is a lot of flash and exuberance in these songs with their counterparts in 'Foxy Lady' and 'Purple Haze' from an earlier era. 'Drifting', 'Angel', 'Nightbird Flying' and 'Pali Gap' veer more towards the more delicate construction of sound tapestries exemplified by 'Little Wing', 'May This Be Love' and the aquatic suite on *Electric Ladyland*.

'Pali Gap' is interesting because Jimi rarely recorded purely instrumental tracks for release. The song, a dedication to the Hawaiian goddess of the volcanoes, Pali or Pele, is a good example of how Mitch had to change his style whereby it was now less appropriate for him to 'free float' behind the guitar. On certain types of song, Jimi was going for a more integrated sound, meshing together the

437

various rhythmic devices to achieve an overall effect decidedly African in its concept and execution. Jimi uses lots of jazz chording and wailing double-octave bends plus chromatic runs in the style of Les Paul which are unique to this track.

Lyrically 'Drifting', 'Angel' and 'Night Bird Flying' hang together with 'In From The Storm' as further evidence of how important to Jimi was the idea of a mother-figure who would save him from isolation.

In May, Jimi had recorded Dylan's 'Drifter's Escape', but had his own idea for a song, based on the traditional blues lyric: 'You know, I'm drifting just like a ship out on the sea / Well, you know I ain't got nobody in this world to care for me.' Jimi's verse is rather more hopeful: 'Drifting / on a sea of forgotten teardrops / On a lifeboat sailing for your love / Sailing home'. The guitar parts are beautifully constructed with imaginative and tasteful use of backwards guitar. With its intricate *mélange* of harmony and unison guitars, 'Night Bird Flying' appears to operate on two levels. First as an ode to a one-night stand:

> So all we got, baby, is one precious night
> All we got is one precious night
> Throw your blues and shoes and things
> and lay it down under the bed.

But the lines 'Well, she's flying down to me' and 'Just wrap me up in your beautiful wings' make the connection with arguably Jimi's finest ballad, 'Angel', written back in 1968 after he had dreamt of Lucille. He had the lyric with him when he spoke to Freddie Mae in Seattle about Lucille and her family, just a few days after recording the song. He read it out to Freddie Mae as a piece of poetry: 'It was very deep, it was what was in him.' As a religious person, Freddie Mae wanted Jimi to believe that God would help him through his troubles. 'He said, "I don't know whether I want to talk about God, but I know there's a Supreme Being." I said, "Well, that's all you have to rely on, whatever you want to call it, somebody you can rely on, someone who's going to be there win, lose or draw."'

> Angel came down from heaven yesterday
> She stayed with me just long enough to rescue me
> And she told me a story yesterday,
> about the sweet love between the moon and the deep blue sea
> And then she spread her wings high over me
> She said she's gonna come back tomorrow

438

And I said 'fly on my sweet Angel,
fly on through the sky,
fly on my sweet Angel,
tomorrow I'm gonna be by your side'

Sure enough this morning came unto me
Silver wings silhouetted against the child's sunrise
And my Angel she said unto me
'today is the day for you to rise,
take my hand,
you're gonna be my man,
you're gonna rise'
And then she took me high over yonder (Lord)

And I said 'fly on my sweet Angel,
fly on through the sky,
fly on my sweet Angel,
forever I will be by your side'

As well as recording songs for the album, Jimi had been working with a four-track cassette player in private at his apartment on an autobiographical suite of eight songs called 'Black Gold'. After Jimi died, the set of tapes disappeared, but Alan Douglas, who knew about 'Black Gold', says that one of the songs was 'Astro Man', possibly the only one Jimi managed to record. To be honest, it was the least convincing of the songs from this period. It begins very weakly and one cannot imagine that Jimi wouldn't have improved on that had he been given the chance. 'Astro Man' is an example of the 'cartoon' material Jimi mentioned to John Burks of *Rolling Stone*. The 'little boy inside a dream' is Jimi as he runs through the streets of Seattle, cape streaming behind him re-enacting the adventures of his Saturday movie idol, Flash Gordon, or as he sits glued to the TV in 1966 watching Batman. But Jimi's not content with second-hand heroes – he has his own alter-ego, Astro Man – 'flying higher than that old faggot Superman' and 'Twice as fast as Donald Duck'. Mildly amusing (apart from the unnecessary 'faggot') but dispensable.

Jimi chose a simple country blues with no accompaniment for a very personal and original song entitled 'Belly Button Window'.

Well, I'm up here in this womb
I'm looking all around (hmm, hmm, hmm)
Well, I'm looking out my Belly Button Window
And I see a whole lot of frowns
And I'm wondering if they don't want me around

What seems to be the fuss out there?
Just what seems to be the hang?
'Cause you know if ya just don't want me this time around,
yeah I'll be glad to go back to Spirit Land
And even take a longer rest,
before I'm coming down the chute again
Man I sure remember the last time, baby,
they were still hawkin' about me then
So if you don't want me now,
make up your mind, where or when
If you don't want me now,
give or take, you only got two hundred days
'Cause I ain't coming down this way too much more again

You know they got pills for ills and thrills and even spills,
but I think you're just a little too late
So I'm coming down into this world, Daddy,
regardless of love and hate
And I'm gonna sit up in your bed, Mama (huh),
and just a-grin right in your face
And then I'm gonna eat up all your chocolates (huh),
and say 'I hope I'm not too late'

So if there's any questions,
make up your mind
'Cause you better give or take
questions in your mind
Give it a take,
you only got two hundred days

Way up into this womb,
looking all around
Sure's dark in here!
And I'm looking out my Belly Button Window
And I swear I see nothing but a lot of frowns
And I'm wondering if they want me around . . .

Although Jimi injects a brief element of humour about eating all
his mother's chocolates, 'Belly Button Window' is very poignant as
Jimi reflects on the childhood unhappiness of his broken home. He
tries to imagine having the chance to talk to his parents before he
was born and saying, 'Okay, make up your mind – do you want me,
or not?' Instinctively, as the song relates, he feels something is wrong
with the family background he is about to be born into.

Incidentally, the line 'you only got two hundred days' raised up
a chorus of significant 'ah-aahs' when the song was released after

Jimi's death as if he was using the song to make the announcement. However, the lyric is clear enough; in the context of the song Jimi was a three-month-old baby, telling his parents 'you've got about six months (about 200 days) to sort yourselves out'.

The First Rays of the New Rising Sun never appeared. Instead, the tracks listed above, plus others, became the first posthumously released albums, *The Cry of Love* and *Rainbow Bridge* (see Discography). Which songs Jimi would have included is impossible to say – probably not 'Astro Man' if that was supposed to be part of 'Black Gold', but 'Izabella', 'Stepping Stone' and 'Room Full of Mirrors' might well have been considered. One very early song, 'Look Over Yonder', *was* included. Jimi had been playing this song under the title 'Mr Bad Luck' back in his Greenwich Village days. The lyric of the song had gained in significance over the period to its recording in October 1968 (with Noel and Mitch) because of the police violence that Jimi had witnessed in Europe the previous summer.

> Look over yonder here come the blues . . .
> I can see 'em comin'
> Wearing a blue armoured coat . . .
> You're sittin' there with your violins
> Hittin' wrong notes . . .
> Look over yonder, he's comin' my way
> When he's around, I never have a happy day
> (You even bust my guitar strings)
>
> Look over yonder
> Well, he's talkin' to my baby
> They found my peace pipe on her
> Now they're draggin' her away
> Lord knows we don't need a devil like him beatin' us around
> Well, he's knockin' on my door
> Now my house is tumbling down.

Jimi had other songs in the development stage such as 'Valleys of Neptune' recorded in early 1970, 'Coming Down Hard On Me, Baby', 'Beginning' and unrecorded material like 'Eyes and Imagination'. But this would only have been a fragment of what he was planning; he took notebooks with him everywhere, there were miles of tapes in studios all over America and snatches of song lyrics strewn about wherever he laid his head.

The following appeared in 1970 in a book entitled *Rock: A World*

Bold As Love, or *Superstars in Their Own Words*, much of which was devoted to Jimi, including quotes by him and about him from other musicians such as John Mayall and John Sebastian.

Three or four different worlds went by within the wink of an eye. Things were happening. There was this cat came around called Black Gold. And there was this other cat came around called Captain Coconut. Other people came around. I was all these people. And finally when I went back home, all of a sudden I found myself bein' a little West Coast Seattle boy – for a second. Then all of a sudden when you're back on the road again, there he goes, he starts goin' back. That's my *life* until somethin' else comes about.

I wish they'd had electric guitars in cotton fields back in the good old days. A whole lot of things would have been straightened out. Not just only for the black and white, but I mean for the *cause!*

It's time for a new national anthem. America is divided into two definite divisions. And this is good for one reason because like somethin' has to happen or else you can just keep on bein' dragged along with the program, which is based upon the past and is always dusty. And the grooviest part about it is not all this old-time thing that you can cop out with. The easy thing to cop out with is sayin' black and white. That's the easiest thing. You can see a black person. But now to get down to the nitty-gritty, it's gettin' to be old and young – not the age, but the way of thinking. Old and new, actually. Not old and young. Old and new because there's so many even older people that took half their lives to reach a certain point that little kids understand now. They don't really get a chance to express themselves. So therefore they grab on to what is happening. That's why you had a lot of people at Woodstock. You can say all the bad things, but why keep elaboratin'? You have to go to the whole balls of it. That's all you can hold on to, in the arts, which is the actual earth, the actual soul of earth. Like writing and sayin' what you think. Gettin' into your own little thing. Doin' this and doin' that. As long as you're off your ass and on your feet some kind of way. Out of the bed and into the street, you know, blah-blah, woof-woof-crackle-crackle – we can tap-dance to that, can't we? That's old hat.

We was in America. We was in America. The stuff was over and starting again. You know, like after death is the end and the beginning. And it's time for another anthem and that's what I'm writin' on now.

Wednesday 26 August was the official opening date of the Electric Lady studio. It was a night out for the rock fraternity – Noel Redding, members of Fleetwood Mac, Yoko Ono and Johnny Winter all attended. But the atmosphere was not good; people were getting absolutely out of their heads and throwing up the Japanese buffet food. Mike Quashie hosted the event, but didn't like what he saw. Jimi arrived, but left early, disgusted and upset that his beautiful studio, his chapel, should have been so violated. A reporter from *Rock* magazine who had enjoyed a free night out at Jimi's expense later wrote, 'Imagine about 100 very stoned freaks getting thrown out into the wilds of the streets of New York! The studio was totally fucked up, but I didn't really care too much. Jimi's only spent a million on it, and I'm sure there's more where that came from.'[9] Enough said.

Jimi had another reason for leaving early. He was due in England for the Isle of Wight Festival, his first official visit to that country for nearly eighteen months.

Fourteen *Tomorrow, I'm Gonna Be By Your Side*

I'm not sure I will live to be twenty-eight years old. (*Morgenposten* [Denmark], 6 September 1970)

I've been doing like Yogi Bear, I've been hibernating.... we've received a lot of static in New York, a lot of aggravation.... most of the time we play like a whole vacuum, you know, a wall of sound, a wall of feeling, that's what we try to get across.... You get to realise how important a friend is in this world. (Radio interview, Stockholm, 31 August 1970)

Can you imagine all those people who died beforehand, and all of us, all up in heaven? All over the top of each other ... 'Hey, man, move over, man, I don't have no room up here!' 'Well, hey, you didn't have no business dyin', did ya?' (Interview, London, December 1967)

Jimi was happy to play the Isle of Wight Festival as a one-off. After that, he wanted to get back to New York to finish his new album. Instead he was booked on a European tour through Sweden, Denmark and West Germany. With the benefit of hindsight, Jimi's performance on the Isle of Wight and the subsequent dates in Europe have been loaded down with a ton of symbolic baggage around premonitions and omens presaging future events. But what must be borne in mind is that Jimi was a very temperamental artist – acutely sensitive to all the circumstances surrounding any particular gig. This was the guitarist who actually stopped playing and cried on stage in Greenwich Village when the music didn't go right. But, even though he didn't want to be on the tour, there was no reason why the individual gigs should not have been a success, if they had not been jeopardised by a number of circumstances beyond Jimi's control. His spontaneous and improvisational approach to live performances meant that the songs he sang and how he sang them were a gut reaction to how he felt at that precise moment – a sum total of what that concert was doing for him emotionally whether that experience was negative or positive. More than that, when you are trying to create, night after night, sometimes even the beautiful things can be painful.

Important, too, in assessing the events of the coming weeks is the fact that Jimi was physically very run down. His glandular problems earlier in the year were a testament to that and he never had or gave himself the time to recover fully. Jimi's poor state of physical health was primarily a product of the lifestyle he led. When he wasn't touring, he was spending long hours in the studio; then there were the press receptions, the parties, the clubs and the jam sessions often accompanied by precious little food or sleep. Jimi had been living variations on that kind of life since he left the army in 1962. He now also had to cope with the psychological stress of being a famous rock star and behind-the-scenes problems with his business affairs, his personal life, finding the right musicians to play with and so on. The body can only take that kind of punishment for so long before it begins to protest.

He arrived in London on 27 August. He was very tired – he had been working at Electric Lady almost non-stop since he got back from Hawaii. He went straight to his suite at the Londonderry to catch up on some sleep, before spending the evening at the Speakeasy. Throughout the morning of the 28th, the press were camped in Jimi's bedroom while he gave interviews. Later on, he had other visitors to his hotel suite; Kirsten Nefer was a 24-year-old Danish actress-model, living in London. 'I was taken to meet Jimi by my friend Karen Davies who had known Jimi in New York. I was really into the music, but I didn't like the man. He looked small and ugly in his pictures and there was all this stuff about girls and everything. We knocked on Jimi's door, he opened it and I couldn't believe it – he was tall, he was skinny and he was BEAUTIFUL!'

The three of them talked for several hours and later Kirsten received a note from Jimi detailing the arrangements he had made for her and Karen to join him on the Isle of Wight.

Those journalists who spoke to Jimi that morning found him in buoyant mood. Although he was nursing a cold, he was relaxed and full of ideas. Norman Jopling's interview for *Record Mirror* was headlined, 'JIMI HENDRIX IS BACK, AND HAPPY, AND TALKING . . .' Jopling wrote:

> The 'superstar' aura that has always surrounded Jimi isn't at all apparent in an interview or conversation. How much of it is hype? How much is it a part that Jimi plays?

'I wouldn't know how to play that part. But I get a lot of people
trying to make me play it. I'm here to communicate, that's my reason
for being around, it's what it's all about. I want to turn people on and
let them know what's happening. Even if they have nine-to-five jobs and
come back to the family and TV, that's what counts, to keep turned on.'

He explained some of the options under consideration to Roy
Hollingsworth of *Melody Maker*. It is clear that Jimi was contemplating
a radical rethink of his musical direction:

It's all turned full circle. I'm back right now where I started. I've
given this era of music everything. I still sound the same, my music's
the same and I can't think of anything new to add to it in its present
state.
    When the last American tour finished earlier this year, I just wanted
to go away for a while and forget everything. I wanted to just do
recording and see if I could write something. Then I started thinking.
Thinking about the future. Thinking that this era of music – sparked off
by the Beatles – has come to an end. Something new has got to come
and Jimi Hendrix will be there.
    I want a big band. I don't mean three harps and fourteen violins.
I mean a big band full of competent musicians that I can conduct and
write for. And with the music we will paint pictures of Earth and space,
so that the listener can be taken somewhere.

Jimi tried to explain the nature of his new music as a 'new form
of classical music' whereby 'Strauss and Wagner . . . are going to
form the background of my music. Floating in the sky above it will
be the blues – I've still got plenty of blues – and then there will be
Western sky music and sweet opium music (you'll have to bring your
own opium).'
    Trying to equate it with anything currently happening, Jimi agreed
that 'it could be on similar lines to what Pink Floyd are tackling. They
don't know it, you know, but they are the mad scientists of this day and
age.' Jimi said he was happy to go with the trio format if people liked
it, so long as they didn't expect him to 'do a visual thing' on demand,
and he reiterated that 'I can only freak when I feel like doing so.'
    When he finally got round to expanding the band 'I don't want to
be playing as much guitar. I want other musicians to play my stuff.
I want to be a good writer. I still can't figure out what direction my
writing is going at the moment, but it'll find a way.'

He landed by helicopter on the Isle of Wight at 8.30 p.m. His friend

Vishwa was there to greet him and thought Jimi seemed depressed in spirit beyond mere tiredness. However, Noel Redding's mother Margaret was backstage in Jimi's caravan/dressing-room and says he was fine. They had a laugh and a joke over the fact that the zip of his orange stage suit wouldn't stay up. Eventually, Margaret pinned it together at the top.

All festivals ran late and the curse of the headlining act was always to go on at some ridiculous time when half the audience were asleep and the rest had left. By the time Jimi was on, it was the early hours of Monday morning. All he could see was blackness punctuated by bonfires eerily illuminating stoned faces.

'Yeah, thank you very much for showing up, man, Y'all really beautiful and outtasight and thanks for waiting. It has been a long time, hasn't it . . . Give us about a minute to tune up. It's so good to be back in England. We'd like to start off with a thing that everybody knows of out there. You can join in and start singing. Matter of fact, it'd sound better if you'd stand up for your country and your beliefs and start singing. [Quietly] If you don't, fuck ya.' Those who heard it share the joke with Jimi as he hits the British national anthem. Unfortunately, the band needed more than just a minute to tune up. The American tour was a month ago and they had lost the tightness of some of those concerts, as Mitch confirms: 'Strange thing was that before the band had been playing really, really well in my opinion and it would have been a smarter move to have had a day's rehearsal.' As it is, the concert gets off to a very shaky start. From the national anthem, Mitch thumps out a sloppy drum intro segue to a brief snatch of 'Sergeant Pepper's Lonely Hearts Club Band' before the first real song 'Spanish Castle Magic'. The sound is messy and uncontrolled as Jimi rushes through the song improvising lyrics as he goes.

'As I said before, thanks a lot for coming. Like to get into another song we did in the year of 1833. I think it's pretty true still today, if you can dig it.'

The song is 'All Along The Watchtower', but the solo is spoilt by some equipment trouble and Jimi again rushes through it with indecent haste, leaving Mitch and Billy to catch up as best they can. Jimi partly adapts the rap for 'Machine Gun' for an English audience, pronouncing Bournemouth, like all Americans, as if it were two words – Bourne Mouth. 'There's a whole lot of head games going on some-times. Sometimes they leak out . . . and play head games with other people which we call war. And so I'd like to dedicate this one to all the soldiers fighting in Birmingham, all the skinheads, all the soldiers fighting in Bournemouth, London and, oh yes, all the soldiers fighting in Vietnam. So many wars going on.'

Jimi is getting deeply into the song, fighting his own personal war against the equipment, his guitar, which is going out of tune, and the festival security communications system coming loud and clear through the band's Marshall speakers during quiet passages. Mitch all but stops playing, wondering where Jimi is going to take the song. Jimi begins the riff of 'Race With the Devil', a UK hit single for Gun in 1968, then some twelve bar and a sidestep into Elmore James's 'Dust My Broom'. Mitch and Billy try to follow, but 'Machine Gun' is falling apart. Included in this half-hour version of the song are some fine guitar parts, but eventually Jimi hits some final chords and stops.

Jimi knows it isn't going well. 'If you can hold on a little bit, I think we can all get it together. Awright? 'Cos I'm goin' to stay here all night until somebody moves.'

Voices scream out somewhere, 'Shut the camera off!' 'Get rid of that camera, you idiot!' There is a very long interval, Mitch and Billy just kill time busking while Jimi tries to bring the amps, fuzz box and guitar under his normally impeccable control. He plays through 'Lover Man', but it doesn't sound right and he stops again.

'Okay, we're gonna start all over again. How ya doin', England? Glad to see ya. We'll do a thing called "Freedom".' At last things are beginning to happen on stage – the playing is crisp and even, Jimi laying down well-rounded funk chords with plenty of bite. Having got one good song out, Jimi catches his breath with a smooth, calm 'Red House' delivered with verve and conviction. Encouraged, Jimi tries out 'Dolly Dagger', which is less convincing because, as with 'Room Full of Mirrors' live on stage, Jimi cannot play the lead lines and solo *and* the rhythm which underpins them. Consequently, when Jimi stops playing rhythm to switch to lead on certain songs like 'Dolly Dagger', a big hole is left in the sound which Billy Cox on his own cannot fill. It demonstrated that Jimi was moving ahead in the studio with more complex material that would not always work in concert without the presence of additional musicians.

A longish pause while Jimi retunes. 'Outtasight, y'all have patience, 'cos I haven't.' He backtracks slightly, changes the mood to a safe, slow blues, 'Midnight Lightnin' ', followed by 'Foxy Lady'. The audience latch on to 'Foxy Lady' and press Jimi for more blasts from the past. He feels caught in a dilemma, not having played a concert in England for so long.

448

'Y'all wanna hear those old songs, man? Damn, man, we're tryin' to get some other things together. I just woke up about two minutes ago. We was recordin' some little things, but I think . . . er . . . I dunno. I think we'll play something a little more familiar.' The compromise is 'Message to Love', a relatively new song but from an album which charted in Britain. The less driven songs seem to be working best – a gentle instrumental acappella, then an opening figure which could have been 'All Along The Watchtower' as Dylan played it, but is in fact 'Hey Baby (The Land of the New Rising Sun)'. The rest of the concert is a mixture of old and new: 'Hey Joe' (with improvised lyrics – 'I'm goin' way down south / way down where I can be free / ain't nobody knows me / Aint' nobody gonna fuck with me either / ain't no redneck, man / gonna fool around with me' – and a touch of 'I Feel Fine' and a traditional song ('English Country Garden'), 'Purple Haze', 'Voodoo Chile' and 'Ezy Ryder', with 'In From The Storm' to finish.

Not one of Jimi's best concerts. He was tired from the start, took ages to get into it, playing and singing out of tune as he tried to find some kind of groove to slot into. And there were four long drum intro/solos – always a bad sign, especially as Mitch was rather stiff that night. Inevitably, the equipment was playing up; at one point Jimi had to replace the fuzz unit. But the set had its bright moments and was not the disastrous débâcle written about since.

Jimi stepped forward to thank the crowd for their patience – his words lost in the cheers, although as Kirsten Nefer recalls, there was some booing as well, 'the whole atmosphere was very weird . . . he was so afraid of going on stage in the first place, now there was a fire backstage, people were trying to break into the ground and there were just crowds everywhere backstage'. Jimi came off stage exhausted. The security was hopeless, people pushed themselves forward. Jimi, slumped in the caravan, responded with mechanical smiles. He escaped for a few hours to the Seagrove Hotel, where all the musicians were staying, until it was time for the helicopter flight to Southampton and then on to Stockholm. Vishwa, who always seemed to be around Jimi these days as kind of general factotum and gofer, was expecting to travel with him to Europe. But Jimi, probably tired of people tagging along for the ride, however well meaning they might have been, just cold-shouldered him: 'Who are you, my old lady?' Vishwa was left standing in a field staring into the early-morning sky as the chopper whirled away.

It wasn't long ago . . .
But it seems like years ago since I felt the warm hello of the Sun
Lately things seem a little colder
The wind, it seems to get a little bolder

(written early September 1970, London)

Jimi and the daughter of 'King' George Clemons, Ditta, who now works with Neneh Cherry
Stora Scenen, Gröna Lund, Tivoli Gardens, Stockholm, 31 August 1970

First stop was the Stora Scenen in Stockholm. Jimi was a demi-god in
Sweden – the backstage dressing-room was awash with disciples. Jimi
grabbed a small bottle of whisky and drank it like water. He appeared
very drunk on stage. While he was in Stockholm, he apparently met Eva
Sundqvist. She had written to tell him she was pregnant and had written
again in October 1969 to say that James Daniel Sundqvist (whom she
called Little Jimi) had been born. She sent photos to Jimi's flat in London.
Kathy Etchingham remembers them arriving, but doesn't think Jimi ever
saw them. Eva said later that Jimi asked about the baby – in which case,
he must have seen some of Eva's correspondence, but he couldn't get

450

away from journalists, photographers and so on. So Jimi never got to see Little Jimi, whom Eva claimed was his son. From Stockholm, the band travelled to Gothenburg. After the gig, there was a party, but Billy Cox, always very quiet and reserved, decided to go back to his room instead. There, he was tempted into trying some acid which sent him into alternate states of paranoia and catatonia where he couldn't speak. Jimi had his suspicions that this was part of the same tactic as buying off Juma to desert him, to isolate him and make him more malleable. Billy was a close friend, somebody Jimi would confide in. But as he had shown before when Gypsy, Suns and Rainbows was being put together, Billy was not strong enough to survive in the environment of intrigue and subterfuge so common in the music business.

She said she comes from Iceland
I told her I was from the West
She took me to the snow capped mountains
and then she put me through the test
We walked across the glacier, the horses stayed behind
And as we laid between the frozen vallies [sic]
we kissed for the very first time
And now we're stuck together

(written early September 1970, London)

On 2 September, the band flew to Denmark. By now, the cold that Jimi had had in England had turned feverish; he was trembling and shaking as he arrived at the Vejlby Risskov Hallen in Arhus. He was thinking of cancelling the concert even before he arrived at the venue. An acquaintance, Anne Bjørndal, met him at his hotel: 'He was saying, "I don't think it's fair towards the audience as I don't feel up to it today."'

Kirsten arrived at the hotel to see Jimi and met Mitch coming out of the lift: 'He told me that Jimi was in a very funny mood.' Apparently, Jimi had taken a handful of pills; he was staggering around his hotel room and quite upset that she should see him in this state. The press were there in force, particularly interested that Jimi knew a Danish girl. Kirsten said she wanted to leave, but Jimi wouldn't let her.

At the concert hall, Jimi was still in a very confused state from the effects of sleeping tablets. Kirsten was with him in the dressing room, 'there was this whole scene where he couldn't decide what to wear and he couldn't tune his guitar. He was throwing people out of the dressing room and calling them back in again. It was crazy. In the end I was alone with him and he was going on and on about his guitar, about how he didn't want to play . . . Eventually he got up there, but I could see on his face there was something really, really wrong.'

With Billy off in outer space somewhere and Jimi hardly able to stand, they stumbled through 'Freedom', 'Message to Love' and 'Hey Baby', before Jimi left the stage unable to continue. He was helped, virtually bent double, back to his dressing room. The concert was called off, everyone got their money back and Jimi promised to do a free concert as well. Anne Bjørndal, who had first met Jimi in London in 1968, interviewed him for a Danish newspaper after the concert. She said he was 'exhausted and scared. I mean that's how he appeared to me, scared, like a frightened child.' They spoke back at his hotel. Jimi was admiring the view of the harbour from his hotel bedroom window.

> He said, 'This is the pity about touring, you don't get to see the places where you tour.' He didn't eat or anything, just drank some orange juice and talked a lot about supernatural things, mentioning Jesus, saying, 'Well, obviously religion must come from inside', and calling himself a traveller in electric religion. He was also talking about harmony and peace of mind – obviously that was the one thing he was looking for so badly. He said that he spoke through his guitar. 'I sacrifice part of my soul every time I play.'

He told Anne he didn't think he would live to see twenty-eight: 'The moment that I feel that I don't have anything more to give musically, that's when I won't be found on this planet unless I have a wife and children, because if I don't have anything to communicate through my music, then there is nothing for me to live for.' Jimi said he had been dead for a long time and been resurrected in a new musical body, and he'd been on this death trip for quite a while.'

Jimi travelled to Copenhagen for the concert at the K.B. Hallen. Before the concert, he spent some time at Kirsten's house with her family, catching up on some sleep and eating dinner. While they were eating, press photographers arrived and they posed for some photos. Just before Jimi died, the Danish press ran a story that Jimi was engaged to Kirsten, something she vehemently denied at the time.

In the taxi on the way to the concert, Jimi was once again struck by nerves and didn't want to play. He locked himself in the dressing room with Kirsten and it took a lot of persuading for him finally to emerge.

Jimi and Anne Bjørndal
Hotel Atlantic, Arhus, 2 September 1970

Meanwhile Mitch had flown to London to see his new baby daughter, Aysha. He took Billy Cox with him because the bassist couldn't be left alone. They arrived back in time for the concert and under the circumstances, the playing was remarkably good, particularly the extended passages of melodic, ethereal guitar.

The next two dates were in Germany – one in Berlin and then the biggest German festival of the year at the Isle of Fehmarn on 6 September. It was dubbed a 'Love and Peace' festival; German bikers and the weather ensured it was anything but.

The band travelled to Fehmarn by train from Berlin. As usual Gerry Stickells was with them: 'The train had some sleeping compartments, but they were locked, so we got one open 'cos Jimi wanted to go to sleep. The guard freaked out, stopped the train and was gonna have us thrown off. But the wife of the guy who owned the railway was on the train and she told the guard, "Don't be stupid. Let him sleep in there. *And get this train on its way!*"'

453

They needn't have worried about being late. The weather was appalling – torrential rain and a howling gale off the Baltic Sea were causing major problems both for the audience and for the performers. Meanwhile, German bikers went berserk. Along with most of the crowd, the bikers were stoned on booze and barbiturates. They robbed the box office at gunpoint and took over the car parking, waving guns at anyone who thought they were charging too much. Looking out across the audience from the stage, it looked like anybody who wasn't sleeping was fighting. Jimi wanted to play straight away, but the organisation was atrocious and he delayed going on stage for a day to wait for better weather. On the morning of the 6th, Jimi still hadn't appeared. The mood out front was tense as many had braved further batterings from the wind and rain just to see Jimi play. Alexis Korner was one of two comperes; the other had fled in holy terror of the bikers and it was left to Alexis to tell the crowd in fluent German that they would have to be patient a little longer and listen to him playing acoustic guitar.

Eventually Jimi got on stage and spent the first part of the set battling against four-part-harmony booing and cries of 'Go home!' from disgruntled fans.

'I don't give a fuck if you boo – so long as you boo in key,' Jimi retaliated, but went on to apologise for not coming on the previous day. 'It was just unbearable, man.'

Significantly perhaps he started with 'Killin' Floor', with its opening line, 'I should have quit you, a long time ago.' The crowd calmed down; the boos turned to cheers and the band played out their set. But offstage trouble was escalating; Gerry was attacked by bikers and a stagehand was shot. As soon as the set was finished, the band fled the stage. It was the last concert Jimi ever played.

Billy Cox was getting worse – he was seeing conspiracy and threats at every turn. Mitch says Billy firmly believed they would never get off the island alive. Thorazine, the standard treatment for a bad LSD trip, could only do so much. Billy needed peace and quiet and time to recuperate, but he was in no fit state to travel back to America. Jimi was very concerned for his friend's well-being; he took him back to London with him after the Fehmarn fiasco and hid him away in an apartment until he was fit to make the journey. Arriving in London on the evening of the 6th, Jimi booked into the Cumberland Hotel. The next couple of days were spent looking after Billy in the company of Kirsten, 'Billy would be groaning, "Oh, I'm gonna die, I'm gonna die" and Jimi would say, "NOBODY is going to die!!"' For some respite, Jimi, Kirsten and her friend Karen went off to see Antonioni's film *Red Desert*.

Meanwhile, Monika Dannemann had come to London. She moved into the garden flat of a private hotel, the Samarkand, at 22 Lansdowne Crescent, Notting Hill. The first she knew that Jimi had returned from Europe was on 10 September, down at the Speakeasy, when she met Eric Barratt with Billy Cox. Billy looked awful, slumped in a chair clutching a handful of pills, talking in meandering muted tones about how 'they' wouldn't let him near Jimi. The next day, Billy flew home to the care of his parents in Pennsylvania. Concerts had been planned in Vienna, Paris and Rotterdam. All were cancelled. The Dutch promoter Barry Visser received a letter from Jimi's physician Dr J.M. Robertson stating, 'I have examined Mr Billy Cox. He is suffering from an acute phobic anxiety state with paranoia and is totally unfit to work.'

Now that Jimi was back in England, he was having second thoughts about returning to America. He told *NME*, 'Not my scene, man! I don't want to go back until I really have to. I've been away from this country and Europe for such a long time, I want to show them all over again what it's all about.'[1]

The frenetic pace of New York city life was driving Jimi crazy:

New York's killing me at the moment. It's positively claustrophobic! Things go so fast, you might as well get ready to step on a roller coaster every time you move outside your door . . . and America is inclined to bring out the rebel in me. And I'm not really like that at all. I wanted once to stay forever in California. But I hear God's even going to reclaim that soon . . . I'm so glad the mini-skirt hasn't gone out of style. There's no place like London![2]

London was where Jimi had first found acceptance and it made sense to him to stay in England while he thought through his new musical direction, which, if it was as radical as he had been suggesting, would require a whole new kind of acceptance from his fans. In England, he could more easily rest both physically and mentally, consolidating his energies for the next big push.

Much against Jimi's wishes, Devon followed Jimi to London. Other New York friends of Jimi, Stella and Alan Douglas, were also in London. Pat Hartley had a London address at Elvaston Place; staying there was another of Jimi's women friends, a beautiful tall black girl, Alvinia Bridges, whom Jimi hadn't seen for about two years. Jimi spent time with all these people reminiscing, catching up with the news and generally hanging out. Jimi never stayed at the Cumberland to sleep – instead he spent the first week or so back in London at the Fulham flat of yet another friend, Debbie Toomey, an American who had been living in London for several years. Jimi had met her through a girl called Pam, who worked as a waitress at the Speakeasy.

On 10 September, Keith Altham invited Jimi to a party for ex-Monkee Mike Nesmith at the Inn on the Park Hotel. Next day, he interviewed Jimi for *Record Mirror* at the Cumberland Hotel. Keith says he found Jimi 'Fragile, I would say, but not in a depressed state. In fact he was very positive about what he wanted to do.' Keith began asking Jimi about the Isle of Wight – the last interview Jimi ever gave, from which the following is an extract:

'You were quoted prior to the Isle of Wight, that if it happened really big for you, you'd carry on for a while. Were you satisfied with the results of the Isle of Wight?'

'Well, I was so mixed up there and at that time it got so confused, like eh . . . I didn't have a chance to base any of my future on that one gig, you know. Except when I played "God Bless the Queen" ha ha ha . . . if you know what I mean . . .'

'Do you intend to form another small unit or are you hoping to get something bigger together?'

'It's hard to decide what I'll do next. I'd like to have a small group and a large one, and maybe go touring with one of them. It's hard to know what people want around here sometimes . . .'

'Do you feel any compulsion to prove yourself as King Guitar, which is the kind of label that people have slapped on you?'

'I don't know. Well, I was just playing loud, that's the only difference [laughs]. No, I don't really let that bother me, 'cause they say a lot of things, people, that if they let that bother them, they wouldn't even be around today, you know . . . King Guitar, now that's a bit heavy!'

Keith explored the fact that Jimi's onstage image had become less wild, and wondered, 'So the anger has maybe dispersed a little?'

'Oh yeah, that's always happening, though. But like, I didn't know that was anger till they told me it was, you know, with destruction and all that. But I believe everybody should have like a room, where they get rid of all their . . . you know, all their releases . . . So my room was the stage [laughs].'

'Do you personally feel the excitement has gone out of things?'

'No, I was going like that before, because I was thinking too fast, you know. It seems like, you know, a person has a tendency to get bored,

456

because like, you always want to try to do all these accomplishments, you know, like starting an idea or something like that and never quite finishing them, you know. Some people should just be let, you know, to start ideas and others should carry them out.'

'I remember Alvin Lee of Ten Years After some weeks ago said you'd never been truly appreciated or analysed as a writer. Do you feel you've never been truly criticised as a songwriter?'

'Well, probably it's a good thing, because I'm still trying to get that together, you know. All I write is just what I feel, that's all . . . I don't round it off too good. I just keep it almost naked, you know . . . But there again, I hate to be in one corner, I hate to be put only as a guitar player, or either only as a songwriter, or only as a tap-dancer, or something like this [laughs]. You know, I like to move around.'

'Is there any moral or political intent in the kinds of things you want to write?'

'Music is getting too heavy, almost to the state of unbearable . . . I have this one little thing, when things get too heavy, just call me helium, the lightest gas known to man [laughs].'

'Was your music originally intentionally psychedelic?'

'I really don't know. I have to tell the truth. "Are You Experienced?", I just heard that recently . . . I said, "Damn, I wonder where my head was at when I said all of those things . . . But, like, I don't consider that . . . the invention of psychedelic, it is just asking a lot of questions . . . like most curious people do . . . And I just happened to put that on "Purple Haze". The way I write things, I just write them in . . . with a clash between reality and fantasy mostly. You have to use fantasy in order to show different sides to reality. That's how it can bend.'

'Do you feel that you've got enough money to live comfortably?'

'Ah, I don't think so, not the way I live. Because like, I want to get up in the morning and just roll over my bed into an indoor swimming pool and then swim into the breakfast table, you know, come up for air and maybe get a drink of orange juice or something like that, and then just flap over from a chair and swim into the bathroom, and you know, go on and shave and whatever.'

'You don't want to live comfortably, you want to live luxuriously!'

'Nooo, is that luxurious? I was thinking about a tent, overhanging . . . a mountain stream [laughs].'

In several interviews, including the one for this book, Monika Danne-mann has related how Jimi had declared his total and undying love for her. 'He had already told his father in Seattle when he went to a concert there in the summer that we were getting married. And he asked me to get a house in England in the country because he wanted to come and live in England . . . I was everything to him . . . I had complete trust in him. And the way he behaved when I was with him, there seemed to be nothing more important than me.'

457

According to Monika, Jimi planned to announce his new life with her at a press conference when he got back from Scandinavia. Instead he told *Disc and Music Echo*, 'Marriage is a bit risky now . . . I'd really hate to get hurt. That would completely blow my mind. But I must admit I'd like to meet a quiet little girl now – probably one from the country. But someone who doesn't know anything about me and my "reputation" . . . I'd really like to settle down. Though one can never tell if the time's right. I can fall in love – really in love – with one girl. And I can also fall in love with someone else – but in a different way – at the same time. I guess I confuse myself sometimes.'3

There were a number of women in Jimi's life, some lovers, others friends, lovers who became friends afterwards, and casual acquaintances. He related far better to women than men – even in 'straight' society it is hard for men to confide in other males their thoughts, feelings and insecurities, let alone in the self-obsessed macho world of rock. Jimi needed female company like he needed to breathe – to comfort him, listen to him, look after and shelter him. However, just by listening to his songs and reading what he had to say in interviews, it was abundantly clear that the idea of having his freedom restricted in any way whatsoever was anathema to Jimi. Any woman who seriously believed that, irrespective of what he might have said in private, Jimi could truly give himself entirely to one relationship, to the exclusion of all others, was heading for a lot of heartache. Jimi had learnt through bitter experience as a child that the more you loved somebody, the more chance there was of being betrayed. He desperately wanted meaningful personal relationships, but was scared of the commitment that went with them – the lessons of childhood are not easily forgotten.

Late on Sunday 13 September, Monika received her first call from Jimi since he'd arrived from Germany. He came to the flat at the Samarkand on the Monday and again the next day, Tuesday. Most of his luggage remained at the Cumberland. Monika says that the idea was that he would conduct business and give interviews at the Cumberland, while using the Samarkand as a bolt-hole.

On Tuesday night, Jimi and Monika visited Ronnie Scott's club in Frith Street to see Eric Burdon's new band, War. All the American contingent were there with Angie Burdon. Jimi came in with Monika, horsed around a bit with Devon and then disappeared backstage. While he was gone, Devon tried some mind games on Monika, telling her how great Jimi was in bed. Monika had no experience in dealing with such a gregarious and pushy person as Devon and says she was shocked to

Jimi and Kirsten Nefer
Copenhagen, 3 September 1970

overhear Devon talking to some others about the techniques of getting rock stars into bed.

Back at the flat, Jimi and Monika spent the rest of the evening talking. Monika says Jimi spoke to her of many things – astrology, cosmology, art, music, religion – often expressed as an ethereal stream

459

of consciousness which could be difficult to follow.

He very much believed in Jesus, in God, but he didn't believe in the
Church itself. There were two very important things in Jimi's life, his
music, and his spiritual beliefs. He had some psychic powers, he could
see visions; he could recall astral travels – some of the songs he had
written had nothing to do with Earth, it had to do with his astral travels.
He saw different past lives. He could see the auras of people. He could
also give healing. He was very good in telepathy, he was picking up on
my thoughts and did quite a lot of meditation. He could just switch on
and off, all of a sudden he would switch, he would have a spacey look
as if something overtook him, some inspiration. When he composed or
if he wrote a lyric, he didn't think for one moment, it just went through
him and he just wrote things down. He did believe he was here for
a special mission, opening up people's consciousness, waking up their
sleepy souls. It all came from within him, the real drive was his faith.
His main purpose as a musician was to give certain messages to people.
He had found a lot of answers and wanted to pass them on.

He encouraged her to continue her own painting, and together they
sketched out artwork ideas for the next album cover. He also warned
her off drugs and told her to beware of those who might want to harm
her because she was with him.

On Wednesday 16 September Jimi spent the whole day with Monika,
returning to the Cumberland to pick up any messages. Later, a hotel
spokesman said that Jimi was served a meal in his room – the last time
he was seen by the staff.

Jimi had an engagement that night which he didn't keep. Ed Chalpin
told the *Sun* newspaper in 1984 that 'Jimi was having problems with
his career. He wanted to pull out of the music business and called
me in New York begging me to join him in London.' A number of
business engagements were allegedly scheduled for the coming few
days. The first was that very night; according to Ed Chalpin, Jimi
phoned him and asked him to come to London to help sort out his
business affairs. Monika confirms that Jimi was due to meet Chalpin
on the evening of the 16th, but never showed up. Chalpin was due in
anyway, because Friday 18 September was the date set for the preliminary court hearing of his case against Track Records and Polydor. Jimi
was also supposed to be visiting Track Records to discuss the release
of his new single 'Dolly Dagger'. Another visitor to London was Jimi's
lawyer, Henry Steingarten, who flew in to discuss with Jimi a paternity
suit brought by Diane Carpenter who Jimi had lived with in New York

for six months in 1966.

Instead of meeting Ed Chalpin, Jimi went off to the Lyceum to see Sly and the Family Stone. Eric Clapton says he was due to meet Jimi there.

'I brought with me a left-handed Stratocaster . . . I just found it in Orange Music, I think. I'd never seen one before and I was gonna give it to him. He was in a box over there and I was in a box over here and I could see him, but I couldn't . . . we never got together.'

From the Lyceum, Jimi took Monika to Ronnie Scott's. It had been arranged that Jimi would get up and jam with War. Eric recalled later: 'He started off badly as Jimi the Sound Freak, did one solo which died and was very bad. Later he became better, real loose, but when the break came he wasn't in such a good mood. In the dressing-room he said he wouldn't go back on, but after a bit of talking he did and after some good playing, he really got into the last number "Tobacco Road". He wasn't sound freaking, he was just gelling nicely with the band.'4 Jimi apparently shocked Howard Scot, War's guitarist, into playing the best solo anyone had ever heard him play. Jimi then traded off solos with Scot until they ran over time.

Monika says that Jimi spent the night with her, although both Chas Chandler and Alan Douglas recall a different sequence of events.

Monika says that Jimi had given Chas the phone number of his 'secret' address because he wanted to discuss yet again the idea of Chas managing him. This would take on a new significance because Jimi's contract with Mike was up for renewal in October and it was becoming almost public knowledge that Jimi didn't want to re-sign. He probably also realised that he did need a personal manager who was in tune with his music rather than one for whom commercial considerations were uppermost.

Chas says that on Wednesday night, 'He came up to our apartment, the same one we used to share. He came up to see my son, because he hadn't seen the baby and we sat and talked. He wasn't satisfied with the stuff he had done in the studio. He had come to the conclusion, "I grudgingly have to admit you were right about producing the band." I said, "If you got stuff, we'll bring it over here, we'll do it in London away from the fuckin' crowd." And he was gonna go to New York on Friday and come back on the Monday with all the twenty-four tracks. We ended up having a game of Risk. There was lots of laughter, "Have you heard such and such recording?" He left about three or four in the morning.' Later Chas was quoted in both *Disc* and *Record Mirror* as not having seen Jimi since March. Now he says that these quotes were made up, that he never spoke to either paper. In Chris Welch's biography of Jimi, Chas said, 'I never heard any more about him for three months until two days before he died. He asked me to produce for him again. He rang me again on the Thursday and we got to discussing the design for a cover.'[5]

Alan, Stella, and Devon were staying at the home of Daniel Secunda, a cousin of pop manager Tony Secunda. Alan Douglas maintains that 'Wednesday night, Jimi stayed over at Danny's house with us.'

Although Mike Jeffery reluctantly went along with Alan producing Jimi in the studio in late 1969, he soon changed his mind when he suspected that Alan was trying to come between him and Jimi. Eventually Jimi asked Alan if *he* would consider becoming his manager. Alan declined, saying he wasn't the management type, but on that Wednesday night, 'We just talked all night long. And the plan was that I would leave next morning and go back and tell Steingarten and that whole attorneys' group that it was over, that we were terminating. I was gonna personally talk to all of the business relationships and tell them what we were about to do. Instead of touring, we would do four concerts a year, film those concerts and bicycle the prints around the country to all the theatres. He loved that idea, it was all part of the plan.' Jimi also wanted Alan to tell Mo Ostin of Warners that he would deliver a double album and not the single LP they were expecting and that Mike had been pushing him towards. He had more than enough material for a double and he didn't want any reduction in the length of songs to make them fit a single album. Also part of 'the plan' was a recording session with Gil Evans, the world's foremost jazz composer/arranger/conductor. A meeting had been set up for Monday 21 September. Gil told *Guitar World*, 'We were talking about doing a guitar album . . . all new material.'[6]

Alan remembers that Jimi took him to the airport the following morning, Thursday 17 September.

That afternoon, Monika took a number of photos of Jimi in the garden before they went off to the bank. From there they went to Kensington Market to do some shopping. He bumped into Kathy Etchingham. 'I was looking at some things and he came up behind me. He said, "I'm staying at the Cumberland Hotel. Come over later." I went home, but Ray was terribly jealous and I couldn't go.' Monika and Jimi then headed off for the King's Road where Jimi saw Devon and Stella walking along the pavement. He jumped out of the car and went over to have a few words. They suggested he come with them to a dinner party that evening at the home of Englishman David Saloman in Great Cumberland Place W1. Jimi said he would. On the drive back to the hotel, Jimi got talking to some people, complete strangers in another car, who invited him and Monika for a drink. They seemed nice people and, very typically, Jimi (who never played being an 'unapproachable rock star') accepted. Later that afternoon, he called Henry Steingarten from his hotel suite to discuss again his position in relation to Mike. Hotel business and socialising over, they drove back to the Samarkand flat around 8 p.m. Jimi had a bath, Monika cooked them a meal and they drank some wine. Monika says Mitch and Chas both phoned that evening, but that Jimi wouldn't speak to either of them.*

In fact Mitch denies phoning Jimi there; he says he never even had the number. According to Mitch, a jam session had been arranged for Sly Stone at the Speakeasy. Mitch arrived at Gerry Stickells' flat around 7 p.m. to be told that Jimi had just phoned. Mitch returned the call – not at the Samarkand Hotel, but at the Cumberland Hotel, and says he got straight through. Jimi said he would be there for the jam, 'but he didn't show up, which we all thought was very, very strange, 'cos no matter what situation was going on, for Hendrix to miss a chance of a play was very out of character – really completely out of character'.

According to Monika, some time after 1 a.m., Jimi said he was going to the dinner party. She says he asked her to drive him there and call him at the number he gave her in half an hour to pick him up again. Monika says that Jimi's sole reason for going was to tell Devon to leave them alone. When it came time to pick Jimi up, Monika couldn't find the flat. All she had was the number, so she called from a nearby hotel. 'That is how he had to stay longer than he wanted to be.'

Not so, says Angie Burdon, who was at the party. She says Jimi arrived *mid-evening* and 'seemed jumpy'. When Monika arrived to pick Jimi up, 'He got Stella to put her off. She called up on the intercom twice more, and he got angry because she wouldn't leave him alone. In fact she was bugging him. Period. Well, he asked Stella to put her off again. Stella was rude to her and she [Monika] asked to speak to Jimi. When he finally got to the intercom, he mumbled something and then without saying anything, he just got into the lift and split.'

*It was during this evening that Jimi allegedly wrote his last song, reproduced on page 507.

Alvinia Bridges has said that after Monika and Jimi left the party, they drove to where she was staying in Elvaston Place. They all went for drinks in Soho before Alvinia was dropped off at Ronnie Scott's. Monika says that she and Jimi got back to the Samarkand about 3 a.m. on Friday morning. She says that she made Jimi a tuna fish sandwich, he drank some wine and they continued talking until about 6 a.m., when they got into bed. When she fell asleep around 7 a.m., Jimi was still awake. Monika says that she took a sleeping pill, but never saw Jimi take any himself. She says she woke up around 10 a.m., Jimi was fast asleep. Realising she needed some cigarettes, she left the flat around 10.15. The interview she gave for this book continues,

'When I returned from getting the cigarettes, I went to Jimi, tiptoeing, because I didn't want to wake him up . . . I knew he had a meeting with the record company that day, so I thought he has to have as much sleep as possible. So I went to see if he was awake . . . He was completely sleeping alright, there was nothing wrong with him . . . At twelve o'clock he had the meeting. I sat down on one of the chairs and I was thinking "Shall I wake him up or not?" And while I was trying to make up my mind, maybe three or four minutes, and watching him at the same time, all of a sudden I saw something came out of his mouth. So he wasn't sick when I came back. What I noticed when I left the flat was that he was sleeping on one side and when I came back he had changed himself on the other side. He was still quite alright.

'So when I saw he was sick, I tried immediately to wake him up and I just couldn't wake him up. And I tried all different ways, shaking and everything and I just couldn't. So, not to forget he was a star, I thought I'd better call quickly his doctor. I knew the name of Jimi's doctor in London, but I only knew the name, Roberts[on], I didn't know the telephone number. I looked up the name and there were so many "Roberts[on]s", that I thought "forget that". I called up somebody I knew to ask her about a good doctor because I thought I needed a doctor and not a hospital. She wasn't there, but funnily enough, which I didn't know, she was staying with Eric Burdon. That is how I got Eric Burdon.

'When I reached her, I asked her if she knew the number, because she also knew Jimi or if she knew somebody else who was good as a doctor. She said, "no", so I said, "Well, I'll call an ambulance quick". Then Eric Burdon took the telephone and asked me what was happening. I said that Jimi was sick, I can't wake him up and that I'm going to get an ambulance. He said no way I should get an ambulance and I said, "I'm going to get one and I must stop [talking] now". He said, "Well then, call your so-and-so ambulance." He really was mad.'

The girl Monika spoke to was Alvinia Bridges, whom Eric had known back in Los Angeles. In his autobiography, Eric's account of that phone call is quite different. After playing with War at Ronnie Scott's, Eric went home with Alvinia and they went to bed.

'Then the phone rang. Alvinia answered. "It's Monika Dannemann. She is with Jimi and he's so stoned he won't wake up." Half asleep, I suggested she give him hot coffee and slap his face. If she needed any more help to call me back. My girlfriend, Alvinia told me: "Monika's a good kid, she'll look after him." That made me feel better and I slid back under the covers. I don't know how long I dozed, but alarm bells began ringing in my mind. The first light of dawn was coming through the window . . . "Monika's number, Alvinia, give me Monika's number, quickly!"
   "Monika, it's Eric. Listen, just do what I say and don't ask any questions. Phone an ambulance now, quickly." She came back at me with, "I can't have people round here now, there's all kind of stuff in the house." "I don't care, get the illegal stuff and just throw it down the toilet, do anything you can, but get an ambulance now, we're on our way over".'[7]

The ambulance was called at 11.18. 'In the meantime,' says Monika,

I tried to wake him and didn't succeed. I stumbled across at the side of the bed a packet of sleeping tablets. And out of this packet were ten, or rather nine. I found one under the bed. Nine were missing. There were some more sleeping tablets in the cupboard and I looked and they were all there. So he definitely didn't try to commit suicide because there were much more tablets there. And these tablets were not very strong. He had tried them out before and he couldn't sleep with them.

The ambulance arrived at 11.27. As far as Monika remembers, 'They checked his heart, his pulse, his breathing and said it's all right, it's fine, nothing to worry about, especially as he'd only taken them at the most three hours ago. They were not worried one bit. They said this afternoon, you will walk out of the hospital with him. So I started to get more relaxed because I trusted the ambulancemen that they knew what they were talking about.'
   The ambulance left the Hotel Samarkand at 11.45. 'They got Jimi in the ambulance and I drove with them. They didn't put the siren on and it took about eighteen minutes to get to the hospital, it was just a normal drive. What I found out later was that there was a hospital just around the corner. But they didn't take him there, but to one further away, to St Mary's. They sat Jimi up in a chair. Because Jimi was asleep, his head was falling down and this guy always pushed it back.

I didn't think anything was wrong, because I thought they knew what they were doing.'

The ambulance arrived at St Mary Abbots Hospital, Marloes Road, Kensington at just after twelve noon. Monika alleges the following sequence of events:

Just as we entered the entrance to the hospital, the ambulancemen started to move fast and put an oxygen mask on Jimi. So I knew there was something wrong there. They immediately got him into wherever and I went to one of the doctors. I had taken the packet with me to show what kind they are, what's in it and so on. And he was not so concerned about the tablets, he was more concerned seeing me and Jimi – black and white – he didn't like it. He wanted to know who I am, what I'm doing, why I'm with him and everything. I couldn't believe it. I said, 'We are getting married, if you want to know.' I really got uptight. But he kept on asking me questions. I said, 'From now I want him treated privately – everything.' This doctor said, 'Okay.' But as I found out later, this hospital didn't treat any patients privately.

I got such a bad feeling from this doctor that when he went away I called up a friend to let Gerry Stickells know. I felt if I had a man there, he would do the pushing to make sure Jimi got the right treatment. Then a sister came to me over half an hour later – I tried in between to go in this room and each time they stopped me. She said to me I shouldn't worry at all, his heart had stopped, but they got it all right again, nothing to worry about. Around that time Gerry Stickells and Eric Barrett came.

About ten minutes later [the sister] came back and told me that he had died. Again I spoke with doctors later – if somebody is sick and the air pipe is getting blocked, what they do is they cut the air pipe, so the person can breathe and there's no problem any more. They had him one hour in the hospital. He died through the vomiting, through suffocation. So they easily could have saved him – and they bloody didn't.

I demanded to see him because there were certain things that Jimi had told me that if ever he died that I have to do certain things for him. One of these was to take care of him for three days because there are cases where if somebody goes on an astral travel, their body can appear to be dead. Some people he said have been buried alive because of this. Naturally this request was immediately denied. But after a lot of pushing I was able to see him and I was completely stunned because he had this smile on his face.

Monika is very clear and direct about what happened at the hospital that day. However, one member of the hospital staff on duty that day, equally certain of his facts, offers a very different albeit far briefer recollection of the sequence of events. Walter Price was the Accident and Emergency admissions officer: 'The ambulance turned into the hospital, the two ambulancemen jumped out and rushed into Casualty. Two doctors went out there, tried to revive him but couldn't. I heard them say later that he had died in the ambulance. They took him straight down to the mortuary. He never left the ambulance. That's definite.'

As the admissions officer, Mr Price would have made out a patient's admission card if Jimi had been brought into the hospital. No such card was made out because officially Jimi was never admitted to the hospital. In his jargon he was DOA – Dead On Arrival.

Dr Martin Seifert was the medical registrar on call that day in charge of the 'crash' team. He, too, confirms that Jimi was not formally admitted to the hospital, but says that he *was* taken into casualty in a last ditch attempt to revive him. Dr Seifert recalls that:

> He was brought in and seen by the casualty officers. As a matter of routine when somebody is brought in dead or dying, they would call the medical registrar. [This would have happened within five or ten minutes of arrival.] I came down there . . . I remember seeing him lying there, not knowing who he was and hearing a woman screaming in the background (I vividly remember that). They had a monitor on him and as far as I remember that monitor was 'flat', showing that he wasn't alive. But just as a matter of routine [we] pounded away at the chest, trying to revive him.

However it was clear that there was no sign of life and the medical team 'just called it a day'.

It is one of the duties of the Coroner's Officer to make out a report to the Coroner giving some essential details about the death in question. On the form, Dr Seifert is cited as the 'legally qualified medical man' to have seen Jimi 'before and after death' but no one interviewed Dr Seifert for the coroner's report. In fact, the wording of the report is not meant to imply that Dr Seifert necessarily saw Jimi alive. All it means is that Dr Seifert attended Jimi before the point that the crash team officially stopped trying to resuscitate him. Only after they gave up could Jimi be *formally* certified dead, even though there were no signs of life while the attempt to revive him continued. Thus although death was officially recorded at 12.45 p.m. an hour after arriving at the hospital, this was merely the time when a medically qualified person (i.e. Dr Seifert) was present to certify death.

Additional evidence for the fact that Jimi did not revive at hospital comes from a number of other sources. Firstly, most of the news reports of the time quoted the ubiquitous 'hospital spokesman' as saying that Jimi died on the way to hospital rather than after admission. Secondly, there is

467

the evidence of the two policemen who were called to the hotel by the ambulancemen. Already out on patrol, they arrived within a few minutes. One of the policemen, Ian Smith, now a publican, was interviewed by a journalist from his local newspaper, the *Bucks Advertiser*, in November 1990.

> We went to a basement flat in Lansdowne Crescent . . . Hendrix was on the floor, lumped out. The ambulance people were already there and as far as they were concerned he was dead.

The final source comes from Monika herself. Shortly after Jimi died, the press contacted Monika's brother Herbert in Dusseldorf. The *Daily Telegraph* (24 September 1970) reported Herbert as saying that Monika had phoned him the day after Jimi died. 'She said Jimi told her he wanted to sleep for a day and a half before he went to America . . . She said he died in the ambulance.'

* * *

> I was at home – Madeline Bell rang me and said, 'Have you heard the news?' (Kathy Etchingham)

> I was in New York. Somebody phoned me. 'A friend of yours has just died.' (Noel Redding)

> Noel phoned me. I phoned Mitch and Mitch was crying and I was crying. It seemed like the end of the world really . . . (Margaret Redding)

> I got on the train to Newcastle on the Friday morning. When I arrived my father was waiting for me, which he never usually did. 'I came to get you away from all the reporters.' 'Reporters?' 'Don't you know?' 'Know what?' 'Jimi's dead.' (Chas Chandler)

> There was a freak storm across Majorca and all the phone lines were down. Somebody told Mike later that Jimi had been trying to phone him. The first call that got through was to say Jimi was dead. Mike was terribly upset at the thought of Jimi not being able to get through to him. (Trixie Sullivan)

Back in Seattle, Jimi's family had just heard. They were all gathered together in sadness. Slowly the rocking chair in the corner began to rock gently. Rose, a friend of the family, turned and screamed, 'There's Jimi!' Jimi's dog wouldn't stop howling.

468

'Newport 69', Devonshire Downs, California, 22 June 1969

'Woodstock Music And Art Fair', Bethel, New York, 18 August 1969

Jazz street festival, Harlem, New York City, 5 September 1969

Billy, Jimi and Larry
Shokan house, upstate New York, August/September 1969

Fillmore East, New York City, 31 December 1969 (2nd show)

'Second Atlanta International Pop Festival', Byron, Georgia, 4 July 1970

Yes, this is printed correctly . . .
Isle of Fehmarn, W. Germany, 6 September 1970

The news flashed around the world: 'JIMI HENDRIX DIES AT 24 [sic] – "OVERDOSE"'; 'JIMI HENDRIX IN LONDON OVERLEDEN'; 'JIMI HENDRIX, ROCK STAR IS DEAD IN LONDON AT 27'; 'MORT DU GUITARISTE POP JIMI HENDRIX'. Reverential obituaries followed quickly in both the mainstream and music press. For Michael Lydon writing for the *New York Times*, Jimi Hendrix was 'a genius black musician, a guitarist, singer and composer of brilliantly dramatic power. He spoke in gestures as big as he could imagine and create; his willingness for adventure knew no bounds. He was wild, passionate and abrasive, yet all his work was imbued with his personal gentleness. He was an artist extravagantly generous with his beauty.'[8] For the more sober-minded London *Times* Jimi was simply 'A key figure in the development of popular music' who was 'largely responsible for whatever musical metamorphosis [pop music] has undergone in the last three years.'[9]

There were several personal tributes from journalists who had followed Jimi from his earliest days in New York and London. The praise was fulsome and generous, the sadness tangible. Most were at pains to point out how much of a hype 'The Wild Man of Pop' image really was and how fame had not changed his personality over the years. Under the banner headline 'GENTLEMAN JIM – INVENTOR OF PSYCHEDELIC POP', Mike Ledgerwood wrote for *Disc and Music Echo*, 'Despite his fame and fortune – plus the inevitable hang-ups and hustles which beset his incredible career – he remained a quiet almost timid individual. He was naturally helpful and honest answering questions, somewhat reluctant to talk about himself – yet always excited about his music.'[10] Bob Dawbarn of *Sounds* 'found a man of quite remarkable charm, an almost old-world courtesy and quite overpowering personality,'[11] while Richard Green, who also did PR for Jimi, expressed the feelings of many in his tribute: 'Everyone who knew Jimi is still sad and numb. They have lost a friend. It is hard, too, for the fans, who will never be able to see him again. Only his memory and his music live on as an everlasting monument to a truly great man of music and person.'[12] But perhaps the most poignant observation was made by another good friend, Keith Altham, when he wrote that the contradiction between Jimi on and offstage 'was further emphasised by his close friends who often referred to him as Hendrix rather than Jimi'.[13]

New York journalist Al Aronowitz went back even further with Jimi. He recalled seeing him with Carl Holmes and the Commanders in 1966 when 'even then the word was out in the music underground that you had to see this flashing, graceful black giant who could play the electric guitar with his teeth, who could play it faster than you ever heard'. Aronowitz's eulogy was published in the *New York Post*: 'JIMI HENDRIX, EXILE, IS COMING HOME', the thrust of the article being to remind Americans of Jimi's roots, even though he had found fame in England. After the press conference in the Copter Club at the top of the Pan-Am building in January 1968, 'We went out for soul food on Seventh Av, the first thing Jimi wanted to eat in America because he could never get any in England.' Aronowitz concluded, 'They will be bringing Jimi back to New York. . . . He lived here too, even though he never really had a home.'[14]

Less scrupulous English newspapers were quick to seize on the chance to exploit Jimi's 'reputation' and publish sleazy kiss-and-tell stories. Kathy Etchingham was tricked into giving a story to a press friend who then sold it to a Sunday newspaper, where it was rewritten by another journalist. Allegedly in Kathy's own words, Jimi was portrayed as a violent, drug-addled satyr. She later received an apology in writing from the editor, who acknowledged the deception, but no retraction was printed.

Equally damaging was a story purporting to describe Jimi's last few days. The source of the story was a twenty-one-year-old employee of the Chelsea Drugstore in the King's Road. She alleged that on the last evening of his life, Jimi toured round various flats out of his head on marijuana, made love to two girls until 5 a.m. and witnessed a man leap over a staircase and break his arm. 'When all this commotion happened, Jimi went mad and ran round the house shouting his head off.'[15] An insurance investigator finally exposed the story as a hoax, although again this was never made public.

Since the death of Otis Redding in 1967, it had become customary for record companies and managers to take out insurance policies on the lives of rock stars. Warner Brothers and Mike Jeffery both had insurance policies on Jimi's life to the value of $2 million. When the press reports indicated that Jimi's death had been drug related, the insurance company was looking for a way not to pay on the grounds that drug abuse was deliberate, self-destructive behaviour and if somebody died as a result of this, it was tantamount to suicide, which invalidated the insurance. An investigator went round checking all the stories and under some severe questioning the Drugstore girl confessed that she'd made the whole thing up to earn some money and get herself in the paper alongside Jimi's name. Monika, meanwhile, was forbidden by the coroner to talk about what had happened until after the inquest, by which time it was too late to undo the damage caused by the gutter press.

Also anxious to prove that Jimi was a junkie were the police. As we have seen, this was an era when the police both in Britain and America were looking for any opportunity to implicate musicians in illegal drug use. The autopsy was carried out on Monday 21 September. But the inquest, which opened on Wednesday the 23rd, was adjourned for 'further tests' until the 28th. Mike Jeffery flew to London and phoned back to Trixie to say that during that time the police were doing everything they could to prove Jimi had died as a result of drug abuse.

Much, too, was made of the 'Help me, man' message Jimi was alleged to have left on Chas's office answer-phone the night before he died. Chas denies ever getting such a message: 'I've never had an answer-phone in my life'.

At the inquest Professor Donald Teare, one of the country's leading forensic scientists, presented his autopsy report. He identified the sleeping tablets as Vesperax, a German compound barbiturate containing a fairly high dose of short-acting quinalbarbitone (150 mg) and a smaller dose (50 mg) of intermediate-acting Brallobarbitone. The normal dose was half a tablet to be taken half an hour before retiring. However Monika stated that she usually took a whole tablet and on that basis, the coroner concluded that Jimi had taken nine times the normal dose. Even so, in Professor Teare's opinion, Jimi had not ingested a fatal dose. Teare also estimated Jimi had 100 mg per 100 ml of alcohol in his blood at the time he took the pills. Of itself, the amount of alcohol was not significant – enough to fail a breathalyser test, but only the equivalent of about four pints of beer. However, the forensic literature shows that this amount, taken with the (at least) 1.8 gms of barbiturate that Jimi took, would potentiate the effects of the drugs enormously. In addition, Professor Teare identified 20 mgs of amphetamine and another barbiturate Seconal.

Professor Teare also searched for needle tracks, the 'stigmata of drug addiction' – none were found. He identified some whole rice grains in the stomach, almost certainly the remnants of the Polynesian food laid on at the party (where Jimi possibly consumed the amphetamine).

Three other witnesses were called: Gerry Stickells, Monika and the coroner's officer, Station Sergeant John Shaw, based at Notting Dale Police Station, who interviewed Monika during the afternoon of the day Jimi died. The line of questioning taken by the coroner, Dr

471

Gavin Thurston, makes it clear that his prime intention was to establish the extent of Jimi's drug use and whether or not Jimi committed suicide. From what they said, both Gerry and Monika satisfied the coroner that Jimi was not given to fits of temperament, that he was not depressed, nor a regular consumer of so-called 'hard drugs'.

During the course of the interview for this book, Monika said, '. . . after it happened, I wrote everything down in complete detail. It was just after his death, so everything was fresh.' However, Monika's evidence as presented to the coroner pertaining to the events of the morning of the 18th does appear contradictory. One written statement made by Monika before the inquest and lodged in the coroner's records maintains:

> I woke about 10.20 a.m., he was sleeping normally. I went round the corner to get cigarettes, when I came back he had been sick, he was breathing and his pulse was normal, but I could not wake him.

There was also the newspaper coverage of the inquest. Reporters from two very diverse newspapers, the *Daily Sketch* (29.9.70) and *Rolling Stone* (29.10.70) both noted yet another version of events:

> I wanted some cigarettes, but as Jimi did not like me going out without me telling him, I looked to see if he was awake. He was sleeping normally. *Just before* [author's italics] I was about to go out, I looked at him again and there was sick on his mouth and nose.

And as we read above, Monika now says that Jimi was not sick until *after* she came back with the cigarettes.

Did Monika go out to buy cigarettes? In most accounts, Monika says she did, except in that noted here by the *Daily Sketch* and *Rolling Stone*. Neither paper goes on to say that Monika did go out – hardly surprising if she had discovered Jimi had vomited.

When did she go out? In most accounts Monika says she woke up around 10.15–10.20 a.m. and went out shortly afterwards and bought cigarettes 'around the corner'. This would have been the local shops just off Clarendon Road, about five minutes' walk from the hotel. No other shops were nearer on foot. However, in 1982, Monika had a meeting with Noel Redding, Mitch Mitchell, Kathy Etchingham and her husband which took place at Kathy's house. During the course of that meeting, Kathy says that Monika told them all that she had to drive her car down to Queensway to buy cigarettes because she

472

couldn't find any local shops open. Which brings us to the question of timing.

From everything that Monika has said, no problem was noticed with Jimi much before 10.45 a.m. Yet in his autobiography, Eric Burdon talks about receiving the call from Monika at 'the crack of dawn' and 'the first light of dawn coming through the window'. Admittedly, a musician's 'crack of dawn' could be anything up to midday. However, Gerry Stickells says he received a call from Terry Slater 'fairly early . . . between 8 and 9'. Terry Slater was a former roadie with The Animals and a close friend of both Eric Burdon and Jimi. At the time, Terry was on tour with Eric Burdon and War. Apparently Terry said only that there was 'a problem with Jimi at the hotel'. Although Gerry was living only minutes away from the Samarkand, in Elgin Crescent, he apparently knew nothing about it and when Terry said 'hotel', Gerry thought he meant the Cumberland. Gerry's immediate thought was that Jimi had been busted for drugs and went straight to the Cumberland Hotel.

Mitch Mitchell left the Speakeasy around 4 a.m. on Friday morning and took about two hours to make the journey back to East Sussex. His daughter Aysha was just over two weeks old and it was Mitch's practice to take her from his wife Lynn when he got in from playing. When he got home, the baby was asleep. Mitch says he never went to bed, but pottered around the house waiting for Aysha to wake up. When the call came from Noel's mother Margaret to say Jimi was dead, Aysha was still asleep. Mitch says it was no later than 9.30 a.m.

In summing up the case for the benefit of the jury, the coroner said that for a verdict of suicide to be given there must be definite evidence of the intention to end life. In Jimi's case, the evidence showed that he had taken a large dose of pills, but not one large enough to have been fatal – he would normally have been expected to recover. The cause of death was officially established as inhalation of vomit due to barbiturate intoxication, but as there was no evidence of an intention to commit suicide the coroner advised the jury that an open verdict would be proper; they duly complied.

So did Jimi commit suicide? Eric Burdon seemed to think so. In a controversial television interview by Kenneth Allsop for the BBC's *24 Hours* programme, Burdon stated: 'He made his exit when he wanted to. His death was deliberate. He was happy dying . . . and he used the drug to phase himself out of this life and go someplace else.' He went on to cite the song Jimi wrote on the night before he died as evidence. Eric lived to regret his statements that night. He said in his autobiography:

'In defiance of everybody and everything and all that Jimi stood for, I got stoned before the interview. Allsop took me apart, fried me . . . my ego was stupid enough to allow me to speak publicly about the death of a friend . . . As I left the TV studio, I recognised an executive from Polydor Records . . . He grabbed me by the arm, "For that, for what you've just said, you'll never ever work again in England, son."'[16]

There had been some rumours that Jimi had tried to cut his wrists in New York in the very early days when he had little or no work and the autopsy report did indeed reveal a quarter-inch scar on the wrist of his left hand although this could easily have been caused during his encounter with the Swedish bedroom, among other possibilities. Interviewed for a film on Jimi's life, Stella Douglas said, 'He fluctuated so fast from great joy to intense unhappiness . . . I mean suicidal, not interested in life, completely disinterested in his body.'

The decision to kill or not to kill yourself can be taken in an instant. The comedian Jerry Lewis said that he once had the gun in his hand all ready to shoot, but then he heard his young child laugh in the hallway and he couldn't do it. People have been known to stop in the middle of a simple chore like the washing up – and commit suicide. Jimi seemed so positive about the future, all his plans – how could he have wanted to die? Unfortunately, this by itself is no proof. Those who are severely depressed (as Jimi was during late 1969/early 1970) feel nothing inside, there is no emotion, no motivation to do anything at all. However, when the depression begins to lift and the feelings return, any crisis counsellor knows that by the cruellest of ironies, this is the most dangerous time. Jimi was a very private person. There wasn't one person who could be sure they knew what he was thinking. Nobody who knew Jimi wants to believe he killed himself because accompanying such knowledge is a whole burden of guilt which many find impossible to deal with. 'If only I had . . . then perhaps it would never have happened.' Under such unexplained circumstances, it is only right to examine all possibilities, if only to knock them down. Nobody interviewed for this book believes Jimi did commit suicide nor is there any real evidence to suggest this. As Monika said, there were other tablets in the cupboard which he could have taken, if he had wanted to do the job properly. He didn't even finish the packet of ten pills – one was found under the bed.

'Murder' was on the lips of a few people – he was killed by the CIA, the FBI, the Black Panthers and the mystical 'they', normally meant to indicate Mike Jeffery. Again, there is no evidence for such conspiracy theories. As in life, so in death, there were too many people wanting to hold Jimi up as a 'victim', a martyr to his genius, done in by evil managers, record companies, hangers-on, dope-dealers, political militants and so on. True, like anybody in the public eye, Jimi was under inordinate amounts of stress. But to deny him any inner resources of strength to win through, the belief in the power of his own vision and the ability to gain control over his life, is to do Jimi Hendrix a grave disservice.

So where does this leave us? Why did Jimi take so many tablets? One possible clue is the quote from Herbert Dannemann cited above – that Monika told him Jimi took a handful of pills because he 'wanted to sleep for a day and a half'. The biggest problem with barbiturates is that the margin between a normal or therapeutic dose and a fatal dose is perilously small. Taken with alcohol, the danger becomes even more acute. In the year Jimi died, there were nearly 1000 other accidental deaths in England resulting from taking too many barbiturates. In Gerry Stickells' words, Jimi's death was 'an unfortunate accident'. And almost certainly that is what it was.

However there are puzzling aspects of the Coroner's handling of the inquest, not least the fact that some key witnesses were not called to give evidence, namely the two ambulance drivers, the two policemen who arrived at the scene just as Jimi was being taken away, and Dr Seifert. During 1991, after some painstaking efforts, these witnesses have been located. The research continues and hopefully one day, the full story of the circumstances surrounding Jimi's death will be told.

* * *

If Hendrix had taken all the drugs the papers and rock books say he took, he'd never have lived as long as he did. Jimi *was* the kind of person who'd push things to the nth degree, but I never saw suicidal tendencies there. He's painted as this tragic figure, but he wasn't. He died tragically, but that's *not* the same thing. (Mitch Mitchell, *Hot Press*, 30 November 1989)

When I die I want people to just play my music, go wild and freak out and do anything they wanna do. (*Daily Mirror*, 11 January 1969)

I'll probably get busted at my own funeral. (*Melody Maker*, 8 March 1969)

The next time I go to Seattle will be in a pine box. (To Chuck Wein, July 1970)

On Tuesday 22 September, four days after Jimi had died, Buddy Miles flew into Seattle to see Jimi's family about having an 'all-star jam' instead of a standard funeral. This would take place in New York rather than Seattle, involving a host of top names – Eric Clapton, Mick Jagger and the Beatles among others would all be approached. Al was away in New York consulting with Jimi's lawyer Henry Steingarten about the estate, and the family felt they could not make a decision on this until he got back. On his return, although apparently in favour of a concert, he was persuaded by Mike Jeffery and the press agent Mike Goldstein that such an event could turn Jimi's funeral into a rock 'n' roll circus, especially as radical groups like the Black Panthers had said they wanted to be involved. The family also vetoed a plan to switch the concert to Seattle, much to the relief of the city authorities, who had visions of another Woodstock. Buddy Miles claims that Mike Jeffery had an ulterior motive in not wanting a 'show funeral'. Miles had confronted Jeffery with demands for money he said he was owed from his membership of the Band of Gypsys, plus a number of general allegations concerning the misappropriation of Jimi's earnings. He said he had made a detailed deposition to *Rolling Stone* (who denied this) and claimed that Mike feared he would use the opportunity of a funeral concert to 'go public'.

Jimi would never have wanted to be buried in Seattle, but it was inevitable that, unless it had been stipulated otherwise in a signed will, that was where he would be taken. The day after the inquest on 28 September, Jimi's body was flown to Seattle for what would now be a private family affair.

Seattle had been enjoying something of an Indian summer, but by 1 October, the day of Jimi's funeral, it was a weak winter sun that shone. In the morning, parties of Jimi's friends and acquaintances flew in from New York, Los Angeles and London: John Hammond, Johnny Winter, Steve Paul from the Scene club, Miles Davis, Noel and Mitch, Buddy Miles, Alan Douglas, Devon, Eric Barrett and Gerry Stickells, Chuck Wein, Eddie Kramer. The service took place at the Dunlap Baptist Church, a small, simple chapel on Rainier Avenue South. Just one reporter and one photographer were allowed in – some 200 others plus local fans of Jimi stood respectfully outside behind the ropes. A half-dozen police cars and about a dozen police motorcycles stood by, lined up with twenty-four limos standing black and silent at the kerb. All of Jimi's close family were in attendance – Al, his wife June, Jimi's nine-year-old stepsister Janie and his brother Leon. Against the back-drop of a floral arrangement dominated by a large guitar-shaped wreath, the Reverend Harold Blackburn conducted the service. Patronella Wright, a family friend, sang three hymns backed by a gospel piano, 'His Eye Is on the Sparrow', 'The Angels Keep Watch Over Me' and 'Just a Closer Walk With Thee', which Jimi had sung as a boy with Dorothy Harding on the back porch of her house all those years ago. Freddie Mae Gautier stepped forward to read the eulogy. She read out 'Angel' and Jimi's own liner notes to Buddy Miles' album *Expressway to Your Skull*:

> The express had made the bend, he is coming on down the tracks, shaking steady, shaking funk, shaking feeling, shaking life . . . the conductor says as we climb aboard . . . 'We are going to the electric church.' The express took them away and they lived happily and funkily ever after and – uh – excuse me, I think I hear my train coming . . .

Leon had written a poem. Freddie Mae had marvelled that given his upbringing Jimi had not 'gone bad', as she put it. But Jimi had a wondrous gift. Leon was not so fortunate and sadly had drifted off the tracks, serving time for grand larceny in 1968. Jimi had become disillusioned with Leon and had refused to visit him in jail when he was in Seattle. However, Leon was playing guitar and he claims Jimi was going to help him get started, so perhaps there had been some kind of reconciliation. Leon wrote: 'He knew peace and love he'd find somewhere, so he made the music to guide us there.'

The coffin was opened for invited guests to pay their last respects. Mitch wiped the tears from his eyes, Buddy was near to collapse. With the exception of Herbert Price, Jimi's chauffeur and valet on Maui during the filming of *Rainbow Bridge*, all the pallbearers were friends from Jimi's childhood, including James Thomas, who gave Jimi his first chance in a band. They carried the coffin out to the waiting cars for the twenty-minute drive to Greenwood Cemetery, where Lucille was buried – and there, Jimi Hendrix, aged twenty-seven, was laid to rest.

There are those who come before the public eye and are commercialised into the consciousness of the masses. We are told they are popular, and we echo, they are popular. Then there are a few who are so intuitively tuned into the universe that they are still influential even though they are beyond sight. This is immortality, and Jimi Hendrix is immortal. It is exciting to know that the world has yet to truly be exposed to Jimi's genius. Maybe the overshadowing rumours that are used by some to cloud his image will be replaced by an understanding of the man *I* knew – a child of the universe, a guitar master, a warm and gentle soul. (Billy Cox, *Guitar Player*, May 1989)

Fifteen *Ain't No Telling*

The story of the Jimi Hendrix 'industry' after his death is an unedifying tale of litigation, exploitation and the rubbishing of Jimi's memory by his home town, Seattle.

The saga of the posthumous recordings is set out in the Discography. Of the hundreds of albums released, less than a dozen deserve to carry Jimi's name – even then it is unlikely that any of these would have appeared in the form they did had Jimi lived. Much of the rest is plain awful.

With Jimi's body hardly cold, anything of value was removed from his apartment in New York. Mike sent in two of his employees to gather up all Jimi's tapes, guitars, home movies and photos of Jimi with various women. Apparently these employees hung on to the unfinished tapes of Jimi's autobiographical suite 'Black Gold', alleging that Mike owed them money. Those tapes were never handed over nor have they surfaced since. According to Angie Burdon, Mike also gave Devon Wilson permission to 'take what she wanted from the flat – rugs, clothes and ornaments'.*

Since Jimi died, many people who have legitimately or otherwise been in possession of his belongings have collectively made considerable sums of money from their sale at auction. The temptation to do so is obvious and understandable. However, it would have been a happier state of affairs if such items had no market value, so that the new owners could do little with them other than keep them or donate them to a permanent exhibition of popular music.

Meanwhile, just after Jimi's death, there were press reports that Al Hendrix stood to inherit about $500,000, which to most people

---

*After Jimi died, Devon's heroin habit ran out of control; she died in mysterious circumstances at the Chelsea Hotel in New York during February 1971.

in the know seemed a very small amount. Worse still, it was also alleged that Al had been informed by Mike that only a measly $20,000 had been located in the accounts. A local Seattle lawyer went to New York to see Jimi's lawyers at Steingarten, Weiss and Weden, but he wasn't up to dealing with smart East Coast attorneys. At this point another lawyer, Leo Branton, came on to the scene, recommended to Al by Jimi's sometime valet, Herbert Price. Branton was an aggressive, self-assured black advocate who had represented Nat King Cole among others (who Price had also worked for) and defended the black activist Angela Davis. He took on Steingarten & Co. head-on and cleared them out of the way under threat of a conflict-of-interest suit because different partners in the firm represented both Jimi and Mike.

At the same time, Branton engaged the services of two other black lawyers, Ed Howard and Kenny Hagood, who have since stated that Jimi came to see them himself as early as April 1969, seeking a way out of his contract with Mike Jeffery. It was agreed that Hagood would administer the estate, Howard would be the attorney of record while Branton would deal with any court work and generally oversee the operation of finding out what had happened to Jimi's money. Branton struck a deal with Mike, whereby Jeffery bought out Jimi's share of Electric Lady for $240,000 and took on the remaining obligations of the loan from Warner Brothers.

Then Branton turned his attention to the unresolved lawsuit involving Ed Chalpin. Negotiations had been rumbling on since Jimi died, but it wasn't until March 1973 that the case finally came to trial in London – Ed Chalpin (PPX) versus Track Records and Polydor, with Leo Branton representing the record companies. At the same time, Mike, Chas and Jimi's estate, represented by Branton, were suing Track, presumably over unpaid royalties. All together there were forty-two separate points of contention between PPX and Track/Polydor. Branton says he tried to settle out of court, but that Chalpin refused. Once the case was underway, it became clear, he says, that the judge, Mr Justice Mars-Jones, was very antipathetic to Chalpin's case. Chalpin himself realised and tried to settle during the proceedings. Branton could see they were winning and told him to get lost. According to both Leo Branton and Chris Stamp of Track, Mars-Jones threw the case out; Chalpin agreed to pay over $150,000, which the judge ordered to be paid in sterling, plus costs. Ed Chalpin denies he lost the case. He bases this claim partly on the fact that he was allowed to continue promoting the albums already on the market, which in truth gives some technical legality to his contract with Jimi – otherwise surely he would have been ordered to withdraw those recordings already out. There was a bizarre and tragic twist to the end of the court case. On 5 March 1973, just as the judgement was about to be handed down, Mike Jeffery was killed in an air crash.

At the time, Mike was also being sued over monies due to the Animals and the plaintiff's counsel tried to get Mike's passport confiscated, but the judge refused the request, even granting a recess so that Mike could fly to Majorca for business reasons. Mike was on his way back to Britain, both for his trial and to hear the verdict in the Chalpin case. If Track won, then all Jimi's UK royalties, which had been held up pending the outcome since 1968, would be released. As Jimi's personal manager and through the contract with Track, Mike stood to make a lot of money. French air-traffic controllers (ATC) were on strike as he boarded an Iberian Airways DC-9 in Majorca. Military ATCs were brought in, operating from different centres to their civilian counterparts. Somehow, the DC-9 found itself on the same flight path as a Spantax Coronado over Nantes. The DC-9 was late, the Coronado early. Inexplicably, the Spantax pilot did a right turn and collided with the DC-9. The Spantax survived the impact and was able to carry on, but the DC-9 was knocked out of the air and crashed, killing all the forty-seven British passengers on board. Mike Jeffery was one of them. Recriminations flew back and forth: the Coronado pilot, the military ATCs and faulty radar equipment were all blamed in turn.

Given Mike's reputation as a shady will o' the wisp, there were plenty of people who liked to imagine that Mike had faked his own death and was living in luxury in South America or somewhere equally exotic. However, Gerry Stickells flew to France to make an identification. 'I identified him by his jewellery. They said *you* don't want to see a photograph.' Nobody ever really believed Mike Jeffery when he said he had 'heavy connections', but the inclusion of Vanilla Fudge on the 1968 tour, the resolution of Jimi's kidnap and the circumstances surrounding the gig at the Salvation all indicate that at least circumstantially this was no mere fantasy. As if to reinforce his claims, among his papers was a clipping from the *Los Angeles Times* dated 21 July 1972. It concerned the murder of Mafia boss Tommy Eboli and the subsequent rise to absolute power of Carlo Gambino over all the crime families of New York. Nobody asked can offer an explanation for why Mike had bothered to keep the cutting.*

*In Fredric Dannen's book **Hit Men** (Muller 1990), a link *is* established between Eboli and the music business via Morris Levy who founded the Roulette label.

481

Leo Branton's efforts had realised well in excess of $1 million dollars for the estate, but he drew a blank trying to recover funds from a British offshore company based in the Bahamas called Yameta, into which sums estimated at between $1 million and $5 million allegedly disappeared. He was advised that even if they could ascertain what had happened to the money, the account was empty, so it would be a waste of time mounting an expensive case in London. In Chapter Six, we saw how Jimi, Mitch and Noel signed a production contract with Mike and Chas in October 1966. (This, incidentally, could have been challenged later, because neither Mitch nor Noel was twenty-one years old when the contract was signed.) Then, in December, Jimi *alone* signed an employment contract, not directly with Chas or Mike, but with Yameta.

The man who masterminded the setting up of Yameta was a solicitor specialising in revenue and private international law named John Hillman. He had an office in the prestigious law firm of Clinton's, who were based in Pall Mall.

In 1965, when Mike Jeffery was still the manager of the Animals, Hillman says, 'He came to see me and said that he had heard that there was a way to mitigate the tax of artists' income using tax havens.' And so there was. John Hillman had the idea that the overseas earnings of artists could be channelled into a specially created overseas fund to avoid such earnings being taxed at crippling rates at source in the UK. This would only apply to income earned abroad, not that earned solely in the UK. From a business point of view, the Bahamas was a good choice; not only was it politically stable, but under Bahamian company law a company like Yameta could operate in almost total secrecy. It wouldn't have to disclose its real ownership; the named directors could be kept secret; and there was no obligation to submit accounts for scrutiny or keep any company information in the Bahamas at all save for a record of the directors and the minutes of meetings. In other words, for a few hundred dollars' registration fee, it was possible to incorporate a company potentially handling millions of dollars with no general accountability whatsoever.

Mike thought it sounded like a good idea and so $50,000 belonging to the Animals was transferred to a Bahamian company incorporated by John Hillman in January 1966. The company was called Yameta, after a tribe of Indians who had formerly inhabited some of the Caribbean islands. The new company had bank accounts with the Nassau branch of the Bank of Nova Scotia and the Chemical Trust Bank in New York.

However, Yameta did not stand alone; it was a subsidiary of another company, the Caicos Trust Company, which was renamed the Bank of New Providence Trust Company, of which John Hillman was also a director. It was the trust which owned the shares in Yameta and provided it with the officers (company secretary, treasurer and so on) required under Bahamian law. As well as Yameta Co., there was also Yameta Music and Yameta Publishing. The directors of Yameta included the former Chief Justice for the Bahamas, Sir Guy Henderson; another solicitor, and for a short while John Hillman himself.

The deal with Yameta was that all overseas earnings would come to Yameta, which would take between 5 and 10 per cent for administration. Increasingly Yameta, which was in effect an artists' management company, became responsible for paying all the expenses which accrue to an artist – promoter, agents, hotels, travel, publicity, legal and accounting fees, management and production fees and so on – in which case up to 40 per cent would be sliced off the gross income. Once all the expenses had been paid out and the musicians' personal expenses covered, the balance would be kept in trust for the band, earning interest.

The Animals broke up in late 1966 and, according to Eric Burdon, somebody travelled to Nassau on their behalf to collect the money but, when he got there, there were no little nest-eggs gathering interest.

However, by then, Chas at least had changed sides. He was now in partnership with Mike, who brought him into the Yameta scheme. At the beginning, Mike had been a major shareholder of Yameta, but for the lawful tax-avoidance scheme to work (as opposed to unlawful tax evasion), everybody had to be an employee of the company on a salary. So Mike and Chas signed employment contracts with Yameta, and John Hillman relinquished his directorship to become a 'representative' of the company along with Yameta's lawyer Lee Dicker. At one time Yameta had on its books the Who as well as the Animals, and later signed Soft Machine and Blue Mink. But once the Animals split up, not much was happening, until Jimi came along. Once he did, says John Hillman, Mike and Chas were 'effectively the day-to-day managers of Yameta'.

Jimi was signed as an employee of Yameta, but the question immediately arises – how was Jimi, as an American citizen, supposed to benefit from a British tax haven? As a US citizen, Jimi could be taxed by the Internal Revenue Service wherever he was in the world. There was no provision for a US citizen to have overseas earnings taxed in the country where the money was earned or to have earnings rerouted to an offshore company to avoid taxation at source. It would appear that the only way Jimi could have avoided some of the taxes due from foreign income was to be resident outside the USA in the country where the money was being earned for an entire tax year – and this never happened. The question of non-residence in the USA may explain why in official documents Jimi's address was always given as either in Nassau or Mike's office or Gerry Stickells' flat in London. In truth, Jimi did not have a permanent US address, which conceivably might have been quite convenient when the question of taxes arose.

This was why it was important for Jimi to have an employment contract with Yameta. It meant he was an employee of a Bahamian company. It also meant that, strictly speaking, none of the money he earned was his – it all belonged to Yameta, which paid him a salary, however large that might have been. However, this only worked for Jimi's earnings outside America, but it was America where he earned most of his money and there, says Hillman, 'You're getting into the area of tax evasion,' although some of this might have been mitigated by for example a record company rerouting some of Jimi's royalties through an overseas subsidiary instead of making payments directly from an American parent company.

And what of Noel and Mitch in all this? John Hillman says neither of them wanted any part of the tax-saving scheme: 'They would never sign anything – those guys chose not to be within that structure and nobody encouraged them hard to be in there, because there was always the thought, certainly in Mike's mind, that they would be transient.' Hillman says Yameta did not want a situation where they were drawing up employment contracts for new musicians every few months. During the seventies, Noel employed an American lawyer, Micky Shapiro, to try and track down the money Noel claimed he was owed. Shapiro went to see Sir Guy Henderson. He came away with an armful of documents including one sheet which itemised several cheques to a number of individuals, some in excess of $50,000, but nowhere did the names of Noel, Mitch or for that matter Jimi appear.

'And quite right!' says Hillman, who goes on to point out that as neither Noel nor Mitch were Yameta employees, it should come as no surprise to discover that Yameta never wrote out any cheques to them. As far as Yameta was concerned, either Jimi or Mike was responsible for paying any other musicians, and Jimi himself was invariably paid in cash via Mike's office. This is partly borne out by extant receipts signed by Jimi, which show that, for example, between August and December 1969 he received about $16,000 in cash. The rent on his Shokan house which he had for about half this period would have been paid directly by the office. Also on the list of cheque payments unearthed or compiled by Noel Redding's lawyer were a number of cheques to Lee Dicker. Apart from his fees for work done, John Hillman explains that some of this money was reimbursement for the amounts paid out by Dicker personally to continue the financing of the Experience, after Chas's money ran out, but before any real income was earned. Similar monies were paid out and later recouped, says Hillman, by Yameta itself.

Jimi with
Mike Jeffery
Fillmore East,
New York City,
10 May 1968

It would seem that, unfortunately, many (but not all) roads lead back to Mike Jeffery. Unfortunate because, as John Hillman says, 'He's dead, he can't answer and so he's an easy target, which is what I don't like about it. All I know is what happened.'

By the time Jimi got to Monterey in June 1967, all the basic agreements had been signed – a production contract, a management contract, publishing and agency deals plus contracts with Track, Warners and the French company Barclay.

Then in 1968, Warners stepped in to settle Ed Chalpin's lawsuit, and after that things got really complicated. It is only possible to open a small window on proceedings and offer a tentative scenario as to what may have taken place. Financially, everything that Warners had conceded to Chalpin, they would want to claw back from Mike, Jimi and Yameta, because as Jimi had already signed with Ed Chalpin, all three were in clear breach of their contract with Warners. Warners would thus invoke the indemnity clause in the contract to recoup monies signed away to Chalpin. But the contract that Jimi signed with Yameta also had an indemnity clause in it. 'We always had that indemnity', says John Hillman, 'because we never believed them when they said they had never signed with anybody else.' So this left Jimi high and dry: he was already in the red to Warners because of the advance paid out on signing the contract – now they would be clawing back money through the royalties Jimi would be owed. Mike was in a similarly tricky situation, but he tried to do a deal with Warners effectively to cut out Yameta and give him and Warners the biggest slice of earnings from the Experience. But somewhat prematurely, he also got Jimi, Noel and Mitch to sign letters to their agent, to their music publisher and to Warners, instructing each agency not to pay any more money to Yameta, but instead send it to Jeffery and Chandler Inc. This was the company Mike had set up in New York, at the same time closing down his London office just ahead of the bailiffs.

That was in August 1968. Yameta didn't find out what was going on until December during an audit of the company being conducted by the accounting firm of Price Waterhouse. John Hillman had called for the audit himself, in the wake of various allegations that Yameta had misappropriated funds belonging to the Animals. The Price Waterhouse report did identify some confusion in the accounting, monies sent from one place to another, which according to the books never arrived, but nothing that could be construed as fraud or embezzlement. In fact, the audit showed Yameta was out of pocket and when Hillman found out why, 'It was the subject of potential litigation where we threatened to bury Jeffery.' But Mike shrugged his shoulders, admitted he'd been caught with his hand in the till and paid up. But it didn't end there; John Hillman says that virtually none of the gig money ever found its way to the Bahamas in the first place and that includes most if not all of nearly $1.3 million from the 1969 American tour. 'What I couldn't put up with was that the structure was there, but the funds were being diverted all the time. Somebody picked up the cash at the gig and off they went.'

Hillman says of Mike, 'Part of his trouble was that he was untidy. He did a whole lot of side deals, some on behalf of Yameta, some not. He did divert funds, there's no question of that, but that doesn't necessarily mean he stole anything.' If John Hillman did ask Mike where certain monies were,

He'd say, 'I'm distributing it to the boys' or 'They owe me money and I'm deducting it and I will pay you Yameta's proportion.' But it should have happened the other way round – Yameta receives the money, deducts its ten per cent and pays the guys. He was a rogue, but I could forgive him a lot. There are thousand of singers – virtually all of them get nowhere. It's only people like Mike, with all their shortcomings, that bring them into the public eye, take a chance on them, pay their expenses, sweat and steal to get them into the position they finish up in. And that costs money. And the average artist when he gets there doesn't really want to know what it has cost. He just wants to say, 'Where's my money?' The Animals without Mike Jeffery were nothing. They made money and they spent money.

Mike's habit of hopping from one country to the next with suitcases full of money fuelled speculation that he was fraudulently siphoning off funds to pay for his other ventures, like the clubs in Spain. However, his personal assistant Trixie Sullivan will not accept that Mike could have been a crook. 'I wouldn't have worked for him for all those years if I thought anything like that was going on.' She gives one example of how the clubs could financially support one another. In June 1966, a Spanish singing group called Los Bravos had a worldwide smash hit called 'Black Is Black'. Just before the record broke, Mike had signed them up to play one of his clubs for six months. As a result of the hit record, the club was packed every night and Mike made a fortune. Proceeds from this happy accident went into the Sergeant Pepper's Club, which Jimi opened in July 1968.

When both Noel and Mitch discovered that nothing was coming to them from Yameta, they turned to Leo Branton and the estate for restitution under the terms of the oral agreement they had with Jimi whereby they split everything on a 50–25–25 basis. Writs were also issued against Warners for non-payment of royalties. Eventually,

487

with funds running out, both had to settle with the estate for amounts totalling $400,000. However, Noel in particular has continued trying to this day to discover what happened to all the money. When they settled with the estate, there was little or no interest in Jimi's music among the general record-buying public. However, with the advent of compact discs and videos, Jimi's selling power has soared. Noel calculates that he is at least £6 million out of pocket. The value of the estate has been estimated at anything from $50 million to $80 million. It all goes back to the status of Noel and Mitch in the band and the agreement between the members on how the money should be split. Chas is adamant that Noel and Mitch did get paid according to the agreed split – 'It certainly worked like that when I was around' – and, given the amount that was legitimately deducted before the band saw a penny, perhaps it did. But the cake on offer (and therefore the slices) became enormous once the band became famous, and astronomical twenty years on from Jimi's death. Leo Branton's view is that the estate paid out a considerable sum of money (for 1972) on the strength of an oral agreement which had no basis in law. End of discussion. Noel and Mitch would not agree.

Ironically, if they had both remained high earners in their own right during the seventies and eighties, as many of their peers did (like the Who) who went to court and won settlements over bad deals, they would have had the money to pursue their alleged missing income from the sixties. Unfortunately, personal problems kept Mitch off the road while Noel went from one management disaster to another and now mainly plays around the clubs and bars of southern Ireland where he lives. Of course, their point is that, with Jimi's estate worth millions, they *should* be high earners now.

So what can be said about allegations that Yameta was some kind of Bahama Triangle into which untold millions vanished?

There were a number of reasons why, when he died, there seemed so little money available for Jimi to pass to Al – and subsequently why the cupboard was bare for Noel and Mitch.

In the first place, most contracts that musicians signed in those days, including the Experience (usually with no independent legal advice) were diabolical. For example, Yameta had the right to sell Jimi's songs to a music publisher. They chose a large American company solely owned by Mr and Mrs Aaron Schroeder. As a matter of course, Jimi's entire output would have been signed away for anything up to five years with renewable long-term options at the

The Experience with Chas Chandler
Hamburg between 17 and 19 March 1967

publisher's discretion. The practice of allowing the overseas subsidiaries of the publishing companies to take their cut first meant that the standard 50–50 deals struck then were often meaningless. What the artist was left with was half of what was left, not half of the gross amount. It was even worse for Jimi – he wasn't even signed directly to Schroeders. His cut came after Schroeders, Yameta and the managers had taken theirs. Publishing is where the real money is in music – not selling records or touring. Considering that every single and album was a hit either in the UK or in America or both, not forgetting Europe, the income generated must have been significant. What Jimi saw of this or any of the advances paid out on record deals is anybody's guess.

The second reason is that trying to prise royalty cheques out of record companies was notoriously difficult. Yameta's New York

489

lawyer, Lee Dicker, once went into MGM to collect some royalties for the Animals. The receptionist told him the person he wanted to see was 'unavailable'. 'That's okay, I'll wait.' 'He's out of town right now.' 'No problem, I'll wait.' He then stationed himself in the lobby and waited. When he could see nothing would be happening, he began to buttonhole every single person who came in, including the boy delivering sandwiches, telling them in loud detail just how terrible it was trying to get money out of MGM. Before long, the receptionist was making feverish whispered conversation into her telephone and out of his office came an irate company executive: 'Lee, for Christ's sake – whadda ya think ya doin'?'

John Hillman had similar experiences with just about every company he has ever dealt with. 'The record companies as a matter of business practice retained the funds for as long as they could in order to use them for cash-flow purposes – they were using them to run their businesses.' In Jimi's case, with Ed Chalpin's litigation going on from 1968 to 1973, the record companies had all the reason they needed to hold up payments pending the outcome.

As John Hillman indicated, the money that went in expenses and the money that the musicians themselves spent meant a severe drain on the money that was available. With reference to the Animals, Hillman says, 'They were spending like crazy. One time in New York, Eric Burdon, Hilton Valentine and John Steele spent $17,000 in a week on limousines.' And of course any business providing services to pop stars would multiply the bills by as much as they could get away with. Most of the bills the musicians never even saw – hotels (including any damage), bar bills, travel costs for themselves, girlfriends and the hangers-on, restaurants, cars, houses – the list goes on. And all of this was coming out of what was left after everything else had been paid out, from agents' fees to the lawyers' bills. Even so, in August 1969, Noel could say to Ritchie Yorke of the *Toronto Globe and Mail*, just after leaving the Experience, 'The problem with Mitch, and with Jimi too, is that they never saved any money. As fast as they got it, it was spent. But not me, mate. I've got me Rolls and quite a kitty in the bank.'

Finally there is the question of diverted funds. Certainly, John Hillman asserts that nothing like the amount of money that should have passed through Yameta actually did. This particularly applied to concert money which was invariably paid out in cash. There isn't any firm evidence that any member of the Experience was systematically de-

490

frauded by anybody acting directly on behalf of Yameta, but – personal spending aside – it does appear that, wherever the fault lies, no member of the band actually received all the money to which he was entitled. Even lawyers and accountants get embroiled in litigation to recoup fees for work done, but from a musician's point of view the question of who ultimately gets paid was best summed up by the American writer Ogden Nash when he wrote 'Professional people have no cares. Whatever happens, they get theirs.'

Since 1970, everybody seems to have taken everybody else to court or at least threatened to. An economy tour through the rest of the litigation might look something like this:

1972: Diane Carpenter loses her fight to have her daughter Tamika recognised as Jimi's heir on the grounds of the time taken to bring the suit and the lack of a blood test to identify the father. Had she won, her daughter would have inherited the lot. At one point, however, Al had obtained a court decision naming him as sole heir because Jimi had left no will.

1973: Noel sues Warner Brothers for $350,000 in damages plus an accounting of royalties.

1974: A $10 million lawsuit is filed against Warner Brothers, Polydor and the estates of Jimi and Mike Jeffery by a company called Last Experience which claims it owns the production rights to two songs performed by Jimi at the Royal Albert Hall on 24 February 1969. The songs 'Little Wing' and 'Voodoo Child (slight return)' appeared on the *Hendrix in the West* album. The whole concert was filmed by Steve Gold and Jerry Goldstein (manager–producers of War) and the rights passed over to Last Experience.

1975: A Swedish court rules in Eva Sundqvist's favour that Little Jimi was the son of Big Jimi. She says she would never have brought the suit had she not been threatened with losing her welfare benefits if she refused to name the father. But the suit fails in an American court again on the grounds that a blood test could not be carried out to establish paternity. However, Al chose to recognise the boy as his grandson.

After a five-year battle with Capitol, Ed Chalpin wins back rights on two Curtis Knight/Hendrix albums, *Flashing* and *Get That Feeling*.

1976: Noel files another suit against Warner Brothers and Chas Chandler for a combined sum of $3 million.

1978: It is announced in the Swedish press that the Hendrix estate has agreed to pay Eva Sundqvist about $1 million.

1979: After five years of wrangling, an out-of-court settlement is reached between Warners and Last Experience over the inclusion of the two songs on the *Hendrix in the West* album.

1982: Once more with feeling. The Hendrix estate sue Last Experience and Gold and Goldstein to prevent them releasing the film of the Albert Hall concert. The company are also sued for planning to release a soundtrack of the concert. Last Experience respond with a $50 million suit against Warners over the double live album, *The Jimi Hendrix Concerts*, because 'Stone Free' and 'Bleeding Heart' also come from that Albert Hall concert. To this day the film has never been released.

1989–90: Alan Douglas was brought in by Warner Brothers to sift through the several hundred hours of tape that the estate had gathered in. Mike Jeffery's lawyer Maxwell Cohen, who handled Mike's estate and took over the running of Electric Lady, has claimed that those tapes housed at the studio were originally removed under false pretences (prior to Leo Branton's and Alan Douglas' involvement) to a place of 'safekeeping'. Ultimately under Alan Douglas' supervision came 'Crash Landing' and 'Midnight Lightnin',' (both released in 1975) and the opportunity for Douglas to oversee all estate-sanctioned Hendrix releases – a position he has held ever since. However, what the estate can and cannot sanction seems to be in question. The BBC and a record label Castle Communications both struck deals with Alan Douglas over the release of two albums. The first was the Experience Radio One sessions from 1967 and the second was a triple CD edition of a six-hour American radio show, *Live & Unreleased*. Polydor have challenged the right of the estate to issue these releases in the UK. The estate in turn have challenged Chas Chandler's stated intention to release Hendrix material discovered at Olympic when the studio was recently demolished. And, finally, the estate of Alexis Korner are suing the BBC for piracy in allowing Jimi's song with Alexis, 'Hoochie Coochie Man', to appear on the Radio One set, without permission.

Interest in Jimi's music has never been greater. And no doubt this will be the cue for further flurries of courtroom activity.

Seattle had held nothing but bad memories for Jimi – he couldn't get away quick enough, didn't like going back and most certainly didn't want to be buried there. But the memories linger on . . .

Only days after Jimi had died, his father and Freddie Mae Gautier were approached by a lawyer known to the family, William Lockett.

He said that he had some friends who wanted to start the Jimi Hendrix Memorial Foundation (JHMF), a non-profitmaking organisation which would donate land to the City of Seattle. On that land, they would hold rock concerts, establish a Jimi Hendrix Museum and hold summer camps for underprivileged children. All that was needed was Al's authorisation to use Jimi's name.

Lockett's partners in this show of altruism were: two other attorneys, Gary Culver and Buck Austin; Howard Greenlin, a Los Angeles porno cinema owner; and one of his theatre managers, twenty-one-stone Raymond 'Tiny' Becker. Greenlin also owned the Rivoli Theater in Seattle. Culver had represented Becker on a charge of showing obscene films in 1969. On 20 November 1970, when Al still didn't know if he would get any money at all from Jimi's estate, he signed the necessary contract for $1000 with promises of a further $100 a week, but he only saw about another $400. Al was also made Vice-President of the JHMF, and Freddie Mae a director. But Becker was the President and in charge of the whole operation. Offices were rented in the Lyon Building on Third Avenue and a deposit paid on twenty telephone lines. Businessmen were called up to sponsor (through buying advertising space) *The Official Jimi Hendrix Memorial Foundation Souvenir Photograph Album* with a guaranteed circulation of 500,000. Potential sponsors were told that the charity was going to donate a 146-acre site to fulfil its charitable aims. All kinds of merchandising was sold, and the charity sold memberships to the JHMF and staged four concerts. But the whole thing was set up to finance the purchase of land from one Charles Bollingford. Culver and Austin had helped Bollingford to buy the site on Lake Roosevelt waterfront land in eastern Washington State. Bollingford had stumbled into financial difficulties and now wanted to get rid of it. The JHMF was set up specifically to buy the land with the money raised from unsuspecting business sponsors and fans. Then the edifice began to crack.

The guy who was running the phone lines had a fight with Becker, quit the job and went off to tell the police that, contrary to the laws of charitable status, he and his band of salesmen were getting a commission on telephone sales. Someone else complained to the Department of Labor that the charity was breaking minimum-wage laws. Then the charity-licensing office discovered that Tiny Becker had a police record for, among other things, theft of airline tickets. The JHMF lost its charitable status. A year after Al had signed the contract in good faith, the JHMF was in ruins. One day, Al walked into the offices in Third

Avenue to find everything gone – right down to the Jimi Hendrix candy bars. Nowadays, nobody involved talks about what happened. The two lawyers Austin and Culver claim they lost their investment, although there is no evidence that there was any investment. William Lockett, the lawyer who first approached Al and Freddie Mae, shot himself after an indictment in connection with armed robbery. On 3 November 1973, Tiny Becker's Mormon wife shot him dead with a .38 revolver after a family argument at their home in Tucson, Arizona.

Back in 1970 then, Seattle was the unwitting dupe of an unscrupulous fraud perpetrated in Jimi's memory. One might have thought that, since then, the city would have been at pains to find ways of properly commemorating the life of its most famous son. Not so – in fact quite the reverse.

This sorry tale began in September 1980. To commemorate the tenth anniversary of Jimi's death, a local radio station KZOK launched the Hendrix Memorial Project. The idea was to raise funds for a statue of Jimi to stand in one of the city's parks, which perhaps might in turn be renamed in Jimi's honour. Seward Park was mentioned, which would have been a nice touch, as Jimi had played there as a kid. By July 1981, over $20,000 had been raised from fans nationwide.

Enter the Seattle Parks Department. It was clear from the start that they baulked at the idea of any permanent landmark as homage to Jimi. And they were not alone in this – the city's Arts Committee decided that a statue would be 'inappropriate' – a decision the Parks board heartily endorsed. In fact one board member went so far as to call the idea of a statue 'unimaginative' and instead proposed a 'living memorial'. This would be a concert or similar one-off event which would be inevitably forgotten soon after it had taken place and leave no nasty blot on the landscape. Why the opposition? Racism offers itself as a tempting theory, but first comes the question of drugs.

In July 1981, the First National Anti-Drug Coalition met in Seattle to 'mobilise a counterattack against the Aquarians moving in to take over their city'. The Coalition was backed by the now defunct US Labor Party, which despite its name was an extreme right-wing organisation whose leading light was Lyndon LaRouche. He had been engaged in all kinds of covert political activity and once wrote a book which implicated the whole of the British royal family in drug-trafficking. He was later jailed for tax evasion. LaRouche's Coalition press release continued: 'Members of the Seattle City Council have been under pressure, instigated by a local radio station, to build a memorial to acid rocker Jimi Hendrix who died

494

of a drug overdose in 1970. Hendrix, remembered for his perversion of the National Anthem at the 1968 [sic] Woodstock dopefest, hails from the city.' At the meeting handouts were distributed bearing the legend 'Stop the Jimi Hendrix memorial to LSD'. The city authorities never came clean on why they objected to having a memorial to Jimi and they could not publicly endorse the Coalition's views, though they undoubtedly supported them. As the months rolled by, the organisers of the Memorial Project were in despair of ever cutting through the red tape strewn in their path. Local TV weighed in on the side of the anti-Hendrix lobby. One station commented:

> America is under siege of every kind of drug abuse. The horror stories are never ending. The President of the United States of America has declared all-out war on drug smuggling and illegal drug abuse. Cuba, Soviet puppet, is doing all it can to flood and thus undermine America with the terrorism of illegal drugs.
> And now Seattle is going to honor a drug addict who died of a drug overdose by using the taxpayers' public land for a memorial . . . and thus contribute to perverted hero worship . . . of Jimi Hendrix. Legal action must be taken to stop this corruption of public land.

In despair of finding any location for a memorial, one of the organisers from KZOK, Jane Wainwright, went to see David Hancocks, director of the Woodland Park Zoo. Hancocks was delighted at being approached, although later he admitted that the zoo was not 'the best or most obvious choice' of venue. KZOK must surely have been among the first to agree.

And so it happened that on 9 June 1983 a memorial was unveiled in the African Savannah exhibit, a twelve-inch-square rock inscribed: 'This viewpoint [the Savannah] was funded by worldwide contributions to KZOK Radio in memory of Jimi Hendrix and his music.'

In an article headlined 'HENDRIX SOLD OUT', Matt Dentino of the *Seattle Rocket* commented:

> I felt that many questions needed answering about the way in which Jimi's memory had been honored. The first and most obvious, is that of the zoo site. The compromise of the zoo for the tribute is an outrageous insult to the man and his music, not only because of the racist connotations of the African Savannah site . . . but more importantly for the way the establishment (in this case the park department and civic leaders) has put the memory of Seattle's most famous man within the confines of a zoo . . . exactly where it thinks he and his music belonged in the first place.

Why no statue? Is the image of a black man with a guitar (even if he was a recognised genius) too threatening to the average Seattleite?. . .

And finally the puny plaque . . . surrounded by a mosaic walkway, climbing rocks and purple flowers. The energy of Jimi and his incredible contribution to music have been watered down and tamed to satisfy those who oppose the statue . . . a complete sellout.

Dentino ended the article by quoting from 'If 6 Was 9' about 'white-collar conservatives, flashing down the street, pointing their plastic at me' and noting that (in the American style) the ceremony took place on 6/9/83.

And still it goes on . . . In January 1990, it was reported once again by the *Rocket* that students at a school in Connecticut had suggested a mural of Jimi be covered up because, they claimed, it 'glorified drug abuse'. To his eternal credit, the school principal dismissed the claims as ridiculous.

The *Rocket* went on to observe: 'Hendrix let his guitar do the talking and if we are to erase every aspect of his history because he also did drugs, perhaps we should no longer honor such founding fathers as George Washington and Thomas Jefferson, both of whom grew pot on their plantations.'

The paper recounted briefly the saga of a Hendrix memorial in Seattle and then announced a scholarship fund in Jimi's name to award grants to highly promising young musicians to Seattle public schools. Somewhere down the line the veil may be lifting from the blind eyes of prejudice.

Sixteen *Can You See Me?*

I am what I am, thank God. Some people just don't understand. ('Message to Love')

The greatness of any artist is invariably measured by the extent of the shadow they cast over those who follow. Indeed, Jimi's shadow loomed as large over his peers and contemporaries as over those who were later inspired by his example. In that respect, he was truly a living legend, much of whose music sounds as fresh today as the moment it was released. There are a number of reasons for this, when so many recordings by other artists from that period now sound hopelessly dated.

First, Jimi took a world view of music, appreciating with even-handedness all the forms of music with which he came into contact, from George Frederick Handel to Charlie Mingus and the ragas of India by way of John Coltrane. Just a cursory listen to the range of material across the first three albums reveals a scintillating melting-pot of sounds, incorporating the whole world of music – African rhythms, European harmony and polyphony and melodies or modalities derived from Asiatic sources. Jimi never allowed himself to be hidebound by the limitations of rock 'n' roll, or constrained by the limitations of subjective preference, and always resisted any categorisation of his music.

It is perhaps instructive to list the diversity of musicians who have recorded cover versions of Jimi's songs: Blood, Sweat and Tears, the Cure, Joan Jett, Stevie Ray Vaughan, the Kronos Quartet, Gil Evans, Roy Buchanan, Stanley Jordan, Keith Levine, Todd Rundgren, the Pretenders, Sting and Yngwie Malmsteen. To all these and other artists Jimi has offered a panoply of possibilities from which to choose a particular aspect of his music to recreate.

Jimi inspired musicians irrespective of the instrument they played;

the late Jaco Pastorius, arguably one of the best electric bass players of all time, once commented 'All I gotta say is . . . "Third Stone from the Sun". And for anyone who doesn't know about that by now, they should've checked Jimi out a lot earlier.'[1] But, obviously, it is the guitar players who most idolised the man who wrote the book of modern electric guitar playing. For Al Dimeola's generation of fusion guitarists, 'Jimi was a leader,' while for John McLaughlin 'Jimi single-handedly shifted the whole course of guitar playing and he did it with such finesse and real passion.'[2] But beyond these 'respectable' guitarists there are a whole host of others like Robin Trower and Frank Marino who have been the subject of many a cheap shot from critics who decry what they regard as mindless mimickry. Jimi touched souls – who is in a position to pass judgement on the quality or validity of individual inspiration, even if you don't like what it actually inspires? What one can say, perhaps, is that while many of these guitarists could recreate the force of Jimi's music, their music lacked power and dynamic.

It is compelling also to spread the Hendrix legacy across a whole slew of artists from George Clinton and Run DMC through Weather Report, James Blood Ulmer, Robert Cray and ZZ Top who did not cover any of Jimi's songs. However, the slight danger here is that the legacy becomes too diffuse and Jimi, the wellspring, the epicentre, becomes lost. It is perhaps safer to test the legacy directly against his own achievements.

Another source of Jimi's enduring influence was the spiritual conviction, the sense of mission that gave the music its strength. Jimi firmly believed that he had a divine message to impart, that it was his duty to bring a vision of love and healing to the world through the medium of music. One could argue that he imbued music with a promise of human salvation way beyond its capacity to deliver, but this does not detract from the crusading spirit with which Jimi came to approach his life's work. The universality of Jimi's music is linked directly to this spirit and to the single-minded way in which he harnessed it in the service of his obligations to mankind as he saw them.

Then there was the incredible energy and passion which is sublimated in the music. From his earliest playing days in Seattle, Jimi carried around sounds, dreams, images, poetry and visions which he hadn't a hope of making manifest in music. He had no proper equipment, no money, and, even if he had, the technology was unavailable. His frustration can only be imagined. Then in 1966–67, it all came together. Jimi found himself in a studio environment with sympathetic technicians who built the whole architecture of modern electronic rock music as we know it today, just to realise the sounds in Jimi's head. In an incredibly creative spell during 1967, in between touring and all the demands made of a high-profile pop star, Jimi wrote and recorded two albums and a clutch of singles which are milestones in the history of popular music.

Into that and his subsequent recordings were poured all the contradictions and paradoxes of his life: the American who was 'sold back' to America; the black musician with a predominantly white audience; the man portrayed as a symbol of the sixties who played funky R&B and country blues; the composer of highly structured, orchestrated music with often only three people to play it; the quiet man who smashed up equipment; the pacifist and anti-establishment symbol who believed in 'just wars' against Communism; the polite charmer who had explosions of temper; and the humble musician who once told an audience 'I am the bus driver, you are my passengers.' To Alan Douglas, 'He was a baby'; to Mitch Mitchell 'He was not a naive man.' Jimi lived much of the time in his head, a semi-dreamworld of science fiction, fantasy and cartoon imagery peopled by Flash Gordon, Batman, Winnie the Pooh and the characters from Hans Christian Andersen fairy stories, all of which he loved. Yet, at the same time, he was very centred, aware of the world around him and, rarely for a musician, prepared to make public statements about sensitive issues like black nationalism, ghetto violence and war. Not only that, but what he said was often at odds with the prevailing ethos of his contemporaries.

Everything Jimi was could be found in his music, igniting a high-octane mixture of invention and drive which seems as if it will burn for as long as music is played. A Finnish musicologist has written, in an unpublished essay, about the intensity of Jimi's concerts 'The *whole man* vibrates with feeling like a perfectly tuned string. Many people who have seen live performances of Jimi Hendrix have been amazed by this unity of musical content and visual appearances and at the feeling of mastery and freedom that was conveyed just by watching him play. What we were seeing was a direct manifestation of pure creative energy. . . . This made him free and his listeners feel free in themselves. Such artistic achievements are rare and precious gifts.'[3]

The passion in Jimi's playing transcended even his death, like a building which might hold an imprint of all the life that has gone on within its walls. Like all of the greatest musicians he had his own distinctive cry which is there, in the records, music which is

K.B. Hallen, Copenhagen, 3 September 1970

still evolving, which still catches you unawares with something you hadn't heard before.

Then there was the sheer invention of his playing: Jimi strapped on a guitar virtually every night of his adult life and he never repeated himself. Charlie Parker once told Gil Evans that music was all about editing – a whole series of 'yes' and 'no' decisions taken in a split second hundreds or even thousands of times during the course of a concert. Just think about the notes Jimi Hendrix *didn't* play!

And, finally, Jimi was a revolutionary; as we have said, many of the effects that came out of a Hendrix recording session had never been heard before. He was the first to harness sound to electricity and the first to bring under control all the technological accoutrements of guitar playing (guitar, amps, fuzz-box, wah-wah and so on) to sculpt a whole new aural landscape.

500

For all these reasons, the music of Jimi Hendrix has the timeless quality inherent in all significant art.

However, interviewed by a Seattle paper, *Pulse*, in March 1989, Brian Eno could justifiably pose the question: 'Why isn't Jimi Hendrix regarded as one of the century's great composers? By musicologists, I mean. . . . why is he not spoken of like John Cage. . . .? He is somebody who defined the way people think about music. . . . You mustn't be popular, because anything that's popular automatically can't possibly be interesting musically.'

Some well-meaning but ultimately misguided attempts have been made to turn Jimi into a 'serious musician', by for example suggesting that at the time of his death he was moving away from 'just' being a rock guitarist to joining the community of jazz musicians. Other commentators have tried to 'reclaim' Jimi for black music. But this kind of revisionism, while understandable, is also perhaps misplaced.

Jimi has been the catalyst for action among a generation of black musicians (most notably Vernon Reid of Living Colour) trying to break down the barriers which seem to prevent the acceptance of black rock musicians. Part of this stems from the blatant racism of the white-dominated music industry.

However, if it is undeniable that black rock musicians have been discriminated against, it is equally true that there exists a credibility gap between black rock musicians and the majority of those black people who listen to music. And this was a gap that Jimi, much as he wanted to and much as he paid due homage to his musical roots in country blues and jazz, could never bridge. As black music critic and author Nelson George has said, the problem with Jimi's music for a black audience was 'You just couldn't dance to it. . . . To the audience of Stax and Motown and James Brown, "Purple Haze" and "Hey Joe" just didn't do the do. . . . Like [Chuck] Berry, his success with guitar-based music made him an outcast on Black Main Street.'[4] It is worth remembering, too, that the early to mid-sixties were very lean times for the likes of Muddy Waters and B.B. King until they were introduced to white audiences by their white acolytes like Eric Clapton. Conversely, Jimi was no 'honorary' white; in fact, he was raised up and put down in equal measure by both black and white. He might have been frozen out in Harlem, but some of the finest black musicians in the world, such as Miles Davis, recognised something very special in Jimi. By the same token, Jimi was revered by white musicians and frustrated by white audiences who wouldn't let him progress beyond 'Wild Thing' and a scorched Fender.

501

Jimi wanted his music to be accepted by everyone, and would probably have done more to win over black audiences had the opportunities presented themselves. He had his sensibilities about race; he once fired a roadie in Sweden for making what he deemed to be offensive racial remarks. Jimi wrote and spoke on black issues and supported the work and ideas of Martin Luther King, but he was never going to make a profession out of being black.

So we are back with Jimi and the question posed by Brian Eno. It is not just a question of popularity – Eric Clapton and Nigel Kennedy are both popular, but it does not diminish their stature as musicians. A reviewer for the *Daily Mail* saw a preview of the *South Bank Show* documentary on Jimi, screened in October 1989. Seeing mostly footage of Jimi doing fifteen sorts of damage to his guitar instead of playing it, the reviewer dismissed any notion that Jimi could possibly be designated the greatest guitarist that ever lived. And who can blame him?

But it does highlight the problem. For the past twenty years, the symbols of Jimi's pop-culture heritage have stood defiantly between him and any clear sight of just what an important musician he was. Nor has the task been made any easier by excessive concentration on the more peripheral and/or negative aspects of Jimi's life: drugs, sex, business problems, which government agency had him killed and the like.

It is misleading to try and divorce the ideas of an artist from his/her environment and personality; *all* Jimi's experiences informed his music. Even so, just how unimportant all this stuff really is for the elevation of Jimi to some kind of status once again as a musician of world renown is abundantly clear by simply switching on the stereo and listening to the music.

In any attempt to redress such imbalance, there is a danger of over-intellectualising the music, of analysing it into sterility. Even more dangerous is the temptation to romanticise Jimi as some extraterrestrial superbeing or a victim of circumstance cut down in his prime to join other dead rock stars in the 'live fast die young' hall of fame. All this does is deify Jimi – something he never would have wanted. As he said himself, 'Don't raise me up, I am but a messenger.' What is written here is biography, not hagiography. But, in writing about somebody, their position in the world is to a greater or lesser degree altered, new perspectives may be offered, new correspondences made between events which seemed before unconnected, and above all new opportunities arise for re-evaluation.

Perhaps it is a forlorn hope that art can win out over prurience and pop iconography. But it would be a fitting tribute to Jimi's memory if his substance could begin to predominate over his image, if claims on his legacy could be set aside, and, above all, if through more careful appreciation of his work he could receive due recognition as a genius of twentieth-century contemporary music.

K.B. Hallen, Copenhagen, 3 September 1970

A musician, if he is a messenger, is like a child who hasn't been handled too many times by man, hasn't had too many fingerprints across his brain. That's why music is so much heavier than anything you ever felt. (Jimi Hendrix interview, April 1969).

503

The story of life (slow)

The story of Jesus
so easy to explain
After they crucified him,
a woman, she claimed his name
The story of Jesus
the whole bible knows
went all across the desert
and in the middle, he found a rose

There should be no questions
there should be no lies
He was married ever happily after
All the tears we cry
No use in arguing
all the use to the man that moans
When each man falls in battle,
his soul it has to roam
Angels of heaven
flying saucers to some,
made Easter Sunday
the name of the rising sun

The story is written
by so many people who dared,
to lay down the truth
to so very many who cared
to carry the cross
of Jesus and beyond
We will guide the light
this time with a woman in our arms
We as men
can't explain the reason why
the woman's always mentioned
at the moment that we die
All we know
is God is by our side,
and he says the word
so easy yet so hard

I wish not to be alone,
so I must respect my other heart
Oh, the story
of Jesus is the story
of you and me
No use in feeling lonely,
I am you searching to be free

The story
of life is quicker
than the wink of an eye
The story of love
is hello and goodbye
Until we meet again.

(Jimi's last song – composed in London, 17 September 1970)

Reference Notes

The following abbreviations apply:

NME	= *New Musical Express*
MM	= *Melody Maker*
Disc	= *Disc and Music Echo*
RM	= *Record Mirror*
RS	= *Rolling Stone*
BI	= *Beat Instrumental*

Chapter One: Cherokee Mist

1. David Henderson, *'Scuse Me While I Kiss the Sky: The Life of Jimi Hendrix* (Bantam, 1981), p. 8.

Chapter Two: The Night I Was Born, the Moon Turned A Fire Red

1. Interview with Meatball Fulton, London, December 1967.
2. Jerry Hopkins, *The Jimi Hendrix Story* (Sphere, 1984), p. 14.
3. *Disc* 28/1/67.
4. *Observer* 3/12/67.
5. *International Times* 28/3/69.
6. *NME* 9/9/67.
7. Fulton, op. cit.
8. *Rave* 8/67.
9. *Music Maker* 2/68.

Chapter Three: Spanish Castle Magic

1. Charles Keil, *Urban Blues* (University of Chicago Press, 1966), p. 32.
2. William Ferris, *Blues from the Delta* (Da Capo Press, 1984), p. 37.
3. *Pacific* 30/4/89.
4. *BI* 3/67.
5. Ibid.
6. *MM* 28/10/67.
7. *Humo* 18/3/67.
8. Ray Charles and David Spitz, *Brother Ray* (Macdonald & Jane, 1978), p. 97.
9. *MM* 22/2/69.
10. *RS* 9/3/68.
11. Giles Oakley, *The Devil's Music: A History of the Blues* (BBC Books, 1983), p. 49.
12. Robert Palmer, *Deep Blues* (Macmillan, 1982), p. 60.
13. Peter Guralnick, *Sweet Soul Music* (Virgin Books, 1986), p. 148.
14. *Life* 1/4/68.
15. *Humo*, op. cit.
16. Henderson, op. cit., p. 39.
17. *Sunday Mirror* 11/2/68.
18. *Daily Mirror* 11/1/69.
19. *Humo*, op. cit.

Chapter Four: Hope You Brought Your Parachute With You

1. *NME* 28/1/67.
2. *A Film About Jimi Hendrix*, Warner Brothers 1973 (hereafter WB).
3. *Jackie* 25/11/67.
4. *Music Maker* 2/68.
5. *Rave* 6/67.
6. Ibid.
7. *Disc* 28/1/67.
8. *BI* 3/67.
9. *Rave* 6/67.
10. *Rave* 6/67.
11. *Guitar Player* 9/87.

12. *Rave* 6/67.
13. *Guitar Player* 9/87.
14. *LA Free Press* 25/8/67.
15. *Guitar Player* 9/87.
16. *MM* 1/3/69.
17. *LA Free Press* 25/8/67.
18. Keil, op. cit., p. 77.
19. *MM* 22/2/69.
20. Charles Shaar Murray, *Crosstown Traffic: Jimi Hendrix and Post-War Pop* (Faber & Faber, 1989), p. 37.
21. *Rave* 6/67.

Chapter Five: Dusty Boots Cadillac

1. John Henrik Clarke (ed.), *Harlem USA* (Macmillan, 1971), pp. 3–5.
2. *Gallery* 9/82.
3. *Sepia* 9/75.
4. Interview in unidentified UK publication, London 1/69.
5. Sleeve notes *In the Beginning*, Isley Brothers, Teaneck, 1970.
6. Ibid.
7. WB.
8. *Guitar World* 9/85.
9. *Guitar Player* 9/75.
10. *RS* 9/3/68.
11. Charles White, *The Life and Times of Little Richard: The Quasar of Rock* (Pan, 1985), p. 124.
12. Ibid, pp. 126–7.
13. *Rave* 6/67.
14. WB.
15. Ibid.
16. White, p. 129.
17. *Cheltenham Chronicle* 11/2/67.
18. WB.
19. *New York Times* 25/2/68.
20. *Guitar Player* 9/75.
21. *Rave* 6/67.
22. *Guitar Player* 9/75.

23. *West One* 2/67.
24. Chris Welch, *Hendrix: A Biography* (Omnibus, 1982), p. 57.

Chapter Six: If My Daddy Could See Me Now

1. 'Tribute to Jimi Hendrix', BBC Radio One, September 1980.
2. Philip Norman, *The Stones* (Elm Tree, 1984), p. 234.
3. *L'Eure Eclair* 22/10/66.
4. Radio One, op. cit.
5. *NME* 23/11/68.
6. *Humo* 18/3/67.
7. *RM* 10/12/66.
8. Johnny Rogan, *Starmakers and Svengalis: The History of British Pop Management* (Queen Anne Press, 1988), p. 94.

Chapter Seven: Are You Experienced?

1. *RS* 11/5/68.
2. *Disc* 28/1/67.
3. *RM* 14/1/67.
4. *NME* 28/1/67.
5. *RS* 25/8/88.
6. *Musician* 8/86.
7. *Disc* 17/6/67.
8. *West One* 2/67.
9. *Observer* 3/9/89.
10. *Plaza Bulletin* 11/2/67.
11. Fulton, op. cit.
12. Radio One, op. cit.
13. *NME* 28/1/67.
14. *Dundee Recorder* 7/4/67.
15. Unpublished concert review by Lorraine Walsh.
16. *NME* 6/5/67.
17. *Disc* 13/5/67.
18. *Bravo* 26/6/67.
19. *Oz* 10/70.
20. *Fabulous 208* 14/10/67.
21. Evan Eisenberg, *The Recording Angel: Music, Records and Culture from Aristotle to Zappa* (Picador, 1988), p. 69.

22. *West One* 2/67.
23. Stockholm radio interview, 25/5/67.
24. Nelson George, *The Death of Rhythm and Blues* (Omnibus, 1988), p. 19.
25. *West One* 2/67.
26. *Music Maker* 6/67.
27. John Litweiler, *The Freedom Principle: Jazz After 1958* (Blandford, 1985), p. 32.
28. Quoted in notes accompanying limited edition boxed CD.

Chapter Eight: No More Surf Music

1. Eric Burdon, *I Used to Be an Animal, But I'm All Right Now* (Faber & Faber 1986), p. 172.
2. Ibid.
3. Ellen Sander, *Trips: Rock Life in the Sixties* (Scribners, 1973), p. 97.
4. *Musician* 8/86.
5. Hopkins, op. cit., p. 96.
6. *NME* 9/9/67.
7. *West One* 2/67.
8. *History of Rock 1982*, vol. 5, p. 990 (Orbis, 1982).
9. Hopkins, op. cit., p. 96.
10. *Guitar World* 3/88.
11. *NME* 29/7/67.
12. *Guitar Player* 9/75.
13. *Open City* 24/8/67.
14. *NME* 9/9/67.
15. *MM* 19/8/67.
16. *MM* 26/8/67.
17. *Nottingham Guardian Journal* 26/8/67.
18. Unit One (Manchester University), 2/68.
19. *Disc* 2/9/67.
20. *Live & Unreleased*, US Radio Show 1988.
21. *Recording Engineer and Producer* 12/76.
22. Ibid.
23. *Guitar World* 9/85.
24. Ibid.
25. Ibid.

26. *MM* 9/12/67.
27. Douglas Kent Hall and Sue Clark, *Rock: A World Bold as Love* (Cowles Book Co., 1970), p. 131.
28. *Eye* 7/68.
29. *Downbeat* 10/82.
30. Stockholm radio interview, 8/1/68.
31. *RS* 6/4/68.
32. *NME* 23/11/68.
33. *Disc* 25/11/67.
34. *Chatham Standard* 5/12/67.
35. *Disc* 2/9/67.
36. *Manchester Independent* 5/12/67.
37. *MM* 23/12/67.

Chapter Nine: Alive, But the War Is Here to Stay

1. *Hitparader* 1/68.
2. Palmer, op. cit., p. 18.
3. *NME* 23/8/75.
4. *Guitar Player* 9/75.
5. *Pop* 10/67.
6. Interview with Pat O'Day, *Straight Ahead* 3/89.
7. *Time* 5/4/68.
8. Interview shown in *See My Music Talking*.
9. Pamela Des Barres, *I'm With the Band* (Jove Books, 1988), p. 98.
10. Ibid., p. 109.
11. *Time* 5/4/68.
12. *Time* 5/4/68.
13. Interview *South Bank Show*. LWT. 1/10/89.

Chapter Ten: Have You Ever Been . . . to Electric Ladyland?

1. *Guitar World* 9/85.
2. Ibid.
3. *Eye* 7/68.
4. *Guitar Player* 9/75.
5. *RS* 2/3/72.
6. *Live & Unreleased.*
7. *Modern Drummer* 12/81.

8. Interview WLIR FM 18/9/80.
9. Richard Neville, *Playpower* (Paladin, 1971), p. 38.
10. *NME* 8/6/68.
11. *RS* 9/3/68.
12. *Guitar World* 9/85.
13. *MM* 20/7/68.
14. Marc Eliot, *Rockonomics* (Franklin Watts, 1989), p. 45.
15. *Hullabaloo* 8/68.
16. *Dallas Notes* 15/8/68.
17. *MM* 9/11/68.
18. *Downbeat* 4/4/68.
19. *Metanoia* 12/68.
20. *Circus* 4/69.
21. *History of Rock*, vol. 6, p. 1372 (Orbis).
22. *Live & Unreleased.*

Chapter Eleven: Electric Church

1. *MM* 1/3/69.
2. Unidentified interview, January 1969.
3. *Eye* 1/69.
4. *Top Pops* 11/1/69.
5. *MM* 1/3/69.
6. *International Times* 28/3/69.
7. Eisenberg, op. cit., p. 123.
8. *Distant Drummer* 17/4/69.
9. *LA Image* 2/5/69.
10. *LA Times* 29/4/69.

Chapter Twelve: House Burning Down

1. *Charleston Gazette* 17/5/69.
2. *Guitar Player* 9/75.
3. *Creem* 9/74.
4. Interview by Paul Zimmerman, New York, May 1969.
5. *Seattle Post-Intelligencer* 24/5/69.
6. *San Diego Door* 5/6/69.
7. WB.
8. *LA Image* 27/6/69.

9. *Disc* 19/7/69.
10. *MM* 28/1/67.
11. *MM* 11/2/67.
12. *Kink* 25/2/67.
13. *Aftonbladet* 9/1/68.
14. *New York Times* 6/9/69.
15. *RS* 15/11/69.
16. Arthur Taylor, *Notes and Tones* (Quartet, 1983), p. 35.
17. *Rock Scene* 7/87.
18. *Guitar Player* 1/88.

Chapter Thirteen: New Rising Sun

1. Michael Herr, *Dispatches* (Picador, 1978), p. 148.
2. Kent Hall and Clark, op. cit. p 22–25.
3. *MM* 20/12/69.
4. *RM* 3/1/70.
5. *Guitar Player* 9/75.
6. *RM* 19/9/70.
7. Neville, op. cit., p. 20.
8. *International Times* 14/6/73.
9. *Rock* 2/11/70.

Chapter Fourteen: Tomorrow, I'm Gonna Be by Your Side

1. *NME* 5/9/70.
2. *Disc* 12/9/70.
3. *Disc* 12/9/70.
4. *MM* 26/9/70.
5. Welch, op. cit., p. 50.
6. *Guitar World*, 3/88.
7. Burdon, op. cit., p. 216.
8. *New York Times* 27/9/70.
9. *The Times* 19/9/70.
10. *Disc* 26/9/70.
11. *Sounds* 10/10/70.
12. *NME* 26/9/70.
13. *Rave* 11/70.
14. *New York Post* 19/9/70.

15. *News of the World* 20/9/70.
16. Burdon, op. cit., p. 218.

Chapter Sixteen: Can You See Me?

1. *Downbeat* 10/82.
2. Ibid.
3. Arto Koskinen, 'The Music of Jimi Hendrix as a Spiritual Phenomenon', unpublished, 1989.
4. George, op. cit., p. 109.

Bibliography of Secondary Sources

These books were referred to in addition to the articles, cuttings, reviews and additional documentation supplied by the Hendrix Information Centre, which it would be impractical to list.

Victoria Balfour, *Rock Wives* (Virgin Books, 1986).
Pamela Des Barres, *I'm With the Band* (Jove Books, 1988).
Eric Burdon, *I Used to Be an Animal, But I'm All Right Now.* (Faber & Faber, 1986).
Evan Eisenberg, *The Recording Angel: Music, Records and Culture from Aristotle to Zappa* (Picador, 1988).
Marc Eliot, *Rockonomics* (Franklin Watts, 1989).
David Evans, *Tommy Johnson* (Studio Vista, 1971).
John Fahey, *Charlie Patton* (Studio Vista, 1970).
William Ferris, *Blues from the Delta* (Da Capo Press, 1978).
Julio Finn, *The Bluesman* (Quartet, 1986).
Ted Fox, *Show Time at the Apollo* (Quartet, 1985).
Simon Garfield, *Expensive Habits: The Dark Side of the Music Industry* (Faber & Faber, 1986).
Paul Garon, *The Devil's Son-in-Law: The Story of Peetie Wheatstraw* (Studio Vista, 1971).
Nelson George, *The Death of Rhythm and Blues* (Omnibus, 1988).
John Gibbens, 'Be in My Dream: Bob Dylan Through the Needle's Eye', unpublished.
Charlie Gillett, *The Sound of the City* (Souvenir, 1983).
Michael Gray, *The Art of Bob Dylan* (Hamlyn, 1981).
Jonathon Green, *Days in the Life: Voices from the English Underground 1961–1971* (Heinemann, 1988).

Peter Guralnick, *Sweet Soul Music* (Virgin, 1986).

Douglas Kent Hall and Sue Clark, *Rock: A World Bold as Love* (Cowles Book Co., 1970).

David Henderson. *'Scuse Me While I Kiss the Sky: The Life of Jimi Hendrix* (Bantam, 1981).

John Herdman, *Voice Without Restraint: Bob Dylan's Lyrics and Their Background* (Paul Harris, 1982).

Gerry Hershey, *Nowhere to Run: The Story of Soul Music* (Pan, 1985).

Jerry Hopkins, *The Jimi Hendrix Story* (Sphere, 1984).

Leroi Jones, *Blues People: Negro Music in White America* (MacGibbon & Kee, 1965).

Charles Keil, *Urban Blues* (University of Chicago Press, 1966).

Curtis Knight, *Jimi Hendrix* (Star Books, 1975).

Michael Lydon, *Boogie Lightning* (Da Capo, 1974).

Dave Marsh, *Before I Get Old: The Story of the Who* (Plexus, 1983).

Richard Middleton, *Pop Music and the Blues: A Study of the Relationship and Its Significance* (Gollancz, 1972).

Andrew Motion, *The Lamberts* (Chatto & Windus, 1986).

Charles Shaar Murray, *Crosstown Traffic: Jimi Hendrix and Post-War Pop* (Faber & Faber, 1989).

Richard Neville, *Playpower* (Paladin, 1971).

Giles Oakley, *The Devil's Music: A History of the Blues* (BBC Books, 1983).

Paul Oliver, *The Meaning of the Blues* (Collier, 1963).

Robert Palmer, *Deep Blues* (Macmillan, 1981).

Johnny Rogan, *Starmakers and Svengalis: The History of British Pop Management* (Queen Anne Press, 1988).

The Rolling Stone Encyclopaedia of Rock & Roll (Michael Joseph, 1983).

Victor Sampson, *Hendrix: An Illustrated Biography* (Proteus, 1984).

Ellen Sander, *Trips: Rock Life in the Sixties* (Scribners, 1973).

Carl Seashore, *The Psychology of Music* (Dover, 1967).

Harry Shapiro, *Waiting for the Man: The Story of Drugs and Popular Music* (Quartet, 1988).

Robert Spitz, *Barefoot in Babylon: The Creation of the Woodstock Music Festival 1969* (Viking, 1979).

Arthur Taylor, *Notes and Tones: Musician to Musician Interviews* (Quartet, 1983).

Frank Waters, *Book of the Hopi* (Ballantine, 1963).

517

Chris Welch, *Hendrix: A Biography* (Omnibus, 1982).

Charles White, *The Life and Times of Little Richard: The Quasar of Rock* (Pan, 1985).

APPENDICES

1 *Music, Sweet Music: The Discography*

INTRODUCTION

During Jimi's lifetime, there were only five official album releases: *Are You Experienced? Axis: Bold As Love, Electric Ladyland, Smash Hits* and *Band Of Gypsys*. In addition half of the album *Historic Performances Recorded At The Monterey International Pop Festival* was devoted to Jimi – the other half to Otis Redding. Of these albums, Jimi had most control over the production of *Electric Ladyland*, but even here he was unhappy with the way the album was cut, feeling that much of the depth of sound captured on the original masters was lost. Nonetheless, all these albums are essential listening for anybody wanting to build a collection of Jimi Hendrix releases.

The quality of much of the posthumously released material is an insult to Jimi's memory. However, the diamonds in the dust for any prospective collection would be: *The Cry Of Love, Rainbow Bridge, Isle Of Wight, Hendrix In The West, Jimi Plays Monterey, Radio One,* and both *Woodstock* releases. Additionally, there is some fine playing on the *Jimi Hendrix Concerts* and *Live At Winterland*. They were a breath of fresh air after so much dross, although overall the performances on the latter were not quite so earth-shattering as the reviews would have us believe.

To the best of our knowledge, what follows is the most comprehensive discography of Jimi's recording history ever published. However, we have refrained from the endless repetition inherent in all compilation releases. In Jimi's case, these run into hundreds ranging across all formats (LP's, CD's, cassettes, reels, and eight-track cartridges) and so only a selection is included.

The discography is divided into four separate sections: Experience Releases; Miscellaneous Releases; Jimi Hendrix As Guest and/or Producer (including all Jimi's early recordings before he became famous); and Bootlegs. Singles are obviously listed, but not in a separate section as all the songs appeared on albums.

The following conventions operate throughout:
A) Each time a recording is mentioned for the first time it is given a unique number and retains that number for any subsequent mentions.
B) Each entry has a prefix letter: I = interview, L = live concert recording, P = private or home recording, S = studio recording. Thus S001 is the studio version of 'Hey Joe'.
C) The first entry for a song contains all the known recording details listed once only.
D) As far as the information on covers, labels, booklet inserts etc. is concerned, the rule is forget everything you've ever read and start again here, because much of it is wrong. It would be too tedious to cite all the errors, however some of the more gross examples are mentioned.

E) All compositions are by Jimi Hendrix unless otherwise stated.
F) In general, the studio recording dates given refer to when the basic track was laid down. However, given Jimi's persistent striving for perfection, there may have been any number of trips into the studio after the creation of the basic track, before a song was deemed finished – if it ever was!
G) *Music Week* (Top 40 for LP's and Top 50 for singles) and *Billboard* (Top 200 for LP's, and Top 100 for singles) are the sources for chart information in England and America respectively.
H) All dates are stated in the European way: Day/Month/Year.
I) All LP and CD releases are single unit releases unless otherwise stated.
J) Some technical information is included on guitars, effects etc., but these are primarily covered in the technical appendix (pages 622 to 647).
K) 'Getting My Heart Back Together Again' is preferred throughout to its alternative title 'Hear My Train A Comin''.

Finally, the following abbreviations apply:

INSTRUMENTS & VOCALS

ba	=	bass guitar
dr	=	drums
fl	=	flute
gi	=	guitar
gs	=	guitars
ha	=	harmonica
hv	=	harmony vocals
lv	=	lead vocals
or	=	organ
pe	=	percussion
pi	=	piano
sa	=	saxophone
ta	=	tambourine
vo	=	all vocals

NAMES OF MUSICIANS

Billy	=	Billy Cox
Buddy	=	Buddy Miles
Jerry	=	Jerry Velez
Jimi	=	Jimi Hendrix
Juma	=	Juma Sultan
Larry	=	Larry Lee
Mitch	=	Mitch Mitchell
Noel	=	Noel Redding

STUDIO PERSONNEL

Chas	=	Chas Chandler
Dave	=	Dave Siddle
Eddie	=	Eddie Kramer
Gary	=	Gary Kellgren

RECORDING INFORMATION

a.k.a.	= also known as
Brc:	= broadcast during
Comp:	= composed by
Engi:	= engineered by
Prod:	= produced by
Rec:	= recorded at
I	= interview
L	= live (concert) recording
P	= private 'home' recording
S	= studio recording
*	= suggested listening/highlights

COUNTRY OF RELEASE AND/OR PRESSING

CAN	= Canada
ENG	= England
FRA	= France
GER	= West Germany
HOL	= Holland
ITA	= Italy
JAP	= Japan
LUX	= Luxembourg
SWE	= Sweden
USA	= United States of America

RECORDING STUDIOS

| BBCA | = BBC Broadcasting House, Portland Place, London W1. Note: all recordings were done on 4-track mono tape recorders |
| BBCB | = BBC Theatre The Playhouse, Northumberland Avenue, London WC2. |

Note: all recordings were done on 4-track mono tape recorders

CBS = CBS Recording Studios, 73 New Bond Street, London W1 – Note: all recordings were done on Studer J37 4-track tape recorders at 15 i.p.s.

CEN = Sound Center, 247 West 46th Street, New York City

DLL = De Lane Lea Music Ltd. (a.k.a.: Kingsway studio), 129 Kingsway, London WC2 – Note: all recordings were done on 4-track tape recorders at 15 or 30 i.p.s. Tapes used: Scotch 202. Monitoring: VU meters.

ELE = Electric Lady Studios, 52 West 8th Street, New York City – Note: the majority of the recordings were done on 16-track tape recorders, 2 inch

HIT = The Hit Factory, 6 West 20th Street, New York City – Note: the majority of the recordings were done on 16-track tape recorders, 2 inch

MAY = Mayfair Recording Studio Inc., 701 7th Avenue, New York City Note: all recordings were done on Ampex 8-track tape recorders, 1 inch at 15 i.p.s.

OLM = Olmstead Sound Studios, New York City – Note: all recordings were done on 8-track tape recorders, 1 inch

OLY = Olympic Sound Studios, 117 Church Road, Barnes, London SW13 – Note: all 1967 and 1968 recordings were done on 4-track at 15 i.p.s. 4-track tape recorders: Ampex 8300. Tapes used: Basf LR56, ½ inch. Console: custom designed by Dick Swetenham. Monitoring: PPM (peak program meters). Limiters: Pye. Bass (in general) recorded: DI (direct inject) in conjunction with live miking. Mikes used: Neumann U67, Neumann U87, Neumann KM84, Neumann KM86, AKG D20, AKG D30, AKG C12, AKG C12A, Beyer M160 (among others).

PLA = Record Plant, 321 West 44th Street, New York City – Note: up to March 1969 all recordings were done on 12-track tape recorders, 1 inch; from 18 March 1969 the majority of the recordings were done on 16-track tape recorders, 2 inch.

REG = Regent Sound (studio A), 163–166 Tottenham Court Road, London W1 – Note: all 1967 recordings were done on 4-track tape recorders

TTG = T.T.G. Inc. Sunset-Highland Recording Studios, 1441 North McCadden Place, Hollywood, California – Note: all recordings were done on 8- (1 inch) and 16-track (2 inch) tape recorders

EXPERIENCE RELEASES

There is little consistency between recordings released in different countries as far as the quality of the mixing, stereo effects and pressings is concerned. The songs are even different lengths. For example, the American releases of *Are You Experienced* and *Smash Hits* are superior in all these respects to their European counterparts. The same can apply to CD's. For example on the CD of *The Cry Of Love* released by Polydor [GER] you will miss the instrumental introduction for the song 'Freedom'. Moreover, Reprise [USA] have been 'upgrading' the Jimi Hendrix CD catalogue. These upgraded CD's have been marked on the discs' small inner circle with 'RE-1'. This is the only way you can tell if you are buying an old or upgraded CD version. One could argue that record companies (who continue to make an awful lot of money from Jimi Hendrix products) should offer a refund for old CD versions when you purchase an upgraded version – as is customary when buying upgraded computer programmes. In general the record company CD message is simply, 'you bought it and you're stuck with it . . . '

HEY JOE b/w STONE FREE
>   – Polydor 56139 [ENG] – Released 16/12/66 – Single
>   Charts – entry: 41 (05/01/67); top position: 6; weeks in chart: 10
>   – Also on: Polydor 59061 [GER]

S001:   **Hey Joe** – Jimi (gs, lv), Mitch (dr), Noel (ba), The Breakaways [Gloria George, Barbara Moore, Margaret Stredder] (hv). Comp: William M. Roberts. Rec: DLL, 23/10/66. Engi: Dave. Prod: Chas.

NOTE: Noel was borrowing Chas Chandler's Gibson EB-2 bass, as he did not own a bass guitar himself at this point, and used this on some of the early recordings (up to mid 02/67) like 'Hey Joe'.

S002:   **Stone Free** – Jimi (gs, vo), Mitch (dr, cow-bell), Mitch? (ta), Noel (ba). Rec: DLL, 02/11/66. Engi: Dave. Prod: Chas.

Note: This is the first song Jimi wrote when he moved to England in late 1966.

PURPLE HAZE b/w 51ST ANNIVERSARY
>   – Track 604001 [ENG] – Released 17/03/67 – Single
>   Charts – entry: 39 (23/03/67); top position: 3; weeks in chart: 14
>   – Also on: Polydor 59 072 [GER]

S003:   **Purple Haze** – Jimi (gs, lv, voice, tongue-click, coughing just before the first singing), Mitch (dr), Noel (ba, hv, voice). Special effect: Jimi (octavia). Rec: DLL, 11/01/67 (basic track); OLY, 03/02/67 (gi overdub with octavia); DLL, 11/01/67 (vo) or OLY, 07/02/67 (vo). Engi: Dave (DLL). Engi: unknown (OLY). Prod: Chas.

NOTES: <1> Composed by Jimi in the dressing-room of The Upper Cut club in London, 26/12/66. <2> Chas denies that originally 'Purple Haze' contained anything else and/or more lyrics ('it was done exactly as it was recorded, no edits or anything'), however Jimi stated that 'it had about a thousand, thousand words . . . you should have heard it man. I had it written out . . . ' <3>'Purple Haze' has been recorded by other artists more than any other Jimi Hendrix composition. At last count 40 cover versions have been released. The funniest version is a 1968 take-off (single: Warner Brothers 7096; LP: Warner Brothers WS 1728) by Bill Cosby. Containing the music of 'Purple Haze' with new lyrics by Cosby, it's re-named 'Hooray For The Salvation Army', with no credit to Jimi whatsoever. The most mysterious version (copyrighted in October 1968, but probably unreleased) is one by Frank Metis with 'words, music, and piano arrangements by Jimi Hendrix' . . .

S004:   **51st Anniversary** – Jimi (gs, vo), Mitch (dr), Noel (ba). Rec: DLL, probably 11/01/67. Engi: Dave. Prod: Chas.

THE WIND CRIES MARY b/w HIGHWAY CHILE
>   – Track 604004 [ENG] – Released 05/05/67 – Single
>   Charts – entry: 27 (11/05/67); top position: 6; weeks in chart: 11
>   – Also on: Polydor 59078 [GER]; Barclay 060840 [FRA]

S005:   **The Wind Cries Mary** – Jimi (gs, vo), Mitch (dr), Noel (ba). Rec: DLL, 11/01/67. Engi: Dave. Prod: Chas.

NOTE: Jimi: 'Mary is a girlfriend of mine. She is a girl who is slightly taken to talking about me to her friends, you know. One moment she will talk about me like I was a dog, and the next moment she says the complete opposite . . . we did that number in about two takes, we never do more than four or five takes in a recording studio, it's too expensive . . . '

S006:   **Highway Chile** – Jimi (gi, vo), Mitch (dr), Noel (ba). Rec: OLY, 03/04/67. Prod: Chas.

ARE YOU EXPERIENCED?
>   – Track 612 001 [ENG] – Released 12/05/67 – *:entire release
>   Charts – entry: 21 (25/05/67); top position: 2; weeks in chart: 33

- Also on: Polydor 184 085 [GER]; Polydor 2459 390 [GER]; Barclay 820 143 [FRA]
- CD: not released (see next entry)

<1> The recordings for the first Jimi Hendrix Experience LP were made during 16 recording sessions in London (first day of recording 23/10/66, last day of recording 04/04/67). <2> Jimi: 'First off I don't want people to get the idea it's a collection of freak-out material. I've written songs for teeny boppers like "Can You See Me" and blues things. "Manic Depression" is so ugly you can feel it and "May This Be Love" is a kind of "get your mind together" track. Imagination is very important, our music cannot be categorised. Free form is the best way to explain our sound, unrestricted and uninhibited creative expression . . . ' <3> Chas: 'The *Are You Experienced* album was the first time where we found ourselves with a bit of time. We just fucked about with the equipment really. We tried putting two and three instruments through a compressor and see what the hell would come out the other end, things like that. If it worked we'd edit it into the track or something. We'd do anything we could think of just for the fun of it, any daft idea that came along, we'd try it.' <4> Although Dave Siddle is credited as engineer at DLL, it is possible that other engineers at this studio were also involved. <5> All mixing: OLY.

S007: **Foxy Lady** – Jimi (gs, lv, hv), Mitch (dr), Noel (ba, hv). Special effect: Jimi (slide with gi at end). Rec: CBS, 13/12/66. Engi: Mike Ross. Prod: Chas.

NOTE: It is said that this song was inspired by Heather Taylor (who later married Roger Daltrey).

S008: **Manic Depression** – Jimi (gs, vo, faint throat-clearing sounds), Mitch (dr), Noel (ba). Rec: DLL, 29?/03/67. Engi: Dave. Prod: Chas.

NOTES: <1> 'The fastest raw-nerves waltz on record!' <2> The idea for this song was conceived during a press reception, when Chas told Jimi he sounded like a manic depressive. While Jimi was answering the questions, he wrote the lyrics down.

S009: **Red House** – Jimi (gi, vo, voice), Mitch (dr), Noel (bass strings of a normal 6-string gi, probably owned by Alexis Korner), Chas (voice from control-room). Rec: CBS, 13/12/66. Engi: Mike Ross. Prod: Chas.

S010: **Can You See Me?** – Jimi (gs, vo), Mitch (dr, ta), Noel (ba). Rec: DLL or REG, 11/66 or 12/66. Prod: Chas.

S011: **Love Or Confusion** – Jimi (gs, vo, voice), Mitch (dr), Noel (ba). Rec: DLL or REG or OLY, 11/66 (basic track); OLY, 03/04/67 (possible additional recordings). Prod: Chas.

NOTE: This song was originally selected to be the second Jimi Hendrix Experience single, however 'Purple Haze' was chosen instead.

S012: **I Don't Live Today** – Jimi (gs, hand wah-wah, vo, voice), Jimi? (hand claps), Mitch (dr), Noel (ba, voice). Rec: DLL, 02/67. Engi: Dave. Prod: Chas.

NOTES: <1> This is Jimi's first recording with a wah-wah effect. <2> When performing this song during live concerts Jimi frequently dedicated this song to 'the American Indians'.

S013: **May This Be Love** – Jimi (gs, vo, turning a page with lyrics), Mitch (dr), Mitch? (ta), Noel (ba). Rec: OLY, 03/04/67. Prod: Chas.

NOTE: Song a.k.a: Waterfall.

S014: **Fire** – Jimi (gs, lv), Mitch (dr, hv), Noel (ba, hv). Special effect: Jimi (octavia). Rec: OLY, 03/02/67. Prod: Chas.

NOTES: <1> Song a.k.a.: Let Me Stand Next To Your Fire. <2> The basic idea for this song stems, in part, from a party held on 31/12/66 in Folkestone, Kent, England. Jimi asked Noel's mother, Margaret Redding, 'is it all right if I stand next to your fireplace?'

525

S015: **3rd Stone From The Sun** – Jimi (gs, vo, voices, voice of 'Star Fleet'), Mitch (dr), Noel (ba), unknown male person (voice of 'Scout Ship'). Rec: CBS, 13/12/66 (basic track); OLY, likely 03/04/67 (additional recordings, including the 'Star Fleet' and 'Scout Ship' overdub). Engi: Mike Ross (CBS); unknown (OLY). Prod: Chas.

NOTES: <1> Jimi wrote this song in the Hyde Park Towers hotel, London, which was Jimi's residence between 24/09/66 and 06/12/66. <2> When playing this song at 66⅔ r.p.m. you will hear an exchange of messages between a 'Star Fleet' and a 'Scout Ship'. Refer to page 177 for the text of the 'transmission'. This transmission sparked off a Donald Duck story titled 'Officer For A Day' by script writer Carl Barks in late 1968 (first published in the *Donald Duck* comic issue 126, 07/69, in the USA). In the story Donald is playing a substitute policeman and is being faced with, among other problems, visitors from a flying saucer who believe chickens are the only inhabitants of the Earth worth talking to . . .

S016: **Remember** – Jimi (gs, vo, tongue-clicks), Mitch (dr, ta), Noel (ba). Rec: DLL, 02/67. Engi: Dave. Prod: Chas.

S017: **Are You Experienced?** – Jimi (gs, pi, vo), Mitch (dr), Noel (ba). Special effects: Jimi (backward gi); Mitch (backward dr); Noel (backward ba). Rec: OLY, 03/04/67. Prod: Chas.

NOTES: <1> George Chkiantz on the backward guitar parts: 'The original idea was to do a loop, but that gave a problem . . . we tried looping it and then we couldn't get it to loop . . . in the end Jimi got so impatient doing this, he said "look, it's quite easy, we're just gonna play" and played it in.'<2> It is possible that Jimi did some of the backward drums.

ARE YOU EXPERIENCED?
   – CD: Polydor 825 416–2 [GER]

S018: **Can You See Me** – Jimi (gs, vo), Mitch (dr, ta), Noel (ba). Rec: DLL or REG, 11/66 or 12/66. Prod: Chas.

NOTE: This is the same basic version as S010. Differences: different vocal take by Jimi; some ADT plus delay on vocals.

Plus: Foxy Lady [S007]; Manic Depression [S008]; Red House [S009]; Love Or Confusion [S011]; I Don't Live Today [S012]; May This Be Love [S013]; Fire [S014]; 3rd Stone From The Sun [S015]; Remember [S016]; Are You Experienced [S017].

HEY JOE b/w 51ST ANNIVERSARY
   – Reprise 0572 [USA] – Released 01/05/67 – Single
     Charts – never
Contains: Hey Joe [S001]; 51st Anniversary [S004].

ARE YOU EXPERIENCED?
   – Reprise RS 6261 [USA] – Released 08/67 – *: entire release
     Charts – entry: 190 (26/08/67); top position: 5; weeks in chart: 106 (!)
   – CD: Reprise 6261–2 [USA]
Contains: Purple Haze [S003]; Manic Depression [S008]; Hey Joe [S001]; Love Or Confusion [S011]; May This Be Love [S013]; I Don't Live Today [S012]; The Wind Cries Mary [S005]; Fire [S014]; Third Stone From The Sun [S015]; Foxy Lady [S007]; Are You Experienced [S017].

PURPLE HAZE b/w THE WIND CRIES MARY
   – Reprise 0597 [USA] – Released 19/06/67 – Single
     Charts – entry: 94 (26/08/67); top position: 65; weeks in chart: 8
Contains: Purple Haze [S003]; The Wind Cries Mary [S005].

THE BURNING OF THE MIDNIGHT LAMP b/w THE STARS THAT PLAY WITH LAUGHING SAM'S DICE

– Track 604007 [ENG]
– Released 19/08/67 – Single
   Charts – entry: 32 (02/09/67); top position: 18; weeks in chart: 9
– Also on: Polydor 59.117 [GER]

S019: **The Burning Of The Midnight Lamp** – Jimi (gs, electric harpsichord, lv, mellotron for hv effects), Mitch (dr), Noel (ba), unknown (ta). Rec: MAY, 06 and 07/07/67 (basic track); MAY, 20/07/67 (additional recordings, very likely including the harpsichord and mellotron); MAY, 20/07/67 (final mix). Engi: Gary. Prod: Chas.

NOTES: <1> Written by Jimi during a plane trip between Los Angeles and New York (03/07/67). <2> Jimi: 'I really don't care what our record does as far as chart-wise. We had this one ['The Burning Of The Midnight Lamp'] that only made number 11 . . . which everybody around here [in England] hated. They said that was the worst record, you know. But to me that was the best one we ever made. Not as far as recording, 'cause the recording technique was really bad, you know, you couldn't hear the words so good. Probably that's what it was . . .'

S020: **The Stars That Play With Laughing Sam's Dice** – Jimi (gs, vo, voice of 'friendly neighbourhood experience maker'), Mitch (dr), Noel (ba), 'the Milky Way express' (voices, whistles, cheers). Rec: MAY, 18/07/67 (basic track) and 29/07/67. Engi: Gary. Prod: Chas.

NOTES: <1> Song a.k.a.: STP with LSD. <2> A lot of people attended the recording sessions, including Frank Zappa, so they all very likely made up 'the Milky Way express'. <3> This is the first released recording where Jimi used a wah-wah foot pedal.

AXIS: BOLD AS LOVE
– Track 613003 [ENG] – Released 01/12/67 – *: entire release
   Charts – entry: 22 (13/12/67); top position: 5; weeks in chart: 16
– Reprise RS 6281 [USA] – Released 01/68
   Charts – entry: 140 (10/02/68); top position: 3; weeks in chart: 53
– Also on: Track 2407 011 [ENG]; Polydor 184110 [GER];
   Polydor 2343 097 & 2486 029 [HOL];   Barclay 0820 167 [FRA]
– CD: Polydor 813 572–2 [GER]; Reprise 6281–2 [USA];
   Polydor P33P 25023 [JAP]

<1> The recordings for this second Jimi Hendrix Experience LP were made during 14 or 15 recording sessions (first day of recording 04/05/67, last day of recording 30/10/67). <2> Tape operator and ideas for ADT and phasing: George Chkiantz. A few other special effects and electronic devices built by: Roger Mayer. Although we credit Eddie Kramer as engineer for all the songs on the LP, it is understood that on some songs engineer Andy Johns was in charge instead. <3> All mixing: OLY. <4> The cover drawing was done by Roger Law. Jimi: 'When I first saw the design I thought, it's great, but maybe we should have an American Indian. The three of us have nothing to do with what's on that Axis cover . . .' <5> Eddie: 'I set up a drum platform . . . I remember miking Mitch by raising him on that platform about a foot and using distant miking and close miking – with that D30 on the bass drum and, more than likely, 67's or C12's on the cymbals. Probably C12's and 87's on the floor toms . . .' <6> Chas: 'There's more Hendrix solos ended up on the floor at Olympic in the cutting-room than was ever put out. Jimi had a tendency to ramble when he got into solos . . . you can't have a three-minute single with a three-minute guitar solo. I used to change his lyrics and everything . . . George Chkiantz was basically tape op, and he was really into thinking up sounds. There was another young lad [Roger Mayer] and it ended up where he would turn up in the studio and he and George Chkiantz would

sit huddled in the corner thinking up ideas about sound and how you could misuse the equipment . . .' <7> Jimi: '. . . it was mixed beautifully, but we lost the original mix so we had to re-mix it. Chas and I and the engineer, Eddie Kramer, all of us had to re-mix it the next morning within 11 hours and it's very hard to do that. We're going to take more time . . .'

S021: **EXP** – Jimi (voice of 'Mr. Paul Caruso'), Mitch (voice of the Radio Station EXP 'Announcer'). Rec: OLY, 05/0567. Engi: Terry Brown? Prod: Chas.

NOTE: There's no real bass in this song. The Experience did set up a couple of guitars, turned the volume up full and smashed them against the amplifiers and that's all the noises in 'part B'. This part was originally recorded under the title 'Symphony Of Experience', and was mixed by Terry Brown.

S022: **Up From The Skies** – Jimi (gi, vo), Mitch (dr, brushes), Noel (ba). Rec: OLY, 29/10/67. Engi: Eddie. Prod: Chas.

S023: **Spanish Castle Magic** – Jimi (gs, pi, vo), Mitch (dr), Noel (Hagstrom 8-string bass). Rec: OLY, 27/10 and 28/10/67. Engi: Eddie. Prod: Chas.

NOTE: The song title refers to the Spanish Castle club in Seattle, Washington, where Jimi used to play in his early days.

S024: **Wait Until Tomorrow** – Jimi (gs, lv), Mitch (dr, ta, hv), Noel (ba, hv). Rec: OLY, 26/10/67. Engi: Eddie. Prod: Chas.

S025: **Ain't No Telling** – Jimi (gs, lv), Mitch (dr, hv), Noel (ba, hv). Special effect: Jimi (octavia). Rec: OLY, 26/10/67. Engi: Eddi. Prod: Chas.

S026: **Little Wing** – Jimi (gi, glockenspiel, vo), Mitch (dr, ta), Noel (ba). Special effect: Leslie speaker (used for gi); Pultec filter (on some of Jimi's vo). Rec: OLY, 25/10/67 (basic track); OLY, 28/10/67 (additional recordings, very likely including glockenspiel). Engi: Eddie. Prod: Chas.

S027: **If Six Was Nine** – Jimi (gs, wooden flute, lv), Mitch (dr, pe), Noel (ba, hv), Gary Leeds (foot-stamping), Graham Nash (foot-stamping), Michael Jeffery ('heavy foot-thumping'), unknown (voice). Rec: OLY, 04 or 05/05/67 (basic track); OLY, 09/05/67 (hv by Noel plus all foot-stamping and foot-thumping). Engi: Eddie. Prod: Chas.

S028: **You've Got Me Floating** – Jimi (gs, lv), Mitch (dr, hv), Noel (Hagstrom 8-string ba, hv), Trevor Burton (hv), Chris Kefford or Roy Wood (hv), unknown (ta). Special effect: Jimi (backward gi). Rec: OLY, 03/10/67. Engi: Eddie. Prod: Chas.

S029: **Castles Made Of Sand** – Jimi (gs, vo, turning a page with lyrics), Mitch (dr), Noel (ba). Special effect: Jimi (backward gi). Rec: OLY, last week 10/67. Engi: Eddie. Prod: Chas.

S030: **She's So Fine** – Jimi (gs, hv), Mitch (dr, hv), Noel (ba, lv). Comp: Noel Redding. Rec: OLY, 04/05/67 (basic track); OLY, 30/10/67 (all hv plus very likely lv by Noel). Engi: Eddie. Prod: Chas.

NOTE: Song a.k.a.: She's So Fine (She's In With Time).

S031: **One Rainy Wish** – Jimi (gs, vo), Mitch (dr), Noel (ba). Rec: OLY, 10/67. Special effects: Jimi (octavia); ADT (on some of Jimi's vo); Engi: Eddie. Prod: Chas.

NOTE: Song a.k.a.: Golden Rose.

S032: **Little Miss Lover** – Jimi (gs, lv), Jimi? (ta), Mitch (dr, hv), Noel (Hagstrom 8-string ba, hv). Special effect: Jimi (octavia); Pultec filter (on Jimi's lv). Rec: OLY, first week 10/67. Engi: Eddie. Prod: Chas.

S033: **Bold As Love** – Jimi (gs, harpsichord, vo), Mitch (dr), Noel (ba). Special effect: phasing (particularly on dr). Rec: OLY, 29/10/67. Engi: Eddie. Prod: Chas.

528

FOXY LADY b/w HEY JOE
> – Reprise 0641 [USA] – Released 27/11/67 – Single
>> Charts – entry: 80 (23/12/67); top position: 67; weeks in chart: 4

Contains: Foxy Lady [S007]; Hey Joe [S001].

UP FROM THE SKIES b/w ONE RAINY WISH
> – Reprise 0665 [USA] – Released 26/02/68 – Single
>> Charts – entry: 94 (16/03/68); top position: 82; weeks in chart: 4
> – Also on: Barclay 060959 [FRA]

Contains: Up From The Skies [S022]; One Rainy Wish [S031].

SMASH HITS
> – Track 613004 [ENG] – Released 04/68 – *: entire release
>> Charts – entry: 32 (24/04/68); top position: 4; weeks in chart: 25
> – Also on: Polydor 2310 268 [ENG]
> – CD: not released (but see next entry)

Contains: Purple Haze [S003]; Fire [S014]; The Wind Cries Mary [S005]; Can You See Me [S010]; 51st Anniversary [S004]; Hey Joe [S001]; Stone Free [S002]; The Stars That Play With Laughing Sam's Dice [S020]; Manic Depression [S008]; Highway Chile [S006]; The Burning Of The Midnight Lamp [S019]; Foxy Lady [S007].

SMASH HITS
> – CD: Polydor 825 255–2 [GER]

Contains: Purple Haze [S003]; Fire [S014]; The Wind Cries Mary [S005]; Can You See Me [S018]; 51st Anniversary [S004]; Hey Joe [S001]; Stone Free [S002]; The Stars That Play With Laughing Sam's Dice [S020]; Manic Depression [S008]; Highway Chile [S006]; The Burning Of The Midnight Lamp [S019]; Foxy Lady [S007].

ALL ALONG THE WATCHTOWER b/w THE BURNING OF THE MIDNIGHT LAMP
> – Reprise 0767 [USA] – Released 02/09/68 – Single
>> Charts – entry: 66 (21/09/68); top: 20; weeks in chart: 9

S034: **All Along The Watchtower**– Jimi (gs, vo), Mitch (dr), Dave Mason (ba, acoustic gi), Mitch? (temple block), unknown (ta). Comp: Bob Dylan. Special effect: Jimi (slide-effect via the back of his cigarette lighter with the gi on his lap). Rec: OLY, 21/01/68 (basic track); PLA, 04/68 or 05/68 (transfer from 4 to 12 track, plus additional recordings). Eng: Eddie (OLY); Gary (PLA). Prod: Chas (OLY); Jimi (PLA). Wiped (at PLA) in 1968: Dave Mason (ba). Added (at PLA) in 1968: Jimi (ba).

NOTE: <1> Jimi, Dave Mason and Viv Price were at a small party where they all listened to Bob Dylan's *John Wesley Harding* LP for the very first time. When it got to 'All Along The Watchtower' Jimi said, 'we gotta record that, I gotta do that.' That same evening Jimi recorded the song at Olympic. Brian Jones and Linda Keith among others attended this session. <2> Jimi: 'I felt like "Watchtower" was something I had written but could never get together. I often feel like that about Dylan.' <3> Refer to S138 for a slightly different mixed version. <4> Refer to S816 for the version with the original bass take.

Plus: The Burning Of The Midnight Lamp [S019].

ELECTRIC LADYLAND (double)
> – Reprise 2RS 6307 [USA] – Released 10/68 – *: entire release
>> Charts – entry: 179 (19/10/68); top position: 1; weeks in chart: 37
> – Track 613 008/9 [ENG] – Released 25/10/68
>> Charts – entry: 23 (13/11/68); top position: 6; weeks in chart: 12
> – Double CD: Reprise 6307–2 [USA]; Polydor 823 359–2 [GER]; Polydor P58P 25001/2 [JAP]
> – Single CD: Reprise 6307–2 [USA] – upgraded version

<1> The Warner Brothers tape box that contains the master reels has the following message: 'Note: special phase effects on this tape. Do not change phase!' <2> All mixing: PLA. Jimi: 'Some of the mix came out kind of muddy, not exactly muddy, but kind of bassy, because we didn't get a chance to do it completely till the end. We mixed it all and produced it and all this mess. But then when it was time for them to press it quite naturally they screwed up, 'cause they didn't know what we wanted. There's 3-D sound on there that's been used that you can't appreciate because like they didn't know how to cut it properly. They thought it was out of phase [laughs]!' <3> The American and English covers are completely different. Jimi: 'People have been asking me about the English cover and I don't know anything about it. I didn't know it was going to be used.' – Mitch: 'We thought it was a load of rubbish. We didn't know anything about it until we came back from the States.' <4> On several of the songs on this release Jimi also plays bass guitar. Mitch: 'There were some things where it was just faster to work just Jimi and myself. Some were cut guitar and drums, some just bass and drums, there was no set gauge for that.'

S035: **. . . And The Gods Made Love** – Jimi? (timpani), Jimi (ba, gs?). Special effects: Jimi (backward vo at half speed); tape manipulations. Rec: PLA, 29?/06/68. Engi: Eddie or Gary. Prod: Jimi.

NOTE: <1> This song was originally recorded with the title: At Last The Beginning. <2> Jimi: '. . . a 90-second sound painting of the heavens. I know it's the thing people will jump on to criticise so we're putting it right at the beginning to get it over with. It's typifying what happens when the Gods make love or whatever they spend their time on.' <3> Jimi's backward vocal (including the line 'Okay, one more time') comes from a studio rehearsal session of 'Voodoo Child' (Rec: PLA, 01?/05/68).

S036: **Have You Ever Been (To Electric Ladyland)** – Jimi (gs, ba, vo), Jimi or Mitch (ta), Mitch (dr). Special effect: phasing (on dr). Rec: PLA, between 04/68 and 06/68. Engi: Eddie or Gary. Prod: Jimi.

NOTE: Refer to S153 for a completely different studio recording known as: Electric Lady Land.

S037: **Crosstown Traffic** – Jimi (gs, pi, kazoo, lv), Mitch (dr, hv on 'Crosstown' parts), Noel (ba, hv on 'Crosstown' parts), Dave Mason (hv on 'Traffic' parts). Special effect: Pultec filter (on Jimi's vo). Rec: OLY, 20 and 21/12/67 (basic track); PLA, 04/68 or 05/68 (4-track to 12-track transfer, plus additional recordings). Eng: Eddie (OLY); Gary (PLA). Prod: Chas (OLY); Jimi (PLA).

S038: **Voodoo Chile** – Jimi (gi, vo), Mitch (dr), Jack Casady (ba), Steve Winwood (or), unknown (crowd noises). Rec: PLA, 01 or 02/05/68; PLA, 10?/06/68 (final mix). Engi: Eddie. Prod: Jimi.

NOTE: <1> Steve Winwood: 'Out in the corridor were all these musicians waiting to be given their chance to play. Jimi came out and said "Hi, come in." There were no chord sheets, no nothing. He just started playing. It was a one-take job, with him singing and playing at the same time.' <2> The crowd noises during this song were recorded separately and overdubbed.

S039: **Little Miss Strange** – Jimi (gs), Mitch (dr, hv), Noel (gi, ba, acoustic gi, lv). Comp: Noel Redding. Rec: PLA, 22/04/68 (basic track); PLA, 25/04/68 (additional recordings); PLA, 28/04/68 (mixing). Engi: Gary & Eddie. Prod: Jimi & Noel. Wiped on 05/05/68: Noel (ba). Added on 05/05/68: Noel (new ba take).

S040: **Long Hot Summer Night** – Jimi (gs, ba, lv, hv, voice), Mitch (dr), Al Kooper (pi), unknown (hv). Rec: PLA, 18/04/68; PLA, 26/07/68 (final mix). Engi: Gary. Prod: Jimi.

S041: **Come On (Part I)** – Jimi (gi, vo), Mitch (dr), Noel (ba). Comp: Earl King (real name: Solomon Johnson). Rec: PLA, 27/08/68. Engi: Eddie or Gary. Prod: Jimi.

NOTE: <1> Song a.k.a.: Let The Good Times Roll. <2> Jimi recorded 14 takes in total of this song. This is take 14.

S042: **Gypsy Eyes** – Jimi (gs, ba, vo), Mitch (dr). Rec: PLA, last week 04/68 or first week 05/68. Engi: Eddie or Gary. Prod: Jimi.

NOTE: This song is about Jimi's mother Lucille.

S043: **Rainy Day, Dream Away** – Jimi (gs, vo, coughs and sniffs, talking), Jimi? (ba), Buddy (dr), Larry Faucette (congas), Freddie Smith (sa), Mike Finnigan (or). Rec: PLA, 10/06/68. Engi: Eddie or Gary. Prod: Jimi.

NOTE: The idea for the lyric line 'Hey man, it's raining' (by Jimi in a funny voice) came from a Bill Cosby story which was on the Bill Cosby LP (*Revenge* – Warner Bros. WS 1691 [USA]) Jimi had in his record collection. Bill Cosby does his lyric line ('Hey man') in that same funny voice, which Jimi adapted for his song.

S044: **1983 . . . (A Merman I Should Turn To Be)** – Jimi (gs, ba, dr, pe, vo), Chris Wood (fl). Special effects: Jimi (backward gi); Chris Wood (bit of backward fl); seagulls sound created via microphone feedback from Jimi's headphones while 'squeaking', with added delay, echo etc.; heavy delay on vo; slowed down and speeded up tape manipulations. Rec: PLA, 23?/04/68. Engi: Gary or Eddie. Mixing: Jimi & Eddie. Prod: Jimi.

S045: **Moon, Turn The Tides . . . Gently Gently Away** – Jimi (gs). Special effects: slowed down and speeded up tape manipulations. Rec: PLA, 23?/04/68. Engi: Gary or Eddie. Mixing: Jimi & Eddie. Prod: Jimi.

S046: **Still Raining, Still Dreaming** – Jimi (gs, vo, voice), Jimi? (ba), Buddy (dr), Mike Finnigan (or). Rec: PLA, 10/06/68. Engi: Eddie or Gary. Mixing: Jimi and Eddie. Prod: Jimi.

NOTE: Written 19/05/68 in Hallandale, Florida.

S047: **House Burning Down** – Jimi (gs, ba, vo, voice), Mitch (dr). Special effect: phasing (on gi). Rec: PLA, 01/05/68 (basic track); PLA, 08/68 (additional recordings); PLA, 23/08/68 (final mix). Engi: Eddie or Gary. Prod: Jimi.

NOTE: Jimi: 'We made the guitar sound like it was on fire. It's constantly changing dimensions, and up on top that lead guitar is cutting through everything.'

S048: **Voodoo Child (slight return)** – Jimi (gi, vo), Mitch (dr), Jimi or Mitch (maracas), Noel (ba). Rec: PLA, 03/05/68 (basic track); PLA, 05/68 (maracas overdub). Engi: Eddie. Prod: Jimi.

NOTE: <1> Jimi recorded eight takes in total of this song. This is take eight. <2> Jimi: 'Somebody was filming us as we started doing that . . . it was like, Okay, boys, look like you're recording. It was in the studio and they *were* recording it . . . so it was one-two-three and then we went into "Voodoo Child".'

Plus: The Burning Of the Midnight Lamp [S019]; All Along The Watchtower [S034].

ELECTRIC JIMI HENDRIX

    – Track 2856 002 [ENG] – Released end 68

    – Charts: never

    – Not released [USA]

This was an alternative kind of 'best of' compilation set and was upon its release immediately withdrawn. Hardly any copies made it to the shops, if any at all.

Contains: Still Raining, Still Dreaming [S046]; House Burning Down [S047]; All Along The Watchtower [S034]; Voodoo Child (slight return) [S048]; Little Miss Strange [S039]; Long Hot Summer Night [S040]; Come On (Part 1) [S041]; Gypsy Eyes [S042]; The Burning Of The Midnight Lamp [S019].

Jimi's flat, London, first week of January 1969

ALL ALONG THE WATCHTOWER b/w LONG HOT SUMMER NIGHT
    – Track 604025 [ENG] – Released 18/10/68 – Single
        Charts – entry: 48 (23/10/68); top position: 5; weeks in chart: 11
    – Also on: Barclay 060 993 [FRA]
Contains: All Along The Watchtower [S034]; Long Hot Summer Night [S040].
CROSSTOWN TRAFFIC b/w GYPSY EYES
    – Reprise 0792 [USA] – Released 18/11/68 – Single
        Charts – entry: 73 (30/11/68); top position: 52; weeks in chart: 8
    – Track 604029 [ENG] – Released 04/04/69 – Single
        Charts – entry: 37 (16/04/69); top position: 37; weeks in chart: 3
    – Also on: Polydor 59 256 [GER]; Barclay 061 038 [FRA]
Contains: Crosstown Traffic [S037]; Gypsy Eyes [S042].
SMASH HITS
    – Reprise MS 2025 [USA] – Released 07/69 – *: entire release
        Charts – entry: 81 (02/08/69); top position: 6; weeks in chart: 35
    – CD: not released [USA], but see next entry
Originally this release also included a colour poster showing the JHE dressed up as
cowboys (from a 29/04/69 photo session on Warner Bros. film location, Hollywood).
S049:   **Red House** – Jimi (gi, vo), Mitch (dr), Noel (bass strings of a normal
       6-string gi, probably owned by Alexis Korner). Rec: CBS, 13/12/66. Engi:
       Mike Ross. Prod: Chas.
NOTE: This is a slightly different version of S009. Differences: different vocal

take by Jimi; different mix containing much more echo on the guitar; studio chat introduction by Jimi and Chas mixed out.
Plus: Purple Haze [S003]; Fire [S014]; The Wind Cries Mary [S005]; Can You See Me [S018]; Hey Joe [S001]; Stone Free [S002]; Manic Depression [S008]; Foxy Lady [S007]; Crosstown Traffic [S037]; All Along The Watchtower [S034]; Remember [S016].

SMASH HITS
> – Reprise 2276–2 [USA] – Released 11/89 – CD (only)
> – Not released [ENG]

Contains: Purple Haze [S003]; Fire [S014]; The Wind Cries Mary [S005]; Can You See Me [S018]; Hey Joe [S001]; Stone Free [S002]; Manic Depression [S008]; Foxy Lady [S007]; Crosstown Traffic [S037]; All Along The Watchtower [S034]; Red House [S049]; Remember [S016]; 51st Anniversary [S004]; Highway Chile [S006].

STONE FREE b/w IF 6 WAS 9
> – Reprise 0853 [USA] – Released 15/09/69 – Single
> Charts – never
> – Not released [ENG]

Contains: Stone Free [S002]; If 6 Was 9 [S027].

FIRE b/w THE BURNING OF THE MIDNIGHT LAMP
> – Track 604033 [ENG] – Released 14/11/69 – Single
> Charts – never
> – Also on: Polydor 59375 [GER]
> – Not released [USA]

Contains: Fire (stated as: Let Me Light Your Fire) [S014]; The Burning Of The Midnight Lamp [S019].

STEPPING STONE b/w IZABELLA
> – Reprise 0905 [USA] – Released 13/04/70 – Single – *: Stepping Stone
> Charts – never
> – Not released [ENG]

<1> Only a few copies of this single were ever released, and only for a very short time. The single was presumably taken off the market as it wasn't mixed properly and/or released without Jimi's approval. <2> Juma Sultan: 'Heaven Research Unlimited, that was all of us, Jimi, Arthur and Albert Allen etc. We all had it, and we would come together as a unit, we all had certain skills. Jimi was trying to surround himself with people with open ears. It was based on feeling. Jimi was working on some material on my album, and that was all about Heaven Research Unlimited.'

S050: Stepping Stone – Jimi (gs, vo), Buddy (dr), Billy (ba), Bob Hughes? (voice from control-room). Rec: PLA, 14/11/69. Engi: Bob Hughes. Prod: Heaven Research Unlimited.

NOTE: Jimi: 'I don't know how good it is – I can't tell any more. Some of the copies out here have no bass on them. I had to go out somewhere and told the guy to remix it but he didn't. Sure it matters . . .'

S051: Izabella – Jimi (gs, lv, hv), Buddy (dr, hv), Billy (ba), Juma and Jerry (ta, pe, maracas), unknown (hv).
Rec: HIT, 28 and 29/08/69. Prod: Jimi or Heaven Research Unlimited.

NOTE: This song was written at Jimi's house, Tavor Hollow Road, near Shokan, New York, early 08/69.

BAND OF GYPSYS
> – Capitol STAO-472 [USA] – Released 04/70 – *: entire release
> Charts – entry: 18 (02/05/70); top position: 5; weeks in chart: 61
> – Track 2406 002 [ENG] – Released 12/06/70
> Charts – entry: 6 (04/07/70); top position: 6; weeks in chart: 16

- Also on: Polydor 2480 005 [GER]; Polydor 2491 507 [HOL]; Barclay 0920. 221 [FRA]
  - CD: Polydor 821 933–2 [GER]; not released [USA]

<1> This is the release that Jimi Hendrix 'owed' PPX/Capitol for releasing him over to Reprise. <2> There are three entirely different covers in circulation. The Capitol version shows Band Of Gypsys photographs. The first Track version had a photograph showing various dolls. Music Now 20/06/70: 'Jimi Hendrix plus Brian Jones, John Peel and Bob Dylan gets the same treatment on his sleeve as the Labour Party gave their opponents in pre-election ads; he's been turned into a doll.' Mike Jeffery: 'If ever there is an award for the worst taste album cover it must go to this.' After deleting this, the second Track cover shows photographs of Jimi's performance at the Isle Of Wight Festival, 30/08/70. <3> Concert introduction: Bill Graham. <4> All songs rec (by Wally Heider): Fillmore East, New York City. Engi: Eddie. Mixing: Eddie. Prod: Heaven Reseach Unlimited. <5> Jimi: 'I wasn't too satisfied with the album. If it had been up to me I would have never put it out .. not enough preparation went into it and it came out a bit "grizzly". The thing was we owed the record company an album and they were pushing us – so here it is.'

L052: **Who Knows** – Jimi (gi, lv), Buddy (dr, hv), Billy (ba). Special effect: Jimi (octavia). Rec: 01/01/70, 1st show.

L053: **Machine Gun** – Jimi (gi, lv), Buddy (dr, hv), Billy (ba, hv). Special effect: Jimi (Uni-Vibe with chorus setting; octavia; flicking the guitar springs). Rec: 01/01/70, 1st show.

NOTE: The flicking of the guitar springs occurs almost at the very end of the song, during the very fast guitar bits (imitating bombs etc. exploding).

L054: **Changes** – Jimi (gi, hv), Buddy (dr, lv), Billy (ba). Comp: Buddy Miles. Rec: 01/01/70, 2nd show.

L055: **Power Of Soul** – Jimi (gi, lv), Buddy (dr, hv), Billy (ba), Billy? (hv). Special effect: Jimi (octavia). Rec: 01/01/70, 2nd show.

L056: **Message To Love** – Jimi (gi, lv), Buddy (dr, hv), Billy (ba), Billy? (hv). Rec: 01/01/70, 2nd show.

NOTE: There is clearly a suspiciously blurry sounding part during this song, which seems to indicate censorship of Jimi's lyrics. The line which seems to be censored comes before the line 'They'll never understand'. For example, during the Isle Of Wight (30/08/70) concert Jimi sings 'Forget about that pig, they'll never understand,' while during the concert in Copenhagen (03/09/70) he sings 'Never mind the policeman, they'll never understand.'

L057: **We Gotta Live Together** – Jimi (gi, hv), Buddy (dr, lv), Billy (ba), Billy? (hv). Special effect: Jimi (octavia). Comp: Buddy Miles. Rec: 01/01/70, 2nd show.

BAND OF GYPSYS 2

- Capitol SJ-12416 [USA] – Released 10/86 – *: Getting My Heart Back Together Again; Hey Baby (The Land Of The New Rising Sun)
  Charts – never
  - Also on: Capitol/EMI 1A 064–26 1174 1 [HOL]
  - CD: not released.

<1> There are 2 different pressings of the USA release in circulation. However, the cover and the labels are all identical. <2> Although this release is called a Band Of Gypsys album, there are in fact only 3 songs (L058, L059, L060) on this release that were performed by the original Band Of Gypsys. <3> The sound recordings (in poor quality) of 'Foxy Lady' and 'Stop' were lifted from a video tape; and 'Getting My Heart Back Together Again' was lifted from a ¼ inch soundboard tape. <4>

The 31/12/69 and all 01/01/70 songs rec: Fillmore East, New York City. <5>
All 30/05/70 songs rec (by Wally Heider on 8 track, 1 inch): Berkeley Community
Theatre, Berkeley, California. Engi: Abe Jacobs. <6> The Atlanta song recorded on
8 track, 1 inch.
ORDINARY PRESSING
L058:   **Getting My Heart Back Together Again** – Jimi (gi, lv), Buddy (dr,
hv), Billy (ba). Rec: 31/12/69, 1st show.
L059:   **Foxy Lady** – Jimi (gi, lv), Buddy (dr, hv), Billy (ba). Rec: 01/01/70,
1st show.
L060:   **Stop** – Jimi (gi, hv) Buddy (dr, lv, hv), Billy (ba, hv). Comp: Jerry
Ragavoy & Mort Shuman. Rec: 01/01/70, 1st show.
NOTE: Incomplete.
L061:   **Voodoo Child (slight return)** – Jimi (gi, vo), Mitch (dr), Billy (ba).
Rec: 2nd Atlanta Pop Festival/Middle Georgia Raceway, Byron, Georgia,
04/07/70.
L062:   **Stone Free** – Jimi (gi, vo), Mitch (dr), Billy (ba). Rec: 30/05/70, 2nd show.
L063:   **Ezy Ryder** – Jimi (gi, vo), Mitch (dr), Billy (ba). Rec: 30/05/70, 1st show.
ALTERNATIVE PRESSING
L064:   **Hey Joe** – Jimi (gi, vo), Mitch (dr), Billy (ba). Comp: William M. Roberts.
Rec: 30/05/70, 2nd show.
L065:   **Hey Baby (The Land Of The New Rising Sun)** – Jimi (gi, vo), Mitch
(dr), Billy (ba). Special effect: Jimi (Uni-Vibe with vibrato setting at slow
speed). Rec: 30/05/70, 2nd show.
L066:   **Lover Man** – Jimi (gi, vo), Mitch (dr), Billy (ba). Rec: 30/05/70, 2nd show.
Plus: Getting My Heart Back Together Again [L058]; Voodoo Child (slight return)
[L061]; Stone Free [L062]; Ezy Ryder [L063].
WOODSTOCK (triple)
– Cotillion SD 3500 [USA] – Released 06/70 – *: entire release
Charts – entry: 4 (06/06/70); top position: 1; weeks in chart: 68
– Atlantic K60001 [ENG] – Released 06/70
Charts – entry: 35 (08/08/70); top position: 35; weeks in chart: 8
– Double CD: Mobile Fidelity Sound Lab 4–816–1/2 [USA];
Atlantic SD 500–2 [USA, also available in ENG]
<1> The rest of this release contains performances of other artists at Woodstock.
<2> All listed songs rec (by Hanley Sound Inc. on 8 track, 1 inch): Woodstock Music
& Art Fair Festival, Bethel, New York, early morning of 18/08/69. Location engi:
Eddie Kramer & Lee Osborne. Prod: Eric Blackstead. <3> Jimi called this band 'Sky
Church'. <4> Star Spangled Banner, Purple Haze and Instrumental Solo is actually a
medley. <5> Instrumental Solo was not the final song performed as the Woodstock
film and this release may suggest.
L067:   **Star Spangled Banner** – Jimi (gi), Mitch (dr), Billy (bits of ba). Comp:
Francis Scott Key.
NOTE: This song is preceded by a few seconds of 'Voodoo Child (slight return)'.
L068:   **Purple Haze** – Jimi (gi, vo), Mitch (dr), Billy (ba), Larry (rhythm gi),
Juma (pe), Jerry (pe).
L069:   **Instrumental Solo** – Jimi (gi), Mitch (dr), Billy (ba), Larry (rhythm
gi), Juma (ta), Jerry (pe).
NOTE: Incomplete (instrumental introduction leading into the song edited out).
Refer to L625 for the complete version.
WOODSTOCK TWO (double)
– Cotillion SD 2400 [USA] – Released 04/71 – *: entire release

Charts – entry: 28 (10/04/71); top position; 8; weeks in chart: 17
- Atlantic K60002 [ENG] – Released 04/71
    Charts – never
- Double CD: Mobile Fidelity Sound Lab 4–816–3/4 [USA];
    Atlantic 781 981–2 [GER]

<1> More from Woodstock (refer to the previous release for additional information).
<2> The rest of this release contains performances of other artists at Woodstock.

L070: **Jam Back At The House** – Jimi (gi), Mitch (dr), Billy (ba), Larry (rhythm gi), Juma (cow-bell, pe), Jerry (pe). Comp: Mitch Mitchell.

NOTE: <1> Song a.k.a.: Beginning. <2> Incomplete. Refer to L620 for the complete version.

L071: **Izabella** – Jimi (gi, vo), Mitch (dr), Billy (ba), Larry (rhythm gi), Juma (pe), Jerry (pe).

NOTE: Incomplete. Refer to L621 for the complete version.

L072: **Getting My Heart Back Together Again** – Jimi (gi, vo), Mitch (dr), Billy (ba), Larry (rhythm gi), Juma (maracas, pe), Jerry (congas).

NOTE: Incomplete. Refer to L614 for the complete version.

JIMI PLAYS MONTEREY
- Reprise 25358–1 [USA] – Released 02/86 – *: entire release
- Also on: Polydor 827 990–1 [GER]
- CD: Polydor 827 990–2 [GER]; Reprise 9 25358–2 [USA]

<1> This release contains the complete performance (in correct order) at the Monterey International Pop Festival, Monterey, California, 18/06/67 (rec: by Wally Heider on 8 track, 1 inch). 1967 Engi: Eric Weinbang. <2> The Reprise CD version is of somewhat better sound quality and is also 4:37 longer (contains complete tune-ups and complete chat between the songs), when compared with any of the other releases listed. <3> Concert introduction: Brian Jones.

L073: **Killin' Floor** – Jimi (gi, vo), Mitch (dr), Noel (ba). Comp: Howlin' Wolf (real name: Chester Burnett).

L074: **Foxy Lady** – Jimi (gi, lv), Mitch (dr), Noel (ba, hv).

L075: **Like A Rolling Stone** – Jimi (gi, vo), Mitch (dr), Noel (ba). Comp: Bob Dylan.

L076: **Rock Me, Baby** – Jimi (gi, vo), Mitch (dr), Noel (ba). Comp: B.B. King & Joe Josea.

L077: **Hey Joe** – Jimi (gi, vo), Mitch (dr), Noel (ba). Comp: William M. Roberts.

L078: **Can You See Me** – Jimi (gi, vo), Mitch (dr), Noel (ba).

L079: **The Wind Cries Mary** – Jimi (gi, vo), Mitch (dr), Noel (ba).

L080: **Purple Haze** – Jimi (gi, vo), Mitch (dr), Noel (ba).

L081: **Wild Thing** – Jimi (gi, lv, tongue-click), Mitch (dr), Noel (ba, hv). Comp: Chip Taylor.

HISTORIC PERFORMANCES RECORDED AT THE MONTEREY INTERNATIONAL POP FESTIVAL
- Reprise MS 2029 [USA] – Released 09/70
    Charts – entry: 53 (19/09/70); top position: 16; weeks in chart: 20
- Also on: Atlantic 40 430 [FRA]; not released [ENG]
- CD: not released

<1> The rest of this release contains part of Otis Redding's performance. <2> Refer to the previous entry for the complete JHE performance at Monterey.

Contains: Like A Rolling Stone [L075]; Rock Me, Baby [L076]; Can You See Me [L078]; Wild Thing [L081].

VOODOO CHILD (SLIGHT RETURN) b/w *HEY JOE* b/w *ALL ALONG THE WATCHTOWER*
> – Track 2095 001 [ENG] – Released 23/10/70 – Maxi Single
> Charts – entry: 15 (07/11/70); top position: 1; weeks in chart: 13
> – Not released [USA]

Contains: Voodoo Child (slight return) [S048]; Hey Joe [S001]; All Along The Watchtower [S034].

THE CRY OF LOVE
> – Reprise MS 2034 [USA] – Released 03/71 – *: entire release
> Charts – entry: 18 (06/03/71); top position: 3; weeks in chart: 39
> – Track 2408 101 [ENG] – Released 05/03/71
> Charts – entry: 2 (03/04/71); top position: 2; weeks in chart: 13
> – Also on: Polydor 2480 027 [GER]; Barclay 080.433 [FRA]
> – CD: Reprise 2034–2 [USA]; Polydor 829 926–2 [GER];
> Polydor P33P 25011 [JAP]

<1> Most of the recordings on this release plus most of the studio recordings on the *Rainbow Bridge* release were planned by Jimi for a double-LP titled *First Rays Of The New Rising Sun*. <2> Posthumous: Mitch re-recorded and corrected small drum parts, while Eddie Kramer did some more mixing and re-mixing. <3> The Polydor [GER] CD release contains a slightly incomplete version of 'Freedom'. All other CD's contain the complete version.

S082: **Freedom** – Jimi (gs, lv), Mitch (dr), Billy (ba), Arthur Allen & Albert Allen (hv), Juma (congas), unknown (pi). Rec: ELE, 06/70. Engi: Eddie. Prod: Jimi.

NOTE: This song refers (in part) to Devon Wilson.

S083: **Drifting** – Jimi (gs, vo), Mitch (dr), Bill (ba). Special effect: Jimi (backward gi). Rec: ELE, 06/70 or 07/70. Engi: Eddie. Prod: Jimi. Added in late 1970: Buzzy Linhart (vibraphone).

NOTE: Buzzy Linhart: 'That was [recorded] posthumous[ly], it was very emotional for me . . . most of the things had been done, but he was telling Eddie and Mitch that he didn't know whether to add on "Drifting" another rhythm guitar or vibes. We rented some vibes and there were no charts written out.'

S084: **Ezy Ryder** – Jimi (gs, lv, hv), Buddy (dr), Buddy? (hv), Billy (ba), Juma (cow-bell), Juma or Jerry (congas), Steve Winwood? (hv), Chris Wood? (hv), unknown (ta). Rec: PLA, 18/12/69. Engi: Tony Bongiovi? Prod: Heaven Research Unlimited.

S085: **Night Bird Flying** – Jimi (gs, vo), Mitch (dr), Billy (ba), Juma (cow-bell, pe). Rec: ELE, 16/06/70. Engi: Eddie. Prod: Jimi.

S086: **My Friend** – Jimi (gi, vo), Buddy (dr), Noel? (ba), Paul Caruso (ha), Stephen Stills (pi), Ken Weaver (12-string gi). Other musicians present included Jimmy Mayes, Lonnie Youngblood and members of Mitch Ryder's Detroit Wheels. Rec: CEN, 13/03/68. Prod: Chas.

NOTE: Paul Caruso (*Rolling Stone* 10/06/71): 'Since the truth always seems to out in its simple way, let me simply say this, the harp on "My Friend" from *The Cry Of Love* was not played by any such Gers person, but by me . . . I tried to get the credits changed diplomatically, avoiding legal channels taken by another musician involved with this record, but neither of us has gotten anywhere, Michael Jeffery once again.'

S087: **Straight Ahead** – Jimi (gs, vo, voice), Mitch (dr), Billy (ba), Eddie (faint voice from control-room). Rec: ELE 16?/06/70. Engi: Eddie. Prod: Jimi.

S088: **Astro Man** – Jimi (gs, vo), Mitch (dr), Billy (ba), Juma (cow-bell, pe). Special effect: Jimi (Uni-Vibe with vibrato setting at very slow speed –2nd gi); phased cymbals. Rec: ELE, 24?/06/70. Engi: Eddie. Prod: Jimi.

S089: **Angel** – Jimi (gs, vo, voice), Mitch (dr), Billy (ba). Special effect: Jimi (unknown kind of organ effect on gi). Rec: ELE, 23/07/70. Engi: Eddie. Prod: Jimi.

NOTE: Written by Jimi in early 68 after he had a dream about Lucille, his mother.

S090: **In From The Storm** – Jimi (gs, lv, hv, voice), Mitch (dr), Billy (ba), Emeretta Marks (hv). Rec: ELE, 21 and 22/07/70. Engi: Eddie. Prod: Jimi.

NOTE: Emeretta Marks: 'Originally Eddie tried the four of us, but the voices didn't blend [so instead] I sang with Jimi, I sang all these high parts.'

S091: **Belly Button Window** – Jimi (gs, vo, whistles). Rec: ELE, 22/08/70. Engi: Eddie. Prod: Jimi.

NOTE: This appears to be Jimi's very last studio recording. Recorded on 4 track, ½ inch.

FREEDOM b/w ANGEL
- Reprise 1000 [USA] – Released 08/03/71 – Single
    Charts – entry: 99 (03/04/71); top position: 59; weeks in chart; 8
- Not released [ENG]

Contains: Freedom [S082]; Angel [S089].

EXPERIENCE
- Ember 5057 [ENG] – Released 08/71
    Charts – never
- Also on: Ariola 85 087TT [GER]; Sonet SLPS 1526 [SWE]; Entertainment International SLDEI 782 [FRA]
- Not released [USA]
- CD: not released

<1> All songs rec: Royal Albert Hall, London, 24/02/69, on 4 track, ½ inch, Engi: Glyn Johns. <2> The songs on this release are very poorly mixed. <3> The motion picture *Experience* has thus far never been released. <4> The liner notes of this release give an incorrect date for the concert, and incorrectly claim that the recordings were '. . . probably the last recorded sounds of Jimi Hendrix' (!).

L092: **The Sunshine Of Your Love** – Jimi (gi), Mitch (dr), Noel (ba). Comp: Pete Brown & Jack Bruce & Eric Clapton.

NOTE: This song was not the 'opening jam' of the concert, as the liner notes may suggest ('Lover Man' was the first song).

L093: **Room Full Of Mirrors** – Jimi (gi, vo), Mitch (dr, cow-bell), Noel (ba), Dave Mason (gi), Chris Wood (fl), Kwasi 'Rocky' Dzidzournu (bongos)

L094: **Bleeding Heart** – Jimi (gi, vo), Mitch (dr), Noel (ba). Comp: Elmore James.

NOTE: Refer to L183 for a much better sound quality version of this same song.

L095: **Smashing Of Amps** – Jimi (gi), Mitch (dr), Noel (ba).

MORE EXPERIENCE
- Ember NR 5061 [ENG] – Released 03/72
    Also on: Sonet SLPS 1535 [SWE]; Entertainment International LDM 30.148 [FRA]; Kaleidoscope KAL 19026 [FRA]
- Not released [USA]
- CD: not released

NOTES: <1> All songs rec: Royal Albert Hall, London, 24/02/69. <2> See previous release for additional information.

L096: **Little Wing** – Jimi (gi, vo), Mitch (dr), Noel (ba).
NOTES: <1> Stated incorrectly as: Little Ivey. <2> Refer to L125 for a much better sound quality version of this same song.
L097: **Voodoo Child (slight return)** – Jimi (gi, vo), Mitch (dr), Noel (ba).
NOTE: Refer to L122 for a much better sound quality version of this same song.
L098: **Fire** – Jimi (gi, vo), Mitch (dr), Noel (ba).
L099: **Purple Haze** – Jimi (gi, vo), Mitch (dr), Noel (ba).
L100: **Wild Thing** – Jimi (gi, tongue-click), Mitch (dr), Noel (ba). Comp: Chip Taylor.
NOTES: <1> Incomplete. <2> 'Purple Haze' and 'Wild Thing' is a medley.
Plus: part of Room Full Of Mirrors [L093]: part of Bleeding Heart [L094].
THE LAST EXPERIENCE
  – CD: Bescol CD-42 [GER or ITA] – Released 80's
  – Also on CD (titled: Experience): Bulldog Records BDCD 40023 [ENG]
The Bescol release incorrectly states: His Final Live Performance.
Contains: Little Wing [L096]; Voodoo Child (slight return) [L097]; part of Room Full Of Mirrors [L093]; Fire [L098]; Purple Haze [L099]; Wild Thing [L100]; part of Bleeding Heart [L094]; The Sunshine Of Your Love [L092]; Room Full Of Mirrors [L093]; Bleeding Heart [L094]; Smashing Of Amps [L095].
GYPSY EYES; REMEMBER b/w PURPLE HAZE; STONE FREE
  – Track 2094 010 [ENG] – Released 10/71 – Maxi single
    Charts – entry: 50 (30/10/71); top position: 35; weeks in chart: 5
  – Not released [USA]
Contains: Gypsy Eyes [S042]; Remember [S016]; Purple Haze [S003]; Stone Free [S002].
ISLE OF WIGHT
  – Polydor 2302 016 [ENG] – Released 11/71 – *: entire release
    Charts – entry: 17 (20/11/71); top position: 17; weeks in chart: 2
  – Also on: Polydor 2310 139 [GER]; Barclay 80 462 [FRA]; not released [USA]
  – CD: Polydor 831 313–2 [GER]; Polydor P33P 25010 [JAP]; not released [USA]
<1> Concert introduction: Jeff Dexter. <2> All songs rec: Isle Of Wight Festival, England, 30/08/70, by Pye mobile, Mixing (1971): Carlos Olms. <3> 'Midnight Lightning' and 'Foxy Lady' is actually a medley. <4> The LP version released (Polydor 2310 151) in Spain was censored: 'Freedom' was completely removed!
L101: **Midnight Lightnin'** – Jimi (gi, vo), Mitch (dr), Billy (ba).
NOTES: <1> Jimi: 'I like to watch the lightning. Especially on the fields and flowers when I'm on my own.' <2> Refer to S765 for the first recorded version of this song. <3> Refer to S163 for a completely different song with the same title.
L102: **Foxy Lady** – Jimi (gi, vo), Mitch (dr), Billy (ba).
L103: **Lover Man** – Jimi (gi, vo), Mitch (dr), Billy (ba).
L104: **Freedom** – Jimi (gi, vo), Mitch (dr), Billy (ba).
L105: **All Along The Watchower** – Jimi (gi, vo), Mitch (dr), Billy (ba). Comp: Bob Dylan.
L106: **In From The Storm** – Jimi (gi, vo), Mitch (dr), Billy (ba).
THE FIRST GREAT ROCK FESTIVALS OF THE SEVENTIES: ISLE OF WIGHT/ATLANTA POP FESTIVAL (double)
  – *: Message To Love
  – Columbia G3X 30805 [USA] – Released 09/71

Charts – entry: 91 (18/09/71); top position: 47; weeks in chart: 9
– CBS 66311 [ENG] – Released 10/71
Charts – never
– CD: not released

<1> All listed songs rec: Isle Of Wight Festival, 30/08/70. <2> The rest of this release contains material by other artists.

L107:   Message To Love – Jimi (gi, vo), Mitch (dr), Billy (ba).
NOTE: Stated incorrectly as: Power To Love.
L108:   Midnight Lightnin' – Jimi (gi, vo), Mitch (dr), Billy (ba).
NOTE: This is the same version as L101. Differences: incomplete; different mix.
L109:   Foxy Lady – Jimi (gi, vo), Mitch (dr), Billy (ba).
NOTE: This is the same version as L102. Differences: incomplete; different mix.

RARE TRACKS
– Polydor 2482 274 [ENG] – Released 04/76
Charts – never
– Also on: Polydor MPF 1009 [JAP]; not released [USA]
– CD: not released

<1> One more song from Isle Of Wight Festival, 30/08/70. <2> The rest of this release contains material by other artists.

L110:   Dolly Dagger – Jimi (gi, vo), Mitch (dr), Billy (ba).

RAINBOW BRIDGE
– Reprise MS 2040 [USA] – Released 10/71 – *: entire release
Charts – entry: 69 (09/10/71); top position: 15; weeks in chart: 21
– Reprise K44159 [ENG] – Released 11/71
Charts – entry: 16 (04/12/71); top position: 16; weeks in chart: 10
– Also on: Reprise REP 54004 [GER]; Reprise 54004 [FRA]
– CD: not released

<1> Although the cover and labels state 'Original Motion Picture Sound Track', none of the recordings on this release is actually from the two live shows performed by Jimi, Mitch and Billy in Hawaii on 30/07/70. <2> In order to 'make room' for the *Crash Landing, Midnight Lightning* and *Nine To The Universe* releases, Reprise deleted this release in the USA (consequently this release is so far not available on CD). Unforgivable, as most of the studio recordings on this release, together with most of the songs on *The Cry Of Love* plus a few additional songs, were planned *by Jimi* to be released on a double-LP titled *The First Rays Of The New Rising Sun*.

S111:   Dolly Dagger – Jimi (gs, lv, hv), Mitch (dr), Billy (ba, fuzz bass), Juma (congas), unknown (pe), Arthur Allen & Albert Allen (hv), unknown (footstamping). Special effect: Jimi (Uni-Vibe with vibrato setting). Rec: ELE, 01/07/70. Engi: Eddie. Prod: Jimi.
NOTES: <1> This song was inspired by Devon Wilson (=Dolly Dagger). <2> Arthur Allen & Albert Allen a.k.a.: The Ghetto Fighters.
S112:   Earth Blues – Jimi (gs, lv, hv, voice), Buddy (dr, hv), Billy (ba), The Ronettes [Veronica Bennett & Estelle Bennett & Nedra Talley] (hv), Juma? (pe, maracas), unknown (ta), unknown (cow-bell). Special effect: Jimi (Uni-Vibe with vibrato setting). Rec: PLA, 19/12/69 (basic recording): PLA, 20/01/70 (additional recordings). Prod: Heaven Research Unlimited.
S113:   Pali Gap – Jimi (gs, voice), Mitch (dr), Billy (ba), Juma (pe, congas), unknown (ta), unknown (cow-bell). Special effect: Jimi (Uni-Vibe with vibrato setting). Rec: ELE, 01/07/70. Engi: Eddie. Prod: Jimi.
NOTE: Pali is the Goddess of the volcanoes in Hawaii.
S114:   Room Full Of Mirrors – Jimi (gs, vo), Buddy (dr), Billy (ba), Juma (pe, congas), unknown (cow-bell). Special effects: Jimi (slide via his ring

or bracelet; octavia). Rec: PLA, 17/11/69. Engi: Tony Bongiovi? Prod: Heaven Research Unlimited.

S115: **Star Spangled Banner** – Jimi (gs). Comp: Francis Scott Key. Special effect: Jimi (octavia). Rec: PLA, 18/03/69. Prod: Jimi.

NOTE: Jimi first recorded the basic track, then overdubbed more rhythm and solo guitar while the basic track was played at half speed, so when listening to this song at the normal speed, the guitar overdubs are at double speed.

S116: **Look Over Yonder** – Jimi (gs, vo, voice), Mitch (dr), Noel (ba). Rec: TTG, 22/10/68. Prod: Jimi.

NOTE: <1> Song a.k.a.: 'Mr Bad Luck'. <2> Jimi used to play 'Mr Bad Luck' during the live performances with his group Jimmy James & The Blue Flames in the Summer of 1966 in New York City. <3> Refer to S236 for 'Mr Bad Luck'.

L117: **Getting My Heart Back Together Again** – Jimi (gi, vo), Mitch (dr), Billy (ba). Rec: Berkeley Community Theatre, Berkeley, California, 30/05/70, 1st show.

S118: **Hey Baby (The Land Of The New Rising Sun)** – Jimi (gi, vo, voice), Mitch (dr), Bill (ba), Juma (pe). Special effect: Jimi (Uni-Vibe with vibrato setting at high speed). Rec: ELE, 01?/07/70. Engi: Eddie. Prod: Jimi.

NOTE: Song a.k.a.: 'Gypsy Boy (New Rising Sun)'.

DOLLY DAGGER b/w STAR SPANGLED BANNER
– Reprise 1044 [USA] – Release 10/71 – Single
Charts – entry: 89 (23/10/71); top position: 74; weeks in chart: 7
– Not released [ENG]

Contains: Dolly Dagger [S111]; Star Spangled Banner [S115].
Note: other singles on Reprise after this release did not chart . . .

HENDRIX IN THE WEST
– Polydor 2302 018 [ENG] – Released 01/72 – *: Johnny B. Goode; Little Wing; Red House
Charts – entry: 8 (12/02/72); top position: 7; weeks in chart: 12
– Reprise MS 2049 [USA] – Released 02/72
Charts – entry: 43 (04/03/72); top position: 12; weeks in chart: 19
– Also on: Polydor 2310 161 [GER]; Barclay 80 448 [FRA]
– CD; Polydor 831 312–2 [GER]; Polydor P33P 25004 [JAP]; not released [USA]

<1> All 24/02/69 songs rec (on 4 track, ½ inch): Royal Albert Hall, London. Engi: Glyn Johns. <2> The 24/05/69 song rec (by Willy Heider) on 8 track, 1 inch. Engi: Abe Jacobs. <3> All 30/05/70 songs rec: Berkeley Community Theatre, Berkeley, California. <4> All 30/08/70 songs rec: Isle Of Wight Festival, England.

L119: **Johnny B. Goode** – Jimi (gi, vo), Mitch (dr), Billy (ba). Comp: Chuck Berry. Rec: 30/05/70, 1st show.

L120: **Lover Man** – Jimi (gi, vo), Mitch (dr), Billy (ba). Rec: 30/05/70, 2nd show.

L121: **Blue Suede Shoes** – Jimi (gi, vo), Mitch (dr), Billy (ba). Comp: Carl Lee Perkins. Rec: 30/05/70, afternoon rehearsals.

NOTE: Slightly incomplete. Refer to L825 for the complete version.

L122: **Voodoo Child (slight return)** – Jimi (gi, vo), Mitch (dr), Noel (ba). Rec: 24/02/69.

L123: **God Save The Queen** – Jimi (gi), Mitch (dr), Billy (ba). Comp: Dr. John Ball. Rec: 30/08/70.

L124: **Sergeant Pepper's Lonely Hearts Club Band** – Jimi (gi, vo), Mitch (dr), Billy (ba). Comp: John Lennon & Paul McCartney. Rec: 30/08/70.

L125: **Little Wing** – Jimi (gi, vo), Mitch (dr), Noel (ba). Rec: 24/02/69.

L126: **Red House** – Jimi (gi, vo), Mitch (dr), Noel (ba). Rec: Sports Arena, San Diego, California, 24/05/69.

JOHNNY B. GOODE b/w LITTLE WING
- Polydor 2001–277 [ENG] – Released 01/72 – Single
  Charts – entry: 50 (12/02/72); top position: 35; weeks in chart: 5
- Also on: Polydor 2001 277 [GER]

Contains: Johnny B. Goode [L119]; Little Wing [L125].

MUSIQUE ORIGINALE DU FILM JIMI PLAYS BERKELEY
- Barclay 80.555 [FRA] – Released late 70's
- Not released [ENG]; not released [USA]
- CD: not released

This is not a soundtrack from the film *Jimi Plays Berkeley* as the title of this release may suggest. In fact only 'Johnny B. Goode' and 'Lover Man' are from Berkeley.

Contains: Johnny B. Goode [L119]; Purple Haze [S003]; Star Spangled Banner [L067]; Little Wing [L125]; Voodoo Child (slight return) [L122]; Machine Gun [L053]; I Don't Live Today [S012]; Lover Man [L120].

WAR HEROES
- Polydor 2302 020 [ENG] – Released 01/10/72 – *: Bleeding Heart; Tax Free; Midnight; Beginning
  Charts – entry: 40 (11/11/72); top position: 23; weeks in chart: 3
- Also on: Polydor 2310208 [GER]; Barclay 80467 [FRA]
- CD: Polydor 813 573–2 [GER]

S127: **Bleeding Heart** – Jimi (gs, vo), Mitch or Buddy (dr), Billy (ba), Juma and/or Jerry (cow-bell, pe), unknown (ta), unknown (rhythm gi). Comp: Elmore James. Rec: PLA, 18/12/69 and/or 24/03/70. Prod: Jimi.

S128: **Tax Free** – Jimi (gs), Mitch (dr), unknown – unlikely Noel – (ba), Steve Winwood? (or). Special effect: organ sound via Jimi's gi (unknown how this was achieved). Comp: Bo Hansson & Janne Karlsson. Rec: PLA, 01/05/68. Engi: Eddie? Prod: Jimi.

S129: **Peter Gunn** – Jimi (gi, voice), Mitch (dr), Billy (ba), Eddie (voice from control-room). Comp: Henry Mancini. Rec: PLA or ELE, mid 70. Engi: Eddie. Prod: Jimi.

NOTE: <1> 'Peter Gunn' was the first song Jimi learned to play during his Seattle childhood days. <2> 'Peter Gunn' and 'Catastrophe' is actually a medley.

S130: **Catastrophe** – Jimi (gi, vo, voice), Mitch (dr, voice), Billy (ba), Eddie (voice from control-room). Rec: PLA or ELE, mid 70. Engi: Eddie. Prod: Jimi.

NOTE: This song is in reality a take-off by Jimi of the song 'Jealousy' (comp: V. Bloom & Gade), popularised by Frankie Laine in late 1951. During the improvisation of 'Castastrophe' Jimi invents his own lyrics.

S131: **Stepping Stone** – Jimi (gs, vo), Buddy (dr), Billy (ba), Bob Hughes? (voice from control-room). Rec: PLA, 14/11/69. Engi: Bob Hughes. Prod: Heaven Research Unlimited. Wiped in 1972: Buddy (dr), Bob Hughes? (voice from control-room). Added in 1972: Mitch (dr).

NOTE: This is the same basic version as S050. Differences: new drum take; somewhat different mix. Refer to S050 for the unaltered and original version with Buddy (drums).

S132: **Midnight** – Jimi (gi), Mitch (dr), Noel (ba). Special effect: heavy phasing (on gi). Comp: Noel Redding. Rec: OLM, possibly 04/69. Prod: Jimi.

NOTE: Song a.k.a.: Trashman. Refer to S162 for Trashman.

S133: **3 Little Bears** – Jimi (gs, vo), Mitch (dr), Noel? (ba), unknown (cow-bell). Rec: PLA, 02/05/68. Engi: Gary or Eddie. Prod: Jimi.
NOTE: <1> Refer to S136 for the same version, but censored! <2> Incomplete. Refer to S782 for the complete version.
S134: **Beginning** – Jimi (gi), Mitch (dr), Billy (ba), Juma (bongos), Juma? (temple block). Comp: Mitch Mitchell. Rec: ELE, 16/06/70 and/or 01/07/70. Engi: Eddie. Prod: Jimi. Wiped in 1972: Juma (bongos), Juma? (temple block).
NOTE: <1> Song a.k.a.: 'Jam Back At The House'. <2> Slightly incomplete. <3> Refer to S738 for the complete and unaltered version.
S135: **Izabella** – Jimi (gs, lv, hv, voice), Buddy (dr, hv), Billy (ba), Juma and Jerry (ta, pe, maracas), unknown (hv). Rec: HIT, 28 and 29/08/69. Prod: Jimi or Heaven Research Unlimited.
NOTE: This is the same version as S051. Differences: slightly different mix; Jimi's voice mixed up front.
Plus: Highway Chile [S006].
WAR HEROES
   – Reprise MS 2103 [USA] – Released 12/72
     Charts – entry: 171 (09/12/72); top position: 48; weeks in chart: 18
   – CD: not released (see previous entry)
S136: **3 Little Bears** – Jimi (gs, vo), Mitch (dr), Noel? (ba), unknown (cow-bell). Rec: PLA, 02/05/68. Engi: Gary or Eddie. Prod: Jimi.
NOTE: On this release only, some of Jimi's lyrics ('oh fuck me, fuck me' and 'stop that shit, stop it' plus a few other words) were (in 1972) wiped out or remixed down very low. All European releases (see previous entry) contain the full lyrics, as originally sung and recorded by Jimi.
Plus: Bleeding Heart [S127]; Tax Free [S128]; Peter Gunn [S129]; Catastrophe [S130]; Stepping Stone [S131]; Midnight [S132]; Beginning [S134]; Izabella [S135].
WATERFALL b/w 51ST ANNIVERSARY
   – Barclay 61 389 [FRA] – Released 72 – Single
   – Not released [ENG]; not released [USA]
This is a re-release subtitled: Jimi Hendrix Story Vol 7.
S137: **Waterfall** – Jimi (gs, vo, turning a page with lyrics), Mitch (dr), Mitch? (ta), Noel (ba). Rec: OLY, 03/04/67. Prod: Chas.
NOTE: <1> Song a.k.a.: May This Be Love. <2> This is the same basic version as S013. Difference: slightly different mix. <3> This version has never been issued on any other release.
Plus: 51st Anniversary [S004].
ALL ALONG THE WATCHTOWER b/w CROSSTOWN TRAFFIC
   – Reprise 0742 [USA] – Released 83? – Single (stereo)
This is a re-release subtitled as: 'Back To Back Hits'.
Contains: All Along The Watchtower [S034]; Crosstown Traffic [S037].
ALL ALONG THE WATCHTOWER b/w CROSSTOWN TRAFFIC
   – Reprise GRE 0742 [USA] – Released 83? – Single (mono)
This is a re-release subtitled as: 'Back To Back Hits.'
S138: **All Along The Watchtower** – Jimi (gs, vo), Mitch (dr), Dave Mason (ba, acoustic gi), Mitch? (temple block), unknown (ta). Comp: Bob Dylan. Special effect: Jimi (slide-effect using the back of his cigarette lighter with the gi on his lap). Rec: OLY, 21/01/68 (basic track); PLA, 04/68 or 05/68 (transfer from 4 to 12 track, plus additional recordings). Eng: Eddie (OLY); Gary (PLA). Prod: Chas (OLY); Jimi (PLA). Wiped in (at PLA) 1968: Dave

Mason (ba). Added (at PLA) in 1968: Jimi (ba).
NOTE: This is the same basic version as S034. Difference: different mono mix. This version has never been released on any other release.
Plus: Crosstown Traffic [S037].
SOUND TRACK RECORDINGS FROM THE FILM JIMI HENDRIX (double)
- Reprise K 64017 [ENG] – Released 14/06/73 – *: Red House; Getting My Heart Back Together Again
  Charts – entry: 37 (21/07/73); top position: 37; weeks in chart: 1
- Reprise 2RS 6481 [USA] – Released 07/73
  Charts – entry: 150 (14/07/73); top position: 89; weeks in chart: 18
- Also on: Reprise REP 64 107 [GER]
- CD: not released

<1> There are 12 other short interviews with various other people on this release. <2> All 19/12/67 items rec: Bruce Fleming's photo studio, 12 Great Newport Street, London WC2. <3> All listed 30/08/70 songs rec: Isle Of Wight Festival, England.

L139: Machine Gun – Jimi (gi, vo), Mitch (dr), Billy (ba). Rec: 30/08/70.
NOTE: Incomplete. Refer to L698 for the complete version.
I140: Interview with Jimi – by Meatball Fulton. Rec: Jimi's flat, Upper Berkeley Street, London W1, mid 12/67.
NOTE: <1> This is on Side One (3rd item). <2> Refer to I295 for the complete interview.
L141: Purple Haze – Jimi (gi, vo), Mitch (dr), Billy (ba). Rec: Berkeley Community Theatre, Berkeley, California, 30/05/70, 1st show.
I142: Interview with Jimi – from the film *See My Music Talking* (a.k.a. *Experience*). Rec: 19/12/67.
NOTE: <1> This is on Side Two (1st item). <2> More of the interview can be seen in the film.
I143: Interview with Jimi – by unknown person. Rec: possibly Copter Lounge, Pan Am building, Manhattan, New York City, 30/01/68.
NOTE: This is on Side Two (4th item).
S144: Getting My Heart Back Together Again – Jimi (1960 Zemaitis 12-string acoustic gi, vo). Rec: 19/12/67.
I145: Interview with Jimi – by unknown person(s) or Hugh Curry. Rec: either Copter Lounge, Pan Am building, Manhattan, New York City, 30/01/68 or at Jimi's flat in Brook Street, London, 07/01/69 (by Hugh Curry).
NOTE: This is on Side Three (2nd item).
L146: Red House – Jimi (gi, vo), Mitch (dr), Billy (ba). Rec: 30/08/70.
Plus: Rock Me, Baby [L076]; Wild Thing [L081]; Johnny B. Goode [L119]; Hey Joe [L077]; Like A Rolling Stone [L075]; Star Spangled Banner [L067]; Machine Gun [L053]; In From The Storm [L106].
HEAR MY TRAIN A' COMIN' b/w ROCK ME, BABY
- Reprise K 14286 [ENG] – Released 08/73 – Single
  Chart – never
- Not released [USA]
Contains: Getting My Heart Back Together Again [S144]: Rock Me, Baby [L076].
LOOSE ENDS
- Polydor 2310 301 [ENG] – Released 02/74 – *: Electric Lady Land
  Charts – never
- Also on: Polydor 2310 301 [GER]; Barclay 80 491 [FRA]; not released [USA]

– CD: Polydor 837 574–2 [GER]; not released [USA]

S147: **Coming Down Hard On Me Baby** – Jimi (gs, vo), Mitch (dr), Billy (ba). Rec: ELE, 14?/07?/70. Engi: Eddie. Prod: Jimi.

S148: **Blue Suede Shoes** – Jimi (gi, vo, voice, drum, tongue-clicks), Buddy (dr, voice, coughing), Billy (ba). Comp: Carl Lee Perkins. Rec: PLA, 23/01/70. Engi: Jack Adams? Prod: Jimi.

NOTE: <1>Incomplete. This is the first part of a jam, which includes Jimi improvising on the opening lyrics of the song 'Heartbreak Hotel' (comp: Mae Boren Axton & Tommy Durden & Elvis Presley). The complete jam lasted well over 11 minutes and features Don – surname unknown – (harmonica). <2> Refer to S779 for another part of the complete jam.

S149: **Jam 292** – Jimi (gi), Dallas Taylor? (dr), unknown – not Noel – (ba). Stephen Stills? (pi). Rec: PLA, 14/05/69. Prod: Jimi.

NOTE: This jam was recorded without a title, and the tape number was simply used for the title.

S150: **Drifter's Escape** – Jimi (gs, vo), Mitch (dr), Mitch? (ta), Billy (ba), unknown (cow-bell). Special effect: Jimi (octavia). Comp: Bob Dylan. Rec: ELE, 15?/05?/70. Engi: Eddie. Prod: Jimi.

S151: **Burning Desire** – Jimi (gi, lv, voice), Buddy (dr, cow-bell, hv), Billy (ba, hv). Rec: PLA, between 15/12/69 and 23/01/70. Prod: Jimi.

S152: **I'm Your Hoochie Coochie Man** – Jimi (gi, lv, voice), Buddy (dr, hv, voice, laughing), Billy (ba). Comp: Willie Dixon. Rec: PLA, between 15/12/69 and 23/01/70. Prod: Jimi.

S153: **Electric Lady Land** – Jimi (gi, voice), Buddy (dr), Gary (voice from control-room). Special effect: Jimi (tremolo). Rec: PLA, 14/06/68. Engi: Gary. Prod: Jimi. Wiped in 1973: Buddy (dr).

Plus: The Stars That Play With Laughing Sam's Dice [S020].

CRASH LANDING

– Reprise MS 2204 [USA] – Released 03/75 – *: Message To Love; With The Power; lyrics of Somewhere

Charts – entry: 61 (22/03/75); top position: 5; weeks in chart: 20

– Polydor 2310 398 [ENG] – Released 08/75

Charts – entry: 36 (30/08/75); top position: 35; weeks in chart: 2

– CD: Polydor 827 932–2 [GER]; Reprise 2204–2 [USA]; Polydor P33P 25024 [JAP]

<1> This is the first of the 'Douglas albums'. Apart from Jimi, almost all of the instrumentation of the musicians who made the original recordings with Jimi was subsequently wiped out in 1974/75 by Alan Douglas, and replaced by several session musicians trying to play along with tape recordings of Jimi's original guitars and vocals. None of these session musicians ever played with Jimi. <2> On some of the releases credit as composer for 5 of the 8 songs is stated incorrectly as: Hendrix-Douglas. When asked for an explanation for this, Alan Douglas said 'that's a political problem' . . . <3> Thanks to a massive publicity campaign of several months before its release promising 'here comes the new Jimi Hendrix', coupled with the fact that in those days listening to LP's in USA shops before buying wasn't common, *Crash Landing* may have been a commercial success but that's no measure of artistic quality. Some reviewers liked the stuff (*Billboard* 22/03/75: 'Jimi at his best') but most others did question the exercise of taking off original musicians – from 'Is there morality in rock and roll?' (*Melody Maker* 30/08/75) to 'The release of this album stinks' (*Sounds* 04/10/75).

S154: **Message To Love** – Jimi (gs, lv, hv), Buddy (dr, hv), Billy (ba), Billy? (hv), Juma? (cow-bell), unknown (ta). Rec: PLA, 12/69 or 01/70. Engi:

Tony Bongiovi? Prod: Jimi. Wiped in 1974: Buddy (his drum ending).

NOTE: <1> Slightly incomplete. <2> Credit is given on the cover to Jimmy Maeulen for percussion (added in 1974), however all percussion appears to be from the original recording session. <3> Refer to S724 for the complete unaltered and original version.

S155: **Somewhere** – Jimi (gi, vo), Buddy (dr), Noel? (ba), unknown (rhythm gi). Rec: CEN, 13/03/68 (basic track). Prod: Chas. Wiped in 1974: Buddy (dr), Noel? (ba). Added in 1974: Jeff Mironov (gi), Alan Schwartzberg (dr), Bob Babbit (ba).

NOTE: <1> Stated incorrectly as: 'Somewhere Over The Rainbow'. <2> Slightly incomplete. Refer to S768 for the complete and unaltered version.

S156: **Crash Landing** – Jimi (gi, vo), unknown – not Mitch or Buddy – (dr), unknown – not Noel or Billy – (ba), unknown (or). Rec: PLA, 24/04/69. Prod: Jimi. Wiped in 1974: Jimi (bits of vo), unknown – not Mitch or Buddy – (dr), unknown – not Noel or Billy – (ba), unknown (or). Added in 1975: Jeff Mironov (gi/gs?), Alan Schwartzberg (dr), Bob Babbit (ba), Jimmy Maeulen (cow-bell, pe), Linda November (hv), Vivian Cherry (hv), Barbara Massey (hv).

NOTE: <1> This song was (partly) inspired by Devon Wilson. <2> Refer to S820 for the unaltered and original version.

S157: **Coming Down Hard On Me Baby** – Jimi (gs, vo), Mitch (dr), Billy (ba). Rec: ELE, 14?/07/70. Engi: Eddie. Prod: Jimi. Wiped in 1974: Mitch (dr), Billy (ba). Added in 1974: Jeff Mironov (gi), Alan Schwartzberg (dr), Bob Babbit (ba).

NOTE: Refer to S147 for the unaltered and original version.

S158: **Peace In Mississippi** – Jimi (solo gi, rhythm gi), Mitch (dr), Noel (ba). Rec: TTG, 24/10/68. Prod: Jimi. Wiped in 1974: Jimi (rhythm gi), Mitch (dr), Noel (ba), delay effects. Added in 1974: Jeff Mironov (rhythm gi), Alan Schwartzberg (dr), Bob Babbit (ba), Jimmy Maeulen (pe).

NOTE: Refer to S769 for a slightly less altered version.

S159: **With The Power** – Jimi (gs, lv, hv), Buddy (dr, hv), Billy (ba), Billy? (hv), Juma (cow-bell). Rec: PLA, 21/11/69. Engi: Tony Bongiovi? Prod: Jimi. Wiped in 1974: Jimi (bits of several guitar solos/overdubs, bits of lv), Buddy (drum break), Juma (cow-bell). Added in 1974; Jimmy Maeulen (pe).

NOTE: <1> Incomplete. Refer to S798 for the complete unaltered and original version. <2> Originally recorded with the working title: Paper Airplanes. <3> With The Power a.k.a.: Power Of Soul. <4> Emeretta Marks: Jimi missed the turn-around. So they emptied the studio and I sat down on the carpet and Jimi would play and I would nod to Jimi and count the bars, 'cause I don't think Jimi ever counted the bars . . .'

S160: **Stone Free** – Jimi (gs, lv), Mitch (dr, voice), Noel (ba, hv), Andy Fairweather Low (hv), Roger Chapman (hv), unknown (ta), unknown (cow-bell), unknown (coughing), unknown (2 hand-claps). Rec: PLA, 07 and 08/04/69. Engi: Gary. Prod: Jimi. Wiped in 1974: Jimi (bits of several gi solos/overdubs, bits of lv), Mitch (dr, voice), Noel (ba), unknown (ta), unknown (cow-bell), unknown (coughing), unknown (2 hand-claps). Added in 1974: Jeff Mirinov (gs), Alan Schwartzberg (dr), Bob Babbit (ba), Jimmy Maeulen (pe); compresser (used on Jimi's lv).

NOTE: Incomplete. Refer to S725 for the complete unaltered and original version.

S161: **M.L.K.** – Jimi (gi), Buddy (dr, cow-bell), Billy (ba). Special effect: Jimi (Uni-Vibe with chorus setting). Rec: PLA, late 69 or early 70. Engi: Jack

546

Adams. Prod: Jimi. Added in 1970 (by Jimi): some backward gi. Mixed (in 1972): Alex Trevor (ELE). Wiped in 1974: Buddy (dr, cow-bell), Billy (small bits of ba). Added in 1974: Alan Schwartzberg (dr), Jimmy Maeulen (slinky). Added in 1974: heavy echo delay in order to create a sound of more than 1 lead guitar.

NOTE: <1> Incomplete. <2> The original basic track contains only 1 lead guitar. Refer to S777 for the complete and unaltered basic track version. <3> 'M.L.K.' for (Martin Luther King) is incorrectly titled as: 'Captain Coconut'.<4>Les Kahn (one of the 1974 engineers): 'That came from 3 different things, we found the master for that whole center part, but not the beginning or the end, which was a compositive. We had to work with the mix, though, we didn't have the masters . . . the title that was on the box was "M.L.K." and that showed up here and there and we couldn't find out what the fuck that meant.'

MIDNIGHT LIGHTNIN'
- Reprise MS 2229 [USA] – Released 11/75 – *: Gypsy Boy (The New Rising Sun)
  Charts – entry: 96 (29/11/75); top position: 43; weeks in chart: 11
- Polydor 2310 415 [ENG] – Released 11/75
  Charts – never
- CD: Polydor 825 166–2 [GER]; Polydor P33P 25025 [JAP]; not released [USA]

<1> This is the second of the 'Douglas albums' with original musicians wiped and replaced by musicians Jimi never played with. <2> Considered by many to be the worst commercial Jimi Hendrix release ever put out on the market. *Melody Maker* 22/11/75: 'Let us be rid of these turbulent producers.' *Stereo Review* 03/76: 'It proves only that the commercial necrophilia about Hendrix is of the most relentless and nauseating type, and that the producers of this jerk-puppet series are perhaps of the family Frankenstein. The public should boycott such body-snatching.' *The Cincinnati Enquirer* 07/12/75: 'Douglas has assumed the presumptuous roles of producer and artist. He is not Hendrix. Douglas has no right or wit to edit and refine what to Hendrix were formative musical investigations. "Midnight Lightning" shows that in the eyes of Douglas and Warner records, Jimi Hendrix still is not an artist. He remains a commodity to be exploited.'

S162: **Trashman** – Jimi (gi), Mitch (dr), Noel (ba). Comp: Noel Redding. Rec: OLM, possibly 04/69. Prod: Jimi. Wiped in 1975: Mitch (dr), Noel (ba). Added in 1975: Jeff Mironov (gi), Alan Schwartzberg (dr), Bob Babbit (ba).

NOTE: Song a.k.a.: 'Midnight'. Refer to S132 for 'Midnight'.

S163: **Midnight Lightnin'** – Jimi (gi, vo), Mitch (dr), Billy? (ba), Juma? (congas). Rec: PLA, likely 23/03/70. Prod: Jimi. Wiped in 1975: Jimi (bit of vo), Mitch (dr), Billy? (da), Juma? (congas). Re-arranged in 1975: song order and some of Jimi's vocals. Added in 1975: Jeff Mironov (gi), Lance Quinn (gi), Alan Schwartzberg (dr), Bob Babbit (ba), Jimmy Maeulen (pe), Maeretha Stewart (hv), Hilda Harris (hv), Vivian Cherry (hv).

NOTE: <1> The lyrics include bits of various nursery rhymes. <2> Incomplete. Refer to S718 for most of the unaltered and original version. <3> This 'Midnight Lightnin'' is an entirely different song with the same title as L101.

S164: **Getting My Heart Back Together Again** – Jimi (gi, vo), Mitch (dr), Noel (ba). Rec: OLM, 02?/04/69. Prod: Jimi. Wiped in 1975: Noel (ba). Added in 1975: Jeff Mironov (gi), Bob Babbit (ba), Alan Schwartzberg (shaker).

S165: **Gypsy Boy (New Rising Sun)** – Jimi (gi, vo, voice), Buddy (dr), Billy (ba). Special effect: Jimi (Uni-Vibe with chorus setting at slow speed). Rec:

PLA, 16/02/70. Prod: Jimi. Wiped in 1975: Jimi (voice), Buddy (dr), Billy (ba). Added in 1975: Lance Quinn (gi), Alan Schwartzberg (dr, pe), Bob Babbit (ba), Maeretha Stewart (hv), Hilda Harris (hv), Vivian Cherry (hv).

NOTE- Song a.k.a.: 'Hey Baby (The Land Of The New Rising Sun)'.

S166: **Blue Suede Shoes** – Jimi (gi, vo, voice, drum teaching, tongue-clicks), Buddy (dr, voice, coughing), Billy (ba). Don – surname unknown – (ha). Comp: Carl Lee Perkins. Rec: PLA, 23/01/70. Engi: Jack Adams? Prod: Jimi. Wiped in 1975: Jimi (voice, drum teaching), Buddy (dr, voice, coughing), Billy (ba), Don – surname unknown – (ha). Added in 1975: Jeff Mironov (gi), Alan Schwartzberg (dr), Bob Babbit (ba). 1975: song order re-arranged.

NOTE: Incomplete. Refer to S148 for a small first part of the unaltered and original jam. Refer to S779 for another unaltered part.

S167: **Izabella/Machine Gun** – Jimi (gs, vo), Buddy? (dr), Billly (ba), Larry (rhythm gi), Juma? (cow-bell), Jerry (pe), unknown (ta). Rec: HIT, 29/08/69. Prod: Jimi. Wiped in 1975: Buddy? (dr), Billy (ba), Larry (rhythm gi), Juma? (cow-bell), Jerry (pe). Added in 1975: Lance Quinn (gi), Alan Schwartzberg (dr), Bob Babbit (ba).

NOTE: <1> The medley of 'Izabella'/'Machine Gun' is given only as: 'Machine Gun'. <2> Incomplete. Refer to S719 for the complete unaltered and original version.

S168: **Once I Had A Woman** – Jimi (gi, vo), Buddy (dr), Billy (ba), Don – surname unknown – (ha). Rec: PLA, 23/01/70. Engi: Jack Adams? Prod: Jimi. Wiped in 1975: Buddy (dr), Billy (ba), Don – surname unknown – (ha). Added in 1975: Lance Quinn (gi), Alan Schwartzberg (dr), Bob Babbit (ba), Buddy Lucas (ha), Maeretha Stewart (hv), Hilda Harris (hv), Vivian Cherry (hv). 1975: song order re-arranged.

NOTE: <1> Incomplete. Refer to S775 for a part of the unaltered version. <2> The song title was made up in 1975, Jimi didn't give it a name while recording the jam.

S169: **Beginning** – Jimi (gi), Mitch (dr), Billy (ba), Juma (bongos), Juma? (temple block). Comp: Mitch Mitchell. Rec: ELE, 16/06/70 and/or 01/07/70. Engi: Eddie. Prod: Jimi. Wiped in 1975: Mitch (dr), Billy (ba), Juma (bongos), Juma? (temple block). Added in 1975: Jeff Mironov (gi), Alan Schwartzberg (dr), Bob Babbit (ba), Jimmy Maeulen (pe).

NOTE: <1> Song a.k.a.: 'Jam Back At The House'. <2> Refer to S134 for most of a less altered version. Refer to S738 for the complete unaltered and original version.

THE ESSENTIAL JIMI HENDRIX (double)
    – Reprise 2RS 2245 [USA] – Released 07/78
        Charts – entry: 144 (12/08/78); top position: 114; weeks in chart: 15
    – Polydor 2612 034 – labels state 2335–134 and 2335–135– [ENG]
    – Released 08/78
        Charts – never
    – Also on: Polydor MPZ 8109/10 [JAP]
    – CD: not released (but see two entries down)

<1> 'Gloria' comes on a separate one-sided single, but is not included with the Reprise release. <2> The voice of the engineer ('you made it') on 'Stepping Stone' has been edited out.

S170: **Gloria** – Jimi (gi, vo), Mitch (dr), Noel (ba). Comp: Van Morrison. Rec: TTG, 10/68. Prod: Jimi.

NOTE: Incomplete.

548

Plus: Are You Experienced [S017]; Third Stone From The Sun [S015]; Purple Haze [S003]; Little Wing [S026]; If Six Was Nine [S027]; Bold As Love [S033]; Little Miss Lover [S032]; Castles Made Of Sand [S029]; Gypsy Eyes [S042]; The Burning Of The Midnight Lamp [S019]; Voodoo Child (slight return) [S048]; Have You Ever Been (To Electric Ladyland) [S036]; Still Raining, Still Dreaming [S046]; House Burning Down [S047]; All Along The Watchtower [S034]; Room Full Of Mirrors [S114]; Izabella [S135]; Freedom [S082]; Dolly Dagger [S111]; Stepping Stone [S131]; Drifting [S083]; Ezy Ryder [S084].

THE ESSENTIAL JIMI HENDRIX VOLUME TWO
- Reprise 2RS 2293 [USA] – Released 07/79
  Charts – entry: 180 (18/08/79); top position: 156; weeks in chart: 7
- Polydor 2311 014 [ENG] – Released 01/81
  Charts – never
- CD: not released (but see next entry)
'Gloria' comes on a separate one-sided single, but is not included with the Polydor release.
Contains: Hey Joe [S001]; Fire [S014]; Foxy Lady [S007]; The Wind Cries Mary [S005]; I Don't Live Today [S012]; Crosstown Traffic [S037]; Wild Thing [L081]; Machine Gun [L053]; Star Spangled Banner [L067]: Gloria [S170].

THE ESSENTIAL JIMI HENDRIX VOLUMES ONE AND TWO
- Double CD (only): Reprise 26035–2 [USA] – Released 11/89
Contains: Are You Experienced [S017]; Third Stone From The Sun [S015]; Purple Haze [S003]; Hey Joe [S001]; Fire [S014]; Foxy Lady [S007]; The Wind Cries Mary [S005]; Little Wing [S026]; If 6 Was 9 [S027]; Bold As Love [S033]; Little Miss Lover [S032]; Castles Made Of Sand [S029]; Gypsy Eyes [S042]; The Burning Of The Midnight Lamp [S019]; Voodoo Child (slight return) [S048]; Crosstown Traffic [S037]; Still Raining, Still Dreaming [S046]; Have You Ever Been (To Electric Ladyland) [S036]; All Along The Watchtower [S034]; House Burning Down [S047]; Room Full Of Mirrors [S114]; Izabella [S135]; Freedom [S082]; Dolly Dagger [S111]; Stepping Stone [S131]; Drifting [S083]; Ezy Ryder [S084]; Wild Thing [L081]; Machine Gun [L053]; Star Spangled Banner [L067]: Gloria [S170].

NINE TO THE UNIVERSE
- Reprise HS 2299 [USA] – Released 03/80 – *: Young/Hendrix; Easy Blues
  Charts – entry: 181 (26/04/80); top position: 127; weeks in chart: 7
- Polydor 2344 155 [ENG] – Released 06/80
  Charts – never
- Also on: Polydor KI 8007 – labels state MPF 1311 – [JAP]
- CD: not released
<1> This is what one could call a jam session album. During Jimi's career he would jam with just about anybody. Frequently Jimi would also take those musicians into the studio with him, either just for fun or to try out his musical ideas. Jack Adams (engineer at the Record Plant in 1969): 'They would come in and jam all night. One song would blend right into the next one, but later on he'd remember every single one.' <2> All song titles (except 'Message From Nine To The Universe') were made up in 1979/80. Jimi didn't give any of the jams a name while recording them. <3> This release came out in Brazil in late 1979 with a different cover and a different song order as: *Message From Nine To The Universe* (on WEA 38.023).

S171:   **Message From Nine To The Universe** – Jimi (gi, lv, voice), Buddy (dr), Billy (ba), Devon Wilson (hv). Rec: PLA, 22/05/69. Prod: Jimi. Wiped in 1979/80: Devon Wilson (hv).

NOTE: <1> Incomplete. Refer to S790 for the complete version. <2> This is an early try-out version of 'Message To Love'.
S172:   **Jimi/Jimmy Jam** – Jimi (gi), Mitch or Buddy (dr), Dave Holland (ba), Jim McCarty (gi). Special effect: Jimi (octavia). Rec: PLA, 25/03/69. Prod: Jimi.
NOTE: Incomplete. Refer to S789 for the complete version.
S173:   **Young/Hendrix** – Jimi (gi), Buddy? (dr), Billy (ba), Larry Young (or). Rec: PLA, 14/05/69. Prod: Jimi.
NOTE: Incomplete.
S174:   **Easy Blues** – Jimi (gi, voice), Mitch (dr), Billy (ba), Larry (rhythm gi), unknown (ta). Special effect: Jimi (Uni-Vibe with chorus setting at slow speed). Rec: HIT, Autumn 69. Prod: Jimi.
NOTE: <1> The tambourine appears to have been added via an overdub in 1969.
<2> Incomplete. Refer to S848 for the complete version, without the tambourine.
S175:   **Drone Blues** – Jimi (gi), unknown – not Mitch or Buddy – (dr), unknown – not Noel or Billy – (ba). Rec: PLA, 24/04/69. Prod: Jimi.
NOTE: Incomplete. Refer to S781 for the complete version.
THE JIMI HENDRIX CONCERTS (double)
       – Reprise 2306–1 [USA] – Released 08/82 – *: Stone Free; Are You Experienced; Little Wing; Bleeding Heart
       – CBS 88592 [ENG, pressed in HOL] – Released 08/82
       Charts – entry: 16 (21/08/82); top position: 16; weeks in chart: 5
       – Also on: Frituna FRIX-178 [SWE]
       – Single CD: Media Motion Media CD 1 [ENG]; Polydor P33P 25038 [JAP]; not released [USA], but see next entry
<1> All listed 10/68 songs rec (on 8 track, 1 inch): Winterland, San Francisco, California. <2> All 24/02/69 songs rec: Royal Albert Hall, London. <3> 'New York Pop' song recorded on 8 track, 1 inch. <4> The Media Motion Media CD [ENG] omits all the song introductions by Jimi. All other CD releases include these introductions.
L176:   **Fire** – Jimi (gi, lv), Mitch (dr), Noel (ba, faint hv). Rec: 12/10/68, 1st show.
L177:   **I Don't Live Today** – Jimi (gi, lv), Mitch (dr), Noel (ba, hv). Rec: Sports Arena, San Diego, California, 24/05/69.
L178:   **Red House** – Jimi (gi, vo), Mitch (dr), Billy (ba). Rec: 'New York Pop', Downing Stadium, Randall's Island, New York, 17/07/70.
L179:   **Stone Free** – Jimi (gi, vo), Mitch (dr, cow-bell), Noel (ba). Rec: 24/02/69.
NOTE: Incomplete (part of drum solo wiped in 1982). Refer to L709 for the complete version.
L180:   **Are You Experienced** – Jimi (gi, vo), Mitch (dr), Noel (ba). Rec: 10/10/68, 1st show.
L181:   **Little Wing** – Jimi (gi, vo), Mitch (dr), Noel (ba). Rec: 12/10/68, 2nd show.
L182:   **Voodoo Child (slight return)** – Jimi (gi, vo), Mitch (dr), Noel (ba). Rec: 10/10/68, 1st show.
L183:   **Bleeding Heart** – Jimi (gi, vo), Mitch (dr), Noel (ba). Comp: Elmore James. Rec: 24/02/69.
NOTE: This is the same version as L094, now in much better quality.
L184:   **Wild Thing** – Jimi (gi, tongue-click, vo), Mitch (dr), Noel (ba). Comp: Chip Taylor. Rec: 12/10/68, 1st show.
L185:   **Getting My Heart Back Together Again** – Jimi (gi, vo), Mitch (dr), Noel (ba). Rec: 10/10/68, 2nd show.
NOTE: Incomplete (edited in 1982). Refer to L801 for the completed version.
Plus: Hey Joe [L064].

550

THE JIMI HENDRIX CONCERTS
- Reprise 9 2306–2 [USA] – Released 11/89 – Single CD (only)
- Castle Communications CCSCD 235 [FRA, available in ENG] – Single CD (only)

L186: **Foxy Lady** – Jimi (gi, lv), Mitch (dr), Noel (ba, hv). Rec: The Forum, Los Angeles, California, 26/04/69.

Plus: Fire [L176]; I Don't Live Today [L177]; Red House [L178]; Stone Free [L179]; Are You Experienced [L180]; Little Wing [L181]; Voodoo Child (slight return) [L182]; Bleeding Heart [L183]; Hey Joe [L064]; Wild Thing [L184]; Getting My Heart Back Together Again [L185].

THE SINGLES ALBUM (double)
- Polydor PODV 6 [ENG] – Released 02/83
Charts – never
- Also on: Polydor 2625 047 – labels state 2335 267 and 2335 268 – [HOL] Not released [USA]
- Double CD: Polydor 827 369–2 [GER]; not released [USA]

Contains: Hey Joe [S001]; Stone Free [S002]; Purple Haze [S003]; 51st Anniversary [S004]; The Wind Cries Mary [S005]; Highway Chile [S006]; The Burning Of The Midnight Lamp [S019]; The Stars That Play With Laughing Sam's Dice [S020]; All Along The Watchtower [S034]; Long Hot Summer Night [S040]; Crosstown Traffic [S037]; Fire [S014]; Voodoo Child (slight return) [S048]; Angel [S089]; Night Bird Flying [S085]; Gypsy Eyes [S042]; Remember [S016]; Johnny B. Goode [L119]; Little Wing [L125]; Foxy Lady [S007]; Manic Depression [S008]; 3rd Stone From The Sun [S015]; Gloria [S170].

KISS THE SKY
- Reprise 25119 [USA] – Released 10/84
Charts – entry: 182 (17/11/84); top position: 148; weeks in chart: 5
- Polydor 823 704-1 [ENG, pressed in GER] – Released 11/84
Charts – never
- CD; Reprise 9 25119-2 [USA]; Polydor 823 704-2 [GER]

S187: **Red House** – Jimi (gi, vo, voice), Mitch (dr), Noel (bass strings of a normal 6-string gi, probably owned by Alexis Korner). Rec: CBS, 13/12/66. Engi: Mike Ross. Prod: Chas.

NOTE: This is the same version as S049. Difference: addition of a few seconds of studio chat by Jimi.

Plus: Are You Experienced? [S017]; I Don't Live Today [L177]; Voodoo Child (slight return) [S048]; Stepping Stone [S050]; Castle Made Of Sand [S029]; Killin' Floor [L073]: Purple Haze [S003]; Crosstown Traffic [S037]; Third Stone From The Sun [S015]; All Along The Watchtower [S034].

JOHNNY B. GOODE
- Capitol MLP 15022 [USA] – Released 06/86 – Mini LP – *: Machine Gun
Charts – never
- Capitol/EMI FA 3160 [ENG] – Released 86 – Mini LP
Charts – never
- CD: not released

All 04/07/70 songs rec: 2nd Atlanta Pop Festival, Middle Georgia Raceway, Byron, Georgia.

L188: **All Along The Watchtower** – Jimi (gi, vo), Mitch (dr), Billy (ba). Comp: Bob Dylan. Rec: 04/07/70.

NOTE: The liner notes incorrectly state that Jimi 'so often' forgot the lyrics of this song.

L189: **Star Spangled Banner** – Jimi (gi). Comp: Francis Scott Key. Rec: 04/07/70.

London,
December 1967

L190: **Machine Gun** – Jimi (gi, vo), Mitch (dr), Billy (ba). Rec: Berkeley
Community Theatre, Berkeley, California, 30/05/70, 2nd show.
NOTE: This song cannot be seen in the *Johnny B. Goode* video as the liner
notes may suggest.
Plus: part of Voodoo Child (slight return) [L061]; Johnny B. Goode [L119].
LIVE AT WINTERLAND
- Single CD: Rykodisc RCD 20038 [USA] – Released 05/87 – *: Manic
Depression; Red House; Tax Free
Charts (*Billboard* CD Top-30) – entry 29: (23/05/87); top position:
11; weeks in chart: 15
- Also on: Polydor 833 004–2 [GER] – Single CD
- Also on: Ryko 0038 [USA] – Double LP; Polydor 833–004–1 [GER]
- Double LP
<1> The songs on the LP releases are actually on three sides (plus 1 blank). <2>
All songs rec: Winterland, San Francisco, California. <3> Concert introduction: Bill
Graham.

552

L191: **Fire** – Jimi (gi, vo), Mitch (dr), Noel (ba), Herbie Rich (or). Rec: 11/10/68, 2nd show. Wiped in 1986: Herbie Rich (or).

NOTE: Refer to L807 for the unaltered and original version.

L192: **Manic Depression** – Jimi (gi, vo), Mitch (dr), Noel (ba). Rec: 12/10/68, 2nd show.

L193: **The Sunshine Of Your Love** – Jimi (gi), Mitch (dr), Noel (ba). Comp: Pete Brown & Jack Bruce & Eric Clapton. Rec: 10/10/68, 2nd show.

NOTE: Jimi's spoken introduction rec: 12/10/68, 2nd show.

L194: **Spanish Castle Magic** – Jimi (gi, vo), Mitch (dr), Noel (ba). Rec: 12/10/68, 2nd show.

L195: **Red House** – Jimi (gi, vo), Mitch (dr), Noel (ba). Rec: 11/10/68, 1st show.

L196: **Killin' Floor** – Jimi (gi, vo), Mitch (dr), Jack Casady (ba). Comp: Howlin' Wolf. Rec: 10/10/68, 2nd show.

197: **Tax Free** – Jimi (gi), Mitch (dr), Noel (ba). Comp: Bo Hansson & Janne Karlsson. Rec: 11/10/68, 2nd show.

NOTE: Slightly incomplete (bass solo edited in 1986).

L198: **Foxy Lady** – Jimi (gi, vo), Mitch (dr), Noel (ba), Herbie Rich (or). Rec: 11/10/68, 2nd show. Wiped in 1986: Herbie Rich (or).

NOTE: Refer to L808 for the unaltered and original version.

L199: **Hey Joe** – Jimi (gi, vo), Mitch (dr), Noel (ba). Comp: William M. Roberts. Rec: 12/10/68, 1st show.

L200: **Purple Haze** – Jimi (gi, lv), Mitch (dr), Noel (ba, faint hv). Rec: 12/10/68, 1st show.

Plus: Wild Thing [L184].

RADIO ONE (double)

– Ryko Analogue RALP 0078–2 [USA] – Released 11/88 – *: entire release
– Also on: Castle Communications CCSLP 212 [ENG] – Released early 89
– Single CD: Rykodisc RCD 20078 [USA]; Castle Communications CCSCD 212 [ENG]

<1> All songs are mono. <2> The CD alone sold well over 300,000 copies in the USA, while in the UK the 100,000 mark was reached (figure for all formats together).

S201: **Stone Free** – Jimi (gi, lv, hv), Mitch (dr), Noel (ba, hv). Rec: BBCA, 13/02/67. Prod: Bill Bebb & Jimmy Grant. First brc: 'Saturday Club', BBC Light, 18/02/67.

S202: **Radio One** – Jimi (gi, vo), Mitch (dr), Noel (ba). Rec: BBCB, 15/12/67. Engi: Pete Ritzema. Prod: Bernie Andrews & Bev Phillips. First brc: 'Top Gear', BBC Radio 1, 24/12/67.

NOTE: <1> Slightly incomplete (some studio chat wiped out). Refer to S480 for the complete version. <2> This song was worked out by the Experience in advance and was not, as the liner notes state, an 'impromptu' jingle recorded 'at the end of a session' with 'five minutes to kill'. In fact this song was the first one recorded during the recording session.

S203: **Day Tripper** – Jimi (gi, lv), Mitch (dr, hv), Noel (ba, hv). Comp: John Lennon & Paul McCartney. Rec: BBCB, 15/12/67. Engi: Pete Ritzema. Prod: Bernie Andrews & Bev Phillips. First brc: 'Top Gear', BBC Radio 1, 24/12/67.

NOTE: The liner notes incorrectly hint that the Beatles were involved on harmony vocals.

S204: **Killin' Floor** – Jimi (gi, vo, tongue-clicks), Mitch (dr), Mitch? (hand-claps), Noel (ba). Comp: Howling Wolf. Rec: BBCA, 28/03/67. Prod: Bill Bebb & Jimmy Grant. First brc: 'Saturday Club', BBC Light, 01/04/67.

S205: **Love Or Confusion** – Jimi (gi, vo), Mitch (dr), Noel (ba). Rec: BBCB, 13/02/67. Prod: Bill Bebb & Jimmy Grant. First brc: 'Saturday Club', BBC Light, 18/02/67.

S206: **Drivin' South** – Jimi (gi), Mitch (dr), Noel (ba). Rec: BBCB, 06/10/67. Engi: Pete Ritzema. Prod: Bernie Andrews & Bev Phillips.

NOTE: <1> The liner notes incorrectly state that this song was first broadcast on 'Top Gear' in 1967. This song is an alternate version which in fact was never broadcast by the BBC until the release of *Radio One* itself. <2> 'Drivin' South' was copyrighted on 25/02/70 at the United States Copyright Office (Alexandria, Virginia), and credited as its composer: Curtis McNear [a.k.a.: Curtis Knight]. However, the true composer of 'Drivin' South' according to Curtis Knight himself is Jimi Hendrix! During a live concert of Jimi (when he was known as Jimmy James) with the group Curtis Knight & The Squires on 26/12/65 at George's Club 20, Hackensack, New Jersey – as released on the LP *Welcome Home* on Astan 201020 [GER] – Curtis Knight introduced 'Drivin' South' as follows: 'Right now we're gonna feature Jimmy James, Jimmy's gonna do a little tune for you, one of his own selection.' After the song is finished Curtis Knight even adds more evidence: 'How about it ladies and gentleman? . . . That's an original tune wrote by Jimmy, a little thing entitled, written I should say, wrote-written-written-wrote, called "Drivin' South" . . .'

S207: **Catfish Blues** – Jimi (gi, vo), Mitch (dr), Noel (ba). Comp: Muddy Waters. Rec: BBCB, 06/10/67. Engi: Pete Ritzema. Prod: Bernie Andrews & Bev Phillips. First brc: 'Top Gear', BBC Radio 1, 15/10/67.

NOTE: <1> This song is actually a combination of parts from several blues songs: 'Rollin Stone' (comp: Muddy Waters), and 'Two Trains Running' (comp: L.J. Welch) which is a.k.a.: 'Still A Fool'. Jimi himself called his treatment: 'Experiencing The Blues'. <2> Surprisingly enough some of the lyrics must have escaped the Beeb's Censorship department in 1967!

S208: **Wait Until Tomorrow** – Jimi (gi, lv), Mitch (dr, hv), Noel (ba, hv, voice). Rec: BBCB, 15/12/67. Engi: Pete Ritzema. Prod: Bernie Andrews & Bev Phillips. First brc: 'Top Gear', BBC Radio 1, 24/12/67.

S209: **Getting My Heart Back Together Again** – Jimi (gi, lv), Mitch (dr, hv, voice), Mitch? (ta), Noel (ba), studio guests (hand-claps, voices, foot-stamping). Rec: BBCB, 15/12/67. Engi: Pete Ritzema. Prod: Bernie Andrews & Bev Phillips. First brc: 'Top Gear', BBC Radio 1, 24/12/67.

NOTE: The liner notes incorrectly state that this song was first broadcast on 'Top Gear' in 1967. This song is an alternate version which in fact was never broadcast by the BBC until the release of *Radio One* itself.

S210: **Hound Dog** – Jimi (gi, lv), Mitch (dr), Noel (ba), Jimi & Mitch & Noel (cat and dog sounds, laughing). Comp: Jerry Leiber & Mike Stoller. Rec: BBCB, 06/10/67. Engi: Pete Ritzema. Prod: Bernie Andrews & Bev Phillips. First brc: 'Top Gear', BBC Radio 1, 15/10/67.

S211: **Fire** – Jimi (gi, lv), Mitch (dr), Noel (ba, hv), Jimmy Leverton (hv), Trevor Burton (hv), Brian Mathew (introduction – overdub). Rec: BBCA, 28/03/67. Prod: Bill Bebb & Jimmy Grant. First brc: 'Saturday Club', BBC Light, 01/04/67.

S212: **I'm Your Hoochie Coochie Man** – Jimi (gi, vo), Mitch (dr), Noel (Hagstrom 8-string ba), Alexis Korner (slide gi). Comp: Willie Dixon. Rec: BBCB, 17/10/67. Prod: Jeff Griffin. First brc: 'Rhythm And Blues', BBC World Service, 13/11/67.

S213: **Purple Haze** – Jimi (gi, lv, tongue-clicks), Mitch (dr), Noel (ba, hv). Rec: BBCA, 28/03/67. Prod: Bill Bebb & Jimmy Grant. First brc: 'Saturday Club', BBC Light, 01/04/67.

S214: **Spanish Castle Magic** – Jimi (gi, lv, hv), Mitch (dr, hv, voice), Noel (ba, hv). Rec: BBCB, 15/12/67. Engi: Pete Ritzema. Prod: Bernie Andrews & Bev Phillips. First brc: 'Top Gear', BBC Radio 1, 24/12/67.

S215: **Hey Joe** – Jimi (gi, vo), Mitch (dr), Noel (ba). Comp: William M. Roberts. Rec: BBCA, 13/02/67. Prod: Bill Bebb & Jimmy Grant. First brc: 'Saturday Club', BBC Light, 18/02/67.

S216: **Foxy Lady** – Jimi (gi, vo), Mitch (dr), Noel (ba). Rec: BBCA, 13/02/67. Prod: Bill Bebb & Jimmy Grant. First brc: 'Saturday Club', BBC Light, 18/02/67.

S217: **The Burning Of The Midnight Lamp** – Jimi (gi, vo), Mitch (dr), Noel (ba). Rec: BBCB, 06/10/67. Engi: Pete Ritzema. Prod: Bernie Andrews & Bev Phillips, First brc: 'Top Gear', BBC Radio 1, 15/10/67.

DAY TRIPPER
- Rykodisc RCD31-008 [USA] – Released late 88 – CD single (only)
- *: entire release
  Not released [ENG]

S218: **Driving South** – Jimi (gi), Mitch (dr), Noel (ba). Rec: BBCB, 06/10/67. Engi: Pete Ritzema. Prod: Bernie Andrews & Bev Phillips. First brc: 'Top Gear', BBC Radio 1, 15/10/67.

NOTE: <1> Incomplete (drum solo missing). Refer to S478 for the complete version. <2> The liner notes incorrectly state that this version is an alternate version. Refer to S206 for the alternate version.

S219: **Getting My Heart Back Together Again** – Jimi (gi, lv), Mitch (dr, hv, voice), Mitch? (ta), Noel (ba), studio guest (hand-claps). Rec: BBCB, 15/12/67. Engi: Pete Ritzema. Prod: Bernie Andrews & Bev Phillips. First brc: 'Top Gear', BBC Radio 1, 24/12/67.

NOTE: The liner notes incorrectly state that this version is an alternate version. Refer to S209 for the alternate version.

Plus: Day Tripper (S203).

THE PEEL SESSIONS: THE JIMI HENDRIX EXPERIENCE
- Strange Fruit Records SFPSO65 [ENG] – Released: 88 – 12 inch EP
- CD: Strange Fruit Records SFPSCDO65 [ENG]

Contains: Radio 1 [S202]; Day Tripper [S203]; Wait Until Tomorrow [S208]; Getting My Heart Back Together Again [S209]; Spanish Castle Magic [S214].

21 YEARS OF ALTERNATIVE RADIO 1 (double)
- Strange Fruit Records SFRLP200 [ENG] – Released 09?/88
- Single CD: Strange Fruit Records SFRCD200 [ENG]

The rest of this release contains BBC material by other artists.

Contains: Hey Joe [S215].

PURPLE HAZE
- Polydor PZCD 33 [ENG] – Released 88 – CD single (only)
  Not released [USA]

Contains: Purple Haze [S003]; 51st Anniversary [S004]; All Along The Watchtower [S034]; Hey Joe [S001].

GLORIA
- Polydor 887 585–2 [GER] – Released 88 – CD single (only)
  Not released [USA]

Contains: Gloria [S170]; Hey Joe [S001]; Voodoo Child (slight return) [S048]; Purple Haze [S003].

CROSSTOWN TRAFFIC
- Polydor PZCD 71 [ENG] – Released 04/90 – CD single (only)
  Not released [USA]

Contains: Crosstown Traffic [S037]; Voodoo Child (slight return) [S048]; All Along The Watchtower [S034]; Have You Ever Been (To Electric Ladyland) [S036].
LIVE & UNRELEASED (5 LP's)
- Castle Communications HBLP 100 [FRA] - Released 20/11/89 - *: Mr. Bad Luck; One Rainy Wish; Machine Gun; Room Full Of Mirrors; Send My Love To Linda; Night Bird Flying
- Triple CD: Castle Communications HBCD 100 [FRA]
- Not released [USA]

<1> Although pressed in France, this release is available all over Europe. <2> This is all part of a six-hour radio show, first broadcast in the USA on 02 and 03/09/88. The general concept might work for radio, but as a commercial release it's nothing but a disaster. And what you are actually getting is very, very little: 12 more or less new songs or alternate versions of previously released songs that are complete. That's it really, as the rest is just snatches of songs (and a lot of material was released elsewhere long before), or fades out after 1 or 2 minutes, or the song is drowned out by an irritating voice-over. <3> The information in the booklet that goes with this release contains many factual errors and misspellings of names. <4> The listing below is the full running order of all items (except non-Jimi Hendrix interviews) on this release. <5> All interviews with Jimi are only very short. <6> All 26/12/65 songs rec: George's Club 20, Hackensack, New Jersey. <7> All early 68 songs rec: Jimi's flat, New York City, between 02 and 04/68.
Part of Purple Haze [S213].

I220: **Interview with Jimi** – by Lennart Wretlind. Rec: Stockholm, Sweden, 09/01/69.

NOTE: Incomplete.

L221: **I Don't Live Today** – Jimi (gi, lv), Mitch (dr), Noel (ba, hv). Rec (by Wally Heider, on 8 track, 1 inch): The Forum, Los Angeles, California, 26/04/69.

NOTE: <1> Track 1. <2> Incomplete (drum intro cut). Refer to L598 for the complete version.
Part of Remember [S016].
Part of Stone Free [S002].

P222: **Cherokee Mist** – Jimi (gi). Rec: early 68.

NOTE: <1> Track 2. <2> Incomplete.

I223: **Interview with Jimi** – by Meatball Fulton. Rec: Jimi's flat, Upper Berkeley Street, London W1, mid 12/67.

NOTE: Incomplete. Refer to I295 for the complete interview.

S224: **Star Spangled Banner** – Jimi (gs). Comp: Francis Scott Key. Special effect: Jimi (octavia). Rec: PLA, 18/03/69. Prod: Jimi.

NOTE: <1> Incomplete. <2> This is the same basic version as S115. Difference: slightly different mix.

I225: **Interview with Jimi** – from the film *See My Music Talking* (a.k.a.: *Experience*). Rec: Bruce Fleming's photo studio, 12 Great Newport Street, London WC2, 19/12/67.

NOTE: Incomplete.

S226: **Bleeding Heart** – Jimi (gs), Juma? (ta). Rec: PLA, 18/12/69. Comp: Elmore James. Prod: Jimi.

NOTE: Incomplete.

I227: **Interview with Jimi** – by Klas Burling. Rec: Stockholm, Sweden, 25/05/67.

NOTE: Incomplete.

S228: **Testify Part I** – Jimi (gi), Isley Brothers (vo), unknown (rest). Comp:

Ronald Isley & O'Kelly Isley & Rudolph Isley. Rec: unknown studio, New York City (on 4 track), 03/64.
NOTE: <1> Track 3. <2> Incomplete. Refer to S339 for the complete version. <3> The liner notes incorrectly state that this version was released as a single. Refer to S331 for the single version.
Part of Tutti Frutti by Little Richard.
NOTE: This does not get an entry number, for the simple reason that Jimi is NOT playing a single note in this song! Besides, this Little Richard song contains guitar with wah-wah, an effect which wasn't available until mid 1967 . . . See page 574 for more details.
Another part from the Interview with Jimi – by Klas Burling (I227).
Part of Lawdy Miss Claudy by Little Richard, Track 4.
NOTE: Again this does not get an entry number, as Jimi is not on this song, See page 574 for more details.
L229: **Drivin' South** – Jimi (gi, voice), Curtis Knight (vo, voice), Curtis Knight & The Squires (rest). Rec: 26/12/65.
NOTE: Incomplete. Refer to L406 for the complete version.
L230: **I'm a Man** – Jimi (gi, lv), Curtis Knight & The Squires (rest). Comp: Bo Diddley. Rec: 26/12/65.
NOTE: <1> Track 5. <2> Incomplete. Refer to L407 for the complete version.
Another part from the Interview with Jimi – by Klas Burling (I227).
L231: **Like A Rolling Stone** – Jimi (gi, vo), Phillip Wilson (dr), Buzzy Feiten (ba), Al Kooper (or). Comp: Bob Dylan. Rec: Generation, 54 West 8th Street, New York City, mid/04/68.
NOTE: <1> Track 6. <2> Incomplete. <3> Jimi recorded the complete jam (which also included B.B. King) on his own tape recorder.
S232: **Little One** – Jimi (gs), Mitch (dr), Mitch? (cow-bell), Jimi or Dave Mason (ba), Dave Mason (sitar), unknown (pe), unknown(tongue-clicks), unknown (faint hv bits). Rec: OLY, 26/01/68. Engi: Eddie. Prod: Chas.
NOTE: <1> Incomplete. <2> It's possible that Brian Jones was involved in this song.
L233: **Red House** – Jimi (gi, vo), Mitch (dr), Noel (ba). Rec: L'Olympia, Paris, France, 09/10/67.
NOTE: <1> Track 7. <2> Incomplete (2:16 cut out in the middle). Refer to L524 for the complete version.
Hey Joe [S001]. Track 8.
S234: **Instrumental** – Jimi (gs), Mitch (dr, cow-bell), Noel (ba). Special effect: Jimi (octavia – with gi overdub). Rec: TTG?, 10?/68? Prod: Jimi.
NOTE: Incomplete.
Part of I'm Your Hoochie Coochie Man [S212]. Track 9.
Purple Haze [S003].
S235: **Instrumental** – Jimi (gs), Mitch (dr), Noel (ba). Special effect: Jimi (octavia – with gi overdub). Rec: TTG?, 10?/68? Prod: Jimi.
NOTE: <1> Incomplete. <2> This is an outtake of S234.
The Wind Cries Mary [S005]. Track 10.
Part of Love Or Confusion [S205].
Foxy Lady [S216]. Track 11.
Part of Third Stone From The Sun [S015]. Track 12.
Another two parts from the Interview with Jimi – by Klas Burling [I227].
Another part of Third Stone From The Sun [S015]. Track 12.
Part of Killin' Floor [L073].
Wild Thing [L081]. Track 13.
Part of Tax Free [S128].

Part of May This Be Love (S013).
S236:   Mr Bad Luck – Jimi (gs, lv), Mitch (dr), Noel (ba), Mitch or Noel
(hv), unknown (ta). Rec: OLY, 04/05/67. Engi: Eddie. Prod: Chas.
NOTE: <1> Track 14. <2> Mr Bad Luck a.k.a.: Look Over Yonder. Refer
to S116 for Look Over Yonder.
S237:   The Burning Of The Midnight Lamp – Jimi (gi), Mitch (dr). Rec:
MAY, 06?/07/67. Engi: Gary. Prod: Chas.
NOTE: Incomplete.
I238:   Interview with Jimi – by Klas Burling. Rec: Stockholm, Sweden,
05/09/67.
NOTE: Incomplete.
The Burning Of The Midnight Lamp [S019].
NOTE: <1> Track 15. <2> The liner notes incorrectly state that a part of
this song was recorded in London, and that 'backing vocals are by The Sweet
Inspirations.'
Part of You've Got Me Floating [S028].
Spanish Castle Magic [S023]. Track 16.
Bold As Love [S033]. Track 17.
I239:   Interview with Jimi – by Leif H. Andersson. Rec: Stockholm, Sweden,
08/01/68.
NOTE: Incomplete.
S240:   One Rainy Wish – Jimi (gs, vo), Mitch (dr), Noel (ba). Rec: OLY,
10/67. Special effect: Jimi (octavia); ADT (on some of Jimi's vo). Engi:
Eddie. Prod: Chas.
NOTE: <1> Track 18. <2> One Rainy Wish a.k.a.: Golden Rose. <3> This is the
same basic version as S031. Differences: few extra guitar licks; somewhat different
mix. <4> The liner notes incorrectly state that this version is one of the stolen or
'missing mixes'.
Little Wing [S026]. Track 19.
Drivin' South [S206].
NOTE: <1> Track 20. <2> The liner notes incorrectly state that this version
was recorded 17/10/67 at the BBC. Another part from the Interview with Jimi
– by Meatball Fulton [I223].
I241:   Interview with Jimi – by Tony Glover. Rec: Auditorium, Minneapolis,
Minnesota, 02/11/68.
NOTE: Incomplete.
S242:   The Things I Used To Do – Jimi (gi, vo), Johnny Winter (slide gi),
Stephen Stills (ba), Dallas Taylor (dr). Comp: Guitar Slim. Rec: PLA,
15/05/69. Prod: Jimi.
NOTE: <1> Track 21. <2> Incomplete. <3> Refer to S761 for a somewhat
different (but complete) version.
All Along The Watchtower (S034). Track 22.
S243:   Drifter's Escape – Jimi (gs, vo), Mitch (dr), Mitch? (ta), Billy (ba).
Comp: Bob Dylan. Rec: ELE, 15?/05?/70. Engi: Eddie. Prod: Jimi.
NOTE: <1> Track 23. <2> This is the same basic version as S150. Differences:
other guitar parts; no cow-bell; different mix.
S244:   Cherokee Mist – Jimi (gs), Jimi? (sitar), Mitch (dr). Rec: PLA, 02/05/68.
Engi: Eddie? Prod: Jimi.
NOTE: <1> Track 24. <2> Incomplete. Refer to S710 for the complete version.
Another three parts from the Interview with Jimi – from the film *See My Music
Talking* (a.k.a.: *Experience*) [I224].

P245: **Voodoo Chile** – Jimi (gi, vo). Rec: early 68.
NOTE: <1> Track 25. <2> Incomplete. Refer to P736 for the complete version.
S246: **Voodoo Child (slight return)** – Jimi (gi, vo), Mitch (dr), Noel (ba). Rec: PLA, 03/05/68 (take 4). Engi: Eddie. Prod: Jimi. Track 26.
Part of . . . And The Gods Made Love [S035].
S247: **1983 . . . (A Merman I Should Turn To Be)** – Jimi (gs, ba, dr, pe, vo), Chris Wood (fl). Special effects: Jimi (bit of backward gi); heavy delay on vo; slowed down and speeded up tape manipulations. Rec: PLA, 23/04/68. Engi: Gary or Eddie. Mixing: Jimi & Eddie. Prod: Jimi.
NOTE: <1> Track 27. <2> Incomplete, <3> Some of the instrumentation (such as one of Jimi's guitar takes) although differently mixed on this version, is similar to that of S044.
Part of Have You Ever Been (To Electric Ladyland) [S036].
S248: **Voodoo Chile** – Jimi (gi, vo, voice), Mitch (dr), Jack Casady (ba), Steve Winwood (or), unknown (voice). Rec: PLA, 01 or 02/05/68. Engi: Eddie. Prod: Jimi.
NOTE: Incomplete (2 bits only).
Part of Voodoo Chile [S038]. Track 28.
S249: **Rainy Day, Dream Away** – Jimi (gi), Buddy (dr), Freddie Smith (sa), Mike Finnigan (or), Larry Faucette (congas). Rec: PLA, 10/06/68. Engi: Eddie or Gary. Prod: Jimi.
NOTE: Incomplete (bit only).
Another part from the Interview with Jimi – by Lennart Wretlind [I220].
S250: **Come On (Part 1)** – Jimi (gi, vo, voice), Mitch (dr), Noel (ba). Comp: Earl King. Rec: PLA, 27/08/68 (take 9). Track 29.
Part of Fire [L191].
I251: **Interview with Jimi** – by Hugh Curry. Rec: Jimi's (Handel) flat, 25 Brook Street, London W1, 07/01/69.
NOTE: <1> Incomplete (one line only). Lifted from *A Film About Jimi Hendrix*.
Manic Depression [L192]. Track 30.
S252: **Astro Man** – Jimi (gi), Mitch (dr), Billy (ba). Rec: PLA, 20/01/70. Prod: Jimi.
NOTE: Incomplete. Refer to S721 for the complete version.
Another part from the Interview with Jimi – by Lennart Wretlind [I220].
Part of The Stars That Play With Laughing Sam's Dice [S020].
L253: **Machine Gun** – Jimi (gi, vo), Buddy (dr, cow-bell), Billy (ba). Rec: Fillmore East, New York City, 31/12/69, 2nd show.
NOTE: <1> Track 31. <2> Incomplete.
Part of Stepping Stone [S050].
S254: **Room Full Of Mirrors** – Jimi (gs, vo), Buddy (dr), Billy (ba), Juma (pe, congas), unknown (cow-bell). Special effect: Jimi (octavia; slide via his ring or bracelet). Rec: PLA, 17/11/69. Engi: Toni Bongiovi? Prod: Heaven Research Unlimited.
NOTE: <1> Track 32. <2> This is the same basic version as S114. Differences: extra rhythm guitar take; more and different guitar solo takes; some extra congas at times; different mix; slide guitar take only at the end.
P255: **Angel** – Jimi (gi, vo). Rec: early 68. Track 33.
S256: **Rainy Day Shuffle** – Jimi (gi), Jimi (ba), Buddy (dr), Mike Finnigan (or), unknown (ta). Rec: PLA, 10/06/68. Engi: Eddie or Gary. Prod: Jimi.
NOTE: <1> Track 34. <2> Incomplete.
S257: **Valleys Of Neptune** – Jimi (gi, vo, voice), Mitch (dr, voice), unknown

(ba), Juma? or Jerry? (congas), Juma? (pe). Rec: PLA, 21?/01?/70 (basic track); PLA?, 70 (ba and pe overdub). Comp: Hamilton Camp (music); Jimi Hendrix (words). Prod: Jimi.

NOTE: <1> Track 35. <2> Incomplete. <3> The original version of Hamilton Camp's instrumental songs was titled 'Pride Of Man'. This song was made popular by Quicksilver Messenger Service who released (in mid 67) their version on their debut LP of the same name, and again released (in 05/68) the song as the b-side of one of their singles. It's very likely that this is where Jimi picked it up from, and re-named it 'Valleys Of Neptune'.

S258: **Drifting** – Jimi (gi), Billy (ba). Rec: ELE, 06 or 07/70. Engi: Eddie. Prod: Jimi.

NOTE: Incomplete. Refer to S745 for a more complete version.

S259: **Send My Love To Linda** – Jimi (gi, vo, voice). Rec: HIT? 09?/69? Prod: Jimi. Track 36.

S260: **Send My Love To Linda** – Jimi (gi, vo). Rec: HIT? 09?/69? Prod: Jimi.

NOTE: Incomplete.

S261: **South Saturn Delta** – Jimi (gs), Jimi? (ba), Buddy? (dr), Freddie Smith? (horns), Larry Faucette (congas). Rec: PLA, 14/06/68 (basic track). Engi: Gary? (basic track). Prod: Jimi.

NOTE: <1> Track 37. <2> Incomplete. <3> Liner notes incorrectly state the involvement of the Brecker Brothers.

S262: **God Save The Queen** – Jimi (acoustic gi, gs). Comp: Dr. John Ball, Rec: PLA? 69 or 70. Prod: Jimi.

NOTE: Incomplete. Refer to S812 for the complete version.

Dolly Dagger [L110].

S263: **Can I Whisper In Your Ear** – Jimi (gi, vo), Billy (ba). Rec: PLA or HIT, Autumn 69, or ELE, Summer 70. Prod: Jimi.

NOTE: <1> Incomplete. <2> The real song title is unknown.

S264: **Night Bird Flying** – Jimi (gs, vo), Mitch (dr), Billy (ba), Juma (cow-bell, pe). Rec: ELE, 16/06/70. Engi: Eddie. Prod: Jimi.

NOTE: <1> Track 39. <2> This is the same basic version as S085. Differences: bit more percussion; different guitar bits; different mix.

Part of Getting My Heart Back Together Again [S209 and S219].

NOTE: This 'new' version was made up (in 1988) from the beginning part of S209 and spliced together with the end part of S219. How inventive can you get?

MISCELLANEOUS RELEASES

LITTLE MISS LOVER
> – Emidisc [ENG] – Pressed: late 67 – Acetate single (mono)

<1> One-sided acetate by: Jimi Hendrix Experience. <2> This version has never appeared on any other release.

S265: **Little Miss Lover** – Jimi (gs, vo, wolf-whistle), Mitch (dr), Mitch? (ta), Noel (ba). Rec: OLY, 10?/67. Engi: Eddie? Prod: Chas.

DREAM b/w DANCE
> – Emidisc [ENG] – Pressed: early 68 – Acetate single (mono)

<1> Acetate by: Jimi Hendrix Experience. <2> These songs have never appeared on any other release.

S266: **Dream** – Jimi (ba, hv), Mitch (dr, hv), Noel (gi, lv). Comp: Noel Redding. Rec: OLY, 20/12/67 (basic track); OLY, 30/12/67 (additional recordings). Prod: Chas.

S267: **Dance** – Jimi (gi, hv), Mitch (dr, lv), Noel (ba). Comp: Noel Redding & Mitch Mitchell. Rec: OLY, 21/12/67. Prod: Chas.

THE IN SOUND
> – United States Army USA-IS 67 [USA] – Pressed: late 67.
> – Public Service LP

<1> Amazing ditty, with Harry Harrison trying to recruit people into the army – 'your future, your decision, choose army!' – via short 5-minute radio spots. <2> The rest of this release contains music and short interviews with other artists. <3> The label states: For Broadcast Week of October 30, 1967.

I268: **Interview with Jimi** – by Harry Harrison. Rec: unknown radio location, likely Los Angeles, California, 06?/67.

Plus: part of Purple Haze [S003].

THE IN SOUND

$– United States Army USA-IS51 [USA] – Pressed: early 68 – Public Service LP

<1> More army stuff. <2> The rest of this release contains music and short interviews with other artists. <3> The label states: For Broadcast Week of February 5, 1968.

I269: **Interview with Noel (with Jimi giggling in the background)** – by Harry Harrison. Rec: unknown radio location, likely Los Angeles, California, 06?/67.

Plus: part of Foxy Lady [S007].

THE BURNING OF THE MIDNIGHT LAMP b/w HOUSE BURNING DOWN

– Bell Sound Studios Inc. [USA] – Pressed: 08?/68 – Acetate single

<1> Acetate by: Jimi Hendrix Experience. <2> The version of 'House Burning Down' has never appeared on any other release.

S270: **House Burning Down** – Jimi (gs, ba, lv, hv, voice), Mitch (dr), Mitch? (hv). Rec: PLA, 01/05/68 (basic recording); PLA, 08/68 (additional recordings); PLA, 23?/08/68 (final mix). Engi: Eddie or Gary. Prod: Jimi.

NOTE: This is a somewhat different version of S047. Differences: some of the guitar solos and part of the drums are different; completely different mix.

Plus: The Burning Of The Midnight Lamp [S019].

THE STARS THAT PLAY WITH LAUGHING SAM'S DICE

– Mayfair Recording Studio Inc. [USA] – Pressed: 67 – Acetate single

<1> One-sided acetate by: Jimi Hendrix Experience. <2> This version has never appeared on any other release.

S271: **The Stars That Play With Laughing Sam's Dice** – Jimi (gs), Mitch (dr), Noel (ba, 12-string gi with wah-wah), unknown (or). Rec: unknown studio, Los Angeles, California, very likely 28/06/67. Prod: Chas.

WOKE UP THIS MORNING AND FOUND MYSELF DEAD

– Red Lightnin' RLOO15 [ENG] – Released 10/80 – LP

– Also on: Red Lightnin' RL0048 [ENG] – Picture LP;
    Surprise JTUAL 77 [FRA] – LP

– Also (as: Tomorrow Never Knows) on: Happy Bird B/90166 [GER] – LP

– Red Lightnin' RLCD 0068 [ENG] – CD

– Also (as: New York Sessions) on: Tradit. Line CD 1301 [GER] – CD

<1> All song rec: The Scene, 301 West 46th Street, New York City, 06?/03/68, Jimi recorded the jam with his own tape recorder. <2> It has been wrongly implied that Noel Redding (bass) and Johnny Winter (second guitar) were involved in the jam. In fact, Johnny Winter was still living in Texas when this jam took place. As the McCoys were more or less the house-band at The Scene during this period it's possible that some members of this group were playing during the jam. Possibly it's Randy Hobbs (bass), and Randy Zherringer (drums). Buddy Miles (drums) may be another possibility on some of the songs. As for the other guitarist, this may remain a mystery forever . . . <3> Most of the jam was originally released in 1972 on the bootleg LP *Sky High* prior to all these listed releases.

L272: **Red House** – Jimi (gi, vo) Jim Morrison (screaming), unknown (rest).

L273: **I'm Gonna Leave This Town/Everything's Gonna Be Allright** – Jimi (gi, vo), Jim Morrison (ha, screaming), unknown (rest). Comp: Walter Jacobs ('Everything's Gonna Be Allright').

L274: **Bleeding Heart** – Jimi (gi, lv), Jim Morrison (ha, hv, screaming), unknown (rest). Comp: Elmore James.

562

L275:   **Tomorrow Never Knows** – Jimi (gi, voice), Jim Morrison (obscenities), unknown (rest). Comp: John Lennon & Paul McCartney,
NOTE: Incomplete, Refer to L277 for a somewhat longer version.
L276:   **Outside Woman Blues/The Sunshine Of Your Love** – Jimi (gi), Jim Morrison (faint screaming), unknown (rest). Comp: Reynolds (Outside Woman Blues); Pete Brown & Jack Bruce & Eric Clapton (The Sunshine Of Your Love).
NOTE: Incomplete.
HIGH, LIVE 'N DIRTY
    – Nutmeg NUT-1001 [USA] – Released 11/78 – LP
In case anyone is interested, Jim Morrison's screaming and obscenities can be heard better on this release than on any of those previously listed . . .
L277:   **Tomorrow Never Knows** – Jimi (gi, voice), Jim Morrison (obscenities), unknown (rest). Comp: John Lennon & Paul McCartney.
NOTE: <1> This is the more complete version of L275. <2> During this jam somebody (probably Jim Morrison) knocks over Jimi's mike-stand . . .
Plus: part of Tomorrow Never Knows [L275]; part of Bleeding Heart [L274]; Outside Woman Blues/The Sunshine Of Your Love [L276]; Bleeding Heart [L274].
EXPERIENCE
    – Signal CD 88110 [HDL] – Released 80's – CD
    – Also on: Galaxis CD 9006 [GER] – Released 86 – CD
PURPLE HAZE
    – Success 2101CD [GER?] – Released 80's – CD
All releases contain the same songs, but in a different order.
Contains: part of Red House [L272]; Voodoo Child (slight return) [L097]; Bleeding Heart [L094]; Fire [L098]; Purple Haze [L099]; part of Room Full Of Mirrors [L093]; Smashing Of Amps [L095]; Wild Thing [L100]; The Sunshine Of Your Love [L092].
Plus fake: She's So Fine; Suspicious; Something You Got.
JIMI HENDRIX AT HIS BEST VOLUME 1
    – Saga 6313 [ENG] – Released 06/72 – LP
    Also on: Joker SM 3271 [ITA] – LP
<1> Part of the material on the following five releases first became available in 04/70 on the bootleg LP 'This Flyer'. From 1971 onwards a steady stream of 'official' releases on record labels such as Saga and Joker appeared. <2> All jams rec: Jimi's rented house, Tavor Hollow Road, near Shokan, New York, 22?/09/69. The covers incorrectly state and/or imply a recording date in 1964 or 'while Hendrix was in his teens.' The labels also incorrectly credit Mike Ephron as the composer of all the improvisations, and all titles of these improvisations are given on the covers and labels under fictitious titles.
P278:   **Stepping Stone** – Jimi (gi, vo), Mike Ephron (keyboards), Juma (pe).
NOTE: Stated incorrectly as: 'She Went To Bed With My Guitar'.
P279:   **Instrumental 1** – Jimi (gi), Mike Ephron (keyboards), Juma (pe).
NOTE: Stated as: 'Free Thunder'.
P280:   **Instrumental 2** – Jimi (gi), Mike Ephron (keyboards), Juma (pe).
NOTE: Stated as: 'Cave Man Bells'.
P281:   **Instrumental Solo** – Jimi (gi), Mike Ephron (keyboards), Juma (pe).
NOTE: Stated incorrectly as: 'Strokin' A Lady On Each Hip'.
P282:   **Instrumental 3** – Jimi (gi), Mike Ephron (keyboards), Juma and Jerry (pe, ta).
NOTE: Stated as: 'Baby Chicken Strut'.

JIMI HENDRIX AT HIS BEST VOLUME 2
        – Saga 6314 [ENG] – Released 06/72 – LP
        – Also on: Joker SM 3272 [ITA] – LP
P283:   Instrumental 4 – Jimi (gi), Mike Ephron (keyboards), Juma (pe).
NOTE: Stated as: 'Down Man Blues.'
P284:   Flying (Here I Go) – Jimi (gi, vo, voice), Mike Ephron (keyboards, voice), Juma (fl, pe), Jerry (pe).
NOTE: Stated as: 'Feels Good'.
P285:   Instrumental 5 – Jimi (gi), Mike Ephron (keyboards), Juma and Jerry (pe).
NOTE: Stated as: 'Fried Cola'.
P286:   Monday Morning Blues – Jimi (gi, vo, voice), Mike Ephron (keyboards), Juma (pe).
P287:   Key To The Highway – Jimi (gi), Mike Ephron (keyboards, voice), Juma and Jerry (pe, ta). Comp: Charles Segar & Willy 'Big Bill' Broonzy.
NOTE: <1> Stated incorrectly as: 'Jimi Is Tender Too'. <2> Possibly Charles Segar should be Charles Seeger (father of Pete Seeger).
P288:   Instrumental 6 – Jimi (gi), Mike Ephron (keyboards), Juma and Jerry (pe, ta, marimba?).
NOTE: Stated as: 'Madagascar'.
JIMI HENDRIX AT HIS BEST VOLUME 3
        – Saga 6315 [ENG] – Released 06/72 – LP
        – Also on: Joker SM 3273 [ITA] – LP
P289:   Instrumental 7/Gypsy Boy (New Rising Sun) – Jimi (gi), Mike Ephron (keyboards), Juma and Jerry (pe).
NOTE: Stated incorrectly as: 'Young Jim'.
P290:   Instrumental 8 – Jimi (gi, voice), Mike Ephron (keyboards), Juma (pe, fl, voice), Jerry? (maracas).
NOTE: Stated as: 'Lift Off'.
P291:   Instrumental 9 – Jimi (gi), Mike Ephron (keyboards), Juma and Jerry (pe).
NOTE: Stated as: 'Swift's Wing'.
P292:   Earth Blues – Jimi (gi), Mike Ephron (keyboards), Juma and Jerry (pe).
NOTE: Stated incorrectly as: 'Giraffe'.
Plus: Flying (Here I Go) [P284], stated as 'Spiked With Heady Dreams'.
JIMI HENDRIX
        – Pantonic Pan 6307 [ENG] – LP – Released 04/71 – LP
<1> The fictitious titles of the improvisations are this time stated as: 'Impromptu No 1. "Baroque I"', 'Impromptu No 2 "Baroque II"'; 'Impromptu No 3, "Virtuoso" Part 1. Berceuse – Part 2. Flying – Part 3. Perpetuum Mobile.' <2> *Melody Maker* 17/04/71: '. . . the release of this album is a con of the worst order, doing nothing for Jimi except pick the pennies off his dead eyes.'
Contains: Instrumental 7/Gypsy Boy (New Rising Sun) [P289]; Instrumental 9 [P291]; Flying (Here I Go) [P284].
JIMI HENDRIX '64
        – Boulevard 4106 [ENG] – Released 01/75 – LP
Contains: Stepping Stone [P278]; Instrumental 8 [P290]; Instrumental 4 [P283]; Instrumental 6 [P288]; Monday Morning Blues [P286]; Earth Blues [P292]; Key To The Highway [P287].
. . . AND A HAPPY NEW YEAR
        – Reprise PRO 595 [USA] – Released 12/74 – Promo single
        – Also on: Reprise PRO-A 840 [USA] – Released 12/79 – 12 inch promo single
The 12 inch release contains all the songs twice, on side A and B.
S293:   The Little Drummer Boy/Silent Night – Jimi (gi), Buddy (dr), Billy

(ba). Comp: David Onorati & Harry Simeone & Katherine Davis (The Little Drummer Boy); Father Joseph Mohr & Franz Gruber (Silent Night). Rec: PLA, 12/69. Engi: Toni Bongiovi? Prod: Jimi.

S294: **Auld Lang Syne** – Jimi (gi), Buddy (dr, vo), Billy (ba). Comp: Robert Burns. Rec: PLA, 12/69. Engi: Toni Bongiovi? Prod: Jimi.

THE INTERVIEW
> – Rhino Records RNDF 254 [USA] – Released 80's – Picture LP
> – Also on: CID Productions CID 006 [ENG] – CD

The LP release also contains several spoken observations by Meatball Fulton, which are not included on the CD.

I295: **Interview with Jimi** – by Meatball Fulton. Rec: Jimi's flat, Upper Berkeley Street, London W1, mid 12/67.

NOTE: This is the complete interview of I140 and I223.

JIMI HENDRIX
> – British Broadcasting Corporation LP 37480 [ENG] – Pressed 02/76
> – Transcription LP

<1> This release contains various interview material partly used during the programme 'Insight', BBC Radio 1, 22/02/76.

I296: **Interview with Jimi** – by Keith Altham. Rec: Hotel Cumberland, Rooms 507 & 508, London W1, 11/09/70.

NOTE: <1> Slightly incomplete. <2> This was Jimi's last recorded interview.

I297: **Interview with Jimi** – by Klas Burling. Rec: Stockholm, Sweden, 25/05/67.

NOTE: <1> Incomplete. <2> This is from the same interview as I227.

I298: **Interview with Jimi** – by Lennart Wretlind. Rec: Stockholm, Sweden, 09/01/69.

NOTE: <1> Incomplete. <2> This is from the same interview as I220.

Plus: various short interviews with Chas Chandler, Chris Welch, Alan Douglas, and Paul McCartney.

RED HOUSE: VARIATIONS ON A THEME
> – Hal Leonard HL00660040 [USA] – Released 11/89 – CD – *: versions S300; L301; L302; L303
> Not released [ENG]

This release (and the following two) are only available (on CD and cassette) in music and instrument stores.

L299: **Red House** – Jimi (gi, vo), Mitch (dr), Billy (ba). Rec: Berkeley Community Theatre, Berkeley, California, 30/05/70, 1st show.

S300: **Red House** – Jimi (gi, vo, introduction), Mitch (dr), Buddy (dr), Noel (ba), Lee Michaels (or), unknown (ta). Rec: TTG, 29/10/68, Prod: Jimi.

L301: **Red House** – Jimi (gi, vo), Mitch (dr), Noel (ba). Rec: The Forum, Los Angeles, California, 24/04/69.

L302: **Red House** – Jimi (gi, vo), Mitch (dr), Noel (ba). Rec: Royal Albert Hall, London, 24/02/69.

L303: **Red House** – Jimi (gi, vo), Mitch (dr), Noel (ba). Rec: Winterland, San Francisco, California, 10/10/68, 1st show.

Plus: Red House (stated incorrectly as being from Newport, 20/06/69) [L178].
Plus: Red House by John Lee Hooker (no Jimi involvement).

FUZZ, FEEDBACK & WAH-WAH
> – Hal Leonard HL00660036 [USA] – Released 11/89 – CD
> Not released [ENG]

This release contains 42 snippets of songs.
Contains: 1:08 of Drivin' South [S206]; 0:16 of Drivin' South [S206]; 0:17 of Freedom

[S082]; 0:45 of Peace In Mississipi [S158]; 0:32 of Purple Haze [S003]; 0:45 of Manic Depression [S008]; 0:34 of Love Or Confusion [S011]; 0:50 of Bold As Love [S033]; 0:14 of Spanish Castle Magic [S023]; 0:27 of Spanish Castle Magic [S023]; 1:03 of If 6 Was 9 [S027]; 0:19 of Little Miss Lover [S032]; 3:51 of Stone Free [L179 and L709]; 0:12 of Foxy Lady [S007];

L304: **Foxy Lady** – Jimi (gi), Mitch (dr), Noel (ba). Rec: Winterland, San Francisco, California, 10/10/68, 1st show.

NOTE: Only 0:42 of this version.

Contains: 0:47 of Third Stone From The Sun [S015]; 0:28 of EXP [S021]; 0:19 of Wild Thing [L184]; 0:51 of Look Over Yonder [S116]; 0:32 of Ezy Ryder [S084]; 0:38 of Red House [L302]; 0:39 of Stone Free [L179]; 1:25 of Are You Experienced [L180]; 0:28 of The Burning Of The Midnight Lamp [S019]; 0:15 of Up From The Skies [S022]; 0:31 of Up From The Skies [S022]; 0:19 of Little Miss Lover [S032]; 0:35 of Voodoo Child (slight return) [S048]; 0:12 of Still Raining, Still Dreaming [S046]; 0:08 of Belly Button Window [S091]; 0:16 of Tax Free [L197]; 0:44 of Changes [L054]; 0:16 of Who Knows [L052]; 0:44 of Are You Experienced [L180]; 0:28 of Straight Ahead [S087]; 0:21 of In From The Storm [S090]; 1:04 of Red House [L301]; 0:51 of Red House [L299]; 1:05 of Red House [L301]; 0:37 of Message To Love [L056]; 2:28 of Tax Free [L197]; 0:39 of 1983 . . . (A Merman I Should Turn To Be) [S044].

WHAMMY BAR & FINGER GREASE
– Hal Leonard HL00660038 [USA] – Released 11/89 – CD
Not released [ENG]

<1> This release contains 40 snippets of songs. <2> All 10/10/68 and 11/10/68 songs rec: Winterland, San Francisco, California.

Contains: 1:23 of Star Spangled Banner [L067]; 0:27 of Third Stone From The Sun [S015]; 0:23 of Machine Gun [L053].

L305: **Star Spangled Banner** – Jimi (gi). Comp: Francis Scott Key. Rec: 10/10/68, 2nd show.

NOTE: <1> Only 0:06 of this version. <2> Stated as: This Is America. <3> Refer to L803 for the complete version.

Contains: 0:27 of Pali Gap [S113]: 0:12 of Look Over Yonder [S116]; 0:40 of I Don't Live Today [S012]; 0:31 of Tax Free [L197]; 1:04 of Cherokee Mist [S244 and S710].

L306: **Star Spangled Banner** – Jimi (gi), Mitch (dr). Comp: Francis Scott Key. Rec: 10/10/68, 2nd show.

NOTE: <1> Another 0:32 of this version. <2> Stated as: 'This Is America'. <3> Refer to L803 for the complete version.

0:45 of Machine Gun [L053]; 0:40 of Machine Gun [L139 and L698]; 0:12 of Ain't No Telling [S025]; 0:10 of Machine Gun [L053]; 0:24 of Machine Gun [L139 and L698]; 0:47 of House Burning Down [S047]; 1:07 of Hey Joe [L199]; 0:27 of Hey Joe [S001]; 0:19 of Red House (the booklet states incorrectly that this version is on the *Live At Winterland* release) [L303]; 0:24 of Foxy Lady [S007]; 0:29 of Astro Man [S252 and S721]; 0:54 of Drivin' South [S206]; 0:35 of Machine Gun [L139 and L698]; 0:33 of Spanish Castle Magic [L194]; 0:29 of Manic Depression [S008]; 1:16 of Bold As Love [S033]; 0:38 of Third Stone From The Sun [S015]; 0:49 of Third Stone From The Sun [S015]; 0:31 of Astro Man [S252 & S721]; 0:48 of Drivin' South [S206]; 0:25 of Machine Gun [L139 and L698]; 0:58 of God Save The Queen [S262 and S812]; 0:27 of Spanish Castle Magic [L194]; 0:27 of Machine Gun [L053]; 0:37 of The Wind Cries Mary [S005]; 1:17 of May This Be Love [S013]; 0:11 of Third Stone From The Sun [S015]; 1:07 of Astro Man [S252 and S721].

L307: **Star Spangled Banner** – Jimi (gi), Mitch (dr). Comp: Francis Scott Key. Rec: 10/10/68, 2nd show.

NOTE: <1> Another 0:29 of this version. <2> Stated as: 'This is America'.
<3> Refer to L803 for the complete version.
L308: **Spanish Castle Magic** – Jimi (gi), Mitch (dr), Noel (ba). Rec: 11/10/68,
2nd show.
NOTE: <1> Only 4:03 of this version. <2> Refer to L806 for the complete version.

JIMI HENDRIX AS GUEST AND/OR PRODUCER

<1>Many of the very early releases listed may prove very hard to obtain, or have long
ago been deleted. <2>Where known, other musicians involved in the various sessions
are listed. Unfortunately it's impossible to determine who is playing what on each song
– in particular for Jimi's early studio periods, as most of these bands and performers
had line-ups that could change from day to day. <3>None of the early listed releases
charted, unless otherwise stated.

Lonnie Youngblood

<1>Lonnie Youngblood's real name is Lonnie Thomas. In 1986 Audiofidelity Enter-
prises was sued (by PPX) under the U.S. Lanham Act for the distributing and marketing
of eight different 'patently fraudulent' albums 'allegedly featuring Mr. Hendrix but which
did not contain such performances.' On May 5, 1987, the U.S. Court of Appeals for the
Second Circuit in New York upheld the damage claim. These LP's had been distributed
and licensed by Audiofidelity Enterprises to such record companies as Nutmeg, Trip,
and many others all over the world. The sessions included on these LP's were
supposedly recorded in 1966 in New York City (according to liner notes that is)
with saxophonist Lonnie Youngblood and guitarist Herman Hitson. In an interview
for CBS Television, Lonnie Youngblood had this to say about the material: 'You think
you're buying Hendrix. You're not buying Hendrix, you're buying Lonnie Youngblood
. . . even the voice, that's not Hendrix singing . . . that's not Hendrix playing.' Since
there are around 100 (!) different releases world-wide containing these fake songs, we
will not list them all. Instead here's a listing of all these fake songs, followed by a listing
of the LP's where they pop up:
SONGS: A Mumblin' Word (also stated as: Funky); All Alone; Be My Baby;
Bring My Baby Back; Edda Mae; Every Little Bit Hurts (also stated as: Gotta
Find Someone); Everything You Got; Feel That Soul; Find Someone; Free Spirit;
From This Day On (also stated as: She's So Fine); Gangster Of Love; Get Down
(also stated as: Git Down, and Down Now); Girl So Fine; Gonna Take A Lot; Good
Feeling; Good Time; Good Times; Groove; Hey LeRoy; Hot Trigger (also stated as:
Not Trigger, and Walking With Bessie Mae); House Of The Rising Sun; Human Heart
(also stated as: Let Me Go, and Louisville); Interlude; Let Me Thrill Your Soul; Let
The God Sing; Miracle Worker; Nite Life; Psycho; So Called Friend (also stated as:
Backroom Lady); Something You Got; Suspicious (also stated as: I Love My Baby);
Voice In The Wind; Win Your Love; You Got It; You Say You Love Me (also stated
as: Freedom And You); Young Generation.
*LP'S: Attention Jimi Hendrix!; Jimi Hendrix!; Before London; Cosmic Turnaround;
Faces and Places Vol. 12; Free Spirit; Gangster of Love; Good Times; Hendrix &
Youngblood; Hendrix 66; In The Beginning; Jimi Hendrix; Jimi Hendrix at His
Best (double); Jimi Hendrix in Concert; Jimi Hendrix 1966; Jimmy Hendrix (double);
Kaleidoscope; La Grande Storia Del Rock Vol. 31; La Grande Storia Del Rock Vol. 56; La
Grande Storia Del Rock Vol. 60; Moods; Original Sessions; Purple Haze; Rare Hendrix;
Rock Guitar Greats; Rock Guitar Greats Vol. 2; Rock Guitar / Original Jimi Hendrix;*

Original Hendrix / Roots of Hendrix; 16 Greatest Classics; 16 Greatest Hits; Strange Things; Superpak; That Unforgettable Jimi Hendrix; The Greatest Original Sessions (double); The Very Best of (The World of) Jimi Hendrix.

<2> However, most the above listed releases also contain several songs which are in fact genuine recordings of Jimi with Lonnie Youngblood. The genuine songs pop up between all the fake stuff and are listed below only once as all songs are the same on all these releases. <3> These recordings with Lonnie Youngblood are almost certainly the very first studio recordings Jimi ever made. <4> Note that some of the above listed releases also contain material by other artists, as well as songs from the so called 'Sky High' jam session. <5> All listed songs by Jimi with Lonnie Youngblood rec: unknown studio. Philadelphia?, Pennsylvania, late 63.

GO GO SHOES b/w GO GO PLACE
> – Fairmount Records F-1002 [USA]
> Released late 63 – Single (mono)

S309: **Go Go Shoes** – Jimi (gi), Lonnie Youngblood (sa, lv), unknown female person (hv), unknown (rest). Comp: M. Thomas & Lonnie Youngblood & A. Hall. Prod: Lonnie Youngblood.

NOTE: Slightly incomplete. Refer to S324 for the complete version.

S310: **Go Go Place** – Jimi (gi), Lonnie Youngblood (sa, vo), unknown (rest). Comp: M. Thomas & Lonnie Youngblood & A. Hall. Prod: Lonnie Youngblood.

NOTE: Slightly incomplete. Refer to S330 for the complete version.

SOUL FOOD (THAT'S A WHAT I LIKE) b/w GOODBYE, BESSIE MAE
– Fairmount Records F-1022 [USA] – Released early? 64 – Single (mono)

S311: **Soul Food (That's A What I Like)** – Jimi (gs), Jimi? (ba), Lonnie Youngblood (sa, vo), unknown (rest). Comp: Lonnie Youngblood & Hank Anderson, Prod: Lonnie Youngblood.

NOTE: Refer to S317 for a somewhat different version.

S312: **Goodbye, Bessie Mae** – Jimi (gi), Lonnie Youngblood (sa, lv), unknown (rest). Comp: Lonnie Youngblood. Prod: Lonnie Youngblood.

NOTE: Refer to S316 for a somewhat different version.

TWO GREAT EXPERIENCES TOGETHER
> – Maple Records LPM 6004 [USA] – Released 03/71 – LP
> Charts: entry 132 (20/03/71); top position: 127; weeks in chart: 4
> – Also on: Joker SM 3536 [ITA]

It appears that the songs on this release which are in mono are the original recorded versions, while most of the stereo versions contain the basic recorded versions in mono, plus (in 1971) added overdubs in stereo.

S313: **Wipe The Sweat I** – Jimi (gi), Lonnie Youngblood (sa, bits of vo), unknown (rest). Comp: Lonnie Youngblood? Added in 1971: unknown (gi – high/cleaner sound).

NOTE: <1> Stated as: Wipe The Sweat (vocal). <2> Stereo.

S314: **Wipe The Sweat II** – Jimi (gi), Lonnie Youngblood (sa, vo), unknown (rest). Comp: Lonnie Youngblood?

NOTE: <1> Stated as: Segway II. <2> Stereo.

S315: **Wipe The Sweat III** – Jimi (gi, lv during 2nd half of the song), Lonnie Youngblood (sa, lv during 1st half of the song, hv), unknown (rest). Special effect: reverb. Comp: Lonnie Youngblood?

NOTE: <1> Stated as: Segway III. <2> Mono.

S316: **Goodbye, Bessie Mae** – Jimi (gi), Lonnie Youngblood (sa, vo), unknown (rest). Comp: Lonnie Youngblood. Prod: Lonnie Youngblood.

NOTE: <1> This is the same basic version as S312. Differences: without harmony vocals; with tambourine; Jimi's guitar solo during the fade-out edited out. <2> Mono.

S317: **Soul Food (That's A What I Like)** – Jimi (gi), Jimi? (ba), Lonnie Youngblood (sa, vo), unknown (rest). Comp: Lonnie Youngblood & Hank Anderson. Prod: Lonnie Youngblood.

NOTE: <1> Stated as: All I Want. <2> This is the same basic version as S311: Differences: different vocal take; different organ take; less guitar; different guitar; longer version. <3> Stereo.

S318: **Under The Table I** – Jimi (gi), Lonnie Youngblood (sa), unknown (rest). Comp: Lonnie Youngblood?

NOTE: <1> Short 'false start' version. <2> Mono.

S319: **Under The Table II** – Jimi (gi), Lonnie Youngblood (sa), unknown (rest). Comp: Lonnie Youngblood?

NOTE: <1> This starts with the same guitar intro as S318. Includes a break in the song, someone (engineer?) says 'this is two', continues with some funny guitar bits, and starts off again with the same guitar intro as S318. <2> Stereo.

S320: **Under The Table III** – Jimi (gi), Lonnie Youngblood (sa), unknown (rest). Comp: Lonnie Youngblood? Added in 1971: unknown (gi – high/distorted sound).

NOTE: Stereo.

Plus: Two In One Goes (no Jimi involvement, or fake). Plus fake: Psycho.

THE GENIUS OF JIMI HENDRIX
– Trip TLP-9523 [USA] – Released 09/74 – LP

All listed songs are enhanced mono.

S321: **Sweet Thang** – Jimi (gi), Lonnie Youngblood (sa, vo), unknown (rest). Comp: Nathan W. Stuckey.

S322: **Groovemaker** – Jimi (gi), Lonnie Youngblood (sa, vo), unknown (rest). Comp: Lonnie Youngblood?

S323: **Fox** – Jimi (gi), Lonnie Youngblood (vo, sa), unknown (rest). Special effect: Jimi (tremolo). Comp: Lonnie Youngblood?

NOTE: Song a.k.a.: She's A Fox.

Plus: Red House [L272]; I'm Gonna Leave This Town/Everything's Gonna Be Allright (stated incorrectly as: Blue Blues) [L273]; Bleeding Heart [L274]; two parts of Tomorrow Never Knows (stated incorrectly as: Whoa' Ech; Lime Lime) [L275].

Plus fake: Gonna Take A Lot.

FOR REAL!
– DJMMD 8011 [ENG] – Released 11/75 – Double LP

All listed songs are mono.

S324: **Go Go Shoes** – Jimi (gi), Lonnie Youngblood (sa, lv), unknown female person (hv), unknown (rest). Comp: M. Thomas & Lonnie Youngblood & A. Hall. Prod: Lonnie Youngblood.

NOTE: This is the complete version of S309.

S325: **Wipe The Sweat IV** – Jimi (gi), Lonnie Youngblood (sa, bits of vo), unknown (rest). Comp: Lonnie Youngblood? Added in 1971: unknown (gi – clean sounding).

NOTE: <1> Stated as: Wipe The Sweat. <2> This is the same basic version as S313. Difference: no stereo overdubs.

S326: **Under The Table Part IV** – Jimi (gi), Lonnie Youngblood (sa), unknown (rest). Comp: Lonnie Youngblood?

NOTE: <1> Stated as: Under The Table Pt. 1. <2> This is the same basic version as S318 and S319 presented as one song. Differences: without someone (engineer?) saying 'this is two'; without guitar overdub.

S327: **Wipe The Sweat V** – Jimi (gi), Lonnie Youngblood (sa, vo), unknown (rest). Comp: Lonnie Youngblood?

NOTE: <1> Stated as: More Sweat. <2> This is the same basic version as S314. Difference: mono mix.

S328: **Under The Table V** – Jimi (gi), Lonnie Youngblood (sa), unknown (rest). Comp: Lonnie Youngblood?

NOTE: <1> Stated as: Under The Table Pt. 2. <2> This is the same basic version as S320. Difference: mono mix.

Plus: Goodbye, Bessie Mae [S316]; Sweet Thang [S321]; Groovemaker [S322]; Fox [S323].

Plus: Red House [L272]; Bleeding Heart [L274]; I'm Gonna Leave This Town/Everything's Gonna Be Allright (stated incorrectly as: Blue Blues) [L273].

Plus fake: Good Time; Bring My Baby Back; Suspicious; Hot Trigger; Voice In The Wind; Psycho; Good Feeling.

RARE HENDRIX
     – Enterprise ENTF 3000 [ENG] – Released 07/72 – LP
      Also on: Trip TLP-9500 [USA] – LP
      Also (subtitled: Jimi Hendrix Vol. 4) on: Joker Records CSM 3535 [ITA] – LP

All releases contain the same songs, but in a different order.

S329: **Go Go Shoes** – Jimi (gi), Lonnie Youngblood (sa, lv), unknown female person (hv), unknown (rest). Comp: M. Thomas & Lonnie Youngblood & A. Hall. Prod: Lonnie Youngblood.

NOTE: <1> Stated as: Go Go Shoes Part I. <2> This is the same version as S324. Difference: stereo mix.

S330: **Go Go Place** – Jimi (gi), Lonnie Youngblood (sa, vo), unknown (rest). Comp: M. Thomas & Lonnie Youngblood & A. Hall. Prod: Lonnie Youngblood.

NOTE: <1> Stated as: Go Go Shoes Part II. <2> This is the complete version of S310, now in a stereo mix.

Plus fake: Good Feeling; Voice In The Wind; Good Times; Hot Trigger; Bring My Baby Back; Suspicious.

ORIGINAL JIMI HENDRIX ROOTS OF HENDRIX
     – Musidisc 30 CV 1315 [FRA] – Released 80's – LP

Contains: Wipe The Sweat I [S313]; Wipe The Sweat II [S314]; Goodbye, Bessie Mae [S316]; Soul Food (That's A What I Like) [S317]; part of Under The Table II [S319]; Under The Table III (stated as: 'Under The Table II') [S320].

Plus: Two In One Goes (no Jimi involvement, or fake). Plus fake: Psycho.

JIMI HENDRIX IN CONCERT
     – Springboard SPB-4031 [USA] – Released 80's – LP

Contains: part of Under The Table III (stated as: Under The Table Part 2) [S320]; Plus: Sweet Thang [S321].

Plus: Bleeding Heart [L274]; part of Tomorrow Never Knows (stated incorrectly as: 'Whoa Eeh') [L275]; Outside Woman Blues/ The Sunshine Of Your Love (stated incorrectly as: 'Lime Lime') [L276];

Plus fake: Miracle Worker; From This Day On; Human Heart.

The Isley Brothers

All songs comp: Ronald Isley & O'Kelly Isley & Rudolph Isley. All songs recorded on 8 track, 1 inch, unless otherwise stated. The 3 Isley brothers: Ronald, O'Kelly and Rudolph. All listed 05/08/65 songs: Arranged & Conducted by Teacho Wilshire (orchestra leader).

TESTIFY (PART I) b/w TESTIFY (PART II)
- T-Neck 45–501 [USA] – Released early 64 – Single
- Not released [ENG]

Both songs rec: unknown studio, New York City (on 4 track), 03/64.

S331: **Testify (Part I)** – Jimi (gi), Isley Brothers (vo), unknown (rest).
S332: **Testify (Part II)** – Jimi (gi), Isley Brothers (vo), unknown (rest).

THE LAST GIRL b/w LOOKING FOR A LOVE
- Atlantic 45–2263 [USA] – Released late 64 – Single
- Atlantic AT 4010 [ENG] – Released 11/64 – Single

Both songs rec: Atlantic Studios, New York City, 23/09/64.

S333: **The Last Girl** – Jimi (gi), Isley Brothers (lv, hv), Dionne Warwick (hv), unknown (rest, including a second guitarist).
S334: **Looking For A Love** – Jimi (gi), Isley Brothers (vo), unknown (rest, including acoustic gi). Special effect: Jimi (tremolo).

MOVE OVER AND LET ME DANCE b/w HAVE YOU EVER BEEN DISAPPOINTED?
- Atlantic 45–2303 [USA] – Released late 65 – Single
- Not released [ENG]

Both songs rec: Atlantic Studios, New York City, 05/08/65.

S335: **Move Over And Let Me Dance** – Jimi (gi), Isley Brothers (vo), Al Lucas (ba), James Brown or Bobby Gregg (dr), Jimmy Nottingham, Eddie Williams, Quentin Jackson, Dickie Harris, Seldon Powell, Haywood Henry (horn section), unknown (ta).
S336: **Have You Ever Been Disappointed?** – Jimi (gi), Isley Brothers (vo), Al Lucas (ba), James Brown or Bobby Gregg (dr), Paul Griffin (pi), Jimmy Nottingham, Eddie Williams, Quentin Jackson, Dickie Harris, Seldon Powell, Haywood Henry (horn section), unknown (ta).

IN THE BEGINNING
- T-Neck TNS 3007 [USA] – Released early 70's – LP
- Also on: Polydor 2310 105 [GER]; Brunswick 2911 508 [GER]; not released [ENG]
- CD: not released

S337: **Move Over Let Me Dance Part 1** – Jimi (gi), Isley Brothers (vo), Al Lucas (ba), James Brown or Bobby Gregg (dr), Jimmy Nottingham, Eddie Williams, Quentin Jackson, Dickie Harris, Seldon Powell, Haywood Henry (horn section), unknown (ta). Rec: Atlantic Studios, New York City, 05/08/65.

NOTE: This is the same basic version as S335. Differences: different vocal take; echo on some vocals; sax almost totally mixed down; guitar mixed up front.

S338: **Have You Ever Been Disappointed?, Part 1 & Part 2** – Jimi (gi), Isley Brothers (vo), Al Lucas (ba), James Brown or Bobby Gregg (dr), Paul Griffin (pi), Jimmy Nottingham, Eddie Williams, Quentin Jackson, Dickie Harris, Seldon Powell, Haywood Henry (horn section), unknown (ta). Special effect: Jimi (tremolo). Rec: Atlantic Studios, New York City, 05/08/65.

NOTE: This is the same basic version as S336. Differences: over twice as long; different vocal take; piano almost totally mixed down; guitar and drums mixed up front.

S339: **Testify, Part 1** – Jimi (gi), Isley Brothers (vo), unknown (rest). Rec: unknown studio, New York City (on 4 track), 03/64.

NOTE: <1> This is the complete version of S228. <2> This is a completely different version from S331.

S340: **Testify, Part 2** – Jimi (gi), Isley Brothers (vo), unknown (rest). Rec: unknown studio, New York City (on 4 track), 03/64.
NOTE: This is a completely different version from S332, and is actually a continuation of S339.
S341: **Move Over Let Me Dance, Part 2** – Jimi (gi), unknown (rest). Rec: Atlantic Studios, New York City, 05/08/65.
NOTE: <1> This is the same basic version as S335. Differences: no vocals; sax almost totally mixed down; guitar mixed up front. <2> This is actually a continuation of S337.
S342: **The Last Girl** – Jimi (gi), Isley Brothers (lv, hv), Dionne Warwick (hv), unknown (rest, including a second guitarist). Rec: Atlantic Studios, New York City, 23/09/64.
NOTE: This is the same basic version as S333. Differences: slightly longer; different mix (guitar more up front); bits of extra guitar.
S343: **Looking For A Love** – Jimi (gi), Isley Brothers (vo), unknown (rest, including acoustic gi). Special effect: Jimi (tremolo). Rec: Atlantic Studios, New York City, 23/09/64.
NOTE: This is the same basic version as S334. Difference: different vocal take.
Plus: Wild Little Tiger (no Jimi involvement); Simon Says (no Jimi involvement).

Little Richard & The Upsetters

Up to now, there has been a great deal of confusion about the period that Jimi actually played and recorded with Little Richard. After extensive research (also see the 1965 diary entries) it became clear that Jimi, calling himself Maurice James at this time, only performed and recorded with Little Richard between January 1965 to July 1965. Thus, Jimi is not on any of the following Little Richard releases:
Little Richard Is Back – Vee Jay Records VJS-1107 – Released 08/64 – LP
Friends From The Beginning – Ala Records ALA 1972 [USA] – Released 72 – LP
Together – Pickwick SPC-3347 [USA] – Released 72 – LP
Friends From The Beginning – EMI Stateside 5C 054–93 762 [HOL] – Released 72? – LP
Friends From The Beginning – Ember EMB 3434 [ENG] – Released 02/77 – LP
Friends From The Beginning – Disques Espérance ESP 155 566 [FRA] – Released 77? – LP
Rock 'N' Roll Special – PMC CD 926 [GER] – Released 88? – CD
The songs 'Whole Lotta Shakin' Goin' On', 'Hound Dog', 'Going Home Tomorrow', 'Goodnight Irene', 'Money Honey' and 'Lawdy Miss Claudy' were rec: Los Angeles, California, 06/64, 'Blueberry Hill', 'Cherry Red', 'Only You', 'Memories Are Made Of This', 'Groovy Little Suzie' and 'Short Fat Fanny' were rec: Los Angeles?, Summer 64, 'Belle Stars', 'Funky Dish Rag' and 'Why Don't You Love Me' contains guitar by Black Arthur. Nobody knows anything about these 3 songs, and Richard experts labelled these songs 'suspect with regard their origin and personnel.' And finally, 'Keep A Knockin', 'Tutti Frutti', and 'Lucille' all contain guitar with wah-wah! Maybe someone can explain how it's possible that Jimi would have played in '1964–1965' (source: liner notes of the Pickwick release) on these songs, with a wah-wah effect unit that wasn't available until mid 1967! Having said all the above, the following releases do contain Jimi in the grooves. All listed songs rec: unknown studio, New York City or Los Angeles, between 02/65 and 07/65. All songs were recorded during the same session.
I DON'T KNOW WHAT YOU'VE GOT BUT IT'S GOT ME PART I b/w *I DON'T KNOW WHAT YOU'VE GOT BUT IT'S GOT ME PART II*
 – Vee Jay Records VJ-698 [USA] – Released 11/75 – Single

Charts – entry 92 (27/11/65); top position: 92; weeks in chart: 1
– Not released [ENG]
S344: **I Don't Know What You've Got But It's Got Me Part I** –Jimi (gi), Little Richard (pi, lv), Don Covay (or), unknown (rest). Special effect: Jimi (tremolo). Comp: Don Covay. Prod: Calvin Carter.
S345: **I Don't Know What You've Got But It's Got Me Part II** – Jimi (gi), Little Richard (pi, lv), Don Covay (or), unknown (rest). Special effect: Jimi (tremolo). Comp: Don Covay. Prod: Calvin Carter.
MR BIG – Joy 195 [ENG] – Released 06?/71 – LP
S346: **I Don't Know What You've Got But It's Got Me Part I** – Jimi (gi), Little Richard (pi, vo), Don Covay (or), unknown (rest). Special effect: Jimi (tremolo). Comp: Don Covay. Prod: Calvin Carter.
NOTE: This is a completely different version from S344. Actually it is a version consisting of Part I and Part II presented as one complete song.
S347: **Dancin' All Around The World** – Jimi (gi), Little Richard (pi, vo), unknown (rest). Comp: Little Richard?
NOTE: Song recorded with the title: Dance A-Go-Go.
Plus: I Don't Know What You've Got But It's Got Me Part II [S345]. Plus: other Little Richard material.
THE COLLECTION
– Castle Communications CCSLP227 [FRA] – Released 09/89 – LP
– CD: Castle Communications CCSCD227 [FRA]
<1> Although pressed in France these releases are available all over Europe.
<2> Going Home Tomorrow is incorrectly stated as being a 'Hendrix/Richard' composition.
S348: **I Don't Know What You've Got But It's Got Me** – Jimi (gi), Little Richard (pi, lv), Don Covay (or), unknown (rest). Special effect: Jimi (tremolo). Comp: Don Covay. Prod: Calvin Carter.
NOTE: This is actually the same versions of S344 and S345 presented as one complete version, although the end (of S345) fades out about half a minute earlier.
Plus: Dancin' All Around The World [S347]. Plus: other Little Richard material.
RIP IT UP – Chameleon Records D2-74797 [USA] – Released 89 – CD
Contains: I Don't Know What You've Got But It's Got Me [S348].
Plus: other Little Richard material.

Rosa Lee Brooks
MY DIARY b/w UTEE
– Revis Records 1013 [USA] – Released mid 65 – Single
– Not released [ENG]
Arthur Lee: 'I got him to play on this record. The sound was sort of like, well, you take Curtis Mayfield and his riffs and turn up your amps full blast and years later, see what you get.' Both songs rec: unknown studio, Los Angeles, California, between 02 and 04/65.
S349: **My Diary** – Jimi (gi), Rosa Lee Brooks (vo), unknown (rest). Special effect: Jimi (tremolo). Comp: Arthur Lee. Engi: Doc Siegel. Prod: Billy Revis.
S350: **Utee** – Jimi (gi), Rosa Lee Brooks (vo), unknown (rest). Comp: Rosa Lee Brooks & Billy Revis. Engi: Doc Siegel. Prod: Billy Revis.

King Curtis
During a six-month period in 1966 Jimi recorded some sessions and performed briefly

573

with King Curtis. This was mainly in and around New York City. In a 1968 interview published in Sweden the interviewer asked Jimi about a certain King Curtis record, released in Sweden with Jimi's name on the cover. Jimi: 'On that record I'm just one of the several guitar players in the studio. On many of the tracks I don't play one single note on my instrument. It's King Curtis' record all the way through.' Unfortunately the release in question could not be traced. Possibly it's the LP titled *That Lovin' Feeling* (Atco Records 33–189 [USA] – Released 04/66), although there is very little guitar on it at all, and the information sheets about the various studio sessions don't mention Jimi at all. Refer to the 28/04/66 diary entry for an unreleased recording session of Jimi with King Curtis.

HELP ME – PART I b/w HELP ME – PART II
> – Atco Records 45–6402 [USA] – Released early 66 – Single (mono)
> – Not released [ENG]

Single by: Ray Sharpe with the King Curtis Orchestra. Help Me is subtitled as: Get The Feeling. Help Me is musically almost identical to that of 'Gloria' (comp: Van Morrison). Both songs rec: Atlantic Studios, New York City, 21/01/66.

S351: **Help Me – Part I** – Jimi (lead gi), Ray Sharpe (vo), King Curtis (tenor sa), Melvin Lastie (trumpet), Willie Bridges (baritone), Cornell Dupree (rhythm gi), Chuck Rainey (ba), Ray Lucas (dr). Comp: King Curtis & Ray Sharpe & Cornell Dupree. Prod: King Curtis.

S352: **Help Me – Part II** – Jimi (lead gi), Ray Sharpe (vo), King Curtis (tenor sa), Melvin Lastie (trumpet), Willie Bridges (baritone), Cornell Dupree (rhythm gi), Chuck Rainey (ba), Ray Lucas (dr). Comp: King Curtis & Ray Sharpe & Cornell Dupree. Prod: King Curtis.

BLAST OFF b/w PATA PATA
> – Atlantic 45–2468 [USA] – Released Winter 67 – Single (mono)
> – Not released [ENG]

Single by: The Atlantic Sounds with the King Curtis Orchestra. As no recording details were traced, Jimi's involvement is not confirmed.

S353: **Blast Off** – Jimi? (some lead gi), King Curtis (tenor sa), unknown (rest including another guitarist). Rec: Atlantic Studios, New York City, 31/05/66. Comp: King Curtis. Prod: King Curtis & Tom Dowd & Arif Mardin.

Plus: Pata Pata (no Jimi involvement).

Jayne Mansfield

AS THE CLOUDS DRIFT BY b/w SUEY
> – London HL 10147 [ENG] – Released 21/07/67 – Single

S354: **Suey** – Jimi (gi), Jayne Mansfield (vo), unknown (rest). Comp: Ed Chalpin & Doug Henderson. Rec: Studio 76 Inc. (a.k.a.: Dimensional Studio), 1650 Broadway, New York City, between 10/65 and 12/65.

Plus: As The Clouds Drift By (no Jimi involvement).

Curtis Knight & The Squires

<1> There exists an incredible amount of releases world-wide, containing studio and live recordings of Curtis Knight with Jimi. The total figure is well over 100, with hardly any release completely identical to another. That's why it is necessary here to list different versions/mixes/incomplete versions/doctored versions etc. with the addition of version I, II, etc. (going up to VI in some cases!). In reality there are 35 different live songs, and 26 different studio songs released. That's 61 songs in total. Due to lots of 'tricks' (cutting songs short, making up 'new songs' from 'old' songs etc.) the grand total comes to 100. <2> Locating specific details is another nightmare.

Even in Curtis Knight's own book on Jimi there are very few details about the material. For example, apart from a casual mention of Ray Lucas (drums), there's not a single mention of any of the other musicians involved. Jimi in *Melody Maker* 23/12/67: 'They were nothing but jam sessions, man, with a group called the Squires. No, I didn't sing on "Hush Now", that was dubbed on later by Knight trying to copy my voice. And on that one the guitar was out of tune and I was stoned out of my mind . . .'

STUDIO MATERIAL: All songs rec: Studio 76 Inc. (a.k.a.: Dimensional Studio), 1650 Broadway, New York City. Prod: Ed Chalpin (unless otherwise stated). Musicians involved were: Ray Lucas (drums on some of the 1967 material), Marlon Booker? (drums), Ed Dantes (organ, piano), Curtis Knight (vocals, some rhythm guitar), unknown (electric 12-string mandolin), Dick Glass, and Jerry Simon. Possibly also Marvin Held (bass), and Johnny Starr (engineer?). All 65 songs rec: between 10/65 and 12/65 (two sessions spread out over two days). All 07/67 songs rec: late 07/67 two sessions spread out over two days). Fuzz bass = Hagstrom 8-string bass with fuzz unit.

LIVE MATERIAL: All songs appear to have been recorded during two live concerts. The 26/12/65 songs rec: George's Club 20, Hackensack, New Jersey. The Winter 65 songs rec: very likely close to the 26/12/65 date or very early 66 at an unknown location, either in the State of New York or New Jersey again. Musicians involved were: Marlon Booker (drums), Henry Henderson (bass), Curtis Knight (rhythm guitar, lead vocals, harmony vocals, tambourine), Ed Dantes? (organ, piano), unknown (saxophone). All songs were originally recorded in mono. A lot of the songs have drums, rhythm and bass guitar added via overdubs (none of them by Jimi, of course), presumably to suggest it's in stereo. Introductions, by Jimi and/or Curtis, to songs may differ from release to release. By the way, if you put all the different live songs onto a tape, the total running time would be around 151 minutes. In other words, one double LP or double CD would have been enough . . .

HOW WOULD YOU FEEL? b/w WELCOME HOME
    – RSVP 1120 [USA] –
      Released late 65 or early 66 – Single (mono)
      Both labels state: Arr. by Jimmy Hendrix.
S355:   **How Would You Feel** – Jimi (straight gi, fuzz gi), Jimi? (hv), Curtis (lv, hv). Comp: Curtis Knight. Rec: 65.
S356:   **Welcome Home I** – Jimi (straight lead gi, hv), Curtis (lv, hv), unknown (rest including hv). Comp: Curtis Knight & Dick Glass. Rec: 65.
NOTE: Incomplete. Refer to S379 for the complete version.
HORNET'S NEST b/w KNOCK YOURSELF OUT
    – RSVP 1124 [USA] – Released early 66 – Single (mono)
S357:   **Hornet's Nest I** – Jimi (fuzz gi). Comp: Jimmy Hendrix & Jerry Simon. Prod: Jerry Simon. Rec: 65.
NOTE: Incomplete. Refer to S366 for the complete (and slightly different mixed) version.
S358:   **Knock Yourself Out I** – Jimi (fuzz gi). Comp: Jimmy Hendrix & Jerry Simon. Prod: Jerry Simon. Rec: 65.
NOTE: Incomplete. Refer to S370 for the complete version.
HOW WOULD YOU FEEL? b/w YOU DON'T WANT ME
    – London 5.620 [ENG] – Released 11/08/67 – Single (mono)
    – Track 604 009 [ENG] – Released 17/08/67 – Single (mono)
S359:   **You Don't Want Me** – Jimi (fuzz gi). Comp: Curtis Knight. Rec: 65.
Plus: How Would You Feel [S355].
HUSH NOW b/w FLASHING
    – London HL 10160 [ENG] – Released 20/10/67 – Single (mono)

– Also on: London FLX 3197 [HOL]
S360: **Hush Now I** – Jimi (wah-wah gi), Curtis (vo). Comp: Curtis Knight. Rec: 07/67.
NOTE: Incomplete. Refer to S368 for the complete version.
S361: **Flashing I** – Jimi (fuzz ba). Comp: Ed Dantes. Rec: 07/67.
NOTE: Slightly incomplete. Refer to S369 for the complete version.
GET THAT FEELING
– Capitol ST 2856 [USA] – Released 12/67 – LP
Charts – entry 194 (30/12/67); top position: 75; weeks in chart: 12
– Also on: London SH 8349 [ENG]: London LDY 379 256 [HOL]
S362: **Ballad Of Jimi I** – Jimi (wah-wah gi), Curtis (vo). Comp: Curtis Knight. Rec: 07/67.
S363: **No Business I** – Jimi (fuzz ba), Curtis (vo). Comp: Curtis Knight. Rec: 07/67.
S364: **Future Trip** – Jimi (fuzz ba). Comp: Ed Dantes. Rec: 07/67.
NOTE: This song is musically very similar to Day Tripper (comp: John Lennon & Paul McCartney) . . .
S365: **Gotta Have A New Dress** – Jimi (straight gi). Comp: Sampson Horton & Curtis Knight. Rec: 65.
S366: **Hornet's Nest II** – Jimi (fuzz gi). Comp: Jimmy Hendrix & Jerry Simon. Prod: Jerry Simon. Rec: 65.
NOTE: This is the same basic version as S357. Differences: complete version of S357; some of the screaming has been mixed more up front.
S367: **Don't Accuse Me I** – Jimi (straight gi, some hv), Curtis (lv, hv). Comp: Curtis Knight. Rec: 65.
S368: **Hush Now II** – Jimi (wah-wah gi), Curtis (vo). Comp: Curtis Knight. Rec: 07/67.
NOTE: This is the complete version of S360.
S369: **Flashing II** – Jimi (fuzz ba). Comp: Ed Dantes. Rec: 07/67.
NOTE: This is the complete version of S361.
S370: **Knock Yourself Out II** – Jimi (fuzz gi). Comp: Jimmy Hendrix & Jerry Simon. Prod: Jerry Simon. Rec: 65.
NOTE: This is the complete version of S358.
S371: **Happy Birthday I** – Jimi (wah-wah gi). Curtis (vo). Comp: Curtis Knight. Rec: 07/67.
FLASHING / JIMI HENDRIX PLAYS CURTIS KNIGHT SINGS
– Capitol ST 2894 [USA] – Released late 68 – LP
Down Beat 26/12/68: 'Everything about this record is shoddy: the lack of information about the performers, the repertoire, the brevity, the performances themselves, the sound quality . . .'
S372: **Gloomy Monday I** – Jimi (gi – main riff). Comp: Curtis Knight. Rec: 07/67.
S373: **Fool For You Baby** – Jimi? (straight rhythm gi). Comp: Curtis Knight. Rec: 65.
S374: **Day Tripper I** – Jimi (fuzz ba), Curtis (vo). Comp: John Lennon & Paul McCartney. Rec: 07/67.
NOTE: Incomplete. Refer to S387 for the complete (and somewhat different) version.
S375: **Odd Ball I** – Jimi (fuzz ba). Comp: Ed Dantes. Rec: 07/67.
NOTE: Slightly incomplete. Refer to S386 for the complete version.
S376: **Love Love I** – Jimi (wah-wah gi), Curtis (vo). Comp: Curtis Knight. Rec: 07/67.
Plus: Hornet's Nest II (S366); Happy Birthday I (S371); Flashing II (S369); Don't Accuse Me I (S367).

576

THE GREAT JIMI HENDRIX IN NEW YORK (double)
  – London 379 008 XNU [HOL] – Released 12/68 – LP
S377: **Get That Feeling I** – Jimi (fuzz ba), Curtis (vo). Comp: Curtis Knight
  & Gregory (?). Rec: 07/67.
S378: **Hush Now III** – Jimi (wah-wah gi). Comp: Curtis Knight. Rec: 07/67.
NOTE: <1> Stated incorrectly as: 'Level'. <2> This is a different (slow try-out)
version of Hush Now. This is also an edited version, taking out a mistake by Jimi,
and splicing it up with another take. Refer to S454 for a small part of the version that
includes this mistake.
S379: **Welcome Home II** – Jimi (straight lead gi, hv), Curtis (lv, hv), unknown
  (rest including hv). Comp: Curtis Knight & Dick Glass. Rec: 65.
NOTE: This is the complete version of S356.
S380: **Simon Says I** – Jimi (fuzz gi, straight gi). Special effect: Jimi (tremolo
  – on straight gi). Comp: Curtis Knight. Rec: 65.
S381: **Simon Says II** – Jimi (fuzz gi, straight gi). Special effect: Jimi (tremolo
  – on straight gi). Comp: Curtis Knight. Rec: 65.
NOTE: This is the same basic version as S380. Differences: with horns; slightly
different mix.
S382: **Love Love II** – Jimi (wah-wah gi). Comp: Curtis Knight. Rec: 07/67.
NOTE: This is the same basic version as S376. Differences: no vocals; somewhat
longer; slightly different mix.
S383: **U.F.O. I** – Jimi (straight Hagstrom ba). Comp: Curtis Knight. Rec. 07/67.
NOTE: Refer to S446 for a completely different version.
S384: **Hush Now IV** – Jimi (wah-wah gi). Comp: Curtis Knight. Rec: 07/67.
NOTE: <1> Incomplete. Refer to S390 for the complete version. <2> This
(version 2 on the release) is the same basic version as S368. Differences: no
vocals; cut in length; less guitar overdubs; slightly different mix.
S385: **Strange Things I** – Jimi (fuzz gi). Curtis (vo). Comp: Curtis Knight. Rec: 65.
S386: **Odd Ball II** – Jimi (fuzz ba). Comp: Ed Dantes. Rec: 07/67.
NOTE: This is the complete version of S375.
Plus: Future Trip [S364]; part of Flashing II [S369]; Ballad Of Jimi I [S362];
My Heart Is Higher (no Jimi involvement); Love Love I [S376]; Gloomy Monday
I [S372]; part of Hush Now II [S368]; Day Tripper I [S374].
MY BEST FRIEND
  – Astan 201017 [GER] – Released 81? – LP
S387: **Day Tripper II** – Jimi (fuzz ba). Comp: John Lennon & Paul McCartney.
  Rec: 07/67.
NOTE: This is the same basic version as S374. Differences: no vocals; 6 minutes
longer.
S388: **No Business II** – Jimi (fuzz ba). Comp: Curtis Knight. Rec: 07/67.
NOTE: <1> Stated incorrectly as: Sleepy Fate. <2> This is the same basic
version as S363. Difference: no vocals.
S389: **Ballad Of Jimi II** – Jimi (wah-wah gi). Comp: Curtis Knight. Rec: 07/67.
NOTE: <1> Stated as: My Best Friend. <2> This is the same basic version
as S362. Difference: no vocals.
Plus: Get That Feeling I [S377]; Happy Birthday I [S371]; part of Hush Now
II [S368]; Odd Ball I [S375].
SECOND TIME AROUND
  – Astan 201018 [GER] – Released 81? – LP
S390: **Hush Now V** – Jimi (wah-wah gi). Comp: Curtis Knight. Rec: 07/67.
NOTE: <1> Stated incorrectly as: 'Torture Me, Honey'. <2> This is the same
basic version as S384. Difference: 2 minutes longer; slightly different mix.

577

S391: **Love Love III** – Jimi (wah-wah gi). Comp: Curtis Knight. Rec: 07/67.
NOTE: <1> Stated incorrectly as: 'Mercy Lady Day'. <2> This the same basic version as S382. Difference: somewhat different mix.
L392: **Let The Good Times Roll** – Jimi (gi, faint vo, voice), Curtis (faint hv). Comp: Earl King. Rec: 26/12/65.
NOTE: <1> Stated incorrectly as: 'Hard Night'. <2> Let The Good Times Roll a.k.a.: 'Come On' (Part 1).
S393: **Get That Feeling II** – Jimi (fuzz ba). Comp: Curtis Knight & Gregory (?). Rec: 07/67.
NOTE: <1> Stated incorrectly as: 'Second Time Around'. <2> This is the same basic version as S377. Differences: no vocals; somewhat shorter; slightly different mix. <3> Refer to S449 for a slightly longer version.
S394: **Happy Birthday II** – Jimi (wah-wah gi). Comp: Curtis Knight. Rec: 07/67.
NOTE: <1> Stated incorrectly as: 'Got To Have It'. <2> This is the same basic version as S371. Differences: vocals have been mixed down; much shorter.
HUSH NOW
　　　Astan 201021 [GER] – Released 81? – LP
S395: **Love Love IV** – Jimi (wah-wah gi). Comp: Curtis Knight. Rec: 07/67.
NOTE: This is the same basic version as S376. Differences: a few bits of vocals mixed down very low; few bits of guitar slightly differently mixed.
S396: **Hornet's Nest III** – Jimi (fuzz gi). Comp: Jimmy Hendrix & Jerry Simon. Prod: Jerry Simon. Rec: 65.
NOTE: Stated incorrectly as: Level. This is the same basic version as S366. Differences: no organ; cat howls mixed more up front.
S397: **Gloomy Monday II** – Jimi (gi -main riff-). Comp: Curtis Knight. Rec: 07/67.
NOTE: This is a somewhat different version of S372. Differences: less guitar overdubs; different vocal take.
Plus: Hush Now II [S368]; No Business I [S363]; U.F.O. I [S383]; Simon Says I [S380]; My Heart Is Higher (no Jimi involvement); Day Tripper I [S374].
BALLAD OF JIMI b/w GLOOMY MONDAY
　　　– Decca DL 25 430 [GER] – Released 10/70 – Single (stereo)
This release includes a re-print of a studio sheet. The sheet gives recording information about some songs done by Curtis Knight with Jimi Hendrix. However, this studio sheet with 18/09/65 as the recording date for 'Ballad Of Jimi', is very odd: Once again, there was no wah-wah effect (used on 'Ballad Of Jimi', and given on the sheet as 'wow guitar') available in 1965 . . .
S398: **Ballad Of Jimi III** – Jimi (wah-wah gi); Curtis (vo). Comp: Curtis Knight. Rec: 07/67.
NOTE: This is a somewhat different version of S362. Differences: small bit of wah-wah guitar introduction (by Jimi) extra; different mix; contains an almost totally different vocal take by Curtis (recorded likely after 18/09/70). Towards the end of this version with new vocals you'll hear a clear tape cut, at which point you'll also hear some of the original vocals of version S362 in the background.
Plus: Gloomy Monday I [S372].
NO SUCH ANIMAL PART 1 b/w NO SUCH ANIMAL PART 2
　　　– RCA 2033 [ENG] – Released 02/71 – Single (mono)
　　　– Also on: Audio Fidelity Records AF 167 [USA]; Bellaphon BF 18019 [GER]; Audio Fidelity AF 45.003H [HOL]; Audio Fidelity Records AF 11.002 [FRA]
S399: **No Such Animal Part 1** – Jimi (fuzz gi). Rec: 65. Comp: Jimi Hendrix?
S400: **No Such Animal Part 2** – Jimi (fuzz gi). Rec: 65. Comp: Jimi Hendrix?

LOOKING BACK WITH JIMI HENDRIX
        Ember EMB 3428 [ENG] – Released 02/75 – LP
S401:   Ballad Of Jimi IV – Jimi (wah-wah gi), Curtis (vo). Rec: 07/67.
NOTE: This is the same basic version as S398. Differences: added rhythm guitar take
(recorded likely after 18/09/70); no drums; slightly different mix: no cut in the tape
with some of the original vocals.
S402:   Don't Accuse Me II – Jimi (straight gi), Curtis (vo). Comp: Curtis
        Knight. Rec: 65.
NOTE: This is the same basic version as S367. Differences: no harmony vocals;
different and better mix (guitar more up front).
L403:   Hang On Sloopy – Jimi (gi, lv in 2nd half of song), Curtis (rhythm gi,
        rest of lv). Comp: Bert Russell (a.k.a.: Bert Berns) & Wes Farrell. Rec:
        26/12/65.
L404:   Twist & Shout – Jimi (gi, hv). Curtis (hv). Comp: Phil Medley & Bert
        Russell. Rec: 26/12/65.
L405:   Bo Diddley – Jimi (gi, lv), Curtis (hv). Special effect: Jimi (tremolo).
        Comp: Bo Diddley. Rec: 26/12/65.
Plus: Hush Now V [S390]; Knock Yourself Out II [S370]; No Business I [S363];
Gotta Have A New Dress [S365]; Flashing II [S369].
BALLAD OF JIMI b/w GLOOMY MONDAY
        – London HLZ 10321 [ENG] – Released 16/10/70 – Single (mono)
Melody Maker 17/10/70: 'You can't even die in peace these days –
there's always someone with some old tapes ready to make a quick penny.
Rest in peace Jimi, this old disc won't sell.'
Contains: Ballad Of Jimi IV [S401]; Plus: Gloomy Monday I [S372].
EARLY JIMI HENDRIX
        – Stateside 5C 054–91962 [HOL] – Released early 70's – LP
L406:   Drivin' South – Jimi (gi, voice), Curtis (vo, voice). Rec: 26/12/65.
NOTE: This is the complete version of L229.
L407:   I'm A Man I – Jimi (gi, lv). Comp: Bo Diddley. Rec: 26/12/65.
NOTE: <1> This is the complete version of L230. <2> Refer to L452 for
a completely different version.
L408:   Killin' Floor I – Jimi (gi, vo, voice), Curtis (voice). Comp: Howlin'
        Wolf. Rec: 26/12/65.
NOTE: Refer to L439 for a completely different version.
L409:   California Night I – Jimi (gi, vo). Comp: Memphis Slim & additional
        lyrics by Jimi Hendrix. Rec: 26/12/65.
NOTE: <1> This appears to be a re-make of the song 'Everyday I Have The Blues'
(comp: Memphis Slim). <2> This is a 'doctored' version. The vocal verse that starts
with 'On my way forward, I got a friend I used to know' plus the following guitar solo
has been edited into this version twice. Refer to L447 for the original non-doctored
version. <3> Refer to L448 for a completely different version.
L410:   Ain't That Peculiar? – Jimi (gi, some hv), Curtis (lv), unknown (hv).
        Comp: Bobby Rogers & William 'Smokey' Robinson & Pete Moore & Marv
        Tarplin. Rec: 26/12/65.
L411:   What'd I Say I – Jimi (gi, lv, introduction), Curtis (hv). Comp: Ray
        Charles. Rec: 26/12/65.
NOTE: Slightly incomplete. Refer to L441 for the complete version.
L412:   Bright Lights, Big City I – Jimi (gi, vo), Curtis (introduction). Comp:
        Jimmy Reed. Rec: likely 26/12/65.
NOTE: Jimi is imitating the voice of Jimmy Reed!

EARLY JIMI HENDRIX VOL II
- Stateside 5C 052–92031 [HOL] – Released early 70's – LP

S413: **Last Night I** – Jimi (lead gi). Comp: Charles 'Packy' Axton & Jerry Lee 'Smoochie' Smith with the help of Chips Moman. Rec: 65?
NOTE: Despite the added crowd noises, this appears to be a studio recording. Refer to S450 for the basic (and somewhat different) version.

L414: **Get Out Of My Life Woman** – Jimi (gi, vo). Comp: Allen Toussaint. Rec: 26/12/65.

L415: **I'll Be Doggone** – Jimi (gi, hv), Curtis (lv). Comp: William Robinson & Pete Moore & Marv Tarplin. Rec: 26/12/65.

L416: **(I Can't Get No) Satisfaction** – Jimi (gi). Comp: Mick Jagger & Keith Richard. Rec: 26/12/65.

L417: **Sugar Pie, Honey Bunch (I Can't Help Myself) I** – Jimi (gi). Comp: Eddie Holland & Lamont Dozier & Brian Holland. Rec: 26/12/65.

L418: **Land Of A Thousand Dances** – Jimi (gi, lv), Curtis (hv). Comp: Chris Kenner & Fats Domino. Rec: 26/12/65.

Plus: California Night I [L409]; U.F.O. I [S383].

IN THE BEGINNING
- Ember NR 5068 [ENG] – Released 73 – LP
This release has irritating applause added (before, after, and sometimes during) the songs, none of which was part of the original recording . . .

L419: **You Got Me Running I** – Jimi (gi, hv), Curtis (lv). Comp: Jimmy Reed. Rec: 26/12/65.

L420: **Money** – Jimi (gi). Comp: Barry Gordy & Janie Bradford. Rec: 26/12/65.

L421: **Let's Go, Let's Go, Let's Go I** – Jimi (gi). Comp: Hank Ballard. Rec: 26/12/65.

L422: **You Got What It Takes I** – Jimi (gi, hv shouting), Curtis (lv). Comp: Joe Tex. Rec: 26/12/65.
NOTE: Incomplete. Refer to L451 for the complete version.

L423: **Sweet Little Angel I** – Jimi (gi). Comp: B.B. King. Rec: 26/12/65.

L424: **Walkin' The Dog I** – Jimi (gi, lv), Jimi or Curtis (wolf-whistles). Comp: Rufus Thomas. Rec: 26/12/65.

L425: **There Is Something On Your Mind** – Jimi (gi). Special effect: Jimi (tremolo). Comp: unknown. Rec: Winter 65.

Plus: Let The Good Times Roll (stated incorrectly as: 'Hard Night') [L392].

WHAT'D I SAY?
- Music For Pleasure MFP 5278 [USA] – Released (in ENG) 07/72 – LP
The labels state the release title as: Early Jimi Hendrix.
Contains: Driving South [L406]; California Night I [L409]; Killin' Floor I [L408]; What'd I Say? [L411]; I'll Be Doggone [L415]; Bright Lights, Big City I [L412].

LAST NIGHT
- Astan 201016 [GER] – Released 81? – LP

L426: **Let's Go, Let's Go, Let's Go II** – Jimi (gi). Comp: Hank Ballard. Rec: 26/12/65.
NOTES: <1> Stated incorrectly as: 'Running Slow'. <2> This is a 'doctored' song, taking various guitar solos from L421 and spliced together into a 'new' song. For example, one of these solos appears three times in this 'new' song!

L427: **Sweet Little Angel II** – Jimi (gi). Comp: B.B. King. Rec: 26/12/65.
NOTE: This is the same basic version as L423. Differences: faster; heavy echo added.

L428: **You Got What It Takes II** – Jimi (gi, hv shouting), Curtis (lv). Comp: Joe Tex. Rec: 26/12/65.
NOTE: This is the same version as L422, but faster.

L429: **Walkin' The Dog II** – Jimi (gi, lv), Jimi or Curtis (wolf-whistle). Comp: Rufus Thomas. Rec: 26/12/65.
NOTE: This is the same version as L424, but faster.
L430: **Bright Lights, Big City II** – Jimi (gi, vo), Curtis (introduction). Comp: Jimmy Reed. Rec: likely 26/12/65.
NOTE: This is the same version as L412, but slower.
L431: **Sweet Little Angel III** – Jimi (gi). Comp: B.B. King. Rec: 26/12/65.
NOTE: <1> Stated incorrectly as: 'My Fault'. <2> This is a 'doctored' song, taking various guitar solos from L423 and spliced together into a 'new' song.
Plus: Money [L420]; You Got Me Running I [L419]; Hang On Sloopy [L403]; Last Night I [L413].
MR. PITIFUL
          – Astan 201019 [GER] - Released 81? – LP
L432: **Wooly Bully** – Jimi (gi, hv), Curtis (lv). Comp: Sam The Sham (real name: Domingo Samudio). Rec: 26/12/65.
L433: **Bleeding Heart I** – Jimi (gi, lv). Comp: Elmore James. Rec: 26/12/65.
NOTE: Stated incorrectly as: 'Left Alone'.
L434: **Mercy Mercy** – Jimi (gi, hv), Curtis (lv, introduction). Comp: Don Covay & Horace Ott. Rec: 26/12/65.
NOTE: Song a.k.a.: 'Have Mercy Baby'.
L435: **Something You've Got** – Jimi (gi, lv, introduction), Curtis (hv). Comp: Alvin Robinson. Rec: 26/12/65.
L436: **Just A Little Bit** – Jimi (gi). Comp: Roscoe Gordon or Roy Head. Rec: 26/12/65.
NOTE: Just A Little Bit is incorrectly stated as: 'Itsy Bitsy Teenie Weenie Yellow Polka Dot Bikini'.
L437: **Stand By Me** – Jimi (gi). Special effect: Jimi (tremolo). Comp: Ben E. King. Rec: 26/12/65.
L438: **Hold (On To) What You've Got** – Jimi (gi). Special effect: Jimi (tremolo). Comp: Joe Tex. Rec: 26/12/65.
L439: **Killin' Floor II** – Jimi (gi, vo). Comp: Howlin' Wolf. Rec: Winter 65.
NOTE: This is a completely different version from L408.
Plus: part of California Night I (stated incorrectly as: 'Mr. Pitiful') [L409].
WELCOME HOME
          – Astan 201020 [GER] – Released 81? – LP
L440: **You Got Me Running II** – Jimi (gi). Comp: Jimmy Reed. Rec: 26/12/65.
NOTE: <1> Stated incorrectly as: 'Not This Time'. <2> This is a 'doctored' song, taking various guitar solos from L419 several times, and spliced together into a 'new' song.
L441: **What'd I Say? II** – Jimi (gi, lv, introduction), Curtis (hv). Comp: Ray Charles. Rec: 26/12/65.
NOTE: This is the complete version of L411.
L442: **Bleeding Heart II** – Jimi (gi, lv). Comp: Elmore James. Rec: 26/12/65.
NOTE: <1> Stated incorrectly as: 'It's Not My Gig'. <2> This is a 'doctored' song, taking various guitar solos from L433 several times, and spliced together into a 'new' song.
Plus: Sugar Pie, Honey Bunch (I Can't Help Myself) I [L417]; Get Out Of My Life Woman [L414]; Ain't That Peculiar? [L410]; Welcome Home II [S379]; I'll Be Doggone [L415]; Drivin' South [L406].
IN THE BEGINNING
          – Everest CBR 1031 [ENG] – Released 80's – LP

L443: Sugar Pie, Honey Bunch (I Can't Help Myself) II – Jimi (gi). Comp: Eddie Holland & Lamont Dozier & Brian Holland. Rec: 26/12/65.
NOTE: This is the same version as L417. Differences: without added echo effect.
L444: Day Tripper – Jimi (gi, lv), Curtis (lv). Comp: John Lennon & Paul McCartney. Rec: 26/12/65.
L445: Mr. Pitiful – Jimi (gi). Comp: Otis Redding. Rec: Winter 65.
Plus: Stand By Me [L437]; Bright Lights, Big City I [L412]; (I Can't Get No) Satisfaction [L416]; You Got What It Takes I [L422]; Land Of A Thousand Dances [L418]; I'm A Man I [L407]; Hold (On To) What You've Got [L438]; Twist & Shout [L404]; What'd I Say II [L441]; Wooly Bully [L432]; Walkin' The Dog I [L424]; Hang On Sloopy [L403].
THE LEGENDS OF ROCK (double)
    – Strand 6.28530 DP [GER] – Released 80's – LP
S446: U.F.O. II – Jimi (straight Hagstrom ba). Comp: Curtis Knight. Rec: 07/67.
NOTE: This is a completely different version from S383.
Plus: Get That Feeling I [S377]; Drivin' South [L406]; How Would You Feel? [S355]; Ballad Of Jimi II (stated as: My Best Friend) [S389]; Gloomy Monday I [S372]; I'm A Man I [L407]; Hush Now IV [S384]; California Night I [L409]; Land Of A Thousand Dances [L418]; Love Love III (stated incorrectly as: Mercy Lady Day) [S391]; Get Out Of My Life Woman [L414]; Don't Accuse Me I [S367].
GUITAR GIANTS VOL I (double)
    – Babylon DB 80020 [GER] – Released 80's – LP
L447: California Night II – Jimi (gi, vo). Comp: Memphis Slim & additional lyrics by Jimi Hendrix. Rec: 26/12/65.
NOTES: <1> Stated incorrectly as: 'Mr Pitiful'. <2> This is the original, non-doctored version of L409. This version also includes the original backing instruments. <3> Refer to L448 for a completely different version.
L448: California Night III – Jimi (gi, vo, introduction). Comp: Memphis Slim & additional lyrics by Jimi Hendrix. Rec: Winter 65.
NOTE: This is a completely different version from L447.
S449: Get That Feeling III – Jimi (fuzz ba). Comp: Curtis Knight & Gregory (?). Rec: 07/67.
NOTE: <1> Stated incorrectly as: 'Second Time Around'. <2> This is the same version as S393. Difference: somewhat longer.
Plus: Wooly Bully [L432]; Bleeding Heart I (stated incorrectly as: 'Left Alone') [L433]; Killin' Floor II [L439]; Welcome Home II [S379]; Sugar Pie, Honey Bunch (I Can't Help Myself) II [L443]; Get Out Of My Life Woman [L414]; Ain't That Peculiar [L410]; Bleeding Heart II (stated incorrectly as: 'Not This Time') [L442]; Fool For You Baby (stated as: 'Fool About You') [S373]; Killin' Floor I [L408]; Land Of A Thousand Dances [L418]; Twist & Shout [L404]; Knock Yourself Out II [S370]; Let The Good Times Roll (stated incorrectly as: 'Hard Night') [L392].
GUITAR GIANTS VOL 2 (double)
    – Babylon DB 80021 [GER] – Released 80's – LP
S450: Last Night II – Jimi (lead gi, voice), Curtis (voice). Comp: Charles 'Packy' Axton & Jerry Lee 'Smoochie' Smith with the help of Chips Moman. Rec: 65?
NOTE: This is the basic version of S413. Difference: shorter; no guitar overdub; different drums; different mix.
L451: You Got What It Takes III – Jimi (gi, hv shouting), Curtis (lv). Comp: Joe Tex. Rec: 26/12/65.
NOTE: This is the complete version of L422.
L452: I'm A Man II – Jimi (gi, lv, voice). Comp: Bo Diddley. Rec: Winter 65.

NOTE: This is a completely different version of L407.
Plus: Don't Accuse Me II [S402]; part of Hush Now II [S368]; Odd Ball I [S375]; No Business II (stated incorrectly as: 'Sleepy Fate') [S388]; Ballad Of Jimi II (stated as: My Best Friend) [S389]; Strange Things I [S385]; You Got Me Running I [L419]; Walkin' The Dog I [L424]; Flashing I [S361]; Hush Now V [S390]; No Business I [S363]; U.F.O. I [S383]; part of Love Love I [S376]; Hornet's Nest II [S366]; Ballad Of Jimi IV [S401]; How Would You Feel? [S355].

JIMI HENDRIX INSTRUMENTAL
    – Music For Pleasure 2M 046/94370 [FRA] – Released 80's – LP
S453:   Strange Things II – Jimi (fuzz gi). Comp: Curtis Knight. Rec: 65.
NOTES: <1> Stated incorrectly as: 'You Can Do It'. <2> This is the same basic version as S385. Differences: somewhat longer; no organ; different mix (vocals almost totally mixed out).
S454:   Hush Now VI – Jimi (wah-wah gi). Comp: Curtis Knight. Rec: 07/67.
NOTES: <1> Stated incorrectly as: 'Wah Wah'. <2> This is the beginning part of the basic version of S378. Differences: includes a mistake by Jimi; different mix (rhythm guitar more up front); shorter; not spliced up with another take.
Plus: Hornet's Nest II [S366]; No Business II (stated incorrectly as: 'Sleepy Fate') [S388]; Hush Now V (stated incorrectly as: 'Torture Me Honey') [S390]; Ballad Of Jimi II (stated as: 'My Best Friend') [S389]; Love Love III (stated incorrectly as: 'Mercy Lady Day') [S391].

HISTORIC HENDRIX
    – Pair Records SPCD2 1155 [USA/pressed in JAP] – Released 86 – CD (only)
Contains: Get That Feeling I [S377]; How Would You Feel [S355]; Hush Now IV [S384]; No Business I [S363]; Simon Says I [S380]; Gotta Have A New Dress [S365]; Strange Things I [S385]; Welcome Home II [S379]; Love Love I [S376]; Day Tripper I [S374]; Gloomy Monday I [S372]; Fool For You Baby [S373]; Happy Birthday I [S371]; Don't Accuse Me II [S402]; Hornet's Nest I [S357]; Flashing I [S361]; Odd Ball I [S375].

16 GREATEST CLASSICS
    – Bigtime 2615252 [GER] – Released 88? – CD (only)
Contains: Strange Things I [S385]; Welcome Home II [S379]; Day Tripper I [S374]; Simon Says I [S380]; Fool For You Baby [S373]; Don't Accuse Me II [S402]; Flashing I [S361]; Odd Ball I [S375]; Hornet's Nest I [S357]; Happy Birthday I [S371].
Plus: part of Tomorrow Never Knows (stated incorrectly as: 'WhoaEeh') [L275].
Plus: Sweet Thang [S321].
Plus fake: Voice In The Wind; Bring My Baby Back; Good Times; Psycho.
STRANGE THINGS – Success 2171CD [GER?] – Released 88? – CD (only)
JIMI HENDRIX THE COLLECTION
    – Object Enterprises OR0071 [FRA] – Released 90 – CD (only)
Althought pressed in FRA the second release is also available in ENG.
Contains: Flashing I [S361]; Hornet's Nest I (stated incorrectly as: 'Homet's Nest') [S357]; Don't Accuse Me II [S402]; Simon Says I [S380]; Day Tripper I [S374]; Welcome Home II [S379]; Strange Things I [S385]; Odd Ball I [S375].
Plus: Soul Food (That's A What I Like) stated as: 'All I Want' [S317].
Plus: part of Tomorrow Never Knows (stated incorrectly as: 'Whoaech' and 'Whoa Ech') [L275].
Plus: Instrumental 4 (stated incorrectly as: Down Mean Blues) [P283]; Monday Morning Blues [P286].
Plus fake: Bring My Baby Back; Suspicious; Good Times; Hot Trigger; Psycho; Good Feeling.

583

McGough & McGear

McGOUGH & McGEAR
- EMI Parlophone PCS 7047 [ENG] – Released 10/04/68 – LP
- Also on: Parlophone PCS 7332 [ENG] – Re-released 89 – LP
- CD: EMI CDP 7 91877 2 [ENG]

Jimi is involved in two songs only. Roger McGough and Mike McGear (real name: Mike McCartney, Paul's brother) of Scaffold fame recorded this delightful LP with the help of a host of stars, such as Mitch Mitchell and Noel Redding, among many others. Both songs rec: DLL, 20?/01/68. One other song with Jimi (playing toy drums!) from this session remains unreleased, the 'Toy Symphony' composed by Joseph Haydn.

S455: **So Much** – Jimi (lead gi), Mike McGear (lv), Gary Leeds? (dr), Barry Fantoni (sa), unknown (ba), unknown (rhythm gi), unknown (hv), unknown (ta). Comp: Roger McGough & Mike McGear. Engi: Mike Weighell? Prod: Paul McCartney.

S456: **Ex Art Student** – Jimi (lead gi), Mike McGear (lv), Roger McGough (lv), Dave Mason? (sitar), Jack Bruce? (ba), unknown (dr), unknown (fl), unknown (pe). Comp: Roger McGough. Engi: Mike Weighell? Prod: Paul McCartney.

Fat Mattress

FAT MATTRESS
- Polydor 583 056 [ENG] – Released 15/08/69 – LP
- Atco SD 33–309 [USA] – Released 10/69 – LP
  Charts – entry: 172 (15/11/69); top position: 134; weeks in chart: 10
- CD: not released

Fat Mattress members: Noel Redding (guitar, vocals), Eric Dillon (drums), Jimmy Leverton (bass, organ, vocals, harpsichord), Neil Landon (vocals). Jimi is involved in one song only. Jimmy Leverton: 'I don't think he played any guitar . . . I got an image of him and Mitch doing some percussion, sort of maracas and tambourines and things like that.' Mitch is playing drums on several other songs (like 'Magic Forest') on this release.

S457: **How Can I Live?** – Jimi (pe), Mitch (pe), Fat Mattress (rest). Comp: Neil Landon & Noel Redding. Rec: PLA, 27/08/68 (basic track). Prod: Fat Mattress.

Robert Wyatt

SLOW WALKING TALK b/w SLOW WALKING TALK
- label unknown [USA] – Pressed: late 68 – Acetate single

Both songs are the same version. 'Slow Walking Talk' was re-named by Robert Wyatt on the acetate label into: But I'm Clean As A Whistle. Years after this recording Robert added his own lyrics and re-recorded it under the title: Soup Song. Robert Wyatt: 'It's a kind of Mose Allison kind of thing, Jimi came in and listened and whispered, "I could try the bass line on that, you wouldn't have to use it". And he got Noel's bass, and you have to remember he's left handed, so he's playing bass the wrong way around. Puts down the first take, a fucking Larry Graham [of Sly And The Family Stone fame] bass line. He heard it once, including the changes, the breaks and all that, and it was staggering.'

S458: **Slow Walking Talk** – Jimi (ba), Robert Wyatt (dr, pi, or, vo). Comp: Brian Hopper. Rec: TTG, 10/68. Prod: Robert Wyatt.

584

Eire Apparent

ROCK 'N' ROLL BAND b/w YES I NEED SOMEONE
- Buddah Records 201039 [ENG] – Released 21/03/69 – Single
- Also on: Buddah Records 2011–117 [USA]

Eire Apparent members: Eric Stewart (bass), Ernie Graham (rhythm guitar, vocals), Mick Cox (lead guitar), David Lutton (drums). Carlos Olms: 'Eire Apparent came in at six o'clock in the afternoon and we messed around to eleven o'clock to get the right sound and then Jimi arrived . . . the boys really had a hard time with him, to please him with the sound. We did about five or six complete versions complete through, but always he found something which he thought was not correct. And we did it again! So it was already three o'clock at night when Jimi started to put his parts on the tape. He had to play the middle A-part and the end [of 'Rock 'N' Roll Band'] . . . we turned the light so much down that I just could see the shadow of his figure. I must say I was very impressed the first time he played, and every time he started to play his parts we thought it was fantastic, only Jimi didn't think so! So it came to five o'clock in the morning he was still playing his parts, never satisfied. We stayed until nine o'clock in the morning and the other people came already into the offices and were very surprised we were still there.'

S459: **Rock 'N' Roll Band** – Jimi (gi), Eire Apparent (rest). Comp: Mick Cox. Rec: Polydor Studio, 13 St. Georges Street, London W2, 1st week 01/69. Mixing: Jimi & Carlos Olms. Engi: Carlos Olms. Prod: Jimi.

S460: **Yes I Need Someone** – Jimi (gi), Eire Apparent (rest). Special effect: Jimi (backward gi). Comp: Eric Stewart & Ernie Graham & Mick Cox & David Lutton. Rec: TTG, 10/68. Prod: Jimi.

SUNRISE
- Buddah Records 203 021 [ENG] – Released 05/69 – LP
- CD: not released

All songs (except '1026') prod: Jimi. 'The Clown' and 'Captive In The Sun' rec: TTG, 31/10/68. Engi: Jack Hunt. All other listed songs rec: TTG, 10/68. Engi: Jack Hunt & Eddie Kramer & Gary Kellgren & Toni Bongiovi. Noel Redding (harmony vocals) and Robert Wyatt (drums?) also contributed to some of the songs. Arranger of orchestration: Vic Briggs. Jimi is playing the heavy sounding lead guitar parts (thus not the rhythm guitar) in the songs listed.

S461: **The Clown** – Jimi (gi), Eire Apparent (rest). Special effect: Jimi (gi at the end: creating the laughing sounds of the clown; backward gi). Comp: Eric Stewart.

NOTE: It took Jimi ten minutes to rehearse the clown laughing parts on his guitar . . .

S462: **Mr. Guy Fawkes** – Jimi (gi after the storm sounds), Eire Apparent (rest). Comp: Mick Cox.

S463: **Someone Is Sure To (Want You)** – Jimi (some gi during the later part of the song), Eire Apparent (rest). Comp: Ernie Graham.

S464: **Morning Glory** – Jimi (some gi), Eire Apparent (rest). Comp: Mick Cox.

S465: **Magic Carpet** – Jimi (possibly gi with wah-wah), Eire Apparent (rest). Comp: Ernie Graham.

S466: **Captive In The Sun** – Jimi (gi with wah-wah), Eire Apparent (rest). Comp: Mick Cox.

Plus: Yes I Need Someone [S460]; Got To Get Away (no Jimi involvement); Rock 'N' Roll Band [S459]; 1026 (no Jimi involvement).

SUNRISE
- Buddah Records BDS 5031 [USA] – Released 69 – LP
- CD: not released

See the previous release for additional information.

S467: **Let Me Stay** – Jimi (gi), Eire Apparent (rest). Comp: Eric Stewart & Ernie Graham & Mick Cox & David Lutton. Rec: TTG, 10/68. Prod: Jimi.

Plus: Yes I Need Someone [S460]; Got To Get Away (no Jimi involvement); The Clown [S461]; Mr. Guy Fawkes [S462]; Someone Is Sure To (Want You) [S463]; Morning Glory [S464]; Magic Carpet [S465]; Captive In The Sun [S466]; 1026 (no Jimi involvement).

Timothy Leary

YOU CAN BE ANYONE THIS TIME AROUND
- Douglas 1 [USA] – Released 04/70 – LP
- Not released [ENG]
- CD: Not released

Jimi is involved in one song only. This was Leary's so-called 'campaign album' made for his bid to run for governor of the state of California in 1970. However, when the LP was released Leary was back in jail again.

S468: **Live And Let Live** – Jimi (ba), Stephen Stills (gi), John Sebastian (gi), Buddy (dr), Timothy Leary (vo). Comp: Timothy Leary. Rec: PLA, 19 or 20/05/69. Prod: Alan Douglas.

Lightnin' Rod

DORIELLA DU FONTAINE b/w DORIELLA DU FONTAINE
- Celluloid CART 232 [USA] – Released 07/84 – 12 inch single
- Carrere Records 332 [ENG] – 12 inch single

<1> Lightnin' Rod (vocalist of The Last Poets) a.k.a: Alafia Pudim. <2> Doriella Du Fontaine was part of a suite titled 'Jail Toasts'. <3> Both songs rec: PLA, 11/69. <4> Both songs prod: Alan Douglas.

S469: **Doriella Du Fontaine** – Jimi (gi, ba), Buddy (dr, or), Lightnin' Rod (vo). Comp: Lightnin' Rod.

S470: **Doriella Du Fontaine** – Jimi (gi, ba), Buddy (dr, or). Comp: Lightnin' Rod.

Stephen Stills

STEPHEN STILLS
- Atlantic 2401 004 [ENG] – Released 11/70 – LP
- Atlantic SD 7202 [USA] – Released 11/70 – LP
  Charts – entry: 59 (28/11/70); top position: 4; weeks in chart: 39
- Also on: Atlantic 940 058 [FRA] – LP
- CD: Atlantic 7202–2 [USA]

Jimi is involved in one song only. Stephen Stills: 'Jimi's guitar was done first take . . . Jimi and I burned . . . we cut a bunch of things, and a lot of them are still in hiding.'

S471: **Old Times Good Times** – Jimi (gi), Stephen Stills (vo, or), Conrad Isedor (dr), Calvin Samuels (ba), Jeff Whittaker (congas). Comp: Stephen Stills. Engi: Andy Johns. Prod: Stephen Stills & Bill Halverson. Rec: Island Studios (the bottom studio), 8–10 Basing Street, London W11, mid 03/70. Recorded on 16 track, 2 inch. Console: Helius.

Love

FALSE START
- Blue Thumb BTS 22 [USA] – Released 12/70 – LP

Charts – entry: 184 (26/12/70); top position: 184; weeks in chart; 3
    – CD: MCAD 22029 [USA] – Released 07/90
It is possible that Jimi is also playing lead guitar on 'Slick Dick' and 'Ride That Vibration'.
S472:   **The Everlasting First** – Jimi (gi), Arthur Lee (vo), George Suranovich
    (dr), Frank Fayad (ba). Comp: Arthur Lee. Rec: OLY, 17/03/70, Prod:
    Arthur Lee.
THE EVERLASTING FIRST b/w KEEP ON SHINING
    – Harvest HAR 5030 [ENG] – Released 11/70 – Single
    – Also on: Blue Thumb 7116 [USA]; Blue Thumb 5C 006–92 011 [HOL]
Contains: The Everlasting First (S472), Plus: Keep On Shining (no Jimi involvement).

Buddy Miles Express

EXPRESSWAY TO YOUR SKULL
    – Mercury 20137 SMLC [ENG] – Released 01/69 – LP
    – Also on: Mercury SR–61196 [USA]
    – CD: not released
Jimi's only involvement in this release was the introductory notes which he wrote
around 10/68 in California. These notes are printed on the inside cover.

ELECTRIC CHURCH
    – Mercury 20163SMCL [ENG] – Released mid 69 – LP
    – Also on: Mercury SR-61222 [USA]
        Charts – entry: 147 (07/06/69); top position: 145; weeks in chart: 4
    – CD: not released
Buddy Miles Express members: Buddy Miles (drums, vocals), Jim McCarty (guitar),
Bill Rich (bass), Duane Hitchings (organ), Tobie Wynn (baritone saxophone), James
Tatum (tenor saxophone), Bobby Rock (tenor saxophone), Peter Carter (trumpet),

587

Tom Hall (trumpet). Jimi's only involvement in this release is that he produced the songs 'Miss Lady', '69 Freedom Special', 'Destructive Love' and 'My Chant'. Rec: unknown studio, New York City, between mid and end 03/69.

Cat Mother And The All Night Newsboys
'THE STREET GIVETH . . . AND THE STREET TAKETH AWAY'
- Polydor 24–4001 [USA] – Released 06/69 – LP
  Charts – entry: 177 (05/07/69); top position; 55; weeks in chart: 15
- Also on: Polydor 184 300 [ENG]
- CD: not released

Cat Mother And The All Night Newsboys members: Roy Michaels (bass, rhythm guitar, vocals), Michael Equine (drums, rhythm guitar, vocals), Larry Packer (lead guitar, violin, mandolin, vocals), Bob Smith (piano, organ, drums, vocals), Charlie Chin (rhythm guitar, banjo, vocals). Jimi produced all the songs. Possibly Jimi plays some rhythm guitar bits during 'Track In "A" (Nebraska Nights)', although this is not confirmed. All songs rec: PLA, 11/68. Engi: Tony Bongiovi & Gary Kellgren. Prod: Jimi & Cat Mother. According to Roy Michaels, Jimi was more involved in the mixing. Both releases contain the same songs, but in a different order.
Contains: Can You Dance To It; Favors; Bad News; Boston Burglar; How I Spent My Summer; Marie; Good Old Rock 'N' Roll (medley: Sweet Little Sixteen/Long Tall Sally/Chantilly Lace/Whole Lotta Shakin' Goin' On/Blues Suede Shoes/Party Doll); Bramble Bush; Probably Won't; Track In 'A' (Nebraska Nights).

BOOTLEGS

LIVE EXPERIENCE 1967–68 – Voodoo Chile [ENG] – Released 70 – LP –
  *: Purple Haze; Wild Thing
LIVE EXPERIENCE – LP
LIVE EXPERIENCE – Pod Records [USA] – LP
J. H. – Voodoo Chile [ENG] – LP
GOODBYE, JIMI – [USA] – LP
BROADCASTS – Trade Mark Of Quality 1841 [USA] – LP
<1> All 15/03/68 songs rec: Atwood Hall, Clark University, Worcester, Massachusetts, 1st or 2nd show. <2> All 04/01/69 songs rec: BBC Television Centre/Studio 4, Wood Lane, Shepherd's Bush, London W12. First brc: Happening For Lulu, BBC 1 TV (live transmission).

L473: **Purple Haze** – Jimi (gi, lv), Mitch (dr), Noel (ba, hv, voice). Rec: 15/03/68.
L474: **Wild Thing** – Jimi (gi, vo), Mitch (dr), Noel (ba). Comp: Chip Taylor. Rec: 15/03/68.
L475: **Voodoo Child (slight return)** – Jimi (gi, vo), Mitch (dr), Noel (ba). Rec: 04/01/69.
L476: **Hey Joe** – Jimi (gi, vo), Mitch (dr), Noel (ba). Comp: William M. Roberts. Rec: 04/01/69.
L477: **The Sunshine Of Your Love** – Jimi (gi, introduction), Mitch (dr), Noel (ba). Comp: Pete Brown & Jack Bruce & Eric Clapton. Rec: 04/01/69.
S478: **Drivin' South** – Jimi (gi), Mitch (dr), Noel (ba). Rec: BBCB, 06/10/67. Engi: Pete Ritzema. Prod: Bernie Andrews & Bev Phillips. First brc: 'Top Gear', BBC Radio 1, 15/10/67.
NOTE: This is the complete version of S218.
S479: **Little Miss Lover** – Jimi (gi, lv), Mitch (dr, cow-bell, hv), Noel (ba, hv), unknown (hand-claps). Rec: BBCB, 06/10/67. Engi: Pete Ritzema.

Prod: Bernie Andrews & Bev Phillips. First brc: 'Top Gear', BBC Radio
1, 15/10/67.
Plus: Catfish Blues [S207]; Hound Dog [S210]; Love Or Confusion [S205]; Foxy
Lady [S216]; Hey Joe [S215]; Stone Free [S201].
10 YEARS AFTER – Weird Sounds [USA] – Released 81? – LP
Contains: Purple Haze [L473]; Wild Thing [L474]; Voodoo Child (slight return) [L475];
Hey Joe [L476]; The Sunshine Of Your Love [L477]; Drivin' South [S478]; Day Tripper
[S203]; Catfish Blues [S207]; Hound Dog [S210]; Little Miss Lover [S479]; Love Or
Confusion [S205]; Foxy Lady [S216]; Stone Free [S201].
LENNON–HENDRIX DAYTRIPPER JAM
    – King Kong Records [USA] – LP
LENNON–HENDRIX DAYTRIPPER JAM
    – Instant Analyses JL 1056/4242 [USA] – LP
WORKING CLASS HERO!
    – Chet Mar Records CMR-75 [USA] – Released 84? – Double LP
Releases by: John Lennon. The rest of these releases contain songs by John Lennon.
Contains: Day Tripper [S203].
THEIR LEGENDS LIVE ON – Jaar Records 83425 [HOL] – Released 80's – Single
The other side of this release contains a song by the Rolling Stones.
Contains: Day Tripper (S203).
GUITAR HERO THE UNRELEASED ALBUM – Stoned Records STD 3 [SWE]
    – Released 77 – LP
GUITAR HERO – K & S Records 011 [USA?] – Released 78 – LP
PRIMAL KEYS – Impossible Recordworks IMP 1–02 [HOL?] – Released 78 – LP
GUITAR HERO – Document Records DR 013 CD [ITA] – Released 88 – CD
All 17/10/67 songs first brc: 'Rhythm And Blues', BBC World Service, 13/11/67.
S480:   **Radio One** – Jimi (gi, vo, voice), Mitch (dr, faint voice), Noel (ba),
     Pete Ritzema (voice from control-room). Rec: BBCB, 15/12/67. Engi:
     Pete Ritzema. Prod: Bernie Andrews & Bev Phillips. First brc: 'Top Gear',
     BBC Radio 1, 24/12/67.
NOTE: This is the complete version of S202. Difference: contains more chat
by Jimi, Mitch and Pete Ritzema.
S481:   **Can You Please Crawl Out Your Window?** – Jimi (gi, vo), Mitch
     (dr), Noel (ba). Comp: Bob Dylan, Rec: BBCB, 17/10/67. Prod: Jeff
     Griffin.
S482:   **Drivin' South** – Jimi (gi), Mitch (dr), Noel (ba). Rec: BBCB, 17/10/67.
     Prod: Jeff Griffin.
Plus: Catfish Blues [S207]; I'm Your Hoochie Coochie Man [S212]; Spanish Castle
Magic [S214]; Day Tripper [S203]; Wait Until Tomorrow [S208]; Stone Free [S201];
Foxy Lady [S216]; Little Miss Lover [S479]; The Burning Of The Midnight Lamp
[S217]; Hound Dog [S210]; Hey Joe [S215]; Getting My Heart Back Together Again
[S209].
THE GUITAR WIZZARD (sic) – Document Records DR 1305 [ITA] – Released
    88 – Single
    Contains: Hound Dog [S210]; Foxy Lady [S216].
JIMI HENDRIX VOLUME 2: A MAN OF OUR TIME
    – Napoleon NLP 11018 [ITA] – Released 70's – LP
The rest of this release contains material by other artists.
Contains: Highway Chile [S006]; Stone Free [S201]; Hound Dog [S210]; Foxy
Lady [S216]; Purple Haze [L473]; Little Miss Lover [S479]; Catfish Blues [S207];
The Sunshine Of Your Love [L477].

589

CAN YOU PLEASE CRAWL OUT YOUR WINDOW?
   – Dragonfly Records 5 [USA] – Released 70's – LP
CAN YOU PLEASE CRAWL OUT YOUR WINDOW?
   – Ruthless Rhymes Ltd. [USA] – LP
All 17/09/70 songs rec: Ronnie Scott's Club, Frith Street, London W1. Jimi's last jam session recorded in the early morning hours . . .

L483: **Mother Earth** – Jimi (solo gi), Eric Burdon & War (rest). Comp: Memphis Slim & Lewis Simpkins. Rec: 17/09/70.

L484: **Tobacco Road** – Jimi (solo gi), Eric Burdon & War (rest). Comp: John D. Loudermilk. Rec: 17/09/70.

Plus: Auld Lang Syne [S294]; Little Drummer Boy/Silent Night [S293]; The Burning Of The Midnight Lamp [S217]; Can You Please Crawl Out Your Window [S481]; Drivin' South [S482]. Plus: short interviews & introductions by Alexis Korner (all from 'Insight', BBC Radio 1, 22/02/76).

LIVE IN LONDON 1967
   – Koiné Records K881104 [ITA] – Released 88 – CD

S485: **Ain't Too Proud To Beg** – Jimi (gi), Noel (ba), Stevie Wonder (dr, faint vo). Comp: Norman Whitfield & Eddie Holland. Rec: BBCB, 06/10/67. Engi: Pete Ritzema. Prod: Bernie Andrews & Bev Phillips. First brc: 'The Friday Rock Show', BBC Radio 1, 25/05/79.

NOTE: Incomplete. The complete version was first brc: 'Night Rockin'', BBC Radio 1, 02/10/88.

Plus: Hey Joe [S215]; Foxy Lady [S216]; Love Or Confusion [S205]; Purple Haze [S213]; Killin' Floor [S204]; The Burning Of The Midnight Lamp [S217]; Hound Dog [S210]; Catfish Blues [S207]; Little Miss Lover [S479]; part of Radio One [S202]; Can You Please Crawl Out Your Window [S481]; I'm Your Hoochie Coochie Man [S212]; Driving South [S482]; Spanish Castle Magic [S214]; Wait Until Tomorrow [S208]; Stone Free [S201]; Day Tripper [S203]; Getting My Heart Back Together Again [S209].

ON THE KILLING FLOOR
   – The Swingin' Pig Records TSP-CD-012–1/2 [LUX] – Released 89 – Double CD – *: entire 2nd show.

<1> All songs rec: Konserthuset, Stockholm, Sweden, 09/01/69. Both shows are complete on this release. <2> Excellent quality CD overall, with the 1st show nothing short of a disaster, and the 2nd show being one of the better JHE concert performances captured on tape.

L486: **Killin' Floor** – Jimi (gi, vo), Mitch (dr), Noel (ba). Comp: Howling Wolf. Rec: 1st show.

L487: **Spanish Castle Magic** – Jimi (gi, vo), Mitch (dr), Noel (ba). Rec: 1st show.

L488: **Fire** – Jimi (gi, lv), Mitch (dr), Noel (ba, hv). Rec: 1st show.

L489: **Hey Joe** – Jimi (gi, vo), Mitch (dr), Noel (ba). Comp: William M. Roberts. Rec: 1st show.

L490: **Voodoo Child (slight return)** – Jimi (gi, vo), Mitch (dr), Noel (ba). Rec: 1st show.

L491: **Red House** – Jimi (gi, vo), Mitch (dr), Noel (ba). Rec: 1st show.

L492: **The Sunshine Of Your Love** – Jimi (gi), Mitch (dr), Noel (ba). Comp: Pete Brown & Jack Bruce & Eric Clapton. Rec: 1st show.

L493: **Instrumental** – Jimi (gi). Rec: 2nd show.

L494: **I Don't Live Today** – Jimi (gi, vo), Mitch (dr), Noel (ba). Rec: 2nd show.

L495: **Spanish Castle Magic** – Jimi (gi, vo), Mitch (dr), Noel (ba). Rec: 2nd show.

L496: **Hey Joe** – Jimi (gi, vo), Mitch (dr), Noel (ba). Comp: William M. Roberts. Rec: 2nd show.

L497: **Voodoo Child (slight return)** – Jimi (gi, vo), Mitch (dr), Noel (ba). Rec: 2nd show.

L498: **The Sunshine Of Your Love** – Jimi (gi), Mitch (dr), Noel (ba). Comp: Pete Brown & Jack Bruce & Eric Clapton. Rec: 2nd show.

NOTE: Includes a bass and drum solo, plus a small continuation of Voodoo Child (slight return).

L499: **Red House** – Jimi (gi, vo), Mitch (dr), Noel (ba). Rec: 2nd show.

L500: **Fire** – Jimi (gi, lv), Mitch (dr), Noel (ba, hv). Rec: 2nd show.

L501: **Purple Haze** – Jimi (gi, lv), Mitch (dr), Noel (ba, hv). Rec: 2nd show.

L502: **Star Spangled Banner** – Jimi (gi), Mitch (dr), Noel (ba). Comp: Francis Scott Key. Rec: 2nd show.

ELECTRONIC CHURCH MUSIC
   – Pyramid Records PY CD 23 [ITA] – Released 88 – CD
Contains: Killin' Floor [L486]; Spanish Castle Magic [L487]; Fire [L488]; Hey Joe [L489]; Red House [L491]; The Sunshine Of Your Love [L492].

JIMI HENDRIX – Released 70's – Single
Contains: Spanish Castle Magic [L495]; Fire [L500], Hey Joe [L496].

LIVE IN STOCKHOLM – Fruit-End C 10 168 [HOL] – Released 70's – LP
LIVE IN STOCKHOLM – Wizardo Records WRM6 333 [USA] – LP
PIPE DREAM – The Amazing Kornyfone Record Label TAKRL 1959 [USA] – LP
LIVE IN STOCKHOLM 1967 – Document Records DR 003 CD [ITA] – Released 88 – CD

All listed songs rec: Studio 4/Radiohuset, Stockholm, Sweden, 05/09/67.

L503: **Sergeant Pepper's Lonely Hearts Club Band** – Jimi, (gi, lv), Mitch (dr), Noel (ba, hv). Comp: John Lennon & Paul McCartney.

L504: **Hey Joe** – Jimi (gi, vo), Mitch (dr), Noel (ba). Comp: William M. Roberts.

L505: **I Don't Live Today** – Jimi (gi, lv), Mitch (dr), Noel (ba, hv).

L506: **The Wind Cries Mary** – Jimi (gi, vo), Mitch (dr), Noel (ba).

L507: **Foxy Lady** – Jimi (gi, lv), Mitch (dr), Noel (ba, hv).

L508: **Fire** – Jimi (gi, lv, tongue-click), Mitch (dr), Noel (ba, hv).

L509: **The Burning Of The Midnight Lamp** – Jimi (gi, vo), Mitch (dr), Noel (ba).

NOTE: First public performance of this song.

L510: **Purple Haze** – Jimi (gi, lv), Mitch (dr), Noel (ba, hv).

Plus: The Sunshine Of Your Love [L498]; Voodoo Child (slight return) [L497].

NEVER FADE
   – Phoenix Records 44775 [USA] – Released 79 – Double LP
Contains: Radio One [S480]; Catfish Blues [S207]; Can You Please Crawl Out Your Window [S481]; I'm Your Hoochie Coochie Man [S212]; Drivin' South [S482]; Spanish Castle Magic [S214]; Day Tripper [S203]; Wait Until Tomorrow [S208]; Stone Free [S201]; Foxy Lady [S216]; Little Miss Lover [S479]; The Burning Of The Midnight Lamp [S217]; Hound Dog [S210]; Hey Joe [S215]; Getting My Heart Back Together Again [S209]; Sergeant Pepper's Lonely Hearts Club Band [L503]; Hey Joe [L504]; I Don't Live Today [L505]; The Wind Cries Mary [L506]; Foxy Lady [L507]; Fire [L508]; The Burning Of The Midnight Lamp [L509]; Purple Haze [L510]; The Sunshine Of Your Love [L498]; Voodoo Child (slight return) [L497].

LIVE IN CONCERT 1967
   – Living Legend Records LLR-CD 001 [ITA] – Released 88 – CD
Contains: Hey Joe [L504]; Voodoo Child (slight return) [L497]; Catfish Blues [S207]; Can You Please Crawl Out Your Window [S481]; I'm Your Hoochie Coochie Man [S212]; Drivin' South [S482]; Spanish Castle Magic [S214]; Day Tripper [S203]; Wait Until Tomorrow [S208]; Stone Free [S201]; Foxy Lady [S216]; Little Miss Lover [S479]; The Burning Of The Midnight Lamp [S217]; part of Hound Dog [S210].

RECORDED LIVE AT MONTEREY POP FESTIVAL 1967
    – Document Records DR 021 CD [LUX] – Released 88? – CD
Contains: Can You See Me [L078]; Hey Joe [L077]; Purple Haze [L080]; The
Wind Cries Mary [L079]; Killin' Floor [L073]; Foxy Lady [L074]; Like A Rolling
Stone [L075]; Rock Me, Baby [L076]; Wild Thing [L081].
THE WILD MAN OF POP PLAYS VOLUME 1
    – Pyramid Records RFT LP 003 [ITA] – Released 88 – LP
THE WILD MAN OF POP PLAYS VOLUME 1
    – Pyramid Records RFT CD 003 [ITA] – Released 88 – CD
<1> All 18/05/67 songs rec: Stadthalle, Offenbach, W. Germany. First brc: *Beat,
Beat, Beat!*, Hessischer Rundfunk, German TV, 29/05/67. <2> All 24/05/67
songs rec: TV Studio, Stockholm, Sweden, First brc: *Popside*, Swedish TV, 11/
06/67.
L511: **Stone Free** – Jimi (gi, lv), Mitch (dr), Noel (ba, hv). Rec: 18/05/67.
NOTE: Incomplete.
L512: **Hey Joe** – Jimi (gi, vo), Mitch (dr), Noel (ba). Comp: William M. Roberts.
    Rec: 18/05/67.
L513: **Purple Haze** – Jimi (gi, lv), Mitch (dr), Noel (ba, hv). Rec: 18/05/67.
L514: **The Wind Cries Mary** – Jimi (gi, vo), Mitch (dr), Noel (ba). Rec:
    24/05/67.
L515: **Purple Haze** – Jimi (gi, lv), Mitch (dr), Noel (ba, hv). Rec: 24/05/67.
Plus: Sergeant Pepper's Lonely Hearts Club Band [L503]; The Wind Cries Mary
[L506]; Foxy Lady [L507]; Fire [L508]; Hey Joe [L504]; I Don't Live Today [L505];
The Burning Of The Midnight Lamp [L509]; Purple Haze [L510].
THE WILD MAN OF POP PLAYS VOLUME 2 – Pyramid Records RFT LP
    004 [ITA] – Released 88 – LP – *: Catfish Blues; Red House
THE WILD MAN OF POP PLAYS VOLUME 2 – Pyramid Records RFT CD
    004 [ITA] – Released 88 – CD
<1> All 10/11/67 songs rec: Vitus Studio, Bussum, Holland. Catfish Blues and
Purple Haze first brc: 'Jimi Hendrix Jams', VPRO, Dutch Radio, 03/08/73, Foxy
Lady first brc: 'Hoepla', VPRO, Dutch TV, 23/11/67. Introductions by: Roselie
Peters. <2> All 25/11/67 songs rec: Opera House, Blackpool, England (1st or
2nd show). <3> All 09/10/67 songs rec: L'Olympia, Paris, France.
L516: **Catfish Blues** – Jimi (gi, vo), Mitch (dr), Noel (ba). Comp: Muddy
    Waters. Rec: 10/11/67.
L517: **Foxy Lady** – Jimi (gi, lv), Mitch (dr), Noel (ba, hv). Rec: 10/11/67.
L518: **Purple Haze** – Jimi (gi, lv), Mitch (dr), Noel (ba, hv). Rec: 10/11/67.
L519: **Purple Haze** – Jimi (gi, lv), Mitch (dr), Noel (ba, hv). Rec: 25/11/67.
L520: **Wild Thing** – Jimi (gi, vo, tongue-clicks), Mitch (dr), Noel (ba). Comp:
    Chip Taylor. Rec: 25/11/67.
L521: **Foxy Lady** – Jimi (gi, lv), Mitch (dr), Noel (ba, hv). Rec: 09/10/67.
L522: **The Wind Cries Mary** – Jimi (gi, vo), Mitch (dr), Noel (ba). Rec:
    09/10/67.
L523: **Rock Me, Baby** – Jimi (gi, vo), Mitch (dr), Noel (ba). Comp: B.B.
    King & Joe Josea. Rec: 09/10/67.
L524: **Red House** – Jimi (gi, vo), Mitch (dr), Noel (ba). Rec: 09/10/67.
NOTE: This is the complete version of L233.
L525: **Purple Haze** – Jimi (gi, lv), Mitch (dr), Noel (ba, hv). Rec: 09/10/67.
NOTE: Preceded by Jimi speaking some French . . .
L526: **Wild Thing** – Jimi (gi, lv, tongue-clicks), Mitch (dr), Noel (ba, hv). Comp:
    Chip Taylor. Rec: 09/10/67.
Plus: Getting My Heart Back Together Again [S144].

592

FIRE – The Swingin' Pig TSP-CD-018 [LUX] – Released 89 – CD
FIRE – The Swingin' Pig TSP-LP-018 [LUX] – Released 89 – LP
Contains: Sergeant Pepper's Lonely Hearts Club Band [L503]; The Wind Cries Mary [L506]; Foxy Lady [L507]; Fire [L508]; Hey Joe [L504]; I Don't Live Today [L505]; The Burning Of The Midnight Lamp [L509]; Purple Haze [L510]; Foxy Lady [L517]; Purple Haze [L518]; Catfish Blues [L516].
PARIS IS SIR JAMESTOWN – Instant Analysis [USA] – Released 87? – LP
PARIS 67 – Instant Analysis BBR 003 [USA] – Released 87? – LP
Contains: Foxy Lady [L521]; The Wind Cries Mary [L522]; Rock Me, Baby [L523]; Red House [L524]; Purple Haze [L525]; Hey Joe [S215]; Purple Haze [S213]; Foxy Lady [S216]; Love Dr Confusion [S205]; Killing Floor [S204]; The Burning Of The Midnight Lamp [S217]; Hound Dog [S210]; Day Tripper [S203].
THE LEGENDARY STARCLUB TAPES
 – The Early Years 02-CD-3309 [GER] – Released 89 – CD
All listed material rec: Studio 1/NDR Radiohouse, Hamburg, W. Germany, 18/03/67. First (live transmission) brc: 'Twenclub', NDR, W. German Radio, Re-brc: 'Hamburg Swings', BBC Light Radio, 01/07/67.
I527: **Interview with Jimi and Noel** – by Jochem Rathmann.
NOTES: <1> Incomplete. <2> Noel's interview is in the German language.
L528: **Foxy Lady** – Jimi (gi, vo), Mitch (dr), Noel (ba).
L529: **Hey Joe** – Jimi (gi, vo), Mitch (dr), Noel (ba). Comp: William M. Roberts.
L530: **Stone Free** – Jimi (gi, lv), Mitch (dr), Noel (ba, hv).
L531: **Fire** – Jimi (gi, lv), Mitch (dr), Noel (ba, hv).
L532: **Purple Haze** – Jimi (gi, lv, hv), Mitch (dr), Noel (ba, hv).
Plus: I Don't Live Today [L494]; Spanish Castle Magic [L495]; part of Voodoo Child (slight return) [L497]; part of The Sunshine Of Your Love [L498].
FUCKIN' HIS GUITAR FOR DENMARK
 – JH CO [ENG] – Released 88 – LP
FUCKIN' HIS GUITAR FOR DENMARK
 – Polymore [HOL] – Released 88 – LP
All songs rec: Tivolis Konsertsal, Copenhagen, Denmark, 07/01/68, likely 2nd show.
L533: **Sergeant Pepper's Lonely Hearts Club Band** – Jimi (gi, vo), Mitch (dr), Noel (ba). Comp: John Lennon & Paul McCartney.
L534: **Fire** – Jimi (gi, lv), Mitch (dr), Noel (ba, hv).
L535: **Hey Joe** – Jimi (gi, vo), Mitch (dr), Noel (ba). Comp: William M. Roberts.
L536: **Catfish Blues** – Jimi (gi, vo), Mitch (dr), Noel (ba). Comp: Muddy Waters.
L537: **The Wind Cries Mary** – Jimi (gi, vo), Mitch (dr), Noel (ba).
NOTE: Incomplete.
L538: **Purple Haze** – Jimi (gi, lv), Mitch (dr), Noel (ba, hv).
L539: **Spanish Castle Magic** – Jimi (gi, vo), Mitch (dr), Noel (ba).
L540: **Wild Thing** – Jimi (gi, vo), Mitch (dr), Noel (ba). Comp: Chip Taylor.
DRIVING SOUTH WITH THE JIMI HENDRIX EXPERIENCE
 – Tan Studio [ENG] – Released 81 – LP
LIVE AT THE OLYMPIA THEATRE
 – JH 68 P [USA?] – Released 87? – LP
All songs rec: L'Olympia, Paris, France, 29/01/68, 2nd show.
L541: **Killin' Floor** – Jimi (gi, vo), Mitch (dr), Noel (ba). Comp: Howlin' Wolf.
L542: **Catfish Blues** – Jimi (gi, vo), Mitch (dr), Noel (ba). Comp: Muddy Waters.
L543: **Foxy Lady** – Jimi (gi, lv), Mitch (dr, voice), Noel (ba, hv).
L544: **Red House** – Jimi (gi, vo), Mitch (dr), Noel (ba strings of a normal 6-string gi, owned by Keith Richard).
L545: **Tune-Up Song (Spanish Castle Magic)** – Jimi (gi), Mitch (dr), Noel (ba).

L546: **The Wind Cries Mary** – Jimi (gi, vo), Mitch (dr), Noel (ba).
L547: **Drivin' South** – Jimi (gi), Mitch (dr), Noel (ba).
L548: **Fire** – Jimi (gi, lv), Mitch (dr), Noel (ba, hv).
L549: **Little Wing** – Jimi (gi, vo), Mitch (dr), Noel (ba).
L550: **Purple Haze** – Jimi (gi, lv), Mitch (dr), Noel (ba, hv).
LIVE IN PARIS
　　　– The Swingin' Pig TSP-CD-016 [LUX] – Release 89 – CD
LIVE IN PARIS
　　　– The Swingin' Pig TSP 016 [LUX] – Released 89 – LP
Contains: Killin' Floor [L541]; Catfish Blues [L542]; Foxy Lady [L543]; Red House [L544]; Drivin' South [L547]; The Wind Cries Mary [L546]; Fire [L548]; Little Wing [L549]; Purple Haze [L550].
GUITARS & AMPS – World Productions of Compact Music WPOCM 0888B005–1
　　　[ITA] – Released 88 – LP
GUITARS & AMPS
　　　– World Productions of Compact Music WPOCM 0888D005–2 [ITA] –
　　　Released 88 – CD
Contains: Killin' Floor [L541]; Catfish Blues [L542]; Foxy Lady [L543]; Red House [L544]; Drivin' South [L547]; Fire [L548]; Little Wing [L549]; Purple Haze [L550].
RECORDED LIVE PARIS OLYMPIA JANUARY 29, 1968
　　　– UFO 201018 [USA] – Released 82 – LP
Contains: Killin' Floor [L541]; Catfish Blues [L542]; Foxy Lady [L543]; Red House [L544]; Drivin' South [L547]; Purple Haze [L550].
RECORDED LIVE IN EUROPE 1967 (sic)
　　　– Bulldog Records – Released 90 – LP
Contains: Sergeant Pepper's Lonely Hearts Club Band [L503]; Hey Joe [L504]; I Don't Live Today [L505]; The Wind Cries Mary [L506]; Foxy Lady [L507]; Fire [L508]; The Burning Of The Midnight Lamp [L509]; Purple Haze [L510]; Killing Floor [L541]; Catfish Blues [L542]; Foxy Lady [L543]; Red House [L544]; The Wind Cries Mary [L546]; Drivin' South [L547]; Fire [L548].
SKY HIGH – [ENG] – Released 70's – LP
SKY HIGH – Kustom Records SPJH1 [ENG] – Released 70's – LP
SKY HIGH – Skydog 2017378 [HOL] – Released 72 – LP
SKY HIGH – Trade Mark Of Quality 73031 [USA] – LP
JAM – Ax Records HHJAM [USA] – LP
Contains: Red House [L272]; I'm Gonna Leave This Town/Everything's Gonna Be Allright [L273]; Bleeding Heart [L274]; Tomorrow Never Knows [L275]; Outside Woman Blues/The Sunshine Of Your Love [L276].
CAFÉ AU GO GO
　　　– Koiné Records K880802 [ITA] – Released 88 – CD
JIMI HENDRIX JAMMING WITH FRIENDS
　　　– Koiné Records V880802 [ITA] – Released 88 – LP
All jam session song rec: Café Au Go Go, 152 Bleecker Street, New York City, 17/03/68.
L551: **Everything's Gonna Be Allright** – Jimi (gi), Elvin Bishop (gi), Phillip Wilson (dr), Harvey Brooks (ba), Paul Butterfield (vo, ha). Comp: Walter Jacobs.
L552: **Stormy Monday** – Jimi (gi), Elvin Bishop (gi), Buddy (dr, vo), Harvey Brooks (ba), Herbie Rich (or). Comp: T-Bone Walker.
L553: **Three Little Bears** – Jimi (gi), Elvin Bishop (gi), Buddy (dr), Harvey Brooks (ba), Herbie Rich (or), James Tatum (sa).

L554: **Instrumental Jam I** – Jimi (gi), Elvin Bishop (gi), Buddy (dr), Harvey Brooks (ba), Herbie Rich (or), James Tatum (sa). Comp: unknown.

L555: **Instrumental Jam II** – Jimi (gi), Elvin Bishop (gi), Phillip Wilson (dr), Harvey Brooks (ba), Paul Butterfield (ha), James Tatum (sa). Comp: unknown.

L556: **Little Wing** – Jimi (gi, voice), Phillip Wilson (dr), Harvey Brooks (ba), Herbie Rich (or), Paul Butterfield (ha), unknown (voice).

CANADIAN CLUB
 – World Productions Of Compact Music WPOCM 0888 B 006–1 [ITA]
 – Released 88 – LP

CANADIAN CLUB
 – World Productions Of Compact Music WPOCM 0888 D 006–2 [ITA]
 – Released 88 – CD

All listed songs rec: Capitol Theatre, Ottawa, Canada, 19/03/68, 2nd show.

L557: **Foxy Lady** – Jimi (gi, lv), Mitch (dr), Noel (ba, hv).

L558: **Fire** – Jimi (gi, lv), Mitch (dr), Noel (ba, hv).

L559: **Killin' Floor** – Jimi (gi, vo), Mitch (dr), Noel (ba). Comp: Howlin' Wolf.

L560: **Red House** – Jimi (gi, vo), Mitch (dr), Noel (ba).

L561: **Spanish Castle Magic** – Jimi (gi, vo), Mitch (dr), Noel (ba).

L562: **Hey Joe** – Jimi (gi, vo), Mitch (dr), Noel (ba). Comp: William M. Roberts.

L563: **Purple Haze** – Jimi (gi, lv), Mitch (dr), Noel (ba, hv).

Plus: Ain't Too Proud To Beg [S485].

LIVE IN OTTAWAY (sic), CANADA – 3/19/68
 – [USA] – Released 81? – LP

LIVE FROM OTTAWA
 – SL 87010 [USA] – LP

Both releases contain the same material, but in a different order.

L564: **Tax Free** – Jimi (gi), Mitch (dr), Noel (ba). Comp: Bo Hansson & Janne Karlsson. Rec: Capitol Theatre, Ottawa, Canada, 19/03/68, 2nd show.

Plus: Fire [L558]; Red House [L560]; Foxy Lady [L557]; Hey Joe [L562]; Spanish Castle Magic [L561]; Purple Haze [L563].

DAVENPORT, IOWA '68
 – Creative Artisty 26K10/55K10 [USA] – Released 82 – Double LP

All songs rec: Col Ballroom, Davenport, Iowa, 11/08/68.

L565: **Are You Experienced?** – Jimi (gi, vo), Mitch (dr), Noel (ba).

NOTE: Incomplete.

L566: **Lover Man** – Jimi (gi, vo), Mitch (dr), Noel (ba).

L567: **Foxy Lady** – Jimi (gi, vo), Mitch (dr), Noel (ba).

L568: **Red House** – Jimi (gi, vo), Mitch (dr), Noel (ba).

L569: **I Don't Live Today** – Jimi (gi, vo), Mitch (dr), Noel (ba).

L570: **Fire** – Jimi (gi, lv), Mitch (dr), Noel (ba, hv).

LIVE AT THE HOLLYWOOD BOWL
 – Continuing Saga Records RSR 251 [USA] – Released 80's – Double LP

LIVE AT THE HOLLYWOOD BOWL
 – Continuing Saga Records/Trade Mark Of Quality [USA] – Released 80's – Double LP

All listed songs rec: Hollywood Bowl, Hollywood, California, 14/09/68.

L571: **Are You Experienced?** – Jimi (gi, vo), Mitch (dr), Noel (ba).

L572: **Voodoo Child (slight return)** – Jimi (gi, vo), Mitch (dr), Noel (ba).

L573: **Red House** – Jimi (gi, vo), Mitch (dr), Noel (ba).

NOTE: Incomplete.

L574: **Fire** – Jimi (gi, lv), Mitch (dr), Noel (ba, hv).

L575: **Hey Joe** – Jimi (gi, vo), Mitch (dr), Noel (ba). Comp: William M. Roberts.

L576: **I Don't Live Today** – Jimi (gi, lv), Mitch (dr), Noel (ba, hv).

L577: **Little Wing** – Jimi (gi, vo), Mitch (dr), Noel (ba).

NOTE: Preceded by a 'false start' of the song, stopped due to too much splashing!

L578: **Star Spangled Banner** – Jimi (gi, voice), Mitch (dr). Comp: Francis Scott Key.

L579: **Purple Haze** – Jimi (gi, lv), Mitch (dr), Noel (ba, hv).

Plus: Sergeant Pepper's Lonely Hearts Club Band [L503]; The Wind Cries Mary [L506]; Foxy Lady [L507]; The Sunshine Of Your Love [L498]; The Burning Of The Midnight Lamp [L509].

LIVE AT PHILHARMONIC HALL
    – Sagittarius Ltd. [USA] – Released 70's – LP

<1> All 28/11/68 songs rec: Philharmonic Hall, New York City, 1st show. <2> All 10/07/69 songs and interview rec: *The Tonight Show* (live transmission from New York City), NBC TV Studio, NBC TV. First public performance of Jimi with Billy Cox on bass. During the interview with Flip Wilson there are also a few comments from Ed McMahon. Jimi's amp blew up during Lover Man, hence the second version.

L580: **I Don't Live Today** – Jimi (gi, lv), Mitch (dr), Noel (ba, hv). Rec: 28/11/68.

L581: **Getting My Heart Back Together Again** – Jimi (gi, vo), Mitch (dr), Noel (ba). Rec: 28/11/68.

L582: **Spanish Castle Magic** – Jimi (gi, vo), Mitch (dr), Noel (ba). Rec: 28/11/68.

I583: **Interview with Jimi** – by Flip Wilson. Rec: 10/07/69.

NOTE: Incomplete.

L584: **Lover Man I & II** – Jimi (gi, vo), Billy (ba), Ed Shaughnessy (dr). Rec: 10/07/69.

ELECTRIC CHURCH MUSIC PART 1
    – Tan Studio [ENG] – Released 81 – LP

All songs rec: Falkoner Centret, Copenhagen, Denmark, 10/01/69, 1st show.

L585: **Fire** – Jimi (gi, vo), Mitch (dr), Noel (ba).

L586: **Tax Free** – Jimi (gi), Mitch (dr), Noel (ba). Comp: Bo Hansson & Janne Karlsson.

L587: **Spanish Castle Magic** – Jimi (gi, vo), Mitch (dr), Noel (ba).

L588: **Red House** – Jimi (gi, vo), Mitch (dr), Noel (ba).

L589: **I Don't Live Today/Star Spangled Banner** – Jimi (gi, vo), Mitch (dr), Noel (ba). Comp: Francis Scott Key (Star Spangled Banner).

NOTE: During the concert, Jimi introduced this medley as: Electric Church Music Part One.

Plus: two small parts of I239.

ELECTRIC CHURCH MUSIC PART ONE
    – Guitar Hero Records 71056 [ENG] – Released 90 – LP

L590: **The Sunshine Of Your Love** – Jimi (gi), Mitch (dr), Noel (ba). Comp: Pete Brown & Jack Bruce & Eric Clapton.

Rec: Falkoner Centret, Copenhagen, Denmark, 10/01/69, 1st show.

Plus: Tax Free [L586]; Red House [L588]; I Don't Live Today/Star Spangled Banner [L589].

GOOD VIBES – Trade Mark Of Quality JH 113/TMQ 71042 [USA] – Released 80's – LP

GOOD VIBES – Mushroom Records Vol.7/1850 [USA] – LP

GOOD VIBES – Ruthless Rhymes 1850 [USA] – LP

Hawaii, first week of October 1968

HE WAS A FRIEND OF YOURS
>   – Out To Lunch Production I [USA] – LP

<1> All 24/02/69 songs rec: Royal Albert Hall, London, afternoon rehearsals. Besides the complete versions of the songs listed this release also contains various bits of try-out's for the same songs throughout the whole release. There are also various voices during the songs, by Jimi, Noel and various film and sound crew members. <2> The late 03/69 backstage interview rec: Teen-Age Fair/Pop Expo '69/The Palladium, Hollywood, California, probably for radio station KAA1. The interview is split up into various small parts throughout the whole release.

I591: **Interview with Jimi** – by Jay Harvey. Rec: late 03/69.

L592: **Hey Joe** – Jimi (gi, vo), Mitch (dr), Noel (ba). Comp: William M. Roberts. Rec: 24/02/69.

L593: **Hound Dog I** – Jimi (gi, vo), Mitch (dr), Noel (ba). Comp: Jerry Leiber & Mike Stoller. Rec: 24/02/69.

L594: **Hound Dog II** – Jimi, (gi), Mitch (dr), Noel (ba). Comp: Jerry Leiber & Mike Stoller. Rec: 24/02/69.

L595: **Voodoo Child (slight return)** – Jimi (gi, vo), Mitch (dr), Noel (ba). Rec: 24/02/69.

NOTE: Two separate small parts.

L596: **Getting My Heart Back Together Again** – Jimi (gi, vo), Mitch (dr), Noel (ba). Rec: 24/02/69.

UNKNOWN WELLKNOWN
>   – Stardust [USA] – Released 72 – LP

Contains: Star Spangled Banner [L067]; Purple Haze [L068]; Instrumental Solo [L069]; Getting My Heart Back Together Again [S144]; Day Tripper [S203]; Hound Dog I [S593].

'EXPERIENCE'
>   – Immaculate Conception Records CBMR-10 [USA] – LP

Contains: The Sunshine Of Your Love [L092]; Room Full Of Mirrors [L093]; Bleeding Heart [L094]; Smashing Of Amps [L095].

'SMASHING AMPS'
>   – Duck Records [USA] – Released 78 – LP

The labels incorrectly state 11 song titles, all containing the word duck, such as: Smoke On The Duck, I Wanna Hold Your Duck, and Voodoo Duck (Slight Return) . . .

Contains: The Sunshine Of Your Love [L092]; Room Full Of Mirrors [L093]; Bleeding Heart [L094]; Smashing Of Amps [L095].

SMASHING AMPS – Trade Mark Of Quality [USA] – Released 70's – LP
SMASHING AMPS – Ruthless Rhymes JHE [USA] – Released 71 – LP
Both releases contain the same songs, but in a different order.

Contains: Bleeding Heart [L094]; Purple Haze [L519]; Getting My Heart Back Together Again [S144]; Wild Thing [L520]; The Sunshine Of Your Love [L092]; Room Full Of Mirrors [L093]; Smashing Of Amps [L095].

LIVE AT THE ALBERT HALL
>   – Jimi Records 2288 [ENG?] – Released 70's – LP

Contains: The Sunshine Of Your Love [L092]; Room Full Of Mirrors [L093]; Bleeding Heart [L094]; Smashing Of Amps [L095].

BLUES
>   – Toasted Records 25 912 [USA] – Released 80? – Double LP

Contains: Bleeding Heart [L094]; Purple Haze [L519]; Getting My Heart Back Together Again [S144]; The Sunshine Of Your Love [L092]; Room Full Of Mirrors [L093]; Smashing Of Amps [L095]; Red House [L272]; I'm Gonna Leave This

Town/Everything's Gonna Be Allright [L273]; Bleeding Heart [L274]; Tomorrow
Never Knows [L275].
ELECTRIC JIMI
     – Jaguarondi Records JAG CD 001/2 [ITA] – Released 89 – Double CD
ELECTRIC JIMI
     – Jaguarondi Records JAG 001/2 [ITA] – Released 89 – Double LP
SPANISH CASTLE MAGIC
     – Toasted Records TRW 1952 [USA] – Released 89 – Double LP
SPANISH CASTLE MAGIC
     – Trade Mark Of Quality [USA] – Released 89 – Double LP
L.A. FORUM
     – Zipper [USA?] – Released 89 – Double LP
<1> All songs rec: The Forum, Los Angeles, California, 26/04/69. <2> All
releases contain the same songs, but in a different order.
L597:   **Tax Free** – Jimi (gi), Mitch (dr), Noel (ba). Comp: Bo Hansson &
        Janne Karlsson.
NOTE: Includes a drum solo.
L598:   **I Don't Live Today** – Jimi (gi, lv), Mitch (dr), Noel (ba, hv).
NOTE: This is the complete version of L221.
L599:   **Spanish Castle Magic** – Jimi (gi, vo), Mitch (dr), Noel (ba).
L600:   **Star Spangled Banner** – Jimi (gi, voice), Mitch (dr). Comp: Francis
        Scott Key.
L601:   **Purple Haze** – Jimi (gi, lv), Mitch (dr), Noel (ba, hv).
L602:   **Voodoo Child (slight return)** – Jimi (gi, vo), Mitch (dr), Noel (ba).
NOTE: Includes a drum solo.
L603:   **The Sunshine Of Your Love** – Jimi (gi), Mitch (dr), Noel (ba). Comp:
        Pete Brown & Jack Bruce & Eric Clapton.
NOTE: Includes the continuation of Voodoo Child (slight reurn).
Plus: Foxy Lady [L186]; Red House [L301].
I DON'T LIVE TODAY, MAYBE TOMORROW
     – Living Legend Records LLRCD 030 [ITA] – Released 89 – CD
Contains: Tax Free [L597]; Spanish Castle Magic [L599]; Star Spangled Banner
[L600]; Purple Haze [L601]; Red House [L301]; Foxy Lady [L186]; I Don't Live
Today [L598]; Voodoo Child (slight return) [L602]; The Sunshine Of Your Love
[L603].
A LIFETIME OF EXPERIENCE
     – Sleepy Dragon 55 10 – Released 88? – Double LP – *: Are You
       Experienced?; Like A Rolling Stone
All listed songs rec: Newport 69, nearby San Fernando, Devonshire Downs, California,
20/06/69.
L604:   **Stone Free** – Jimi (gi, vo), Mitch (dr), Noel (ba).
NOTE: <1> Includes a drum solo. <2> Incomplete.
L605:   **Are You Experienced?/Stone Free** – Jimi (gi, lv), Mitch (dr), Noel
       (ba, hv).
L606:   **The Sunshine Of Your Love** – Jimi (gi), Mitch (dr), Noel (ba). Comp:
       Pete Brown & Jack Bruce & Eric Clapton.
NOTE: Includes a bass and drum solo.
L607:   **Fire** – Jimi (gi, lv), Mitch (dr), Noel (ba, hv).
L608:   **Getting My Heart Back Together Again** – Jimi (gi, vo), Mitch (dr),
       Noel (ba).
NOTE: Incomplete.
L609:   **Red House** – Jimi (gi, vo), Mitch (dr), Noel (ba).
NOTE: Incomplete.

L610: **Foxy Lady** – Jimi (gi, lv), Mitch (dr), Noel (ba, hv).

L611: **Like A Rolling Stone** – Jimi (gi, vo), Mitch (dr), Noel (ba). Comp: Bob Dylan.

L612: **Voodoo Child (slight return)** – Jimi (gi, vo), Mitch (dr), Noel (ba).

NOTE: Includes a short bass and a long drum solo.

L613: **Purple Haze** – Jimi (gi, lv), Mitch (dr), Noel (ba, hv).

Plus: Everything's Gonna Be Allright [L551]; Stormy Monday [L552].

WIZARD'S (sic) VISIONS
    – World Productions Of Compact Music WPOCM 0789 D 026–2 [ITA]
    – Released 89 – CD

Contains: Fire [L607]; Getting My Heart Back Together Again [L608]; Red House [L609]; Stone Free [L604]; Are You Experienced/Stone Free [L605]; The Sunshine Of Your Love [L606]; Foxy Lady [L610]; Like A Rolling Stone [L611]; Voodoo Child (slight return) [L612]; Purple Haze [L613].

THE LORD OF THE STRINGS
    – International Record [USA] – Released 83 – Double LP

THE LORD OF THE STRINGS
    – Continuing Saga Records [USA] – Released 83? – Released 83? – Double LP

WOODSTOCK NATION
    – Wild Bird Records WBR890901/2 [ITA] – Released 89 – Double CD

<1> All songs rec: Woodstock Music & Art Fair, Bethel, New York, early morning of 18/08/69. <2> All songs on this release are mixed differently to some of the same songs which appeared on the official releases. <3> This release contains the songs in the correct order of performance. At least 'Message To Love' was also performed (missing on this release).

L614: **Getting My Heart Back Together Again** – Jimi (gi, vo), Mitch (dr), Billy (ba), Larry (rhythm gi), Juma (maracas, pe), Jerry (congas).

NOTE: This is the complete version of L072.

L615: **Spanish Castle Magic** – Jimi (gi, vo), Mitch (dr), Billy (ba), Larry (rhythm gi), Juma (cow-bell), Jerry (congas).

L616: **Red House** – Jimi (gi, vo), Mitch (dr), Billy (ba), Larry (rhythm gi), Juma (maracas).

L617: **Mastermind** – Jimi (gi, hv), Mitch (dr), Billy (ba), Larry (rhythm gi, lv). Comp: Larry Lee.

L618: **Lover Man** – Jimi (gi, vo), Mitch (dr), Billy (ba), Larry (rhythm gi).

L619: **Foxy Lady** – Jimi (gi, vo), Mitch (dr), Billy (ba), Larry (rhythm gi).

L620: **Jam Back At The House** – Jimi (gi), Mitch (dr), Billy (ba), Larry (rhythm gi), Juma (cow-bell, pe), Jerry (pe). Comp: Mitch Mitchell.

NOTE: <1> Song a.k.a.: Beginning. <2> This is the complete version of L070.

L621: **Izabella** – Jimi (gi, vo), Mitch (dr), Billy (ba), Larry (rhythm gi), Juma (pe), Jerry (pe).

NOTE: This is the complete version of L071.

L622: **Gypsy Woman** – Jimi (gi), Mitch (dr), Billy (ba), Larry (rhythm gi, vo), Juma and Jerry (cow-bell). Comp: Curtis Mayfield.

L623: **Fire** – Jimi (gi, vo), Mitch (dr), Billy (ba), Larry (rhythm gi), Juma (pe).

L624: **Voodoo Child (slight return)** – Jimi (gi, vo), Mitch (dr), Billy (ba), Larry (rhythm gi, plus a solo), Jerry (congas).

L625: **Instrumental Solo** – Jimi (gi), Mitch (dr), Billy (ba), Larry (rhythm gi), Juma (ta), Jerry (pe).

NOTE: This is the complete version of L069.

L626: **Hey Joe** – Jimi (gi, vo), Mitch (dr), Billy (ba), Larry (rhythm gi). Comp: William M. Roberts.

600

Plus: Star Spangled Banner [L067]; Purple Haze [L068].
BEST OF WOODSTOCK
– [ENG] – Released 69/70 – LP
The rest of this release contains material by other artists.
Contains: Star Spangled Banner [L067]; Purple Haze [L068]; part of Instrumental Solo [L069].
WOW – Released 69/70 – LP
Contains: Like A Rolling Stone [L075]; Rock Me, Baby [L076]; Can You See Me [L078]; Wild Thing [L081]; Star Spangled Banner [L067]; Purple Haze [L068]; Instrumental Solo [L069].
JIMI HENDRIX LIVE AT THE LOS ANGELES FORUM 4–25–70
– Rubber Dubber 70–001 [USA] – Released 70 – Double LP –*: [L634]
JIMI HENDRIX LIVE AT THE LOS ANGELES FORUM 4–25–70
– Pod Records [USA] – Double LP
LIVE AT THE FORUM
– Munia Records LPR-28/9 & Munia M1612 [USA] – Double LP
HENDRIX ALIVE!
[USA] – Double LP
L.A. FORUM – LIVE!
– Trade Mark Of Quality – Double LP
LIVE IN L. A. APRIL 1970
– Bread & Circus Records [USA] – Four singles
<1> All songs rec: The Forum, Los Angeles, California, 25/04/70. <2> All releases contain the same songs, but in a different order.
L627: **Spanish Castle Magic** – Jimi (gi, vo), Mitch (dr), Billy (ba).
L628: **Foxy Lady** – Jimi (gi, vo), Mitch (dr), Billy (ba).
L629: **Lover Man** – Jimi (gi, vo), Mitch (dr), Billy (ba).
L630: **Getting My Heart Back Together Again** – Jimi (gi, vo), Mitch (dr), Billy (ba).
L631: **Message To Love** – Jimi (gi, vo), Mitch (dr), Billy (ba).
L632: **Ezy Ryder** – Jimi (gi, vo), Mitch (dr), Billy (ba).
L633: **Machine Gun** – Jimi (gi, vo), Mitch (dr), Billy (ba).
L634: **Room Full Of Mirrors/Hey Baby (The Land Of The New Rising Sun)/Instrumental Solo/Freedom** – Jimi (gi, vo), Mitch (dr), Billy (ba).
NOTE: This medley also includes a drum solo (after Instrumental Solo).
L635: **Star Spangled Banner** – Jimi (gi), Mitch (dr). Comp: Francis Scott Key.
L636: **Purple Haze** – Jimi (gi, vo), Mitch (dr), Billy (ba).
NOTE: Star Spangled Banner and Purple Haze is a medley.
L637: **Voodoo Child (slight return)/Midnight Lightnin'** – Jimi (gi, vo), Mitch (dr), Billy (ba).
JIMI HENDRIX LIVE AT THE L.A. FORUM 4–25–70 'SCUSE ME . . . WHILE I KISS THE SKY . . .
– [USA] – Released 70 – LP
Contains: Spanish Castle Magic [L627]; Foxy Lady [L628]; Lover Man [L629]; Getting My Heart Back Together Again [L630]; Message To Love [L631]; Ezy Ryder [L632]; Machine Gun [L633].
THE BEST OF JIMI HENDRIX LIVE IN CONCERT
– Immaculate Conception Records CBMR-7 [USA] – Released 70's – LP
Contains: Foxy Lady [L628]; Purple Haze [L068]; Instrumental Solo [L069]; Can You See Me [L078]; Voodoo Child (slight return)/Midnight Lightnin' [L637]; Ezy Ryder [L632]; Getting My Heart Back Together Again [L630]; Wild Thing [L081]; Like A Rolling Stone [L075].

GOOD KARMA 1
    – Trade Mark Of Quality TMQ 71060/JH 525 [USA] – LP
GOOD KARMA
    – Trade Mark Of Quality [USA] – Released 70's – LP
All songs rec: Berkeley Community Theatre, Berkeley, California, 30/05/70, 1st show.
L638:   **Fire** – Jimi (gi, vo), Mitch (dr), Billy (ba).
L639:   **Foxy Lady** – Jimi (gi, vo), Mitch (dr), Billy (ba).
L640:   **Machine Gun** – Jimi (gi, vo), Mitch (dr), Billy (ba).
L641:   **Freedom** – Jimi (gi, vo), Mitch (dr), Billy (ba).
Plus: Johnny B. Goode [L119]; Getting My Heart Back Together Again [L117].
GOOD KARMA 2
    – Trade Mark Of Quality JH 549 [USA] – Released 73 – LP
GOOD KARMA VOL 2
    – Trade Mark Of Quality TMQ-71060 [USA] – LP
All songs rec: Berkeley Community Theatre, Berkeley, California, 30/05/70, 1st show.
L642:   **Message To Love** – Jimi (gi, vo), Mitch (dr), Billy (ba).
L643:   **Star Spangled Banner** – Jimi (gi, voice). Comp: Francis Scott Key.
L644:   **Voodoo Child (slight return)** – Jimi (gi, vo), Mitch (dr), Billy (ba).
Plus: Red House [L299]; Ezy Ryder [L063]; Purple Haze [L141].
JIMI HENDRIX LIVE
    – Black Gold Concerts BG-2022 [USA] – Released 80's – Double LP
Contains: Fire [L638]; Johnny B. Goode [L119]; Getting My Heart Back Together Again [L117]; Foxy Lady [L639]; Machine Gun [L640]; Freedom [L641]; Red House [L299]; Message To Love [L642]; Ezy Ryder [L063]; Star Spangled Banner [L643]; Purple Haze [L141]; Voodoo Child (slight return) [L644].
ATLANTA
    – Toasted Records TRW 1946 [USA] – Released 89? – Double LP
All songs rec: 2nd Atlanta International Pop Festival, Middle Georgia Raceway, Byron, Georgia, 04/07/70.
L645:   **Fire** – Jimi (gi, lv), Mitch (dr), Billy (ba, hv).
L646:   **Lover Man** – Jimi (gi, vo), Mitch (dr), Billy (ba).
L647:   **Spanish Castle Magic** – Jimi (gi, vo), Mitch (dr), Billy (ba).
L648:   **Red House** – Jimi (gi, vo), Mitch (dr), Billy (ba).
L649:   **Room Full Of Mirrors** – Jimi (gi, vo), Mitch (dr), Billy (ba).
L650:   **Getting My Heart Back Together Again** – Jimi (gi, vo), Mitch (dr), Billy (ba).
L651:   **Message To Love** – Jimi (gi, vo), Mitch (dr), Billy (ba).
L652:   **Purple Haze** – Jimi (gi, vo), Mitch (dr), Billy (ba).
L653:   **Hey Joe** – Jimi (gi, vo), Mitch (dr), Billy (ba). Comp: William M. Roberts.
L654:   **Stone Free** – Jimi (gi, vo), Mitch (dr), Billy (ba).
L655:   **Hey Baby (The Land Of The New Rising Sun)** – Jimi (gi, vo), Mitch (dr), Billy (ba).
Plus: All Along The Watchtower [L188]; Voodoo Child (slight return) [L061]; Star Spangled Banner [L189].
CAN YOU HERE (sic) ME ROCK
    – Hemero 01/Keri [FRA] – Double LP
All 17/07/70 songs rec: 'New York Pop', Downing Stadium, Randall's Island, New York.
L656:   **Purple Haze** – Jimi (gi, vo), Mitch (dr), Noel (ba). Rec: Marquee, London W1, 02/03/67.

602

L657: **Foxy Lady** – Jimi (gi, lv), Mitch (dr), Noel (ba, hv). Rec: Royal Albert Hall, London, 24/02/69.

L658: **Getting My Heart Back Together Again** – Jimi (gi, vo), Mitch (dr), Billy (ba), Juma? (bongos). Rec: Jimi's rented house, near Shokan, New York, 14/08/69.

L659: **Stone Free** – Jimi (gi, vo), Mitch (dr), Billy (ba). Rec: 17/07/70.

L660: **Fire** – Jimi (gi, vo), Mitch (dr), Billy (ba). Rec: 17/07/70.

L661: **Message To Love** – Jimi (gi, vo), Mitch (dr), Billy (ba). Rec: 17/07/70.

L662: **Lover Man** – Jimi (gi, vo), Mitch (dr), Billy (ba). Rec: 17/07/70.

L663: **All Along The Watchtower** – Jimi (gi, vo), Mitch (dr), Billy (ba). Comp: Bob Dylan. Rec: 17/07/70.

L664: **Ezy Ryder** – Jimi (gi, vo), Mitch (dr), Billy (ba). Rec: 17/07/70.

L665: **Star Spangled Banner** – Jimi (gi, voice), Mitch (dr). Comp: Francis Scott Key. Rec: 17/07/70.

L666: **Purple Haze** – Jimi (gi, vo), Mitch (dr), Billy (ba). Rec: 17/07/70.

L667: **Voodoo Child (slight return)** – Jimi (gi, vo), Mitch (dr), Billy (ba). Rec: 17/07/70.

Plus: Foxy Lady [L528]; Stone Free [L530]; Fire [L531]; Purple Haze [L532]; Spanish Castle Magic [L487]; Manic Depression [L192]; Red House [L178].

LIVE AT RANDALL'S ISLAND
 – Moon Tree Records PH 1692 [USA] – LP

L668: **Foxy Lady** – Jimi (gi, lv), Mitch (dr), Billy (ba, hv). Rec: 'New York Pop', Downing Stadium, Randall's Island, New York, 17/07/70.

Plus: Stone Free [L659]; Fire [L660]; Message To Love [L661]; Lover Man [L662]; Ezy Ryder [L664]; Star Spangled Banner [L665]; Purple Haze [L666].

LAST AMERICAN CONCERT ALIVE AND FLOWING FROM THE CRATER OF THE SUN
 – Jupiter 444 [USA] – Released 81 – LP – *: entire release

<1> Excellent quality. <2> All songs rec: 'Rainbow Bridge Vibratory Color/Sound Experiment', Rainbow Ridge, Haleakala Crater, near Seabury Hall, Island Of Maui, Hawaii, 30/07/70. <3> This was not Jimi's last American concert (01/08/70 was his final official USA concert).

L669: **Hey Baby (The Land Of The New Rising Sun)** – Jimi (gi, vo), Mitch (dr), Billy (ba). Rec: 1st show.

NOTE: Incomplete.

L670: **In From The Storm** – Jimi (gi, vo), Mitch (dr), Billy (ba). Rec: 1st show.

NOTE: <1> Slightly incomplete. <2> Hey Baby (The Land Of The New Rising Sun) and In From The Storm is a medley.

L671: **Getting My Heart Back Together Again** – Jimi (gi, vo), Mitch (dr), Billy (ba). Rec: 1st show.

NOTE: Incomplete. Refer to L680 for the complete version.

L672: **Voodoo Child (slight return)** – Jimi (gi, vo), Mitch (dr), Billy (ba). Rec: 1st show.

L673: **Hey Baby (The Land Of The New Rising Sun)** – Jimi (gi), Mitch (dr), Billy (ba). Rec: 2nd show.

L674: **Midnight Lightning** – Jimi (gi), Mitch (dr), Billy (ba). Rec: 2nd show.

NOTE: <1> Incomplete, Refer to L691 for the complete version. <2> Hey Baby (The Land Of The New Rising Sun) and Midnight Lightnin' is a medley.

L675: **Foxy Lady** – Jimi (gi, vo), Mitch (dr), Billy (ba). Rec: 1st show.

L676: **Red House** – Jimi (gi, vo), Mitch (dr), Billy (ba). Rec: 2nd show.

L677: **Ezy Ryder** – Jimi (gi, vo), Mitch (dr), Billy (ba). Rec: 2nd show.

L678: **Purple Haze** – Jimi (gi, vo), Mitch (dr), Billy (ba). Rec: 1st show.

Plus: small part of I591; introduction to Hawaii songs.
INCIDENT AT RAINBOW BRIDGE
      – [USA] – Released 71 – LP – *: Jam Back At The House/Straight Ahead
HENDRIX LIVE IN HAWAII–1970
      – Hen Records 37 [USA] – LP
J. H. IN HAWAII–1970
      – Trade Mark Of Quality – [USA] – LP
All songs rec: 'Rainbow Bridge Vibratory Sound Color/Sound Experiment', Rainbow Ridge, Haleakala Crater, near Seabury Hall, Island Of Maui, Hawaii, 30/07/70.

L679: **Jam Back At The House/Straight Ahead** – Jimi (gi, vo), Mitch (dr), Billy (ba). Comp: Mitch Mitchell (Jam Back At The House). Rec: 2nd show.

L680: **Getting My Heart Back Together Again** – Jimi (gi, vo), Mitch (dr), Billy (ba). Rec: 1st show.

NOTE: This is the complete version of L671.

L681: **Instrumental Solo** – Jimi (gi), Mitch (dr), Billy (ba). Rec: 2nd show.

NOTE: Added (by the bootleg people): recording of the sound of a seagull.

Plus: introduction to Hawaii songs; small part of Hey Baby (The Land Of The New Rising Sun) [L669]; Red House [L676]; small part of Ezy Ryder [L677].

JIMI HENDRIX RAINBOW BRIDGE
      – Shalom [USA] – LP
Contains: Red House [L676]; Jam Back At The House/Straight Ahead [L679]; Getting My Heart Back Together Again [L680]; Instrumental Solo [L681]; small part of Ezy Ryder [L677].

YOU CAN'T USE MY NAME
      – Rock Folders 2 [USA] – LP – *: entire release
<1> Excellent quality. <2> All Studio 76 Inc. items rec (during the same session): 1650 Broadway, New York City, late 07/67. <3> All 30/07/70 songs rec: 'Rainbow Bridge Vibratory Color/Sound Experiment', Rainbow Ridge, Haleakala Crater, near Seabury Hall, Island Of Maui, Hawaii.

S682: **'You Can't Use My Name'** – studio chat with Jimi, Curtis Knight, Ed Chalpin (from control-room), plus another unknown male person. Rec: Studio 76 Inc.

NOTE: See page 204 for the complete text of this chat.

S683: **Gloomy Monday 1** – Jimi (gi – main riff), Curtis Knight (vo), unknown (rest). Comp: Curtis Knight. Rec: Studio 76 Inc.

S684: **Gloomy Monday 2** – Jimi (gi – main riff), Curtis Knight (vo), unknown (rest). Comp: Curtis Knight. Rec: Studio '76' Inc.

S685: **1983 . . . (A Merman I Should Turn To Be)** – Jimi (gi, vo, voice), Buddy (dr), Stephen Stills or Noel Redding (ba), unknown (rhythm gi). Rec: CEN, 13?/03/68. Prod: Jimi.

S686: **Little Miss Strange** – Jimi (gi), Buddy (dr, count-in), Noel (gi, faint laughing), Stephen Stills (ba). Comp: Noel Redding. Rec: CEN, 13/03/68. Prod: Chas.

NOTE: This is an early try-out version, which at this point sounds actually in parts more like the song 'I Can't Turn You Loose' (comp: Otis Redding).

L687: **Dolly Dagger** – Jimi (gi, vo), Mitch (dr), Billy (ba). Rec: 30/07/70, 2nd show.

L688: **Instrumental Solo** – Jimi (gi), Mitch (dr), Billy (ba). Rec: 30/07/70, 2nd show.

NOTE: This is the same version as L681. Differences: much better quality; without the seagull.

NOTE: Dolly Dagger and Instrumental Solo is a medley.

604

L689: **Freedom** – Jimi (gi, vo), Mitch (dr), Billy (ba). Rec: 30/07/70, 2nd show.

L690: **Stone Free/Hey Joe** – Jimi (gi, vo, voice), Mitch (dr), Billy (ba). Rec: 30/07/70, 2nd show. Comp: William M. Roberts (Hey Joe).

L691: **Midnight Lightnin'** – Jimi (gi), Mitch (dr), Billy (ba). Rec: 30/07/70, 2nd show.

NOTE: This is the complete version of L674.

Plus: Catfish Blues (L516); Hey Baby (The Land Of The New Rising Sun) (L673).

UNKNOWN WELLKNOWN
- Raven Records JH 6146 [USA?] – LP

Contains: Hey Baby (The Land Of The New Rising Sun) [L669]; In From The Storm [L670]; Getting My Heart Back Together Again [L671]; Voodoo Child (slight return) [L672]; Hey Baby (The Land Of The New Rising Sun) [L673]; Midnight Lightnin' [L674]; Foxy Lady [L675]; Red House [L676]; Ezy Ryder [L677]; Purple Haze [L678].

BROADCASTS MAUI
- Trade Mark Of Quality JH-106/7 [USA] – Released 70's – Double LP

BROADCASTS MAUI
- Trade Mark Of Quality TMQ 7502 [USA] – Double LP

Contains: Purple Haze [L473]; Wild Thing [L474]; Voodoo Child (slight return) [L475]; Hey Joe [L476]; The Sunshine Of Your Love [L477]; Drivin' South [S478]; Catfish Blues [S207]; Hound Dog [S210]; Little Miss Lover [S479]; Love Or Confusion [S205]; Foxy Lady [S216]; Hey Joe [S215]; Stone Free [S201]; introduction for Hawaii songs; Hey Baby (The Land Of The New Rising Sun] [L673]; Red House [L676]; Jam Back At The House/Straight Ahead [L679]; Getting My Heart Back Together Again [L680]; Instrumental Solo [L681]; small part of Ezy Ryder [L677].

LAST BRITISH CONCERT
- [USA] – Released 80 – LP – *: Hey Baby (The Land Of The New Rising Sun)
<1> Excellent quality. <2> All songs rec: Isle Of Wight Festival, England, 30/08/70.

L692: **Spanish Castle Magic** – Jimi (gi, vo), Mitch (dr), Billy (ba).

L693: **Hey Baby (The Land Of The New Rising Sun)** – Jimi (gi, vo), Mitch (dr), Billy (ba).

L694: **Ezy Ryder** – Jimi (gi, vo), Mitch (dr), Billy (ba).

L695: **Hey Joe** – Jimi (gi, vo), Mitch (dr), Billy (ba). Comp: William M. Roberts.

L696: **Purple Haze** – Jimi (gi, vo), Mitch (dr), Billy (ba).

L697: **Voodoo Child (slight return)** – Jimi (gi, vo), Mitch (dr), Billy (ba).

LAST BRITISH CONCERT ISLE OF WRIGHT [sic] 3/8/70 [sic] LAST AMERICAN MAUI
- Postcard Records [USA] – Released 80's – Double LP

Contains: Spanish Castle Magic [L692]; Hey Baby (The Land Of The New Rising Sun) [L693]; Ezy Ryder [L694]; Hey Joe [L695]; Purple Haze [L696]; Voodoo Child (slight return) [L697]; small part of [I591]; introduction to Hawaii songs; Hey Baby (The Land Of The New Rising Sun) [L669]; In From The Storm [L670]; Getting My Heart Back Together Again [L671]; Voodoo Child (slight return) [L672]; Hey Baby (The Land Of The New Rising Sun) [L673]; Midnight Lightnin' [L674]; Foxy Lady [L675]; Red House [L676]; Ezy Ryder [L677]; Purple Haze [L678].

JIMI HENDRIX LIVE ISLE OF WIGHT 30–08–70 VOL. 1
- [ENG] – Released 70 – LP

J. H. ISLE OF WIGHT VOL. I
- Space [HOL] – Released 70 – LP

L698: **Machine Gun** – Jimi (gi, vo), Mitch (dr), Billy (ba), Rec: Isle Of Wight Festival, England, 30/08/70.

NOTES: <1> This is the complete version of L139 <2> Includes a drum solo.

Plus: Lover Man [L103]; Freedom [L104]; Red House [L146].

JIMI HENDRIX LIVE ISLE OF WIGHT 30–08–70 VOL. 2
    – [ENG] – Released 70 – LP
J. H. ISLE OF WIGHT VOL. II
    – Space [HOL] – Released 70 – LP
Contains: Foxy Lady [L109]; Hey Baby (The Land Of The New Rising Sun) [L693]; Ezy Ryder [L694]; Voodoo Child (slight return) [L697]; In From The Storm [L106].
KRALINGEN ISLE OF WIGHT
    – Westcoast Recordings WCR 001–S [HOL] – Released 70 – LP
The rest of this release contains material by other artists.
God Save The Queen [L123]; Sergeant Pepper's Lonely Hearts Club Band [L124]; Spanish Castle Magic [L692].
JAM THE NIGHT
    – Trade Mark Of Quality TMQ 71116 [USA] – Released 89 – LP
Contains: Doriella Du Fontaine [S469]; Doriella Du Fontaine [S470]; part of Purple Haze [L473]; Wild Thing [L474]; Message To Love (stated incorrectly as: Power to Love) [L107]; Midnight Lightnin' [L108]; Foxy Lady [L109].
WINK OF AN EYE
    – Fan Records [USA] – Released 79 – LP
WINK OF AN EYE
    – Loma Records M-105 [USA?] – LP
All songs rec: Love And Peace Festival, Isle Of Fehmarn, W. Germany, 06/09/70. This release contains part of Jimi's last official concert performance.
L699: **Killin' Floor** – Jimi (gi, vo), Mitch (dr), Billy (ba), Comp: Howlin' Wolf.
L700: **Spanish Castle Magic** – Jimi (gi, vo), Mitch (dr), Billy (ba).
L701: **Foxy Lady** – Jimi (gi, lv), Mitch (dr), Billy (ba, hv).
L702: **Room Full Of Mirrors** – Jimi (gi, vo), Mitch (dr), Billy (ba).
L703: **All Along The Watchtower** – Jimi (gi, vo), Mitch (dr), Billy (ba). Comp: Bob Dylan.
L704: **Hey Joe** – Jimi (gi, lv), Mitch (dr), Billy (ba, hv). Comp: William M. Roberts.
L705: **Hey Baby (The Land Of The New Rising Sun)** – Jimi (gi, vo), Mitch (dr), Billy (ba). Special effect: Jimi (Uni-Vibe with chorus setting at slow speed).
L706: **Message To Love** – Jimi (gi, vo), Mitch (dr), Billy (ba).
FOXY HENDRIX
    – [USA] – Released 80 – Double LP
Contains: Killin' Floor [L699]; Spanish Castle Magic [L700]; Foxy Lady [L701]; Room Full Of Mirrors [L702]; All Along The Watchtower [L703]; Hey Joe [L704]; Hey Baby (The Land Of The New Rising Sun) [L705]; Message To Love [L706]; Sergeant Pepper's Lonely Hearts Club Band [L503]; Hey Joe [L504]; I Don't Live Today [L505]; The Wind Cries Mary [L506]; Foxy Lady [L507]; Fire [L508]; The Burning Of The Midnight Lamp [L509]; Purple Haze [L510]; The Sunshine Of Your Love [L498]; Voodoo Child (slight return) [L497].
JIMI – INSIDE THE RAINBOW
    – Blue Records SX501 [USA] – Released 80 – Double LP
Contains: Killin' Floor [L699]; Spanish Castle Magic [L700]; Foxy Lady [L701]; Room Full Of Mirrors [L702]; All Along The Watchtower [L703]; Hey Joe [L704]; Hey Baby (The Land Of The New Rising Sun) [L705]; Message To Love [L706]; Spanish Castle Magic [L692]; Hey Baby (The Land Of The New Rising Sun) [L693]; Ezy Ryder [L694]; Hey Joe [L695]; Purple Haze [L696]; Voodoo Child (slight return) [L697].

606

THE GOOD DIE YOUNG
  – White Knight Records WK22 [USA] – Released 81 – Double LP
L707: **Pass It On** – Jimi (gi, vo), Mitch (dr), Billy (ba). Rec: Berkeley Community Theater, Berkeley, California, 30/05/70, 2nd show.
NOTE: 'Pass It On' is an early try-out version for 'Straight Ahead'.
L708: **Lover Man** – Jimi (gi, vo), Mitch (dr), Noel (ba). Rec: Royal Albert Hall, London, 24/02/69.
L709: **Stone Free** – Jimi (gi, vo), Mitch (dr, cow-bell), Noel (ba). Rec: Royal Albert Hall, London, 24/02/69.
NOTE: This is the complete version of L179.
S710: **Cherokee Mist** – Jimi (gs), Jimi? (sitar), Mitch (dr). Rec: PLA, 02/05/68. Engi: Eddie? Prod: Jimi.
NOTE: This is the complete version of S244.
L711: **Are You Experienced?** – Jimi (gi, vo), Mitch (dr), Noel (ba). Rec: The New York Rock Festival, Singer Bowl, Flushing Meadow Park, Queens, New York, 23/08/68.
L712: **Come On (Part 1)** – Jimi (gi, vo), Mitch (dr), Billy (ba). Rec: Stora Scenen, Gröna Lund, Tivoli Garden, Stockholm, Sweden, 31/08/70.
NOTE: Includes a short drum solo.
L713: **Stop** – Jimi (gi, hv), Buddy (dr, lv), Billy (ba, hv). Comp: Jerry Ragavoy & Mort Schuman, Rec: Fillmore East, New York City, 31/12/69, 1st show.
Plus: I Don't Live Today [L598]; The Wind Cries Mary [L514]; Killin' Floor [L073]; All Along The Watchtower [L188]; part of Fire [L660]; Spanish Castle Magic [L487]; Freedom [L104].
THE EXPERIENCE
  – Towne Records RG-2001 [USA] – Released 81 – Double LP
S714: **Dolly Dagger** – Jimi (gs, lv, hv), Mitch (dr), Billy (ba, fuzz ba), Juma (congas), unknown (pe), Arthur & Albert Allen (hv), unknown (footstamping). Special effect: Jimi (Uni-Vibe with vibrato setting). Rec: ELE, 01/07/70. Engi: Eddie, Prod: Jimi.
NOTE: This is the same version as S111 and is a break-down mix of the original 16-track master, explained with examples by Eddie Kramer.
Plus: Foxy Lady [L557]; Fire [L558]; Killin' Floor [L559]; Red House [L560]; Spanish Castle Magic [L561]; Hey Joe [L562]; Tax Free [L564]; Purple Haze [L563]; I Don't Live Today [L598]; Ain't Too Proud To Beg [S485].
THIS FLYER
  – [USA] – Released 04/70 – LP
P715: **Instrumental Jam 10** – Jimi (gi), Mike Ephron (keyboards), Juma and Jerry (pe).
NOTE: This long jam is the first jam on the side with the most grooves. This jam starts off in a similar fasion as P288.
P716: **Instrumental Solo Jam** – Jimi (gi), Mike Ephron (keyboards), Juma and Jerry (pe).
Plus: Instrumental 4 [P283]; Flying (Here I Go) [P284]; part of Instrumental 6 [P288].
. . . AND A HAPPY NEW YEAR
  – Warner Bros. Records [USA] – Released late 70's – Picture single
Contains: The Little Drummer Boy/Silent Night [S293]; Auld Lang Syne [S294].
T'ANKS FOR THE MAMMARIES
  – The Amazing Kornyfone Record TAKRL Anthology Bozo 1 [USA] – Released 77? – Double LP
The rest of this release contains material by other artists.

Contains: The Little Drummer Boy/Silent Night [S293]; Auld Lang Syne [S294].

JIMI HENDRIX EXPERIENCE – ERIC CLAPTON – GINGER BAKER – JOHN MAYALL – JACK BRUCE
– Munia MBR 707 [USA] – Released 70's – LP

JIMI HENDRIX EXPERIENCE – ERIC CLAPTON – GINGER BAKER – JOHN MAYALL – JACK BRUCE
– Munia MBR 1 [USA] – LP

The rest of this release contains material by other artists.
Contains: The Stars That Play With Laughing Sam's Dice [S020]; Highway Chile [S006].

JIMMY JAMES & HIS BLUE FLAMES
– Blue Flame Records 5205 [USA] – Released 89 – Single

Contains: Bright Lights, Big City I [L412]; I'm A Man I [L407]; No Such Animal Pt. 1 [S399]; No Such Animal Pt. 2 [S400].

GYPSY SUNS, MOONS AND RAINBOWS
– Sidewalk Music JHX 8868 [ITA] – Released 88 – CD – *: Astro Man; Country Blues

JAMES MARSHALL: MIDNIGHT LIGHTNING
– Marshall Records JMH/L32641 [USA] – Released 89 – LP

S717: **Crash Landing** – Jimi (gs, vo, voice), unknown – not Mitch or Buddy – (dr), unknown – not Noel or Billy – (ba), unknown (or), unknown engi (voice from control-room). Rec: PLA, 24/04/69. Prod: Jimi. Wiped in 1974: unknown – not Mitch or Buddy – (some dr), unknown (or).

NOTE: This is a somewhat less altered version of S156. Refer to S820 for the original and unaltered version.

S718: **Midnight Lightnin'** – Jimi (gi, vo), Mitch (dr), Billy? (ba), Juma? (congas). Rec: PLA, likely 23/03/70. Prod: Jimi.

NOTE: This is (most of) the unaltered version of S163.

S719: **Izabella/Machine Gun** – Jimi (gs, vo), Buddy? (dr), Billy (ba), Larry (rhythm gi), Juma (cow-bell), Jerry (pe), unknown (ta). Rec: HIT, 29/08/69. Prod: Jimi or Heaven Research Unlimited.

NOTE: This is the complete and unaltered version of S167.

S720: **Further Up On The Road** – Jimi (gi, vo, voice), Mitch (dr), Billy (ba), Eddie Kramer (voice from control-room). Comp: Joe Nedwick Veasey & Don G. Robey. Rec: ELE, 24/06/70. Engi: Eddie. Prod: Jimi.

S721: **Astro Man** – Jimi (gi), Mitch (dr), Billy (ba). Rec: PLA, 20/01/70. Prod: Jimi.

NOTE: This is the complete version of S252.

S722: **Country Blues** – Jimi (gi), Buddy (dr), Billy (ba). Rec: PLA, 23/01/70. Engi: Jack Adams? Prod: Jimi.

S723: **Lord I Sing The Blues For Me And You** – Jimi (gi, vo), Buddy or Mitch (dr), Billy (ba), Larry (rhythm gi), Juma and/or Jerry (pe). Rec: HIT, 06/09/69. Engi: Bob Hughes? Prod: Heaven Research Unlimited.

NOTE: Incomplete.

S724: **Message To Love** – Jimi (gi, lv, hv), Buddy (dr, hv), Billy (ba), Billy? (hv), Juma? (cow-bell), unknown (ta). Rec: PLA, 12/69 or 01/70. Engi: Tony Bongiovi? Prod: Jimi.

NOTE: This is the unaltered version of S154.

S725: **Stone Free** – Jimi (gs, lv), Mitch (dr, voice), Noel (ba, hv), Andy Fairweather Low (hv), Roger Chapman (hv), unknown (ta), unknown (cow-bell), unknown (coughing), unknown (2 hand-claps). Rec: 07 and 08/04/69, Engi: Gary. Prod: Jimi.

NOTE: This is the complete and unaltered version of S160.

608

S726: **Untitled Rock & Roll jam** – Jimi (gi), Mitch (dr), Noel (ba). Rec: OLM, 04/69. Prod: Jimi.

S727: **Izabella** – Jimi (gs, vo), Buddy (dr), Billy (ba), Juma and Jerry (ta, pe, maracas). Rec: HIT, 28 and 29/08/69. Prod: Jimi or Heaven Research Unlimited.

NOTE: This is the same basic version as S051. Differences: different guitar solos; no harmony vocals by Buddy; different mix.

THE FIRST RAYS OF THE NEW RISING SUN
– Living Legend LLRCD 023 [ITA] – Released 89 – CD

S728: **Voodoo Chile** – Jimi (gi, vo), Mitch (dr), Jack Casady (ba), Steve Winwood (or). Rec: PLA, 01 or 02/05/68. Engi: Eddie. Prod: Jimi.

NOTE: <1> Incomplete. <2> This is the same version as S038. Difference: hardly any crowd noises.

Plus: Angel [P255]; part of Cherokee Mist [S710]; The Things I Used To Do [S242]; Like A Rolling Stone [L231]; I'm A Man [L230]; Cherokee Mist (stated incorrectly as: 'First Rays Of The New Rising Sun') [P222]; Little Wing [S026]; Mr Bad Luck [S236]; One Rainy Wish [S240]; Manic Depression [L192]; Are You Experienced [L180]; Red House [L303]; Machine Gun [L253]; Send My Love To Linda [S259].

ACOUSTIC JAMS
– Sphinx Records SXCD 001 [ITA] – Released 89 – Double-sided CD
– *: Belly Button Window

<1> All early 68 songs rec: Jimi's flat, New York City, between 02/68 and 04/68. <2> All Autumn 69 songs rec: Jimi's Shokan house.

P729: **Long Hot Summer Night I** – Jimi (acoustic gi, vo). Rec: early 68.

P730: **Long Hot Summer Night II** – Jimi (acoustic gi, vo, voice). Rec: early 68.

P731: **1983 . . . (A Merman I Should Turn To Be)** – Jimi (gi, vo). Rec: early 68.

P732: **Cherokee Mist** – Jimi (gi). Rec: early 68.

P733: **Astro Man/Valleys Of Neptune** – Jimi (gi, vo). Rec: Autumn 69. Comp of Valleys Of Neptune – originally titled 'Pride Of Man': Hamilton Camp (music) & Jimi Hendrix (words).

P734: **Money** – Jimi (gi), Taj Mahal? (gi), unknown (coughing). Comp: Berry Gordy & Janie Bradford. Rec: Autumn 69.

P735: **Getting My Heart Back Together Again** – Jimi (gi, vo). Rec: early 68.

P736: **Voodoo Chile** – Jimi (gi, vo, voice). Rec: early 68.

NOTE- This is the complete version of P245.

P737: **Gypsy Eyes** – Jimi (acoustic gi, vo). Rec: early 68.

S738: **Beginning** – Jimi (gi), Mitch (dr), Billy (ba), Juma (bongos), Juma? (temple block). Comp: Mitch Mitchell. Rec: ELE, 16/06/70 and/or 01/07/70. Engi: Eddie. Prod: Jimi.

NOTE: This is the unaltered and complete version of S134.

S739: **Little Miss Strange** – Jimi (gs), Mitch (dr, hv), Noel (gi, ba, acoustic gi, lv, hv). Comp: Noel Redding. Rec: PLA, 22/04/68 (basic track); PLA, 25/04/68 (additional recordings); PLA, 28/04/68 (mixing). Engi: Gary & Eddie. Prod: Jimi.

NOTE: This is the same basic version as S039. Differences: several other guitar solos; with the original bass take; different mix.

S740: **South Saturn Delta** – Jimi (gi). Rec: PLA?, Spring? 68.

NOTE: Stated incorrectly as: 'Three Little Bears'.

P741: **Three Little Bears** – Jimi (gi). Rec: early 68.

P742: **Gypsy Eyes** – Jimi (gi). Rec: early 68.

P743: **1983 . . . (A Merman I Should Turn To Be)** – Jimi (gi). Rec: early 68.

P744: **Gypsy Eyes** – Jimi (gi). Rec: early 68.

NOTE: This is a continuation of S742.

S745: **Drifting** – Jimi (gi), Mitch (dr), Billy (ba), Eddie (voice from control-room). Rec: ELE, 06 or 07/70. Engi: Eddie. Prod: Jimi.

NOTE: <1> This is a more complete version of S258. <2> This version also includes a 'false start' and a few instrumental bits of 'Midnight Lightnin''.

S746: **Drifting** – Jimi (gi, vo, voice), Mitch (dr), Billy (ba). Rec: ELE, 06 or 07/70. Engi: Eddie. Prod: Jimi.

S747: **Belly Button Window** – Jimi (gi), Mitch (dr, brushes), Billy (ba). Rec: ELE, 23/07/70. Engi: Eddie. Prod: Jimi.

S748: **Freedom** – Jimi (gs, vo, voice), Mitch (dr), Billy (ba). Special effect: phasing (on gi). Rec: ELE, 06/70. Engi: Eddie. Prod: Jimi.

NOTE: Preceded by tune-up bits by Mitch, Eddie (voice from control-room), Jimi (voice, tune-up bit).

S749: **Cherokee Mist/In From The Storm/Valleys Of Neptune** – Jimi (gi, voice), Mitch (dr), Billy (ba), unknown (voice). Comp of 'Valleys Of Neptune' (originally titled 'Pride Of Man'): Hamilton Camp (music). Rec: ELE, 06 or 07/70. Engi: Eddie. Prod: Jimi.

P750: **Untitled acoustic jam** – Jimi (acoustic gi), Mitch (pe, clapping, faint voice). Rec: Jimi's flat?, New York City?, 69?

Plus: Angel [P255]; Voodoo Child (slight return) [S246]; Come On (Part 1) [S250]; Mr Bad Luck [S236]; Send My Love To Linda [S259].

TWO SIDES OF THE SAME GENIUS

– Amazing Kornyfone Record Label TAKRL H-6770 [USA] – Released 80's – LP

All listed Autumn 69 songs probably rec: Jimi's Shokan house.

P751: **Room Full Of Mirrors Jam** – Jimi (gi, lv), Taj Mahal? (gi, faint bit of hv). Rec: Autumn 69.

NOTE: Stated incorrectly as: 'Afternoon Blues Jam'.

P752: **Instrumental Jam** – Jimi (gi), Taj Mahal? (gi). Rec: Autumn 69.

NOTE: Stated incorrectly as: 'Night Blues Jam.'

Plus: The Wind Cries Mary [L506]; Foxy Lady [L508]; Fire [L508]; Sergeant Pepper's Lonely Hearts Club Band [L503]; Hey Joe [L504]; I Don't Live Today [L505]; The Burning Of The Midnight Lamp [L509]; Purple Haze [L510]; Astro Man/Valleys Of Neptune (stated incorrectly as: They Call Me Extra Man) [P733]; part of Money (stated incorrectly as: TaJimi Boogie) [P734].

THIS ONE'S FOR YOU

– Veteran Music Inc. MF-243 [USA] – Released 87 – LP

S753: **Lover Man** – Jimi (gi), Mitch (dr), Billy (ba), Juma (cow-bell). Rec: ELE, 20?/07/70. Engi: Eddie. Prod: Jimi.

S754: **Untitled Instrumental** – Jimi (gi). unknown (dr), unknown (ba), unknown (pi), unknown (trumpet), unknown (gi). Rec: unknown studio, probably New York City, 69 or 70.

S755: **Peace In Mississippi** – Jimi (gi), Mitch (dr), Noel (ba). Rec: TTG, 24/10/68. Prod: Jimi.

S756: **The Little Drummer Boy/Silent Night** – Jimi (gi, voice), Buddy (dr), Billy (ba). Comp: David Onorati & Harry Simeone & Katherine Davis (The Little Drummer Boy); Father Joseph Mohr & Franz Gruber (Silent Night). Rec: PLA, 12/69. Engi: Tony Bongiovi? Prod: Jimi.

NOTE: This is the same basic version as S293. Difference: added (in 1974?): unknown females (vocals, voice).

S757: **Calling All Devil's Children** – Jimi (gi), Mitch (dr), Noel (ba, gi). Comp: Jimi Hendrix & Noel Redding. Rec: TTG, 21/10/68. Prod: Jimi.

S758: **Jungle** – Jimi (gi), Buddy (dr). Rec: PLA, 14?/11/69. Special effect:

Jimi (Uni-Vibe turned on, but not used with any setting). Prod: Jimi.

S759: **Ezy Ryder** – Jimi (gi, lv, hv), Buddy (dr, hv), Billy (ba, hv). Rec: PLA, 18/12/69. Prod: Jimi.

NOTE: Incomplete.

S760: **Message To Love** – Jimi (gi, lv, hv), Buddy (dr, hv), Billy (ba, hv). Rec: PLA, 18/12/69. Prod: Jimi.

S761: **The Things I Used To Do** – Jimi (gi, vo, voice), Johnny Winter (slide gi), Stephen Stills (ba), Dallas Taylor (dr). Comp: Guitar Slim. Rec: PLA, 15/05/69. Prod: Jimi.

NOTE: This is the same basic version as S242. Difference: longer; partly different solo guitar by Jimi, particularly during the middle part of the song.

S762: **Lover Man** – Jimi (gi, vo), Mitch (dr), Noel (ba). Rec: TTG, 10/68. Prod: Jimi.

S763: **Midnight Lightnin'** – Jimi (gi, vo), Mitch (dr), Billy (ba). Rec: PLA, 23/03/70. Prod: Jimi.

HOOCHIE COOCHIE MAN
– Waggle Records/Toasted TRW 1953 [USA] – Released 89 – Double LP
Contains: Cherokee Mist [P222]; I'm A Man [L230]; Like A Rolling Stone [L231]; Red House [L233]; part of I'm Your Hoochie Coochie Man [S212]; Foxy Lady [S216]; Lover Man [S753]; Mr. Bad Luck [S236]; One Rainy Wish [S240]; Drivin' South [S206]; The Things I Used To Do [S242]; Drifter's Escape [S243]; Cherokee Mist [S244]; Voodoo Child (slight return) [S246]; 1983 . . . (A Merman I Should Turn to Be) [S247]; Come On (Part 1) [S250]; Room Full of Mirrors [S254]; Angel [P255]; Valleys Of Neptune [S257]; Send My Love To Linda [S259]; South Saturn Delta [S261]; Dolly Dagger [L110]; Hey Joe [L064]; Hey Baby (The Land Of The New Rising Sun) [L065]; Lover Man [L066].

FIRST RAYS OF THE RISING SUN
– RSJ 02 [USA] – Released 87 – LP

S764: **Untitled guitar improvisation** – Jimi (gi). Rec: PLA, 69 or ELE, 70. Prod: Jimi.

NOTE: Stated incorrectly as: 'Electric Ladyland'.

S765: **Midnight Lightnin'** – Jimi (gi, vo, voice), Kathy Etchingham (faint voice). Rec: OLY, likely 14/02/69.

S766: **Instrumental improvisation** – Jimi (gi), Billy (ba). Rec: ELE, 70. Prod: Jimi.

S767: **Earth Blues** – Jimi (gi), Buddy (dr), Billy (ba). Rec: Fillmore East, New York City, 01/01/70, 2nd show.

NOTE: Incomplete.

S768: **Somewhere** – Jimi (gi, vo), Buddy (dr), Noel? (ba), unknown (rhythm gi). Rec: CEN, 13/03/68 (basic track). Special effect: heavy delay on vo. Prod: Chas.

NOTES: <1> Stated incorrectly as: 'Somewhere Over The Rainbow'. <2> This is the unaltered version of S155.

S769: **Peace In Mississippi** – Jimi (solo gi, rhythm gi), Mitch (dr), Noel (dr). Rec: TTG, 24/10/68. Prod: Jimi. Wiped in 1974: Jimi (some rhythm gi), Mitch (dr), Noel (dr). Added in 1974: Jeff Mironov (rhythm gi), Allan Schwartzberg (dr), Bob Babbit (ba), Jimmy Maeulen (pe).

NOTE: This is a slightly less altered version of S158. Difference: contains most of Jimi's rhythm guitar; more delay effects; different mix.

Plus: Angel [P255]; Cherokee Mist [S710]; Further Up On The Road [S720]; Mr. Bad Luck [S236]; Little Miss Strange [S686]; 1983 . . . (A Merman I Should Turn To Be) [S685].

ELECTRIC BIRTHDAY JIMI
   – EBJ 01 [USA] – Released 87 – LP
S770:   **Valleys Of Neptune** – Jimi (gi), Mitch (dr), Billy (ba), Larry (rhythm gi).
   Comp (originally titled 'Pride Of Man'): Hamilton Camp (music). Rec: HIT,
   08 or 09/69. Prod: Jimi.
NOTE: Stated incorrectly as: 'Lonely Avenue'.
S771:   **World Traveler** – Jimi (gi, vo), Mitch (dr), Billy (ba), Larry Young
   (or). Rec: PLA, 14/05/69. Prod: Jimi.
S772:   **It's Too Bad** – Jimi (gi, vo), Mitch (dr), Billy (ba), Larry Young (or).
   Rec: PLA, 14/05/69. Prod: Jimi.
S773:   **Message From Nine To The Universe** – Jimi (gi, voice), Buddy
   (dr), Billy (ba). Rec: PLA, 22/05/69. Prod: Jimi.
NOTES: <1> Stated incorrectly as: 'Strato Strut'. <2> Incomplete. <3> This is
from the same version as S171. The part on this release is actually the start of the
song, part of which is not included in the S171 version. <4> Refer to S790 for the
complete version.
Plus: introduction and interview with Alan Douglas by Alexis Korner; Cherokee
Mist [S710]; Untitled guitar improvisation [S764]; Midnight Lightnin' [S765].
LADYLAND IN FLAMES
   – Marshall Records L30640 [USA] – Released 88 – Double LP
Contains: introduction and interview with Alan Douglas by Alexis Korner; Valleys
Of Neptune (stated incorrectly as: 'Lonely Avenue') [S770]; World Traveler [S771];
It's Too Bad [S772]; Message From Nine To The Universe [S773]; Cherokee Mist
[S710]; Untitled guitar improvisation [S764]; Midnight Lightnin' [S765]; Angel [P255];
Cherokee Mist [S710]; Untitled guitar improvisation (stated incorrectly as: Electric
Ladyland) [S764]; Midnight Lightnin' [S765]; Further Up On The Road [S720]; Instru-
mental improvisation [S766]; Earth Blues [L767]; Mr. Bad Luck [S236]; Little Miss
Strange [S686]; Somewhere (stated incorrectly as: Somewhere Over The Rainbow)
[S768]; 1983 . . . (A Merman I Should Turn To Be) [S685]; Peace In Mississippi
[S769]
SIR JAMES MARSHALL – GYPSY ON CLOUD NINE
   – [USA] – Released 80's – Double LP – *: M.L.K.; Instrumental Jam
S774:   **Astro Man** – Jimi (gi, vo), Mitch (dr), Billy (ba), Juma (cow-bell, pe).
   Rec: ELE, 24?/06/70. Engi: Eddie. Prod Jimi.
NOTE: <1> Slightly incomplete. <2> This is the same basic version as S088.
Differences: some extra guitar bits; different mix (mellow effect on rhythm and bass
guitar).
S775:   **Once I Had A Woman** – Jimi (gi, vo), Buddy (dr), Billy (ba), Don –
   surname unknown – (ha). Rec: PLA, 23/01/70. Engi: Jack Adams? Prod:
   Jimi.
NOTE: Incomplete. This is a part of the unaltered version of S168.
S776:   **Ezy Ryder** – Jimi (gs), Mitch (dr), Noel (ba). Rec: OLM or PLA,
   04?/69. Prod: Jimi.
S777:   **M.L.K.** – Jimi – (gi, voice), Buddy (dr, cow-bell), Billy (ba). Special effect:
   Jimi (Uni-Vibe with chorus setting). Rec: PLA, late 69 or early 70. Engi: Jack
   Adams. Prod: Jimi.
NOTES: <1> Stated incorrectly as: Captain Coconut. <2> This is the complete,
unaltered basic track version of S161. And ten times better too!
S778:   **Instrumental Jam** – Jimi (gi), Buddy (dr), Billy (ba). Rec: PLA,
   18?/12/69. Prod: Jimi.
S779:   **Blue Suede Shoes** – Jimi (gi, vo, voice, tongue-clicks), Buddy (dr),

612

Billy (ba), Don – surname unknown – (ha). Comp: Carl Lee Perkins. Rec: 23/01/70. Engi: Jack Adams? Prod: Jimi.
NOTES: <1> Stated as: Blue Suede Shoes Pt.1. <2> This is another part of version S148.
Plus: Further Up On The Road [S720]; The Things I Used To Do [S761]; Ezy Ryder [S759]; Message To Love [S760]; Peace In Mississippi [S755]; The Little Drummer Boy/Silent Night [S756]; Izabella/Machine Gun [S719]; part of Midnight Lightnin' (stated incorrectly as: 'Blue Suede Shoes Pt.2') [S718].

HELLS SESSION
– BGR 001 [ITA] – Released 88 – LP

All song titles given on this release are fake.
S780: **Instrumental Jam** – Jimi (gi), John McLaughlin (gi), Buddy (dr), Dave Holland (ba). Rec: PLA, mid 69.
S781: **Drone Blues** – Jimi (gi), unknown – not Mitch or Buddy – (dr), unknown – not Noel or Billy – (ba). Rec: PLA, 24/04/69. Prod: Jimi.
NOTE: This is the complete version of S175.
Plus: Young/Hendrix [S173]; part of It's Too Bad [S772]; Jimi/Jimmy Jam [S172].

SWEET ANGEL
– World Productions Of Compact Music WOC 022CD [ITA] – Released 89 – CD

Contains: Stone Free [L511]; Hey Joe [L512]; Purple Haze [L513]; Catfish Blues [L516]; Foxy Lady [L517]; Purple Haze [L518]; Voodoo Child (slight return) [L502]; Hey Joe [L503]; The Sunshine Of Your Love [L504]; Angel [P255]; Like A Rolling Stone [L230].

THE THINGS I USED TO DO
– Golden Memories GM 890738 [ITA] – Released 89 – CD

S782: **Three Little Bears** – Jimi (gs, vo), Mitch (dr), Noel? (ba), unknown (cow-bell). Rec: PLA, 02/05/68. Engi: Gary or Eddie. Prod: Jimi.
NOTE: This is the complete version of S133.
S783: **Gypsy Eyes** – Jimi (gs, ba, vo), Mitch (dr). Rec: PLA, last week 04/68 or first week 05/68. Engi: Eddie or Gary. Prod: Jimi.
NOTE: This is (in part) the basic version of S042. Differences: longer; some more and different guitar solos; different mix.
S784: **Who Knows?** – Jimi (gi, lv, voice), Buddy (dr, hv, bit of voice), Billy (ba). Rec: PLA, 19?/12/69. Prod: Jimi.
S785: **Who Knows?** – Jimi (gi, lv, voice), Buddy (dr, hv, voice), Billy (ba). Rec: PLA, 19?/12/69. Prod: Jimi.
S786: **Message To Love** – Jimi (gi, lv), Buddy (dr, hv, voice), Billy (ba). Rec: PLA, 19?/12/69. Prod: Jimi.
NOTE: Very short false start.
S787: **Message To Love** – Jimi (gi, lv, voice), Buddy (dr, hv, voice), Billy (ba). Rec: PLA, 19?/12/69. Prod: Jimi.
S788: **Izabella I, II, III, IV** – Jimi (gi, voice), Mitch (dr, voice), Billy (ba), Larry (rhythm gi), Bob Hughes? (voice from control-room). Rec: HIT, Autumn 69. Prod: Jimi or Heaven Research Unlimited.
NOTE: Contains various try-outs, false starts, tune-ups, talk between Jimi and the engineer.
Plus: The Things I Used To Do [S242]; Izabella (stated as: Izabella V) [S727].

ELECTRIC LADY JAMS
– Sure Nice Shoes Records H-3600 [USA] – Released 83 – LP

LET'S DROP SOME LUDES AND VOMIT WITH JIMI
– Sure Nice Shoes Records H-3600 [USA] – LP

S789: **Jimi/Jimmy Jam** – Jimi (gi), Mitch or Buddy (dr), Dave Holland (ba), Jim McCarty (gi). Special effect: Jimi (octavia). Rec: PLA, 25/03/69. Prod: Jimi.

NOTE: This is the complete version of S172.

Plus: Instrumental Jam [S780]; part of Drone Blues [S175].

RECORD PLANT JAMS
   – Tam Studio [ENG] – Released 81 – LP

Contains: Jimi/Jimmy Jam [S789]; Young/Hendrix [S173]; part of Drone Blues [S781]; Valleys Of Neptune [S770]; Instrumental Jam [S780]; part of The Things I Used To Do [S242].

MUSIC FOR FANS VOL. I
   – QCS-1447 [USA] – Released 80's – LP

MUSIC FOR FANS
   – Music Of Distinction MOD 1003 [USA] – Released 80's – LP

S790: **Message From Nine To The Universe** – Jimi (gi, lv, voice), Buddy (dr), Billy (ba), Devon Wilson (hv). Rec: PLA, 22/05/69. Prod: Jimi.

NOTE: This is the complete and unaltered version of S171.

S791: **Strato Strut** – Jimi (gi), Mitch (dr), Billy (ba). Rec: ELE, Summer 70. Engi: Eddie. Prod: Jimi.

Plus: Cherokee Mist [S710]; Drone Blues [S781].

TURN 'ER ON!
   – APEJH-818169 [USA] – Released late 80's – LP

In From The Storm [L106]; Johnny B. Goode [L119]; Hey Joe [L077]; Purple Haze [L141]; Machine Gun [L139]; Getting My Heart Back Together Again [S144]; Rock Me, Baby [L076]; Wild Thing [L081]; Like A Rolling Stone [L075]; Red House [L146].

LOADED GUITAR
   – Starlight Records SL 87013 [USA] – Released 88 – LP

<1> All 22/12/67 songs rec: 'Christmas On Earth Continued', Olympia, Kensington Road, London W8. <2> The late 07/69 or 08/69, and 09/09/69 songs rec: ABC studio, New York City (*Dick Cavett Show*, both live transmissions).

L792: **Getting My Heart Back Together Again** – Jimi (gi, vo), unknown (dr), unknown (ba), Dick Cavett (introduction). Rec: late 07/69 or 08/69.

L793: **Izabella/Machine Gun** – Jimi (gi, vo), Mitch (dr), Billy (ba), Juma (jaw-bone, congas), Dick Cavett (introduction). Rec: 08/09/69.

S794: **Purple Haze** – Jimi (gi, lv, tongue-click), Mitch (dr), Noel (ba, hv). Rec: BBC Lime Grove Studios, London W12, 30/03/67, for *Top Of The Pops*, BBC 1 TV.

NOTE: This is the normal studio version of Purple Haze [S004], minus all the original vocals but with added live vocals.

L795: **Hey Joe** – Jimi (gi, vo), Mitch (dr), Noel (ba). Comp: William M. Roberts. Rec: Marquee, London W1, 02/03/67.

L796: **Sergeant Pepper's Lonely Hearts Club Band** – Jimi (gi, lv), Mitch (dr), Noel (ba, hv). Comp: John Lennon & Paul McCartney. Rec: 22/12/67.

L797: **Foxy Lady** – Jimi (gi, lv), Mitch (dr), Noel (ba, hv). Rec: 22/12/67.

Plus: Purple Haze [L656]; Hey Joe [L476]; The Sunshine Of Your Love [L477]; Getting My Heart Back Together Again [S144]; I Don't Live Today [L505]; The Wind Cries Mary [L506]; Fire [L508]; The Burning Of The Midnight Lamp [L509].

AMERICAN DREAM
   – World Productions Of Compact Music WPOCM 0589D023-2 [ITA] – Released 89 – CD

Contains: Tax Free [L564]; part of Purple Haze [L473]; Wild Thing [L474]; Earth

Blues [L767]; Hey Joe [L064]; Hey Baby (The Land Of The New Rising Sun) [L065]; Lover Man [L066]; Hound Dog I [L593].

SHINE ON EARTH, SHINE ON
- Sidewalk Music SW 89010/89011 [ITA] – Released 89 – Double CD

S798: **With The Power** – Jimi (gs, lv, hv), Buddy (dr, hv), Billy (ba), Billy? (hv), Juma (cow-bell). Rec: PLA, 21/11/69. Engi: Tony Bongiovi? Prod: Jimi.

NOTE: This is the complete and unaltered version of S159.

S799: **Freedom** – Jimi (gi, vo, voice), Mitch (dr), Billy (ba), Eddie (voice from control-room). Rec: ELE, 06/70. Engi: Eddie. Prod: Jimi.

L800: **Trying To Be** – Jimi (gi, vo), Buddy (dr), Billy (ba). Rec: Fillmore East, New York City, 01/01/70, 1st show.

NOTE: Song a.k.a.: Stepping Stone.

Plus: Little Wing [L556]; Everything's Gonna Be Allright [L551]; Three Little Bears [L553]; Instrumental Jam I [L554]; Peace In Mississippi (stated incorrectly as: Somewhere Over The Rainbow) [S755]; Stone Free [S725]; Crash Landing [S717]; part of Drone Blues [S781]; Once I Had A Woman [S775].

THE WINTERLAND DAYS
- Manic Depression Records MDR 001/002 [ITA] – Released 89 – Double CD

All songs rec: Winterland, San Francisco, California.

L801: **Getting My Heart Back Together Again** – Jimi (gi, vo), Mitch (dr), Noel (ba). Rec: 10/10/68, 2nd show.

NOTE: This is the complete version of L185.

L802: **Hey Joe** – Jimi (gi, vo), Mitch (ba), Jack Casady (ba). Comp: William M. Roberts. Rec: 10/10/68, 2nd show.

L803: **Star Spangled Banner** – Jimi (gi, faint voice), Mitch (dr), Noel (ba). Comp: Francis Scott Key. Rec: 10/10/68, 2nd show.

NOTE: This is the complete version of L305, L306, and L307.

L804: **Purple Haze** – Jimi (gi, lv), Mitch (dr), Noel (ba, hv). Rec: 10/10/68, 2nd show.

L805: **Are You Experienced?** – Jimi (gi, vo), Mitch (dr), Noel (ba), Virgil Gonsales (fl). Rec: 11/10/68, 1st show.

L806: **Spanish Castle Magic** – Jimi (gi, vo), Mitch (dr), Noel (ba). Rec: 11/10/68, 2nd show.

NOTE: This is the complete version of L308.

L807: **Fire** – Jimi (gi, vo), Mitch (dr), Noel (ba), Herbie Rich (or). Rec: 11/10/68, 2nd show.

NOTE: This is the original version of L191.

L808: **Foxy Lady** – Jimi (gi, vo), Mitch (dr), Noel (ba), Herbie Rich (or). Rec: 11/10/68, 2nd show.

NOTE: This is the original version of L198.

L809: **Lover Man** – Jimi (gi, vo), Mitch (dr), Noel (ba). Rec: 12/10/68, 1st show.

L810: **Like A Rolling Stone** – Jimi (gi, vo), Mitch (dr), Noel (ba). Comp: Bob Dylan. Rec: 12/10/68, 1st show.

L811: **Tax Free** – Jimi (gi), Mitch (dr), Noel (ba). Comp: Bo Hansson & Janne Karlsson. Rec: 12/10/68, 1st show.

Plus: Voodoo Child (slight return) [L182]; Red House [L303]; The Sunshine Of Your Love [L193]; Little Wing [L181].

THE MASTER'S MASTERS
- Rockin' Records JH-01 [USA] – Released 89 – CD – *: God Save The Queen; Bold As Love

S812: **God Save The Queen** – Jimi (acoustic gi, gs). Comp: Dr. John Ball. Rec: PLA?, 69 or 70. Prod: Jimi.

NOTE: This is the complete version of S262.

S813: **Seven Dollars In My Pocket** – Jimi (gi, vo), Buddy (dr), Billy (ba), Don – surname unknown – (ha). Rec: PLA, 23/01/70. Engi: Jack Adams? Prod: Jimi.

S814: **Jungle Jam** – Jimi (gi), Mitch? (dr), Billy (ba), Juma and Jerry (congas, pe). Rec: HIT, 09?/69. Prod: Jimi.

S815: **Calling All Devil's Children** – Jimi (gi), Mitch (dr), Noel (ba, gi), Jimi & Mitch & Noel & guests (crowd noises re-creating a fake bust). Comp: Jimi Hendrix & Noel Redding. Rec: TTG, 21/10/68. Prod: Jimi.

NOTES: <1> Slightly incomplete. <2> This is the same basic version as S757. Difference: added bust noises via an overdub.

S816: **All Along The Watchtower** – Jimi (gs, vo), Mitch (dr, congas), Dave Mason (ba, acoustic gi), Mitch? (temple block), unknown (ta). Comp: Bob Dylan. Special effect: Jimi (slide-effect via the back of his cigarette lighter with the gi on his lap). Rec: OLY, 21/01/68. Engi: Eddie. Prod: Chas.

NOTE: This is the original basic track version of S034. Differences: with the original bass take; with congas; different mix.

S817: **Bold As Love** – Jimi (gi, vo), Mitch (dr), Noel (ba). Special effect: phasing (on dr). Rec: OLY, 29/10/67. Engi: Eddie. Prod: Chas.

S818: **Jazz Jimi Jam** – Jimi (gi), Buddy (dr), Jack Bruce? (ba). Rec: PLA, 69. Prod: Jimi.

S819: **Electric Lady Land** – Jimi (gi), Buddy (dr), unknown (ba). Special effect: Jimi (tremolo). Rec: PLA, 14/06/68. Engi: Gary. Prod: Jim.

NOTE: This is an outtake from S153.

S820: **Crash Landing** – Jimi (gi, vo), unknown – not Mitch or Buddy – (dr), unknown – not Noel or Billy – (ba), unknown (or). Rec: PLA, 24/04/69. Prod: Jimi.

NOTE: This is the original and unaltered version of S156, without guitar overdubs.

Plus: Mr. Bad Luck [S236]; Red House [S300].

Plus fake: Midnight (by clone-band 'Rainbow Bridge').

STAR SPANGLED BLUES

– Waggle Records WAG 1935 [USA] – Released 88 – Double LP

All listed 10/68 songs rec: Winterland, San Francisco, California.

L821: **Like A Rolling Stone** – Jimi (gi, vo), Mitch (dr), Noel (ba), Herbie Rich (or). Comp: Bob Dylan. Rec: 11/10/68, 2nd show.

L822: **Lover Man** – Jimi (gi, vo), Mitch (dr), Noel (ba), Herbie Rich (or). Rec: 11/10/68, 2nd show.

NOTE: Stated incorrectly as: Rock Me, Baby.

L823: **Hey Joe** – Jimi (gi, vo), Mitch (dr), Noel (ba), Herbie Rich (or). Comp: William M. Roberts. Rec: 11/10/68, 2nd show.

L824: **Purple Haze** – Jimi (gi, lv, tongue-click), Mitch (dr), Noel (ba, hv), Herbie Rich (organ bits). Rec: 11/10/68, 2nd show.

L825: **Blue Suede Shoes** – Jimi (gi, vo), Mitch (dr), Billy (ba). Comp: Carl Lee Perkins. Rec: Berkeley Community Theatre, Berkeley, California, 30/05/70, afternoon rehearsals.

NOTE: This is the complete version of L121.

L826: **Foxy Lady** – Jimi (gi, vo), Mitch (dr), Noel (ba). Rec: 12/10/68, 1st show.

L827: **Bass And Drum Jam** – Jimi (introduction), Mitch (dr), Noel (ba). Comp: Noel Redding & Mitch Mitchell. Rec: 12/10/68, 1st show.

NOTES: <1> Incomplete, <2> Stated as: Blown' Amp Blues.

Plus: Fire [L807]; Foxy Lady [L808]; Ezy Ryder [L063]; Hey Joe [L064]; Hey Baby (The Land Of The New Rising Sun) [L065]; Lover Man [L066]. Plus fake: Star Spangled Banner (by clone-band 'Rainbow Bridge').

STAR SPANGLED BLUES
– Neutral Zone Records NZCD 89011 [USA] – Released 89 – CD
Contains: Like A Rolling Stone [L821]; Lover Man (stated incorrectly as: Rock Me, Baby) [L822]; Hey Joe [L823]; Fire [L807]; Foxy Lady [L808]; Purple Haze [L824]; Blue Suede Shoes [L825]; Foxy Lady [L826]; Bass And Drum Jam (stated as: Blown' Amp Blues) [L827]. Plus fake: Star Spangled Banner (by clone-band 'Rainbow Bridge').

MIDNIGHT MAGIC
– Waggle Records WAG 1936 [USA] – Released 88 – Double LP
All listed 24/05/69 songs rec: Sports Arena, San Diego, California.
L828: **Fire** – Jimi (gi, lv), Mitch (dr), Noel (ba, hv). Rec: 24/05/69.
L829: **Hey Joe** – Jimi (gi, vo), Mitch (dr), Noel (ba). Comp: William M. Roberts. Rec: 24/05/69.
L830: **Spanish Castle Magic** – Jimi (gi, vo), Mitch (dr), Noel (ba). Rec: 24/05/69.
NOTE: Includes a small part of The Sunshine Of Your Love (comp: Pete Brown & Jack Bruce & Eric Clapton).
L831: **Foxy Lady** – Jimi (gi, lv), Mitch (dr), Noel (ba, hv), concert crowd (hv). Rec: 24/05/69.
L832: **Purple Haze** – Jimi (gi, lv), Mitch (dr), Noel (ba, hv). Rec: 24/05/69.
L833: **Voodoo Child (slight return)** – Jimi (gi, vo), Mitch (dr), Noel (ba). Rec: 24/05/69.
S834: **Midnight Lightnin'** – Jimi (gi, vo). Rec: PLA, early 70? Prod: Jimi.
S835: **Drivin' South** – Jimi (gi), Mitch (dr), Noel (ba). Rec: unknown studio location, 68. Prod: Jimi.
S836: **Sergeant Pepper's Lonely Hearts Club Band** – Jimi (gi), Mitch (dr), Noel (ba). Comp: John Lennon & Paul McCartney. Rec: unknown studio location, 68. Prod: Jimi.
NOTE: 'Driving South' and 'Sergeant Pepper's Lonely Hearts Club Band' is a medley.
Plus: I Don't Live Today [L177]; Red House [S300]; God Save The Queen (stated incorrectly as: 'Jimi & John Jam') [S812].
Plus fake: Midnight (by clone-band 'Rainbow Bridge').

MIDNIGHT MAGIC
– Neutral Zone Records 89012 [FRA] – Released 89 – CD
Contains: Fire [L828]; Hey Joe [L829]; Spanish Castle Magic [L830]; I Don't Live Today [L177]; Foxy Lady [L831]; Purple Haze [L832]; Voodoo Child (slight return) [L833]; Ezy Ryder [L063]; Hey Joe [L064]; Hey Baby (The Land Of The New Rising Sun) [L065]; Lover Man [L066].

BAND OF GYPSYS HAPPY NEW YEAR, JIMI
– Cops and Robbers Records JTYM 01 [USA?] – Released 90 – LP
All songs rec: Fillmore East, New York City, 31/12/69, 1st show.
L837: **Power Of Soul** – Jimi (gi, vo), Buddy (dr), Billy (ba).
L838: **Lover Man** – Jimi (gi, vo), Buddy (dr), Billy (ba).
L839: **Machine Gun** – Jimi (gi, lv), Buddy (dr, hv), Billy (ba, hv).
L840: **Bleeding Heart** – Jimi (gi, vo), Buddy (dr), Billy (ba). Comp: Elmore James.
L841: **Earth Blues** – Jimi (gi, lv), Buddy (dr, hv), Billy (ba).
L842: **Burning Desire** – Jimi (gi, lv), Buddy (dr, hv), Billy (ba, hv).

UNFORGETABLE [sic] EXPERIENCE
– RAH-2469 [USA] – Released 90 – LP
The cover shows a photograph of Jimi in the garden of the Samarkand Hotel,

Lansdowne Crescent, London W11, taken in the early afternoon of 17/09/70 . . .

L843: **Hey Joe** – Jimi (gi, vo), Mitch (dr), Noel (ba). Comp: William M. Roberts. Rec: Marquee, London W1, 02/03/67.

NOTE: This is an outtake version of L795.

L844: **Purple Haze** – Jimi (gi, vo), Mitch (dr), Noel (ba). Rec: Marquee, London W1, 02/03/67.

NOTE: This is an outtake version of L656.

L845: **Getting My Heart Back Together Again** – Jimi (gi, vo), Mitch (dr), Noel (ba). Rec: Royal Albert Hall, London, 24/02/69.

Plus: part of I Don't Live Today [L221]; The Wind Cries Mary [L514]; Foxy Lady [L657]; Red House [L302].

LORD, I CAN SEE THE BLUES
> – Humphrey Records EC1333 [USA?] – Released 89 – LP – *: Easy Blues

MANNISH BOY
> – Contraband Records CBM 88 [USA?] – Released 90 – LP

S846: **Mannish Boy** – Jimi (gi, vo), Buddy (dr), Billy (ba). Comp: Muddy Waters & Bo Diddley & Mel London. Rec: PLA, 07/01/70. Prod: Jimi.

S847: **Instrumental** – Jimi (gi), Mitch (dr), Noel (ba). Rec: TTG, 10/68. Prod: Jimi.

S848: **Easy Blues** – Jimi (gi, voice), Mitch (dr), Billy (ba), Larry (rhythm gi), unknown engi (voice from control-room). Special effect: Jimi (Uni-Vibe with chorus setting at slow speed). Rec: HIT, Autumn 69. Prod: Jimi.

NOTE: This is the complete basic track version of S174, without the added tambourine.

Plus: Lord I Sing The Blues For Me And You [S723]; Country Blues [S722]; Catfish Blues [L516]; Pass It On [L707].

GYPSY SUN AND RAINBOWS
> – Manic Depression Records MOCD 05/06 – Released 90 – Double CD
> All 14/08/69 songs rec: Jimi's Shokan house.

I849: **Interview with Jimi** – Rec: 18/08/69, shortly after finishing his Woodstock performance.

L850: **Lover Man** – Jimi (gi, vo), Mitch (dr), Billy (ba), Larry (rhythm gi), Juma? (ta). Rec: 14/08/69.

L851: **Lover Man** – Jimi (gi, vo), Mitch (dr), Billy (ba), Larry (rhythm gi). Rec: 14/08/69.

L852: **Spanish Castle Magic** – Jimi (gi, vo), Mitch (dr), Billy (ba), Larry (rhythm gi). Rec: 14/08/69.

Plus: Getting My Heart Back Together Again [L614]; Spanish Castle Magic [L615]; Red House [L616]; Mastermind [L617]; Lover Man [L618]; Foxy Lady [L619]; Jam Back At The House [L620]; Izabella [L621]; Gypsy Woman [L622]; Fire [L623]; Voodoo Child (slight return) [L624]; Star Spangled Banner [L067]; Purple Haze [L068]; Instrumental Solo [L625]; Hey Joe [L626]; Getting My Heart Back Together Again [L658].

GIMMIE THE GLAD EYE
> – World Productions Of Compact Music DTD 003 [ITA] – Released 04/90 – Double CD

The release title is stated on the labels as: *The Best Of Jimi Hendrix Live In Concert 1968–1969*.

Contains: Stone Free [L511]; Hey Joe [L512]; Purple Haze [L513]; Catfish Blues [L516]; Foxy Lady [L517]; Purple Haze [L518]; Voodoo Child (slight return) [L475]; Hey Joe [L476]; The Sunshine Of Your Love [L477]; Angel [P255]; Like A Rolling Stone [L231]; Fire [L607]; Getting My Heart Back Together Again [L608];

Red House [L609]; Stone Free [L604]; Are You Experienced/Stone Free [L605]; Foxy Lady [L610]; Like A Rolling Stone [L611]; part of Voodoo Child (slight return) [L612]; Purple Haze [L613].

UPDATE
Since the book was first published, there have been several new releases, both official and unofficial. The following is a select listing.

OFFICIAL RELEASES

Title	Title/Label No.	Contents
ALBUMS		
Cornerstones	Polydor 847 231-1	Compilation of released material
Live At The Isle Of Wight	Polydor 847 236-1	Isle Of Wight festival
COMPACT DISCS		
Introspective	Baktaback CINT 5006	John Burke interview 04-02-70
		Scene Club, March 1968
The Best + Rest Of	Action Replay CDAR 1022	Scene Club, March 1968
Hendrix Speaks	Rhino R-2 70771	Nancy Carter interview 1969
		Meatball Fulton interview 67-69
Lifelines	Reprise 9 26435-2	Repackage of Live And Unreleased
		Los Angeles Forum 26-04-69
Between the Lines	Reprise PRO CD-4541	Sampler for Lifelines
Rarities On CD Vol 1	On The Radio releases	Compilation of released material
Rarities On CD Vol 3	On The Radio releases	Compilation of released material
Johnny B. Goode	Capitol 432018-2	Video soundtrack
Sessions [box set]	Polydor 847 232-2	Are You Experienced?
		Axis: Bold As Love
		Electric Ladyland
		Cry Of Love
Footlights [box set]	Polydor 847 235-2	Monterey
		Live At The Isle Of Wight
		Band Of Gypsys
		Winterland
Jimi Hendrix 1970	Merman-1983	John Burke interview 04-02-70
Jimi Hendrix 1967	If 6 was 9 CD	Compilation of Swedish interviews
Masterpieces	Pulsar PULS. 008	Lonnie Youngblood material
Experiences	Pulsar PULS. 004	Lonnie Youngblood material
SINGLES		
Voodoo Chile [12″]	Polydor	Cornerstones material
Crosstown Traffic [CD]	Polydor POL 940	Cornerstones material
Berlin 69 [7′]	If 6 Was 9 C.D.	Berlin conversations 23-01-69
Jimi Hendrix 1970 [7″]	If 6 Was 9 C.D.	John Burke interview
		04-01-70

UNOFFICIAL

ALBUMS

Unforgettable Experience	RAH-2469-A-B	Royal Albert Hall 24-02-69
Electric Jimi	Jaguarondi JAG 0001	Los Angeles Forum 26-04-69
Last American Concert Vol 1	Swinging Pig TSP 062	Maui, Hawaii 30-07-70 1st show
Last American Concert Vol 2	Swinging Pig TSP 072	Maui, Hawaii 30-07-70 1st show
Paris 67	TMQ	Paris, L'Olympia, 29-01-68

COMPACT DISCS

Isle of Wight Incident at Rainbow Bridge	Triangle PYCD 060-2	Isle Of Wight / Maui, Hawaii
Last American Concert Vol 1	Swinging Pig TSP-CD-062	Maui, Hawaii 30-07-70 1st show
Last American Concert Vol 2	Swinging Pig TSP-CD-062	Maui, Hawaii 30-07-70 2nd show
Rare Masters Series Vol 3	Genuine Pig TGP-CD-134	Maui, Hawaii 30-07-70 both shows
Things I Used To Do	Early Years Releases 02-CD-3334	Studio outakes
Black Devil	Great Dane Records	Paris, L'Olympia, 29-01-68
Historic Performances	Aquarius AQ 67-JH-080	Royal Albert Hall 24-02-69 B.B. King Jam Lulu Show 04-01-69
Atlanta Special	Genuine Pig TGP-CD-121	Atlanta 04-07-70
It Never Takes An End	Genuine Pig TGP-CD-118	Newport 22-06-69
Jimi Hendrix and Traffic	Oh Boy 1-9027	Hendrix / Traffic, jam
Musicorama	Triangle PYCD 042	Paris, L'Olympia, 20-01-68
Message To Love	Triangle, PYCD 043	Randalls Isle 17-07-70
Cafe Au Go Go	Koine K880802	Jimi Hendrix and Paul Butterfield

2 *Move Over Rover and Let Jimi Take Over: The Technical File*

JIMI'S EARLY GUITARS – 1959 TO 1966*

The first guitar Jimi ever owned was bought for him by his father Al Hendrix in 1959 from Myers Music Store in Seattle. It was a Supro *'Ozark'* solid electric guitar, model 1560 S, made around 1957. This was the cheapest and most basic in the Supro range, retailing at $89. The Ozark had a single pick-up mounted by the bridge, set on a panel which included the volume and tone controls, plus jack socket. The guitar had

The Rocking Kings at the Washington Hall in Seattle, 20 February 1960. Line-up (from left to right): Lester Exkano, Jimi (with Supro *Ozark*), Webb Lofton, Walter Harris, Robert Green.

* All guitars mentioned in this Appendix are right-handed models (unless otherwise stated) which Jimi would simply turn upside down and re-string: guitar prices quoted are for new instruments, valid during the period Jimi obtained each listed guitar

21 frets, rare for such a cheap guitar as they usually contained one fret less. The Supro brand was part of the Valco company which produced many other makes and models including 'National' and 'Dobro'. The Supro Jimi had was a white model with a black scratch plate. Jimi used it up to the end of 1960, when it was stolen from the bandstand during a gig at the Birdland club in Seattle.

After Jimi's Supro guitar was stolen, he obtained another guitar from Myers Music. This was a Danelectro which had a single 'lipstick' pick-up, and was made around 1956/57 and sold for around $75. The guitar was available in two colours, black (model 3011) and bronze (model 3012) and was the cheapest in its range. The brand and model names weren't on the guitar. This was mainly done so that the giant Sears mail-order company in the States could offer guitars like the Danelectro and Silvertone in their catalogues under their own brand name. This was common practice in those days, as many guitar manufacturers supplied instruments to mail-order companies. The Danelectro had a white scratch plate, and at some point Jimi painted the guitar red.

The Tomcats at Bors Brumo, Seattle, early 1961. Line-up: Perry Thomas (piano), Leroy Toots (bass), James Thomas (vocals), Jimi (with Danelectro), Bill Rinnick and Richard Grayswood (drums and sax – unknown who played what).

When Jimi went into the army in May 1961 he left the above guitar at his girlfriend's house (Betty Jean Morgan) and played up to around February 1962 on a Japanese-made guitar. With money always a problem in the army, this was the cheapest guitar Jimi ever played on – costing no more than $20. The guitar was either a Kay or an Eko, manufactured in 1961, available also in England under various brand names such as 'Star'.

Jimi (with Kay or Eko), Billy Cox and 2 others on stage at the Pink Poodle Club, Clarksville, Tennessee, November 1961. The name of this band is unknown, possibly it was The King Kasuals.

On 17 January 1962 Jimi wrote a letter to his father asking him to send his red Danelectro, which was gathering dust at Betty Jean's house in Seattle. Around Spring 1962 the Danelectro was traded in at a music store in Clarksville, Tennessee, for a slightly better guitar. The guitar of his choice was the Epiphone *'Wiltshire'*, model SB432. At that time Jimi had a bit more money to invest; he bought the guitar brand new for around $65. The guitar came in cherry finish and had a black scratch plate. The Epiphone company was bought out by Gibson in 1957, and Gibson produced the Epiphone guitars at their factory from 1958 to 1969. Many former Epiphone craftsmen moved to the Guild company. The Epiphone name has survived since 1969 on inexpensive Japanese-made guitars, although it should be noted that these guitars have nothing in common with the finely crafted instruments of the original Epiphone company.

Around this time Jimi did another paint job to his Epiphone *'Wiltshire'*, changing the scratch plate's original colour from black to white.

During Jimi's spell with the Isley Brothers from March to November 1964, Jimi got his first Fender guitar – a blond Fender *Duo-Sonic*. The *Duo-Sonic* range was introduced by Fender in 1959 and was fitted with a single-coil bar pick-up encased in black plastic with a white scratch plate. The one Jimi got was manufactured after 1959/60, a short-scale guitar (22½ inch), selling for $160. The common blond finish was available up to 1964. An interesting feature of this guitar was that Jimi fitted it with an Epiphone 'Tremtone' Vibrato unit. As the story goes, Jimi's guitar was stolen after a gig in Seattle, but it's unknown if this in fact was the blond Duo-Sonic or not.

623

The King Kasuals at Jolly Roger, Nashville, Tennessee, Spring 1962. Line-up: Jimi (with Epiphone standard finish), Billy Cox (bass), Harold Nesbit (drums), Leonard Moses (guitar), Buford Majors (sax), Harry Batchelor (vocals).

The King Kasuals at Club Del Morocco, Nashville, Tennessee, 19 May 1962. Line-up: Jimi (with painted Epiphone), Billy, Harry Batchelor (vocals), Babe Boo (guitar), Tee Howard Williams (sax). Two remaining musicians (who also played at this gig) aren't in this photo: Frank Sheffield (drums) and part-time member Tommy Lee Williams (sax).

Jimi (on a Fender *Duosonic*) with the Isley Brothers' backing band, USA, 1964 (no full line-up known).

During Jimi's playing days with Little Richard (as a permanent member of the Upsetters) from January to July 1965, Jimi used a sunburst Fender *Jazzmaster*. The *Jazzmaster* was launched in 1957. The guitar featured two large single-coil pick-ups mounted under black-coloured plastic covers (cream covers were used from 1959). The guitar was fitted with a so-called 'Floating Tremolo', with the standard sunburst finish, while the laminated-shell plastic scratch plate was added in 1959/60. The retail price of the guitar was about $220.

After Jimi left Little Richard, he either kept the Fender *Jazzmaster* guitar as a reserve or he had to return the guitar to Little Richard, because during Jimi's on and off period with Curtis Knight & The Squires (from September 1965 to May 1966) Jimi played on yet another Fender *Duo-Sonic*, with sunburst finish. This model, which retailed at around $95, was made around 1963/64, and had a white scratch plate and standard black pick-ups.

During a brief period in mid 1966, Jimi switched back once again to playing a Fender *Jazzmaster*. It's not known if this was the same *Jazzmaster* he had before, or if he had bought or borrowed another one.

In order to 'free' him finally from Curtis Knight, Jimi's girlfriend at that time, Carol Shiroky, gave him the money to buy a fairly new Fender (trading in the *Duo-Sonic*) from Manny's in New York City. This was Jimi's first Fender *Stratocaster*, which in those days retailed for $289. Jimi's model was manufactured around 1964. The *Stratocaster* was developed in 1954 by Fred Tavares. It has three alnico pole magnet single-coil pick-ups and features a floating tremolo system and contoured body styling,

625

Jimi (on Fender *Duosonic*) with Curtis Knight & The Squires, New York City, late 1965/early 1966.

Jimi playing on a Fender Jazzmaster with Wilson Pickett during a party thrown by Atlantic Records in New York City for all the Atlantic artists, mid 1966. Jimi was actually playing for and with King Curtis at this time, as an official member of Curtis' backing band The Kingpins.

for a more comfortable playing position. When Jimi flew out from New York City to London in September 1966 it was probably this Strat which he took with him.

JIMI'S GUITARS – 1966 TO 1970

Jimi would invariably use right-handed guitars, simply because there were very few left-handed models made at all. Thus, out of necessity, Jimi had to use right-handed models and re-string them. This meant that the volume and tone controls were now at the top of the guitar and therefore easy to adjust while he was actually playing. However, using a right-handed guitar also presented him with a few problems. Firstly he needed to reverse the nut which caused a problem with the bass E string. Due to the position of the machine head, the bass E string would slip out of the nut. In order to prevent this, Jimi would wind the bass E string the opposite way around the machine head, which seemed to eliminate the problem. Countless photographs show that Jimi applied this technique throughout his career.

In general, Jimi's guitars weren't modified in any way, although Roger Mayer stated that he did sometimes re-wire Jimi's guitars to by-pass the tone controls. Roger also re-surfaced and profiled the frets in order to eliminate any fret buzz, while he also improved the sustain of Jimi's guitars by making sure of a clean joint where the neck joined the body. Roger: 'Sometimes during the original spraying process, if paint accumulated in that area, the neck would not be a perfect match to the body, which in turn would cause a loss of sustain. So by making sure that the neck was joined to the body perfectly the sustain of the guitar would increase.' It should be noted that this was mainly done to the guitars Jimi used in the studio. If none of the equipment people were around, Jimi would do the re-fretting and so on himself. The guitars Jimi used on stage while on long tours (particularly in the States) would be standard stock models, often purchased on the road: 'I use a Fender *Stratocaster*. Everybody's screaming about the seven-year-old *Telecaster*, and the 12-year-old Gibson, and the 92-year-old Les Paul. They've gone into an age bag right now, but it's nothing but a fad. The guitars nowadays play just as good. Y'know the salesman is always telling you that Chuck Berry took this one to the bathroom with him and he didn't have no toilet paper, so watch out for the pickguard . . . The *Stratocaster* is the best all-round guitar for the stuff we're doing. You can get the very bright trebles and the deep bass sound. I tried *Telecaster* and it only has two sounds, good and bad, and a very weak tone variation. The Guild guitar is very delicate but it has one of the best sounds. I tried one of the new Gibsons, but I literally couldn't play it at all, so I'll stick with Fender. I really like my old Marshall tube amps, because when it's working properly there's nothing can beat it, nothing in the whole world. It looks like two refrigerators hooked together . . .'

1966–1968 – Jimi was using a large variety of Fender *Stratocasters*. They were mainly rosewood neck models during this period, although he did use a maple neck on a few occasions.

1968–1970 – In October 1968, Jimi started using a black maple-neck *Stratocaster* and in November a blond maple-neck *Stratocaster* – the guitar with which Jimi is chiefly associated. These two models remained Jimi's main choice of guitar for the rest of his career.

The *Stratocaster* was a new model from Fender and featured a laminated maple neck, a larger headstock and a much larger logo. The models with the laminated maple fingerboard were made in the same way as the rosewood models, and did not have the normal stripe down the back of the neck or the truss-rod fillet on the headstock. As far as could be determined, these models were only available on special order and only for a short period of time, which is why these models are nearly impossible to find today.

Make	Model	Serial	Year	Colour	Neck	Owner/comments
Supro	Ozark	?	1957	White	r/wood	stolen at Birdland, Seattle, in 1960
Danelectro		?	1956	Red	r/wood	sold in Nashville, 1962
Kay or Eko		?	1961	White	r/wood	used during Jimi's army days, possibly loaned to him
Epiphone	Wiltshire	?	1961	Cherry	r/wood	used during Nashville days
Fender	Duo-Sonic	?	1964-	White	r/wood	used during Isley Brothers period, fitted with 'Tremtone' vibrato unit
Fender	Jazzmaster	?	1965-	Sunburst	r/wood	used during Little Richard period
Fender	Duo-Sonic	?	1964-	Sunburst	r/wood	used during Curtis Knight period, later traded in for the next guitar
Fender	Stratocaster	?	1964	Sunburst	r/wood	bought at Manny's, probably the Strat Jimi took to England with him
Fender	Stratocaster	?	1964	Red?	r/wood	–
Fender	Stratocaster	?	1964-	Blue	r/wood	owner unknown [ex-Oliver Keen/Eire]
Fender	Stratocaster	?	1965-	Sunburst	r/wood	used in early 1967 in studio and for concerts up to around May 1967
Fender	Stratocaster	?	1965-	Sunburst	r/wood	used during gig at Saville Theatre, London (07/05/67)
Fender	Stratocaster	?	1959-	Red	maple	used during TV rehearsal (18/05/67); black PU selector & controls
Fender	Stratocaster	?	1965-	Red?	r/wood	used in Stockholm (24/05/67) and at Spalding (29/05/67)
Fender	Stratocaster	?	1965-	Black	maple	used Saville Theatre (04-06/67)
Fender	Stratocaster	?	1965-	White	r/wood	used and smashed during 2nd show at Saville Theatre (04/06/67)
Fender	Stratocaster	?	1965-	Black	r/wood	used at Monterey (18/06/67) and at Golden Gate (25/06/67)
Fender	Stratocaster	?	1965-	Black	r/wood	Al Kooper/USA; possibly the same guitar as in the previous entry
Fender	Stratocaster	?	1965-	Red	r/wood	painted white by Jimi; used and burned at Monterey (18/06/67)
Fender	Stratocaster	?	1965+	White	r/wood	used in Central Park (05/07/67)
Fender	Stratocaster	?	1959-	White	r/wood	used at Hollywood Bowl (14/09/67)

628

Make	Model	Serial	Year	Colour	Neck	Owner/comments
Gibson	Flying V	?	?	Cherry	r/wood	used from 15/08/67 to 01/69; painted by Jimi
Fender	Jaguar	?	1967-	Blue	r/wood	used at *Top Of The Pops* TV Show (24/08/67) for BBC
Epiphone	Acoustic	?	1967-	Sunburst	r/wood	bought during first USA tour
Fender	Stratocaster	?	1965+	White	r/wood	used at Dutch TV show (10/11/67); with black PU switch
Fender	Stratocaster	?	1967	White	r/wood	used at Rotterdam gig (10/11/67); with tortoiseshell pick guard
Fender	Stratocaster	?	1968-	M/Blue	r/wood	used in Zurich (31/05/68) and Singer Bowl (23/08/68); metallic blue
Fender	Stratocaster	?	1959-	Red	maple	Billy Gibbons/USA
Goya		?	1968-	?	r/wood	probably loaned to Jimi
Guild	SF-V Starfire DeLuxe	?	1966	Red	r/wood	Bob Terry/USA; used at jam session in Miami 05/68; left-handed model
Fender	Stratocaster	?	1968-	Sunburst	r/wood	Frank Zappa/USA; burned at Miami (19/05/68); restored by Rex Bouge
Gibson	SG Custom	?	1968-	White	r/wood	used in 1968 and 1969
Gibson	SG Custom	899617	1969	White	r/wood	Hard Rock Café, London; this guitar has wear and tear from a right-handed guitar player, which makes it very doubtful Jimi ever even owned the guitar. . .
Washburn	Acoustic	A33191	?	?	r/wood	owner unknown (sold by Mitch Mitchell at the 05/08/87 Sotheby's auction); ¾ scale guitar; possibly used on the studio recording of 'All Along The Watchtower'
Fender	Stratocaster	240981	1968	White	maple	Red Rodney, Italy (sold by Mitch Mitchell at the 25/04/90 Sotheby's auction for £198,000); used from 10/68 to 09/70, including the European September 1970 tour
Fender	Stratocaster	222625	1968	Black	maple	Monika Dannemann/UK; used from 10/68 to 09/70, including at the Isle of Wight Festival
Gibson	Les Paul	?	1968-	Black	r/wood	owner unknown; used from 05/68
Gibson	ES-335	847084	1968	Sunburst	r/wood	Hard Rock Café, Dallas; left handed model; no photographs exist with Jimi playing this guitar. . .

Make	Model	Serial	Year	Colour	Neck	Owner/comments
Epiphone	Casino	8508423?	?	?	?	bought by Jimi at Manny's 07/11/69; the serial number mentioned on the invoice has one number too many
Gibson	Les Paul	1042?	?	?	?	bought by Jimi at Manny's 07/11/69; the serial number mentioned on the invoice has one number too few
Fender	Stratocaster	40281	1968	Sunburst	maple	Hard Rock Café, Dallas (sold by Velvert Turner/USA)
Gibson	Flying V	SN-849476	1970	Black	r/wood	Hard Rock Café, Dallas (sold by Eric Barrett/USA); left-handed model with Trini Lopez Fingerboard and 3 gold pick-ups
Fender LH	Stratocaster	285705	1968	Black	maple	owner unknown (sold at Sotheby's 17/06/88 auction)
Fender	Stratocaster	240981	1968	White	?	–
Fender	Stratocaster	244458	1968	Sunburst	?	–
Fender	Mustang	L45185	1964	Red	r/wood	withdrawn from Sotheby's 28/08/86 auction, so possibly a fake. . .
Fender	Stratocaster	?	1965-	White	r/wood	owner unknown (sold by Brian Eno/UK); has EXP sticker on the back
Fender	Jazz Bass	116544	1965	Sunburst	r/wood	Al Hendrix/USA
Gibson	Acoustic J-200	?	1968-	Sunburst	r/wood	Dave Brewis/UK (sold by Chas Chandler/UK)
Fender	Stratocaster	L39720	1964	Sunburst	r/wood	fake
Fender	Stratocaster	L66347	1965	Red	maple	fake
Fender	Stratocaster	186781	1966	Sunburst	r/wood	fake
Fender	Stratocaster	135306	1967	Sunburst	r/wood	fake
Fender	Stratocaster	217373	1967	Black	maple	fake
Fender	Stratocaster	247724	1968	?	?	fake
Fender	Stratocaster	252238	1968	?	?	fake
Fender	Stratocaster	236326	1968	?	?	fake

NOTE: During recent years the prices paid at UK and USA auctions for guitars owned (or claimed to have been owned) by Jimi have soared. Extreme caution should be applied to any possible purchases; the money that can be made nowadays has seen a proliferation of guitars being offered which Jimi never laid a finger on. If you're planning to buy something, be sure to have the guitar examined by a guitar and/or Jimi Hendrix expert. Also pieces of paper, offered as authenticity, should be examined by an expert. There's a well-known case of a sales receipt printed with the address of a guitar shop in New York, which turned out to be fake. The street number would have been right in the middle of the Hudson river!

OTHER GUITARS USED BY JIMI

When Jimi lived in New York, he would often visit Manny's Musical Instruments on 48th Street and try out guitars and new effect units. Jimi bought loads of different guitars, anything from a Rickenbacker, Firebird, Mosrite electric dobro, to a Guild and a Martin acoustic with pearl inlay. Some of these he hung on to, others he gave away to friends, or as Henry Goldrich (of Manny's) puts it, 'I'd see kids come in the store with guitars I'd sold Jimi the week before. If he liked a kid, he gave him his guitar, brand new.' The following is a very brief summary of some of the more unusual guitars Jimi played and/or owned.

Hofner 'Club 40' – made in 1959
This April 1967 photograph shows Jimi during an interview with Alan Freeman for *Rave* magazine. It is a right-handed electric Hofner, strung right-handed, with a single pick-up. All this suggests the guitar was not Jimi's. However, it appears that Jimi did own a Hofner at some early stage, but no other details are available. By the way, it has been incorrectly suggested in several magazines that Jimi used a very old Hofner during the studio recording of 'Red House'. In fact he was playing a Stratocaster.

Epiphone 'Acoustic'
See page 227 for a photograph of Jimi with this guitar.

Gretch 'Corvette' – made in 1967
During a warm-up session in late July 1967 for a studio day with Curtis Knight in New York City, Jimi played this cherry-red guitar. At the same session Jimi played a red 1967 Hagstrom 8-string bass that either belonged to Jimi or Noel Redding (they both had one). Jimi in fact used the Hagstrom on some of the recordings with Curtis Knight (see discography for details).

Gibson 'Flying V'
Bought by Jimi between June and August 1967 in the States. Originally it was in cherry red, but Jimi painted very colourful psychedelic designs all over the body. Jimi kept the guitar until early January 1969 when he gave it to Mick Cox, guitarist with Eire Apparent. Cox later sold the guitar; the last known owner was Mick Box of Uriah Heep. The first photographic evidence of Jimi using the Flying V was at the Fifth Dimension Club, Ann Arbor, Michigan, 15 August 1967. See page V for a photograph of Jimi with this guitar.

631

Fender 'Jaguar'
This rare photograph shows Jimi during a performance on *Top Of The Pops* for BBC Television (24 August 1967) while doing a version of 'The Burning Of The Midnight Lamp'. The vocals were done live, but the guitar wasn't plugged in, and in fact the guitar is still strung right handed!

Zamaitis – made in 1960
This is the 12-string acoustic Jimi is playing in the movie *See My Music Talking* (a.k.a.: *Experience*) during 'Getting My Heart Back Together Again' (19 December 1967). The guitar was made by Tony Zamaitis. Jimi didn't own the right-handed guitar; film director Peter Neal borrowed it from a friend for the occasion and re-strung it.

Fender 'Jazzmaster'
Jimi rarely played this guitar in concert with the Experience. The photograph was taken around March 1968 during a concert in the States.

Goya – probably made in early 1968
This photograph (taken around March 1968 in the USA) shows Jimi playing this Italian-manufactured guitar – the first psychedelic guitar available on the market.

Gibson 'Les Paul'
Sometime in mid 1968 Jimi got a black Les Paul. The first photographic evidence of Jimi using it was on 10 May 1968 at the Fillmore East in New York City. The photograph shows Jimi with this guitar at the Hallenstadion in Zurich, Switzerland, 30 May 1968.

Guild 'SF-V Starfire Deluxe'
– made around 1966
This left-handed guitar had a Guild Bigsby Vibrato unit fitted. The guitar was beautifully custom-painted by an unknown admirer who gave Jimi the guitar as a present during a jam session at the Wreck Bar in Miami, Florida, on 20 May 1968.

Gibson SG Custom type 2
– made in 1968
The first photographic evidence of Jimi using this guitar was at Hollywood's TTG studio in October 1968. After Jimi gave his Gibson 'Flying V' to Mick Cox in early January 1969, Jimi used the Gibson SG as a replacement guitar for his blues numbers during concerts. He continued to use it until he obtained his second Gibson 'Flying V' in 1970. The photograph here is from a concert at the Musikhalle, Hamburg, W. Germany, 11 January 1969.

633

Gibson 'Flying V' – likely made in 1970

This one is a black, left-handed 'Flying V', with a rosewood neck, boasting gold pick-ups, machine-heads etc. It is believed that this guitar was especially made for Jimi by Gibson, which could explain why it's a left-handed model. Jimi got the guitar in the States in 1970. The first photographic evidence of Jimi actually playing it dates from the Temple University Stadium, Philadelphia, Pennsylvania, 16 May 1970. Jimi went on to use this guitar mainly for blues numbers and the more melodic songs such as 'Hey Baby (The Land Of The New Rising Sun)'. After Jimi died, Eric Barrett acquired the guitar stating that he 'would never sell it, even if I was starving.' Guess what? Eric sold the guitar in 1986 to the Hard Rock Café in Dallas, Texas, for $11,000.

JIMI'S PLAYING TECHNIQUES

A lot of what Jimi achieved on a guitar still remains a mystery. However, through carefully studying films and video recordings and listening to and researching his musical legacy it is possible to work out some of the things he did. The following is a brief guide of some of his techniques . . .

Tremolo Arm

It has been said that Jimi spent hours bending his tremolo arm by hand, so that he could tap each string with the tremolo bar. This is not the case. The real reason why Jimi spent so much time bending his tremolo arm was because, by playing a right-handed guitar left-handed, the tremolo arm would be in line with the bass E string which would make it awkward to use the tremolo while playing. So, Jimi bent the arm down across the strings so that the tremolo arm was in line with the high E string – the conventional position for a right-handed player.

Finger Tremolo

Also known as vibrato, this is applied by moving the string across the fret while slightly shaking one's wrist. Jimi had a very distinctive finger vibrato which in some ways was his trademark. Finger vibrato is unique to each player and therefore very hard to copy.

Rhythm Guitar

Jimi was an extremely accomplished rhythm guitarist, for which he rarely got any credit. Jimi crafted his rhythm-guitar technique during his years performing as a backing musician to soul and R&B artists. In concert, Jimi was also one of the very few guitarists who could play rhythm parts and lead solos at the same time. Sometimes Jimi would also play the rhythm on dead strings: he would damp the strings with his fingers and produce a kind of scratchy rhythm using his pick. A classic example of this is in the guitar intro during the studio version of 'Voodoo Child (slight return)'.

String-Bending

Most rock guitarists use string-bending nowadays. Jimi would frequently bend the strings upwards, as opposed to the downward bend that most guitarists use. According to Eric Barrett, Jimi's strength enabled him to 'bend the first string on a bass all the way to the top.' Jimi would also play a bent note on one string bent up and then play the second note on another string on the way down from the first bend. A good example of this technique can be heard during 'Message From Nine To The Universe' (*Nine To The Universe* LP). Another bend technique was to bend one string and fret on a note on second string, but play both notes together during the actual bend – like during the introduction to 'Highway Chile'.

634

Octave Playing

Jimi played a great deal in octaves: he would play a note on one string and play the same note on another string an octave higher. The effect was that the note would sound more like a chord. To hear this kind of fingering to its full effect, listen to 'Third Stone From The Sun', 'Instrumental Solo' (live at Woodstock) or 'Earth Blues' and 'Pali Gap' on the *Rainbow Bridge* LP.

Chording

Jimi played most of his chords using his thumb, so that he was able to play a chord, keep the rhythm going and play lead licks all at the same time. Jimi's ability could make it sound as if you were hearing two guitars rather than just one. Jimi had great knowledge of chords, but didn't read a single note of music. One can only guess at what he could have accomplished if he had been able to read music; he was sometimes very frustrated that he was unable to play the things he heard in his head. He also mastered the very difficult technique of singing while he was playing (as opposed to singing a line, playing a few guitar licks, singing again, etc.). Most guitarists never manage this at all!

Harmonics

Apart from playing the strings, Jimi also used almost every part of his guitar to obtain effects. He would tap the back of the headstock, different parts of the guitar neck and even tap the body of his guitar to obtain various harmonic effects. At the back of a *Stratocaster*, there is a plastic plate covering the springs which operate the tremolo system. Jimi would remove this plate so that he could tap the springs with his fingers to create different effects, and he would use this in conjunction with his tremolo arm to obtain searing dive-bombing sounds. It was also easier to change the strings with the plastic cover removed.

Slide

Jimi never used the conventional metal bottle-neck for slide-playing. Sometimes he would use one of his rings, or for more dramatic slide effects he would use the edge of a speaker cabinet or the microphone stand. Some examples of Jimi playing slide include 'Room Full Of Mirrors' (*Rainbow Bridge*) and 'All Along The Watchtower' (*Electric Ladyland*). On this photograph, taken backstage at Hunter College, New York City (2 March 1968) Jimi is performing the old trick of using a beer can for slide effect . . .

Showmanship

Jimi did tricks with his guitar that go back almost half a century: he played the guitar behind his head, between his legs, behind his back and of course with his teeth. A few other 'tricks' and 'effects' are worth a mention here. Here's Mick Cox talking about a jam session by Jimi (bass) and Jeff Beck (guitar) at the Scene club in New York City in June 1968: 'They did "Superstition". It's one of those that has a break of two seconds. As it came to the break they threw each other's guitars, Beck caught the bass and Jimi caught the guitar and they carried straight on into the song. People weren't even noticing that you know!'

Hugh Hopper on a concert where Jimi was frustrated by defective equipment: 'At the end he didn't do the business with the guitar on the amplifier, what he did was get the head of the guitar and ride along the footlights at the bottom of the stage and popped them all. It looked good but the theatre did not like it at all. I remember the stagehands, all sort of straight, shaking their heads . . .'

A couple of times Jimi also stuck his guitar in amps and ceilings. Chas: 'It was in Newcastle City Hall (4 December 1967) and it was one of them nights when everything had gone wrong. No matter what happened, an amp was breaking down, there was crackling coming over, and at one point, half-way through the act, he was getting so uptight because the world was falling down around him out on the stage, and he took this guitar he was playing [Gibson Flying V] and he threw it at the amp. And this is where the good luck comes into it, the guitar went into the amp like that and stuck, it was just like an enormous arrow sticking out. The audience thought it was part of the act, rose as a man and from that minute nothing went wrong. It was just one of them little magic seconds.'

Lastly, a little story about the opening gig at Sgt. Pepper's in Palma, Majorca, Spain (15 July 1968), the club then owned by Mike Jeffery and Chas Chandler. Keith Altham: 'Jimi opened it and he brought down the new ceiling in the process. Chas didn't know whether to laugh or cry. Jimi was sticking his guitar head through the newly polystyrene-tiled ceiling . . . coming down in great clouds of asbestos . . .'

Destruction

Auto-destruction in music wasn't new when Jimi did it. The Who were very much into smashing up everything in sight during their stage act in the 60's. In Jimi's case, Chas Chandler stated that this all started when the Jimi Hendrix Experience performed for four days in November 1966 at the Big Apple club in Munich, W. Germany – Jimi smashed his guitar to pieces after he was pulled off stage by some enthusiastic fans. Although Jimi became (unfortunately) associated with smashing and burning guitars (we suggest a total ban on showing Jimi performing 'Wild Thing' at Monterey!) in reality he only ever burned a guitar on a couple of occasions. Out of the 527 official performances Jimi gave during the peak of his career, the number of guitars he completely smashed up can be counted on two hands. Usually Jimi would only harpoon the speaker cabinets with his guitar, or throw the guitar at the stacks. Roadies would then re-build the guitar from all the pieces for the next performance. As a matter of fact, Jimi lost far more guitars from people stealing them . . .

JIMI'S AMPLIFIERS

Jimi Hendrix used a variety of different makes of amplifier. Here's a guide to the main amplifiers he used.

Silvertone

During Jimi's early days in and around Tennessee (1961 etc.) – when he actually possessed his own amplifier – Jimi had a Silvertone with a 2 × 12 cabinet. Mostly Jimi borrowed amplifiers from other musicians, club owners, etc.

Fender (1965/66)
From 1965 and up until the beginning of 1966 Jimi used a Fender Twin Reverb amplifier. This amp had a rated power output of 85 watts RMS, and a peak power output of 187 watts. The self-contained unit (combo amp) contained two 12-inch J. B. Lansing D120F speakers. It also featured Reverb and Vibrato (Tremolo). The tremolo unit on these amplifiers had two controls, one for 'depth' of effect, and one for 'speed'. The effect it created in sounds was much like a rotating speaker sound which could be slowed down or speeded up as required. All the songs in the discography of this book referred to as 'Special effect: Jimi (tremolo)' refer to Jimi using an amplifier with the Tremolo (Vibrato) effect unit turned on.

Burns
During the first rehearsals of the newly formed Jimi Hendrix Experience in 1966, the band were using small 30-watt Burns amplifiers. Mitch: 'Chas went out and got us a couple of amplifiers. He brought in these little Burns amplifiers, and at the second rehearsal we tried to break the bloody things by throwing them down flights of stairs, and they didn't break! But we knew what we wanted, which was big clout, you know, big amplifiers and make it as dramatic as possible . . .'

Fender (1968)
For the lengthy USA tour that started in February 1968, Jimi got brand new Fender Dual Showman amps. They were nicknamed the 'Piggyback' amp, and had a rated power output of 85 watts RMS, with a peak power output of 187 watts. The speaker cabinets featured two 15-inch J. B. Lansing speakers. Jimi was using two amp tops and two speaker cabinets.

Marshall
The first Marshall amplifier was designed and constructed by Ken Bran in 1962. It was constructed on a 2 inch aluminium chassis. The first models used a pair of American 5880 output valves, a GZ34 receiver and three ECC83 pre-amp valves which produced around 35 watts. Due to the demand of the musicians of the day, Jim Marshall decided to produce an amplifier that could produce 100 watts – which is the amplifier that Jimi Hendrix made popular. The first Marshall 100-watt was fitted with four KT66 output valves and two 50-watt transformers. In early 1966 the KT66 valves were changed in favour of EL34 output valves. Jim Marshall designed the speaker cabinets which would become known as 4 × 12's because each cabinet contained four 12-inch speakers. The speakers used were the Celestion G12 which handled 25 watts each. There are two cabinets to a stack, the bottom cabinet with a straight front, and the top cabinet with a slanted front. Jim Marshall: 'Mitch was working in the [drums] shop as a Saturday-boy and eventually he brought Jimi along to see me. Jimi said he wanted to use Marshall equipment. I thought he was just another one who wanted to have something for nothing. But he seemed to read what I was thinking and he said, almost in his next breath, "well I don't want it for nothing, I wanna pay full price, but I want good service." And that's what we gave him. I built the first hundred-watt stack for Pete Townshend, that must have been 1965 . . . I think Jimi bought, as far as I can remember, four stage set-ups, which he had put in strategic places, so that they didn't have to transport it around. He had more than one set-up you see . . . standard hundred-watt heads and standard 1960 [model number] four by twelves . . .'

Jimi experimented with different formats of Marshall, starting off with just one stack, which comprised one Marshall 100-watt amp and two 4 × 12 speaker cabinets, up to using three stacks comprised of three 100-watt amps and six 4 × 12 speaker cabinets. The Marshall 100-watt Super Lead amplifier had four inputs: input 1 (high treble); input 2 (low treble); input 3 (high normal) and input 4 (low normal). So in order to link up three stacks of Marshall, Jimi would plug his guitar into input 1 of the first stack and, using a cord, link between input 2 of the first stack into input 1 of the second stack and so on, so it was possible to link as many amps up in this way as was required.

All Jimi Hendrix Marshall equipment was stencilled 'J.H. EXP' in January 1969 by the late John 'Upsy' Downing, one of Jimi's roadies at that time.

Below is a listing of amplifiers and cabinets once owned and used by Jimi Hendrix. As it is not possible to date Marshall equipment accurately purely from the serial number, only known items have been dated by the 'passed' stickers inside the amplifier, which were always signed and dated by the test person at the Marshall factory. The SLAs (Super Lead Amplifiers) listed below were made in March 1969 and shipped over to the West Coast Organ and Amp Service company in the States for the start of Jimi's Spring 1969 tour there.

Some of Jimi Hendrix's Marshall cabinets had J.B. Lansing 120F–6 Signature speakers fitted into them. The changing of Celestion speakers to JBL's (which came out of the Sunn amps) was carried out by Eugene McFadden during recordings at the Electric Lady studio, Summer 1970. The reason for this change over was that the Celestion speakers were constantly cracking up – no doubt again due to being switched to position 10 on the amp.

Make	Model	Serial No.	Manufacture date	Present owner
Amplifiers				
Marshall	100 watt lead	SLA 10032	03/69	Tony Brown/UK
Marshall	100 watt Lead	SLA 10045	?	?
Marshall	100 watt Lead	SLA 10047	?	?
Marshall	100 watt Lead	SLA 10590	03/69	Marcel Aeby/Switzerland
Marshall	100 watt Lead	SLA 12361	?	?
Marshall	100 watt Lead	SL/A 5273A	?	?
Marshall	100 watt Lead	ST/A 4329A	?	?
Marshall	100 watt Lead	ST/A 4360A	?	?
Fender	Duel Showman TFL 5000D	99110624	?	Al Hendrix/USA
Fender	Champ 5F1	C11239	?	? (sold by Mitch Mitchell at Sotheby's 05/08/87 auction)
Speaker cabinets				
Marshall	4 × 12s	10133	?	?
Marshall	4 × 12s	11244	?	?
Marshall	4 × 12s	11252	?	Tony Brown/UK
Marshall	4 × 12s	11368	?	?
Marshall	4 × 12s	17649	?	?
Marshall	4 × 12s	29127	?	?
Marshall	4 × 12s	29573	?	?
Marshall	4 × 12s	30023	?	?
Marshall	4 × 12s	30036	?	John Gregg/UK

Fender (1970)

Jimi used a Fender Twin Reverb amplifier and a so-called '½ stack' Marshall (one amp and one speaker with 4 × 12's) for most of his recordings at the Electric Lady studio.

Sound City

In November 1967 Jimi started using a Sound City stack for concert performances, it comprised one 100-watt amplifier and two 4 × 12 speaker cabinets. These were in addition to the Marshall stacks. It seems that Sound City was the equipment that Jimi was most likely to 'attack' with his guitar as part of his stage act. Jimi used the set-up with the Sound City gear until the end of January 1968, although he still continued to use Sound City on occasions as a monitor system. During recordings for the *Axis* LP, Sound City was used quite regularly in order to obtain a much cleaner sound (as opposed to the Marshall amps with their more distorted sound).

Sunn

During the early part of the USA tour which started in February 1968, Sunn came into the amp picture. A case of 'right time, right place' as, just at that moment, the Fender amps started to cause problems. Buck Munger explains: 'My basic mandate was to find one or two artists that the company could support wholly with equipment for nothing, in exchange for the endorsement. And I saw Jimi play and it was obvious that he played his amplifier even more than he was playing his guitar, so my company got involved . . . I walked up to Jimi, saying "I work for an amplifier company in Oregon, and I see you have a bunch of mixed-up, beaten-up, burned-up shit, and we'll give you whatever you want for nothing" . . . basically it was Jimi saying to me, "bring the equipment and we'll give it a try." They were brand new [but] they were still really poor. We signed a five year contract, what turned out to be one of one and a half years.' However, Roger Mayer offers a different view about the Sunn amps: 'basically they gave us an incredible amount of trouble. We didn't have burned-out shit, we had brand new Fenders that were given to us right at the beginning of the tour. We weren't really quite getting the sound out of the Fenders, probably because of the fifteens. But these Sunn amplifiers, you know, the transformers were falling off the chassis. I was rebuilding these and it was a completely wrong design. Jimi was most unsatisfied with these amps. In fact I actually had to go out to the factory to see if we could do anything about it, because the output transformers, when in transportation, were falling off the chassis, and mashing up everything. Also, they were constantly burning up. This guy [Buck Munger] is in "la-la-land" about that. We got totally rid of them as soon as we could. In fact when we got back to New York, Jimi had some of the original Marshalls from England flown over to finish up the tour . . .'

Jimi started using the Sunn 100-F speaker cabinets for the first time during a concert at the Shrine Auditorium in Los Angeles (10 February 1968). They contained one J. B. Lansing D-30 at the bottom and a L-E 100-S driver horn in the top. As there wasn't much mid-range, they were combined with the other amps Jimi used in order to get a somewhat better blend. He then tried a different set-up of Sunn which featured two 'Coliseum' PA tops altered for guitar with a power output of 120 watts RMS, driving five speaker cabinets each of which contained two 12-inch J. B. Lansing D-130 F speakers. The Sunn amp itself used 4 KDAD88 tubes, an ultra-linear design, which was more like a hi-fi design, and as a result didn't stand up to the continuous overdrive that Jimi subjected them to.

Buck Munger again: 'The only specifications that Jimi ever really dealt with, usually had to do with power and speaker configuration: "I want this many watts and

I want this many twelve-inch speakers and clusters" . . . and at that time actually Sunn had experimented with a cabinet called the 100S which had a high-frequency horn and crossover network and a fifteen-inch JBL speaker. Sunn's approach from the engineering point-of-view was to give him a big stack of speakers that on one hand had these high frequency horns and at the other end had big fifteen-inch big deep speakers and in the middle had all the twelves, but Jimi just discounted that, he did not want anything to do with it. So basically what happened in that case, which became a joke, was that the engineers at Sunn said, "OK fine, we will give him the maximum clear power before it starts becoming distorted, we will give him two thirds of it, so when he opens it all the way up he's actually getting 100% of the clear power." So that sounded intelligent to everyone concerned. So they did that, shipped it Jimi, Jimi wired it all up, turned it all the way up, and immediately knew exactly what was happening, and shook his head and said, "You are not getting the message, right?" So it didn't work at all, and that was the beginning of the end . . . Nobody ever got far away from Marshall, Jimi went for the Moon as far as the sound went . . .'

Jimi used Sunn just for a very short period and by April 1968 he was back to using all Marshall amplifiers again. From that point on, Sunn was only used as a monitor system, although Noel Redding continued to use Sunn gear for a much longer period.

Wem
Jimi used Wem 4 × 12 column speaker cabinets for a few gigs, like at the Royal Albert Hall, London, in February 1969, and at the Isle Of Wight Festival on 30 August 1970. The Wem gear was used only as a monitor system.

JIMI'S GUITAR EFFECTS
The main effect units Jimi used were: Fuzz Face, Mosrite Fuzzrite, Uni-Vibe, Wah-Wah, and Octavia. Here's a brief history of these effects.

Fuzz
The first photographs of Jimi Hendrix using a Fuzz box were taken when he played with Curtis Knight & The Squires at the Cheetah, New York City, May 1966. Possibly this was a Maestro fuzz unit.

Arbiter Fuzz Face
The Fuzz Face was designed and manufactured in England and distributed by the Arbiter Company in London. It became available in late 1966, and at that time sold for seven guineas (seven pounds and seven shillings). The Dallas Musical Instruments Company merged with Arbiter some time in the late 60's and they started to produce the Dallas Arbiter Fuzz Face. The Fuzz Face came in a die-cast metal disc-shaped box and had a rotary volume control, a rotary sustain control, and a foot switch situated in the middle of the unit. The way the controls were set out resembled a face; that's why it was called the Fuzz Face. They came in a variety of colours, but the early units Jimi used were red with black controls. The first Fuzz Face used two PNP germanium transistors, but shortly after that the PNP transistors became hard to obtain so NPN-type transistors were used instead. Unfortunately this meant the unit would now pick up radio signals during live work. The first photographs of Jimi using a Fuzz Face were taken at the Marquee, London, 24 January 1967. Jimi continued to use the Arbiter Fuzz Face throughout his career, mainly for concerts.

640

'Axis' fuzz

This was a special fuzz unit built for Jimi by Roger Mayer. It was used frequently during the 1967 recordings at Olympic studios. It was also used during the Band Of Gypsys concerts at the Fillmore East in New York City.

Mosrite Fuzzrite

The Mosrite Fuzzrite was manufactured in California. It was a very simple design and produced a sound very like the Arbiter Fuzz Face. It's not clear during which period Jimi used the Mosrite, but it would only have been used in the studio during 1969 or 1970.

Vox wah-wah pedal

The Vox wah-wah was manufactured in Kent, England by Jennings Musical Industries Ltd. Jimi: 'On the first LP *Are You Experienced?*, you know, well, eh, on this track "I Don't Live Today" there's a guitar taking a solo and it's wah-wah, like, but see we're doing it like by hand then you know, so then Vox and this other company in the States, in California, they made this . . . the first record I heard with the wah-wah was *Tales Of Brave Ulysses* by the Cream, yeah, which is one of my favourite records, but, eh, beforehand, you know, like we used to use a hand wah-wah then, you know which sounds very good . . .'

There are lots of songs in which Jimi used this effect, such as 'The Burning Of The Midnight Lamp' and 'Voodoo Child (slight return)' both on *Electric Ladyland*. The first photographs of Jimi using the wah-wah pedal live on stage were taken at the Fifth Dimension Club, Ann Arbor, Michigan, 15 August 1967. Jimi continued to use the Vox wah-wah throughout his career, although he also used the Jennings 'Cry Baby' for a short time. Nowadays the Dunlop Manufacturing Inc., California, and the Italian company JEN Elettronica manufacture the 'Cry Baby' unit, which is identical to the original. During the recordings for the *Axis: Bold As Love* LP, Roger Mayer modified Jimi's wah-wah pedals, in order to optimise the filter range and to interface better with the fuzz unit.

Leslie Speaker cabinet

The Leslie Speaker was primarily designed for use with the Leslie organ, but Jimi was so keen to experiment with many different sounds on the guitar, he used it for the studio recording of 'Little Wing' (*Axis: Bold As Love*).

Jimi: 'Well, there's one song on there we did a lot of sound on, you know. We put the guitar through the Leslie speaker of an organ, and it sounds like "Jelly Bread", you know . . .'

The technical staff at Olympic also built a smaller speaker cabinet based on the original Leslie, which had a smaller speaker operating on the rotating-drum principle, but without the high frequency horns the original Leslie had. This custom unit gave a better high-frequency response, and it was used on some of the *Axis* recordings.

Uni-Vibe

The Uni-Vibe was developed and manufactured by the Uni-Vox company, Long Island, New York, and sold by Merson Musical Products, Westbury, New York. The unit came on the market in early 1969 for $110. The Uni-Vibe is a device that simulates a rotating-speaker sound with a wide-band variable speed control. It was initially designed for use with electronic organs, but was found to be quite adaptable to guitars. It comes in two units, the first unit – the heart of the effect – was constructed in a metal box which measures $10\frac{1}{2} \times 7$ inches. The second part is the foot control, which resembles a wah-wah pedal and is used to speed the effect up by pushing the foot plate down. The top panel of the main unit has two inputs and one output, a five-pin socket for the foot control, a rotary control for the volume, another rotary control for the intensity of the effect and a rocker switch for the two different effects that the Uni-Vibe gives. The first effect was the chorus which simulates the sound of a rotating speaker made famous by the Leslie Company. It gives an irregular swirling effect and this was the main effect that Jimi used on such songs as 'Hey Baby (The Land Of The New Rising Sun)' and 'Machine Gun'. The second effect was the vibrato which gave a more regular sound. Jimi can be heard using this effect on 'Earth Blues' on the *Rainbow Bridge* LP.

Roger Mayer on the Uni-Vibe: 'it's a four-stage swept filter, almost like a kind of phaser sort of filter. It's controlled by four photo cells driven by one lightbulb which is modulated with a variable oscillator . . . basically what we used to do with them is a very similar situation as with the wah-wah; you had to make sure that the actual filters are optimised because there is quite a bit of a spread on the photo cells when you buy them . . . and then you had to play around also with the actual modulation signal that went to the lightbulb to optimise that. So basically I just used to tune them up. When you get them working right, they really sound very musical.'

Apart from using it in the studio, Jimi seems to have started using the Uni-Vibe for live work around August 1969. The first time Jimi used the Uni-Vibe was during a jam session at the Tinker Street Cinema, Woodstock, 10 August 1969. The first official live concert where Jimi used it was at Woodstock itself, 8 days later. Here he used it for almost every song. From that moment on it became a permanent part of his stage set-up but restricting its actual use mainly to 'Machine Gun' and 'Hey Baby (The Land Of The New Rising Sun'). However, even when the Uni-Vibe wasn't used *per se* (but still plugged in and part of the set-up), the effect still gave a more mellow sound. Since the unit which Jimi used was American-made, it ran on 110 volts. When Jimi toured Europe in August and September 1970, the Uni-Vibe effect had a much more prominent sound because there it ran instead on 240 volts. If you happen to collect unofficial tapes of concerts, have a listen to 'Hey Baby (The Land Of The New Rising Sun)' or 'Machine Gun' from the Isle Of Wight performance on 30 August 1970, or in fact to any of the European concerts Jimi gave in September 1970, you can hear how much different and stronger the effect sounded compared to, for example, the concerts in America, like Berkeley (30 May 1970) and Hawaii (30 July 1970).

The Uni-Vibe was later also manufactured by the Shin-ei Companion Company in Japan – model number SM.NO 49.2 – and was available into the mid 70's. These units were made for the European markets and available in 240 volts. These Japanese units looked and also sounded identical to the original American units.

Uni-Drive

According to a statement from Merson Musical Products published in *Melody Maker* (11 September 1971) they also gave Jimi another effect in mid 1970; the Uni-Drive, selling for $49.50. No other information can be obtained. It's possible that this effect created a kind of organ effect when hooked up with a guitar, such as on 'Angel' (*The Cry Of Love* LP).

Octavia

This effect was designed and made by Roger Mayer in early 1967. Roger: 'Basically it's a frequency doubler, it produces the octave up. If you put a sound wave into it and look at it, you'd see that you get double the frequency out. It gives the effect of a multiple mirror image of the actual sound, but phased inverted. So really it produces a sound that absolutely multiplies all the harmonics up, almost to infinity, so you get an extremely high tone out of it. There is another point about the Octavia, the circuit is designed to be touch-sensitive, so it uses some of the input from the player to actually

642

change the characteristics of how the device works, so it does adapt to how you play, but it is basically a frequency doubler.' Jimi limited the use of the Octavia to the studio in the early days. The first song Jimi cut using the Octavia was 'Purple Haze'. He went on to record many other songs using the unit such as 'One Rainy Wish'. Roger Mayer made several other effect units for Jimi, most of which were simply called Octavia, with identification numbers on them.

Shortly before the Band Of Gypsys made its debut at the Fillmore East in New York, Roger Mayer made some new Octavias for Jimi. He used it on a lot of the songs he played, most notably during 'Machine Gun'. Nowadays, the Octavia is again available from Roger Mayer, after many years of absence from the market.

EQUIPMENT SET-UP

The usual way Jimi set up his equipment for live performances was as follows: Fender Stratocaster, into Vox wah-wah, into Octavia (if used), into Arbiter Fuzz Face, into the Uni-Vibe and finally into his Marshall stack.

STRINGS

Jimi: 'I play a Fender Stratocaster, with light-gauge strings, using a regular E string for a B and sometimes a tenor A string for a little E. To get my kind of sound on the Stratocaster, [I] put the strings on slightly higher, so they can ring longer. I use two 100-watt Marshall speaker cabinets with one 100-watt Marshall amplifier, although we have to change the valves every week due to loss of power . . .'

It seems that Jimi almost always used Fender Rock 'N' Roll light-gauge strings (.010, .013, .015, .026, .032, .038), although he might have used Esquier strings a couple of times, as he endorsed their strings during late 1968 in some advertisements in American publications.

TUNING

From September 1966 until June 1967, Jimi used the standard tuning of E, A, D, G, B, E, but after returning from the first American tour, he virtually always tuned his guitar down a half step to B-flat, A-flat etc. D-tuning, of course, would make string bending that much easier to do, but in reality this had much more to do with his singing, as by going down half a step less strain was put on his voice. Because of the way Jimi used the tremolo arm, he had constant problems keeping his guitar in tune, and he would tune up after almost every single song during concerts – 'we really care for your ears.' During the live TV performance of the Lulu show in January 1969, he even tuned up during the performance of 'Hey Joe' with a laugh and a smile. At other times he became extremely annoyed with the tuning and showed his frustration; a classic example is the video of the first concert in Stockholm (9 January 1969), where simply nothing went right for him.

NOEL REDDING'S EQUIPMENT

When Noel Redding went along for his first audition with Jimi, he borrowed Chas Chandler's Gibson 'EB-2' semi-acoustic one-pick-up bass guitar. This bass was used by him until mid February 1967, when Noel purchased his own bass guitar, a 1964 Fender Jazz Bass in sunburst. Noel: 'I used a six-string bass for a while. That made the change-over from lead easier, but I could only seem to get a trebly sound of it. Later I moved on to the four-string.' The Jazz bass was used for the remainder of Noel's career with the Jimi Hendrix Experience. Noel also got a Hagstrom eight-string bass, which he used for some studio recordings (details in the discography) and during live concerts (mainly for 'Spanish Castle Magic'). A few years ago, the Fender Jazz bass (although in poor condition) was sold privately for a cool £10,000. Lastly, Noel always used 'Rotosound Swing Bass' strings on his bass guitars.

MITCH MITCHELL'S EQUIPMENT

Mitch mainly used Ludwig, Premier and Gretch drums. He used a very small kit for almost all his studio work with Jimi. Mitch had various goes with a double bass drum during live performances (as early as November 1966 in Munich, borrowing the second bass drum from the support act). You can hear Mitch's excellent double bass drum work on *The Cry Of Love* LP.

STUDIO EFFECTS

Jimi applied a variety of different effects on his recordings. Here's a brief description of some of the effects he used.

ADT

Automatic (or Artificial) Double Tracking, ADT for short, is a process whereby a recording signal is taken from the playback head of a tape machine, recorded onto a separate tape machine which has a variable oscillator (enabling the speed to be altered) and then fed back into the first tape machine to be combined with the original signal. The true origin of ADT, even today, remains something of a mystery. In at least three different London studios (Abbey Road, EMI, and Olympic) the technical boffins were working on this technique independently of each other. According to Mark Lewisohn, author of *The Beatles' Recording Sessions*, it was Ken Townsend who came up with ADT, here labelled as Artificial Double Tracking. Eddie Kramer thinks that Beatles producer George Martin (who gained technical knowledge and experience while he worked in the sound laboratories at the BBC in the late 50's and early 60's) got the basic idea from the BBC Radiophonic Workshop Manual. George Chkiantz (present at most of the recordings at Olympic Sound Studios) thinks that possibly the original basic idea for ADT came from an even older source: the 1930's British Navy Signals manual, nick-named the 'Blue Book'! Whoever came up with it first, its basic use on Jimi's studio recordings was to simulate the effect of a double-tracked voice from only one track or source. Examples of this technique can be heard on 'One Rainy Wish' (*Axis: Bold As Love*).

Phasing

This 'jet sound' effect was produced by feeding a signal into two tape recorders and recording the combined outputs onto another machine. The effect produced a kind of swirling tonal sweep, achieved by varying the speed of one of the input tape recorders and altering the frequency response (EQ) of the audio signal to obtain the desirable sound. Eddie Kramer has said that Jimi told him he heard this sound in his dreams, being an 'underwater sound'. As Eddie was 'messing about' in the studio one day, they stumbled onto phasing and when Jimi came into the studio, Eddie played Jimi the track using the phasing they had been experimenting on. According to Eddie, Jimi cried, 'That's the sound, that's the sound I heard in my dream!' Nice story, but in reality George Chkiantz should be credited with phasing. Chas Chandler: 'George created things like the phasing, he was quite a boffin on how to misuse the equipment . . . So although he was sort of the tape operator, it would be horrible to say he was the tape-op, 'cause he wasn't, he was responsible for a lot of the noise that went on there . . .'

644

George: 'It was certainly a parallel invention. During recordings by the Beatles for the *Sgt Pepper* LP at EMI they were using an old BTR-2 tape recorder running at 30 i.p.s. This is a multi-track machine, which has a self-mixing output that came off the machine's recording head which was present all the time. And the Beatles had found out if they would take the output and mix that back in they got this effect. It probably didn't run at the full correct speed, and they got the effect largely by accident, because of this. This is how it was described to us. Now we couldn't do this because we didn't have the same equipment, so I was basically trying to get a simulation of this Beatles effect together. This produced the phasing effect, and I was mucking around as it happened with P.P. Arnold's "The First Cut Is The Deepest", and I got this effect together. I was doing a session with Glyn Jones that evening and said, "Hey, you got to listen to this effect." He said, "Hmm, yeah, that's a good trick you should keep to yourself," and then proceeded to suggest to the Small Faces that they should use it on "Itchycoo Park", which they did. That is what I know about it, and it was regarded as my effect, at this point in time. Eddie [Kramer], meanwhile, was absolutely livid that I had given the effect to Glyn, he was furious that I had given it to this external engineer when it should have been an "in-house trick", and what he really meant was that I should have given it to him. And I told him that when you have an idea, you can't hold it back, the minute you do that you stop having ideas in my opinion, so it was practically total war for a while between us, but we became quite close friends.'

Good examples of phasing are on 'Midnight' (a.k.a. 'Trashman') and 'House Burning Down': or listen to the effect in full flight on Mitch's drumming during 'If Six Was Nine'. Today, phasing is created by electronic effects and is much easier to obtain, however it still doesn't capture the original phasing sound of the 1960's.

Pultec Filter
This filter created the kind of 'telephone vocals' you can hear on 'Little Wing' and 'Little Miss Lover' (both on the *Axis* LP). George Chkiantz: 'This is a flat topped band-pass filter made all of transformers which would adjust the top frequency. We used to call this the "top hat" filter.' The filter was manufactured by the Pulse Techniques company in England and was mainly used during the sessions at Olympic Sound.

Panning
Panning is created by using pan pots on the control desk and gives the effect of the recorded signal moving backwards and forwards across the speakers (in stereo mode). By using LFO (Low Frequency Oscillator) on a slow rate, the signal would drift from left to right, while using LFO at a high rate, it might sound like a Leslie Speaker Cabinet (a mechanical means of producing a chorus effect by placing rotating baffles in front of the speaker). Today panning is achieved using an 'Autopanner' – a kind of electronic pan pot controlled by an LFO.

Echoplex
Tape echo was pioneered by Les Paul in the early 1950's. It's a tape device which uses a tape loop and five recording heads to create an echo effect (note: musicians call this echo, while engineers call it reverb). The recording heads are movable to enable echo to be produced with any desired delay. At Olympic they used EMT echoplates, which was a simulator echo chamber, used for special effects.

Reversed Tape
Or backwards tape. This is a simple effect that Jimi experimented with on various

tracks. He would record the basic track, turn the tape over so it would play backwards, then overdub another guitar track on top of the already recorded track, so when the tape was played the right way, it would include the track that Jimi had overdubbed, but backwards. Eddie Kramer has said that Jimi would know exactly where he was at any point in a track and would know exactly where to insert the backward guitar solo even to the point of knowing how the finished track would sound. Outtake tapes with studio talk between Jimi and Eddie (with Jimi instructing Eddie, by the way!) back this up. As a result, Jimi was able to record a backwards guitar solo which would blend in perfectly with the track . . . The first time Jimi used backward guitar was on 'Are You Experienced?' from the album of the same name (refer to the discography for all other songs with backward tapes).

DI

This stands for Direct Inject, whereby an instrument is plugged directly into the mixing board when recording in a studio. This was more commonly used for bass rather than guitar, however Jimi did use DI for 'Dolly Dagger' (*Rainbow Bridge* album). In this case his guitar signal was split in two: one input fed directly into the mixing board which gave a very clean sound, while the other signal went into Jimi's effect and into his amplifier which gave a heavy fuzz sound. The two signals were then mixed together, resulting in an almost stereo effect from the two signals.

Beyer M160

Although loads of different microphones were used during the various sessions, Eddie Kramer frequently used Beyer M160's at Olympic and also at Electric Lady Studios (there used for Jimi's vocals, for example) – doubtless some small aspects of the sounds created there could be attributed to this.

To capture the Hendrix sound there was no one formula . . .

George Chkiantz

My own thing is in my head. I hear sounds and if I don't get them together nobody else will . . .

Jimi Hendrix

If I tried to test his equipment, all I got was feedback. Jimi could control it all with his fingers, and I still don't understand to this day how he did it. It was all part of his genius . . .

Eric Barrett

I've been imitated so well I've heard people copy my mistakes . . .

Jimi Hendrix

3 *Jimi Hendrix – A Life in Music: A Chronology*

1942–1966

NOTE: All events in this section took place in Seattle (unless otherwise stated).

1942 Nov 27	Johnny Allen Hendrix born at 10.15 am at King County Hospital (a.k.a.: Harborview) Note: for other family details see the family tree on pages 700 and 701
1942 Dec 07	Name registration by Lucille Hendrix of Johnny Allen Hendrix
1945 Jul 04	Johnny gets pneumonia, and goes into hospital for a short period
1945 Nov 11	Al Hendrix gets discharged from the Army on Armistice Day
1945 Nov 19	Al obtains a copy of Johnny's birth certificate
1945 Nov	Al collects Johnny from Mrs Champ in Berkeley, California, and they go by train back to Seattle
1946 Sep 11	Al renames Johnny Allen Hendrix as James Marshall Hendrix
1946?	James gets his first instrument, a harmonica
1948 Sep 08	James starts his kindergarten period at the Rainier Vista School, 3100 Alaska Street S.
1949 Jun?	Goes to Vancouver, British Columbia, for his summer holiday (the first of many)
1949 Sep 05	Starts attending Dawson Annex School, Dawson Street, Vancouver
1949 Nov?	Returns to Seattle
1949 Nov?	Re-enters Rainier Vista School
1950 or 1951	Leaves Rainier Vista School Up to the age of eight or so, James' nickname was Buster, after that he wanted to be called Jimmy . . .
1950 or 1951	Jimmy starts attending Horace Mann Elementary School, 2410 East Cherry Street/23rd Avenue
1951 Dec 17	Al and Lucille get divorced, and Al gets custody of Jimmy, Leon Morris Hendrix, and Joseph Allen Hendrix
1952 Jun	Leaves Horace Mann Elementary School
1952 Sep 05	Re-enters Rainier Vista School
1953 Apr 24	Leaves Rainier Vista School
1953 Apr 27	Starts attending Leschi Elementary School, 135 32nd Avenue S.
1953	Joins the Boy Scouts
1954	Starts to play football for two years with 'The Fighting Irish' youth league team

1955 Jun 17	Leaves Leschi Elementary School
1955 Sep 07	Starts attending Meany Junior High School, 301 Jackson Street S.
1955/1956	Plays football for the 'Capitol Hill Rough Riders' team
1956 Feb 20	Leaves Meany Junior High School
1956 Feb 23	Starts attending Washington Junior High School, 1600 Columbian Way S.
1956 Jun 15	Leaves Washington Junior High School
1956 Sep 05	Re-enters Meany Junior High School
1957 Sep 01	Attends the Elvis Presley performance at Sicks Stadium
1958 Feb 02	Lucille dies at the King County Hospital (a.k.a.: Harborview)
1958 Feb 05	Lucille is buried at Greenwood Cemetery, Renton, Washington
1958 Jun 06	Jimmy leaves Meany Junior High School
1958	Al gets a ukulele for Jimmy
1958	Jimmy buys a second-hand acoustic guitar for $5 from a friend of Al
1958 Sep 04	Starts attending Asa Mercer Junior High School, 1600 Columbian Way S.
1958 Dec 09	Leaves Asa Mercer Junior High School, and re-enters Washington Junior High School
1956/1958	According to Leon Hendrix, Jimmy designed cars (sent to Ford), and won some awards for these . . .
1959 Sep 09	Jimmy starts attending Garfield High School, 400 23rd Avenue S.
1959	Al buys himself a C Melody saxophone and buys Jimmy his first electric guitar, from Myers Music, 1204 1st Avenue S.
1959	Jimmy plays his first official gig at the Washington National Guard Armory, 36th Avenue, near Kent, Washington Note: the first group Jimmy joined was possibly called The Velvetones
1959	Joins The Rocking Kings – line-up: Lester Exkano (drums); Walter Harris (saxophone); Ulysses Heath Jr. (guitar); Jimmy (bass on a normal 6-string guitar); Webb Lofton (saxophone); James Woodberry (piano & vocals)
1959	Jimmy and other members of The Rocking Kings walk by the house of James Thomas at 21st Avenue, and join in during a rehearsal of James Thomas and his nephew Perry Thomas. James Thomas acts from now on as the 'manager' of The Rocking Kings, while Jimmy shortly after this switched from playing bass to lead guitar
1959	The Rocking Kings play at Polish Hall, 1714 18th Street S.
1960 Feb 20	The Rocking Kings play at Washington Hall, 153 14th Street S. The line-up of the band now is: Lester Exkano (drums); Robert Green (piano); Walter Harris (saxophone); Jimmy (guitar); Webb Lofton (saxophone)
1960	The Rocking Kings play at a teenage dance in Yesler Terrace
1960	The Rocking Kings play at Birdland, 21st Avenue/Madison Street E. for 3 nights (Wednesday, Thursday and Sunday) a week for quite some time until the Summer vacations
1960	During a gig at Birdland, Jimmy's guitar gets stolen Mary Hendrix buys him another guitar from Myers Music, but Al makes Jimmy bring this back to the shop. Shortly after that Al himself buys Jimmy another guitar . . .
1960	The Rocking Kings play in Ballard (part of Seattle) during an All State Tournament and win a trophy for becoming the second 'All State Band Of The Year'

648

1960 Summer	The Rocking Kings play near Cottage Lake (east of Woodinville), Washington, during an outdoor picnic for the Annual Fair of L.C.I.O. Union, Local 242 with 2000 people attending
1960	The Rocking Kings play on the streets near the campus of Western Washington State College, Bellingham, Washington during that afternoon and in the evening play in the auditorium of the College. Shortly after these events some of the members of the group became discouraged, resulting in a new line-up: Lester Exkano (drums); Jimmy (guitar); Webb Lofton (saxophone)
1960	A new group is formed by James Thomas, called The Tomcats – line-up: Lester Exkano (drums); Rolland Green (bass); Jimmy (guitar); Webb Lofton (saxophone); James Thomas (vocals); Perry Thomas (piano)
1960 Jul 22	The Tom Cats play at the American Legion Hall, 620 University Street, billed as a Cabaret Summer Style Dance
1960 Winter	Other gigs by The Tom Cats: Paine Field Airport base, Everett, Washington; Larson Air Force Base, near Moses Lake, eastern Washington; Fort Lewis army base, Washington; U.S. Naval Reservation, Pier 91, near Magnolia Bridge, west Seattle
1960	Together with a friend, Jimmy breaks into Wilner's Clothing Store, stealing some sweaters, shirts and slacks, depositing the clothing anonymously in the 'Needy Box' outside the principal's office at Garfield High School the next day . . .
1960 Oct 31	Jimmy leaves Garfield High School on Halloween without graduating . . .
1960	Tries several times to get a daytime job, but finally Jimmy joins Al, who is now doing landscape gardening (on his own)
1961	The line-up for The Tomcats now becomes: Richard Gayswood (saxophone or drums); Jimmy (guitar); Bill Rinnick (saxophone or drums); James Thomas (vocals); Perry Thomas (piano); Leroy Toots (bass)
1961 beg	The Tomcats play at Bors Brumo nightclub
1961 May 02	Jimmy gets arrested by the Seattle Police Department for 'taking a motor vehicle without permission'
1961 May 05	Gets arrested a second time by the Seattle Police Department, this time for 'taking and riding in a motor vehicle without permission of owner' Jailed at: Rainier Vista 4-H Youth Centre, 12th Avenue/Terrace Street
1961 May	Appears in Seattle Court House, 12th Avenue/Terrace Street, and is given a suspended sentence with the two charges remaining on his permanent record
1961 May 26	Copy of Jimmy's birth certificate obtained for army enlistment
1961 May 31	Jimmy enlists in the army at Fort Ord, California, for eight weeks of basic training. He signs up for a period of three years
1961 Aug 05	The Tomcats are booked for the Annual Seattle Seafair Picnic & Dance in Vassa Park, to play on the 5th, 6th and 12th, but of course Jimmy is in the army by this time . . .
1961 Sep	Jimmy visits Seattle while on a furlough Note: during his entire army period he only makes two furloughs to Seattle

1961 Sep 11	Returns from his furlough via San Francisco, California
1961 Oct 31	Receives his army orders
1961 Nov 08	Enlists at the 101st Airborne Division, Fort Campbell, Kentucky
1961 Nov	Jimmy meets Billy Cox at Fort Campbell (Billy Cox born in Wheeling, West Virginia, 16 October 1941)
1961 Nov	Jimmy, Billy and three others play at the Pink Poodle Club, Clarksville, Tennessee
1962 Jan 17	Jimmy writes a letter to Al from Fort Campbell asking him to send his guitar
1962 Jan	Jimmy teams up with Billy Cox and starts the group The King Kasuals. Line up: Billy Cox (bass); Gary Ferguson (drums); Jimmy (guitar) Note: for a very short time the line-up also included Major Charles Washington (saxophone)
1962 Jan 30	Jimmy gets promoted to Private First Class
1962	During his army time, Jimmy was once dropped in Hawaii
1962 May 19	The King Kasuals play at Club Del Morocco, Nashville, Tennessee The line-up by this time is: Harry Batchelor (vocals); Babe Boo (guitar); Billy Cox (bass); Jimmy (guitar); Frank Sheffield (drums); Tee Howard Williams (saxophone); Tommy Lee Williams (saxophone) Note: Tommy was a 'part-time' member
1962	The King Kasuals backed several other artists while playing at the Club Del Morocco, like Nappy Brown, School Boy, Carla Thomas, and Ironing Board Sam . . .
1962 Jul 02	Jimmy gets discharged from the army because of 'medical unsuitability' after he breaks his right ankle in a parachute jump (his 26th?)
1962 Sep	After Billy Cox is discharged, Jimmy and Billy briefly rent a house in Clarksville, Tennessee
1962	Jimmy and Billy Cox move to Indianapolis, Indiana, for a short time and move back to Clarksville again
1962	Jimmy meets Larry Lee at the Club Del Morocco, Nashville, Tennessee (Lawrence H. Lee Jr. born in Memphis, Tennessee, 7 March 1943)
1962	Jimmy and Billy Cox move to Nashville, Tennessee and live upstairs at Joyce's House of Glamour
1962	The King Kasuals line-up now becomes: Harry Batchelor (vocals); Billy Cox (bass); Jimmy (guitar); Buford Majors (sax); Leonard Moses (guitar); Harold Nesbit (drums)
1962	The King Kasuals play at Jolly Roger, Nashville, Tennessee
1962?	Jimmy, Billy Cox and Larry Lee team up with Bob Fisher & The Barnevilles. They tour for one month, doing backing for The Marvelettes and for Curtis Mayfield And The Impressions
1962?	Jimmy and Billy Cox tape a recording session with Bill 'Hoss' Allen for Starday-King Records in Nashville. Allen: 'It was Billy's session for King Records . . . Jimi's guitar playing was so wild that I couldn't use it at all. I had to shut him up on the record!'
1962 Winter	Jimmy moves to Vancouver, living with his grandmother Nora and her family, and joins Bobbie Taylor & The Vancouvers (with lead singer Tommie Chong, Bobby Taylor, among others) and plays at Dante's Inferno nightclub regularly

1963 Mar?	Jimmy leaves Vancouver again and works his way back to Tennessee, where he meets 'Gorgeous' George Odell in Nashville when a big tour headed by Sam Cooke and Jackie Wilson came through. Jimmy starts playing with and for George, touring with him all over the States. Jimmy did backing work behind countless performers, including Jackie Wilson, Sam Cooke, Slim Harpo, Tommy Tucker, The Supremes, The Valentinos (with the Womack brothers) etc. During intervals Jimmy and George also work for Henry Wynne, a tour promotor
1963 Mar 13	Jimmy plays in Columbia, South Carolina
1963 Mar	Jimmy and Gorgeous George join up with yet another package tour with Hank Ballard And The Midnighters and Little Richard and George asks if Jimmy can come on the Little Richard tour.
	The next day, in Greenville, South Carolina, due to Gorgeous George's efforts, Jimmy sits in (using a guitar with 5 strings) with The Upsetters, the backing band for Little Richard. On some occasions Jimmy is allowed to play with The Upsetters during the so-called 'after-hours-gigs'. . .
	Note: this period is unconnected with the later period when Jimmy became Little Richard's permanent guitar player . . .
1963	Jimmy, Gorgeous George, The Valentinos (among others) play in Minneapolis, Minnesota
1963 end	Jimmy records with Lonnie Youngblood, likely in Philadelphia, Pennsylvania
1964 beg	Jimmy arrives in New York City
1964 beg	Wins first place ($25) in the Wednesday-night Amateur Contest at the Apollo Theatre, NYC
1964	Moves into Hotel Theresa, 125th Street/Seventh Avenue, NYC
1964 Mar	Jimmy meets and joins the Isley Brothers in NYC
1964 Mar	Recordings with the Isley Brothers in NYC
1964	Tours with the Isley Brothers in Canada and Bermuda (playing in a baseball stadium)
1964	Plays with the Isley Brothers at the Upton Club in Montreal and meets Buddy Miles there
	(George Allen Buddy Miles born in Omaha, Nebraska, 5 September 1947)
1964	Plays with the Isley Brothers in Seattle. Jimmy stays a day extra and his guitar gets stolen, a week later he makes his way up to NYC again . . .
1964 Aug 05	Recordings with the Isley Brothers in NYC
1964 Sep	Embarks with the Isley Brothers on a 35-day tour of cities in the mid West, East and South
1964 Sep 23	Recordings with the Isley Brothers in NYC
1964 Sep 28	Plays with the Isley Brothers in Columbus, Ohio
1964 Oct	Plays with the Isley Brothers in Jacksonville, Tampa and Miami, all in Florida
1964 Oct	Plays with the Isley Brothers in Cincinnati, Ohio
1964 Nov?	Jimmy quits the Isley Brothers in Nashville, Tennessee
1964	Jimmy meets Steve Cropper in a soul food restaurant in Memphis, Tennessee and makes a demo with him
1964	Jimmy went on yet another package tour playing with Sam Cooke again for a short time until he missed the tour bus in Kansas City,

	Missouri, but managed to make his way up to Atlanta, Georgia
	Note: Sam Cooke died on 11 December 1964 in Los Angeles
1965 Jan	Jimmy meets Little Richard again in Atlanta, Georgia. This time around he becomes his regular guitar player (staying with him for 5 to 6 months)
1965 Jan 25	Jimmy writes a postcard to Al from Lafayette, Louisiana saying that he's playing with Little Richard now . . .
	While on tour with Little Richard, Jimmy once got mobbed by fans after a concert thinking he was Little Richard . . .
1965 Feb	Jimmy takes up rooms at the Wilcox Hotel, 6500 Selma Avenue, Hollywood, California, calling himself Maurice James
1965	Jimmy meets Arthur Lee in Los Angeles and records with him for Rosa Lee Brooks
1965	Plays with Little Richard at Cyril's, Los Angeles
1965	Jimmy auditions for Ike and Tina Turner
1965	Jimmy plays with Little Richard at the Fillmore Auditorium, San Francisco
1965	Jimmy jams with Albert Collins at the Club 500 in Houston, Texas
1965	Jimmy plays with Ike and Tina Turner in Amarillo, Texas
	Note: after the few shows with the Turners, Jimmy went back to play again with Little Richard
1965	Jimmy, Buddy & Stacey (two singers from Long Island, New York), plus members of the Upsetters, tape a live version of 'Shotgun' in a TV studio in Dallas, Texas, for Nashville's Channel 5 TV show the *Night Train*
1965 Feb/Apr	Recordings with Little Richard in Los Angeles or NYC
1965 Apr?	Jimmy plays with Little Richard at the Whiskey A Go Go in Atlanta, Georgia
1965 Apr	Arrives back in New York City and takes up rooms at the Theresa Hotel, 2090 7th Avenue
1965 Apr 17	Plays with Little Richard at the Paramount Theater, Broadway, NYC. Line-up: Soupy Sales (comedian); Little Richard & The Upsetters; King Curtis & The Kingpins; The Hallabaloos (dancers); The Detergents; Shirley Ellis; The Hollies; Joe Stampley And The Uniques; The Vibrations; Dee Dee Warwick; Sandie Shaw; The Exciters
1965 Apr 18	Plays with Little Richard at the Paramount Theater, Broadway, NYC (same line-up as the previous day)
	Note: Jimmy should have played the next day too, but Little Richard got fired from the show . . .
1965 May	Plays with Little Richard at Union College, Schenectady, New York
1965 May	Plays with Little Richard at Syracuse College, Syracuse, New York
1965 Jun/Jul	Jimmy quits playing with Little Richard in NYC
1965 Jul 27	Jimmy signs a 2-year contract (with an option for another 3 years) with Sioux Records and Copa Management in NYC
	Note: Chas Chandler bought this contract up for $50 in 1966 . . .
1965 Aug 05	Jimmy records with the Isley Brothers in NYC
1965 Oct	Jimmy joins Curtis Knight and The Squires, with whom he plays on and off (between many other playing jobs) until the beginning of 1966. Some of the places they play in NYC:
	Purple Onion, 4th Street, Greenwich Village;
	Queen's Inn, Queens Boulevard;

	Ondine's, 59th Street/3rd Avenue;
	The Lighthouse
1965 Oct 15	Jimmy signs a 3-year contract with Ed Chalpin for PPX Inc. in NYC
1965 Oct/Dec	Jimmy records with Curtis Knight & The Squires in NYC
1965 Oct/Nov	Jimmy joins Joey Dee And the Starlighters
1965 Nov	Embarks on a 10-day tour in Massachusetts with Joey Dee (playing in Beverly, Boston, and Lynn among other cities)
1965 Nov	Plays at the Arena, Cleveland, Ohio with Joey Dee in a package show which also included Chuck Jackson
1965 Dec 26	Plays with Curtis Knight & The Squires in George's Club 20, Hackensack, New Jersey
1965 end	Jimmy records with Jayne Mansfield (!) in NYC
1966 Jan	Jimmy joins the King Curtis band, and plays with him (on and off) for about 6 months. His first gig with them was at Smalls Paradise, 135th Street/7th Avenue, Harlem, NYC
1966 Jan 21	Jimmy records with King Curtis and Ray Sharpe in NYC
1966 Jan end	Jimmy plays (with King Curtis?) in Texas (Houston, Dallas and Ft. Worth)
1966 Febr	Jimmy plays (with King Curtis?) around Tulsa, Oklahoma and Louisiana
1966 Febr	Jimmy plays (with King Curtis?) in California
1966 Apr 28	Jimmy records with King Curtis (saxophone), Ray Sharpe (vocals), Cornell Dupree (rhythm guitar), Chuck Rainey & Al Lucas (bass), and Bernard Purdie (drums) in NYC. They record 'Linda Lou', 'I Can't Take It' and 'Baby How About You'. These songs were never released on any record, and the tapes don't exist anymore, due to a fire at the ATCO/Atlantic warehouse
1966 May?	Plays with King Curtis during a party thrown by Atlantic Records in NYC, during which Jimmy also plays with Percy Sledge and Wilson Pickett . . .
1966 May 13	Plays with Curtis Knight & The Squires (advertised as: Curtiss Night) at the Cheetah, 53 Broadway, NYC, for almost 2 weeks Note: Jimi's final gigs with Curtis Knight . . .
1966 May end	Jimmy joins Carl Holmes & The Commanders in NYC
1966 May end	Plays with Carl Holmes & The Commanders in Gettysburg, Pennsylvania
1966 May 27	Plays for 1 week with Carl Holmes & The Commanders at the Cheetah, NYC
1966	Jimmy meets Bob Dylan at the The Kettle of Fish, MacDougal Street, Greenwich Village, NYC
1966 Jun	Jimmy buys a guitar at Manny's, NYC, and meets Randy California there
1966 Jun	Jimmy plays at the Night Owl Café, 118 West 3rd Street, NYC
1966 Jun/Jul	Jimmy forms his first own band Jimmy James And the Blue Flames (a.k.a.: The Rainflowers), line up: Jimmy (guitar); Randy California (guitar); Randy – surname unknown, from Texas – (bass); unknown (drums) Note: Jeff Baxter plays occasional bass as well
1966 Jul 05	The Animals fly from London to NYC for a USA tour
1966 Jul 05	Chas Chandler sees Jimmy James And The Blue Flames perform at the Café Wha?, MacDougal Street, Greenwich Village, NYC

653

1966 Aug	John Hammond Jr. sees Jimmy James And The Blue Flames play at the Café Wha? and joins the band after a few rehearsals
1966 Aug	Jimmy James And The Blue Flames play at the Café Au Go Go, 152 Bleecker Street, NYC, for a couple of weeks
	Note: several keyboard players, such as Al Kooper and Barry Goldberg would drift in and out of the band
1966 Aug	Jimmy plays some solo dates with Ellen McIlwaine (piano), in NYC
1966 Sep 05	The US Animals tour ends with a gig at Central Park, NYC
1966 Sep 09	Chas Chandler works out details with Jimmy in NYC
	A birth certificate is ordered from Seattle for his passport . . .
1966 Sep 19	Copy of birth certificate supplied
1966 Sep 23	Passport (G 1044108) issued in NYC. Jimmy flies immediately from Kennedy International Airport, New York, to London . . .

1966

Note: Starting with the entry for 13 October 1966 up to 6 September 1970 *all* the official concert performances Jimi ever gave are printed in capital letters. Two shows are indicated by: -2-

SEP

24	*ENGLAND*
	Jimi arrives at London Airport in the early morning hours
	Scotch Of St James, London
	Jimi's first public jam
	Jimi moves into Hyde Park Towers hotel, 41–49 Inverness Terrace, London
29	Jimi meets Noel Redding during an audition at the Birdland, London (Noel David Redding born in Folkestone, Kent, 25 December 1945)
	Blaises, London
	Jimi jams with the Brian Auger Trinity with Johnny Halliday in the audience, who invites Jimi to tour France with him
end	Scotch Of St James, London
	Jimi jams with the V.I.P.s

OCT

01	The Polytechnic of Central London
	Jimi jams with The Cream
02	Mitch Mitchell plays his last gig with Georgie Fame And The Blue Flames at the 'Grand Gala Du Disque' in Amsterdam, Holland
05	Les Cousins, London
	Jimi jams with various American blues musicians
06	Mitch Mitchell joins the band and rehearsals of the Jimi Hendrix Experience start (John Mitchell, born Ealing, Middlesex, 9 July 1947)
12	*FRANCE*
13	NOVELTY, EVREUX
	[supporting: Long Chris; The Blackbirds; Johnny Halliday]
14	UNCONFIRMED VENUE, NANCY
	[supporting: Long Chris; The Blackbirds; Johnny Halliday]

654

15	SALLE FÊTES, VILLERUPT
	[supporting Long Chris: The Blackbirds; Johnny Halliday]
18	L'OLYMPIA, PARIS
	[supporting: Long Chris; The Blackbirds; The Brian Auger Trinity; Johnny Halliday]

19	*ENGLAND*
23	De Lane Lea Music Ltd., London – First JHE studio recordings
25	SCOTCH OF ST. JAMES, LONDON SW1
Sep/Oct	Knuckles Club, London
	Jimi jams with Deep Feeling

NOV

| 02 | De Lane Lea Music Ltd., London – Recordings |
| 08 | Gerry Stickells joins as road manager |

	WEST GERMANY
08	BIG APPLE, MUNICH -2-
09	BIG APPLE, MUNICH -2-
10	BIG APPLE, MUNICH -2-
11	BIG APPLE, MUNICH -2-

12	*ENGLAND*
18	Regent Sound, London – Recordings
24	De Lane Lea Music Ltd., London – Recordings
25	BAG O' NAILS, LONDON W1
	Press reception & concert
	Bag O' Nails – First UK interview with Jimi
	by Peter Jones for *Record Mirror* (Dec 10)
26	RICKY TICK, HOUNSLOW, MIDDLESEX
	[supporting: The New Animals]
27	Jimi's 24th birthday
30	Blaises, London
	Jimi attends the Young Rascals concert
end	The Cromwellian Club, London
	Jimi jams with local musicians including Lol Coxhill

DEC

06	Jimi moves into a flat at 34 Montagu Square, London
10	THE RAM JAM CLUB, LONDON SW9
	[supporting: John Mayall's Bluesbreakers]
11	London – Jimi meets Little Richard at his hotel and borrows $50 from him . . .
13	Wembley, Middlesex – TV recordings for *Ready, Steady, Go!*
	'Hey Joe' (live) – JHE TV debut
	CBS Studios, London – Recordings
16	'Hey Joe' b/w 'Stone Free' (1st JHE single) released in the UK on Polydor
	CHISLEHURST CAVES, BROMLEY, KENT
21	CBS Studios, London – Recordings
	BLAISES, LONDON SW7

TV rehearsals for *Ready, Steady, Go!*
Wembley, 13 December 1966

I've heard of people playing by ear . . . but this Jimi Hendrix plays by TEETH !

1967

JAN
04   BROMEL CLUB, BROMLEY COURT HOTEL, BROMLEY, KENT -2-
07   NEW CENTURY HALL, MANCHESTER, LANCASHIRE
[support: The Silverstone Set; DJ Dave Eager]
Twisted Wheel, Manchester
Jimi attends The Spellbinders concert
08   TOLLBAR, MOJO A GO-GO, SHEFFIELD, YORKSHIRE
Advertised as: 'The New Weirdo Trio Jimi Hendrick's Experience'
11   De Lane Lea Music Ltd., London – Recordings
BAG O' NAILS, LONDON W1 -2-
12   National Hall, Olympia, London
JHE appearance at The 1967 International Racing Car Show at the Radio London display on the balcony (mimed), not transmitted
7½ CLUB, LONDON W1
13   7½ CLUB, LONDON W1
14   BEACHCOMBER CLUB, NOTTINGHAM, NOTTINGHAMSHIRE
[support: Jimmy Cliff And Shakedown Sound]
15   COUNTRY CLUB, KIRK LEVINGTON, YORKSHIRE
16   7½ CLUB, LONDON W1
17   Tiles, London – Radio recordings for 'Ready, Steady, Radio!'
(live concert, not transmitted)
7½ CLUB, LONDON W1
18   London – TV recordings
'Hey Joe' (live)
7½ CLUB, LONDON W1

19	SPEAKEASY, LONDON W1
20	HAVERSTOCK HILL COUNTRY CLUB, LONDON NW3
21	REFECTORY, LONDON NW11
22	ASTORIA, OLDHAM, LANCASHIRE
24	MARQUEE, LONDON W1
	[support: Syn]
25	THE ORFORD CELLAR, NORWICH, NORFOLK
	[support: The Orford Discotheque System]
27	CHISLEHURST CAVES, BROMLEY, KENT
28	THE UPPER CUT, LONDON E7
	Advertised as: 'The American Top Soul Singer and guitarist extraordinary'
29	SAVILLE THEATRE, LONDON W1 -2-
	[support: The Who; The Koobas; Thoughts; MC Mike Quinn]
30	London – Radio recordings
	'Hey Joe'; 'Rock Me, Baby'; 'Foxy Lady' (live)
31	Saville Theatre, London – Filming a promo clip for 'Hey Joe' (mimed)

FEB	
01	NEW CELLAR CLUB, SOUTH SHIELDS, CO. DURHAM
	[support: The Bond]
02	IMPERIAL HOTEL, DARLINGTON, CO. DURHAM
	[support: West Coast Promotion]
	Advertised as: 'Don't miss this man who is Dylan, Clapton and James Brown all in one'
03	RICKY TICK, HOUNSLOW, MIDDLESEX
	Olympic Sound Studios, London – Recordings
04	THE RAM JAM CLUB, LONDON SW9
	[support: All Night Workers]
	FLAMINGO, LONDON W1
	[support: All Night Workers]
05	Saville Theatre, London
	Jimi attends The Cream concert
06	STAR HOTEL, CROYDON, SURREY
07	Olympic Sound Studios, London – Recordings
08	Olympic Sound Studios, London – Recordings
	BROMEL CLUB, BROMLEY COURT HOTEL, BROMLEY, KENT
09	LOCARNO, BRISTOL, GLOUCESTER
10	PLAZA, NEWBURY, BERKSHIRE
11	BLUE MOON, CHELTENHAM, GLOUCESTERSHIRE
12	SINKING SHIP CLUBLAND, STOCKPORT, CHESHIRE
13	London – Radio recordings for 'Saturday Club'
	Interview, 'Love Or Confusion', 'Foxy Lady', 'Hey Joe', 'Stone Free' (live)
14	THE CIVIC HALL, GRAYS, ESSEX
	[support: Lot 5]
	'Valentine's Day Massacre', Speakeasy, London
	Jimi attends and jams with Skip Allen (drums) of the Pretty Things
15	DOROTHY BALLROOM, CAMBRIDGE, CAMBRIDGESHIRE
17	RICKY TICK, THAMES HOTEL, WINDSOR, BERKSHIRE

18	YORK UNIVERSITY, YORK, YORKSHIRE
19	BLARNEY CLUB, LONDON W1
20	De Lane Lea Music Ltd., London – Recordings
	THE PAVILION, BATH, SOMERSET

Press reception
Speakeasy, London, around February 1967

22	London – Radio recordings
	'Hey Joe' (live)
	Speakeasy, London
	Jimi attends a press reception for the Soft Machine (launching their first single)
	ROUNDHOUSE, LONDON NW1
	[support: Soft Machine]
23	THE PAVILION, WORTHING, SUSSEX
24	LEICESTER UNIVERSITY, LEICESTER, LEICESTERSHIRE
25	SATURDAY SCENE, CORN EXCHANGE, CHELMSFORD, ESSEX
	[support: The Soul Trinity]
26	CLIFFS PAVILION, SOUTHEND-ON-SEA, ESSEX -2-

659

[support: Dave Dee, Dozy, Beaky, Mick & Tich; Nashville Teens; Koobas; Force Five; MC Pete Murray]

MAR
01   De Lane Lea Music Ltd., London – Recordings
ORCHID BALLROOM, PURLEY, SURREY
02   Marquee, London – TV recordings
'Hey Joe', 'Purple Haze' (live), several versions of each song

03   *FRANCE*
04   SMALL CLUB IN A HOTEL, PARIS
[MC: Robert Ismir]
Note: venue name unconfirmed
Paris – Radio recordings
LAW SOCIETY GRADUATION BALL, FACULTÉ DE DROIT D'ASSAS, PARIS
[support: The Pretty Things]

05   *BELGIUM*
TWENTY CLUB, MOUSCRON

FRANCE
TWENTY CLUB, LENS

06   *BELGIUM*
Zoniewoud (a forest), St. Pieters Woluwe – TV recordings 'Hey Joe' (mimed)
07   Universal Video, Waterloo – TV recordings
'Hey Joe', 'Stone Free' (mimed)

ENGLAND
09   SKYLINE BALLROOM, HULL, YORKSHIRE
[support: The Family; The Small Faces; The Strollers; The Mandrakes]
10   CLUB À GO GO, NEWCASTLE-UPON-TYNE, NORTHUMBER-LAND -2-
11   INTERNATIONAL CLUB, LEEDS, YORKSHIRE
12   GYRO CLUB, TROUTBECK HOTEL, ILKLEY, YORKSHIRE
The concert was stopped by the police due to overcrowding of the club . . .

13   *HOLLAND*
14   Bellevue, Amsterdam – TV recordings for *Fanclub*
'Hey Joe', 'Stone Free' (mimed)

15   *ENGLAND*
16   Speakeasy, London – Jimi attends the launching party of Track Records
17   'Purple Haze' b/w '51st Anniversary' (2nd JHE single) released in the UK

18	*WEST GERMANY* STAR-CLUB, HAMBURG Radiohouse, Hamburg – Radio recordings Two interviews, 'Foxy Lady', 'Hey Joe', 'Stone Free', 'Fire', 'Purple Haze' (live) STAR-CLUB, HAMBURG -2-
19	STAR-CLUB, HAMBURG -2-
20	*LUXEMBOURG* Radio Luxembourg – Radio interviews
21	*ENGLAND*
23	GUILD HALL, SOUTHAMPTON, HAMPSHIRE
25	STARLIGHT ROOM, GLIDERDROME, BOSTON, LINCS [support: Sons And Lovers; Charades; The Steel Band; Ray Bones]
26	TABERNACLE CLUB, STOCKPORT, CHESHIRE
27	Manchester, Lancashire – TV recordings 'Purple Haze' (studio track with live vocals)
28	London – Radio recordings for 'Saturday Club' 'Killin' Floor', 'Fire', 'Purple Haze' (live) ASSEMBLY HALL, AYLESBURY, BUCKS
29	De Lane Lea Music Ltd., London – Recordings
30	London – TV recordings 'Purple Haze' (studio track with live vocals), 2 versions
31	*START OF THE FIRST UK TOUR* Line-up for all the concerts to Apr 30: Walker Brothers; JHE; Cat Stevens; Engelbert Humperdinck; Californians; Quotations; MC Nick Jones THE ASTORIA, LONDON N4 -2-

APR beg/mid	London – Radio interview with Leif H. Andersson
01	GAUMONT, IPSWICH, SUFFOLK -2- Filmed
02	GAUMONT, WORCESTER, WORCESTERSHIRE -2-
03 & 04	Olympic Sound Studios, London – Recordings
05	ODEON, LEEDS, YORKSHIRE -2-
06	ODEON, GLASGOW, SCOTLAND -2-
07	ABC, CARLISLE, CUMBERLAND -2-
08	ABC, CHESTERFIELD, DERBYSHIRE -2-
09	THE EMPIRE, LIVERPOOL, LANCASHIRE -2-
10	London – Radio recordings 'Purple Haze', 'Foxy Lady' (live)
11	GRANADA, BEDFORD, BEDFORDSHIRE -2-
12	GAUMONT, SOUTHAMPTON, HAMPSHIRE -2-
13	GAUMONT, WOLVERHAMPTON, STAFFORDSHIRE -2- Kingfisher, Wolverhampton Jimi jams with the Californians
14	ODEON, BOLTON, LANCASHIRE -2-
15	ODEON, BLACKPOOL, LANCASHIRE -2-

661

Ha, a grey one!
The Astoria, London, 31 March 1967

662

16	DE MONTFORT HALL, LEICESTER, LEICESTERSHIRE -2-
17	London – TV recordings
	'Purple Haze', 'Manic Depression' (live)
mid	Speakeasy, London
	Jimi jams (on bass) with Georgie Fame (organ) and Ben E. King (drums)
19	ODEON, BIRMINGHAM, WARWICKSHIRE -2-
20	ABC, LINCOLN, LINCOLNSHIRE -2-
21	CITY HALL, NEWCASTLE-UPON-TYNE, NORTHUMBERLAND -2-
22	ODEON, MANCHESTER, LANCASHIRE -2-
23	GAUMONT, HANLEY, STAFFORDSHIRE -2-
24	Saville Theatre, London
	Jimi attends the Donovan concert
25	COLSTON HALL, BRISTOL, GLOUCESTERSHIRE -2-
26	CAPITOL, CARDIFF, GLAMORGAN, SOUTH WALES -2-
27	ABC, ALDERSHOT, HAMPSHIRE -2-
28	ADELPHI, SLOUGH, BUCKINGHAMSHIRE -2-
	UFO, London
	Jimi jams (on bass) with Keith West (vocals), John 'Twink' Adler (drums) and Stephen Howe (guitar), all from the group Tomorrow
29	WINTER GARDENS, BOURNEMOUTH, HAMPSHIRE -2-
30	GRANADA, LONDON SW17 -2-

END OF THE FIRST UK TOUR

MAY

04	London – TV recordings
	'Purple Haze' (studio track with live vocals)
	Olympic Sound Studios, London – Recordings
05	'The Wind Cries Mary' b/w 'Highway Chile' (3rd JHE single) released in the UK
	Olympic Sound Studios, London – Recordings
06	BALLROOM OF THE STARS, THE IMPERIAL, NELSON, LANCASHIRE
	[support: The Movement; The Jo De Brown Trust]
07	SAVILLE THEATRE, LONDON W1 -2-
	[support: Garnet Mimms; 1, 2, 3; MC Rick Dane]

'Screaming fans are like a herd of little piglets squealing . . .'
said by Jimi during the show

08	Speakeasy, London
	Jimi attends the Brian Auger Trinity concert
09	Dorchester Hotel, London
	Jimi is one of the guests of honour at the Variety Club Of Great Britain's 'Tribute To The Recording Industry' luncheon
	Olympic Sound Studios, London – Recordings
10	London – TV recordings
	'The Wind Cries Mary' (studio track with live vocals)

11	FRANCE
	Paris – TV recordings
	'Hey Joe' and four other songs (live)
12	ENGLAND
	Are You Experienced? (1st JHE LP) released in the UK
	'BLUESVILLE '67', BLUESVILLE CLUB, THE MANOR HOUSE,
	LONDON N4
mid	Speakeasy, London
	Jimi jams with Amen Corner
13	IMPERIAL COLLEGE, LONDON SW7
14	BELLE VUE, NEW ELIZABETHAN, MANCHESTER, LAN-
	CASHIRE
	[support: DJ Jimmy Savile]
15	WEST GERMANY
	NEUE WELT, BERLIN -2-
	[support: The Beat Cats; Restless Sect; Shatters And Manuela]
16	BIG APPLE, MUNICH -2-
17	Hotel Intercontinental, Frankfurt – Radio interview by Hans Carl
	Schmidt

Neue Welt, Berlin, 15 May 1967

18	Stadthalle, Offenbach – TV recordings
	'Stone Free', 'Hey Joe', 'Purple Haze' (live)
	K 52, Frankfurt
	Jimi jams (on bass) with Noel (guitar), David 'Dave Dee' Harman
	(vocals) and John 'Beaky' Dymond (drums)

18   Stadthalle, Offenbach – TV recordings
          'Stone Free', 'Hey Joe', 'Purple Haze' (live)
          K 52, Frankfurt
          Jimi jams (on bass) with Noel (guitar), David 'Dave Dee' Harman
          (vocals) and John 'Beaky' Dymond (drums)

19   *SWEDEN*
          KONSERTHALLEN, LISEBERG, LISEBERG NÖJESPARK,
          GOTHENBURG -2-
          [support: Mats & Brita; Cat Stevens; DJ Clem Dalton]
20   MARIEBERGSSKOGEN, KARLSTAD
          [support: Metrosextetten; Arnes]

21   *DENMARK*
          FALKONER CENTRET, COPENHAGEN
          [support: Harlem Kiddies with King George; Defenders; Beef-
          eaters]

22   *FINLAND*
          Ratakatu TV Studio, Helsinki – TV recordings
          'Hey Joe' and three other songs (mimed)
          KULTTUURITALO, HELSINKI
          [support: First; Wantons; New Joys; DJ Antti Einiö]

23   *SWEDEN*
          KLUBB BONGO – NEW ORLEANS, MALMÖ, SWEDEN -2-
          [support: Namelosers]
24   Stockholm – TV recordings
          'The Wind Cries Mary', 'Purple Haze' (live)
          STORA SCENEN, GRÖNA LUND, TIVOLI GARDEN,
          STOCKHOLM -1st show-
          DANS IN, GRÖNA LUND, TIVOLI GARDEN, STOCKHOLM
          -2nd show-
          [support: Perhaps; Bread]
          Stockholm – Radio interview by Roger Wallis
24 or 25 En Till, Stockholm
          Jimi jams (on bass) with Noel (guitar) and Mitch (drums) plus
          local musicians
25   Stockholm – Radio interview by Klas Burling

27   *WEST GERMANY*
          STAR PALACE, KIEL -2-
28   JAGUAR-CLUB, SCALA, HERFORD
          [support: The Rivets; The Lions]

29   *ENGLAND*
          'BARBEQUE 67', TULIP BULB AUCTION HALL, SPALDING,
          LINCOLNSHIRE
          [support: The Cream; Geno Washington And The Ram Jam
          Band; Pink Floyd; The Move; Zoot Money And His Big Roll
          Band; Sounds Force Five]

Jam session (Jimi on bass and Noel on lead guitar)
En Till, Stockholm, 24 or 25 May 1967

JUN
beg
        Speakeasy, London
        Jimi attends the Jose Feliciano concert and jams with him
04
        SAVILLE THEATRE, LONDON W1 -2-
        [support: Stormsville Shakers; Procol Harum; Chiffons; Denny
        Laine And His Electric String Band]
        Speakeasy, London
        Jimi attends the Turtles concert
05
        London – Studio recordings

13
        USA
        Cafe A Go Go, NYC
        Jimi attends the Richie Havens concert
14
        Scene, NYC
        Jimi attends The Doors concert
18
        Monterey International Pop Festival
        Jimi watches Ravi Shankar's performance
        MONTEREY INTERNATIONAL POP FESTIVAL, MONTEREY,
        CALIFORNIA

[line-up for this day: Ravi Shankar; Blues Project; Buffalo Springfield; The Who; Grateful Dead; JHE; The Mamas & Papas] Filmed and recorded
Stephen Stills' house in Malibu, California
Jimi jams with Steve Stills, Hugh Masekela (trumpet), Buddy Miles (drums) and Bruce Palmer (bass)

20   FILLMORE WEST, SAN FRANCISCO, CALIFORNIA -2-
[support: Gabor Szabo; Jefferson Airplane]
21   FILLMORE WEST, SAN FRANCISCO, CALIFORNIA -2-
[support: Gabor Szabo]
22   FILLMORE WEST, SAN FRANCISCO, CALIFORNIA -2-
[support: Gabor Szabo]
23   FILLMORE WEST, SAN FRANCISCO, CALIFORNIA -2-
[support: Gabor Szabo]
24   FILLMORE WEST, SAN FRANCISCO, CALIFORNIA -2-
[support: Gabor Szabo]
25   'PANHANDLE', GOLDEN GATE PARK, SAN FRANCISCO, CALIFORNIA
FILLMORE WEST, SAN FRANCISCO, CALIFORNIA -2-
[support: Gabor Szabo]
26   Whisky A Go Go, Los Angeles, California
Jimi attends the Sam And Dave concert
28 to 30   Los Angeles, California – Recordings

JUL
01   EARL WARREN SHOWGROUNDS, SANTA BARBARA, CALIFORNIA
[support: Moby Grape; Tim Buckley]
02   WHISKY A GO GO, LOS ANGELES, CALIFORNIA
03   SCENE, NEW YORK CITY
[support: Tiny Tim; The Seeds]
04   SCENE, NEW YORK CITY
[support: Tiny Tim; The Seeds]
05   RHEINGOLD FESTIVAL, CENTRAL PARK, NEW YORK CITY
[support: Len Chandler; The Young Rascals]
06   Mayfair Recording Studio Inc., NYC – Recordings
07   Mayfair Recording Studio Inc., NYC – Recordings
Garrick Theatre, NYC
Jimi attends the Frank Zappa concert

08   *START OF THE MONKEES TOUR*
Line-up for all concerts to Jul 16:
The Sundowners; Lynne Randell; JHE; The Monkees
COLISEUM, JACKSONVILLE, FLORIDA
09   CONVENTION HALL. MIAMI, FLORIDA
11   COLISEUM, CHARLOTTE, NORTH CAROLINA
12   COLISEUM, GREENSBORO, NORTH CAROLINA
13   FOREST HILLS STADIUM, NEW YORK CITY
14   FOREST HILLS STADIUM, NEW YORK CITY
15   FOREST HILLS STADIUM, NEW YORK CITY
16   FOREST HILLS STADIUM, NEW YORK CITY
During one of the concerts at Forest Hills a girl in the audience disrupts Jimi's performance with the plea 'enough with the psychedelic, already' . . .

667

END OF THE JHE ON THE MONKEES TOUR

mid	The Electric Circus, NYC
	Jimi attends The Seeds concert
18 & 19	Mayfair Recording Studio Inc., NYC – Recordings
20	Mayfair Recording Studio Inc., NYC – Recordings
	SALVATION, NEW YORK CITY
end	Studio 76 Inc, NYC – Recordings (2 days) with Curtis Knight
21	CAFE A GO GO, NEW YORK CITY -2-
22	CAFE A GO GO, NEW YORK CITY -2-
23	CAFE A GO GO, NEW YORK CITY -2-
end	Gaslight Café, NYC
	Jimi jams on several days with John Hammond And His Screaming Nighthawks, and Eric Clapton
29	Mayfair Recording Studio Inc, NYC – Recordings

AUG

03	SALVATION, NEW YORK CITY
04	SALVATION, NEW YORK CITY
05	SALVATION, NEW YORK CITY
07	SALVATION, NEW YORK CITY
08	SALVATION, NEW YORK CITY
09	AMBASSADOR THEATRE, WASHINGTON DC -2- [support: Natty Bumpo]
10	AMBASSADOR THEATRE, WASHINGTON DC -2- [support: Natty Bumpo]
	Mitch was ill, and another drummer (unknown) sat in
11	AMBASSADOR THEATRE, WASHINGTON DC -2- [support: Natty Bumpo]
12	AMBASSADOR THEATRE, WASHINGTON DC -2- [support: Natty Bumpo]
13	'KEEP THE FAITH FOR WASHINGTON YOUTH FUND', AMBASSADOR THEATRE, WASHINGTON DC -2- [support: Natty Bumpo]
mid	Jimi gets arrested in Washington DC for jaywalking!
15	FIFTH DIMENSION CLUB, ANN ARBOR, MICHIGAN -2-
18	HOLLYWOOD BOWL, HOLLYWOOD, CALIFORNIA -2- [support: The Mamas And The Papas; Scott McKenzie]
19	'The Burning Of The Midnight Lamp' b/w 'The Stars That Play With Laughing Sam's Dice' (4th JHE single) released in the UK EARL WARREN SHOWGROUNDS, SANTA BARBARA, CALIFORNIA [support: Moby Grape; Captain Speed; Tim Buckley]

21	*ENGLAND*
22	Manchester, Lancashire – TV recordings 'The Burning Of The Midnight Lamp' (live)
24	London – TV recordings 'The Burning Of The Midnight Lamp' (studio track with live vocals), two versions
27	SAVILLE THEATRE, LONDON W1 [support: Crazy World Of Arthur Brown; Tomorrow featuring Keith West]

668

The second show was cancelled due to the death of Brian Epstein
Speakeasy, London
Jimi jams with Fairport Convention

29   NOTTINGHAM BLUES FESTIVAL, SHERWOOD ROOMS, NOTTINGHAM, NOTTINGHAMSHIRE
[support: Jimmy James & Vagabonds; Jimmy Cliff; Wynder K. Frogg; Long John Baldry]

end   Speakeasy, London
Jimi attends the Dantalians Chariot concert

31   *WEST GERMANY*
Berlin – Radio recordings (live)

SEP
02   Berlin – TV recordings
'Can You See Me?', 'The Burning Of The Midnight Lamp' (mimed)

03   *SWEDEN*
KONSERTHALLEN, LISEBERG, LISEBERGS NÖJESPARK, GOTHENBURG -2-
[support: Outsiders; Lucas]

04   STORA SCENEN, GRÖNA LUND, TIVOLI GARDEN, STOCKHOLM -1st show-
DANS IN, GRÖNA LUND, TIVOLI GARDEN, STOCKHOLM -2nd show-

05   Radiohuset, Stockholm – Radio recordings (live show)
Stockholm – Radio interview by Klas Burling

06   VÄSTERÅS IDROTTSHALL, VÄSTERÅS -2-
[support: Mersy Sect; AB Musik; Deejays; Outsiders]

08   Stockholm – TV recordings
'Hey Joe', 'Foxy Lady', 'Purple Haze', 'The Wind Cries Mary', 'I Don't Live Today' (mimed)
POPLADEN, HÖGBO BRUK, HÖGBO -2-
[support: Midnighters; Halifax Team; Outsiders]

09   MARIEBERGSSKOGEN, KARLSTAD -2-
[support: Jörgen Reinholds]

10   STORA SALEN, AKADEMISKA FÖRENINGEN, LUND -2-
[support: Bread; Hansson & Karlsson]

11   STORA SCENEN, GRÖNA LUND, TIVOLI GARDEN, STOCKHOLM -1st show-
Stockholm – Radio interview with Leif H. Andersson
DANS IN, GRÖNA LUND, TIVOLI GARDEN, STOCKHOLM -2nd show-

11?   Club Filips, Stockholm
Jimi jams (on bass) with Janne Karlsson (drums), and George Wadenius (guitar) of Blood, Sweat And Tears
Recorded

12   STJÄRNSCENEN, LISEBERG, LISEBERGS NÖJESPARK, GOTHENBURG -2-

13   *ENGLAND*
15   Bluesville '67, Bluesville Club, The Manor House, London
Jimi jams with Eric Burdon & The Animals

Unknown clergyman and girl, Jimi and his trophy, and DJ Jimmy Savile
Europa Hotel, London, 16 September 1967

670

16	Europa Hotel, London
	Jimi is voted 'World Top Musician' by *Melody Maker* (UK),
	and collects the award for this. Filmed.
23	Royal Albert Hall, London
	Jimi attends the Frank Zappa concert
24	Saville Theatre, London
	Jimi attends the Traffic concert
25	'GUITAR-IN', ROYAL FESTIVAL HALL, LONDON SW1
	[support: see poster opposite]

OCT

01 to 05	Olympic Sound Studios, London – Recordings
06	London – Radio recordings for 'Top Gear'
	Two interviews, 'Little Miss Lover', 'Drivin' South' (2 versions),
	'The Burning Of The Midnight Lamp,' 'Hound Dog', 'Experiencing
	The Blues'
	London – Radio recordings
	Jimi jams with Stevie Wonder (drums) and Noel (bass)
	'Ain't Too Proud To Beg' (live)
07	THE WELLINGTON CLUB, DEREHAM, NORFOLK
	[support: The Flower People; The Rubber Band]
08	SAVILLE THEATRE, LONDON W1 -2-
	[support: Crazy World Of Arthur Brown; The Herd; Eire
	Apparent; MC Len Marshall]

09	*FRANCE*
	L'OLYMPIA, PARIS
	[support: The Pebbles]
	Filmed and recorded
10	Paris – TV recordings
	'The Burning Of The Midnight Lamp', 'Hey Joe' (mimed)
11	Paris, two outside locations – TV recordings
	2 songs (mimed)
12	Paris – TV recordings
	'The Burning Of The Midnight Lamp', 'The Wind Cries Mary'
	(mimed)
	Jimi mimes on a piano and a violin . . .
	Paris – TV recordings

	ENGLAND
13	Borehamwood, Hertfordshire – TV recordings
	'Little Miss Lover' (pre-recorded live backing track with live vocals)
15	STARLIGHT BALLROOM, CRAWLEY, SUSSEX
17	London – Radio recordings for 'Rhythm And Blues'
	'Can You Please Crawl Out Your Window', 'I'm Your Hoochie
	Coochie Man,' 'Drivin' South' (live)
18	The London Pavilion, London
	Jimi attends the premiere of John Lennon's film *How I Won The War*
	Filmed
22	HASTINGS PIER, HASTINGS, SUSSEX
	[support: The Orange Seaweed]

Guitar-In

The Jimi Hendrix Experience
Bert Jansch   Paco Pena
Sebastian Jorgensen & Tim Walker

The Royal Festival Hall
8pm Monday 25th September
Tickets: 21/- 15/6 12/6 7/6 5/-
available from the Royal Festival Hall box office (telephone 01 928 3191)

The Royal Festival Hall General Manager   John Denison CBE   Published by Liberal International   Director   Ken Woollard   Design   John Holder / Ken Vail   Print   D S M of Cambridge

672

23	De Lane Lea Music Ltd., London – Studio rehearsal & photo session
24	MARQUEE, LONDON W1
	[support: The Nice]
25 to 27	Olympic Sound Studios, London – Recordings
28	CALIFORNIA BALLROOM, DUNSTABLE, BEDFORDSHIRE
	[support: Modes Mode; Canal Street Philharmonic]
	Olympic Sound Studios, London – Recordings
29 & 30	Olympic Sound Studios, London – Recordings

NOV

08	THE UNION, MANCHESTER, LANCASHIRE
	[support: Tamla Express; DJ The Baron]
10	*HOLLAND*
	Vitus Studio, Bussum – TV recordings for *Hoepla*
	'Foxy Lady', 'Catfish Blues', 2 versions of 'Purple Haze' (live)
	'HIPPY HAPPY BEURS VOOR TIENERS EN TWENS', AHOY
	HALLEN, ROTTERDAM
	[support: The Motions]
11	*ENGLAND*
	NEW REFECTORY, SUSSEX UNIVERSITY, BRIGHTON,
	SUSSEX
	[support: Ten Years After]
	JHE fee £500, TYA fee £60 . . .
14	*START OF THE SECOND UK TOUR*
	Support for all the concert dates to Dec 5:
	The Move; Pink Floyd; Amen Corner; Outer Limits; Eire
	Apparent; The Nice; MC Pete Drummond
	ROYAL ALBERT HALL, LONDON SW7
15	Mayfair Hotel, London – Filmed interview
	WINTER GARDENS, BOURNEMOUTH, HAMPSHIRE -2-
17	CITY HALL, SHEFFIELD, YORKSHIRE -2-
18	THE EMPIRE, LIVERPOOL, LANCASHIRE -2-
19	THE COVENTRY THEATRE, COVENTRY, WARKS -2-
22	GUILD HALL, PORTSMOUTH, HAMPSHIRE -2-
23	SOPHIA GARDENS PAVILION, CARDIFF, GLAMORGAN,
	WALES -2-
24	COLSTON HALL, BRISTOL, GLOUCESTERSHIRE -2-
25	OPERA HOUSE, BLACKPOOL, LANCASHIRE -2-
	Filmed and recorded
26	PALACE THEATRE, MANCHESTER, LANCASHIRE -2-
27	'FESTIVAL OF ARTS', WHITLA HALL, QUEEN'S COLLEGE,
	BELFAST, N. IRELAND -2-
	(Jimi receives a birthday cake backstage)

DEC

01	*Axis: Bold As Love* (2nd JHE LP) released in the UK
	CENTRAL HALL, CHATHAM, KENT -2-

02	THE DOME, BRIGHTON, SUSSEX -2-
03	THEATRE ROYAL, NOTTINGHAM, NOTTINGHAMSHIRE -2-
04	CITY HALL, NEWCASTLE-UPON-TYNE, NORTHUMBERLAND -2-
05	GREEN'S PLAYHOUSE, GLASGOW, LANARK, SCOTLAND -2-
	END OF THE SECOND UK TOUR
06	Speakeasy, London
	Jimi attends a party for The Foundations
beg	Speakeasy, London
	Jimi jams with Ainsley Dunbar, Noel Redding and Alan Price
08	Borehamwood, Hertfordshire – TV recordings
	'Spanish Castle Magic' (pre-recorded live backing track with live vocals)
10	Speakeasy, London
	Jimi attends the Moody Blues concert
mid	Speakeasy, London
	Jimi jams with the Fairport Convention
mid	Jimi's flat, London – Interview by Meatball Fulton
	Recorded
13	De Lane Lea Music Ltd., London – Recordings
15	London – Radio recordings for 'Top Gear'
	Interview, Radio One Jingle, 'Day Tripper', 'Spanish Castle Magic', 'Getting My Heart Back Together Again' (2 versions), 'Wait Until Tomorrow'
16	London – TV recordings
	'Purple Haze' (studio track with live vocals)
19	Bruce Fleming Photo Studio, London – Filming for the movie *See My Music Talking* film (a.k.a. *Experience*)
	Interview, 'Getting My Heart Back Together Again' (12-string solo), live
20 &21	Olympic Sound Studios, London – Recordings
22	'CHRISTMAS ON EARTH CONTINUED', GRAND & NATIONAL HALLS, OLYMPIA, LONDON W8
	[support: The Who; Eric Burdon & The Animals; The Move; Pink Floyd; Keith West & Tomorrow; Soft Machine; Paper Blitz Tissue; Traffic; Graham Bond Organisation; Sam Gopal Dream; Jeffrey Shaw & The Plastic Circus; DJ's: Mike Lennox and John Peel]
	Filmed (also backstage)
23	'Christmas Festival', Roundhouse, London
	Rumour has it that Jimi played Santa Claus at a children's party . . .
end?	Speakeasy, London
	Jimi jams with Sam Gopal Dream
	Recorded
25	Noel's flat, London
	Jimi attends Noel's birthday party
26	Bruce Fleming's house, London
	Jimi spends Christmas with Bruce Fleming and his family
end	Speakeasy, London
	Jimi jams with Dave Mason, Eric Burdon, and Harry Hughes of The Clouds

674

30	Olympic Sound Studios, London – Recordings
31	Speakeasy, London
	Jimi attends the New Year's Eve party and during a jam session plays a 30 minute version of 'Auld Lang Syne'

1968

JAN
01	London – Radio interview
02	Klooks Kleek, Railway Hotel, London
	Jimi jams with Al Sykes and John Mayall

03	*SWEDEN*
04	LORENSBERG CIRKUS, GOTHENBURG -2-
	[support: Baby Grandmothers; Mecki Mark Men]
	Jimi arrested by Swedish police for wrecking a hotel room
05	JERNVALLEN SPORTS HALL, SANDVIKEN
	[support: Baby Grandmothers; Mecki Mark Men]

06	*DENMARK*
	Copenhagen – TV recordings
07	TIVOLIS KONSERTSAL, COPENHAGEN -2-
	[support: Hanson & Carlsson]

08	*SWEDEN*
	STORA SALEN, KONSERTHUSET, STOCKHOLM -2-
	[support: Baby Grandmothers; Mecki Mark Men]
	Stockholm – Radio interview by Leif H. Andersson
16	Gothenburg Courthouse – Jimi fined 8,918 Swedish Crowns

17	*ENGLAND*
19	London – Jimi attends the launching party for the group Grapefruit
20?	De Lane Lea Music Ltd., London – Recordings with McGough & McGear
21	Olympic Sound Studios, London – Recordings
26	Olympic Sound Studios, London – Recordings
28	Olympic Sound Studios, London – Recordings

29	*FRANCE*
	Paris – Radio interview
	L'OLYMPIA, PARIS -2-
	[support: Eric Burdon & The Animals]
	Second show recorded

30	*USA*
	Copter Club, Pan Am Building, Manhattan, NYC
	JHE attend the press reception 'The British Are Coming'
	Various interviews for magazines, radio and TV

—	JHE are voted 'Best Group on Stage' by *Beat Instrumental* (UK)
01	FILLMORE AUDITORIUM, SAN FRANCISCO, CALIFORNIA -2- [support: Albert King; John Mayall's Bluesbreakers; Soft Machine]
02	WINTERLAND, SAN FRANCISCO, CALIFORNIA -2- [support: Soft Machine; Albert King; John Mayall's Bluesbreakers]
03	WINTERLAND, SAN FRANCISCO, CALIFORNIA -2- [support: Albert King; John Mayall's Bluesbreakers;
04	WINTERLAND, SAN FRANCISCO, CALIFORNIA -2- [support: Albert King; John Mayall's Bluesbreakers; Big Brother And The Holding Company]
05	SUN DEVILS GYM, ARIZONA STATE UNIVERSITY, TEMPE, ARIZONA [support: Soft Machine]
06	V.I.P. CLUB, TUCSON, ARIZONA [support: Soft Machine]
08	MEN'S GYM, SACRAMENTO STATE COLLEGE, SACRA-MENTO, CALIFORNIA [support: The Creators; Soft Machine]
09	ANAHEIM CONVENTION CENTRE, ANAHEIM, CALIFORNIA -2- [support: Eire Apparent; Soft Machine; Eric Burdon & The Animals]
10	Shrine Auditorium Jimi jams with Buddy Miles (drums), Harvey Brooks (bass) and David Crosby (guitar) SHRINE AUDITORIUM, LOS ANGELES, CALIFORNIA [support: Soft Machine; Blue Cheer; Electric Flag]
11	ROBERTSON GYM, SANTA BARBARA, CALIFORNIA [support: East Side Kids; Soft Machine]
12	CENTER ARENA, SEATTLE, WASHINGTON [support: Soft Machine]
13	Jimi visits Garfield High School, Seattle ACKERMAN UNION GRAND BALLROOM, UCLA, LOS ANGELES, CALIFORNIA [support: Soft Machine]
14	REGIS COLLEGE, FIELDHOUSE, DENVER, COLORADO [support: Soft Machine]
15	MUNICIPAL AUDITORIUM, SAN ANTONIO, TEXAS [support: The Moving Sidewalks; Neal Ford And The Fanatics; Soft Machine]
16	STATE FAIR MUSIC HALL, DALLAS, TEXAS [support: The Moving Sidewalks; Neal Ford And The Fanatics; Soft Machine]
17	Jimi is voted 'World Top Musician' by *Disc And Music Echo* (UK) WILL ROGERS AUDITORIUM, FORT WORTH, TEXAS [support: The Moving Sidewalks; Neal Ford And The Fanatics; Soft Machine]
18	MUSIC HALL, HOUSTON, TEXAS -2- [support: The Moving Sidewalks; Neal Ford And The Fanatics; Soft Machine]
20	Scene, NYC Jimi jams with members of The Electric Flag, Soft Machine and Tremeloes

676

21	ELECTRIC FACTORY, PHILADELPHIA, PENNSYLVANIA -2-
	[support: Woody's Truck Stop]
22	ELECTRIC FACTORY, PHILADELPHIA, PENNSYLVANIA -2-
	[support: Woody's Truck Stop; Soft Machine]
23	MASONIC TEMPLE, DETROIT, MICHIGAN
	[support: Soft Machine; MC5; The Rationals]
24	Jimi is voted 'The Rolling Stone Great Balls of Fire Award'
	for 1967 by *Rolling Stone* (USA)
	CNE COLISEUM ARENA, TORONTO, ONTARIO, CANADA
	[support: The Paupers; Soft Machine]
25	CHICAGO CIVIC OPERA HOUSE, CHICAGO, ILLINOIS -2-
	[support: Soft Machine]
27	THE FACTORY, MADISON, WISCONSIN -2-
	[support: Soft Machine]
28	THE SCENE, MILWAUKEE, WISCONSIN -2-
	[support: Soft Machine]
29	THE SCENE, MILWAUKEE, WISCONSIN -2-
	[support: Soft Machine]

MAR

02	HUNTER COLLEGE, NEW YORK CITY -2-
	[support: John Hammond Jr.; Soft Machine]
	Realrock station, NYC - Radio interview (live transmission)
03	VETS MEMORIAL AUDITORIUM, COLUMBUS, OHIO
	[support: Dantes; 4 O'Clock Balloon; Soft Machine]
06?	Scene, NYC
	Jimi jams with Jim Morrison (harmonica) and others
	Recorded by Jimi
08	MARVEL GYM, BROWN UNIVERSITY, PROVIDENCE, RHODE ISLAND
09	STATE UNIVERSITY OF NEW YORK, STONY BROOK, LONG ISLAND, NEW YORK
	[support: Soft Machine]
10	INTERNATIONAL BALLROOM, WASHINGTON HILTON HOTEL, WASHINGTON DC -2-
	[support: Soft Machine]
13	Sound Center, NYC - Recordings
15	Jimi is voted 'Instrumentalist Of The World' by *Hitweek* (Holland)
	ATWOOD HALL, CLARK UNIVERSITY, WORCESTER, MASSACHUSETTS -2-
	[support: Soft Machine]
	Filmed and recorded
16	LEWISTON ARMORY, LEWISTON, MAINE
	[support: Hanseatic League; Terry And The Telstars]
17	Cafe A Go Go, NYC
	Jimi jams with Elvin Bishop (guitar), Harvey Brooks (bass), Phillip Wilson (drums), Buddy Miles (drums), James Tatum (sax), Herbie Rich (organ) and Paul Butterfield (harmonica)
	Recorded by Jimi
19	CAPITOL THEATRE, OTTAWA, ONTARIO, CANADA -2-
	[support: Soft Machine]
	Second show recorded

21	COMMUNITY WAR MEMORIAL, ROCHESTER, NEW YORK
	[support: Rustics; Soft Machine]
22	BUSHNELL MEMORIAL HALL, HARTFORD, CONNECTICUT
	[support: The Bowl; Soft Machine]
23	BUFFALO MEMORIAL AUDITORIUM, BUFFALO, NEW YORK
	[support: Jesse's First Carnival; Soft Machine]
24	IMA AUDITORIUM, FLINT, MICHIGAN
	[support: Rationals; Fruit Of The Loom; Soft Machine]
25	Otto's Grotto, Cleveland, Ohio
	Jimi jams with Good Earth
26	WKYC, Cleveland, Ohio - Radio interview (live transmission)
	PUBLIC MUSIC HALL, CLEVELAND, OHIO -2-
	[support: Soft Machine]
27	TEEN AMERICA BUILDING, LION'S DELWARE CO. FAIR-GROUNDS, MUNCIE, INDIANA
	[support: The Glass Calendar; Soft Machine]
28	XAVIER UNIVERSITY FIELDHOUSE, CINCINNATI, OHIO -2-
	[support: Soft Machine]
29	Chicago University, Chicago, Illinois
	[support: Soft Machine]
	JHE went on stage after the Soft Machine concert, but the amplifiers were picking up radio signals, so Jimi walked off and refused to play the concert
	The Cheetah, Chicago
	Jimi jams with the Paul Butterfield Blues Band
30	UNIVERSITY OF TOLEDO FIELDHOUSE, TOLEDO, OHIO
	[support: Soft Machine]
31	ARENA, PHILADELPHIA, PENNSYLVANIA
	[support: Woody's Truck Stop; Soft Machine]

APR	
02	PAUL SAUVE ARENA, MONTREAL, QUEBEC, CANADA
	[support: Olivus; Soft Machine]
04	Martin Luther King murdered
	CIVIC DOME, VIRGINIA BEACH, VIRGINIA -2-
05	SYMPHONY HALL, NEWARK, NEW JERSEY
	Second show cancelled due to the death of Martin Luther King
06	WESTCHESTER COUNTY CENTER, WHITE PLAINS, NEW YORK
	[support: Soft Machine]
07	Generation, NYC
	Jimi jams with Roy Buchanan (bass) and others
	Filmed
mid	Generation, NYC
	Jimi jams with Elvin Bishop (guitar), B.B. King (guitar), Buzzy Feiten (bass), Phillip Wilson (drums), Don Martin (guitar), Al Kooper (organ), Paul Butterfield (harmonica) and Stewart Somebody (piano)
	Recorded by Jimi
	Later that night, Jimi jams with Ted Nugent, B.B. King, Al Kooper and others
18	Record Plant, NYC - Recordings

678

19	TROY ARMORY, TROY, NEW YORK
	[support: Soft Machine]
20 to 26	Record Plant, NYC - Recordings
28 to 30	Record Plant, NYC - Recordings

MAY

01 to 05	Record Plant, NYC - Recordings
	(only the 3rd part of the session was filmed)
08	Record Plant, NYC - Recordings
10	FILLMORE EAST, NEW YORK CITY -2-
	[support: Sly & The Family Stone]
	Performs the longest version of 'Red House' (17 minutes)
	Both shows recorded
17	Record Plant, NYC - Recordings
18	MIAMI POP FESTIVAL, GULF STREAM RACE TRACK, HALLANDALE, MIAMI, FLORIDA -2- (cancelled)
	[support: Mothers Of Invention; Crazy World Of Arthur Brown; Blue Cheer; John Lee Hooker]
	Filmed (partly)
19	MIAMI POP FESTIVAL, GULF STREAM RACE TRACK, HALLANDALE, MIAMI, FLORIDA -2- (cancelled)
	[support: same as the previous day]
	Wreck Bar, The Castaways Hotel, Miami
	Jimi jams with Noel, Frank Zappa, Jimmy Carl Black, Arthur Brown and others
20	Wreck Bar, The Castaways Hotel, Miami
	Jimi jams on a Guild 'SF-V Starfire Deluxe'
23	Eric Barrett joins as road manager
	ITALY
	PIPER CLUB, MILAN
	(First show cancelled as the equipment didn't arrive in time)
24	TEATRO BRANCACCIO, ROME -2-
	[support: Pier Franco Colonna; The Triad; Franco Estill Groups – ballet group]
25	TEATRO BRANCACCIO, ROME -2-
	[support: same as the previous day]
24 & 25	Titan, Rome
	Jimi (on bass) jams with Noel (guitar), Mitch (drums) and various local bands, such as The Folks
26	PALASPORT, BOLOGNA -2-
27	*USA*
30	*SWITZERLAND*
	'MONSTER-KONZERT', HALLENSTADION, ZURICH
	[support: The Move; Anselmo Trend; Traffic; Small Faces; Koobas; John Mayall's Bluesbreakers; Eric Burdon & The Animals; Eire Apparent]
31	Hallenstadion, Zurich
	Jimi jams with Chris Wood (flute), Stevie Winwood (organ), Dave

Mason (bass), Trevor Burton (drums), Carl Wayne (bongos) and Vic Briggs (guitar)
Recorded by Chris Wood
'MONSTER-KONZERT', HALLENSTADION, ZURICH
[support: same as the previous day]

JUN

01   *ENGLAND*
05   Borehamwood, Hertfordshire – TV recordings for *It Must Be Dusty!*
      'Stone Free', 'Mockingbird' (also with Dusty Springfield on vocals),
      'Voodoo Child (slight return)', live

07   *USA*
      Fillmore East, NYC
      Jimi jams with the Electric Flag
10 & 11   Record Plant, NYC – Recordings
14   Record Plant, NYC – Recordings
mid   Scene, NYC
          Jimi jams with Eric Clapton and Jeff Beck
mid   Scene, NYC
          Jimi jams with the Jeff Beck Group
16   'Daytop Music Festival', Staten Island, New York
          Jimi jams with the Jeff Beck Group
22   Scene, NYC
          Jimi jams with Larry Coryell
28   'Soul Together', Madison Square Garden, NYC
          Benefit for The Martin Luther King Memorial Fund
          Jimi attends and donates $5,000 to the fund
29   Record Plant, NYC – Recordings

JUL
01   Record Plant, NYC – Recordings

04   *ENGLAND*
06   WOBURN MUSIC FESTIVAL, WOBURN ABBEY, BEDS
      [support: Shirley And Dolly Collins; Pentangle; Geno Washington
      And The Ram Jam Band; Tyrannosaurus Rex; The Family; New
      Formula; Little Women]

15   *SPAIN*
      SGT. PEPPER'S, PALMA, MAJORCA
18   Sgt. Pepper's
      JHE perform a Rock & Roll set (with additional musicians, such as
      Jimmy Leverton and Neil Landon) playing such classics as 'Lucille'
      and 'Johnny B. Goode

19   *ENGLAND*
end   Revolution, London
      Jimi jams (unknown with who)

680

25	*USA*
30	INDEPENDENCE HALL, LAKESHORE AUDITORIUM, BATON ROUGE, LOUISIANA -2-
	[support: Soft Machine]
31	MUNICIPAL AUDITORIUM, SHREVEPORT, LOUISIANA

AUG

01	CITY PARK STADIUM, NEW ORLEANS, LOUISIANA
02	MUNICIPAL AUDITORIUM, SAN ANTONIO, TEXAS
	[support: Soft Machine]
03	MOODY COLISEUM, SOUTHERN METHODIST UNIVERSITY, DALLAS, TEXAS
	[support: Soft Machine]
04	KSMK, Houston – Radio recordings
	SAM HOUSTON COLISEUM, HOUSTON, TEXAS
07	Central Park, NYC – Photo session for *Electric Ladyland* LP cover
10	AUDITORIUM THEATRE, CHICAGO, ILLINOIS -2-
	[support: Soft Machine]
11	COL BALLROOM, DAVENPORT, IOWA
12	'Operation Airlift Biafra Benefit', Scene, NYC
	JHE attend and perform a set
	Record Plant, NYC – Recordings
16	MERRIWEATHER POST PAVILION, COLUMBIA, MARYLAND
	[support: The Soft Machine]
17	ATLANTA MUNICIPAL AUDITORIUM, ATLANTA, GEORGIA -2-
	[support: Eire Apparent; Soft Machine; Amboy Dukes (1st show only); Vanilla Fudge]
18	CURTIS HIXTON HALL, TAMPA, FLORIDA
20	THE MOSQUE, RICHMOND, VIRGINIA -2-
	[support: Eire Apparent; Soft Machine]
21	CIVIC DOME, VIRGINIA BEACH, VIRGINIA -2-
23	THE NEW YORK ROCK FESTIVAL, SINGER BOWL, FLUSHING MEADOW PARK, QUEENS, NEW YORK
	[support: Big Brother And The Holding Company; Chambers Brothers; Soft Machine; MC Scott Muni]
24	BUSHNELL MEMORIAL, HARTFORD, CONNECTICUT
	[support: Eire Apparent]
25	CAROUSEL THEATRE, FRAMINGTON, MASSACHUSETTS -2-
	[support: Soft Machine]
26	KENNEDY STADIUM, BRIDGEPORT, CONNECTICUT
	[support: Eire Apparent; Soft Machine]
27	Record Plant, NYC – Recordings
30	LANGOON OPERA HOUSE, SALT LAKE CITY, UTAH
	[support: Soft Machine]

SEP

01	RED ROCKS PARK, DENVER, COLORADO
	[support: Eire Apparent; Vanilla Fudge; Soft Machine]
03	BALBOA STADIUM, SAN DIEGO, CALIFORNIA
	[support: Eire Apparent; Vanilla Fudge; Soft Machine]

04	MEMORIAL COLISEUM, PHOENIX, ARIZONA
	[support: Eire Apparent; Vanilla Fudge; Soft Machine]
05	SWING AUDITORIUM, SAN BERNARDINO, CALIFORNIA
	[support: Eire Apparent; Vanilla Fudge; Soft Machine]
06	CENTER COLISEUM, SEATTLE, WASHINGTON
	[support: Eire Apparent; Vanilla Fudge; Soft Machine]
07	PACIFIC COLISEUM, VANCOUVER, BRITISH COLUMBIA, CANADA
	[support: Eire Apparent; Vanilla Fudge; Soft Machine]
	Pacific Coliseum – Backstage TV interview
08	COLISEUM, SPOKANE, WASHINGTON
	[support: Eire Apparent; Vanilla Fudge; Soft Machine]
09	MEMORIAL COLISEUM, PORTLAND, OREGON
	[support: Soft Machine; Vanilla Fudge]
mid	Hollywood, California – Radio interviews
13	OAKLAND COLISEUM, OAKLAND, CALIFORNIA
	[support: Eire Apparent; Vanilla Fudge; Soft Machine]
14	HOLLYWOOD BOWL, HOLLYWOOD, CALIFORNIA
	[support: Eire Apparent; Vanilla Fudge; Soft Machine]
15	MEMORIAL AUDITORIUM, SACRAMENTO, CALIFORNIA
	[support: Vanilla Fudge; Eire Apparent]
18	Whisky A Go Go, Los Angeles, California
	JHE attend the Buddy Miles Express concert and later on all jam with Graham Bond (organ), Buddy Miles (guitar and drums) and Eric Burdon (vocals). Filmed.
OCT	Filmed (jam only)
05	HONOLULU INTERNATIONAL CENTER, HONOLULU, ISLAND OF OAHU, HAWAII
	[support: Times Music Co.]
06?	K-POI, Honolulu – Radio interview
10	WINTERLAND, SAN FRANCISCO, CALIFORNIA -2-
	[support: Dino Valente; Buddy Miles Express]
	Jack Casady (bass) joins the JHE on stage during the 2nd show
	Both shows recorded
11	WINTERLAND, SAN FRANCISCO, CALIFORNIA -2-
	[support: Dino Valente; Buddy Miles Express]
	Virgil Gonzales (flute) joins the JHE on stage during the 1st show
	Herbie Rich (organ) joins the JHE on stage during the 2nd show
	Both shows recorded
12	WINTERLAND, SAN FRANCISCO, CALIFORNIA -2-
	[support: Dino Valente; Buddy Miles Express]
	Both shows recorded
18	'All Along The Watchtower' b/w 'Long Hot Summer Night' released in the UK
	T.T.G., 1441 N. McCadden Place, Hollywood, California – Recordings
19	The Forum, Los Angeles, California
	Jimi attends The Cream's farewell concert
	Los Angeles
	Jimi jams with the Lee Michaels group
20 to 24	T.T.G., Hollywood – Recordings
25	*Electric Ladyland* (3rd JHE LP) released in the UK
	T.T.G., Hollywood – Recordings

Radio show at K-POI
Honolulu, probably 6 October 1968

26	CIVIC AUDITORIUM, BAKERSFIELD, CALIFORNIA
27 to 29	T.T.G., Hollywood – Recordings
—	T.T.G., Hollywood – Demo recording with Robert Wyatt
end	T.T.G., Hollywood – Recordings with Eire Apparent

NOV
01   MUNICIPAL AUDITORIUM ARENA, KANSAS CITY, MISSOURI
[support: Cat Mother & The All Night Newsboys]
Note: Cat Mother & The All Night Newsboys abbreviated to Cat Mother from now on
02   AUDITORIUM, MINNEAPOLIS, MINNESOTA
[support: Cat Mother]
Auditorium – Backstage interview by Tony Glover (recorded)
03   KIEL AUDITORIUM, ST LOUIS, MISSOURI
[support: Cat Mother]

Civic Auditorium, Bakersfield, 26 October 1968

06	Record Plant, NYC – Recordings
15	CINCINNATI GARDENS, CINCINNATI, OHIO
16	BOSTON GARDEN, BOSTON, MASSACHUSETTS
	[support: The McCoys; Cat Mother]
17	WOOLSEY HALL, YALE UNIVERSITY, NEW HAVEN, CONNECTICUT
	[support: Cat Mother; Terry Reid]
22	JACKSONVILLE COLISEUM, JACKSONVILLE, FLORIDA
	[support: Cat Mother]
23	CURTIS HIXON HALL, TAMPA, FLORIDA
	[support: Cat Mother]
24	MIAMI BEACH CONVENTION HALL, MIAMI BEACH, FLORIDA
	[support: Cat Mother]
27	RHODE ISLAND AUDITORIUM, PROVIDENCE, RHODE ISLAND
	'The Annual Thanksgiving Blues Bag', Cafe Au Go Go, NYC
	Birthday party for Jimi
28	'AN ELECTRONIC THANKSGIVING', PHILHARMONIC HALL, NEW YORK CITY
	[support: Fernando Valenti: The New York Brass Quintet]
30	COBO ARENA, DETROIT, MICHIGAN
	[support: Cat Mother]

After attending a JHE concert in America an older lady told Eric Barrett 'Isn't it wonderful, all those young people coming out to hear Harry Belafonte' (who was scheduled to appear a week later!)

DEC

01	COLISEUM, CHICAGO, ILLINOIS
24	'Poetry At St. Mark's', NYC – Jimi attends a poetry evening
28	JHE are voted 'Artist Of The Year' by *Billboard* (USA)

1969

JAN

01	Record Plant, NYC – Recordings
02	*ENGLAND*
04	Television Centre, London – TV recordings for *Happening For Lulu* 'Voodoo Child (slight return)', 'Hey Joe', 'The Sunshine Of Your Love' (live) – Live transmission
beg	Polydor Studio, London – Recordings with Eire Apparent
07	Jimi's Handel flat, 25 Brook Street, London – TV interview by Hugh Curry
08	London – Radio interview by Keith Altham

09	*SWEDEN* LORENSBURG CIRKUS, GOTHENBURG -2- [support: Gin House Blues Group; Burning Red Ivanhoe] Stockholm, press reception Stockholm – Radio interview by Lennart Wretlind KONSERTHUSET, STOCKHOLM -2- [support: Jethro Tull] 1st show recorded on video, 2nd show recorded on tape
10	*DENMARK* FALKONER CENTRET, COPENHAGEN -2- [support: Jethro Tull]
11	*WEST GERMANY* MUSIKHALLE, HAMBURG -2- Note: support act for all concerts to Jan 23: Eire Apparent
12	RHEINHALLE, DÜSSELDORF -2- Club 66, Düsseldorf Jimi jams
13	Studio Dumond, Cologne – Filmed interview and autograph session SPORTHALLE, COLOGNE Small club, Cologne Jimi jams (on bass) with Noel (guitar) and others
14	HALLE MÜNSTERLAND, MÜNSTER
15	KONGRESAAL, DEUTSCHES MUSEUM, MUNICH -2-
16	MEISTERSINGERHALLE, NUREMBERG -2-
17	JAHRHUNDERTHALLE, FRANKFURT -2- Lots of soldiers in the audience, so Jimi includes 'Reveille' and the 'Last Post' during songs . . .
19	LIEDERHALLE, STUTTGART -2-
20 21	*FRANCE* 'WACKEN', HALL 16, STRASBOURG
22	*AUSTRIA* 'STIMMEN DER WELT', KONZERTHAUS, VIENNA -2-
23	*WEST GERMANY* Sportpalast, Berlin – Backstage filming SPORTPALAST, BERLIN
24	*ENGLAND*
30	*USA*

686

FEB
01   Jimi is voted 'Performer Of The Year' for 1968 by *Rolling Stone* (USA)

beg   *ENGLAND*
13   Post Office Tower Restaurant, London
               Jimi attends the launching party for Mary Hopkins' LP *Postcard*
14   Seymour Hall, London
               Jimi is voted 'World Top Musician' by *Disc And Music Echo* (UK), and collects the award for this
               Olympic Sound Studios, London – Recordings
15 & 16   Olympic Sound Studios, London – Recordings
18   ROYAL ALBERT HALL, LONDON SW7
               [support: Soft Machine; Mason, Capaldi, Wood & Frog]
mid   London – Jimi attends a recording session by Glass Menagerie
21   Jimi is voted 'Instrumentalist Of The World' by *Hitweek* (Holland)
22   Olympic Sound Studios, London – Recordings
24   ROYAL ALBERT HALL, LONDON SW7
               [support: Van Der Graaf Generator; Fat Mattress]
               Filmed and recorded
               Speakeasy, London
               Jimi jams with Jim Capaldi, Dave Mason and Alan Price
26   Olympic Sound Studios, London – Recordings
28   Speakeasy, London
               Jimi jams with Kwasi 'Rocky' Dzidzournu and others

MAR
beg   Jimi's Handel house, London
               Two-day interview by Jane de Mendelssohn for *IT* (Mar 28)
06   Speakeasy, London
               Jimi jams with Billy Preston
08   Ronnie Scott's, London
               Jimi jams with Roland Kirk
mid   Speakeasy, London
               Jimi jams with The Gods

13   *USA*

15?   Mercury studios, NYC
               Jimi jams with the Buddy Miles Express
               Recorded
18 & 19   Record Plant, NYC – Recordings
25   Record Plant, NYC – Recordings
end   'Teen-Age Fair', 'Pop Expo '69', The Palladium, Hollywood, California
               Backstage radio interview by Jay Harvey for KAA1
               Jimi attends the Delaney & Bonnie concert and jams with them on stage
end   The Factory, Hollywood, California
               Jimi attends a party for Donovan

APR	
beg	NYC – Interview for *Life* (Oct 3 – 'An Infinity of Jimis')
01 to 04	Olmstead Studios, NYC – Recordings
05	Record Plant or Olmstead Studios, NYC – Recordings
06 to 09	Record Plant, NYC – Recordings
11	DORTON ARENA, RALEIGH, NORTH CAROLINA [support: Fat Mattress]
12	SPECTRUM, PHILADELPHIA, PENNSYLVANIA [support Fat Mattress]
14 & 15	Record Plant, NYC – Recordings
16	Scene, NYC
	Jimi jams with Noel and Mitch
17	Record Plant, NYC – Recordings
18	ELLIS AUDITORIUM AMPHITHEATRE, MEMPHIS, TENNESSEE -2- [support: Fat Mattress]
19	SAM HOUSTON COLISEUM, HOUSTON, TEXAS [support: Fat Mattress]
20	MEMORIAL AUDITORIUM, DALLAS, TEXAS [support: Fat Mattress; Cat Mother]
21 & 22	Record Plant, NYC – Recordings
24	Record Plant, NYC – Recordings
26	THE FORUM, LOS ANGELES, CALIFORNIA [support: Cat Mother; Chicago Transit Authority] Recorded
27	OAKLAND COLISEUM, OAKLAND, CALIFORNIA [support: Fat Mattress; Jefferson Airplane] Jimi jams with Noel (guitar), Mitch (drums), and Jack Casady (bass) of Jefferson Airplane during the concert
29	Record Plant, NYC – Recordings
MAY	
02	COBO ARENA, DETROIT, MICHIGAN [support: Fat Mattress; Cat Mother]
03	Toronto International Airport, Toronto, Canada Jimi was arrested at 13.30, later being released on $10,000 bail MAPLE LEAF GARDENS, TORONTO, ONTARIO, CANADA [support: Cat Mother]
04	SYRACUSE WAR MEMORIAL AUDITORIUM, SYRACUSE, NEW YORK [support: Cat Mother]
05	Toronto Court House, Toronto Jimi appears in court for 3 minutes. The preliminary hearing is set for Jun 19
07	Record Plant, NYC – Recordings MEMORIAL COLISEUM, TUSCALOOSA, ALABAMA [support: Fat Mattress; Cat Mother]
09	CHARLOTTE COLISEUM, CHARLOTTE, NORTH CAROLINA [support: Chicago Transit Authority]

688

10	CHARLESTOWN CIVIC CENTER, CHARLESTON, WEST VIRGINIA
	[support: Fat Mattress; Chicago Transit Authority]
	Videotaped
11	FAIRGROUNDS COLISEUM, INDIANAPOLIS, INDIANA
	[support: Chicago Transit Authority]
13 & 14	Record Plant, NYC – Recordings
mid	Scene, NYC
	Jimi jams with Stephen Stills (bass) and Johnny Winter (guitar)
15	Record Plant, NYC – Recordings
16	Record Plant, NYC – Recordings
	CIVIC CENTER, BALTIMORE, MARYLAND
	[support: Buddy Miles Express; Cat Mother]
17	RHODE ISLAND AUDITORIUM,
	PROVIDENCE, RHODE ISLAND
	[support: Buddy Miles Express; Cat Mother]
18	Fillmore East, NYC
	Jimi attends The Who concert
	MADISON SQUARE GARDEN, NEW YORK CITY
	[support: Buddy Miles Express; Cat Mother]
19 or 20	Record Plant, NYC – Recordings with Timothy Leary
21 & 22	Record Plant, NYC – Recordings
23	SEATTLE CENTER COLISEUM, SEATTLE, WASHINGTON
	[support: Fat Mattress]
24	Sports Arena, San Diego (dressing-room)
	Interview by Jim Brodey for *San Diego Free Press* (Jun 13)
	SPORTS ARENA, SAN DIEGO, CALIFORNIA
	[support: Fat Mattress]
	Recorded
25	'POP FESTIVAL', SANTA CLARA COUNTY FAIRGROUNDS, SAN JOSE, CALIFORNIA
	[support: Fat Mattress; Taj Mahal; Loading Zone and others]
	Partly filmed
30	WAIKIKI SHELL, HONOLULU, ISLAND OF OAHU, HAWAII
	[support: Fat Mattress]
31	K-POI, Honolulu – Radio interview
	WAIKIKI SHELL, HONOLULU, ISLAND OF OAHU, HAWAII
	[support: Fat Mattress]
JUN	
01	WAIKIKI SHELL, HONOLULU, ISLAND OF OAHU, HAWAII
	[support: Fat Mattress]
beg	Jimi moves into the Beverly Rodeo Hyatt House, Beverly Hills, California and invites Billy Cox to join him there
beg	Beverly Rodeo Hyatt House – Interview by Nancy Carter (recorded)
08	Beverly Rodeo Hyatt House
	Interview by Jerry Hopkins for *Rolling Stone* (Jul 12)
19	Toronto Court House, Toronto, Canada
	Jimi attends a preliminary hearing. Trial is set for Dec 08
	Interview by Ritchie Yorke for the *Los Angeles Times* (Sep 07)

20	'NEWPORT 69', SAN FERNANDO VALLEY STATE COLLEGE, DEVONSHIRE DOWNS, CALIFORNIA
	[support: Muscle; Southwind; Ike & Tina Turner; Don Ellis; Taj Mahal; Joe Cocker; Edwin Hawkins Singers; Spirit]
22	'Newport 69'
	Jimi jams with Buddy Miles (drums), Brad Campbell (bass) and other members of the Full Tilt Boogie Band, Tracy Nelson (vocals) and other members of Mother Earth, and Eric Burdon
29	DENVER POP FESTIVAL, MILE HIGH STADIUM, DENVER, COLORADO
	[support: Aum; Zephyr; 3 Dog Night; Joe Cocker]
	JHE possibly performed 'Bold As Love' for the first time . . .
	Last official concert of the Jimi Hendrix Experience, as Noel quits the band . . .

JUL

beg	Jimi moves into a rented house, Taver Hollow Road, near Shokan, New York
beg	Jerry Velez and Juma Sultan (both on percussion) join the band (Jerry born in Puerto Rico, 15 August 1947; Juma born in Monrovia, California, 13 April 1942)
10	NBC Studio, NYC – TV recordings for *Tonight Show*
	Interview, 2 versions of 'Lover Man' (live) – live transmission
	First public appearance with Billy Cox as the new bass player
14	Larry Lee (rhythm guitar) joins the band
—	*MOROCCO*
	Jimi, Deering Howe and Michael Jason, go on holiday for about a week (some time between Jul 15 and 23)
end Jul/Aug	*USA*
	ABC Studio, NYC – TV recordings for *Dick Cavett Show*
	Interview, 'Getting My Heart Back Together Again' (live) – live transmission

AUG

10	Tinker Street Cinema, Woodstock, New York
	Jimi jams with Juma, Jerry and various local musicians
	Videotaped
18	'WOODSTOCK MUSIC AND ART FAIR', BETHEL, NEW YORK
	Jimi went on stage at 08.00 and closed the festival with the Gypsy Sons And Rainbows (with Billy Cox, Mitch Mitchell, Larry Lee, Juma Sultan and Jerry Velez)
	Filmed and recorded
28 to 30	Hit Factory, NYC – Recordings

SEP

04	Hit Factory, NYC – Recordings

690

05	139th STREET/LENOX AVENUE, HARLEM, NEW YORK CITY
	[support: Sam & Dave backing band; Big Maybelle; J.D. Bryant;
	Maxine Brown; MC Eddie O'Jay]
	Jazz street festival – benefit for the United Block Association
	Videotaped
	Hit Factory, NYC – Recordings
06	Hit Factory, NYC – Recordings
09	ABC Studio, NYC – TV recordings for *Dick Cavett Show*
	Interview, 'Machine Gun'/'Izabella' medley (live) – live transmission
10	SALVATION, NEW YORK CITY
09 or 11	Ungano's, NYC
	Jimi jams (on bass) with Mountain
15	Record Plant, NYC – Recordings
21?	Jimi's Shokan house
	Jimi jams with Mike Ephron, Juma Sultan and Jerry Velez
22?	Jimi's Shokan house
	Interview by Sheila Weller for *Rolling Stone* (Nov 15)
23 to 25	Record Plant, NYC – Recordings

OCT

—	Hotel Navarro, NYC
	Jimi disbands the Gypsy Sons & Rainbows group and forms the
	Band Of Gypsys with Billy Cox (bass) and Buddy Miles (drums)

NOV

—	Record Plant, NYC – Recordings with Lightnin' Rod
02	Record Plant, NYC – Recordings
07	Record Plant, NYC – Recordings
10	Record Plant, NYC – Recordings
12	Record Plant, NYC – Recordings
14	Record Plant, NYC – Recordings
17	Record Plant, NYC – Recordings
20 to 21	Record Plant, NYC – Recordings
27	Jimi's 27th birthday
	Madison Square Garden, NYC
	Jimi attends the Rolling Stones concert
	Backstage filming
Nov/Dec	Cafe A Go Go, NYC
	Jimi jams with the James Cotton Blues Band

DEC

06	Altamont Pop Festival, San Francisco, California
	Jimi attends the Rolling Stones concert
08	Toronto Court House, Toronto, Canada – Jimi's trial, day 1
09	Toronto Court House – trial, day 2
10	Toronto Court House – trial, day 3
	The jury retires for 8 hours, returning a verdict of not guilty
	and Jimi is cleared of all charges
15	Record Plant, NYC – Recordings
18 & 19	Record Plant, NYC – Recordings
23	Record Plant, NYC – Recordings

31	FILLMORE EAST, NEW YORK CITY -2- [support: Voices Of East Harlem] Debut of the Band Of Gypsys Second show partly filmed

1970

JAN

01	FILLMORE EAST, NEW YORK CITY -2- [support: Voices Of East Harlem] Both shows recorded and the 1st show videotaped
07	Record Plant, NYC – Recordings
16	Record Plant, NYC – Recordings
19 to 21	Record Plant, NYC – Recordings
23	Record Plant, NYC – Recordings
28	'WINTER FESTIVAL FOR PEACE', MADISON SQUARE GARDEN, NEW YORK CITY [support: Harry Belafonte; Dave Brubeck; Judy Collins; Peter, Paul & Mary; Blood, Sweat & Tears; The Rascals; Richie Havens; Mother Earth; Voice Of East Harlem; Hair] Benefit concert in aid of the Vietnam Moratorium Committee Filmed Note: Jimi leaves the stage after playing only 'Who Knows?' and 'Earth Blues', making it the final live performance of the Band of Gypsys
02	Record Plant, NYC – Recordings
04	Michael Jeffery's apartment, NYC Interview with JHE by John Burke for *Rolling Stone* (Mar 19, recorded)
16	Record Plant, NYC – Recordings

MAR

mid	*ENGLAND*
13	Revolution Club, London Jimi attends the Rubber Duck concert
mid	Island Studios, London – Recordings with Stephen Stills
17	Olympic Studios, London – Recordings with Arthur Lee and Love
19	*USA*
23 & 24	Record Plant, NYC – Recordings

APR

25	*START OF 'THE CRY OF LOVE' TOUR* THE FORUM, LOS ANGELES, CALIFORNIA [support: Buddy Miles Express; Ballin' Jack] Videotaped
26	'CAL EXPO', SACRAMENTO, CALIFORNIA [support: Buddy Miles Express; Blue Mountain Eagle]

MAY

01	MILWAUKEE AUDITORIUM, MILWAUKEE, WISCONSIN [support: Oz]

692

02	DANE COUNTY MEMORIAL COLISEUM, MADISON, WISCONSIN
	[support: Savage Grace; Oz]
.03	ST PAUL CIVIC CENTER, ST PAUL, MINNESOTA
	[support: Savage Grace; Oz]
04	'HOLDING TOGETHER', VILLAGE GATE, NEW YORK CITY
	[support: Johnny Winter – with Noel as guest]
	Benefit for Timothy Leary
08	UNIVERSITY OF OKLAHOMA FIELD HOUSE, NORMAN, OKLAHOMA -2-
	[support: Bloodrock]
09	WILL ROGERS COLISEUM, FORT WORTH, TEXAS
10	SAN ANTONIO HEMISPHERE ARENA, SAN ANTONIO, TEXAS
14 & 15	Record Plant, NYC – Recordings
16	TEMPLE UNIVERSITY STADIUM, PHILADELPHIA, PENNSYLVANIA
	[support: Grateful Dead; Steve Miller Band; Cactus]
22	Jimi is ill and cancels three concerts (22nd to 24th)
30	BERKELEY COMMUNITY THEATRE, BERKELEY, CALIFORNIA -2-
	Both shows filmed and recorded

JUN
05	MEMORIAL AUDITORIUM, DALLAS, TEXAS
06	SAM HOUSTON COLISEUM, HOUSTON, TEXAS
	[support: Ballin' Jack]
07	ASSEMBLY CENTER ARENA, TULSA, OKLAHOMA
	[support: Ballin' Jack]
09	MID-SOUTH COLISEUM, MEMPHIS, TENNESSEE
10	ROBERTS MUNICIPAL STADIUM, EVANSVILLE, INDIANA
12	*Band Of Gypsys* LP released in the UK
13	CIVIC CENTER, BALTIMORE, MARYLAND
	[support: Ballin' Jack; Cactus]
15 to 17	Electric Lady Studios, 52 West 8th Street, New York City 10011 – Recordings
19	CIVIC AUDITORIUM, ALBUQUERQUE, NEW MEXICO -2-
20	SWING AUDITORIUM, SAN BERNARDINO, CALIFORNIA
21	VENTURA COUNTY FAIRGROUNDS, VENTURA, CALIFORNIA
	[support: Ballin' Jack; Grin]
23	MAMMOTH GARDENS, DENVER, COLORADO
24 & 25	Electric Lady Studios, NYC – Recordings
27	BOSTON GARDEN, BOSTON, MASSACHUSETTS
	[support: The Illusion; Cactus]

JUL
01 & 02	Electric Lady Studios, NYC – Recordings
04	'2ND ATLANTA INTERNATIONAL POP FESTIVAL', MIDDLE GEORGIA RACEWAY, NEAR BYRON, GEORGIA
	[support: Rare Earth; Chambers Brothers; Lee Michaels; Jethro

Tull; Cactus; Cat Mother; Rotary Connection; The Gypsy]
Filmed and recorded
05   MIAMI JAI ALAI FRONTON, MIAMI, FLORIDA -2-
14   Electric Lady Studios, NYC – Recordings
17   'NEW YORK POP', DOWNING STADIUM, RANDALL'S
ISLAND, NEW YORK
[support: John Sebastian; Grand Funk Railroad; Steppenwolf;
Jethro Tull]
Filmed and recorded
20 to 23   Electric Lady Studios, NYC – Recordings
25   SPORTS ARENA, SAN DIEGO, CALIFORNIA
[support: Cat Mother]
26   SICKS STADIUM, SEATTLE, WASHINGTON
[support: Cactus; Rube Tuben & The Rhondonnas]
30   RAINBOW BRIDGE VIBRATORY COLOR/SOUND EXPERI-
MENT, HALEAKALA CRATER, RAINBOW RIDGE, NEAR
SEABURY HALL, ISLAND OF MAUI, HAWAII -2-
Both shows filmed and recorded

AUG
01   ARENA, HONOLULU INTERNATIONAL CENTER,
HONOLULU, ISLAND OF OAHU, HAWAII
Jimi's last official concert in the USA
END OF 'THE CRY OF LOVE' TOUR
22   Electric Lady Studios, NYC – Recordings
Jimi's last recording session . . .
26   Electric Lady Studios, NYC
Jimi attends the official opening party
27   Flies from New York City, to London Heathrow Airport

ENGLAND
Heathrow Airport – Interview for *The Times* (Sep 01)
Books into the Park Suite at Londonderry Hotel, Park Lane, London
28   Londonderry Hotel, London
Interview by Gillian Saich for *New Musical Express* (Sep 05)
Speakeasy, London
Jimi jams with Billy Cox and Stephen Stills
29   Londonderry Hotel, London
Interviews with Jimi by:
Roy Hollingworth for *Melody Maker* (Sep 05 and Sep 26)
Mike Ledgerwood for *Disc & Music Echo* (Sep 12)
Bob Partridge for *Record Mirror* (Sep 19)
Norman Joplin for *Music Now* (Sep 12)
Steve Clackson for *Bild Am Sonntag* (Sep 20)
30   Travels from London to Stapleford Aerodrome, Stapleford, Wilt-
shire, and flies from there to Bembridge Airport, Isle Of Wight
ISLE OF WIGHT FESTIVAL, EAST AFTON FARM, ISLE
OF WIGHT
[support: Kris Kristofferson; Ralph McTell; Heaven; Free;
Donovan; Pentangle; Moody Blues; Jethro Tull; Joan Baez;

694

Richie Havens; Leonard Cohen]
'God Save The Queen'; 'Sergeant Pepper's Lonely Hearts Club
Band', 'Spanish Castle Magic'; 'All Along The Watchtower';
'Machine Gun'; 'Lover Man'; 'Freedom'; 'Red House'; 'Dolly
Dagger'; 'Midnight Lightnin''; 'Foxy Lady'; 'Message To Love';
'Hey Baby (The Land Of The New Rising Sun)'; 'Ezy Ryder';
'Hey Joe'; 'Purple Haze'; 'Voodoo Child (slight return)'; 'In From
The Storm'
Filmed and recorded
'Isle Of Wight' – Radio interview for French radio

31   Flies from Southampton to Stockholm

SWEDEN
Stockholm – Radio interview by Klas Burling
STORA SCENEN, GRÖNA LUND, TIVOLI GARDEN, STOCK-
HOLM
'Lover Man'; 'Catfish Blues'; 'Midnight Lightnin''; 'Ezy Ryder';
'Red House'; 'Come On (Part 1)'; 'Room Full Of Mirrors'; 'Hey
Baby (The Land Of The New Rising Sun)'; 'Message To Love';
'Machine Gun'; 'Voodoo Child (slight return)'; 'In From The Storm';
'Purple Haze'; 'Foxy Lady' Partly videotaped

SEP
01   Flies from Stockholm to Gothenburg
STORA SCENEN, LISEBURG, GOTHENBURG
'Spanish Castle Magic'; 'Killing Floor'; 'Getting My Heart Back
Together Again'; 'Message To Love'; 'Hey Baby (The Land Of
The New Rising Sun)'; 'In From The Storm;' 'Hey Joe'; 'Foxy
Lady'; 'Red House'; 'Room Full Of Mirrors'; 'Straight Ahead';
'Purple Haze'; 'Voodoo Child (slight return)'

02   *DENMARK*
Books into Hotel Atlantic, Århus
Hotel Atlantic – Interview by Anne Bjørndal for *Morgenposten*
(Sep 06)
VEJLBY RISSKOV HALLEN, ÅRHUS
'Freedom'; 'Message To Love'/'Hey Baby' (The Land Of The
New Rising Sun)' medley
Jimi left the stage after these songs due to total exhaustion

03   Copenhagen – Jimi visits the home of Kirsten Nefer and her
family for dinner
K.B. HALLEN, COPENHAGEN
[support: Blue Sun]
'Stone Free'; 'Foxy Lady'; 'Message To Love'; 'Hey Baby (The
Land Of the New Rising Sun)'; 'All Along The Watchtower'; 'Machine Gun'; 'Spanish Castle Magic'; 'Ezy Ryder'; 'Freedom'; 'Red
House'; 'In From The Storm'; 'Purple Haze'; 'Voodoo Child' (slight
return); 'Hey Joe'; 'Fire'

04   Flies from Copenhagen, via Hamburg, to Berlin

695

Stora Scenen, Gröna Lund, Tivoli Garden, Stockholm, 31 August 1970

WEST GERMANY
Books into Hotel Kempinski, Berlin
Deutschlandhalle, Berlin – Filmed backstage interview by Chris
Bromberg
'SUPER CONCERT '70', DEUTSCHLANDHALLE, BERLIN
[support: Murphy Blend; Procul Harum; Canned Heat; Ten Years
After; Cat Mother]
'Straight Ahead'; 'Spanish Castle Magic'; 'The Sunshine Of Your
Love'; 'Hey Baby (The Land Of The New Rising Sun)'; 'Message
To Love'; 'Machine Gun'; 'Purple Haze'; 'Red House'; 'Foxy Lady';
'Ezy Ryder'; 'Hey Joe'; 'Power Of Soul'; 'Lover Man'

05   Travels by train from Berlin to Puttgarden, Isle Of Fehmarn
Books into Hotel Dania, Puttgarden

06   'LOVE AND PEACE FESTIVAL', ISLE OF FEHMARN
[support: Alexis Korner; Floh de Cologne; Limbus 4; Embryo]
'Killing Floor'; 'Spanish Castle Magic'; 'All Along The Watchtower';
'Hey Joe'; 'Hey Baby (The Land Of The New Rising Sun)'; 'Message
To Love'; 'Foxy Lady'; 'Red House'; 'Ezy Ryder'; 'Freedom'; 'Room
Full Of Mirrors'; 'Purple Haze'; 'Voodoo Child (slight return)'
Jimi's last official concert (partly filmed)

696

Vejlby Risskov Hallen, Århus, 2 September 1970

Flies from the festival site by helicopter to Hamburg, and back to London

ENGLAND
Books into the Cumberland Hotel, Great Cumberland Place, Marble Arch, London – Rooms 507 & 508, but rarely stays there

10   Park Hotel, Hamilton Place, Park Lane, Mayfair, London
Jimi attends a party for Mike Nesmith (ex-Monkees)

11   Cumberland Hotel, London – Interview by Keith Altham for BBC Radio, and *Record Mirror* (Oct 03)
Jimi's final interview

15   Ronnie Scott's, London
Jimi attends the Eric Burdon & War concert

16   Ronnie Scott's, London
Jimi jams with Eric Burdon & War
'Mother Earth', 'Tobacco Road'

17   Samarkand Hotel, London
Jimi writes his last song 'The Story Of Life . . .'

18   An ambulance was called for at 11.18 – arrived at 11.27, left at 11.45 from the Samarkand Hotel and arrived around 12.00 at

St Mary Abbots Hospital, Kensington, London, where Jimi was pronounced dead on arrival

23 An inquest was opened on Jimi, but adjourned for further tests

28 Inquest on James Marshall Hendrix: an open verdict was recorded

29 Gerry Stickells flies Jimi's body back from London to Seattle, Washington

OCT

01 Dunlap Baptist Church, Rainier Avenue S., Renton, Washington
Funeral service
Jimi is buried at Greenwood Cemetery, Renton, Washington
Pallbearers: Dave Anderson, James Thomas, Steve Phillips, Eddy Rye, Donny Howell and Herbert Price
The following people (among others) attend the funeral: Al Aronowitz, Eric Barrett, Reverend Harold Blackburn, Miles Davis, Alan Douglas, Freddie Mae Gautier, Dolores Hall, Eddie Hall, John Hammond Jr., Al Hendrix, Ayako June Hendrix, Janie Hendrix, Leon Hendrix, Nora Hendrix, Tom Hullet, Abe Jacobs, Michael Jeffery, Eddie Kramer, Buddy Miles, Mitch Mitchell, Steve Paul, Noel Redding, Gerry Stickells, Chuck Wein, Devon Wilson, Johnny Winter

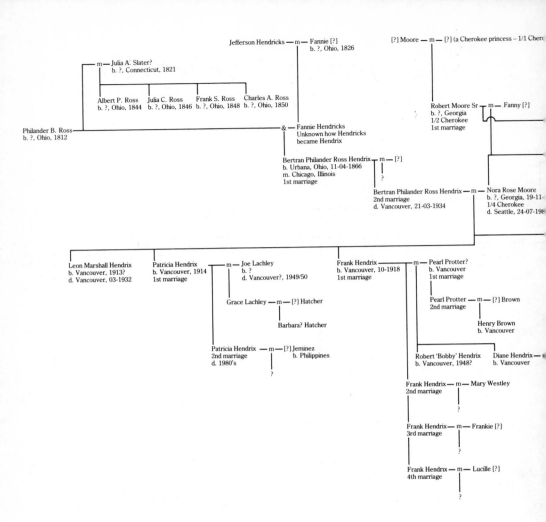

Jefferson Hendricks — m — Fannie [?]
b. ?, Ohio, 1826

[?] Moore — m — [?] (a Cherokee princess – 1/1 Chero

m — Julia A. Slater?
b. ?, Connecticut, 1821

Albert P. Ross   Julia C. Ross   Frank S. Ross   Charles A. Ross
b. ?, Ohio, 1844   b. ?, Ohio, 1846   b. ?, Ohio, 1848   b. ?, Ohio, 1850

Robert Moore Sr — m — Fanny [?]
b. ?, Georgia
1/2 Cherokee
1st marriage

Philander B. Ross
b. ?, Ohio, 1812

& — Fannie Hendricks
Unknown how Hendricks
became Hendrix

Bertran Philander Ross Hendrix — m — [?]
b. Urbana, Ohio, 11-04-1866
m. Chicago, Illinois
1st marriage
                                                ?

Bertran Philander Ross Hendrix — m — Nora Rose Moore
2nd marriage   b. ?, Georgia, 19-11-
d. Vancouver, 21-03-1934   1/4 Cherokee
                                        d. Seattle, 24-07-198

Leon Marshall Hendrix   Patricia Hendrix
b. Vancouver, 1913?   b. Vancouver, 1914 — m — Joe Lachley
d. Vancouver, 03-1932   1st marriage   b. ?
                                                      d. Vancouver?, 1949/50

Frank Hendrix — m — Pearl Protter?
b. Vancouver, 10-1918   b. Vancouver
1st marriage   1st marriage

Grace Lachley — m — [?] Hatcher

Barbara? Hatcher

Pearl Protter — m — [?] Brown
2nd marriage

Henry Brown
b. Vancouver

Patricia Hendrix — m — [?] Jeminez
2nd marriage   b. Philippines
d. 1980's
                    ?

Robert 'Bobby' Hendrix   Diane Hendrix —
b. Vancouver, 1948?   b. Vancouver

Frank Hendrix — m — Mary Westley
2nd marriage
                        ?

Frank Hendrix — m — Frankie [?]
3rd marriage
                        ?

Frank Hendrix — m — Lucille [?]
4th marriage
                        ?

4 *The Jimi Hendrix Family Tree*

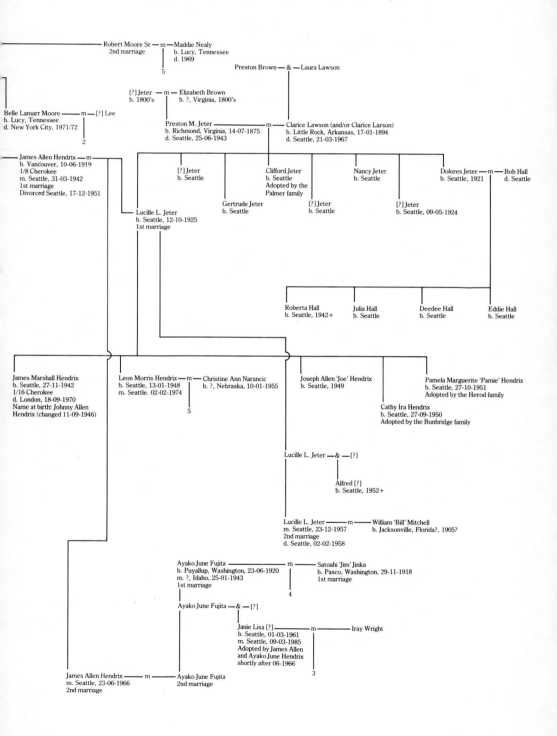

5 *Jimi Hendrix in Print and on Film*

BOOKS

Azderball, Robert, *Jimi Hendrix*, Verlag Azderball, Munich, 1971. Photo book.

Bertoncelli, Riccardo, *Jimi Hendrix*, Arcana Editrice Srl, Milan, 1989. [Italian]

Brown, Tony, *Jimi Hendrix: a visual experience*. (In press Omnibus Books, London 1992)

Dister, Alain, *Jimi Hendrix*, Les Nouvelles Éditions Polaires, Paris, 1972. [French]

Feller, Benoit, *Jimi Hendrix*, Éditions Albin Michel, Paris, 1976. [French]

Gentile, Enzo, *Jimi Hendrix*, Multiplo Edizioni Srl, Milan, 1989. [Italian]

Hatay, Nona, *Jimi Hendrix / The Spirit Lives On . . .* Last Gasp Of San Francisco, San Francisco, 1983.

Henderson, David, *Jimi Hendrix: Voodoo Child of the Aquarian Age*, Doubleday & Company Inc., New York, 1978. Also published by: Bantam Books Inc., New York; Arcana Editrici Srl, Milan; Love Kirjat, Helsinki.

Jimi Hendrix songbook, *Jimi Hendrix / Anthology*, A. Schroeder Int. Ltd, New York, 1975.

Jimi Hendrix songbook, plus text by Pearce Marchbank & Jonathon Green, *Jimi Hendrix: The Forty Greatest*, Wise Publications, London, 1975.

Jimi Hendrix songbook, *Jimi Hendrix*, Ritter Music, Japan, 1977.

Jimi Hendrix songbook, plus text by Richard Daniels, *Jimi Hendrix / Note For Note*, Cherry Lane Music Co. Inc., Greenwich, New York, 1980.

Jimi Hendrix songbook, plus text by Steve Tarshis, *Original Hendrix*, Wise Publications, London, 1982.

Jimi Hendrix lyrics book, plus text by Roger St. Pierre, *Jimi Hendrix / Recorded Poems*, International Music Publications, Woodford Green, England, 1986.

Jimi Hendrix lyrics book, *Jimi Hendrix / Testi Con Traduzione a Fronte / Con Una Testimonianza di Noel Redding*, Arcana Editrice Srl, Milan, 1987. [Italian]

Jimi Hendrix songbook, plus transcriptions by Douglas J. Noble, *Instant Hendrix*, International Music Publications, Woodford Green, England, 1988.

Jimi Hendrix songbook, *Are You Experienced?* Hal Leonard Publishing Corporation, Milwaukee, Wisconsin, 1989.

Jimi Hendrix songbook, *Axis: Bold As Love*, Hal Leonard Publishing Corporation, Milwaukee, Wisconsin, 1989.

Jimi Hendrix songbook, *Electric Ladyland*, Hal Leonard Publishing Corporation, Milwaukee, Wisconsin, 1989.

Herfurtner, Rudolf, *Brennende Gitarre / Ist Jimi Hendrix Wirklich Tot?* Edition Pestum, Munich, 1980. [German]

702

Backstage at BBC TV, London, 18 January 1967

Hopkins, Jerry, *Hit & Run / The Jimi Hendrix Story* Perigee Books/The Putnam
   Publishing Group, New York, 1983. Also published by: Sphere Books Ltd, London;
   B.V. Uitgeverij De Kern, Baarn, Holland.
Knight, Curtis, *Jimi – An Intimate Biography of Jimi Hendrix*, W.H. Allen, London,
   1974. Also published by: Praeger Publishers Inc., New York.
Menn, Don, *Jimi Hendrix*, Player Corporation, Tokyo, 1977. [Japanese]
   A re-print of *Guitar Player*'s special Jimi Hendrix issue of September 1975.
Mitchell, Mitch and John Platt, *The Hendrix Experience*, Pyramid, London, 1990
Murray, Charles Shaar, *Crosstown Traffic / Jimi Hendrix And Post-War Pop*, Faber
   & Faber, London, 1989.
Nolan, Tom, *Jimi Hendrix / A Biography In Words & Pictures*, Sire Books/Chappell
   Music Company, New York, 1977.
Ordovas, Jesús, *Jimi Hendrix*, Ediciones Júcar Madrid, 1974. [Spanish]
Raffaelli, Ron, *Jimi Hendrix / Electric Church / A Visual Experience*, The Visual
   Thing Inc., Beverly Hills, California, 1969. Photo book.
Redding, Noel and Carol Appleby, *Are You Experienced*, Fourth Estate, London 1990
Rotondi, Saverio, *Jimi Hendrix / Nei Dintorni Del Paradiso*, Edizioni Leti Srl,
   Rome, 1972. [Italian]
Rust, Jürgen, *Jimi Hendrix – Der Letzte Auftritt / Das Fehmarn-Festival 1970*,
   Cobra Verlag Hasum/Nordsee, W. Germany, 1988. [German]
Salvatori, Dario, *Jimi Hendrix*, Lato Side Editori Srl, Rome, 1980 [Italian]

Sampson, Victor, *Hendrix / An Illustrated Biography*, Proteus Books Ltd, London, 1984.

Sonderhoff, Achim, *Jimi Hendrix / Voodoo Chile / Die Biographie Einer Rocklegende*, Gustav Lübbe Verlag GmbH, Bergisch Gladbach, W. Germany, 1981. [German]

Welch, Chris, *Hendrix – A Biography*, Ocean Books Ltd, London, 1972. Also published by Flash Books, New York; Shobun-sha Publisher, Tokyo; Gammalibri, Milan.

FILMS

(Rating: ***** excellent; **** very good; *** good; ** poor; * terrible)

JIMI HENDRIX EXPERIENCE: Peter Neal, 33 minutes. ***
Also known as *See My Music Talking*. Mainly a collage of interview bits with and by the Jimi Hendrix Experience; 'Purple Haze' and 'Wild Thing' live from the Opera House, Blackpool, 25 November 1967. The highlight is Jimi's acoustic 12-string version of 'Getting My Heart Back Together Again', filmed on 19 December 1967 in London.
Video: 1987 – Palace Video (UK)

JIMI PLAYS BERKELEY: Peter Pilafian, 55 minutes. ***
Concert footage from rehearsals and extracts from two shows at the Berkeley Community Theatre, Berkeley, California, 30 May 1970. This could have been a five star film if only they had presented some of the songs in their entirety. Quite remarkable how different Jimi looks during the 1st and 2nd show. Highlights: 'Johnny B. Goode' and 'Machine Gun'.
Video: 1971 – Palace Video (UK); Westron Music Video (USA)

RAINBOW BRIDGE: Chuck Wein, 72 minutes. **
Even though the sound is only average, the songs have been heavily edited and the soundtrack is mostly out of sync with the footage, the film's saving grace is Jimi's concert performance with Billy Cox and Mitch Mitchell on 30 July 1970 in Hawaii. The film was originally 103 minutes long; one of the scenes cut showed Jimi leaning out of a window shooting a guy who'd been making a long, rambling speech. As the guy was white, it's a fair guess that the decision to remove this scene was political. It's a pity we don't see much footage with complete songs from the second show, when Jimi played several beautiful instrumentals. Now that would be an interesting film . . .
Video: 1971 – Hendring (UK); Rhino Home Video (USA)

A FILM ABOUT JIMI HENDRIX: Joe Boyd, 102 minutes. ****
A documentary film, with various interviews (but few with Jimi) and film footage of Jimi performing around the world, from the Marquee in March 1967, via Monterey to the Isle Of Wight Festival, 30 August 1970. By no means a definitive documentary, but it shows some of the better moments from the Isle Of Wight performance.
Video: 1973 – Warner Home Video

JOHNNY B GOODE: Alan Douglas, 26 minutes. *
'All Along The Watchtower' and 'Star Spangled Banner' live from the 2nd Annual Atlanta Pop Festival, 4 July 1970. These songs should never have been made available ('Star Spangled Banner' is just awful). Jimi is far from being in top form and he looks very tired. Also included are a promo film/photo collage set to the music of 'Are You Experienced'; 'Johnny B. Goode' from Berkeley; plus an 'arty' ballad set to 'Voodoo Child (slight return)'.
Video: 1985 – Virgin Music Video (UK); Sony (USA)

JIMI PLAYS MONTEREY: Don A. Pennebaker, 50 minutes. ****

704

Almost the complete concert of the Jimi Hendrix Experience at Monterey, 18 June 1967; plus 'Sergeant Pepper's Lonely Hearts Club Band' and 'Wild Thing' live at the 'Christmas On Earth Continued' pop spectacular, Olympia, London, 22 December 1967. Slightly weak colours and irritating to have the film credits on during 'Purple Haze'.
Video: 1987 – Virgin Music Video (UK)
WOODSTOCK 2: Michael Wadleigh, 90 minutes. ***
Jimi's 'Sky Church' is featured in this movie for about 10 minutes, with 'Star Spangled Banner' and 'Purple Haze'. 'Instrumental Solo' is used as background music.
Video: 1979 – Warner Home Video
SUPERSTARS IN CONCERT: Peter Clifton, 104 minutes. **
Jimi can be experienced during almost 11 minutes (the rest of the video contains material with other artists). Contains a mimed promo for 'Hey Joe', shot at the Saville Theatre, London, 31 January 1967; another mimed version of 'Hey Joe' made by Belgium TV, 7 March 1967; an incomplete live version of 'Wild Thing' from 'L'Olympia', Paris, 9 October 1967; plus some silent film footage from 1967 in the USA and the Isle Of Wight Festival, 30 August 1970 with 'Freedom' from the Isle Of Wight used as background music. Some of the footage in this video was previously released in the movies *Rock City* and *The Sound Of The City*.
Video: 1989 – Telstar Video Entertainment (UK)
JIMI HENDRIX CONCERT 27 minutes. **
Mixed bag video with nothing new to offer. 'Purple Haze' (one half from the Marquee and the other half from Berkeley) as released in *A Film About Jimi Hendrix*; 'Wild Thing' from Paris 1967; 'Wild Thing' and 'Hey Joe' from Monterey 1967; and 'Hey Joe' from the Saville 1967.
Video: 1978 – Media-Home Entertainment Inc. (USA)
ISLE OF WIGHT: Murray Lerner, 57 minutes. ***
video: 1990 BMG

UNRELEASED FILMS

WAKE AT GENERATION: Don A. Pennebaker.
This film became recently available on a bootleg video in the USA. Material from Generation club, New York City, 7 April 1968. Included is a six-minute blues jam by Jimi with the late Roy Buchanan (on bass), among others, filmed during a wake for Martin Luther King.
THE LAST EXPERIENCE: Steve Gold & Jerry Goldstein.
Complete concert, Royal Albert Hall, London, 24 February 1969. Legal difficulties throughout the years have so far prevented this film from hitting the screens.
WOODSTOCK
Complete concert, 18 August 1969.
WINTER FESTIVAL FOR PEACE: Michael Jeffery.
Footage from the benefit at the Madison Square Garden in New York City, 28 January 1970. Contains Jimi's short set which turned out to be Band Of Gypsys' final concert.
BERKELEY: Peter Pilafian.
Two complete concerts, 30 May 1970.
ATLANTA
Complete concert, 2nd Atlanta Pop Festival, 4 July 1970.

RANDALL'S ISLAND
Complete concert, 'New York Pop', Downing Stadium, New York, 17 July 1970.
RAINBOW BRIDGE
Two complete concerts, 30 July 1970, Hawaii.

Photo Credits

Index

Reference Notes on pages 509–708 have not been indexed. Page numbers in *italics* indicate photographs.

Wolfe, Randy (Randy California) x,
101–2, 107
Womack, Bobby 78, 156
Womack Brothers (the Valentinos,
Bobby and Harry) 71
Wood, Randy, and Randy's Record
Store, Gallatin 62–3
Woodberry, James 40
Woods, Bobby 393–5
Woods, Chris 277, 342, 376
Woodstock (film) 425
Woodstock Music and Arts Festival
375–88, *386*
Worthington, Herbert x, 372–3, *372*, 374

Wright, Patronella 477
Wyatt, Robert x, 250, 294, 322

Yameta 482–7, 488–91
Yarrow, Peter 412
Yasgur, Max 383
*You Can Be Anything You Want
to Be This Time* 399
'You Got me Floatin'' 226
'You Keep Me Hanging On'
293–4
Young Rascals 199
Youngblood, Gene 253–4
Youngblood, Lonnie 76

Index compiled by Valerie Lewis Chandler BA, ALAA